D1130816

# THE GREAT GOD PAN
## AND OTHER HORROR STORIES

Perhaps no figure better embodies the transition from the Gothic tradition to modern horror than Arthur Machen. In the final decade of the nineteenth century, the Welsh writer produced a seminal body of tales of occult horror, spiritual and physical corruption, and malignant survivals from the primeval past which horrified and scandalized late Victorian readers. Machen's 'weird fiction' has influenced generations of storytellers from H. P. Lovecraft to Guillermo Del Toro, and it remains no less unsettling today.

This new collection, which includes the complete novel *The Three Impostors* as well as such celebrated tales as 'The Great God Pan' and 'The White People', constitutes the most comprehensive critical edition of Machen yet to appear. In addition to the core late-Victorian horror classics, a selection of lesser-known prose poems and later tales helps to present a fuller picture of the development of Machen's weird vision.

ARTHUR MACHEN was born in 1863 in Caerleon, Monmouthshire, the son of a Welsh clergyman. His birthplace, rich in history and legend, was to have a decisive impact on his later fiction. Machen attended Hereford Cathedral School, but his father's poverty precluded a university education. During the 1880s Machen worked in London as a tutor, translator, and cataloguer, while finding his way as a writer. Then, between 1890 and 1900, he produced a body of tales of horror, wonder, and the borderland between the two. The most popular, or notorious, of these in its day was 'The Great God Pan', associated, then and now, with the Decadent movement in literature. 'Pan' and other works written during that decade, including *The Three Impostors*, *The Hill of Dreams*, and 'The White People', are now recognized as classics of weird fiction. At the start of the First World War, Machen caused a stir with a short story about a supernatural rescue of an English company at Mons, 'The Bowmen', which many readers refused to accept as fiction. Despite Machen's very high reputation among other weird writers, his popular appeal, even to fans of horror and the supernatural, has ever waxed and waned. Machen died at St Joseph's Nursing Home in Beaconsfield in 1947.

AARON WORTH is an Associate Professor of Rhetoric at Boston University. He is the author of *Imperial Media: Colonial Networks and Information Technologies in the British Literary Imagination, 1857–1918* (2014), as well as critical essays discussing the work of such Victorian horror writers as Arthur Machen, M. R. James, and Richard Marsh. His own horror fiction has appeared in publications including *Cemetery Dance Magazine* and *Aliterate*.

Cover image: © PictuLandra/Shutterstock

ARTHUR MACHEN

# the great god pan

## and other horror stories

*Edited with an Introduction and Notes by*
AARON WORTH

OXFORD
UNIVERSITY PRESS

# OXFORD
UNIVERSITY PRESS

Great Clarendon Street, Oxford, OX2 6DP,
United Kingdom

Oxford University Press is a department of the University of Oxford.
It furthers the University's objective of excellence in research, scholarship,
and education by publishing worldwide. Oxford is a registered trade mark of
Oxford University Press in the UK and in certain other countries

Selection and editorial material © Aaron Worth 2018

The moral rights of the author have been asserted

First Edition published in 2018

Impression: 3

Published in the United States of America by Oxford University Press
198 Madison Avenue, New York, NY 10016, United States of America

British Library Cataloguing in Publication Data
Data available

Library of Congress Control Number: 2017950098

ISBN 978–0–19–881316–3

Printed in Great Britain by
Clays Ltd, St Ives plc

# ACKNOWLEDGEMENTS

In preparing this edition I have benefited from the generous assistance of several Machen scholars; I must particularly thank Mark Valentine and James Machin for their help on several points of information. I am grateful as well to the following for expert opinion, advice, and aid of various kinds: Millard Baublitz, Mark Bills, Michael Booth, Peter Brabham, Godfrey Brangham, William Charlton, Barry Faulk, Billy Flesch, James Gregory, James Hamill, Gregg Jaeger, Darryl Jones, Roanne Kantor, Valerie Lester, Roger Luckhurst, Natalie McKnight, Jim Mussell, Tom Noel, Bob Patten, Aidan Reynolds, and Justin Willis. Finally, I owe thanks to my editor, Luciana O'Flaherty, for making this book possible; to Kizzy Taylor-Richelieu, Rowena Anketell, Lisa Eaton, and everyone else at Oxford University Press for their expertise and assistance; and to the project's anonymous readers for their perceptive comments and suggestions.

# CONTENTS

# INTRODUCTION

*Readers who are unfamiliar with the stories may prefer to treat
the Introduction as an Afterword.*

IN 1895 the editors of a new magazine, *The Unicorn*, sought to make
a splash by engaging a pair of literary hot properties to contribute parallel series of tales. The two writers were Arthur Machen and H. G. Wells,
both fresh from recent publishing triumphs (perhaps in Machen's case
'scandal' is closer to the mark), and their respective contributions were
to offer readers distinct modes, or flavours, of what we should today call
'genre fiction'. The magazine, unfortunately, folded after a mere three
issues, in which only one of Wells's stories, and none of Machen's,
appeared. Machen related the episode, nearly three decades later, in
characteristically self-deprecating fashion:

> 'The Great God Pan' had made a storm in a Tiny Tot's teacup. And about the
> same time, a young gentleman named H. G. Wells had made a very real, and
> a most deserved sensation with a book called 'The Time Machine'; a book
> indeed. And a new weekly paper was projected by Mr. Raven Hill [*sic*] and Mr.
> Girdlestone, a paper that was to be called 'The Unicorn'. And both Mr. Wells
> and myself were asked to contribute; I was to do a series of horror stories.[1]

This obscure episode in late Victorian publishing history is intriguing
for a number of reasons. It would be interesting to know, for instance,
just how Raven-Hill and Girdlestone phrased their offer; perhaps they
requested 'more stuff in the "Pan" line'. Writing in the 1920s, Machen
speaks of 'horror stories' and 'tales of horror', but it is unlikely that
these were the expressions used at the time[2] (unlikely, too, that the editors asked the young Wells for more 'scientific romances', let alone the
entirely anachronistic designation 'science fiction'). This was, after all,
precisely the period during which the still-fluid conceptual boundaries
of emergent genre categories like 'science fiction', 'fantasy', and 'horror' were themselves beginning to be negotiated, shaped, and defined.
But a more tantalizing question is this: if *The Unicorn*, and its editors'
scheme, had been a success, would the trajectory of Machen's reputation

---

[1] *Things Near and Far* (New York, 1923), 145.
[2] Though not impossible: an early reader of 'Pan' characterized it as a 'clever story of
horror on the Edgar Poe or Sheridan Le Fanu pattern' (John Gawsworth, *The Life of
Arthur Machen* (Carlton, OR, 2005), 119).

have more closely resembled that of Wells, who went on to score triumph after triumph, as well as worldwide celebrity, in the years to come? Machen's star, by contrast, sank slowly back towards the horizon line of relative obscurity, then followed an irregularly wave-like course throughout his later life (and afterlife), ascending and again declining at periodic intervals. For Wells, 1895 marked the beginning of fame; for Machen it meant something like the end of it, until the next century at any rate. But what if Machen had become, as it were, the 'H. G. Wells of horror'?

In one sense, the question is moot for the simple reason that, in the event, Machen found himself quite unable to write anything further in the 'Pan' line. The 32-year-old author of a small body of inventively appalling tales, when pressed to produce more of the same, extruded a quartet of mediocrities, which he was entirely relieved to be able to consign to oblivion. In the short term at least, his imagination led him down less egregiously 'horrific' paths, while the *fin-de-siècle* reading public supped on such fresh terrors as Bram Stoker's *Dracula* and Richard Marsh's *The Beetle*, to say nothing of Wells's own bloodsucking octopus-Martians and surgically transformed beast-men. But it is also moot because in the end Machen would indeed become something very like 'the H. G. Wells of horror'. Today he is widely accepted as a foundational figure—for some *the* foundational figure—in the development of modern horror fiction[3] (though it is worth noting that he would have strenuously, and with justice, resisted the idea that he was simply or solely a 'horror writer'). If, however, Machen is now so recognized, it is less by popular acclaim than by aristocratic consensus. Machen is, as Dante said of Aristotle, a 'maestro di color che sanno'— a master of those who know, a high priest retroactively canonized by later practitioners of his weird art. This process of canonization may be said to have begun with the influential essay *Supernatural Horror in Literature* by H. P. Lovecraft, who wrote:

Of living creators of cosmic fear raised to its most artistic pitch, few if any can hope to equal the versatile Arthur Machen; author of some dozen tales long and short, in which the elements of hidden horror and brooding fright attain an almost incomparable substance and realistic acuteness. . . . his powerful horror-material of the 'nineties and earlier nineteen-hundreds stands alone in its class, and marks a distinct epoch in the history of this literary form.[4]

---

[3] He was, in Brian Stableford's estimation, 'the first British writer of authentically modern horror stories'. David Pringle (ed.), *St James Guide to Horror, Ghost, & Gothic Writers* (London, 1997), 384.

[4] *Supernatural Horror in Literature* (Mineola, NY, 1973), 88.

Whether Machen was in fact a purveyor of 'cosmic fear', as Lovecraft conceived it, is open to dispute; certainly he shared neither Lovecraft's atheism nor his fundamental belief in an amoral, indifferent universe. The point here is that Lovecraft was only the first of a long line of Machen admirers, including Stephen King, Ramsey Campbell, Clive Barker, and Guillermo del Toro, who have drawn upon Machen for inspiration in their own novels, stories, and films, which their own fans have been content to enjoy without necessarily feeling compelled to pursue Machen's distinctive note of weirdness back to the source, his own writing. There are signs, however, that this may be changing. With ever-increasing interest in Machen on the part of both readers and literary scholars—there has been a veritable explosion of critical work on him in recent years— the acolytes of the 'flower-tunicked priest of nightmare' are in some danger of losing their proprietary claims on him and his fiction. And since that fiction represents both a high point in the history of horror and the weird and a fascinating window into the *fin-de-siècle* cultural milieu within which most of it was produced, this is an entirely good thing.

## Life and Work

Machen was pre-eminently a writer of place—of, first of all, his native Monmouthshire (later he would discover London, completing the binary landscape of his imagination). It is significant that in his autobiography Machen privileges geography over genealogy, filling many lyrical pages with evocations of his birthplace before thinking to bring any of his relations onto the stage of memory. He is ever reminding the reader, too, of the decisive impact of the history of Wales—natural as well as human—upon his own. In an often-quoted passage near the beginning of the first of his memoirs, *Far Off Things*, he declares,

I shall always esteem it as the greatest piece of fortune that has fallen to me, that I was born in that noble, fallen Caerleon-on-Usk, in the heart of Gwent. . . . For the older I grow the more firmly am I convinced that anything which I may have accomplished in literature is due to the fact that when my eyes were first opened in earliest childhood they had before them the vision of an enchanted land.[5]

That land was a palimpsest, steeped in both history and legend from Celtic, Roman, and medieval times (for as we will see, if Machen was

---

[5] *Far Off Things* (New York, 1922), 8.

a writer of place, those places were deeply imbued with a sense of temporality):

I am a citizen of what was once no mean city . . . once the splendid Isca Silurum, the headquarters of the Second Augustan Legion. And, then again, a golden mist of legend grew about it; it became the capital of King Arthur's court of faerie and enchantment, the chief city of a cycle of romance that has charmed all the world. . . . wonderful was it to stand in the evening on the green circle of the Roman amphitheatre, and see the sun flame above Twyn Barlwn, the mystic tumulus on the mountain wall of the west. So the old town dreamed the long years away, not forgetful of the Legions and the Eagles, murmuring scraps of broken Latin in its ancient sleep.[6]

Here in 1863 Machen was born, and baptized Arthur Llewellyn Jones. (The 'Machen' came later, from his mother's family, and is a Scottish name, despite there being a village of 'Machen' near his birthplace.) His father was a Welsh clergyman, from a line of Welsh clergymen, and the rectory library furnished the second formative influence on the future writer's life: there the young Machen devoured a heterogeneous collection of books and periodicals, supplemented by such treasured acquisitions as *Don Quixote*, De Quincey's *Confessions of an English Opium Eater*, and *The Arabian Nights*. There was money—for a while—for grammar school in Hereford, but this had entirely evaporated by the time he was to have followed in his father's footsteps—to university and, in all likelihood, the Church.[7] Plan B was a medical career. But a constitutional innumeracy, helped not at all by a preference for sub-Swinburnian versifying over cramming, ensured Machen's failure of the examinations for the Royal College of Surgeons in London. He returned to Wales, where a long, self-published poem on the Eleusinian mysteries suggested to his family—oddly enough—that he might be a journalist; accordingly, he was sent back to London in June 1881, at the age of 18, to become one.

And Machen did, in fact, become a newspaperman, but not for twenty-nine years; in the meantime, he became something else, a 'literary man'. To this end he spent most of the 1880s in severe poverty, serving an idiosyncratic apprenticeship: he translated Marguerite de Navarre's *Heptameron* for a much-needed £20, wrote a pseudo-scholarly

---

[6] Introduction to *Notes and Queries*, quoted in Mark Valentine, *Arthur Machen* (Bridgend, 1995), 10.

[7] Flirtations with occultism aside (see the next paragraphs), Machen was a believing, if somewhat idiosyncratic, Anglican with High Church tendencies throughout life. (In 'The White People' he has the mystic Catholic Ambrose say, 'I am a member of the persecuted Anglican church', p. 264.)

treatise on tobacco and a collection of pseudo-Renaissance tales in archaic English, and read his way through a garret crammed with eso-teric literature to prepare a bookseller's catalogue (entitled *The Literature of Occultism and Archaeology*). This last commission was to provide rich matter for Machen's creative work, exposing him to 'as odd a library as any man could desire to see'. As he would later write:

> Occultism in one sense or another was the subject of [most] of the books. There were the principal and the most obscure treatises on Alchemy or Astrology, on Magic. . . . books about Witchcraft, Diabolical Possession, 'Fascination', or the Evil Eye; here comments on the Kabbala. Ghosts and Apparitions were a large family, Secret Societies of all sorts hung on the skirts of the Rosicrucians and Freemasons. . . . the semi-religious, semi-occult, semi-philosophical sects and schools were represented: we dealt in Gnostics and Mithraists, we harboured the Neoplatonists, we conversed with the Quietists and the Swedenborgians. These were the ancients; and beside them were the modern throng of Diviners and Stargazers and Psychometrists and Animal Magnetists and Mesmerists and Spiritualists and Psychic Researchers. In a word, the collection . . . repre-sented thoroughly enough that inclination of the human mind which may be a survival from the rites of the black swamp and the cave or—an anticipation of a wisdom and knowledge that are to come, transcending all the science of our day.[8]

Most of these subjects would crop up somewhere or other in Machen's later writing (though the 'Ghosts and Apparitions' that were the meat and drink of his contemporary M. R. James appear hardly at all).[9] In particular, the idea of an occult science 'transcending all the science of our day' lay behind the pair of tales which John Lane of The Bodley Head published together in 1894 as part of his 'Keynote Series'. There are superficial resemblances between both 'The Great God Pan' and 'The Inmost Light' and science fiction; in each, a mad scientist figure engages in a forbidden experiment: in the first story, a surgical pro-cedure performed on a woman's brain to make her 'see the god Pan'; in the second, the removal of a woman's soul to a gemstone prison. Yet where science fiction depends upon the presence of what Darko Suvin

---

[8] *Things Near and Far*, 20–1.

[9] Later Machen would become personally involved in the *fin-de-siècle* world of the occult as well, joining the Order of the Golden Dawn after the death of his first wife (his friend the occult scholar Arthur Waite was a leading figure in the Order, which also counted Yeats and Aleister Crowley among its members). He would write disparagingly of the experience and the Order (thinly disguised as the 'Order of the Twilight Star'): 'I supposed that the Order, dimly heard of, might give me some light and guidance...[but] the Twilight Star shed no ray of any kind on my path' (*Things Near and Far*, 218).

has called a 'novum' or 'new thing',[10] consistent with current scientific knowledge (What if time travel were possible? What if robots became smarter than humans?), these tales are premised on what might better be termed an 'antiquum', a recovered piece of older, occult knowledge. Without question Machen's interest in, and treatment of, the brain in both of these stories draws upon contemporary developments in neuroscience; at the same time, however, he suggests that such modern disciplines are only catching up with the 'sciences' of a bygone age. And when the demonic Helen Vaughan in 'Pan' kills herself, her body undergoes a grotesque recapitulation of forms, but it is one which calls to mind less the evolutionary ideas of Darwin or Haeckel than the theories of the seventeenth-century alchemist Thomas Vaughan.[11]

Oscar Wilde called the novella 'un succès fou', but Machen treasured far more, as he would throughout his career, the abuse of critics. 'Pan' was 'gruesome, ghastly, and dull', 'acutely and intentionally disagreeable', 'ludicrous', 'an incoherent nightmare of sex', even—'unmanly'.[12] Some condemned Machen for revealing not too much but too little: Richard le Gallienne wrote in a reader's report that 'The nature of the horror . . . is persistently shirked . . . mainly a dumb-show of ghastly interjections. Terrified asterisks, horrified notes of exclamations are not enough.'[13] Many others echoed this criticism, a fact which points to Machen's pioneering use of a trope which would become a commonplace of twentieth-century horror—that of the 'unspeakable' or 'unnamable' thing which utterly resists representation.[14] This quality of obliqueness extends to other aspects of the novella as well, particularly its narrative structure—the reader pieces together the story from a sequence of seemingly disconnected episodes. H. P. Lovecraft saw the construction of 'Pan' as perhaps its greatest strength: 'But the charm of the tale is in the telling. No one could begin to describe the

---

[10] *Metamorphoses of Science Fiction* (New Haven, 1979), 63.

[11] Who is also her namesake; as far as I know, Machen biographers Aidan Reynolds and William Charlton were the first to make this connection in *Arthur Machen: A Short Account of His Life and Work* (London, 1963).

[12] Introduction, *The Great God Pan and the Hill of Dreams* (Mineola, NY, 2006), 8; D. P. M. Michael, *Arthur Machen* (Cardiff, 1971), 11.

[13] Quoted in Gawsworth, *Life*, 199.

[14] The 1925 story 'The Unnamable' is at least half a parody of this conceit, by one of its greatest purveyors, H. P. Lovecraft; the tale ends with a gloriously futile attempt to articulate the nature of the horror: '*No—it wasn't that way at all.* It was everywhere—a gelatin—a slime—yet it had shapes, a thousand shapes of horror beyond all memory. There were eyes—and a blemish. It was the pit—the maelstrom—the ultimate abomination. Carter, *it was the unnamable!*' *The New Annotated H. P. Lovecraft*, ed. Leslie S. Klinger (New York, 2014), 122.

cumulative suspense and ultimate horror with which every paragraph abounds without following fully the precise order in which Mr. Machen unfolds his gradual hints and revelations.'[15] But this is a minority view; modern readers have tended to be more disturbed by the story's defects of plotting and characterization[16] than by the improprieties which shocked its original audience. Whatever its weaknesses, 'Pan' has exerted an enormous influence on the course of horror fiction in the century and a quarter since its publication.

Despite Machen's later disavowals, 'Pan' was, and remains today, closely associated with the Decadent movement, and benefited, if that is the right way to put it, from the association. The British version of the Decadence was influenced by an earlier French movement, as well as by the Aesthetic school associated with Walter Pater. Machen's personal connection with the central figures of this movement was tangential: he had, for example, a slight and ambivalent relationship with Wilde (the Irishman praised the Welshman's early story 'A Double Return' as well as 'Pan'; for his part Machen considered Wilde a brilliant but superficial conversationalist). Another key figure, Aubrey Beardsley, designed the cover and title page for *The Great God Pan and The Inmost Light*, while the book's publisher, John Lane, was also responsible for the periodical which gave its name to the 'yellow nineties'. Despite these connections, Machen himself, writing in 1916, would have his readers believe that his work owed no debt at all to 'yellow bookery' (as he called it):

'The Great God Pan' was first published in December, 1894. So the book is of full age, and I am glad to take the opportunity of a new edition to recall those early 'nineties when the tale was written and published—those 'nineties of which I was not even a small part, but no part at all. For those were the days of 'The Yellow Book', of 'Keynotes', and the 'Keynotes Series', of Aubrey Beardsley and 'The Woman Who Did', of many portentous things in writing and drawing and publishing. 'The Great God Pan' had the good fortune to issue from The Bodley Head, which was the centre of the whole movement, and no doubt the book profitted by the noise that the movement was making. But this was in a sense an illegitimate profit; since the story was conceived and written in solitude, and came from far off lonely days spent in a land remote from London, and from literary societies and sodalities. So far as it stands for anything, it stands, not for the ferment of the 'nineties, but for the visions that a little boy saw in the late 'sixties and early 'seventies.[17]

---

[15] *Supernatural Horror in Literature*, 90.

[16] As many have noted, Machen looses upon the reader a veritable pack of all but indistinguishable young gentlemen.

[17] Introduction, *The Great God Pan and The Hill of Dreams*, 1.

Machen's attempts to distance himself from that world are understand-
able, given its unsavoury reputation in the public mind, well into the
twentieth century. This does not mean, however, that we are obliged to
accept uncritically his self-portrait of the artist as autocosm. But opinion has divided over the question of just how 'Decadent' his fictions of
this period are, how influenced by the cultural milieu in which Wilde,
Beardsley, and others flourished. On one view (not very different from
Machen's own), the answer would seem to be, 'very little indeed':

for our purpose these dazzling and picturesque figures [of the English Decadent
movement], however tragic, however intriguing, are irrelevant. They are irrelevant because they scarcely affected Machen at all. Although the atmosphere of
the age and the opportunity to experiment had something to do with the themes
he chose for his own stories, he followed no fashion and clung to no coterie.[18]

Even here, however, there is that tantalizing 'something to do with'.
Other critics, seeking to specify the nature and extent of this 'something', have faced first of all the challenge of satisfactorily *defining*
'Decadence', of agreeing on its characteristic qualities. Perhaps the best
way to think about Decadence is in the spirit of what Ludwig Wittgenstein
called 'family resemblances'—as a concept associated with a shifting but
overlapping set of themes, tropes, and techniques. And indeed, Machen
critics have painted various portraits of the Decadence—none exactly
alike, but all bearing a strong likeness to the fiction he produced in the
1890s. Mark Valentine, for instance, has written:

While there has been no succinct and accurate encapsulation of what the
Decadence meant, it may very broadly be considered as implying a devotion to
exquisitely crafted style in literature, and in life to the quest for new sensations,
involving variously the exploration of the occult, the exotic, the sexually
unorthodox, the bohemian way of life, and a taste for strange drugs or drink.[19]

For Wesley Sweetser (thinking along similar but not identical lines),
the 'larger elements of Decadence' are 'intent to shock, emphasis on
sensation, and fascination with evil'.[20] John Simons, warning against
the temptation 'to dismiss Machen as just another of the throng of lit-
erati of the 1890s who have narrowly failed to achieve canonical status',
highlights other qualities:

Certainly, we find throughout Machen's work all of those things which became
the clichés of the 1890s. His work is lushly embroidered with the aureate

---

[18] Reynolds and Charlton, *Arthur Machen*, 42.
[19] Valentine, *Arthur Machen*, 22.
[20] *Arthur Machen* (New York, 1964), 75.

diction of The Yellow Book, it breathes the atmosphere of the study in which a collection of rare erotica is displayed to only the closest friends, it is bathed in the pallid gleam of the Celtic Twilight.[21]

Then there is the *fin-de-siècle* fascination with paganism, and with the figure of Pan (and his various caprine avatars) in particular: '*The Great God Pan* should be seen . . . as a novel of the Decadence, of a piece with . . . [Florence Farr's] *The Dancing Faun*, with Kenneth Grahame's *Pagan Papers* (John Lane, 1893), with Beardsley's sly fauns and lascivious ladies.'[22] One might go on.[23] But these multifarious affinities with the spirit of the movement, and the age, are enough to demonstrate that such works as 'Pan', *The Three Impostors*, and *The Hill of Dreams* deserve to be considered important, perhaps indispensable, works of the English Decadence.

But if the Decadent brand was an asset, albeit an ambivalent one, in 1894, it would prove a liability in 1895—or so Machen believed, blaming the comparative failure of *The Three Impostors* (also published by John Lane) in part on public revulsion at Wilde's trial and conviction on charges of 'gross indecency': 'there had been some ugly scandals... which had made people impatient with reading matter that was not obviously and obtrusively "healthy"; and so, for one reason or another, "The Three Impostors" failed to set the Fleet Ditch on fire'.[24] To be sure, there have always been readers who have recognized its Gothic potency—it scared Conan Doyle to death, and John Betjeman—and today its status as a foundational work of horror fiction is generally acknowledged, among critics at any rate. In the 1980s Jorge Luis Borges included the novel in his 'Personal Library' of a hundred volumes, calling it one of literature's 'short and almost secret masterpieces'. But the text has remained an 'almost secret masterpiece' even to many who have read a fair bit of Machen, for the simple reason that it has so often, and for so long, been chopped up and sold, as it were, for parts. *The Three Impostors*, while to some extent written piecemeal, comprises

[21] 'Horror in the 1890s: The Case of Arthur Machen', in Clive Bloom (ed.), *Creepers* (London, 1993), 35.   [22] Valentine, *Arthur Machen*, 33.

[23] Machen's preoccupation with (physical and spiritual) corruption, for instance, resonates with other Decadent works, as does his depiction of Helen Vaughan in 'Pan' as a man-destroying femme fatale. For Adrian Eckersley, the unifying theme of Machen's 1890s stories is degeneracy, a condition associated with the Aesthetic and Decadent movements (among others), most famously by Max Nordau in his book *Degeneration* (1892, translated into English in 1895) (see 'A Theme in the Early Work of Arthur Machen: "Degeneration"', *ELT* 35/3 (January 1992), 277–87).

[24] *Things Near and Far*, 162.

a gratifyingly perplexing whole. A larger frame narrative—concerning a terrified 'young man with spectacles' fleeing from the occult society he has betrayed—contains a series of interpolated episodes told by unreliable narrators (this is one of those novels which demands a second reading at least).[25] Two of these episodes, however—'The Novel of the Black Seal' and 'The Novel of the White Powder'—have long been treated by anthologists as stand-alone tales.

And they are great tales. But there are losses as well as gains involved when one plucks them from the frame of the novel, which Machen would later describe as

a book which testifies to the vast respect I entertained for the fantastic, 'New Arabian Nights' manner of R. L. Stevenson, to those curious researches in the byways of London which I have described already, and also, I hope, to a certain originality of experiment in the tale of terror, as exemplified in the stories of the Professor who was taken by the fairies, and of the young student of law who swallowed the White Powder.[26]

Interestingly, this passage anticipates—seems even, perhaps, to sanction—the practice of harvesting individual 'stories' from the novel, even as it directs our attention to two fascinating aspects of the text which are almost entirely lost when this is done. The first of these aspects is precisely the narrative complexity noted earlier, for which Machen owes an explicit debt to Stevenson (especially to *The Dynamiter*, the 1885 sequel to his 1882 *New Arabian Nights*), and an implicit one to such works as the original *Arabian Nights* and (very likely) the *Heptameron* which, as we have seen, he had translated during the previous decade—all works using the device of an interlinked series of tales.[27] The second feature is the novel's depiction of London as a potent locus of wonder and terror; the text is in large part the product of a young writer's fascinated urban wanderings—his 'curious researches', as he puts it, 'in the byways of London'. As noted earlier, if Wales stood at one pole of Machen's axial imagination, the great 'City of Resurrections' (as it is called in 'The Great God Pan') was firmly fixed at the other, and

[25] The 'three impostors' of the book's title are liars, spinning fictions within a fiction—but mystery and ambiguity do not necessarily vanish altogether once one realizes this: for example, as Mark Valentine points out, in the case of 'The Novel of the Black Seal' there really *is* a Professor Gregg, and he really *has* vanished, as Phillipps's knowledge independently confirms (Valentine, *Arthur Machen*, 43).

[26] *Things Near and Far*, 144.

[27] Beyond this structural similarity, David Trotter has identified a number of further connections between *The Dynamiter* and *The Three Impostors*, in his introduction to the latter (London, 1995).

was as central to his literary vision as it was to those of Samuel Johnson and Charles Dickens (both favourite authors). Machen's London appears variously as a fantastic 'Baghdad on the Thames', site of impossible coincidences;[28] a source of sudden, transfiguring epiphanies and ecstasies; a network redolent with occult menace; and a disorienting labyrinth. Machen saw himself—how facetiously it is difficult to know for certain—as a solitary practitioner of what he called 'my London science' and 'the Great Art of London': 'I will listen to no objections or criticisms as to the Ars Magna of London, of which I claim to be the inventor, the professor and the whole school. Here I am artist and judge at once, and possess the whole matter of the art within myself.'[29] But of course he was far from the only one 'researching' the city—its seedier side in particular—in the later nineteenth century. Kelly Hurley aligns Machen's treatment of the city in *The Three Impostors* with the work of a host of 'late-Victorian "social explorers" . . . middle-class reformers— sociologists, urban missionaries, government agents, journalists—[who] founded their discussions of urban poverty upon a central conceit: that the slum neighborhoods of London were as little known, mysterious, and fearsome as the more obscure reaches of the colonies'.[30] This wider cultural context should be borne in mind when the reader follows the wanderings of Dyson (a peripatetic stand-in for Machen himself) into 'region[s] as remote as Libya and Pamphylia and the parts about Mesopotamia' (p. 180). However, most readers of Machen's fiction will probably agree that his vision of the metropolis is, ultimately, very much his own.

The second half of the decade was at least as productive for Machen as the first, yet this fact can only be appreciated in retrospect: in 1897 he wrote a novel, *The Hill of Dreams*, and a set of ten prose poems or short fantasies; 1899 saw the completion of 'The White People'—long reckoned, as much as 'Pan' or *The Three Impostors*, a key work of modern horror—and a book of literary criticism, *Hieroglyphics*, at which point the death of Machen's wife interrupted his work on the novella

---

[28] As fantasy writer Lin Carter seemed to recognize, Machen's imaginative Orientalization of London was closely related to his construction of a narrative world shot through with improbability: 'To me it reads rather as if Machen were trying to look at London as Scheherezade [*sic*] looked at Baghdad—through eyes that saw everyday life as a tangle of incredible coincidences, chance meetings, overheard anecdotes, and marvellous encounters'. 'Baghdad on the Thames', Introduction to *The Three Impostors* (New York, 1972), pp. xi–xii.   [29] *Things Near and Far*, 85–6.
[30] *The Gothic Body: Sexuality, Materialism, and Degeneration at the* Fin de Siècle (Cambridge, 1996), 161.

*A Fragment of Life*, and indeed his writing life altogether. But none of these works—among them some of Machen's finest—saw print until 1904 at the earliest; the prose poems would not appear complete until 1924, as *Ornaments in Jade*.

These latter pieces, each of which 'recounts a single incident in which there is an encounter with the celestial or satanic',[31] represent yet another part of Machen's oeuvre which deserves to be better known. While it is easy to dismiss them as derivative or secondary fragments— chips struck from *The Hill of Dreams* during its making, or tentative steps in the direction of 'The White People'—these compressed, ambiguous fictions are powerful in their own right. Reading them, one is particularly struck by their insistence on the ineluctability of rite and ritual, ceremony and mystery, as sources of meaning in an age of religious decline.[32] They explore, too, the abiding appeal of sympathetic magic and other 'primitive' practices. One 'young lady' in these pieces imitates the 'antique immemorial rite' she had seen another girl perform at the flower-decked stone in the wood; another uses a 'loathsome', obscene image to ensnare a gentleman's affection. At midnight the 'quiet modest girls of [an] English village' form a 'writhing' sylvan procession; in a London suburb, a City clerk makes and adores a dubious idol (pp. 254, 250, 260). Kindred scenarios are explored in the fragmentary sketches from this period which did not make it out of Machen's notebooks: there is the 'Story of a man who made for himself a god' of clay, that of the 'ordinary family living in the suburbs [who] shut themselves for certain days in the year to perform some horrible "cave" rites', the 'Girl who danced in the Maze [and] was afterwards beset by the influence she had in that manner invoked', and so on.[33] While Machen's obsession with ritual was hardly new,[34] in his earlier tales such practices had been largely associated with either the unambiguously diabolical or the primitive, subhuman 'other', or both, rather

---

[31] Valentine, *Arthur Machen*, 57. The selections included here have been chosen in part for their greater proximity to the 'satanic', though in Machen it can be difficult to keep these categories separate.

[32] Stephen King's 2008 story 'N' is a self-described 'riff on Arthur Machen's "The Great God Pan"', with a title borrowed from Machen as well, but its most profound connection to Machen may lie in its theme of obsessive-compulsive disorder (a man performs obsessive rituals to keep a monstrous being in its own dimension). It is a striking figure for the irrepressible return of ritual in a secular age.

[33] *The London Adventure* (New York, 1924), 97–100.

[34] As Machen said, he 'chose the mysteries first', and he 'chose them last' (quoted in Gawsworth, *Life*, 31); the Alpha and Omega of his writing career are the poem *Eleusinia* and the story 'Ritual'.

than with ordinary, modern Englishmen and women. It is no accident that these stories, and stories *manqués*, were conceived within a culture still under the spell of James George Frazer's magisterial work of comparative mythology *The Golden Bough* (1890), a book whose core message was deeply troubling to many Victorians: 'when all is said and done our resemblances to the savage are still far more numerous than our differences from him'.[35]

As the Victorian era came to an end, Machen had almost half a century of life ahead of him. It is fair to say that most of his best, and all of his most influential, tales of horror and the weird had been written, if not published, by this time. This is not to say, however, that he produced nothing of interest or value in the twentieth century. During the Great War he performed the remarkable feat of single-handedly, if unintentionally, splicing a myth into the collective imagination of a nation.[36] On 29 September 1914, the *Evening News* carried an account of an embattled English company on the Western Front which is miraculously rescued from annihilation by the spectral bowmen of Agincourt. To say that Machen's tale of providential delivery from the Hun found favour with the British public would be an understatement. Fantasy was taken for reality; Machen's insistence that his tale had no basis in fact provoked angry and elaborate rebuttals in print. It was an object lesson in the kind of deeply rooted human connection to myth and the supernatural he explored in his fiction. The success of 'The Bowmen', published in book form with a few other war stories, led to several commissioned works, including *The Great Return*, one of a number of Machen's writings, fictional and non-fictional, centring upon the Grail legend. Another tale of the War—the mystery-horror novel *The Terror* (1917), which describes a revolt of the animal kingdom against mankind—helped bring about a revival of interest in Machen, which his friend and biographer John Gawsworth called 'the boom'. Collected editions of his work appeared on both sides of the Atlantic (with the American edition, by Knopf, bound in yellow covers: yellow books belatedly invoking the decade of 'yellow bookery'). In the 1920s he wrote a trio of autobiographical books, as well as numerous essays.

[35] *The Golden Bough*, ed. Robert Fraser (Oxford, 2009), 218. Frazer's words might have served as epigraph to Machen's paradigmatically titled story 'Ritual' (1937), in which a group of English boys re-enact, or reinvent, a rite identical to that practised by an African tribe, with the same fatal result.

[36] 'This legend' of the Bowmen, wrote Borges, 'has now become part of popular mythology, and can be heard from the mouths of humble folk who have never heard of Machen'. Introduction, *Los Tres Impostores* (Madrid, 1985).

Finally, in 1936, Machen did what he could not do in 1895—write a sheaf of fresh 'tales of horror' to order. But it is to Machen's distinctive *fin-de-siècle* conception of the Gothic horror tale that we now turn.

## Deep Gothic

The first literary form specifically associated with the generation of extreme sensations of horror and terror—the Gothic romance of the eighteenth century—was inextricably, constitutively bound up with a fascination for the past. The same impulse consciously to revive archaic forms prompted Horace Walpole both to build an imitation medieval castle as his home and to pen the foundational Gothic novel *The Castle of Otranto* (1764); his literary successors, from Clara Reeve and Ann Radcliffe to Edgar Allan Poe, wrote about ancestral curses, restless spirits, ancient houses, ruined abbeys. In large measure this fascination was a historically specific one, part of the same broader interest in antiquity that helped give rise to such modern fields of historical inquiry as archaeology; as Clive Bloom notes, the original Gothic sensibility 'grew from an antiquarian interest in the peoples of the long distant past'.[37] Yet—precisely because of the nascent or non-existent state of such disciplines—the antiquarian imagination was necessarily hampered by what now appears to us as a crude and confused—and, above all, cramped—sense of history, to say nothing of prehistory. Many awoke in the seventeenth and eighteenth centuries to a new sense of wonder at the evidences of past ages to be found throughout Britain—Neolithic barrows, henge monuments, Roman ruins, Saxon artefacts—but lacked a framework for conceptualizing, or differentiating among, these historical periods with anything like the kind of precision which we take for granted today. Sir Thomas Browne's 1658 prose masterpiece, *Urne-Buriall*, was inspired by his discovery of Anglo-Saxon pottery urns which he took to be Roman, and things had not changed much by the time the future author of *The Castle of Otranto* joined the Society of Antiquaries of London in the next century.

Things *had* changed, however, and radically, by the time Machen came to make his own distinctive contributions to the Gothic tradition, and not only in the development of historiography. Above all, the nineteenth century witnessed a revolution—one which would spread very quickly from the confines of scientific circles to the larger culture—in the conceptualization of temporality itself, a revolution whose dramatic—for

---

[37] Clive Bloom, *Gothic Histories* (London, 2010), 2.

some, traumatic—impact is difficult to overstate. The broad contours
of this time revolution, while well known, are worth rehearsing briefly.
Until comparatively recently the world was believed, on the best authority, to be no more than 'Some fifty or sixty centuries' old, a scripturally
sanctioned span which was felt to be quite old enough 'for the unfold-
ing of the whole of known human history and therefore for the natural
world, the stage on which it had been played out'.[38] Famously, in the
middle of the seventeenth century the historian and archbishop James
Ussher, no ignoramus or, in our sense, religious fanatic, fixed a precise
date of 4004 BCE for the Creation. And while subsequent theories of
societal development, as well as discoveries by natural historians, might
have chafed at times against this compressed chronology, it was not
until the nineteenth-century emergence of geology as a science that it
was seriously challenged—and, in rather short order, demolished. The
world was suddenly—overnight, as it were—millions of years old.[39]

The revelation of earth's deep past engendered, variously, feelings
of exhilaration, consternation, and anxiety, but seldom indifference.
Religious faith, especially when rooted in biblical literalism, was often
a casualty; John Ruskin famously lamented: 'If only the Geologists
would let me alone, I could do very well, but those dreadful Hammers!
I hear the clink of them at the end of every cadence of the Bible verses.'
On the other hand, the prospect of an all-but-bottomless well of time
made for exciting possibilities in other sciences. Pioneering works in
evolutionary biology and paleoarchaeology followed in geology's wake,
consolidating the conceptual revolution begun several decades earlier.
Deep time was an indispensable ingredient in Charles Darwin's theory
of natural selection, as well as a spur to new disciplines exploring
human 'prehistory', a word which now appeared for the first time.
Archaeologists proposed the existence of Stone, Bronze, and Iron ages,
while John Lubbock's *Pre-Historic Times as Illustrated by Ancient
Remains* (1865) introduced a further distinction between 'Palaeolithic'
and 'Neolithic' humanity. Meanwhile historians, for their part, largely
shrank back from the challenge of allowing so *longue* a *durée* to cast its
dauntingly attenuated shadow over their discipline, 'fashioning instead
a view of history that begins with the rise of civilization', and accepting
'prehistory' as a kind of conceptual 'buffer zone'.[40]

[38] Martin J. S. Rudwick, *Earth's Deep History* (Chicago, 2014), 10.
[39] Actually billions, as we know now.
[40] Daniel Lord Smail, *On Deep History and the Brain* (Berkeley and Los Angeles,
2008), 1–2.

But what has all this to do with Machen, or the literary form that
originated with *The Castle of Otranto*? One way to characterize Machen's
core contribution to modern horror is to say that he engaged in a thoroughgoing reconceptualization—a 'reboot', as we might say today—of
the Gothic mode in the aftermath of the Victorian time revolution.
Arguably no earlier writer had attempted to inscribe the newly revealed
abysses of deep temporality, with its disconcerting potentialities, within
a recognizably Gothic framework—certainly none so extensively, or so
influentially. Machen's haunted Wales is charged with deep time—it is
not a landscape dotted with ruins of vaguely antique provenance, but
a coded, stratified space preserving traces of the historic, prehistoric,
and prehuman pasts alike (even if these traces have a disconcerting
habit of appearing where they are not supposed to be). And the historical sciences of geology, archaeology, and ethnology, as well as such kindred fields as philology and comparative mythology, are on prominent
display in Machen's fiction, where they are not mere window dressing
but rather central to the articulation of his Gothic vision.

  These disciplines are particularly conspicuous in the stories of the
1890s featuring Machen's recurring character Dyson (a Sherlock
Holmes figure whose mind, unlike that of Conan Doyle's iconic detective,
is ever musing on the mysteries of the deep past). In 'The Shining
Pyramid', for instance, Dyson, seeking to account for the anomalous
presence in Gwent of a number of prehistoric flints, asks casually,
'By the way . . . what is your geological formation down there?' His
friend, while surprised, replies with promptitude and accuracy: 'Old
red sandstone and limestone, I believe. . . . We are just beyond the coal
measures, you know' (p. 227).[41] As for the flints, their appearance
prompts Dyson to deduce the agency of the sinister race which represents one of Machen's favourite conceits—his reimagining of the fairies of Celtic lore as a survival from the prehistoric past. In this and
other tales, Machen clearly draws upon contemporary works of archaeology and anthropology in associating the material culture of the 'Little
People' with the Neolithic period. They possess 'flint arrow-head[s] of
vast antiquity', 'primitive stone axe[s]', a 'primitive stone knife' resembling an 'adze'—all artefacts which might have come straight from
Lubbock's *Pre-Historic Times* (Dyson's ethnologist companion declares

---

[41] Wales, it may be worth noting, had played a prominent role in the development of
geology, with three geological periods of the Palaeozoic Era—the Cambrian, Silurian,
and Ordovician—being named after Welsh tribes because of the important rock strata
found there.

the adze-knife, with authority, to have been 'made about ten thousand years ago. One exactly like this was found near Abury [Avebury], in Wiltshire', p. 200).

Other writers of the time, to be sure, engaged imaginatively with deep time, sometimes to create horrors; H. G. Wells once again comes to mind. Machen once described a sensation of 'travelling in time—backwards, not forwards, as in Mr. Wells's enchantment',[42] and subsequent commentators have imagined his and Wells's countenances as the two faces of Janus—one looking to the past, the other to the future—seeing this as the essential difference between them.[43] This is not quite right—Wells wrote, for instance, a set of 'Stories of the Stone Age' in the 1890s, dramatizing the transition from Palaeolithic to Neolithic culture—but there are indeed fundamental differences between Machen's creative exploitation of deep time and its uses in science fiction. This can be seen quite clearly by simply comparing two subhuman, subterranean races, superficially not dissimilar, which appeared in works of British popular fiction in the same year, 1895: Wells's Morlocks (in *The Time Machine*) and Machen's Little People (in 'The Shining Pyramid', 'The Red Hand', and *The Three Impostors*). While the former are the product of Darwinian evolution, descended from men over the span of hundreds of thousands of years, the latter are, as another of Machen's ethnologists puts it, 'unchanged and unchangeable', perennially 'repeating the evil of Gothic legend' (p. 137)—perpetuating the same rites, propagating the same symbols—throughout the ages. True, Professor Gregg, in a sop to the Darwinian idiom, suggests that they have 'fallen out of the grand march of evolution' (p. 136), but the enduring impression Machen leaves is of an utterly changeless evil, coeval with the geologic timescale itself; the 'chronotope' of these stories, as Russian critic Mikhail Bakhtin would have put it, suggests the presence of a *deep* but not *evolutionary* time (in 'The Red Hand' Dyson, contemplating the inscriptions on one of the Little People's tablets, is struck by 'an impression of vast and far-off ages, and of a living being that had touched the stone with enigmas before the hills were formed, when the hard rocks still boiled with fervent heat' (p. 208); in 'The Novel of the Black Seal' Miss Lally reflects upon 'awful things done long ago, and forgotten before the hills were moulded into form' (p. 129)). Machen

---

[42] *Far Off Things*, 150.
[43] 'If Wells looked forward, Machen looked backward,' wrote William Francis Gekle (*Arthur Machen, Weaver of Fantasy* (Millbrook, NY, 1949), 55)—a phrase echoed later by Machen scholar Wesley Sweetser.

takes care, too, to draw an absolute, unbridgeable boundary line between the speech of these beings ('a jargon but little removed from the inarticulate noises of brute beasts') and that of humans, echoing the anti-Darwinian position of philologist Max Müller, who famously wrote, 'language is our Rubicon, and no brute will dare to cross it'.[44]

And yet. *They write.* These ostensible 'troglodytes' possess systems of symbolic inscription exactly akin to those associated with the first human civilizations (Machen makes pointed reference to Mesopotamian, Egyptian, and Hittite cultures), at just the moment in intellectual history when writing was being conceptualized as *the* defining marker of civilized man.[45] They engrave their 'hieroglyphics' on seals of black stone, and scrawl them with bits of red earth on limestone rocks in Monmouthshire (aeons later, yet 'without alteration of any kind'; they are radically static culturally as well as racially). In one story Machen describes 'a kind of cuneiform character, a good deal altered'; in another, an elaborate system of 'fantastic figures, spirals and whorls' (pp. 139, 208). And this calculated blending of Neolithic and Postlithic cultural forms, and their backwards projection into the fathomless deeps of geologic time, is a good example of the kind of unsettling effect Machen sought to produce in these deep Gothic tales. The chief horror of Darwinism lies in its reminder that we come from beasts, its intimation that 'underneath it all' the respectable vicar or barrister is a savage. But Machen travesties the very categories that were emerging within Victorian intellectual culture, historiography in particular, to distinguish 'civilized' from 'savage', 'history' from 'prehistory' (and both of these from what came before). He articulates, in other words, the 'deep history' which the later Victorian era was keen to repress.[46]

### 'To the Nth and to Infinity'

In the *fin-de-siècle* fictions which earned Machen a measure of evanescent notoriety, he may, again, have sometimes gestured at horrors too awful to be named, but he can hardly be accused of denying his readers horrors of a more explicit, and graphic, nature as well. His 'transmutations'

---

[44] *Lectures on the Science of Language* (London, 1885), i. 403.

[45] There is much more that might be said about Machen's fascinatingly, instructively overdetermined (and, in the context of modern horror and fantasy fiction, extremely influential) Little People. For a brief discussion of their relationship to contemporaneous ideas about race, see explanatory note to p. 240.

[46] See Aaron Worth, 'Arthur Machen and the Horrors of Deep History', *Victorian Literature and Culture* 40/1 (2012), 215–27.

(the subtitle of *The Three Impostors*) of the human form—his depictions of corporeal corruption and deliquescence, of extreme torture, and other figured 'ruinations of the human subject' (in Kelly Hurley's phrase)[47]—evoke shock, disgust, and visceral fear, pointing the way unflinchingly to our contemporary genre of 'body horror'. Yet even in his earlier writings—'The Lost Club' is one example—one can detect another, subtler modality of unease, one which would help to lend a shared, distinctive tone to a number of his later stories in particular, and which often appears in Machen's descriptions of London. The keynote here is one of dislocation, defamiliarization, and dread, rather than acute terror and revulsion. This is the Machen of labyrinthine urban spaces, of uncanny repetition, of bounded infinities; the Machen, perhaps most of all, of the alternate, the parallel, the counterfactual, the lost.

It is a note that has, for us, a distinctly modern, or postmodern, sound, as in an early article he wrote for the *Evening News* and later summarized in *Things Near and Far*:

I said the chief horror of the modern street was not to be sought in the poverty of the design . . . but in the fact that in the street of to-day each house is a replica of the other, so that the effect to the eye is, if the street be long enough, the prolongation of one house to infinity, in an endless series of repetitions. And I pointed out that even if you admired some particular picture or statue immensely, it would be rather awful to traverse a long gallery in which the picture or the statue were repeated again and again as far as the eye could see.[48]

If such passages as this seem to anticipate the imaginative world of Jorge Luis Borges, it is no accident; the Argentine writer whom David Foster Wallace called 'the great bridge between modernism and postmodernism' counted Machen among his influences.[49] Indeed, Machen's impact on postmodern literature, if only through his impact on Borges, has yet to be fully explored. For both writers, the figure of the labyrinth

---

[47] *Gothic Body*, 3.      [48] *Things Near and Far*, 134–5.

[49] Machen's idea of the 'awfulness' of infinite repetition calls to mind, for instance, Borges's conception of Otto Dietrich zur Linde, the Nazi commandant in 'Deutsches Requiem': 'I had realized many years before I met David Jerusalem that everything in the world can be the seed of a possible Hell; a face, a word, a compass, an advertisement for cigarettes—anything can drive a person insane if that person cannot manage to put it out of his mind. Wouldn't a man be mad if he constantly had before his mind's eye the map of Hungary?' *Collected Fictions* (New York, 1998), 232. In his recent discussion of Machen's treatment of the city in *The Hill of Dreams*, Kostas Boyiopoulos invokes the idea of a 'Borgesian *regressus in infinitum*'. ' "The Serried Maze": Terrain, Consciousness and Textuality in Machen's *The Hill of Dreams*', *Victoriographies* 3/1 (2013), 56.

served as a master-trope; both, too, were fascinated with the theme of 'forking paths', in Borges's phrase.[50] In his (itself digressive, reflexive, furcating) book *The London Adventure* Machen would imaginatively populate an entire district of the metropolis, a kind of parallel neighbourhood, with those whose lives had taken a 'wrong' turn:

Here live, I know, the people who are a little aside from all our tracks, and, perhaps some of them have a wisdom of their own or a folly of their own which differs from all our common systems of sapience or stultification. . . . I always look upon this strange, unknown region as the country of the people who have lost their way. . . . I am sure that they are all secret people who live there, to the east of the Gray's Inn Road; secret and severed people. . .[51]

Forking paths and parallel worlds become especially prominent themes in the stories from Machen's last creative period. In 'Out of the Picture', for instance, we encounter a painter whose response to what he sees as the fatuities of modernism is to return, creatively, to the eighteenth century—to one of the branching points in the history of Western art—and from there to take an alternate path forward. Elsewhere Machen explores the prospect of discrete, multiple worlds, and the disconcerting possibility of their intrusion into our own—a theme which has since become a commonplace in science fiction and fantasy, as well as more 'literary' fictions. 'N' is about a parallel reality that can be glimpsed, under certain circumstances, from within the London suburb (as it then was) of Stoke Newington, through a process which Machen, borrowing a term from Christian theology, calls 'a perichoresis, an interpenetration'. This particular world appears as a paradise; but Machen hints that there are others, less pleasant. The story ends as one character, comfortably seated in 'the very heart of London', is struck with a disagreeable thought:

'. . . It is possible, indeed, that we three are now sitting among desolate rocks, by bitter streams.
    . . . And with what companions?' (p. 320)

Written shortly after 'N', the poignant 'The Tree of Life' displays Machen's penchant for articulating counterfactual variants of the reality we know. The story begins prosaically enough, with the young invalid Teilo Morgan talking with his agent about potential improvements to his estate. Only gradually does the reader become aware that his proposed

---

[50] His celebrated story 'El jardin de senderos que se bifurcan', written in 1941, would first appear in English eight months after Machen's death.

[51] *London Adventure*, pp. 158, 160–1.

innovations are insane (there is to be cultivation of eggplants (auber-gines) and arbor vitae, with 'zebras for haulage'); the estate, which had indeed once belonged to his family, is now a madhouse. Yet it is far from clear that Teilo's fantasies are to be understood as lunacy *tout court* (and not only because Machen had himself once advocated the British culti-vation of eggplants[52]); he has, like the denizens of Machen's secret London, 'a wisdom of [his] own or a folly of [his] own'. As a young boy Teilo had been stricken with a brain illness, which changed him utterly. A tutor is hired to humour him:

And . . . young Teilo nearly drove the poor man off his head. He was far sharper in a way than he'd ever been. . . . But then the twist in the brain would come out. Mathematics brilliant; and at the end of the lesson he'd frighten that tutor of his with a new theory of figures, some notion of the figures that we don't know of, the numbers that are between the others, something rather more than one and less than two, and so forth. It was the same with everything: there was the Secret Conquest of England a hundred years ago, that nobody was allowed to mention, and the squares that were always changing their shape in geometry, and the great continent that was hidden because Africa was on top of it, so that you couldn't see it. Then, when it came to the classics, there were fresh cases for the nouns and new moods for the verbs: and all the rest of it. (p. 334)

The phrase 'Tree of Life' refers, among other things, to a Kabbalistic figure, an arrangement of 'Sephiroth [which] tell in a kind of magic shorthand the whole history and mystery of man and all the worlds'.[53] In which of these worlds, we may ask, was Teilo vouchsafed his knowledge of an alternate mathematics, historiography, geography, and grammar?

Machen's fascination with parallel worlds or dimensions shows the convergence of many sources, Christianity and Platonism among them (even such tales as 'Pan' are premised upon the existence of a spiritual world 'beyond the veil'). There are possible antecedents to be found, too, in his favourite reading: the tale of Buluqiya in his beloved *Arabian Nights* has been invoked as an early example of a parallel-worlds fan-tasy, and Isaac D'Israeli and Richard Whately were among the first to explore the theme of counterfactual historiography.[54] Esoteric litera-ture certainly makes a conceptual contribution to 'The Tree of Life' at least. Machen was also intrigued—despite his avowed mathematical

---

[52] Reynolds and Charlton, *Arthur Machen*, 156.
[53] *Things Near and Far*, 30.
[54] D'Israeli's 'Of a History of Events Which Have Not Happened' appeared in *Curi-osities of Literature*, 2nd series (1824), which the young Machen certainly read; Whately, whose *Elements of Logic* had a strong influence on Machen, had written the playful 'Historic Doubts relative to Napoleon Buonaparte' in 1819.

'incompetence'—by the multidimensional speculations of those initiated into the mysteries of what he called 'the high geometry'. He knew (and mentions in *The Terror*) Edwin A. Abbott's pioneering novel of parallel worlds *Flatland* (1884); in *The London Adventure* he writes: 'For we, it is true, live in an illusory world, but there are other spheres of deception, beyond ours, and of a different order . . . the geometers tell us that there is a fourth dimension beyond our three, and so on, as I understand, to the *nth* and to infinity'—perhaps the significance of the cryptic title 'N' lies in that '*nth*'?[55]

Yet it is difficult not to assign some part to Machen's personal ambivalence about his literary achievements as well, one which led him to ruminate about paths not taken, or paths, as he seemed to believe, he was not capable of taking. He was haunted by the gap between vision and execution, the ideal and the real—by a sense of the writer he might have been. Indeed, if Machen had been permitted a glimpse of a world in which he had been transmuted into a 'classic', with his 'shilling shocker' 'Pan' included in a series alongside the masters he revered, he would surely have thought it the most improbable future imaginable. Modern readers of weird fiction, for their part, can be thankful for the particular sequence of forkings in Machen's path which led him to London, unqualified for any vocation but the one he made for himself, in poverty and solitude. If, for instance, the Revd John Edward Jones had been able to send his son to Oxford, some smallish congregation in Monmouthshire might well have been edified by decades of lyrical, allusive sermons, known locally for their unusually vivid depictions of sin, death, and the punishments of hell. But the paths traced by the literature of fear and the uncanny, throughout the twentieth century and beyond, would have been profoundly different—and infinitely less interesting.

[55] *London Adventure*, 126.

# NOTE ON THE TEXT

THE main priority in assembling this collection has been to include as much of Machen's seminal horror fiction from the 1890s as possible, as it originally appeared (hence the inclusion of *The Three Impostors* complete, rather than harvested for individual stories as is usually done), and complemented by seldom-published pieces from this period which throw additional light on these better-known works. But Machen's later fiction is also represented—by two Great War fantasies and a quartet of tales from the 1930s—so that readers can see how he both revisited favourite themes and engaged creatively with the cultural and historical currents of the new century. The texts of all stories have been taken from their first appearance in book form (with earlier periodical appearance, where applicable, discussed in the Explanatory Notes), except in two cases ('The Lost Club' and 'The Shining Pyramid'), where a later but superior edition has been preferred.

# SELECT BIBLIOGRAPHY

## Biography

Gawsworth, John, *The Life of Arthur Machen*, ed. Roger Dobson (Carlton, OR, 2005). (This biography by Machen's friend was written in the 1930s but not published until 2005; it is well worth reading and contains much material not easily available elsewhere, but readers should begin with Machen's own autobiographical books (which are excellent), from which Gawsworth sometimes transcribes verbatim.)

Michael, D. P. M., *Arthur Machen* (Cardiff, 1971). (Very short contribution to *Writers of Wales* series.)

Reynolds, Aidan, and Charlton, William, *Arthur Machen: A Short Account of His Life and Work* (London, 1963).

Valentine, Mark, *Arthur Machen* (Bridgend, 1995).

## Bibliography

Danielson, Henry, *Arthur Machen: A Bibliography* (1923; New York, 1970). (Contains valuable annotations by Machen himself, though it necessarily breaks off in 1922, with Machen's *Far Off Things*.)

Goldstone, Adrian, and Sweetser, Wesley, *A Bibliography of Arthur Machen* (1965; New York, 1973). (Indispensable to anyone writing about Machen.)

## Critical Studies

Boyiopoulos, Kostas, '"The Serried Maze": Terrain, Consciousness and Textuality in Machen's *The Hill of Dreams*', *Victoriographies* 3/1 (2013), 46–63.

Caleb, Amanda Mordavsky, '"A City of Nightmares": Suburban Anxiety in Arthur Machen's London Gothic', in Lawrence Phillips and Anne Witchard (eds.), *London Gothic: Place, Space and the Gothic Imagination* (London, 2010), 41–9.

De Cicco, Mark, '"More than Human": The Queer Occult Explorer of the Fin-de-Siècle', *Journal of the Fantastic in the Arts* 23/1 (2012), 4–24.

Eckersley, Adrian, 'A Theme in the Early Work of Arthur Machen: "Degeneration"', *ELT* 35/3 (January 1992), 277–87.

Ferguson, Christine, 'Reading with the Occultists: Arthur Machen, A. E. Waite, and the Ecstasies of Popular Fiction', *Journal of Victorian Culture* 21/1 (2016), 40–55.

Forlini, Stefania, 'Modern Narratives and Decadent Things in Arthur Machen's *The Three Impostors*', *ELT* 55/4 (2012), 479–98.

Gekle, William Francis, *Arthur Machen: Weaver of Fantasy* (Millbrook, NY, 1949).

Hurley, Kelly, *The Gothic Body: Sexuality, Materialism, and Degeneration at the Fin de Siècle* (Cambridge, 1996).

Jackson, Kimberly, 'Non-Evolutionary Degeneration in Arthur Machen's Supernatural Tales', *Victorian Literature and Culture* 41/1 (2013), 125–35.

Jones, Darryl, 'Borderlands: Spiritualism and the Occult in Fin de Siècle and Edwardian Welsh and Irish Horror', *Irish Studies Review* 17/1 (2009), 31–44.

Joshi, S. T., *The Weird Tale: Arthur Machen, Lord Dunsany, Algernon Blackwood, Ambrose Bierce, H. P. Lovecraft* (Austin, 1990).

Karschay, Stephan, *Degeneration, Normativity and the Gothic at the Fin de Siècle* (New York, 2015).

Leslie-McCarthy, Sage, 'Re-vitalizing the Little People: Arthur Machen's Tales of the Remnant Races', *Australasian Victorian Studies Journal* 11 (2005), 65–78.

Lovatt, Gabriel, 'From Experiment to Epidemic: Embodiment in the Decadent Modernism of Arthur Machen's "The Great God Pan" and "The Inmost Light"', *Mosaic* 49/1 (2016), 19–35.

McCann, Andrew, *Popular Literature, Authorship and the Occult in Late Victorian Britain* (Cambridge, 2014).

Milbank, Alison, 'Huysmans, Machen and the Gothic Grotesque; Or the Way Up Is the Way Down', in Avril Horner and Sue Zlosnik (eds.), *Le Gothic: Influences and Appropriations in Europe and America* (New York, 2008), 83–99.

Rebry, Natasha, '"A Slight Lesion in the Grey Matter": The Gothic Brain in Arthur Machen's *The Great God Pan*', *Horror Studies* 7/1 (2016), 9–24.

Silver, Carole, *A Strange and Secret Peoples: Fairies and Victorian Consciousness* (Oxford, 1999).

Simons, John, 'Horror in the 1890s: The Case of Arthur Machen', in Clive Bloom (ed.), *Creepers: British Horror & Fantasy in the Twentieth Century* (London, 1993), 35–46.

Sweetser, Wesley D., *Arthur Machen* (New York, 1964).

Trotter, David, Introduction to *The Three Impostors* (London, 1995).

Worth, Aaron, 'Arthur Machen and the Horrors of Deep History', *Victorian Literature and Culture* 40/1 (2012), 215–27.

### Further Reading in Oxford World's Classics

Doyle, Arthur Conan, *Gothic Tales*, ed. Darryl Jones.

James, M. R., *Collected Ghost Stories*, ed. Darryl Jones.

*Late Victorian Gothic Tales*, ed. Roger Luckhurst.

Lovecraft, H. P., *The Classic Horror Stories*, ed. Roger Luckhurst.

Wells, H. G., *The Time Machine*, ed. Roger Luckhurst.

# A CHRONOLOGY OF ARTHUR MACHEN

1863   (3 Mar.) Arthur Llewellyn Jones born in Caerleon, in Monmouthshire, Wales, the child of the Revd John Edward Jones and Janet Robina Jones (née Machen).

1874–80   The young Machen boards at Hereford Cathedral School, where he receives a sound classical education. Here he also learns French, laying the groundwork for his later work translating French classics into English.

1880   First visits London, to prepare for examination for the Royal College of Surgeons, which he fails; returns to Wales.

1881   Machen's first work to appear in print, the self-published poem *Eleusinia*. A 'horrible production', as he later called it. Returns to London to prepare for a journalistic career, for which purpose he attempts to learn shorthand. For several years he lives in poverty, wandering the metropolis as he had done the Welsh countryside, and earning a precarious living as a tutor, cataloguer, and translator.

1884   Machen's first book, *The Anatomy of Tobacco*, published by George Redway.

1885   Reads through a substantial library of occult works to prepare a catalogue; death of his mother.

1886   The first of Machen's translations appears: *The Heptameron* of Marguerite de Navarre, which he had begun in 1884.

1887   Marries Amy Hogg; death of his father.

1888   Publishes *The Chronicle of Clemendy*.

1889   Translates *Le Moyen de parvenir*, a seventeenth-century work by François Béroalde de Verville, and has difficulty finding a publisher.

1890   Publishes short stories including 'The Lost Club' and 'A Double Return'; begins acquaintance with Oscar Wilde, who praised the latter tale as having 'fluttered the dovecotes'. Two other pieces from this year would later be incorporated into 'The Great God Pan' and *A Fragment of Life* respectively.

1891   Moves with his wife to Northend, in Buckinghamshire. Here he would complete 'The Great God Pan', and also write 'The Inmost Light', which was commissioned for an annual by Mary Elizabeth Braddon, who 'refused it with lightning speed'.

1894   John Lane of The Bodley Head publishes *The Great God Pan and the Inmost Light* as part of its Keynotes Series (volume v). 'Pan' attracts a great deal of interest, and a great deal of criticism. Machen's translation of *The Memoirs of Casanova* also appears.

1895 Publication of *The Three Impostors*, also as part of the Keynotes Series (volume xix).

1897 Machen writes the prose poems that would eventually (1924) be published in book form as *Ornaments in Jade*. He also completes the novel that would become *The Hill of Dreams*; his ambition is to produce 'a *Robinson Crusoe* of the soul'.

1899 Writes 'The White People', and part of *A Fragment of Life*. His writing life is interrupted by the death of his first wife, Amelia Machen.

1900 Joins the Rosicrucian Order of the Golden Dawn, a secret society whose members included W. B. Yeats and Alastair Crowley; upon initiation he takes the name 'Frater Avallaunius'.

1901 At the age of 38, Machen becomes an actor, joining the Benson Shakespeare Repertory Company.

1902 Machen's work of literary criticism, *Hieroglyphics*, is published by Grant Richards.

1903 (23 June) Marries Dorothie Purefoy Hudleston.

1906 Publication by Grant Richards of *The House of Souls*, a major collection of Machen's work including *A Fragment of Life*, 'The White People', 'The Great God Pan', 'The Inmost Light', a slightly abridged and revised version of *The Three Impostors*, and 'The Red Hand', with cover and frontispiece designed by Sidney H. Sime.

1907 Begins to write *The Secret Glory*; publishes related articles on the Sangraal.

1910 Begins new career as a journalist for the *Evening News*.

1914 First appearance, in the pages of the *Evening News*, of the stories 'The Bowmen' and 'The Soldiers' Rest'; together with 'The Monstrance' and 'The Dazzling Light' these would be published in book form in 1915 as *The Angels of Mons and Other Legends of the War*.

1915 Publishes *The Great Return*.

1916 Serialization of 'The Great Terror' in the *Evening News* (16–31 October); the novel would be published in book form in 1917, as *The Terror*, by Duckworth & Co.; a severe abridgment ('The Coming of the Terror') would also appear in 1917.

1918 Vincent Starrett writes *Arthur Machen: Novelist of Ecstasy and Sin*, a work which helps to fuel a wave of American enthusiasm for Machen's work.

1922 Beginning of what Machen's friend and biographer John Gawsworth would call 'the boom' in interest in Machen and his work. Publication of *The Secret Glory* by Martin Secker in London, and the first of his autobiographies, *Far Off Things*, by both Secker and Alfred A. Knopf in New York; the two publishers would issue parallel series of Machen's collected works on both sides of the Atlantic.

1923 Publication of *Things Near and Far* (the sequel to *Far Off Things*), as well as the first of two collections (this one by Covici-McGee, in Chicago), very different in content, entitled *The Shining Pyramid*.

1924 The third volume of Machen's autobiographical trilogy, *The London Adventure*, appears; also a collection of negative reviews of his work (*Precious Balms*) and a slender volume of prose poems written in 1897, *Ornaments in Jade*.

1925 Martin Secker publishes the second Machen collection to bear the title *The Shining Pyramid*; a quarrel arises over publication rights to story and title.

1926 Publication of *Dreads and Drolls*, a collection of articles which had originally appeared in the *London Graphic* during the previous year. Also *Notes and Queries*, a book of articles from *T.P.'s Weekly*, first published between 1908 and 1910.

1933 Machen publishes his last novel, *The Green Round*.

1936 Two new collections of Machen's short fiction appear: the first, *The Cosy Room*, is made up of previously published material, with the exception of the newly composed 'N'; all six stories in *The Children of The Pool* are new.

1946 Penguin Books issues a new selection of Machen's work, entitled *Holy Terrors*.

1947 (15 Dec.) Machen dies in St Joseph's Nursing Home, Beaconsfield.

1948 Publication of *Tales of Horror and the Supernatural*, with an introduction by Philip Van Doren Stern.

# THE GREAT GOD PAN
# AND OTHER HORROR STORIES

# THE LOST CLUB

ONE hot afternoon in August a gorgeous young gentleman, one would say the last of his race in London, set out from the Circus end, and proceeded to stroll along the lonely expanse of Piccadilly Deserta.* True to the traditions of his race, faithful even in the wilderness, he had not bated one jot or tittle of the regulation equipage; a glorious red-and-yellow blossom in his woolly and exquisitely-cut frock coat proclaimed him a true son of the carnation;* hat and boots and chin were all polished to the highest pitch; though there had not been rain for many weeks his trouser-ends were duly turned up, and the poise of the gold-headed cane was in itself a liberal education. But ah! the heavy changes since June, when the leaves glanced green in the sunlit air, and the club windows were filled, and the hansoms flashed in long processions through the streets, and girls smiled from every carriage. The young man sighed; he thought of the quiet little evenings at the Phœnix, of encounters of the Row, of the drive to Hurlingham,* and many pleasant dinners in joyous company. Then he glanced up and saw a bus,* half-empty, slowly lumbering along the middle of the street, and in front of the 'White Horse Cellars'* a four-wheeler had stopped still (the driver was asleep on his seat), and in the 'Badminton'* the blinds were down. He half expected to see the Briar Rose trailing gracefully over the Hotel Cosmopole; certainly the Beauty, if such a thing were left in Piccadilly, was fast asleep.*

Absorbed in these mournful reflections, the hapless Johnny* strolled on without observing that an exact duplicate of himself was advancing on the same pavement from the opposite direction; save that the inevitable carnation was salmon colour, and the cane a silver-headed one, instruments of great magnifying power would have been required to discriminate between them. The two met; each raised his eyes simultaneously at the strange sight of a well-dressed man, and each adjured the same old-world deity.

'By Jove! old man, what the deuce are you doing here?'

The gentleman who had advanced from the direction of Hyde Park Corner was the first to answer.

'Well, to tell the truth, Austin, I am detained in town on—ah—legal business. But how is it you are not in Scotland?'

'Well, it's curious; but the fact is, I have legal business in town also.'

'You don't say so? Great nuisance, ain't it? But these things must be seen to, or a fellow finds himself in no end of a mess, don't you know.'

'He does, by Jove! That's what I thought.'

Mr Austin relapsed into silence for a few moments.

'And where are you off to, Phillipps?'

The conversation had passed with the utmost gravity on both sides. At the joint mention of legal business, it was true a slight twinkle had passed across their eyes, but the ordinary observer would have said that the weight of ages rested on those unruffled brows.

'I really couldn't say. I thought of having a quiet dinner at Azario's.* The Badminton is closed, you know, for repairs or somethin', and I can't stand the Junior Wilton.* Come along with me, and let's dine together.'

'By Jove! I think I will. I thought of calling on my solicitor, but I dare say he can wait.'

'Ah! I should think he could. We'll have some of that Italian wine—stuff in salad oil flasks—you know what I mean.'

The pair solemnly wheeled round, and solemnly paced towards the Circus, meditating, doubtless, on many things. The dinner in the little restaurant pleased them with a grave pleasure, as did the Chianti, of which they drank a good deal too much; 'Quite a light wine, you know,' said Phillipps, and Austin agreed with him, so they emptied a quart flask between them, and finished up with a couple of glasses apiece of Green Chartreuse.* As they came out into the quiet street smoking vast cigars, the two slaves to duty and 'legal business' felt a dreamy delight in all things, the street glimmered full of fantasy in the dim light of the lamps, and a single star shining in the clear sky above seemed to Austin of exactly the same colour as Green Chartreuse. Phillipps agreed with him. 'You know, old fellow,' he said, 'there are times when a fellow feels all sorts of strange things—you know, the sort of things they put in magazines, don't you know, and novels. By Jove, Austin, old man, I feel as if I could write a novel myself.'

They wandered aimlessly on, not quite knowing where they were going, turning from one street to another, and discoursing in a maudlin strain. A great cloud had been slowly moving up from the south, darkening the sky, and suddenly it began to rain, at first slowly with great heavy drops, and then faster and faster in a pitiless, hissing shower; the gutters flooded over, and the furious drops danced up from the stones. The two walked on as fast as they could, whistling and calling 'Hansom!'* in vain; they were really getting very wet.

'Where the dickens are we?' said Phillipps. 'Confound it all, I don't know. We ought to be in Oxford Street.'

They walked on a little farther, when suddenly, to their great joy, they found a dry archway, leading into a dark passage or courtyard. They took shelter silently, too thankful and too wet to say anything. Austin looked at his hat; it was a wreck; and Phillipps shook himself feebly, like a tired terrier.

'What a beastly nuisance this is!' he muttered; 'I only wish I could see a hansom.'

Austin looked into the street; the rain was still falling in torrents; he looked up the passage, and noticed for the first time that it led to a great house, which towered grimly against the sky. It seemed all dark and gloomy, except that from some chink in a shutter a light shone out. He pointed it out to Phillipps, who stared vacantly about him, then exclaimed:

'Hang it! I know where we are now. At least, I don't exactly know, you know, but I once came by here with Wylliams, and he told me there was some club or somethin' down this passage; I don't recollect exactly what he said. Hullo! why, there goes Wylliams. I say, Wylliams, tell us where we are!'

A gentleman had brushed past them in the darkness and was walking fast down the passage. He heard his name and turned round, looking rather annoyed.

'Well, Phillipps, what do you want? Good evening, Austin; you seem rather wet, both of you.'

'I should think we were wet; got caught in the rain. Didn't you tell me once there was some club down here? I wish you'd take us in, if you're a member.'

Mr Wylliams looked steadfastly at the two forlorn young men for a moment, hesitated, and said:

'Well, gentlemen, you may come with me if you like. But I must impose a condition; that you both give me your word of honour never to mention the club, or anything that you see while you are in it, to any individual whatsoever.'

'Certainly not,' replied Austin; 'of course we shouldn't dream of doing so, should we, Phillipps?'

'No, no; go ahead, Wylliams, we'll keep it dark enough.'

The party moved slowly down the passage till they came to the house. It was very large and very old; it looked as though it might have been an embassy of the last century. Wylliams whistled, knocked twice at the door, and whistled again, and it was opened by a man in black.

'Friends of yours, Mr Wylliams?'

Wylliams nodded and they passed on.

'Now mind,' he whispered, as they paused at a door, 'you are not to recognize anybody, and nobody will recognize you.'

The two friends nodded, and the door was opened, and they entered a vast room, brilliantly lighted with electric lamps. Men were standing in knots, walking up and down, and smoking at little tables; it was just like any club smoking-room. Conversation was going on, but in a low murmur, and every now and then someone would stop talking, and look anxiously at a door at the other end of the room, and then turn round again. It was evident that they were waiting for someone or somebody. Austin and Phillipps were sitting on a sofa, lost in amazement; nearly every face was familiar to them. The flower of the Row was in that strange club-room; several young noblemen, a young fellow who had just come into an enormous fortune, three or four fashionable artists and literary men, an eminent actor, and a well-known canon. What could it mean? They were all supposed to be scattered far and wide over the habitable globe, and yet here they were. Suddenly there came a loud knock at the door; and every man started, and those who were sitting got up. A servant appeared.

'The President is awaiting you, gentlemen,' he said, and vanished.

One by one the members filed out, and Wylliams and the two guests brought up the rear. They found themselves in a room still larger than the first, but almost quite dark. The President sat at a long table and before him burned two candles, which barely lighted up his face. It was the famous Duke of Dartington, the largest landowner in England. As soon as the members had entered he said in a cold, hard voice, 'Gentlemen, you know our rules; the book is prepared. Whoever opens it at the black page is at the disposal of the committee and myself. We had better begin.' Someone began to read out the names in a low distinct voice, pausing after each name, and the member called came up to the table and opened at random the pages of a big folio volume that lay between the two candles. The gloomy light made it difficult to distinguish features, but Phillipps heard a groan beside him, and recognized an old friend. His face was working fearfully, the man was evidently in an agony of terror.

One by one the members opened the book; as each man did so he passed out by another door. At last there was only one left; it was Phillipps's friend. There was foam upon his lips as he passed up to the table, and his hand shook as he opened the leaves. Wylliams had passed out after whispering to the President, and had returned to his friends' side. He could hardly hold them back as the unfortunate man groaned in agony and leant against the table: he had opened the book at the black page.

'Kindly come with me, Mr D'Aubigny,' said the President, and they passed out together.

'We can go now,' said Wylliams, 'I think the rain has gone off. Remember your promise, gentlemen. You have been at a meeting of the Lost Club. You will never see that young man again. Good night.'

'It isn't murder, is it?' gasped Austin.

'Oh no, not at all. Mr D'Aubigny will, I hope, live for many years; he has disappeared. Good night; there's a hansom that will do for you.'

The two friends went to their homes in dead silence. They did not meet again for three weeks, and each thought the other looked ill and shaken. They walked drearily, with grave averted faces down Piccadilly, each afraid to begin the recollection of the terrible club. Of a sudden Phillipps stopped as if he had been shot. 'Look there, Austin,' he muttered, 'look at that.' The posters of the evening papers were spread out beside the pavement, and on one of them Austin saw in large blue letters, 'Mysterious disappearance of a Gentleman.' Austin bought a copy and turned over the leaves with shaking fingers till he found the brief paragraph:—

Mr St John D'Aubigny, of Stoke D'Aubigny, in Sussex, has disappeared under mysterious circumstances. Mr D'Aubigny was staying at Strathdoon, in Scotland, and came up to London, as it is stated, on business, on August 16th. It has been ascertained that he arrived safely at King's Cross, and drove to Piccadilly Circus, where he got out. It is said that he was last seen at the corner of Glasshouse Street, leading from Regent Street into Soho. Since the above date the unfortunate gentleman, who was much liked in London society, has not been heard of. Mr D'Aubigny was to have been married in September. The police are extremely reticent.

'Good God! Austin, this is dreadful. You remember the date. Poor fellow, poor fellow!'

'Phillipps, I think I shall go home.'

D'Aubigny was never heard of again. But the strangest part of the story remains to be told. The two friends called upon Wylliams, and charged him with being a member of the Lost Club, and an accomplice in the fate of D'Aubigny. The placid Mr Wylliams at first stared at the two pale, earnest faces, and finally roared with laughter.

'My dear fellows, what on earth are you talking about? I never heard such a cock-and-bull story in my life. As you say, Phillipps, I once pointed out to you a house said to be a club, as we were walking through Soho; but that was a low gambling club, frequented by German waiters. I am afraid the fact is that Azario's Chianti was rather too strong for you. However, I will try to convince you of your mistake.'

Wylliams forthwith summoned his man, who swore that he and his master were in Cairo during the whole of August, and offered to produce the hotel bills. Phillipps shook his head, and they went away. Their next step was to try and find the archway where they had taken shelter, and after a good deal of trouble they succeeded. They knocked at the door of the gloomy house, whistling as Wylliams had done. They were admitted by a respectable mechanic in a white apron, who was evidently astonished at the whistle; in fact he was inclined to suspect the influence of a 'drop too much.' The place was a billiard-table factory, and had been so (as far as they learnt in the neighbourhood) for many years. The rooms must once have been large and magnificent, but most of them had been divided into three or four separate workshops by wooden partitions.

Phillipps sighed; he could do no more for his lost friend; but both he and Austin remained unconvinced. In justice to Mr Wylliams, it must be stated that Lord Henry Harcourt assured Phillipps that he had seen Wylliams in Cairo about the middle of August; he thought, but could not be sure, on the 16th; and also, that the recent disappearance of some well-known men about town are patent of explanations which would exclude the agency of the Lost Club.

# THE GREAT GOD PAN

## THE EXPERIMENT

'I AM glad you came, Clarke; very glad indeed. I was not sure you could spare the time.'

'I was able to make arrangements for a few days; things are not very lively just now. But have you no misgivings, Raymond? Is it absolutely safe?'

The two men were slowly pacing the terrace in front of Dr Raymond's house. The sun still hung above the western mountain-line, but it shone with a dull red glow that cast no shadows, and all the air was quiet; a sweet breath came from the great wood on the hillside above, and with it, at intervals, the soft murmuring call of the wild doves. Below, in the long lovely valley, the river wound in and out between the lonely hills, and, as the sun hovered and vanished into the west, a faint mist, pure white, began to rise from the banks. Dr Raymond turned sharply to his friend.

'Safe? Of course it is. In itself the operation is a perfectly simple one; any surgeon could do it.'

'And there is no danger at any other stage?'

'None; absolutely no physical danger whatever, I give you my word. You were always timid, Clarke, always; but you know my history. I have devoted myself to transcendental medicine for the last twenty years. I have heard myself called quack, and charlatan and impostor, but all the while I knew I was on the right path. Five years ago I reached the goal, and since then every day has been a preparation for what we shall do to-night.'

'I should like to believe it is all true.' Clarke knit his brows, and looked doubtfully at Dr Raymond. 'Are you perfectly sure, Raymond, that your theory is not a phantasmagoria*—a splendid vision, certainly, but a mere vision after all?'

Dr Raymond stopped in his walk and turned sharply. He was a middle-aged man, gaunt and thin, of a pale yellow complexion, but as he answered Clarke and faced him, there was a flush on his cheek.

'Look about you, Clarke. You see the mountain, and hill following after hill, as wave on wave, you see the woods and orchards, the fields of ripe corn, and the meadows reaching to the reed-beds by the river. You see me standing here beside you, and hear my voice; but I tell you that all these things—yes, from that star that has just shone out in the sky to the solid ground beneath our feet—I say that all these are but dreams and shadows: the shadows that hide the real world from our eyes. There *is* a real world, but it is beyond this glamour and this vision, beyond these "chases in Arras, dreams in a career,"* beyond them all as beyond a veil. I do not know whether any human being has ever lifted that veil; but I do know, Clarke, that you and I shall see it lifted this very night from before another's eyes. You may think all this strange nonsense; it may be strange, but it is true, and the ancients knew what lifting the veil means. They called it seeing the god Pan.'*

Clarke shivered; the white mist gathering over the river was chilly.

'It is wonderful indeed,' he said. 'We are standing on the brink of a strange world, Raymond, if what you say is true. I suppose the knife is absolutely necessary?'

'Yes; a slight lesion in the grey matter,* that is all; a trifling rearrangement of certain cells, a microscopical alteration that would escape the attention of ninety-nine brain specialists out of a hundred. I don't want to bother you with "shop," Clarke; I might give you a mass of technical detail which would sound very imposing, and would leave you as enlightened as you are now. But I suppose you have read, casually, in out-of-the-way corners of your paper, that immense strides have been made recently in the physiology of the brain. I saw a paragraph the other day about Digby's theory, and Browne Faber's discoveries.* Theories and discoveries! Where they are standing now, I stood fifteen years ago, and I need not tell you that I have not been standing still for the last fifteen years. It will be enough if I say that five years ago I made the discovery to which I alluded when I said that then I reached the goal. After years of labour, after years of toiling and groping in the dark, after days and nights of disappointment and sometimes of despair, in which I used now and then to tremble and grow cold with the thought that perhaps there were others seeking for what I sought, at last, after so long, a pang of sudden joy thrilled my soul, and I knew the long journey was at an end. By what seemed then and still seems a chance, the suggestion of a moment's idle thought followed up upon familiar lines and paths that I had tracked a hundred times already, the great truth burst upon me, and I saw, mapped out in lines of light a whole world, a sphere unknown; continents and islands, and great oceans in which no ship has sailed (to my belief) since a Man first lifted up his eyes and beheld the sun, and the stars of heaven, and the quiet earth beneath. You will think all this high-flown language, Clarke, but it is hard to be literal. And yet; I do not know whether what I am hinting at cannot be set forth in plain and homely terms. For instance, this world of ours is pretty well girded now with the telegraph wires and cables;* thought, with something less than the speed of thought, flashes from sunrise to sunset, from north to south, across the floods and the desert places. Suppose that an electrician of to-day were suddenly to perceive that he and his friends have merely been playing with pebbles and mistaking them for the foundations of the world; suppose that such a man saw uttermost space lie open before the current, and words of men flash forth to the sun and beyond the sun into the systems beyond, and the voices of articulate-speaking men* echo in the waste void that bounds our thought. As analogies go, that is a pretty good analogy of what I have done; you can understand now a little of what I felt as I stood here one evening; it was a summer evening, and the valley looked much as it does now; I stood here, and saw before me the unutterable, the unthinkable gulf that yawns profound between two worlds, the world of matter and the world of spirit; I saw the great empty deep stretch dim before me, and in that instant a bridge of light leapt from the earth to the unknown shore, and the abyss was spanned. You may look in Browne Faber's book, if you like, and you will find that to the present day men of science are unable to account for the presence, or to specify the functions of a certain group of nerve-cells in the brain. That group is, as it were, land to let, a mere waste place for fanciful theories. I am not in the position of Browne Faber and the specialists, I am perfectly instructed as to the possible functions of those nerve-centres in the scheme of things. With a touch I can bring them into play, with a touch, I say, I can set free the current, with a touch I can complete the communication between this world of sense and——we shall be able to finish the sentence later on. Yes, the knife is necessary; but think what that knife will effect. It will level utterly the solid wall of sense, and probably, for the first time since man was made, a spirit will gaze on a spirit-world. Clarke, Mary will see the god Pan!'

'But you remember what you wrote to me? I thought it would be requisite that she——'

He whispered the rest into the doctor's ear.

'Not at all, not at all. That is nonsense, I assure you. Indeed, it is better as it is; I am quite certain of that.'

'Consider the matter well, Raymond. It's a great responsibility. Something might go wrong; you would be a miserable man for the rest of your days.'

'No, I think not, even if the worst happened. As you know, I rescued

Mary from the gutter, and from almost certain starvation, when she was
a child; I think her life is mine, to use as I see fit. Come, it is getting late;
we had better go in.'

Dr Raymond led the way into the house, through the hall, and down
a long dark passage. He took a key from his pocket and opened a heavy
door, and motioned Clarke into his laboratory. It had once been a bil-
liard-room, and was lighted by a glass dome in the centre of the ceiling,
whence there still shone a sad grey light on the figure of the doctor as
he lit a lamp with a heavy shade and placed it on a table in the middle
of the room.

Clarke looked about him. Scarcely a foot of wall remained bare; there
were shelves all around laden with bottles and phials of all shapes and
colours, and at one end stood a little Chippendale book-case. Raymond
pointed to this.

'You see that parchment Oswald Crollius?* He was one of the first to
show me the way, though I don't think he ever found it himself. That is
a strange saying of his: "In every grain of wheat there lies hidden the
soul of a star." '

There was not much of furniture in the laboratory. The table in the
centre, a stone slab with a drain in one corner, the two armchairs on
which Raymond and Clarke were sitting; that was all, except an odd-
looking chair at the furthest end of the room. Clarke looked at it, and
raised his eyebrows.

'Yes, that is the chair,' said Raymond. 'We may as well place it in
position.' He got up and wheeled the chair to the light, and began raising and lowering it, letting down the seat, setting the back at various
angles, and adjusting the foot-rest. It looked comfortable enough,
and Clarke passed his hand over the soft green velvet, as the doctor
manipulated the levers.

'Now, Clarke, make yourself quite comfortable. I have a couple of
hours' work before me; I was obliged to leave certain matters to the last.'

Raymond went to the stone slab, and Clarke watched him drearily as
he bent over a row of phials and lit the flame under the crucible. The
doctor had a small hand-lamp, shaded as the larger one, on a ledge
above his apparatus, and Clarke, who sat in the shadows, looked down
the great dreary room, wondering at the bizarre effects of brilliant light
and undefined darkness contrasting with one another. Soon he became
conscious of an odd odour, at first the merest suggestion of odour, in
the room; and as it grew more decided he felt surprised that he was not
reminded of the chemist's shop or the surgery. Clarke found himself
idly endeavouring to analyse the sensation, and, half conscious, he

began to think of a day, fifteen years ago, that he had spent in roaming through the woods and meadows near his old home. It was a burning day at the beginning of August, the heat had dimmed the outlines of all things and all distances with a faint mist, and people who observed the thermometer spoke of an abnormal register, of a temperature that was almost tropical. Strangely that wonderful hot day of 185– rose up in Clarke's imagination; the sense of dazzling all-pervading sunlight seemed to blot out the shadows and the lights of the laboratory, and he felt again the heated air beating in gusts about his face, saw the shimmer rising from the turf, and heard the myriad murmur of the summer.

'I hope the smell doesn't annoy you, Clarke; there's nothing unwholesome about it. It may make you a bit sleepy, that's all.'

Clarke heard the words quite distinctly, and knew that Raymond was speaking to him, but for the life of him he could not rouse himself from his lethargy. He could only think of the lonely walk he had taken fifteen years ago; it was his last look at the fields and woods he had known since he was a child, and now it all stood out in brilliant light, as a picture, before him. Above all there came to his nostrils the scent of summer, the smell of flowers mingled, and the odour of the woods, of cool shaded places, deep in the green depths, drawn forth by the sun's heat; and the scent of the good earth, lying as it were with arms stretched forth, and smiling lips, overpowered all. His fancies made him wander, as he had wandered long ago, from the fields into the wood, tracking a little path between the shining undergrowth of beech-trees; and the trickle of water dropping from the limestone rock sounded as a clear melody in the dream. Thoughts began to go astray and to mingle with other recollections; the beech-alley was transformed to a path beneath ilex-trees, and here and there a vine climbed from bough to bough, and sent up waving tendrils and drooped with purple grapes, and the sparse grey green leaves of a wild olive-tree stood out against the dark shadows of the ilex. Clarke, in the deep folds of dream, was conscious that the path from his father's house had led him into an undiscovered country, and he was wondering at the strangeness of it all, when suddenly, in place of the hum and murmur of the summer, an infinite silence seemed to fall on all things, and the wood was hushed, and for a moment of time he stood face to face there with a presence, that was neither man nor beast, neither the living nor the dead, but all things mingled, the form of all things but devoid of all form. And in that moment, the sacrament of body and soul was dissolved, and a voice seemed to cry 'let us go hence,' and then the darkness of darkness beyond the stars, the darkness of everlasting.

\*    \*    \*    \*    \*

When Clarke woke up with a start he saw Raymond pouring a few drops of some oily fluid into a green phial, which he stoppered tightly.

'You have been dozing,' he said, 'the journey must have tired you out. It is done now. I am going to fetch Mary; I shall be back in ten minutes.'

Clarke lay back in his chair and wondered. It seemed as if he had but passed from one dream into another. He half expected to see the walls of the laboratory melt and disappear, and to awake in London, shuddering at his own sleeping fancies. But at last the door opened, and the doctor returned, and behind him came a girl of about seventeen, dressed all in white. She was so beautiful that Clarke did not wonder at what the doctor had written to him. She was blushing now over face and neck and arms, but Raymond seemed unmoved.

'Mary,' he said, 'the time has come. You are quite free. Are you willing to trust yourself to me entirely?'

'Yes, dear.'

'You hear that, Clarke? You are my witness. Here is the chair, Mary. It is quite easy. Just sit in it and lean back. Are you ready?'

'Yes, dear, quite ready. Give me a kiss before you begin.'

The doctor stooped and kissed her mouth, kindly enough. 'Now shut your eyes,' he said. The girl closed her eyelids, as if she were tired, and longed for sleep, and Raymond held the green phial to her nostrils. Her face grew white, whiter than her dress; she struggled faintly, and then with the feeling of submission strong within her, crossed her arms upon her breast as a little child about to say her prayers. The bright light of the lamp beat full upon her, and Clarke watched changes fleeting over that face as the changes of the hills when the summer clouds float across the sun. And then she lay all white and still, and the doctor turned up one of her eyelids. She was quite unconscious. Raymond pressed hard on one of the levers and the chair instantly sank back. Clarke saw him cutting away a circle, like a tonsure, from her hair, and the lamp was moved nearer. Raymond took a small glittering instrument from a little case, and Clarke turned away shuddering. When he looked again the doctor was binding up the wound he had made.

'She will awake in five minutes.' Raymond was still perfectly cool. 'There is nothing further to be done; we can only wait.'

The minutes passed slowly; they could hear a slow, heavy ticking. There was an old clock in the passage. Clarke felt sick and faint; his knees shook beneath him, he could hardly stand.

Suddenly, as they watched, they heard a long-drawn sigh, and suddenly did the colour that had vanished return to the girl's cheeks, and suddenly her eyes opened. Clarke quailed before them. They shone with an awful light, looking far away, and a great wonder fell upon her face, and her hands stretched out as if to touch what was invisible; but in an instant the wonder faded, and gave place to the most awful terror. The muscles of her face were hideously convulsed, she shook from head to foot; the soul seemed struggling and shuddering within the house of flesh. It was a horrible sight, and Clarke rushed forward, as she fell shrieking to the floor.

Three days later Raymond took Clarke to Mary's bedside. She was lying wide-awake, rolling her head from side to side, and grinning vacantly.

'Yes,' said the doctor, still quite cool, 'it is a great pity; she is a hope-less idiot. However, it could not be helped; and, after all, she has seen the Great God Pan.'

## MR CLARKE'S MEMOIRS

Mr Clarke, the gentleman chosen by Dr Raymond to witness the strange experiment of the god Pan, was a person in whose character caution and curiosity were oddly mingled; in his sober moments he thought of the unusual and the eccentric with undisguised aversion, and yet, deep in his heart, there was a wide-eyed inquisitiveness with respect to all the more recondite and esoteric elements in the nature of men. The latter tendency had prevailed when he accepted Raymond's invitation, for though his considered judgment had always repudiated the doctor's theories as the wildest nonsense, yet he secretly hugged a belief in fantasy, and would have rejoiced to see that belief confirmed. The horrors that he witnessed in the dreary laboratory were to a certain extent salutary; he was conscious of being involved in an affair not altogether reputable, and for many years afterwards he clung bravely to the commonplace, and rejected all occasions of occult investigation. Indeed, on some homœopathic* principle, he for some time attended the séances of distinguished mediums, hoping that the clumsy tricks of these gentlemen would make him altogether disgusted with mysticism of every kind, but the remedy, though caustic, was not efficacious. Clarke knew that he still pined for the unseen, and little by little, the old passion began to reassert itself, as the face of Mary, shuddering and convulsed with an unknowable terror, faded slowly from his memory. Occupied all day in pursuits both serious and lucrative, the temptation to relax in the evening was too great, especially in the winter months, when the fire cast a warm glow over his snug bachelor apartment, and a bottle of some choice claret stood ready by his elbow. His dinner digested, he would make a brief pretence of reading the evening paper, but the mere catalogue of news soon palled upon him, and Clarke would find himself casting glances of warm desire in the direction of an old Japanese bureau, which stood at a pleasant distance from the hearth. Like a boy before a jam-closet, for a few minutes he would hover indecisive, but lust always prevailed, and Clarke ended by drawing up his chair, lighting a candle, and sitting down before the bureau. Its pigeon-holes and drawers teemed with documents on the most morbid subjects, and in the well reposed a large manuscript volume, in which he had painfully entered the gems of his collection. Clarke had a fine contempt for published literature; the most ghostly story ceased to interest him if it happened to be printed; his sole pleasure was in the reading, compiling, arranging, and rearranging what he called his 'Memoirs to prove the Existence of the Devil,' and engaged in this pursuit the evening seemed to fly and the night appeared too short.

On one particular evening, an ugly December night, black with fog, and raw with frost, Clarke hurried over his dinner, and scarcely deigned to observe his customary ritual of taking up the paper and laying it down again. He paced two or three times up and down the room, and opened the bureau, stood still a moment, and sat down. He leant back, absorbed in one of those dreams to which he was subject, and at length drew out his book, and opened it at the last entry. There were three or four pages densely covered with Clarke's round, set penmanship, and at the beginning he had written in a somewhat larger hand:

Singular Narrative told me by my Friend, Dr Phillips. He assures me that all the Facts related therein are strictly and wholly True, but refuses to give either the Surnames of the Persons concerned, or the Place where these Extraordinary Events occurred.

Mr Clarke began to read over the account for the tenth time, glancing now and then at the pencil notes he had made when it was told him by his friend. It was one of his humours to pride himself on a certain literary ability; he thought well of his style, and took pains in arranging the circumstances in dramatic order. He read the following story:

The persons concerned in this statement are Helen V., who, if she is still alive, must now be a woman of twenty-three, Rachel M., since deceased, who was a year younger than the above, and Trevor W., an imbecile, aged eighteen. These persons were at the period of the story

inhabitants of a village on the borders of Wales, a place of some importance in the time of the Roman occupation,* but now a scattered hamlet,
of not more than five hundred souls. It is situated on rising ground, about
six miles from the sea, and is sheltered by a large and picturesque forest.

Some eleven years ago, Helen V. came to the village under rather peculiar circumstances. It is understood that she, being an orphan, was adopted
in her infancy by a distant relative, who brought her up in his own house
till she was twelve years old. Thinking, however, that it would be better
for the child to have playmates of her own age, he advertised in several
local papers for a good home in a comfortable farm-house for a girl of
twelve, and this advertisement was answered by Mr R., a well-to-do
farmer in the above-mentioned village. His references proving satisfac-
tory, the gentleman sent his adopted daughter to Mr R., with a letter, in
which he stipulated that the girl should have a room to herself, and
stated that her guardians need be at no trouble in the matter of education, as she was already sufficiently educated for the position in life
which she would occupy. In fact, Mr R. was given to understand that
the girl was to be allowed to find her own occupations, and to spend her
time almost as she liked. Mr R. duly met her at the nearest station,
a town some seven miles away from his house, and seems to have remarked
nothing extraordinary about the child, except that she was reticent as to
her former life and her adopted father. She was, however, of a very different type from the inhabitants of the village; her skin was a pale, clear
olive, and her features were strongly marked, and of a somewhat foreign character. She appears to have settled down, easily enough, into
farm-house life, and became a favourite with the children, who sometimes went with her on her rambles in the forest, for this was her amusement. Mr R. states that he has known her go out by herself directly
after their early breakfast, and not return till after dusk, and that, feeling uneasy at a young girl being out alone for so many hours, he communicated with her adopted father, who replied in a brief note that
Helen must do as she chose. In the winter, when the forest paths are
impassable, she spent most of her time in her bed-room, where she
slept alone, according to the instructions of her relative. It was on one
of these expeditions to the forest, that the first of the singular incidents
with which this girl is connected occurred, the date being about a year
after her arrival at the village. The preceding winter had been remarkably
severe, the snow drifting to a great depth, and the frost continuing for
an unexampled period, and the summer following was as noteworthy
for its extreme heat. On one of the very hottest days in this summer,
Helen V. left the farm-house for one of her long rambles in the forest,

taking with her, as usual, some bread and meat for lunch. She was seen by some men in the fields making for the old Roman Road, a green causeway which traverses the highest part of the wood, and they were astonished to observe that the girl had taken off her hat, though the heat of the sun was already almost tropical. As it happened, a labourer, Joseph W. by name, was working in the forest near the Roman Road, and at twelve o'clock, his little son, Trevor, brought the man his dinner of bread and cheese. After the meal, the boy, who was about seven years old at the time, left his father at work, and, as he says, went to look for flowers in the wood, and the man, who could hear him shouting with delight over his discoveries, felt no uneasiness. Suddenly, however, he was horrified at hearing the most dreadful screams, evidently the result of great terror, proceeding from the direction in which his son had gone, and he hastily threw down his tools and ran to see what had happened. Tracing his path by the sound, he met the little boy who was running headlong, and was evidently terribly frightened, and on questioning him the man at last elicited that after picking a posy of flowers he felt tired, and lay down on the grass and fell asleep. He was suddenly awakened, as he stated, by a peculiar noise, a sort of singing he called it, and on peeping through the branches he saw Helen V. playing on the grass with a 'strange naked man,' whom he seemed unable to describe further. He said he felt dreadfully frightened, and ran away crying for his father. Joseph W. proceeded in the direction indicated by his son, and found Helen V. sitting on the grass in the middle of a glade or open space left by charcoal burners.* He angrily charged her with frightening his little boy, but she entirely denied the accusation and laughed at the child's story of a 'strange man,' to which he himself did not attach much credence. Joseph W. came to the conclusion that the boy had woke up with a sudden fright, as children sometimes do, but Trevor persisted in his story, and continued in such evident distress that at last his father took him home, hoping that his mother would be able to soothe him. For many weeks, however, the boy gave his parents much anxiety; he became nervous and strange in his manner, refusing to leave the cottage by himself, and constantly alarming the household by waking in the night with cries of 'the man in the wood! father! father!' In course of time, however, the impression seemed to have worn off, and about three months later he accompanied his father to the house of a gentleman in the neighbourhood, for whom Joseph W. occasionally did work. The man was shown into the study, and the little boy was left sitting in the hall, and a few minutes later, while the gentleman was giving W. his instructions, they were both horrified by a piercing shriek and the sound of a fall, and rushing out they found the child lying senseless on the floor, his face contorted with terror. The doctor was immediately summoned, and after some examination he pronounced the child to be suffering from a kind of fit, apparently produced by a sudden shock. The boy was taken to one of the bed-rooms, and after some time recovered consciousness, but only to pass into a condition described by the medical man as one of violent hysteria. The doctor exhibited a strong sedative, and in the course of two hours pronounced him fit to walk home, but in passing through the hall the paroxysms of fright returned and with additional violence. The father perceived that the child was pointing at some object, and heard the old cry, 'the man in the wood,' and looking in the direction indicated saw a stone head of grotesque appearance, which had been built into the wall above one of the doors. It seems that the owner of the house had recently made alterations in his premises, and on digging the foundations for some offices, the men had found a curious head, evidently of the Roman period, which had been placed in the hall in the manner described. The head is pronounced by the most experienced archæologists of the district to be that of a faun or satyr.*[1]

From whatever cause arising, this second shock seemed too severe for the boy Trevor, and at the present date he suffers from a weakness of intellect, which gives but little promise of amending. The matter caused a good deal of sensation at the time, and the girl Helen was closely questioned by Mr R., but to no purpose, she steadfastly denying that she had frightened or in any way molested Trevor.

The second event with which this girl's name is connected took place about six years ago, and is of a still more extraordinary character.

At the beginning of the summer of 188– Helen contracted a friendship of a peculiarly intimate character with Rachel M., the daughter of a prosperous farmer in the neighbourhood. This girl, who was a year younger than Helen, was considered by most people to be the prettier of the two, though Helen's features had to a great extent softened as she became older. The two girls, who were together on every available opportunity, presented a singular contrast, the one with her clear olive skin and almost Italian appearance, and the other of the proverbial red and white of our rural districts. It must be stated that the payments made to Mr R. for the maintenance of Helen were known in the village for their excessive liberality, and the impression was general that she

[1] Dr Phillips tells me that he has seen the head in question, and assures me that he has never received such a vivid presentment of intense evil.

would one day inherit a large sum of money from her relative. The parents of Rachel were therefore not averse to their daughter's friendship with the girl, and even encouraged the intimacy, though they now bitterly regret having done so. Helen still retained her extraordinary fondness for the forest, and on several occasions Rachel accompanied her, the two friends setting out early in the morning, and remaining in the wood till dusk. Once or twice after these excursions Mrs M. thought her daughter's manner rather peculiar; she seemed languid and dreamy, and as it has been expressed, 'different from herself,' but these peculiarities seem to have been thought too trifling for remark. One evening, however, after Rachel had come home, her mother heard a noise which sounded like suppressed weeping in the girl's room, and on going in found her lying, half-undressed, upon the bed, evidently in the greatest distress. As soon as she saw her mother, she exclaimed, 'Ah, mother, mother, why did you let me go to the forest with Helen?' Mrs M. was astonished at so strange a question, and proceeded to make inquiries. Rachel told her a wild story. She said——

Clarke closed the book with a snap, and turned his chair towards the fire. When his friend sat one evening in that very chair, and told his story, Clarke had interrupted him at a point a little subsequent to this, had cut short his words in a paroxysm of horror. 'My God!' he had exclaimed, 'think, think, what you are saying. It is too incredible, too monstrous; such things can never be in this quiet world, where men and women live and die, and struggle, and conquer, or maybe fail, and fall down under sorrow, and grieve and suffer strange fortunes for many a year; but not this, Phillips, not such things as this. There must be some explanation, some way out of the terror. Why, man, if such a case were possible, our earth would be a nightmare.'

But Phillips had told his story to the end, concluding:

'Her flight remains a mystery to this day; she vanished in broad sunlight, they saw her walking in a meadow, and a few moments later she was not there.'

Clarke tried to conceive the thing again, as he sat by the fire, and again his mind shuddered and shrank back, appalled before the sight of such awful, unspeakable elements enthroned as it were, and triumphant in human flesh. Before him stretched the long dim vista of the green causeway in the forest, as his friend had described it: he saw the swaying leaves and the quivering shadows on the grass, he saw the sunlight and the flowers, and far away, far in the long distance, the two figures moved towards him. One was Rachel, but the other?

Clarke had tried his best to disbelieve it all, but at the end of the account, as he had written it in his book, he had placed the inscription:

ET DIABOLUS INCARNATUS EST. ET HOMO FACTUS EST.*

## THE CITY OF RESURRECTIONS

'HERBERT! Good God! Is it possible?'

'Yes, my name's Herbert. I think I know your face too, but I don't remember your name. My memory is very queer.'

'Don't you recollect Villiers of Wadham?'*

'So it is, so it is. I beg your pardon, Villiers, I didn't think I was begging of an old college friend. Good-night.'

'My dear fellow, this haste is unnecessary. My rooms are close by, but we won't go there just yet. Suppose we walk up Shaftesbury Avenue a little way? But how in heaven's name have you come to this pass, Herbert?'

'It's a long story, Villiers, and a strange one too, but you can hear it if you like.'

'Come on, then. Take my arm, you don't seem very strong.'

The ill-assorted pair moved slowly up Rupert Street;* the one in dirty, evil-looking rags, and the other attired in the regulation uniform of a man about town, trim, glossy, and eminently well-to-do. Villiers had emerged from his restaurant after an excellent dinner of many courses, assisted by an ingratiating little flask of Chianti, and, in that frame of mind which was with him almost chronic, had delayed a moment by the door, peering round in the dimly-lighted street in search of those mysterious incidents and persons with which the streets of London teem in every quarter and at every hour. Villiers prided himself as a practised explorer of such obscure mazes and byways of London life, and in this unprofitable pursuit he displayed an assiduity which was worthy of more serious employment. Thus he stood beside the lamp-post surveying the passers-by with undisguised curiosity, and with that gravity only known to the systematic diner, had just enunciated in his mind the formula: 'London has been called the city of encounters; it is more than that, it is the city of Resurrections,' when these reflections were suddenly interrupted by a piteous whine at his elbow, and a deplorable appeal for alms. He looked round in some irritation, and with a sudden shock found himself confronted with the embodied proof of his somewhat stilted fancies. There, close beside him, his face altered and disfigured by poverty and disgrace, his body barely covered by greasy ill-fitting rags, stood his old friend Charles Herbert, who had matriculated on the same day as himself, and with whom he had been merry and wise for twelve revolving terms. Different occupations and varying interests had interrupted the friendship, and it was six years since Villiers had seen Herbert; and now he looked upon this wreck of a man with grief and dismay, mingled with a certain inquisitiveness as to what dreary chain of circumstance had dragged him down to such a doleful pass. Villiers felt together with compassion all the relish of the amateur in mysteries, and congratulated himself on his leisurely speculations outside the restaurant.

They walked on in silence for some time, and more than one passer-by stared in astonishment at the unaccustomed spectacle of a well-dressed man with an unmistakable beggar hanging on to his arm, and, observing this, Villiers led the way to an obscure street in Soho. Here he repeated his question.

'How on earth has it happened, Herbert? I always understood you would succeed to an excellent position in Dorsetshire. Did your father disinherit you? Surely not?'

'No, Villiers; I came into all the property at my poor father's death; he died a year after I left Oxford. He was a very good father to me, and I mourned his death sincerely enough. But you know what young men are; a few months later I came up to town and went a good deal into society. Of course I had excellent introductions, and I managed to enjoy myself very much in a harmless sort of way. I played a little, certainly, but never for heavy stakes, and the few bets I made on races brought me in money—only a few pounds, you know, but enough to pay for cigars and such petty pleasures. It was in my second season that the tide turned. Of course you have heard of my marriage?'

'No, I never heard anything about it.'

'Yes, I married, Villiers. I met a girl, a girl of the most wonderful and most strange beauty, at the house of some people whom I knew. I cannot tell you her age; I never knew it, but, so far as I can guess, I should think she must have been about nineteen when I made her acquaintance. My friends had come to know her at Florence; she told them she was an orphan, the child of an English father and an Italian mother, and she charmed them as she charmed me. The first time I saw her was at an evening party; I was standing by the door talking to a friend, when suddenly above the hum and babble of conversation I heard a voice, which seemed to thrill to my heart. She was singing an Italian song, I was introduced to her that evening, and in three months I married Helen. Villiers, that woman, if I can call her woman, corrupted my soul. The night of the wedding I found myself sitting in her bedroom in the hotel, listening to her talk. She was sitting up in bed, and I listened to her as she spoke in her beautiful voice, spoke of things which even now I would not dare whisper in blackest night, though I stood in the midst of a wilderness. You, Villiers, you may think you know life, and London, and what goes on, day and night, in this dreadful city; for all I can say you may have heard the talk of the vilest, but I tell you you can have no conception of what I know, no, not in your most fantastic, hideous dreams can you have imaged forth the faintest shadow of what I have heard—and seen. Yes, seen; I have seen the incredible, such horrors that even I myself sometimes stop in the middle of the street, and ask whether it is possible for a man to behold such things and live. In a year, Villiers, I was a ruined man, in body and soul,—in body and soul.'

'But your property, Herbert? You had land in Dorset.'

'I sold it all; the fields and woods, the dear old house—everything.'

'And the money?'

'She took it all from me.'

'And then left you?'

'Yes; she disappeared one night, I don't know where she went, but I am sure if I saw her again it would kill me. The rest of my story is of no interest; sordid misery, that is all. You may think, Villiers, that I have exaggerated and talked for effect; but I have not told you half. I could tell you certain things which would convince you, but you would never know a happy day again. You would pass the rest of your life, as I pass mine, a haunted man, a man who has seen hell.'

Villiers took the unfortunate man to his rooms, and gave him a meal. Herbert could eat little, and scarcely touched the glass of wine set before him. He sat moody and silent by the fire, and seemed relieved when Villiers sent him away with a small present of money.

'By the way, Herbert,' said Villiers, as they parted at the door, 'what was your wife's name? You said Helen, I think? Helen what?'

'The name she passed under when I met her was Helen Vaughan,* but what her real name was I can't say. I don't think she had a name. No, no, not in that sense. Only human beings have names, Villiers; I can't say any more. Good-bye; yes, I will not fail to call if I see any way in which you can help me. Good-night.'

The man went out into the bitter night, and Villiers returned to his fireside. There was something about Herbert which shocked him inexpressibly; not his poor rags or the marks which poverty had set upon his face, but rather an indefinite terror which hung about him like a mist. He had acknowledged that he himself was not devoid of blame, the

woman, he had avowed, had corrupted him body and soul, and Villiers
felt that this man, once his friend, had been an actor in scenes evil
beyond the power of words. His story needed no confirmation; he himself was the embodied proof of it. Villiers mused curiously over the
story he had heard, and wondered whether he had heard both the first
and the last of it. 'No,' he thought, 'certainly not the last, probably only
the beginning. A case like this is like a nest of Chinese boxes; you open
one after another and find a quainter workmanship in every box. Most
likely poor Herbert is merely one of the outside boxes; there are stranger
ones to follow.'

Villiers could not take his mind away from Herbert and his story,
which seemed to grow wilder as the night wore on. The fire began to burn
low, and the chilly air of the morning crept into the room; Villiers got
up with a glance over his shoulder, and shivering slightly, went to bed.

A few days later he saw at his club a gentleman of his acquaintance,
named Austin, who was famous for his intimate knowledge of London
life, both in its tenebrous and luminous phases. Villiers, still full of his
encounter in Soho and its consequences, thought Austin might possibly
be able to shed some light on Herbert's history, and so after some casual
talk he suddenly put the question:

'Do you happen to know anything of a man named Herbert—Charles
Herbert?'

Austin turned round sharply and stared at Villiers with some
astonishment.

'Charles Herbert? Weren't you in town three years ago? No; then you
have not heard of the Paul Street case? It caused a good deal of sensation at the time.'

'What was the case?'

'Well, a gentleman, a man of very good position, was found dead,
stark dead, in the area of a certain house in Paul Street, off Tottenham
Court Road. Of course the police did not make the discovery; if you
happen to be sitting up all night and have a light in your window, the
constable will ring the bell, but if you happen to be lying dead in somebody's area, you will be left alone. In this instance as in many others the
alarm was raised by some kind of vagabond; I don't mean a common
tramp, or a public-house loafer, but a gentleman, whose business or
pleasure, or both, made him a spectator of the London Streets at five
o'clock in the morning. This individual was, as he said, "going home,"
it did not appear whence or whither, and had occasion to pass through
Paul Street between four and five A.M. Something or other caught his
eye at Number 20; he said, absurdly enough, that the house had the

most unpleasant physiognomy he had ever observed, but, at any rate, he glanced down the area, and was a good deal astonished to see a man lying on the stones, his limbs all huddled together, and his face turned up. Our gentleman thought this face looked peculiarly ghastly, and so set off at a run in search of the nearest policeman. The constable was at first inclined to treat the matter lightly, suspecting a mere drunken freak; however, he came, and after looking at the man's face changed his tone, quickly enough. The early bird, who had picked up this fine worm, was sent off for a doctor, and the policeman rang and knocked at the door till a slatternly servant girl came down looking more than half asleep. The constable pointed out the contents of the area to the maid, who screamed loudly enough to wake up the street, but she knew nothing of the man; had never seen him at the house, and so forth. Meanwhile the original discoverer had come back with a medical man, and the next thing was to get into the area. The gate was open, so the whole quartet stumped down the steps. The doctor hardly needed a moment's examination; he said the poor fellow had been dead for several hours, and he was moved away to the police-station for the time being. It was then the case began to get interesting. The dead man had not been robbed, and in one of his pockets were papers identifying him as—well, as a man of good family and means, a favourite in society, and nobody's enemy, so far as could be known. I don't give his name, Villiers, because it has nothing to do with the story, and because it's no good raking up these affairs about the dead, when there are relations living. The next curious point was that the medical men couldn't agree as to how he met his death. There were some slight bruises on his shoulders, but they were so slight that it looked as if he had been pushed roughly out of the kitchen door, and not thrown over the railings from the street, or even dragged down the steps. But there were positively no other marks of violence about him, certainly none that would account for his death; and when they came to the autopsy there wasn't a trace of poison of any kind. Of course the police wanted to know all about the people at Number 20, and here again, so I have heard from private sources, one or two other very curious points came out. It appears that the occupants of the house were a Mr and Mrs Charles Herbert; he was said to be a landed proprietor, though it struck most people that Paul Street was not exactly the place to look for county gentry. As for Mrs Herbert, nobody seemed to know who or what she was, and, between ourselves, I fancy the divers after her history found themselves in rather strange waters. Of course they both denied knowing anything about the deceased, and in default of any evidence against them they were discharged. But some very odd things came out about them. Though it was between five and six in the morning when the dead man was removed, a large crowd had collected, and several of the neighbours ran to see what was going on. They were pretty free with their comments, by all accounts, and from these it appeared that Number 20 was in very bad odour in Paul Street. The detectives tried to trace down these rumours to some solid foundation of fact, but could not get hold of anything. People shook their heads and raised their eyebrows and thought the Herberts rather "queer," "would rather not be seen going into their house," and so on, but there was nothing tangible. The authorities were morally certain that the man met his death in some way or another in the house and was thrown out by the kitchen door, but they couldn't prove it, and the absence of any indications of violence or poisoning left them helpless. An odd case, wasn't it? But curiously enough, there's something more that I haven't told you. I happened to know one of the doctors who was consulted as to the cause of death, and some time after the inquest I met him, and asked him about it. "Do you really mean to tell me," I said, "that you were baffled by the case, that you actually don't know what the man died of?" "Pardon me," he replied, "I know perfectly well what caused death. Blank died of fright, of sheer, awful terror; I never saw features so hideously contorted in the entire course of my practice, and I have seen the faces of a whole host of dead." The doctor was usually a cool customer enough, and a certain vehemence in his manner struck me, but I couldn't get anything more out of him. I suppose the Treasury* didn't see their way to prosecuting the Herberts for frightening a man to death; at any rate, nothing was done, and the case dropped out of men's minds. Do you happen to know anything of Herbert?'

'Well,' replied Villiers, 'he was an old college friend of mine.'

'You don't say so? Have you ever seen his wife?'

'No, I haven't. I have lost sight of Herbert for many years.'

'It's queer, isn't it, parting with a man at the college gate or at Paddington, seeing nothing of him for years, and then finding him pop up his head in such an odd place. But I should like to have seen Mrs Herbert; people said extraordinary things about her.'

'What sort of things?'

'Well, I hardly know how to tell you. Every one who saw her at the police court said she was at once the most beautiful woman and the most repulsive they had ever set eyes on. I have spoken to a man who saw her, and I assure you he positively shuddered as he tried to describe the woman, but he couldn't tell why. She seems to have been a sort of enigma; and I expect if that one dead man could have told tales, he would have told some uncommonly queer ones. And there you are again in another puzzle; what could a respectable country gentleman like Mr Blank (we'll call him that if you don't mind) want in such a very queer house as Number 20? It's altogether a very odd case, isn't it?'

'It is indeed, Austin; an extraordinary case. I didn't think, when I asked you about my old friend, I should strike on such strange metal. Well, I must be off; good-day.'

Villiers went away, thinking of his own conceit of the Chinese boxes; here was quaint workmanship indeed.

## THE DISCOVERY IN PAUL STREET

A FEW months after Villiers's meeting with Herbert, Mr Clarke was sitting, as usual, by his after-dinner hearth, resolutely guarding his fancies from wandering in the direction of the bureau. For more than a week he had succeeded in keeping away from the 'Memoirs,' and he cherished hopes of a complete self-reformation; but, in spite of his endeavours, he could not hush the wonder and the strange curiosity that that last case he had written down had excited within him. He had put the case, or rather the outline of it, conjecturally to a scientific friend, who shook his head, and thought Clarke getting queer, and on this particular evening Clarke was making an effort to rationalise the story, when a sudden knock at his door roused him from his meditations.

'Mr Villiers to see you, sir.'

'Dear me, Villiers, it is very kind of you to look me up; I have not seen you for many months; I should think nearly a year. Come in, come in. And how are you, Villiers? Want any advice about investments?'

'No, thanks, I fancy everything I have in that way is pretty safe. No, Clarke, I have really come to consult you about a rather curious matter that has been brought under my notice of late. I am afraid you will think it all rather absurd when I tell my tale, I sometimes think so myself, and that's just why I made up my mind to come to you, as I know you're a practical man.'

Mr Villiers was ignorant of the 'Memoirs to prove the Existence of the Devil.'

'Well, Villiers, I shall be happy to give you my advice, to the best of my ability. What is the nature of the case?'

'It's an extraordinary thing altogether. You know my ways; I always keep my eyes open in the streets, and in my time I have chanced upon some queer customers, and queer cases too, but this, I think, beats all. I was coming out of a restaurant one nasty winter night about three months ago; I had had a capital dinner and a good bottle of Chianti, and I stood for a moment on the pavement, thinking what a mystery there is about London streets and the companies that pass along them. A bottle of red wine encourages these fancies, Clarke, and I daresay I should have thought a page of small type, but I was cut short by a beggar who had come behind me, and was making the usual appeals. Of course I looked round, and this beggar turned out to be what was left of an old friend of mine, a man named Herbert. I asked him how he had come to such a wretched pass, and he told me. We walked up and down one of those long dark Soho streets, and there I listened to his story. He said he had married a beautiful girl, some years younger than himself, and, as he put it, she had corrupted him body and soul. He wouldn't go into details; he said he dare not, that what he had seen and heard haunted him by night and day, and when I looked in his face I knew he was speaking the truth. There was something about the man that made me shiver. I don't know why, but it was there. I gave him a little money and sent him away, and I assure you that when he was gone I gasped for breath. His presence seemed to chill one's blood.'

'Isn't all this just a little fanciful, Villiers? I suppose the poor fellow had made an imprudent marriage, and, in plain English, gone to the bad.'

'Well, listen to this.' Villiers told Clarke the story he had heard from Austin.

'You see,' he concluded, 'there can be but little doubt that this Mr Blank, whoever he was, died of sheer terror; he saw something so awful, so terrible, that it cut short his life. And what he saw, he most certainly saw in that house, which, somehow or other, had got a bad name in the neighbourhood. I had the curiosity to go and look at the place for myself. It's a saddening kind of street; the houses are old enough to be mean and dreary, but not old enough to be quaint. As far as I could see most of them are let in lodgings, furnished and unfurnished, and almost every door has three bells to it. Here and there the ground floors have been made into shops of the commonest kind; it's a dismal street in every way. I found Number 20 was to let, and I went to the agent's and got the key. Of course I should have heard nothing of the Herberts in that quarter, but I asked the man, fair and square, how long they have left the house, and whether there had been other tenants in the meanwhile. He looked at me queerly for a minute, and told me the Herberts had left immediately after the unpleasantness, as he called it, and since then the house had been empty.'

Mr Villiers paused for a moment.

'I have always been rather fond of going over empty houses; there's a sort of fascination about the desolate empty rooms, with the nails sticking in the walls, and the dust thick upon the window-sills. But I didn't enjoy going over Number 20 Paul Street. I had hardly put my foot inside the passage before I noticed a queer, heavy feeling about the air of the house. Of course all empty houses are stuffy, and so forth, but this was something quite different; I can't describe it to you, but it seemed to stop the breath. I went into the front room and the back room, and the kitchens downstairs; they were all dirty and dusty enough, as you would expect, but there was something strange about them all. I couldn't define it to you, I only know I felt queer. It was one of the rooms on the first floor, though, that was the worst. It was a largish room, and once on a time the paper must have been cheerful enough, but when I saw it, paint, paper, and everything were most doleful. But the room was full of horror; I felt my teeth grinding as I put my hand on the door, and when I went in, I thought I should have fallen fainting to the floor. However, I pulled myself together, and stood against the end wall, wondering what on earth there could be about the room to make my limbs tremble, and my heart beat as if I were at the hour of death. In one corner there was a pile of newspapers littered about on the floor and I began looking at them, they were papers of three or four years ago, some of them half torn, and some crumpled as if they had been used for packing. I turned the whole pile over, and amongst them I found a curious drawing; I will show it you presently. But I couldn't stay in the room; I felt it was overpowering me. I was thankful to come out, safe and sound, into the open air. People stared at me as I walked along the street, and one man said I was drunk. I was staggering about from one side of the pavement to the other, and it was as much as I could do to take the key back to the agent and get home. I was in bed for a week, suffering from what my doctor called nervous shock and exhaustion. One of those days I was reading the evening paper, and happened to notice a paragraph headed: "Starved to Death." It was the usual style of thing; a model lodging-house* in Marylebone, a door locked for several days, and a dead man in his chair when they broke in. "The deceased," said the paragraph, "was known as Charles Herbert, and is believed to have been once a prosperous country gentleman. His name was familiar to the public three years ago in connection with the mysterious death in Paul Street, Tottenham Court Road, the deceased being the tenant of the house Number 20, in the area of which a gentleman of good position was found dead under circumstances not devoid of suspicion." A tragic ending, wasn't it? But after all, if what he told me were true, which I am sure it was, the man's life was all a tragedy, and a tragedy of a stranger sort than they put on the boards.'

'And that is the story, is it?' said Clarke musingly.

'Yes, that is the story.'

'Well, really, Villiers, I scarcely know what to say about it. There are no doubt circumstances in the case which seem peculiar, the finding of the dead man in the area of the Herberts' house, for instance, and the extraordinary opinion of the physician as to the cause of death, but, after all, it is conceivable that the facts may be explained in a straight-forward manner. As to your own sensations when you went to see the house, I would suggest that they were due to a vivid imagination; you must have been brooding, in a semi-conscious way, over what you had heard. I don't exactly see what more can be said or done in the matter; you evidently think there is a mystery of some kind, but Herbert is dead; where then do you propose to look?'

'I propose to look for the woman; the woman whom he married. *She* is the mystery.'

The two men sat silent by the fireside; Clarke secretly congratulating himself on having successfully kept up the character of advocate of the commonplace, and Villiers wrapt in his gloomy fancies.

'I think I will have a cigarette,' he said at last, and put his hand in his pocket to feel for the cigarette-case.

'Ah!' he said, starting slightly, 'I forgot I had something to show you. You remember my saying that I had found a rather curious sketch amongst the pile of old newspapers at the house in Paul Street?—here it is.'

Villiers drew out a small thin parcel from his pocket. It was covered with brown paper, and secured with string, and the knots were trouble-some. In spite of himself Clarke felt inquisitive; he bent forward on his chair as Villiers painfully undid the string, and unfolded the outer covering. Inside was a second wrapping of tissue, and Villiers took it off and handed the small piece of paper to Clarke without a word.

There was dead silence in the room for five minutes or more; the two men sat so still that they could hear the ticking of the tall old-fashioned clock that stood outside in the hall, and in the mind of one of them the slow monotony of sound woke up a far, far memory. He was looking intently at the small pen-and-ink sketch of a woman's head; it had evi-dently been drawn with great care, and by a true artist, for the woman's soul looked out of the eyes, and the lips were parted with a strange smile. Clarke gazed still at the face; it brought to his memory one summer evening long ago; he saw again the long lovely valley, the river winding between the hills, the meadows and the cornfields, the dull red sun, and the cold white mist rising from the water. He heard a voice speaking to him across the waves of many years, and saying, 'Clarke, Mary will see the God Pan!' and then he was standing in the grim room beside the doctor, listening to the heavy ticking of the clock, waiting and watching, watching the figure lying on the green chair beneath the lamp-light. Mary rose up, and he looked into her eyes, and his heart grew cold within him.

'Who is this woman?' he said at last. His voice was dry and hoarse.

'That is the woman whom Herbert married.'

Clarke looked again at the sketch; it was not Mary after all. There certainly was Mary's face, but there was something else, something he had not seen on Mary's features when the white-clad girl entered the laboratory with the doctor, nor at her terrible awakening, nor when she lay grinning on the bed. Whatever it was, the glance that came from those eyes, the smile on the full lips, or the expression of the whole face, Clarke shuddered before it in his inmost soul, and thought, unconsciously, of Dr Phillips's words, 'the most vivid presentment of evil I have ever seen.' He turned the paper over mechanically in his hand and glanced at the back.

'Good God! Clarke, what is the matter? You are as white as death.'

Villiers had started wildly from his chair, as Clarke fell back with a groan, and let the paper drop from his hands.

'I don't feel very well, Villiers, I am subject to these attacks. Pour me out a little wine; thanks, that will do. I shall be better in a few minutes.'

Villiers picked up the fallen sketch and turned it over as Clarke had done.

'You saw that?' he said. 'That's how I identified it as being a portrait of Herbert's wife, or I should say his widow. How do you feel now?'

'Better, thanks, it was only a passing faintness. I don't think I quite catch your meaning. What did you say enabled you to identify the picture?'

'This word—Helen—written on the back. Didn't I tell you her name was Helen? Yes; Helen Vaughan.'

Clarke groaned; there could be no shadow of doubt.

'Now, don't you agree with me,' said Villiers, 'that in the story I have told you to-night, and in the part this woman plays in it, there are some very strange points?'

'Yes, Villiers,' Clarke muttered, 'it is a strange story indeed; a strange story indeed. You must give me time to think it over; I may be able to help you or I may not. Must you be going now? Well, good-night, Villiers, good-night. Come and see me in the course of a week.'

## THE LETTER OF ADVICE

'Do you know, Austin,' said Villiers, as the two friends were pacing sedately along Piccadilly one pleasant morning in May, 'do you know I am convinced that what you told me about Paul Street and the Herberts is a mere episode in an extraordinary history. I may as well confess to you that when I asked you about Herbert a few months ago I had just seen him.'

'You had seen him? Where?'

'He begged of me in the street one night. He was in the most pitiable plight, but I recognised the man, and I got him to tell me his history, or at least the outline of it. In brief, it amounted to this—he had been ruined by his wife.'

'In what manner?'

'He would not tell me; he would only say that she had destroyed him body and soul. The man is dead now.'

'And what has become of his wife?'

'Ah, that's what I should like to know, and I mean to find her sooner or later. I know a man named Clarke, a dry fellow, in fact a man of business, but shrewd enough. You understand my meaning; not shrewd in the mere business sense of the word, but a man who really knows something about men and life. Well, I laid the case before him, and he was evidently impressed. He said it needed consideration, and asked me to come again in the course of a week. A few days later I received this extraordinary letter.'

Austin took the envelope, drew out the letter, and read it curiously. It ran as follows:—

MY DEAR VILLIERS,—I have thought over the matter on which you consulted me the other night, and my advice to you is this. Throw the portrait into the fire, blot out the story from your mind. Never give it another thought, Villiers, or you will be sorry. You will think, no doubt, that I am in possession of some secret information, and to a certain extent that is the case. But I only know a little; I am like a traveller who has peered over an abyss, and has drawn back in terror. What I know is strange enough and horrible enough, but beyond my knowledge there are depths and horrors more frightful still, more incredible than any tale told of winter nights about the fire. I have resolved, and nothing shall shake that resolve, to explore no whit further, and if you value your happiness you will make the same determination.

Come and see me by all means; but we will talk on more cheerful topics than this.

Austin folded the letter methodically, and returned it to Villiers.

'It is certainly an extraordinary letter,' he said; 'what does he mean by the portrait?'

'Ah! I forgot to tell you I have been to Paul Street and have made a discovery.'

Villiers told his story as he had told it to Clarke, and Austin listened in silence. He seemed puzzled.

'How very curious that you should experience such an unpleasant sensation in that room!' he said at length. 'I hardly gather that it was a mere matter of the imagination; a feeling of repulsion, in short.'

'No, it was more physical than mental. It was as if I were inhaling at every breath some deadly fume, which seemed to penetrate to every nerve and bone and sinew of my body. I felt racked from head to foot, my eyes began to grow dim; it was like the entrance of death.'

'Yes, yes, very strange, certainly. You see, your friend confesses that there is some very black story connected with this woman. Did you notice any particular emotion in him when you were telling your tale?'

'Yes, I did. He became very faint, but he assured me that it was a mere passing attack to which he was subject.'

'Did you believe him?'

'I did at the time, but I don't now. He heard what I had to say with a good deal of indifference, till I showed him the portrait. It was then he was seized with the attack of which I spoke. He looked ghastly, I assure you.'

'Then he must have seen the woman before. But there might be another explanation; it might have been the name, and not the face, which was familiar to him. What do you think?'

'I couldn't say. To the best of my belief it was after turning the portrait in his hands that he nearly dropped from his chair. The name, you know, was written on the back.'

'Quite so. After all, it is impossible to come to any resolution in a case like this. I hate melodrama, and nothing strikes me as more commonplace and tedious than the ordinary ghost story of commerce; but really, Villiers, it looks as if there were something very queer at the bottom of all this.'

The two men had, without noticing it, turned up Ashley Street, leading northward from Piccadilly. It was a long street, and rather a gloomy one, but here and there a brighter taste had illuminated the dark houses with flowers, and gay curtains, and a cheerful paint on the doors. Villiers glanced up as Austin stopped speaking, and looked at one of these houses; geraniums, red and white, drooped from every sill, and daffodil-coloured curtains were draped back from each window.

'It looks cheerful, doesn't it?' he said.

'Yes, and the inside is still more cheery. One of the pleasantest houses of the season, so I have heard. I haven't been there myself, but I have met several men who have, and they tell me it's uncommonly jovial.'

'Whose house is it?'

'A Mrs Beaumont's.'

'And who is she?'

'I couldn't tell you. I have heard she comes from South America, but, after all, who she is is of little consequence. She is a very wealthy woman, there's no doubt of that, and some of the best people have taken her up. I hear she has some wonderful claret, really marvellous wine, which must have cost a fabulous sum. Lord Argentine was telling me about it; he was there last Sunday evening. He assures me he has never tasted such a wine, and Argentine, as you know, is an expert. By the way, that reminds me, she must be an oddish sort of woman, this Mrs Beaumont. Argentine asked her how old the wine was, and what do you think she said? "About a thousand years, I believe." Lord Argentine thought she was chaffing him, you know, but when he laughed she said she was speaking quite seriously, and offered to show him the jar. Of course, he couldn't say anything more after that; but it seems rather antiquated for a beverage, doesn't it? Why, here we are at my rooms. Come in, won't you?'

'Thanks, I think I will. I haven't seen the curiosity-shop for some time.'

It was a room furnished richly, yet oddly, where every chair and book-case and table, every rug and jar and ornament seemed to be a thing apart, preserving each its own individuality.

'Anything fresh lately?' said Villiers after a while.

'No; I think not; you saw those queer jugs, didn't you? I thought so. I don't think I have come across anything for the last few weeks.'

Austin glanced round the room from cupboard to cupboard, from shelf to shelf, in search of some new oddity. His eyes fell at last on an old chest, pleasantly and quaintly carved, which stood in a dark corner of the room.

'Ah,' he said, 'I was forgetting, I have got something to show you.' Austin unlocked the chest, drew out a thick quarto volume, laid it on the table, and resumed the cigar he had put down.

'Did you know Arthur Meyrick the painter, Villiers?'

'A little; I met him two or three times at the house of a friend of mine. What has become of him? I haven't heard his name mentioned for some time.'

'He's dead.'

'You don't say so! Quite young, wasn't he?'

'Yes; only thirty when he died.'

'What did he die of?'

'I don't know. He was an intimate friend of mine, and a thoroughly good fellow. He used to come here and talk to me for hours, and he was one of the best talkers I have met. He could even talk about painting, and that's more than can be said of most painters. About eighteen months ago he was feeling rather over-worked, and partly at my suggestion he went off on a sort of roving expedition, with no very definite end or aim about it. I believe New York was to be his first port, but I never heard from him. Three months ago I got this book, with a very civil letter from an English doctor practising at Buenos Ayres, stating that he had attended the late Mr Meyrick during his illness, and that the deceased had expressed an earnest wish that the enclosed packet should be sent to me after his death. That was all.'

'And haven't you written for further particulars?'

'I have been thinking of doing so. You would advise me to write to the doctor?'

'Certainly. And what about the book?'

'It was sealed up when I got it. I don't think the doctor had seen it.'

'It is something very rare? Meyrick was a collector, perhaps?'

'No, I think not, hardly a collector. Now, what do you think of those Ainu jugs?'*

'They are peculiar, but I like them. But aren't you going to show me poor Meyrick's legacy?'

'Yes, yes, to be sure. The fact is, it's rather a peculiar sort of thing, and I haven't shown it to any one. I wouldn't say anything about it if I were you. There it is.'

Villiers took the book, and opened it at haphazard. 'It isn't a printed volume then?' he said.

'No. It is a collection of drawings in black and white by my poor friend Meyrick.'

Villiers turned to the first page, it was blank; the second bore a brief inscription, which he read:

*Silet per diem universus, nec sine horrore secretus est; lucet nocturnis ignibus, chorus Ægipanum undique personatur: audiuntur et cantus tibiarum, et tinnitus cymbalorum per oram maritimam.**

On the third page was a design which made Villiers start and look up at Austin; he was gazing abstractedly out of the window. Villiers turned page after page, absorbed, in spite of himself, in the frightful Walpurgis Night* of evil, strange monstrous evil, that the dead artist had set forth in hard black and white. The figures of Fauns and Satyrs and Ægipans* danced before his eyes, the darkness of the thicket, the dance on the mountain-top, the scenes by lonely shores, in green vineyards, by rocks and desert places, passed before him; a world before which the human soul seemed to shrink back and shudder. Villiers whirled over the remaining pages, he had seen enough, but the picture on the last leaf caught his eye, as he almost closed the book.

'Austin!'

'Well, what is it?'

'Do you know who that is?'

It was a woman's face, alone on the white page.

'Know who it is? No, of course not.'

'I do.'

'Who is it?'

'It is Mrs Herbert.'

'Are you sure?'

'I am perfectly certain of it. Poor Meyrick! He is one more chapter in her history.'

'But what do you think of the designs?'

'They are frightful. Lock the book up again, Austin. If I were you I would burn it; it must be a terrible companion, even though it be in a chest.'

'Yes, they are singular drawings. But I wonder what connection there could be between Meyrick and Mrs Herbert, or what link between her and these designs?'

'Ah, who can say? It is possible that the matter may end here, and we shall never know, but in my own opinion this Helen Vaughan, or Mrs Herbert, is only beginning. She will come back to London, Austin, depend upon it, she will come back, and we shall hear more about her then. I don't think it will be very pleasant news.'


## THE SUICIDES

LORD ARGENTINE was a great favourite in London society. At twenty he had been a poor man, decked with the surname of an illustrious family, but forced to earn a livelihood as best he could, and the most speculative of money-lenders would not have intrusted him with fifty pounds on the chance of his ever changing his name for a title, and his poverty for a great fortune. His father had been near enough to the fountain of good things to secure one of the family livings, but the son, even if he had taken orders, would scarcely have obtained so much as this, and moreover felt no vocation for the ecclesiastical estate. Thus he fronted the world with no better armour than the bachelor's gown* and the wits of a younger son's grandson, with which equipment he contrived in some way to make a very tolerable fight of it. At twenty-five Mr Charles Aubernoun saw himself still a man of struggles and of warfare with the world, but out of the seven who stood between him and the high places of his family three only remained. These three, however, were 'good lives,' but yet not proof against the Zulu assegais* and typhoid fever, and so one morning Aubernoun woke up and found himself Lord Argentine, a man of thirty who had faced the difficulties of existence, and had conquered. The situation amused him immensely, and he resolved that riches should be as pleasant to him as poverty had always been. Argentine, after some little consideration, came to the conclusion that dining, regarded as a fine art, was perhaps the most amusing pursuit open to fallen humanity, and thus his dinners became famous in London, and an invitation to his table a thing covetously desired. After ten years of lordship and dinners Argentine still declined to be jaded, still persisted in enjoying life, and by a kind of infection had become recognised as the cause of joy in others, in short as the best of company. His sudden and tragic death therefore caused a wide and deep sensation. People could scarce believe it, even though the newspaper was before their eyes, and the cry of 'Mysterious Death of a Nobleman' came ringing up from the street. But there stood the brief paragraph:

Lord Argentine was found dead this morning by his valet under distressing circumstances. It is stated that there can be no doubt that his lordship committed suicide, though no motive can be assigned for the act. The deceased nobleman was widely known in society, and much liked for his genial manner and sumptuous hospitality. He is succeeded by etc. etc.

By slow degrees the details came to light, but the case still remained a mystery. The chief witness at the inquest was the dead nobleman's valet, who said that the night before his death Lord Argentine had dined with a lady of good position, whose name was suppressed in the newspaper reports. At about eleven o'clock Lord Argentine had returned, and informed his man that he should not require his services till the next morning. A little later the valet had occasion to cross the hall and was somewhat astonished to see his master quietly letting himself out at the front door. He had taken off his evening clothes, and was dressed in a Norfolk coat and knicker-bockers, and wore a low brown hat. The valet had no reason to suppose that Lord Argentine had seen him, and though his master rarely kept late hours, thought little of the occurrence till the next morning, when he knocked at the bedroom door at a quarter to nine as usual. He received no answer, and, after knocking two or three times, entered the room, and saw Lord Argentine's body leaning forward at an angle from the bottom of the bed. He found that his master had tied a cord securely to one of the short bed-posts, and, after making a running noose and slipping it round his neck, the unfortunate man must have resolutely fallen forward, to die by slow strangulation. He was dressed in the light suit in which the valet had seen him go out, and the doctor who was summoned pronounced that life had been extinct for more than four hours. All papers, letters, and so forth, seemed in perfect order, and nothing was discovered which pointed in the most remote way to any scandal either great or small. Here the evidence ended; nothing more could be discovered. Several persons had been present at the dinner-party at which Lord Argentine had assisted, and to all these he seemed in his usual genial spirits. The valet, indeed, said he thought his master appeared a little excited when he came home, but he confessed that the alteration in his manner was very slight, hardly noticeable, indeed. It seemed hopeless to seek for any clew, and the suggestion that Lord Argentine had been suddenly attacked by acute suicidal mania was generally accepted.

It was otherwise, however, when within three weeks, three more gentlemen, one of them a nobleman, and the two others men of good position and ample means, perished miserably in almost precisely the same manner. Lord Swanleigh was found one morning in his dressing-room, hanging from a peg affixed to the wall, and Mr Collier-Stuart and Mr Herries had chosen to die as Lord Argentine. There was no explanation in either case; a few bald facts; a living man in the evening, and a dead body with a black swollen face in the morning. The police had been forced to confess themselves powerless to arrest or to explain the sordid murders of Whitechapel;* but before the horrible suicides of Piccadilly and Mayfair, they were dumfoundered, for not even the mere ferocity which did duty as an explanation of the crimes of the East End, could be of service in the West. Each of these men who had resolved to die a tortured shameful death was rich, prosperous, and to all appearance in love with the world, and not the acutest research could ferret out any shadow of a lurking motive in either case. There was a horror in the air, and men looked at one another's faces when they met, each wondering whether the other was to be the victim of a fifth nameless tragedy.

Journalists sought in vain in their scrap-books for materials whereof to concoct reminiscent articles; and the morning paper was unfolded in many a house with a feeling of awe; no man knew when or where the blow would next light.

A short while after the last of these terrible events, Austin came to see Mr Villiers. He was curious to know whether Villiers had succeeded in discovering any fresh traces of Mrs Herbert, either through Clarke or by other sources, and he asked the question soon after he had sat down.

'No,' said Villiers, 'I wrote to Clarke, but he remains obdurate, and I have tried other channels, but without any result. I can't find out what became of Helen Vaughan after she left Paul Street, but I think she must have gone abroad. But to tell the truth, Austin, I haven't paid very much attention to the matter for the last few weeks; I knew poor Herries intimately, and his terrible death has been a great shock to me, a great shock.'

'I can well believe it,' answered Austin gravely, 'you know Argentine was a friend of mine. If I remember rightly, we were speaking of him that day you came to my rooms.'

'Yes; it was in connection with that house in Ashley Street, Mrs Beaumont's house. You said something about Argentine's dining there.'

'Quite so. Of course you know it was there Argentine dined the night before—before his death.'

'No, I haven't heard that.'

'Oh yes; the name was kept out of the papers to spare Mrs Beaumont. Argentine was a great favourite of hers, and it is said she was in a terrible state for some time after.'

A curious look came over Villiers's face; he seemed undecided whether to speak or not. Austin began again.

I never experienced such a feeling of horror as when I read the account of Argentine's death. I didn't understand it at the time, and I don't now. I knew him well, and it completely passes my understanding for what possible cause he—or any of the others for the matter of that—could have resolved in cold blood to die in such an awful manner. You know how men babble away each other's characters in London, you may be sure any buried scandal or hidden skeleton would have been brought to light in such a case as this; but nothing of the sort has taken place. As for the theory of mania, that is very well, of course, for the coroner's jury, but everybody knows that it's all nonsense. Suicidal mania is not smallpox.'

Austin relapsed into gloomy silence. Villiers sat silent also, watching his friend. The expression of indecision still fleeted across his face, he seemed as if weighing his thoughts in the balance, and the considerations he was revolving left him still silent. Austin tried to shake off the remembrance of tragedies as hopeless and perplexed as the labyrinth of Dædalus,* and began to talk in an indifferent voice of the more pleasant incidents and adventures of the season.

'That Mrs Beaumont,' he said, 'of whom we were speaking, is a great success; she has taken London almost by storm. I met her the other night at Fulham's; she is really a remarkable woman.'

'You have met Mrs Beaumont?'

'Yes; she had quite a court around her. She would be called very handsome, I suppose, and yet there is something about her face which I didn't like. The features are exquisite, but the expression is strange. And all the time I was looking at her, and afterwards, when I was going home, I had a curious feeling that that very expression was in some way or other familiar to me.'

'You must have seen her in the Row.'*

'No, I am sure I never set eyes on the woman before; it is that which makes it puzzling. And to the best of my belief I have never seen anybody like her; what I felt was a kind of dim far-off memory, vague but persistent. The only sensation I can compare it to, is that odd feeling one sometimes has in a dream, when fantastic cities and wondrous lands and phantom personages appear familiar and accustomed.'

Villiers nodded and glanced aimlessly round the room, possibly in search of something on which to turn the conversation. His eyes fell on an old chest somewhat like that in which the artist's strange legacy lay hid beneath a Gothic scutcheon.

'Have you written to the doctor about poor Meyrick?' he asked.

'Yes; I wrote asking for full particulars as to his illness and death. I don't expect to have an answer for another three weeks or a month. I thought I might as well inquire whether Meyrick knew an English-woman named Herbert, and if so, whether the doctor could give me any information about her. But it's very possible that Meyrick fell in with her at New York, or Mexico, or San Francisco; I have no idea as to the extent or direction of his travels.'

'Yes, and it's very possible that the woman may have more than one name.'

'Exactly. I wish I had thought of asking you to lend me the portrait of her which you possess. I might have enclosed it in my letter to Dr Mathews.'

'So you might; that never occurred to me. We might even now do so. Hark! what are those boys calling?'

While the two men had been talking together a confused noise of shouting had been gradually growing louder. The noise rose from the eastward and swelled down Piccadilly, drawing nearer and nearer, a very torrent of sound; surging up streets usually quiet, and making every window a frame for a face, curious or excited. The cries and voices came echoing up the silent street where Villiers lived, growing more distinct as they advanced, and, as Villiers spoke, an answer rang up from the pavement:

'The West End Horrors; Another Awful Suicide; Full Details!'

Austin rushed down the stairs and bought a paper and read out the paragraph to Villiers as the uproar in the street rose and fell. The window was open and the air seemed full of noise and terror.

'Another gentleman has fallen a victim to the terrible epidemic of suicide which for the last month has prevailed in the West End. Mr Sidney Crashaw of Stoke House, Fulham, and King's Pomeroy, Devon, was found, after a prolonged search, hanging from the branch of a tree in his garden at one o'clock to-day. The deceased gentleman dined last night at the Carlton Club* and seemed in his usual health and spirits. He left the Club at about ten o'clock, and was seen walking leisurely up St James's Street a little later. Subsequent to this his movements cannot be traced. On the discovery of the body medical aid was at once summoned, but life had evidently been long extinct. So far as is known Mr Crashaw had no trouble or anxiety of any kind. This painful suicide, it will be remembered, is the fifth of the kind in the last month. The authorities at Scotland Yard* are unable to suggest any explanation of these terrible occurrences.'

Austin put down the paper in mute horror.

'I shall leave London to-morrow,' he said, 'it is a city of nightmares. How awful this is, Villiers!'

Mr Villiers was sitting by the window quietly looking out into the street. He had listened to the newspaper report attentively, and the hint of indecision was no longer on his face.

'Wait a moment, Austin,' he replied, 'I have made up my mind to mention a little matter that occurred last night. It is stated, I think, that Crashaw was last seen alive in St James's Street shortly after ten?'

'Yes, I think so. I will look again. Yes, you are quite right.'

'Quite so. Well, I am in a position to contradict that statement at all events. Crashaw was seen after that; considerably later indeed.'

'How do you know?'

'Because I happened to see Crashaw myself at about two o'clock this morning.'

'You saw Crashaw? You, Villiers?'

'Yes, I saw him quite distinctly; indeed there were but a few feet between us.'

'Where, in heaven's name, did you see him?'

'Not far from here. I saw him in Ashley Street. He was just leaving a house.'

'Did you notice what house it was?'

'Yes. It was Mrs Beaumont's.'

'Villiers! Think what you are saying; there must be some mistake. How could Crashaw be in Mrs Beaumont's house at two o'clock in the morning? Surely, surely, you must have been dreaming, Villiers, you were always rather fanciful.'

'No; I was wide awake enough. Even if I had been dreaming as you say, what I saw would have roused me effectually.'

'What you saw? What did you see? Was there anything strange about Crashaw? But I can't believe it; it is impossible.'

'Well, if you like I will tell you what I saw, or if you please, what I think I saw, and you can judge for yourself.'

'Very good, Villiers.'

The noise and clamour of the street had died away, though now and then the sound of shouting still came from the distance, and the dull, leaden silence seemed like the quiet after an earthquake or a storm. Villiers turned from the window and began speaking.

'I was at a house near Regent's Park last night, and when I came away the fancy took me to walk home instead of taking a hansom. It was a clear pleasant night enough, and after a few minutes I had the streets pretty much to myself. It's a curious thing, Austin, to be alone in London at night, the gas-lamps stretching away in perspective, and the dead silence, and then perhaps the rush and clatter of a hansom on the stones, and the fire starting up under the horse's hoofs. I walked along pretty briskly, for I was feeling a little tired of being out in the night, and as the clocks were striking two I turned down Ashley Street, which, you know, is on my way. It was quieter than ever there, and the lamps were fewer, altogether it looked as dark and gloomy as a forest in winter. I had done about half the length of the street when I heard a door closed very softly, and naturally I looked up to see who was abroad like myself at such an hour. As it happens, there is a street lamp close to the house in question, and I saw a man standing on the step. He had just shut the door and his face was towards me, and I recognised Crashaw directly. I never knew him to speak to, but I had often seen him, and I am positive that I was not mistaken in my man. I looked into his face for a moment, and then—I will confess the truth—I set off at a good run, and kept it up till I was within my own door.'

'Why?'

'Why? Because it made my blood run cold to see that man's face. I could never have supposed that such an infernal medley of passions could have glared out of any human eyes; I almost fainted as I looked. I knew I had looked into the eyes of a lost soul, Austin, the man's outward form remained, but all hell was within it. Furious lust, and hate that was like fire, and the loss of all hope and horror that seemed to shriek aloud to the night, though his teeth were shut; and the utter blackness of despair. I am sure he did not see me; he saw nothing that you or I can see, but he saw what I hope we never shall. I do not know when he died; I suppose in an hour, or perhaps two, but when I passed down Ashley Street and heard the closing door, that man no longer belonged to this world; it was a devil's face that I looked upon.'

There was an interval of silence in the room when Villiers ceased speaking. The light was failing, and all the tumult of an hour ago was quite hushed. Austin had bent his head at the close of the story, and his hand covered his eyes.

'What can it mean?' he said at length.

'Who knows, Austin, who knows? It's a black business, but I think we had better keep it to ourselves, for the present at any rate. I will see if I cannot learn anything about that house through private channels of information, and if I do light upon anything I will let you know.'

## THE ENCOUNTER IN SOHO

THREE weeks later Austin received a note from Villiers, asking him to call either that afternoon or the next. He chose the nearer date and found Villiers sitting as usual by the window, apparently lost in meditation on the drowsy traffic of the street. There was a bamboo table by his side, a fantastic thing, enriched with gilding and queer painted scenes, and on it lay a little pile of papers arranged and docketed as neatly as anything in Mr Clarke's office.

'Well, Villiers, have you made any discoveries in the last three weeks?'

'I think so; I have here one or two memoranda which struck me as singular, and there is a statement to which I shall call your attention.'

'And these documents relate to Mrs Beaumont? it was really Crashaw whom you saw that night standing on the doorstep of the house in Ashley Street?'

'As to that matter my belief remains unchanged, but neither my inquiries nor their results have any special relation to Crashaw. But my investigations have had a strange issue; I have found out who Mrs Beaumont is!'

'Who she is? In what way do you mean?'

'I mean that you and I know her better under another name.'

'What name is that?'

'Herbert.'

'Herbert!' Austin repeated the word, dazed with astonishment.

'Yes, Mrs Herbert of Paul Street, Helen Vaughan of earlier adventures unknown to me. You had reason to recognise the expression of her face; when you go home look at the face in Meyrick's book of horrors, and you will know the sources of your recollection.'

'And you have proof of this?'

'Yes, the best of proof; I have seen Mrs Beaumont, or shall we say Mrs Herbert?'

'Where did you see her?'

'Hardly in a place where you would expect to see a lady who lives in Ashley Street, Piccadilly. I saw her entering a house in one of the meanest and most disreputable streets in Soho. In fact, I had made an appointment, though not with her, and she was precise both to time and place.'

'All this seems very wonderful, but I cannot call it incredible. You must remember, Villiers, that I have seen this woman, in the ordinary adventure of London society, talking and laughing, and sipping her chocolate in a commonplace drawing-room, with commonplace people. But you know what you are saying.'

'I do; I have not allowed myself to be led by surmises or fancies. It was with no thought of finding Helen Vaughan that I searched for Mrs Beaumont in the dark waters of the life of London, but such has been the issue.'

'You must have been in strange places, Villiers.'

'Yes, I have been in very strange places. It would have been useless, you know, to go to Ashley Street, and ask Mrs Beaumont to kindly give me a short sketch of her previous history. No; assuming, as I had to assume, that her record was not of the cleanest, it would be pretty certain that at some previous time she must have moved in circles not quite so refined as her present ones. If you see mud on the top of a stream, you may be sure that it was once at the bottom. I went to the bottom. I have always been fond of diving into Queer Street* for my amusement, and I found my knowledge of that locality and its inhabitants very useful. It is perhaps needless to say that my friends had never heard the name of Beaumont, and as I had never seen the lady, and was quite unable to describe her, I had to set to work in an indirect way. The people there know me, I have been able to do some of them a service now and again, so they made no difficulty about giving their information; they were aware I had no communication direct or indirect with Scotland Yard. I had to cast out a good many lines though, before I got what I wanted, and when I landed the fish I did not for a moment suppose it was my fish. But I listened to what I was told out of a constitutional liking for useless information, and I found myself in possession of a very curious story, though, as I imagined, not the story I was looking for. It was to this effect. Some five or six years ago a woman named Raymond suddenly made her appearance in the neighbourhood to which I am referring. She was described to me as being quite young, probably not more than seventeen or eighteen, very handsome, and looking as if she came from the country. I should be wrong in saying that she found her level in going to this particular quarter, or associating with these people, for from what I was told, I should think the worst den in London far too good for her. The person from whom I got my information, as you may suppose, no great Puritan, shuddered and grew sick in telling me of the nameless infamies which were laid to her charge. After living there for a year, or perhaps a little more, she disappeared as suddenly as she came, and they saw nothing of her till about the time of the Paul Street case. At first she came to her old haunts only occasionally, then more frequently, and finally took up her abode there as before, and remained for six or eight months. It's of no use my going into details as to the life that woman led; if you want particulars you can look at Meyrick's legacy. Those designs were not drawn from his imagination. She again disappeared, and the people of the place saw nothing of her till a few months ago. My informant told me that she had taken some rooms in a house which he pointed out, and these rooms she was in the habit of visiting two or three times a week and always at ten in the morning. I was led to expect that one of these visits would be paid on a certain day about a week ago, and I accordingly managed to be on the look-out in company with my cicerone* at a quarter to ten, and the hour and the lady came with equal punctuality. My friend and I were standing under an archway, a little way back from the street, but she saw us, and gave me a glance that I shall be long in forgetting. That look was quite enough for me; I knew Miss Raymond to be Mrs Herbert; as for Mrs Beaumont she had quite gone out of my head. She went into the house, and I watched it till four o'clock, when she came out, and then I followed her. It was a long chase, and I had to be very careful to keep a long way in the background, and yet not to lose sight of the woman. She took me down to the Strand, and then to Westminster, and then up St James's Street, and along Piccadilly. I felt queerish when I saw her turn up Ashley Street; the thought that Mrs Herbert was Mrs Beaumont came into my mind, but it seemed too improbable to be true. I waited at the corner, keeping my eye on her all the time, and I took particular care to note the house at which she stopped. It was the house with the gay curtains, the house of flowers, the house out of which Crashaw came the night he hanged himself in his garden. I was just going away with my discovery, when I saw an empty carriage come round and draw up in front of the house, and I came to the conclusion that Mrs Herbert was going out for a drive, and I was right. I took a hansom and followed the carriage into the Park. There, as it happened, I met a man I know, and we stood talking together a little distance from the carriage-way, to which I had my back. We had not been there for ten minutes when my friend took off his hat, and I glanced round and saw the lady I had been following all day. "Who is that?" I said, and his answer was, "Mrs Beaumont; lives in Ashley Street." Of course there could be no doubt after that. I don't know whether she saw me, but I don't think she did. I went home at once, and, on consideration, I thought that I had a sufficiently good case with which to go to Clarke.'

'Why to Clarke?'

'Because I am sure that Clarke is in possession of facts about this woman, facts of which I know nothing.'

'Well, what then?'

Mr Villiers leaned back in his chair and looked reflectively at Austin for a moment before he answered:

'My idea was that Clarke and I should call on Mrs Beaumont.'

'You would never go into such a house as that? No, no, Villiers, you cannot do it. Besides, consider; what result . . .'

'I will tell you soon. But I was going to say that my information does not end here; it has been completed in an extraordinary manner.

'Look at this neat little packet of manuscript; it is paginated, you see, and I have indulged in the civil coquetry of a ribbon of red tape. It has almost a legal air, hasn't it? Run your eye over it, Austin. It is an account of the entertainment Mrs Beaumont provided for her choicer guests. The man who wrote this escaped with his life, but I do not think he will live many years. The doctors tell him he must have sustained some severe shock to the nerves.'

Austin took the manuscript, but never read it. Opening the neat pages at haphazard his eye was caught by a word and a phrase that followed it; and, sick at heart, with white lips and a cold sweat pouring like water from his temples, he flung the paper down.

'Take it away, Villiers, never speak of this again. Are you made of stone, man? Why, the dread and horror of death itself, the thoughts who stands in the keen morning air on the black platform, bou tolling in his ears, and waits for the harsh rattle of the bolt, are a compared to this. I will not read it; I should never sleep again.'

'Very good. I can fancy what you saw. Yes; it is horrible enough, but after all, it is an old story, an old mystery played in our day, and in dim London streets instead of amidst the vineyards and the olive gardens. We know what happened to those who chanced to meet the Great God Pan, and those who are wise know that all symbols are symbols of something, not of nothing. It was, indeed, an exquisite symbol beneath which men long ago veiled their knowledge of the most awful, most secret forces which lie at the heart of all things; forces before which the souls of men must wither and die and blacken, as their bodies blacken under the electric current. Such forces cannot be named, cannot be spoken, cannot be imagined except under a veil and a symbol, a symbol to the most of us appearing a quaint, poetic fancy, to some a foolish, silly tale. But you and I, at all events, have known something of the terror that may dwell in the secret place of life, manifested under human flesh; that which is without form taking to itself a form. Oh, Austin, how can it be? How is it that the very sunlight does not turn to blackness before this thing, the hard earth melt and boil beneath such a burden?'

Villiers was pacing up and down the room, and the beads of sweat stood out on his forehead. Austin sat silent for a while, but Villiers saw him make a sign upon his breast.

'I say again, Villiers, you will surely never enter such a house as that? You would never pass out alive.'

'Yes, Austin, I shall go out alive—I, and Clarke with me.'

'What do you mean? You cannot, you would not dare . . .'

'Wait a moment. The air was very pleasant and fresh this morning; there was a breeze blowing, even through this dull street, and I thought I would take a walk. Piccadilly stretched before me a clear, bright vista, and the sun flashed on the carriages and on the quivering leaves in the park. It was a joyous morning, and men and women looked at the sky and smiled as they went about their work or their pleasure, and the wind blew as blithely as upon the meadows and the scented gorse. But somehow or other I got out of the bustle and the gaiety, and found myself walking slowly along a quiet, dull street, where there seemed to be no sunshine and no air, and where the few foot-passengers loitered as they walked, and hung indecisively about corners and archways. I walked along, hardly knowing where I was going or what I did there, but feeling impelled, as one sometimes is, to explore still further, with a vague idea of reaching some unknown goal. Thus I forged up the street, noting the small traffic of the milk-shop, and wondering at the incongruous medley of penny pipes, black tobacco, sweets, newspapers, and comic songs which here and there jostled one another in the short compass of a single window. I think it was a cold shudder that suddenly passed through me that first told me I had found what I wanted. I looked up from the pavement and stopped before a dusty shop, above which the lettering had faded, where the red bricks of two hundred years ago had grimed to black; where the windows had gathered to themselves the fog and the dirt of winters innumerable. I saw what I required; but I think it was five minutes before I had steadied myself and could walk in and ask for it in a cool voice and with a calm face. I think there must even then have been a tremor in my words, for the old man who came out from his back parlour, and fumbled slowly amongst his goods, looked oddly at me as he tied the parcel. I paid what he asked, and stood leaning by the counter, with a strange reluctance to take up my goods and go. I asked about the business, and learnt that trade was bad and profits cut down sadly; but then the street was not what it was before traffic had been diverted, but that was done forty years ago, "just before my father died," he said. I got away at last, and walked along sharply; it was a dismal street indeed, and I was glad to return to the bustle and the noise. Would you like to see my purchase?'

Austin said nothing, but nodded his head slightly; he still looked white and sick. Villiers pulled out a drawer in the bamboo table, and showed Austin a long coil of cord, hard and new; and at one end was a running noose.

'It is the best hempen cord,' said Villiers, 'just as it used to be made for the old trade, the man told me. Not an inch of jute from end to end.'

Austin set his teeth hard, and stared at Villiers, growing whiter as he looked.

'You would not do it,' he murmured at last. 'You would not have blood on your hands. My God!' he exclaimed, with sudden vehemence, 'you cannot mean this, Villiers, that you will make yourself a hangman?'

'No. I shall offer a choice, and leave the thing alone with this cord in a locked room for fifteen minutes. If when we go in it is not done, I shall call the nearest policeman. That is all.'

'I must go now. I cannot stay here any longer; I cannot bear this. Good-night.'

'Good-night, Austin.'

The door shut, but in a moment it was opened again, and Austin stood, white and ghastly, in the entrance.

'I was forgetting,' he said, 'that I too have something to tell. I have received a letter from Dr Harding of Buenos Ayres. He says that he attended Meyrick for three weeks before his death.'

'And does he say what carried him off in the prime of life? It was not fever?'

'No, it was not fever. According to the doctor, it was an utter collapse of the whole system, probably caused by some severe shock. But he states that the patient would tell him nothing, and that he was consequently at some disadvantage in treating the case.'

'Is there anything more?'

'Yes. Dr Harding ends his letter by saying: "I think this is all the information I can give you about your poor friend. He had not been long in Buenos Ayres, and knew scarcely any one, with the exception of a person who did not bear the best of characters, and has since left— a Mrs Vaughan."'

## THE FRAGMENTS

[Amongst the papers of the well-known physician, Dr Robert Matheson, of Ashley Street, Piccadilly, who died suddenly, of apoplectic seizure, at the beginning of 1892, a leaf of manuscript paper was found, covered with pencil jottings. These notes were in Latin, much abbreviated, and had evidently been made in great haste. The MS. was only deciphered with great difficulty, and some words have up to the present time evaded all the efforts of the expert employed. The date, 'xxv Jul. 1888,' is written on the right-hand corner of the MS. The following is a translation of Dr Matheson's manuscript.]

'WHETHER science would benefit by these brief notes if they could be published, I do not know, but rather doubt. But certainly I shall never take the responsibility of publishing or divulging one word of what is here written, not only on account of my oath freely given to those two persons who were present, but also because the details are too loathsome. It is probable that, upon mature consideration, and after weighing the good and evil, I shall one day destroy this paper, or at least leave it under seal to my friend D., trusting in his discretion, to use it or to burn it, as he may think fit.

'As was befitting I did all that my knowledge suggested to make sure that I was suffering under no delusion. At first astounded, I could hardly think, but in a minute's time I was sure that my pulse was steady and regular and that I was in my real and true senses. I ran over the anatomy of the foot and arm and repeated the formulæ of some of the carbon compounds, and then fixed my eyes quietly on what was before me.

'Though horror and revolting nausea rose up within me, and an odour of corruption choked my breath, I remained firm. I was then privileged or accursed, I dare not say which, to see that which was on the bed, lying there black like ink, transformed before my eyes. The skin, and the flesh, and the muscles, and the bones, and the firm struc- ture of the human body that I had thought to be unchangeable, and permanent as adamant, began to melt and dissolve.

'I knew that the body may be separated into its elements by external agencies, but I should have refused to believe what I saw. For here there was some internal force, of which I knew nothing, that caused dissolution and change.

'Here too was all the work by which man has been made repeated before my eyes. I saw the form waver from sex to sex, dividing itself from itself, and then again reunited. Then I saw the body descend to the beasts whence it ascended, and that which was on the heights go down to the depths, even to the abyss of all being. The principle of life, which makes organism, always remained, while the outward form changed.

'The light within the room had turned to blackness, not the darkness of night, in which objects are seen dimly, for I could see clearly and without difficulty. But it was the negation of light; objects were pre- sented to my eyes, if I may say so, without any medium, in such a man- ner that if there had been a prism in the room, I should have seen no colours represented in it.

'I watched, and at last I saw nothing but a substance as jelly. Then the ladder was ascended again . . [*Here the MS is illegible*] . . . for one instant I saw a Form, shaped in dimness before me, which I will not further describe. But the symbol of this form may be seen in ancient sculp- tures, and in paintings which survived beneath the lava,* too foul to be spoken of . . . as a horrible and unspeakable shape, neither man nor beast, was changed into human form, there came finally death.

'I who saw all this, not without great horror and loathing of soul, here write my name, declaring all that I have set on this paper to be true.

'Robert Matheson, Med. Dr'

\*       \*       \*       \*       \*

. . . Such, Raymond, is the story of what I know, and what I have seen. The burden of it was too heavy for me to bear alone, and yet I could tell it to none but you. Villiers, who was with me at the last knows nothing of that awful secret of the wood, of how what we both saw die, lay upon the smooth sweet turf amidst the summer flowers, half in sun and half in shadow, and holding the girl Rachel's hand, called and summoned those companions, and shaped in solid form, upon the earth we tread on, the horror which we can but hint at, which we can only name under a figure. I would not tell Villiers of this, nor of that resemblance, which struck me as with a blow upon my heart, when I saw the portrait, which filled the cup of terror at the end. What this can mean I dare not guess. I know that what I saw perish was not Mary, and yet in the last agony Mary's eyes looked into mine. Whether there be any one who can show the last link in this chain of awful mystery, I do not know, but if there be any one who can do this, you, Raymond, are the man. And if you know the secret, it rests with you to tell it or not, as you please.

I am writing this letter to you immediately on my getting back to town. I have been in the country for the last few days; perhaps you may be able to guess in what part. While the horror and wonder of London was at its height,—for 'Mrs Beaumont,' as I have told you, was well known in society,—I wrote to my friend Dr Phillips, giving some brief outline, or rather hint, of what had happened, and asking him to tell me the name of the village where the events he had related to me occurred. He gave me the name, as he said with the less hesitation, because Rachel's father and mother were dead, and the rest of the family had gone to a relative in the State of Washington six months before. The parents, he said, had undoubtedly died of grief and horror caused by the terrible death of their daughter, and by what had gone before that death. On the evening of the day on which I received Phillips's letter I was at Caermaen,* and standing beneath the mouldering Roman walls, white with the winters of seventeen hundred years, I looked over the meadow where once had stood the older temple of the 'God of the Deeps,' and saw a house gleaming in the sunlight. It was the house where Helen had lived. I stayed at Caermaen for several days. The people of the place, I found, knew little and had guessed less. Those whom I spoke to on the matter seemed surprised that an antiquarian (as I professed myself to be) should trouble about a village tragedy, of which they gave a very commonplace version, and, as you may imagine, I told nothing of what I knew. Most of my time was spent in the great wood that rises just above the village and climbs the hillside, and goes down to the river in the valley; such another long lovely valley, Raymond, as that on which we looked one summer night, walking to and fro before your house. For many an hour I strayed through the maze of the forest, turning now to right and now to left, pacing slowly down long alleys of undergrowth, shadowy and chill, even under the mid-day sun, and halting beneath great oaks; lying on the short turf of a clearing where the faint sweet scent of wild roses came to me on the wind and mixed with the heavy perfume of the elder whose mingled odour is like the odour of the room of the dead, a vapour of incense and corruption. I stood by rough banks at the edges of the wood, gazing at all the pomp and procession of the foxgloves towering amidst the bracken and shining red in the broad sunshine, and beyond them into deep thickets of close undergrowth where springs boil up from the rock and nourish the water-weeds, dank and evil. But in all my wanderings I avoided one part of the wood; it was not till yesterday that I climbed to the summit of the hill, and stood upon the ancient Roman road that threads the highest ridge of the wood. Here they had walked, Helen and Rachel, along this quiet causeway, upon the pavement of green turf, shut in on either side by high banks of red earth, and tall hedges of shining beech, and here I followed in their steps, looking out, now and again, through partings in the boughs, and seeing on one side the sweep of the wood stretching far to right and left, and sinking into the broad level, and beyond, the yellow sea, and the land over the sea. On the other side was the valley and the river, and hill following hill as wave on wave, and wood and meadow, and cornfield, and white houses gleaming, and a great wall of mountain, and far blue peaks in the north. And so at last, I came to the place. The track went up a gentle slope, and widened out into an open space with a wall of thick undergrowth around it, and then, narrowing again, passed on into the distance and the faint blue mist of summer heat. And into this pleasant summer glade Rachel passed a girl, and left it, who shall say what? I did not stay long there.

*     *     *     *     *

In a small town near Caermaen there is a museum, containing for the most part Roman remains which have been found in the neighbourhood at various times. On the day after my arrival at Caermaen I walked over to the town in question, and took the opportunity of inspecting this museum. After I had seen most of the sculptured stones, the coffins, rings, coins, and fragments of tessellated pavement which the place contains, I was shown a small square pillar of white stone, which had been recently discovered in the wood of which I have been speaking, and, as I found on inquiry, in that open space where the Roman road broadens out. On one side of the pillar was an inscription, of which I took a note. Some of the letters have been defaced, but I do not think

there can be any doubt as to those which I supply. The inscript
follows:

DEVOMNODENT*i*
FLA*v*IVSSENILISPOSSV*it*
PROPTERNVP*tias*
*qua*SVIDITSVBVMB*ra*

'To the great god Nodens* (the god of the Great Deep or Abyss),
Flavius Senilis has erected this pillar on account of the marriage which
he saw beneath the shade.'

The custodian of the museum informed me that local antiquaries
were much puzzled, not by the inscription, or by any difficulty in translating it, but as to the circumstance or rite to which allusion is made.

\* \* \* \* \*

...And now, my dear Clarke, as to what you tell me about Helen Vaughan,
whom you say you saw die under circumstances of the utmost and
almost incredible horror. I was interested in your account, but a good
deal, nay, all of what you told me, I knew already. I can understand the
strange likeness you remarked both in the portrait and in the actual
face; you have seen Helen's mother. You remember that still summer
night so many years ago, when I talked to you of the world beyond the
shadows, and of the god Pan. You remember Mary. She was the mother
of Helen Vaughan, who was born nine months after that night.

Mary never recovered her reason. She lay, as you saw her, all the
while upon her bed, and a few days after the child was born, she died.
I fancy that just at the last she knew me; I was standing by the bed, and
the old look came into her eyes for a second, and then she shuddered
and groaned and died. It was an ill work I did that night, when you were
present; I broke open the door of the house of life, without knowing or
caring what might pass forth or enter in. I recollect your telling me at
the time, sharply enough, and rightly enough too, in one sense, that
I had ruined the reason of a human being by a foolish experiment,
based on an absurd theory. You did well to blame me, but my theory was
not all absurdity. What I said Mary would see, she saw, but I forgot that
no human eyes could look on such a vision with impunity. And I forgot,
as I have just said, that when the house of life is thus thrown open, there
may enter in that for which we have no name, and human flesh may
become the veil of a horror one dare not express. I played with energies
which I did not understand and you have seen the ending of it. Helen
Vaughan did well to bind the cord about her neck and die, though the

death was horrible. The blackened face, the hideous form upon the bed, changing and melting before your eyes from woman to man, from man to beast, and from beast to worse than beast, all the strange horror that you witnessed, surprises me but little. What you say the doctor whom you sent for saw and shuddered at I noticed long ago; I knew what I had done the moment the child was born, and when it was scarcely five years old I surprised it, not once or twice but several times with a play-mate, you may guess of what kind. It was for me a constant, an incarnate horror, and after a few years I felt I could bear it no longer, and I sent Helen Vaughan away. You know now what frightened the boy in the wood. The rest of the strange story, and all else that you tell me, as discovered by your friend, I have contrived to learn from time to time, almost to the last chapter. And now Helen is with her companions. . . .

THE END

NOTE.—*Helen Vaughan was born on August 5th, 1865, at the Red House, Breconshire, and died on July 25th, 1888, in her house in a street off Piccadilly, called Ashley Street in the story.*

# THE INMOST LIGHT

## I

ONE evening in autumn, when the deformities of London were veiled in faint blue mist, and its vistas and far-reaching streets seemed splendid, Mr Charles Salisbury was slowly pacing down Rupert Street, drawing nearer to his favourite restaurant* by slow degrees. His eyes were downcast in study of the pavement, and thus it was that as he passed in at the narrow door a man who had come up from the lower end of the street jostled against him.

'I beg your pardon—wasn't looking where I was going. Why, it's Dyson!'

'Yes, quite so. How are you, Salisbury?'

'Quite well. But where have you been, Dyson? I don't think I can have seen you for the last five years?'

'No; I daresay not. You remember I was getting rather hard up when you came to my place at Charlotte Street?'

'Perfectly. I think I remember your telling me that you owed five weeks' rent, and that you had parted with your watch for a comparatively small sum.'

'My dear Salisbury, your memory is admirable. Yes, I was hard up. But the curious thing is that soon after you saw me I became harder up. My financial state was described by a friend as "stone broke." I don't approve of slang, mind you, but such was my condition. But suppose we go in; there might be other people who would like to dine—it's a human weakness, Salisbury.'

'Certainly; come along. I was wondering as I walked down whether the corner table were taken. It has a velvet back, you know.'

'I know the spot; it's vacant. Yes, as I was saying, I became even harder up.'

'What did you do then?' asked Salisbury, disposing of his hat, and settling down in the corner of the seat, with a glance of fond anticipation at the *menu*.

'What did I do? Why, I sat down and reflected. I had a good classical education, and a positive distaste for business of any kind: that was the capital with which I faced the world. Do you know, I have heard people describe olives as nasty! What lamentable Philistinism! I have often thought, Salisbury, that I could write genuine poetry under the influence of olives and red wine. Let us have Chianti; it may not be very good, but the flasks are simply charming.'

'It is pretty good here. We may as well have a big flask.'

'Very good. I reflected, then, on my want of prospects, and I determined to embark in literature.'

'Really, that was strange. You seem in pretty comfortable circumstances, though.'

'Though! What a satire upon a noble profession. I am afraid, Salisbury, you haven't a proper idea of the dignity of an artist. You see me sitting at my desk—or at least you can see me if you care to call—with pen and ink, and simple nothingness before me, and if you come again in a few hours you will (in all probability) find a creation!'

'Yes, quite so. I had an idea that literature was not remunerative.'

'You are mistaken; its rewards are great. I may mention, by the way, that shortly after you saw me I succeeded to a small income. An uncle died, and proved unexpectedly generous.'

'Ah, I see. That must have been convenient.'

'It was pleasant—undeniably pleasant. I have always considered it in the light of an endowment of my researches. I told you I was a man of letters; it would, perhaps, be more correct to describe myself as a man of science.'

'Dear me, Dyson, you have really changed very much in the last few years. I had a notion, don't you know, that you were a sort of idler about town, the kind of man one might meet on the north side of Piccadilly every day from May to July.'

'Exactly. I was even then forming myself, though all unconsciously. You know my poor father could not afford to send me to the University. I used to grumble in my ignorance at not having completed my education. That was the folly of youth, Salisbury; my University was Piccadilly. There I began to study the great science which still occupies me.'

'What science do you mean?'

'The science of the great city; the physiology of London; literally and metaphysically the greatest subject that the mind of man can conceive. What an admirable *salmi** this is; undoubtedly the final end of the pheasant. Yes, I feel sometimes positively overwhelmed with the thought of the vastness and complexity of London. Paris a man may get to understand thoroughly with a reasonable amount of study; but London is always a mystery. In Paris you may say: here live the actresses, here the Bohemians, and the *Ratés;** but it is different in London. You may point out a street, correctly enough, as the abode of washerwomen; but, in that second floor, a man may be studying Chaldee roots,* and in the garret over the way a forgotten artist is dying by inches.'

'I see you are Dyson, unchanged and unchangeable,' said Salisbury, slowly sipping his Chianti. 'I think you are misled by a too fervid imagination; the mystery of London exists only in your fancy. It seems to me a dull place enough. We seldom hear of a really artistic crime in London, whereas I believe Paris abounds in that sort of thing.'

'Give me some more wine. Thanks. You are mistaken, my dear fellow, you are really mistaken. London has nothing to be ashamed of in the way of crime. Where we fail is for want of Homers, not Agamemnons. *Carent quia vate sacro*,* you know.'

'I recall the quotation. But I don't think I quite follow you.'

'Well, in plain language, we have no good writers in London who make a speciality of that kind of thing. Our common reporter is a dull dog; every story that he has to tell is spoilt in the telling. His idea of horror and of what excites horror is so lamentably deficient. Nothing will content the fellow but blood, vulgar red blood, and when he can get it he lays it on thick, and considers that he has produced a telling article. It's a poor notion. And, by some curious fatality, it is the most commonplace and brutal murders which always attract the most attention and get written up the most. For instance, I daresay that you never heard of the Harlesden* case?'

'No; no I don't remember anything about it.'

'Of course not. And yet the story is a curious one. I will tell it you over our coffee. Harlesden, you know, or I expect you don't know, is quite on the out-quarters of London; something curiously different from your fine old crusted suburb like Norwood or Hampstead, different as each of these is from the other. Hampstead, I mean, is where you look for the head of your great China house with his three acres of land and pine-houses, though of late there is the artistic substratum; while Norwood is the home of the prosperous middle-class family who took the house "because it was near the Palace,"* and sickened of the Palace six months afterwards; but Harlesden is a place of no character. It's too new to have any character as yet. There are the rows of red houses and the rows of white houses and the bright green Venetians, and the blistering doorways, and the little backyards they call gardens, and a few feeble shops, and then, just as you think you're going to grasp the physiognomy of the settlement, it all melts away.'

'How the dickens is that? the houses don't tumble down before one's eyes, I suppose!'

'Well, no, not exactly that. But Harlesden as an entity disappears.

Your street turns into a quiet lane, and your staring houses into elm
trees, and the back-gardens into green meadows. You pass instantly
from town to country; there is no transition as in a small country town,
no soft gradations of wider lawns and orchards, with houses gradually
becoming less dense, but a dead stop. I believe the people who live there
mostly go into the city.* I have seen once or twice a laden 'bus* bound
thitherwards. But however that may be, I can't conceive a greater loneliness in a desert at midnight than there is there at mid-day. It is like
a city of the dead; the streets are glaring and desolate, and as you pass it
suddenly strikes you that this too is part of London. Well, a year or two
ago there was a doctor living there; he had set up his brass plate and his
red lamp* at the very end of one of those shining streets, and from the
back of the house, the fields stretched away to the north. I don't know
what his reason was in settling down in such an out-of-the-way place,
perhaps Dr Black as we will call him was a far-seeing man and looked
ahead. His relations, so it appeared afterwards, had lost sight of him for
many years and didn't even know he was a doctor, much less where he
lived. However, there he was, settled in Harlesden, with some fragments of a practice, and an uncommonly pretty wife. People used to see
them walking out together in the summer evenings soon after they
came to Harlesden, and, so far as could be observed, they seemed a very
affectionate couple. These walks went on through the autumn, and then
ceased; but, of course, as the days grew dark and the weather cold, the
lanes near Harlesden might be expected to lose many of their attractions. All through the winter nobody saw anything of Mrs Black; the
doctor used to reply to his patients' inquiries that she was a "little out
of sorts, would be better, no doubt, in the spring." But the spring came,
and the summer, and no Mrs Black appeared, and at last people began
to rumour and talk amongst themselves, and all sorts of queer things
were said at "high teas," which you may possibly have heard are the
only form of entertainment known in such suburbs. Dr Black began to
surprise some very odd looks cast in his direction, and the practice such
as it was fell off before his eyes. In short, when the neighbours whispered about the matter, they whispered that Mrs Black was dead, and
that the doctor had made away with her. But this wasn't the case; Mrs
Black was seen alive in June. It was a Sunday afternoon, one of those
few exquisite days that an English climate offers, and half London had
strayed out into the fields, north, south, east, and west, to smell the
scent of the white May, and to see if the wild roses were yet in blossom
in the hedges. I had gone out myself early in the morning, and had had
a long ramble, and somehow or other as I was steering homeward

I found myself in this very Harlesden we have been talking about. To be exact, I had a glass of beer in the "General Gordon,"* the most flourishing house in the neighbourhood, and as I was wandering rather aimlessly about, I saw an uncommonly tempting gap in a hedgerow, and resolved to explore the meadow beyond. Soft grass is very grateful to the feet after the infernal grit strewn on suburban sidewalks, and after walking about for some time I thought I should like to sit down on a bank and have a smoke. While I was getting out my pouch, I looked up in the direction of the houses, and as I looked I felt my breath caught back, and my teeth began to chatter, and the stick I had in one hand snapped in two with the grip I gave it. It was as if I had had an electric current down my spine, and yet for some moment of time which seemed long, but which must have been very short, I caught myself wondering what on earth was the matter. Then I knew what had made my very heart shudder and my bones grind together in an agony. As I glanced up I had looked straight towards the last house in the row before me, and in an upper window of that house I had seen for some short fraction of a second a face. It was the face of a woman, and yet it was not human. You and I, Salisbury, have heard in our time, as we sat in our seats in church in sober English fashion, of a lust that cannot be satiated and of a fire that is unquenchable,* but few of us have any notion what these words mean. I hope you never may, for as I saw that face at the window, with the blue sky above me and the warm air playing in gusts about me, I knew I had looked into another world—looked through the window of a commonplace, brand-new house, and seen hell open before me. When the first shock was over, I thought once or twice that I should have fainted; my face streamed with a cold sweat, and my breath came and went in sobs, as if I had been half drowned. I managed to get up at last, and walked round to the street, and there I saw the name Dr Black on the post by the front gate. As fate or my luck would have it, the door opened and a man came down the steps as I passed by. I had no doubt it was the doctor himself. He was of a type rather common in London; long and thin, with a pasty face and a dull black moustache. He gave me a look as we passed each other on the pavement, and, though it was merely the casual glance which one foot-passenger bestows on another, I felt convinced in my mind that here was an ugly customer to deal with. As you may imagine I went my way a good deal puzzled and horrified too by what I had seen; for I had paid another visit to the "General Gordon," and had got together a good deal of the common gossip of the place about the Blacks. I didn't mention the fact that I had seen a woman's face in the window; but I heard that Mrs Black had been much admired for her beautiful golden hair, and round what had struck me with such a nameless terror, there was a mist of flowing yellow hair, as it were an aureole of glory round the visage of a satyr. The whole thing bothered me in an indescribable manner; and when I got home I tried my best to think of the impression I had received as an illusion, but it was no use. I knew very well I had seen what I have tried to describe to you, and I was morally certain that I had seen Mrs Black. And then there was the gossip of the place, the suspicion of foul play, which I knew to be false, and my own conviction that there was some deadly mischief or other going on in that bright red house at the corner of Devon Road: how to construct a theory of a reasonable kind out of these two elements. In short, I found myself in a world of mystery; I puzzled my head over it and filled up my leisure moments by gathering together odd threads of speculation, but I never moved a step towards any real solution, and as the summer days went on the matter seemed to grow misty and indistinct, shadowing some vague terror, like a nightmare of last month. I suppose it would before long have faded into the background of my brain—I should not have forgotten it, for such a thing could never be forgotten—but one morning as I was looking over the paper my eye was caught by a heading over some two dozen lines of small type. The words I had seen were simply, "The Harlesden Case," and I knew what I was going to read. Mrs Black was dead. Black had called in another medical man to certify as to cause of death, and something or other had aroused the strange doctor's suspicions and there had been an inquest and *post-mortem*. And the result? That, I will confess, did astonish me considerably; it was the triumph of the unexpected. The two doctors who made the autopsy were obliged to confess that they could not discover the faintest trace of any kind of foul play; their most exquisite tests and reagents failed to detect the presence of poison in the most infinitesimal quantity. Death, they found, had been caused by a somewhat obscure and scientifically interesting form of brain disease. The tissue of the brain and the molecules of the grey matter had undergone a most extraordinary series of changes; and the younger of the two doctors, who has some reputation I believe, as a specialist in brain trouble, made some remarks in giving his evidence which struck me deeply at the time, though I did not then grasp their full significance. He said: "At the commencement of the examination I was astonished to find appearances of a character entirely new to me, notwithstanding my somewhat large experience. I need not specify these appearances at present, it will be sufficient for me to state that as I proceeded in my task I could scarcely believe that the brain before me was that of a human being at all." There was some surprise at this statement, as you may imagine, and the coroner asked the doctor if he meant to say that the brain resembled that of an animal. "No," he replied, "I should not put it in that way. Some of the appearances I noticed seemed to point in that direction, but others, and these were the more surprising, indicated a nervous organisation of a wholly different character from that either of man or of the lower animals." It was a curious thing to say, but of course the jury brought in a verdict of death from natural causes, and, so far as the public was concerned, the case came to an end. But after I had read what the doctor said I made up my mind that I should like to know a good deal more, and I set to work on what seemed likely to prove an interesting investigation. I had really a good deal of trouble, but I was successful in a measure. Though—why, my dear fellow, I had no notion of the time. Are you aware that we have been here nearly four hours? The waiters are staring at us. Let's have the bill and be gone.'

The two men went out in silence, and stood a moment in the cool air, watching the hurrying traffic of Coventry Street pass before them to the accompaniment of the ringing bells of hansoms and the cries of the newsboys; the deep far murmur of London surging up ever and again from beneath these louder noises.

'It is a strange case, isn't it?' said Dyson at length. 'What do you think of it?'

'My dear fellow, I haven't heard the end, so I will reserve my opinion. When will you give me the sequel?'

'Come to my rooms some evening; say next Thursday. Here's the address. Good-night; I want to get down to the Strand.'

Dyson hailed a passing hansom, and Salisbury turned northward to walk home to his lodgings.

## II

MR SALISBURY, as may have been gathered from the few remarks which he had found it possible to introduce in the course of the evening, was a young gentleman of a peculiarly solid form of intellect, coy and retiring before the mysterious and the uncommon, with a constitutional dislike of paradox. During the restaurant dinner he had been forced to listen in almost absolute silence to a strange tissue of improbabilities strung together with the ingenuity of a born meddler in plots and mysteries, and it was with a feeling of weariness that he crossed Shaftesbury Avenue, and dived into the recesses of Soho, for his lodgings were in a modest neighbourhood to the north of Oxford Street. As he walked he speculated on the probable fate of Dyson, relying on literature, unbe-friended by a thoughtful relative, and could not help concluding that so much subtlety united to a too vivid imagination would in all likelihood have been rewarded with a pair of sandwich-boards or a super's banner. Absorbed in this train of thought, and admiring the perverse dexterity which could transmute the face of a sickly woman and a case of brain disease into the crude elements of romance, Salisbury strayed on through the dimly-lighted streets, not noticing the gusty wind which drove sharply round corners and whirled the stray rubbish of the pavement into the air in eddies, while black clouds gathered over the sickly yellow moon. Even a stray drop or two of rain blown into his face did not rouse him from his meditations, and it was only when with a sudden rush the storm tore down upon the street that he began to consider the expedi-ency of finding some shelter. The rain, driven by the wind, pelted down with the violence of a thunderstorm, dashing up from the stones and hissing through the air, and soon a perfect torrent of water coursed along the kennels and accumulated in pools over the choked-up drains. The few stray passengers who had been loafing rather than walking about the street, had scuttered away, like frightened rabbits, to some invisible places of refuge, and though Salisbury whistled loud and long for a hansom, no hansom appeared. He looked about him, as if to discover how far he might be from the haven of Oxford Street, but strolling carelessly along, he had turned out of his way, and found himself in an unknown region, and one to all appearance devoid even of a public-house where shelter could be bought for the modest sum of twopence. The street lamps were few and at long intervals and burned behind grimy glasses with the sickly light of oil lamps, and by this wavering light Salisbury could make out the shadowy and vast old houses of which the street was composed. As he passed along, hurrying, and shrinking from the full sweep of the rain, he noticed the innumerable bell-handles, with names that seemed about to vanish of old age graven on brass plates beneath them, and here and there a richly carved pent-house overhung the door, blackening with the grime of fifty years. The storm seemed to grow more and more furious, he was wet through and a new hat had become a ruin, and still Oxford Street seemed as far off as ever; it was with deep relief that the dripping man caught sight of a dark archway which seemed to promise shelter from the rain if not from the wind. Salisbury took up his position in the driest corner and looked about him; he was standing in a kind of passage contrived under part of a house, and behind him stretched a narrow footway leading between blank walls to regions unknown. He had stood there for some time, vainly endeavouring to rid himself of some of his superfluous moisture, and listening for the passing wheel of a hansom, when his attention was aroused by a loud noise coming from the direction of the passage behind, and growing louder as it drew nearer. In a couple of minutes he could make out the shrill, raucous voice of a woman, threatening and renouncing and making the very stones echo with her accents, while now and then a man grumbled and expostulated. Though to all appearance devoid of romance, Salisbury had some relish for street rows, and was, indeed, somewhat of an amateur in the more amusing phases of drunkenness; he therefore composed himself to listen and observe with something of the air of a subscriber to grand opera. To his annoyance, however, the tempest seemed suddenly to be composed, and he could hear nothing but the impatient steps of the woman and the slow lurch of the man as they came towards him. Keeping back in the shadow of the wall he could see the two drawing nearer; the man was evidently drunk, and had much ado to avoid frequent collision with the wall as he tacked across from one side to the other, like some barque beating up against a wind. The woman was looking straight in front of her, with tears streaming from her eyes, but suddenly as they went by the flame blazed up again, and she burst forth into a torrent of abuse, facing round upon her companion.

'You low rascal, you mean, contemptible cur,' she went on, after an incoherent storm of curses, 'you think I'm to work and slave for you always, I suppose, while you're after that Green Street girl and drinking every penny you've got? But you're mistaken, Sam—indeed, I'll bear it no longer. Damn you, you dirty thief, I've done with you and your master too, so you can go your own errands, and I only hope they'll get you into trouble.'

The woman tore at the bosom of her dress, and taking something out that looked like paper, crumpled it up and flung it away. It fell at Salisbury's feet. She ran out and disappeared in the darkness, while the man lurched slowly into the street, grumbling indistinctly to himself in a perplexed tone of voice. Salisbury looked out after him, and saw him maundering along the pavement, halting now and then and swaying indecisively, and then starting off at some fresh tangent. The sky had cleared, and white fleecy clouds were fleeting across the moon, high in the heaven. The light came and went by turns, as the clouds passed by, and, turning round as the clear, white rays shone into the passage, Salisbury saw the little ball of crumpled paper which the woman had cast down. Oddly curious to know what it might contain, he picked it up and put it in his pocket, and set out afresh on his journey.

## III

SALISBURY was a man of habit. When he got home, drenched to the skin, his clothes hanging lank about him, and a ghastly dew besmearing his hat, his only thought was of his health, of which he took studious care. So, after changing his clothes and encasing himself in a warm dressing-gown, he proceeded to prepare a sudorific* in the shape of hot gin and water, warming the latter over one of those spirit-lamps which mitigate the austerities of the modern hermit's life. By the time this preparation had been exhibited, and Salisbury's disturbed feelings had been soothed by a pipe of tobacco, he was able to get into bed in a happy state of vacancy, without a thought of his adventure in the dark archway, or of the weird fancies with which Dyson had seasoned his dinner. It was the same at breakfast the next morning, for Salisbury made a point of not thinking of anything until that meal was over; but when the cup and saucer were cleared away, and the morning pipe was lit, he remembered the little ball of paper, and began fumbling in the pockets of his wet coat. He did not remember into which pocket he had put it, and as he dived now into one, and now into another, he experienced a strange feeling of apprehension lest it should not be there at all, though he could not for the life of him have explained the importance he attached to what was in all probability mere rubbish. But he sighed with relief when his fingers touched the crumpled surface in an inside pocket, and he drew it out gently and laid it on the little desk by his easy chair with as much care as if it had been some rare jewel. Salisbury sat smoking and staring at his find for a few minutes, an odd temptation to throw the thing in the fire and have done with it, struggling with as odd a speculation as to its possible contents, and as to the reason why the infuriated woman should have flung a bit of paper from her with such vehemence. As might be expected, it was the latter feeling that conquered in the end, and yet it was with something like repugnance that he at last took the paper and unrolled it, and laid it out before him. It was a piece of common dirty paper, to all appearance torn out of a cheap exercise-book, and in the middle were a few lines written in a queer cramped hand. Salisbury bent his head and stared eagerly at it for a moment, drawing a long breath, and then fell back in his chair gazing blankly before him, till at last with a sudden revulsion he burst into a peal of laughter, so long and loud and uproarious that the landlady's baby in the floor below awoke from sleep and echoed his mirth with hideous yells. But he laughed again and again, and took the paper up to read a second time what seemed such meaningless nonsense.

'Q has had to go and see his friends in Paris,' it began. 'Traverse Handel S. "Once around the grass, and twice around the lass, and thrice around the maple tree."'

Salisbury took up the paper and crumpled it as the angry woman had done, and aimed it at the fire. He did not throw it there, however, but tossed it carelessly into the well of the desk, and laughed again. The sheer folly of the thing offended him, and he was ashamed of his own eager speculation, as one who pores over the high-sounding announcements in the agony column* of the daily paper, and finds nothing but advertisement and triviality. He walked to the window, and stared out at the languid morning life of his quarter; the maids in slatternly print dresses washing door-steps, the fishmonger and the butcher on their rounds, and the tradesmen standing at the doors of their small shops, drooping for lack of trade and excitement. In the distance a blue haze gave some grandeur to the prospect, but the view as a whole was depressing, and would only have interested a student of the life of London, who finds something rare and choice in its every aspect. Salisbury turned away in disgust, and settled himself in the easy-chair, upholstered in a bright shade of green, and decked with yellow gimp,* which was the pride and attraction of the apartments. Here he composed himself to his morning's occupation—the perusal of a novel that dealt with sport and love in a manner that suggested the collaboration of a studgroom and a ladies' college. In an ordinary way, however, Salisbury would have been carried on by the interest of the story up to lunchtime, but this morning he fidgeted in and out of his chair, took the book up and laid it down again, and swore at last to himself and at himself in mere irritation. In point of fact the jingle of the paper found in the archway had 'got into his head,' and do what he would he could not help muttering over and over, 'Once around the grass, and twice around the lass, and thrice around the maple tree.' It became a positive pain, like the foolish burden of a music-hall song, everlastingly quoted, and sung at all hours of the day and night, and treasured by the street boys as an unfailing resource for six months together. He went out into the streets, and tried to forget his enemy in the jostling of the crowds, and the roar and clatter of the traffic, but presently he would find himself stealing quietly aside, and pacing some deserted byway, vainly puzzling his brains, and trying to fix some meaning to phrases that were meaningless. It was a positive relief when Thursday came, and he remembered that he had made an appointment to go and see Dyson; the flimsy reveries of the self-styled man of letters appeared entertaining when compared with this ceaseless iteration, this maze of thought from which there seemed no possibility of escape. Dyson's abode was in one of the quietest of the quiet streets that lead down from the Strand to the river, and when Salisbury passed from the narrow stairway into his friend's room, he saw that the uncle had been beneficent indeed. The floor glowed and flamed with all the colours of the East, it was as Dyson pompously remarked, 'a sunset in a dream,' and the lamplight, the twilight of London streets, was shut out with strangely worked curtains, glittering here and there with threads of gold. In the shelves of an oak *armoire* stood jars and plates of old French china, and the black and white of etchings not to be found in the Haymarket or in Bond Street, stood out against the splendour of a Japanese paper. Salisbury sat down on the settle by the hearth, and sniffed the mingled fumes of incense and tobacco, wondering and dumb before all this splendour after the green rep and the oleographs,* the gilt-framed mirror and the lustres of his own apartment.

'I am glad you have come,' said Dyson. 'Comfortable little room, isn't it? But you don't look very well, Salisbury. Nothing disagreed with you, has it?'

'No; but I have been a good deal bothered for the last few days. The fact is I had an odd kind of—of—adventure, I suppose I may call it, that night I saw you, and it has worried me a good deal. And the provoking part of it is that it's the merest nonsense—but, however, I will tell you all about it, by and by. You were going to let me have the rest of that odd story you began at the restaurant.'

'Yes. But I am afraid, Salisbury, you are incorrigible. You are a slave to what you call matter of fact. You know perfectly well that in your heart you think the oddness in that case is of my making, and that it is all really as plain as the police reports. However, as I have begun, I will go on. But first we will have something to drink, and you may as well light your pipe.'

Dyson went up to the oak cupboard, and drew from its depths a rotund bottle and two little glasses, quaintly gilded.

'It's Benedictine,'* he said. 'You'll have some, won't you?'

Salisbury assented, and the two men sat sipping and smoking reflectively for some minutes before Dyson began.

'Let me see,' he said at last, 'we were at the inquest, weren't we? No, we had done with that. Ah, I remember. I was telling you that on the whole I had been successful in my inquiries, investigation, or whatever you like to call it, into the matter. Wasn't that where I left off?'

'Yes, that was it. To be precise, I think "though" was the last word you said on the matter.'

'Exactly. I have been thinking it all over since the other night, and I have come to the conclusion that that "though" is a very big "though" indeed. Not to put too fine a point on it, I have had to confess that what I found out, or thought I found out, amounts in reality to nothing. I am as far away from the heart of the case as ever. However, I may as well tell you what I do know. You may remember my saying that I was impressed a good deal by some remarks of one of the doctors who gave evidence at the inquest. Well, I determined that my first step must be to try if I could get something more definite and intelligible out of that doctor. Somehow or other I managed to get an introduction to the man, and he gave me an appointment to come and see him. He turned out to be a pleasant, genial fellow; rather young and not in the least like the typical medical man, and he began the conference by offering me whisky and cigars. I didn't think it worth while to beat about the bush, so I began by saying that part of his evidence at the Harlesden Inquest struck me as very peculiar, and I gave him the printed report, with the sentences in question underlined. He just glanced at the slip, and gave me a queer look. "It struck you as peculiar, did it?" said he. "Well, you must remember that the Harlesden case was very peculiar. In fact, I think I may safely say that in some features it was unique—quite unique." "Quite so," I replied, "and that's exactly why it interests me, and why I want to know more about it. And I thought that if anybody could give me any information it would be you. What is your opinion of the matter?"

'It was a pretty downright sort of question, and my doctor looked rather taken aback.

' "Well," he said, "as I fancy your motive in inquiring into the question must be mere curiosity, I think I may tell you my opinion with tolerable freedom. So, Mr, Mr Dyson? if you want to know my theory, it is this: I believe that Dr Black killed his wife."

' "But the verdict," I answered, "the verdict was given from your own evidence."

' "Quite so; the verdict was given in accordance with the evidence of my colleague and myself, and, under the circumstances, I think the jury acted very sensibly. In fact, I don't see what else they could have done. But I stick to my opinion mind you, and I say this also. I don't wonder at Black's doing what I firmly believe he did. I think he was justified."

' "Justified! How could that be?" I asked. I was astonished, as you may imagine, at the answer I had got. The doctor wheeled round his chair and looked steadily at me for a moment before he answered.

' "I suppose you are not a man of science, yourself? No; then it would be of no use my going into detail. I have always been firmly opposed myself to any partnership between physiology and psychology. I believe that both are bound to suffer. No one recognises more decidedly than I do the impassable gulf, the fathomless abyss that separates the world of consciousness from the sphere of matter. We know that every change of consciousness is accompanied by a rearrangement of the molecules in the grey matter; and that is all. What the link between them is, or why they occur together, we do not know, and most authorities believe that we never can know. Yet, I will tell you that as I did my work, the knife in my hand, I felt convinced, in spite of all theories, that what lay before me was not the brain of a dead woman—not the brain of a human being at all. Of course I saw the face; but it was quite placid, devoid of all expression. It must have been a beautiful face, no doubt, but I can honestly say that I would not have looked in that face when there was life behind it for a thousand guineas, no, nor for twice that sum."

' "My dear sir," I said, "you surprise me extremely. You say that it was not the brain of a human being. What was it, then?"'

' "The brain of a devil." He spoke quite coolly, and never moved a muscle. "The brain of a devil," he repeated, "and I have no doubt that Black put a pillow over her mouth and kept it there for a few minutes. I don't blame him if he did. Whatever Mrs Black was, she was not fit to stay in this world. Will you have anything more? No? Good-night, good-night."

'It was a queer sort of opinion to get from a man of science, wasn't it? When he was saying that he would not have looked on that face when alive for a thousand guineas, or two thousand guineas, I was thinking of the face I had seen, but I said nothing. I went again to Harlesden, and passed from one shop to another, making small purchases, and trying to find out whether there was anything about the Blacks which was not already common property, but there was very little to hear. One of the tradesmen to whom I spoke said he had known the dead woman well, she used to buy of him such quantities of grocery as were required for their small household, for they never kept a servant, but had a char-woman* in occasionally, and she had not seen Mrs Black for months before she died. According to this man Mrs Black was "a nice lady," always kind and considerate, and so fond of her husband and he of her, as every one thought. And yet, to put the doctor's opinion on one side, I knew what I had seen. And then after thinking it all over, and putting one thing with another, it seemed to me that the only person likely to give me much assistance would be Black himself, and I made up my mind to find him. Of course he wasn't to be found in Harlesden; he had left, I was told, directly after the funeral. Everything in the house had been sold, and one fine day Black got into the train with a small portmanteau, and went, nobody knew where. It was a chance if he were ever heard of again, and it was by a mere chance that I came across him at last. I was walking one day along Gray's Inn Road, not bound for anywhere in particular, but looking about me, as usual, and holding on to my hat, for it was a gusty day in early March, and the wind was making the tree-tops in the Inn rock and quiver. I had come up from the Holborn end, and I had almost got to Theobald's Road when I noticed a man walking in front of me, leaning on a stick, and to all appearance very feeble. There was something about his look that made me curious, I don't know why, and I began to walk briskly with the idea of overtaking him, when of a sudden his hat blew off and came bounding along the pavement to my feet. Of course I rescued the hat, and gave it a glance as I went towards its owner. It was a biography in itself; a Piccadilly maker's name in the inside, but I don't think a beggar would have picked it out of the gutter. Then I looked up and saw Dr Black of Harlesden waiting for me. A queer thing, wasn't it? But, Salisbury, what a change! When I saw Dr Black come down the steps of his house at Harlesden he was an upright man, walking firmly with well-built limbs; a man, I should say, in the prime of his life. And now before me there crouched this wretched creature, bent and feeble, with shrunken cheeks, and hair that was whitening fast, and limbs that trembled and shook together, and misery in his eyes. He thanked me for bringing him his hat, saying, "I don't think I should ever have got it, I can't run much now. A gusty day, sir, isn't it?" and with this he was turning away, but by little and little I contrived to draw him into the current of conversation, and we walked together eastward. I think the man would have been glad to get rid of me; but I didn't intend to let him go, and he stopped at last in front of a miserable house in a miserable street. It was, I verily believe, one of the most wretched quarters I have ever seen: houses that must have been sordid and hideous enough when new, that had gathered foulness with every year, and now seemed to lean and totter to their fall. "I live up there," said Black, pointing to the tiles, "not in the front—in the back. I am very quiet there. I won't ask you to come in now, but perhaps some other day——" I caught him up at that, and told him I should be only too glad to come and see him. He gave me an odd sort of glance, as if he was wondering what on earth I or anybody else could care about him, and I left him fumbling with his latch-key. I think you will say I did pretty well when I tell you that within a few weeks I had made myself an intimate friend of Black's. I shall never forget the first time I went to his room; I hope I shall never see such abject, squalid misery again. The foul paper, from which all pattern or trace of a pattern had long vanished, subdued and penetrated with the grime of the evil street, was hanging in mouldering pennons* from the wall. Only at the end of the room was it possible to stand upright, and the sight of the wretched bed and the odour of corruption that pervaded the place made me turn faint and sick. Here I found him munching a piece of bread; he seemed surprised to find that I had kept my promise, but he gave me his chair and sat on the bed while we talked. I used to go and see him often, and we had long conversations together, but he never mentioned Harlesden or his wife. I fancy that he supposed me ignorant of the matter, or thought that if I had heard of it, I should never connect the respectable Dr Black of Harlesden with a poor garreteer in the backwoods of London. He was a strange man, and as we sat together smoking, I often wondered whether he were mad or sane, for I think the wildest dreams of Paracelsus and the Rosicrucians* would appear plain and sober fact compared with the theories I have heard him earnestly advance in that grimy den of his. I once ventured to hint something of the sort to him. I suggested that something he had said was in flat contradiction to all science and all experience. "No, Dyson," he answered, "not all experience, for mine counts for something. I am no dealer in unproved theories; what I say I have proved for myself, and at a terrible cost. There is a region of knowledge of which you will never know, which wise men seeing from afar off shun like the plague, as well they may, but into that region I have gone. If you knew, if you could even dream of what may be done, of what one or two men have done in this quiet world of ours, your very soul would shudder and faint within you. What you have heard from me has been but the merest husk and outer covering of true science—that science which means death, and that which is more awful than death, to those who gain it. No, Dyson, when men say that there are strange things in the world, they little know the awe and the terror that dwell always within them and about them." There was a sort of fascination about the man that drew me to him, and I was quite sorry to have to leave London for a month or two; I missed his odd talk. A few days after I came back to town I thought I would go and look him up, but when I gave the two rings at the bell that used to summon him, there was no answer. I rang and rang again, and was just turning to go away, when the door opened and a dirty woman asked me what I wanted. From her look I fancy she took me for a plain-clothes officer after one of her lodgers, but when I inquired if Mr Black was in, she gave me a stare of another kind. "There's no Mr Black lives here," she said. "He's gone. He's dead this six weeks. I always thought he was a bit queer in his head, or else had been and got into some trouble or other. He used to go out every morning from ten till one, and one Monday morning we heard him come in, and go into his room and shut the door, and a few minutes after, just as we was a-sitting down to our dinner, there was such a scream that I thought I should have gone right off. And then we heard a stamping, and down he came, raging and cursing most dreadful, swearing he had been robbed of something that was worth millions. And then he just dropped down in the passage, and we thought he was dead. We got him up to his room, and put him on his bed, and I just sat there and waited, while my 'usband he went for the doctor. And there was the winder wide open, and a little tin box he had lying on the floor open and empty, but of course nobody could possible have got in at the winder, and as for him having anything that was worth anything, it's nonsense, for he was often weeks and weeks behind with his rent, and my 'usband he threatened often and often to turn him into the street, for, as he said, we've got a living to myke like other people—and of course that's true: but somehow I didn't like to do it, though he was an odd kind of a man, and I fancy had been better off. And then the doctor came and looked at him, and said as he couldn't do nothing, and that night he died as I was a-sitting by his bed; and I can tell you that, with one thing and another, we lost money by him, for the few bits of clothes as he had were worth next to nothing when they came to be sold." I gave the woman half a sovereign for her trouble, and went home thinking of Dr Black and the epitaph she had made him, and wondering at his strange fancy that he had been robbed. I take it that he had very little to fear on that score, poor fellow; but I suppose that he was really mad, and died in a sudden access of his mania. His landlady said that once or twice when she had had occasion to go into his room (to dun* the poor wretch for his rent, most likely), he would keep her at the door for about a minute, and that when she came in she would find him putting away his tin box in the corner by the window; I suppose he had become possessed with the idea of some great treasure, and fancied himself a wealthy man in the midst of all his misery. *Explicit,** my tale is ended, and you see that though I knew Black, I know nothing of his wife or of the history of her death.—That's the Harlesden case, Salisbury, and I think it interests me all the more deeply because there does not seem the shadow of a possibility that I or any one else will ever know more about it. What do you think of it?'

'Well, Dyson, I must say that I think you have contrived to surround the whole thing with a mystery of your own making. I go for the doctor's solution: Black murdered his wife, being himself in all probability an undeveloped lunatic.'

'What? Do you believe, then, that this woman was something too awful, too terrible to be allowed to remain on the earth? You will remember that the doctor said it was the brain of a devil?'

'Yes, yes, but he was speaking, of course, metaphorically. It's really quite a simple matter, Dyson, if you only look at it like that.'

'Ah, well, you may be right; but yet I am sure you are not. Well, well, it's no good discussing it any more. A little more Benedictine? That's right; try some of this tobacco. Didn't you say that you had been bothered by something—something which happened that night we dined together?'

'Yes, I have been worried, Dyson, worried a great deal. I——But it's such a trivial matter, indeed such an absurdity, that I feel ashamed to trouble you with it.'

'Never mind, let's have it, absurd or not.'

With many hesitations, and with much inward resentment of the folly of the thing, Salisbury told his tale, and repeated reluctantly the absurd intelligence and the absurder doggerel of the scrap of paper, expecting to hear Dyson burst out into a roar of laughter.

'Isn't it too bad that I should let myself be bothered by such stuff as that?' he asked, when he had stuttered out the jingle of once, and twice, and thrice.

Dyson had listened to it all gravely, even to the end, and meditated for a few minutes in silence.

'Yes,' he said at length, 'it was a curious chance, your taking shelter in that archway just as those two went by. But I don't know that I should call what was written on the paper nonsense; it is bizarre certainly, but I expect it has a meaning for somebody. Just repeat it again, will you, and I will write it down. Perhaps we might find a cipher of some sort, though I hardly think we shall.'

Again had the reluctant lips of Salisbury to slowly stammer out the rubbish he abhorred, while Dyson jotted it down on a slip of paper.

'Look over it, will you?' he said when it was done; 'it may be important that I should have every word in its place. Is that all right?'

'Yes; that is an accurate copy. But I don't think you will get much out of it. Depend upon it, it is mere nonsense, a wanton scribble.—I must be going now, Dyson. No, no more; that stuff of yours is pretty strong. Good-night.'

'I suppose you would like to hear from me, if I did find out anything?'

'No, not I; I don't want to hear about the thing again. You may regard the discovery, if it is one, as your own.'

'Very well. Good-night.'

## IV

A GOOD many hours after Salisbury had returned to the company of the green rep chairs, Dyson still sat at his desk, itself a Japanese romance, smoking many pipes, and meditating over his friend's story. The bizarre quality of the inscription which had annoyed Salisbury was to him an attraction, and now and again he took it up and scanned thoughtfully what he had written, especially the quaint jingle at the end. It was a token, a symbol, he decided, and not a cipher, and the woman who had flung it away was in all probability entirely ignorant of its meaning; she was but the agent of the 'Sam' she had abused and discarded, and he too was again the agent of some one unknown; possibly of the individual styled Q, who had been forced to visit his French friends. But what to make of 'Traverse Handel S.' Here was the root and source of the enigma, and not all the tobacco of Virginia seemed likely to suggest any clew here. It seemed almost hopeless, but Dyson regarded himself as the Wellington of mysteries, and went to bed feeling assured that sooner or later he would hit upon the right track. For the next few days he was deeply engaged in his literary labours, labours which were a profound mystery even to the most intimate of his friends, who searched the railway bookstalls in vain for the result of so many hours spent at the Japanese bureau in company with strong tobacco and black tea. On this occasion Dyson confined himself to his room for four days, and it was with genuine relief that he laid down his pen and went out into the streets in quest of relaxation and fresh air. The gas lamps were being lighted, and the fifth edition of the evening papers was being howled through the streets, and Dyson, feeling that he wanted quiet, turned away from the clamorous Strand, and began to trend away to the north-west. Soon he found himself in streets that echoed to his footsteps, and crossing a broad new thoroughfare, and verging still to the west, Dyson discovered that he had penetrated to the depths of Soho. Here again was life; rare vintages of France and Italy, at prices which seemed contemptibly small, allured the passer-by; here were cheeses, vast and rich, here olive oil, and here a grove of Rabelaisian* sausages; while in a neighbouring shop the whole press of Paris appeared to be on sale. In the middle of the roadway a strange miscellany of nations sauntered to and fro, for there cab and hansom rarely ventured; and from window over window the inhabitants looked forth in pleased contemplation of the scene. Dyson made his way slowly along, mingling with the crowd on the cobble-stones, listening to the queer babel of French and German, and Italian and English, glancing now and again at the shop-windows with their levelled batteries of bottles, and had almost gained the end of the street, when his attention was arrested by a small shop at the corner, a vivid contrast to its neighbours. It was the typical shop of the poor quarter; a shop entirely English. Here were vended tobacco and sweets, cheap pipes of clay and cherry-wood; penny exercise-books* and pen-holders jostled for precedence with comic songs, and story papers* with appalling cuts showed that romance claimed its place beside the actualities of the evening paper, the bills of which fluttered at the doorway. Dyson glanced up at the name above the door, and stood by the kennel trembling, for a sharp pang, the pang of one who has made a discovery, had for a moment left him incapable of motion. The name over the little shop was Travers. Dyson looked up again, this time at the corner of the wall above the lamp-post, and read in white letters on a blue ground the words 'Handel Street, W.C.,' and the legend was repeated in fainter letters just below. He gave a little sigh of satisfaction, and without more ado walked boldly into the shop, and stared full in the face the fat man who was sitting behind the counter. The fellow rose to his feet, and returned the stare a little curiously, and then began in stereotyped phrase:

'What can I do for you, sir?'

Dyson enjoyed the situation and a dawning perplexity on the man's face. He propped his stick carefully against the counter and leaning over it, said slowly and impressively:

'Once around the grass, and twice around the lass, and thrice around the maple-tree.'

Dyson had calculated on his words producing an effect, and he was not disappointed. The vendor of miscellanies gasped, open-mouthed like a fish, and steadied himself against the counter. When he spoke, after a short interval, it was in a hoarse mutter, tremulous and unsteady.

'Would you mind saying that again, sir? I didn't quite catch it.'

'My good man, I shall most certainly do nothing of the kind. You heard what I said perfectly well. You have got a clock in your shop, I see; an admirable timekeeper, I have no doubt. Well, I give you a minute by your own clock.'

The man looked about him in perplexed indecision, and Dyson felt that it was time to be bold.

'Look here, Travers, the time is nearly up. You have heard of Q, I think. Remember, I hold your life in my hands. Now!'

Dyson was shocked at the result of his own audacity. The man shrunk and shrivelled in terror, the sweat poured down a face of ashy white, and he held up his hands before him.

'Mr Davies, Mr Davies, don't say that—don't, for heaven's sake. I didn't know you at first, I didn't indeed. Good God! Mr Davies, you wouldn't ruin me? I'll get it in a moment.'

'You had better not lose any more time.'

The man slunk piteously out of his shop, and went into a back parlour. Dyson heard his trembling fingers fumbling with a bunch of keys, and the creak of an opening box. He came back presently with a small package neatly tied up in brown paper in his hands, and still, full of terror, handed it to Dyson.

'I'm glad to be rid of it,' he said. 'I'll take no more jobs of this sort.'

Dyson took the parcel and his stick, and walked out of the shop with a nod, turning round as he passed the door. Travers had sunk into his seat, his face still white with terror, with one hand over his eyes, and Dyson speculated a good deal as he walked rapidly away as to what queer chords those could be on which he had played so roughly. He hailed the first hansom he could see, and drove home, and when he had lit his hanging lamp, and laid his parcel on the table, he paused for a moment, wondering on what strange thing the lamplight would soon shine. He locked his door, and cut the strings, and unfolded the paper layer after layer, and came at last to a small wooden box, simply but solidly made. There was no lock, and Dyson had simply to raise the lid, and as he did so he drew a long breath and started back. The lamp seemed to glimmer feebly like a single candle, but the whole room blazed with light—and not with light alone, but with a thousand colours, with all the glories of some painted window; and upon the walls of his room and on the familiar furniture, the glow flamed back and seemed to flow again to its source, the little wooden box. For there upon a bed of soft wool lay the most splendid jewel, a jewel such as Dyson had never dreamed of, and within it shone the blue of far skies, and the green of the sea by the shore, and the red of the ruby, and deep violet rays, and in the middle of all it seemed aflame as if a fountain of fire rose up, and fell, and rose again with sparks like stars for drops. Dyson gave a long deep sigh, and dropped into his chair, and put his hands over his eyes to think. The jewel was like an opal, but from a long experience of the shop-windows he knew there was no such thing as an opal one quarter or one-eighth of its size. He looked at the stone again, with a feeling that was almost awe, and placed it gently on the table under the lamp, and watched the wonderful flame that shone and sparkled in its centre, and then turned to the box, curious to know whether it might contain other marvels. He lifted the bed of wool on which the opal had reclined, and saw beneath, no more jewels, but a little old pocket-book, worn and shabby with use.

Dyson opened it at the first leaf, and dropped the book again appalled. He had read the name of the owner, neatly written in blue ink:

STEVEN BLACK, M.D.,
   Oranmore,
     Devon Road,
      Harlesden.

It was several minutes before Dyson could bring himself to open the book a second time; he remembered the wretched exile in his garret, and his strange talk, and the memory too of the face he had seen at the window, and of what the specialist had said surged up in his mind, and as he held his finger on the cover, he shivered, dreading what might be written within. When at last he held it in his hand, and turned the pages, he found that the first two leaves were blank, but the third was covered with clear, minute writing, and Dyson began to read with the light of the opal flaming in his eyes.


# V


'EVER since I was a young man'—the record began—'I devoted all my leisure and a good deal of time that ought to have been given to other studies to the investigation of curious and obscure branches of knowledge. What are commonly called the pleasures of life had never any attractions for me, and I lived alone in London, avoiding my fellow-students, and in my turn avoided by them as a man self-absorbed and unsympathetic. So long as I could gratify my desire of knowledge of a peculiar kind, knowledge of which the very existence is a profound secret to most men, I was intensely happy, and I have often spent whole nights sitting in the darkness of my room, and thinking of the strange world on the brink of which I trod. My professional studies, however, and the necessity of obtaining a degree, for some time forced my more obscure employment into the background, and soon after I had qualified I met Agnes, who became my wife. We took a new house in this remote suburb, and I began the regular routine of a sober practice, and for some months lived happily enough, sharing in the life about me, and only thinking at odd intervals of that occult science which had once fascinated my whole being. I had learnt enough of the paths I had begun to tread to know that they were beyond all expression difficult and dangerous, that to persevere meant in all probability the wreck of a life, and that they led to regions so terrible that the mind of man shrinks appalled at the very thought. Moreover, the quiet and the peace I had enjoyed since my marriage had wiled me away to a great extent from places where I knew no peace could dwell. But suddenly—I think indeed it was the work of a single night, as I lay awake on my bed gazing into the darkness—suddenly, I say, the old desire, the former longing, returned, and returned with a force that had been intensified ten times by its absence; and when the day dawned and I looked out of the window, and saw with haggard eyes the sunrise in the east, I knew that my doom had been pronounced; that as I had gone far, so now I must go farther with steps that know no faltering. I turned to the bed where my wife was sleeping peacefully, and lay down again weeping bitter tears, for the sun had set on our happy life and had risen with a dawn of terror to us both. I will not set down here in minute detail what followed; outwardly I went about the day's labour as before, saying nothing to my wife. But she soon saw that I had changed; I spent my spare time in a room which I had fitted up as a laboratory, and often I crept upstairs in the grey dawn of the morning, when the light of many lamps still glowed over London; and each night I had stolen a step nearer to that great abyss which I was to bridge over, the gulf between the world of consciousness and the world of matter. My experiments were many and complicated in their nature, and it was some months before I realised whither they all pointed, and when this was borne in upon me in a moment's time, I felt my face whiten and my heart still within me. But the power to draw back, the power to stand before the doors that now opened wide before me and not to enter in, had long ago been absent; the way was closed, and I could only pass onward. My position was as utterly hopeless as that of the prisoner in an utter dungeon, whose only light is that of the dungeon above him; the doors were shut and escape was impossible. Experiment after experiment gave the same result, and I knew, and shrank even as the thought passed through my mind, that in the work I had to do there must be elements which no laboratory could furnish, which no scales could ever measure. In that work, from which even I doubted to escape with life, life itself must enter; from some human being there must be drawn that essence which men call the soul, and in its place (for in the scheme of the world there is no vacant chamber)—in its place would enter in what the lips can hardly utter, what the mind cannot conceive without a horror more awful than the horror of death itself. And when I knew this, I knew also on whom this fate would fall; I looked into my wife's eyes. Even at that hour, if I had gone out and taken a rope and hanged myself, I might have escaped, and she also, but in no other way. At last I told her all. She shuddered, and wept, and called on her dead mother for help, and asked me if I had no mercy, and I could only sigh. I concealed nothing from her; I told her what she would become, and what would enter in where her life had been; I told her of all the shame and of all the horror. You who will read this when I am dead—if indeed I allow this record to survive,—you who have opened the box and have seen what lies there, if you could understand what lies hidden in that opal. For one night my wife consented to what I asked of her, consented with the tears running down her beautiful face, and hot shame flushing red over her neck and breast, consented to undergo this for me. I threw open the window, and we looked together at the sky and the dark earth for the last time; it was a fine star-light night, and there was a pleasant breeze blowing, and I kissed her on her lips, and her tears ran down upon my face. That night she came down to my laboratory, and there, with shutters bolted and barred down, with curtains drawn thick and close so that the very stars might be shut out from the sight of that room, while the crucible hissed and boiled over the lamp, I did what had to be done, and led out what was no longer a woman. But on the table the opal flamed and sparkled with such light as no eyes of man have ever gazed on, and the rays of the flame that was within it flashed and glittered, and shone even to my heart. My wife had only asked one thing of me; that when there came at last what I had told her, I would kill her. I have kept that promise.'

There was nothing more. Dyson let the little pocket-book fall, and turned and looked again at the opal with its flaming inmost light, and then with unutterable irresistible horror surging up in his heart, grasped the jewel, and flung it on the ground, and trampled it beneath his heel. His face was white with terror as he turned away, and for a moment stood sick and trembling, and then with a start he leapt across the room and steadied himself against the door. There was an angry hiss, as of steam escaping under great pressure, and as he gazed, motionless, a volume of heavy yellow smoke was slowly issuing from the very centre of the jewel, and wreathing itself in snakelike coils above it. And then a thin white flame burst forth from the smoke, and shot up into the air and vanished; and on the ground there lay a thing like a cinder, black and crumbling to the touch.

THE END

# THE THREE IMPOSTORS

## PROLOGUE

'AND Mr Joseph Walters is going to stay the night?' said the smooth, clean-shaven man to his companion, an individual not of the most charming appearance, who had chosen to make his ginger-coloured moustache merge into a pair of short chin-whiskers.

The two stood at the hall door, grinning evilly at each other; and presently a girl ran quickly down the stairs, and joined them. She was quite young, with a quaint and piquant rather than a beautiful face, and her eyes were of a shining hazel. She held a neat paper parcel in one hand, and laughed with her friends.

'Leave the door open,' said the smooth man to the other, as they were going out. 'Yes, by——,' he went on with an ugly oath, 'we'll leave the front door on the jar. He may like to see company, you know.'

The other man looked doubtfully about him.

'Is it quite prudent, do you think, Davies?' he said, pausing with his hand on the mouldering knocker. 'I don't think Lipsius* would like it. What do you say, Helen?'

'I agree with Davies. Davies is an artist, and you are commonplace, Richmond, and a bit of a coward. Let the door stand open, of course. But what a pity Lipsius had to go away! He would have enjoyed himself.'

'Yes,' replied the smooth Mr Davies, 'that summons to the west was very hard on the doctor.'

The three passed out, leaving the hall door, cracked and riven with frost and wet, half-open, and they stood silent for a moment under the ruinous shelter of the porch.

'Well,' said the girl, 'it is done at last. We shall hurry no more on the track of the young man with spectacles.'

'We owe a great deal to you,' said Mr Davies politely; 'the doctor said so before he left. But have we not all three some farewells to make? I, for my part, propose to say good-bye here, before this picturesque but mouldy residence, to my friend Mr Burton, dealer in the antique and curious,' and the man lifted his hat with an exaggerated bow.

'And I,' said Richmond, 'bid adieu to Mr Wilkins, the private secretary, whose company has, I confess, become a little tedious.'

'Farewell to Miss Lally and to Miss Leicester also,' said the girl, making as she spoke a delicious curtsy. 'Farewell to all occult adventure; the farce is played.'

Mr Davies and the lady seemed full of grim enjoyment, but Richmond tugged at his whiskers nervously.

'I feel a bit shaken up,' he said. 'I've seen rougher things in the States, but that crying noise he made gave me a sickish feeling. And then the smell——; but my stomach was never very strong.'

The three friends moved away from the door, and began to walk slowly up and down what had been a gravel path, but now lay green and pulpy with damp mosses. It was a fine autumn evening, and a faint sunlight shone on the yellow walls of the old deserted house, and showed the patches of gangrenous decay, and all the stains, the black drift of rain from the broken pipes, the scabrous blots where the bare bricks were exposed, the green weeping of a gaunt laburnum that stood beside the porch, and ragged marks near the ground where the reeking clay was gaining on the worn foundations. It was a queer, rambling old place, the centre perhaps two hundred years old, with dormer windows sloping from the tiled roof, and on each side there were Georgian wings; bow windows had been carried up to the first floor, and two dome-like cupolas* that had once been painted a bright green were now grey and neutral. Broken urns lay upon the path, and a heavy mist seemed to rise from the unctuous clay; the neglected shrubberies, grown all tangled and unshapen, smelt dank and evil, and there was an atmosphere all about the deserted mansion that proposed thoughts of an opened grave. The three friends looked dismally at the rough grasses and the nettles that grew thick over lawn and flower-beds; and at the sad water-pool in the midst of the weeds. There, above green and oily scum instead of lilies, stood a rusting Triton on the rocks,* sounding a dirge through a shattered horn; and beyond, beyond the sunk fence and the far meadows, the sun slid down and shone red through the bars of the elm-trees.

Richmond shivered and stamped his foot.

'We had better be going soon,' he said; 'there is nothing else to be done here.'

'No,' said Davies; 'it is finished at last. I thought for some time we should never get hold of the gentleman with the spectacles. He was a clever fellow, but, Lord! he broke up badly at last. I can tell you, he looked white at me when I touched him on the arm in the bar. But where could he have hidden the thing? We can all swear it was not on him.'

The girl laughed, and they turned away, when Richmond gave a violent start.

'Ah!' he cried, turning to the girl, 'what have you got there? Look, Davies, look; it's all oozing and dripping.'

The young woman glanced down at the little parcel she was carrying, and partially unfolded the paper.

'Yes, look both of you,' she said; 'it's my own idea. Don't you think it will do nicely for the doctor's museum? It comes from the right hand, the hand that took the Gold Tiberius.'*

Mr Davies nodded with a good deal of approbation, and Richmond lifted his ugly high-crowned bowler, and wiped his forehead with a dingy handkerchief.

'I'm going,' he said; 'you two can stay if you like.'

The three went round by the stable-path, past the withered wilderness of the old kitchen-garden, and struck off by a hedge at the back, making for a particular point in the road. About five minutes later two gentlemen, whom idleness had led to explore these forgotten outskirts of London, came sauntering up the shadowy carriage-drive. They had spied the deserted house from the road, and as they observed all the heavy desolation of the place, they began to moralise in the great style, with considerable debts to Jeremy Taylor.*

'Look, Dyson,' said the one, as they drew nearer; 'look at those upper windows; the sun is setting, and, though the panes are dusty, yet—

"The grimy sash an oriel burns." '*

'Phillipps,' replied the elder and (it must be said) the more pompous of the two, 'I yield to fantasy; I cannot withstand the influence of the grotesque. Here, where all is falling into dimness and dissolution, and we walk in cedarn* gloom, and the very air of heaven goes mouldering to the lungs, I cannot remain commonplace. I look at that deep glow on the panes, and the house lies all enchanted; that very room, I tell you, is within all blood and fire.'


## ADVENTURE OF THE GOLD TIBERIUS

THE acquaintance between Mr Dyson and Mr Charles Phillipps arose from one of those myriad chances which are every day doing their work in the streets of London. Mr Dyson was a man of letters, and an unhappy instance of talents misapplied. With gifts that might have placed him in the flower of his youth among the most favoured of Bentley's favourite novelists,* he had chosen to be perverse; he was, it is true, familiar with scholastic logic, but he knew nothing of the logic of life, and he flattered himself with the title of artist, when he was in fact but an idle and curious spectator of other men's endeavours. Amongst many delusions, he cherished one most fondly, that he was a strenuous worker; and it was with a gesture of supreme weariness that he would enter his favourite resort, a small tobacco-shop in Great Queen Street, and proclaim to any one who cared to listen that he had seen the rising and setting of two successive suns. The proprietor of the shop, a middle-aged man of singular civility, tolerated Dyson partly out of good nature, and partly because he was a regular customer. He was allowed to sit on an empty cask, and to express his sentiments on literary and artistic matters till he was tired, or the time for closing came; and if no fresh customers were attracted, it is believed that none were turned away by his eloquence. Dyson was addicted to wild experiments in tobacco,* he never wearied of trying new combinations; and one evening he had just entered the shop, and given utterance to his last preposterous formula, when a young fellow, of about his own age, who had come in a moment later, asked the shopman to duplicate the order on his account, smiling politely, as he spoke, to Mr Dyson's address. Dyson felt profoundly flattered, and after a few phrases the two entered into conversation, and in an hour's time the tobacconist saw the new friends sitting side by side on a couple of casks, deep in talk.

'My dear sir,' said Dyson, 'I will give you the task of the literary man in a phrase. He has got to do simply this—to invent a wonderful story, and to tell it in a wonderful manner.'

'I will grant you that,' said Mr Phillipps, 'but you will allow me to insist that in the hands of the true artist in words all stories are marvellous, and every circumstance has its peculiar wonder. The matter is of little consequence, the manner is everything. Indeed, the highest skill is shown in taking matter apparently commonplace and transmuting it by the high alchemy of style into the pure gold of art.'

'That is indeed a proof of great skill, but it is great skill exerted foolishly, or at least unadvisedly. It is as if a great violinist were to show us what marvellous harmonies he could draw from a child's banjo.'

'No, no, you are really wrong. I see you take a radically mistaken view of life. But we must thresh this out. Come to my rooms; I live not far from here.'

It was thus that Mr Dyson became the associate of Mr Charles Phillipps, who lived in a quiet square not far from Holborn. Thenceforth they haunted each other's rooms at intervals, sometimes regular, and occasionally the reverse, and made appointments to meet at the shop in Queen Street, where their talk robbed the tobacconist's profit of half its charm. There was a constant jarring of literary formulas, Dyson exalting the claims of the pure imagination; while Phillipps, who was a student of physical science, and something of an ethnologist,* insisted that all literature ought to have a scientific basis. By the mistaken benevolence of deceased relatives both young men were placed out of reach of hunger, and so, meditating high achievements, idled their time pleasantly away, and revelled in the careless joys of a Bohemianism* devoid of the sharp seasoning of adversity.

One night in June Mr Phillipps was sitting in his room in the calm retirement of Red Lion Square.* He had opened the window, and was smoking placidly, while he watched the movement of life below. The sky was clear, and the afterglow of sunset had lingered long about it. The flushing twilight of a summer evening vied with the gas-lamps in the square, had fashioned a chiaroscuro* that had in it something unearthly; and the children, racing to and fro upon the pavement, the lounging idlers by the public, and the casual passers-by rather flickered and hovered in the play of lights than stood out substantial things. By degrees in the houses opposite one window after another leapt out a square of light; now and again a figure would shape itself against a blind and vanish, and to all this semi-theatrical magic the runs and flourishes of brave Italian opera played a little distance off on a piano-organ seemed an appropriate accompaniment, while the deep-muttered bass of the traffic of Holborn never ceased. Phillipps enjoyed the scene and its effects; the light in the sky faded and turned to darkness, and the square gradually grew silent, and still he sat dreaming at the window, till the sharp peal of the house-bell roused him, and looking at his watch, he found that it was past ten o'clock. There was a knock at the door, and his friend Mr Dyson entered, and, according to his custom, sat down in an arm-chair and began to smoke in silence.

'You know, Phillipps,' he said at length, 'that I have always battled for the marvellous. I remember your maintaining in that chair that one has no business to make use of the wonderful, the improbable, the odd coincidence in literature, and you took the ground that it was wrong to do so, because as a matter of fact the wonderful and the improbable don't happen, and men's lives are not really shaped by odd coincidence. Now, mind you, if that were so, I would not grant your conclusion, because I think the "criticism-of-life" theory* is all nonsense; but I deny your premiss. A most singular thing has happened to me to-night.'

'Really, Dyson, I am very glad to hear it. Of course, I oppose your argument, whatever it may be; but if you would be good enough to tell me of your adventure, I should be delighted.'

'Well, it came about like this. I have had a very hard day's work; indeed, I have scarcely moved from my old bureau since seven o'clock last night. I wanted to work out that idea we discussed last Tuesday, you know, the notion of the fetish-worshipper?'

'Yes, I remember. Have you been able to do anything with it?'

'Yes; it came out better than I expected; but there were great difficulties, the usual agony between the conception and the execution. Anyhow, I got it done at about seven o'clock to-night, and I thought I should like a little of the fresh air. I went out and wandered rather aimlessly about the streets; my head was full of my tale, and I didn't much notice where I was going. I got into those quiet places to the north of Oxford Street as you go west, the genteel residential neighbourhood of stucco and prosperity. I turned east again without knowing it, and it was quite dark when I passed along a sombre little by-street, ill-lighted and empty. I did not know at the time in the least where I was, but I found out afterwards that it was not very far from Tottenham Court Road. I strolled idly along, enjoying the stillness; on one side there seemed to be the back premises of some great shop; tier after tier of dusty windows lifted up into the night, with gibbet-like contrivances for raising heavy goods, and below large doors, fast closed and bolted, all dark and desolate. Then there came a huge pantechnicon warehouse;* and over the way a grim blank wall, as forbidding as the wall of a gaol, and then the head-quarters of some volunteer regiment, and afterwards a passage leading to a court where waggons were standing to be hired; it was, one might almost say, a street devoid of inhabitants, and scarce a window showed the glimmer of a light. I was wondering at the strange peace and dimness there, where it must be close to some roaring main artery of London life, when suddenly I heard the noise of dashing feet tearing along the pavement at full speed, and from a narrow passage, a mews or some-thing of that kind, a man was discharged as from a catapult under my very nose, and rushed past me, flinging something from him as he ran. He was gone, and down another street in an instant, almost before I knew what had happened; but I didn't much bother about him, I was watching something else. I told you he had thrown something away; well, I watched what seemed a line of flame flash through the air and fly quivering over the pavement, and in spite of myself I could not help tearing after it. The impetus lessened, and I saw something like a bright halfpenny roll slower and slower, and then deflect towards the gutter, hover for a moment on the edge, and dance down into a drain. I believe I cried out in positive despair, though I hadn't the least notion what I was hunting; and then, to my joy, I saw that, instead of dropping into the sewer, it had fallen flat across two bars. I stooped down and picked it up and whipped it into my pocket, and I was just about to walk on when I heard again that sound of dashing footsteps. I don't know why I did it, but as a matter of fact I dived down into the mews, or whatever it was, and stood as much in the shadow as possible. A man went by with a rush a few paces from where I was standing, and I felt uncommonly pleased that I was in hiding. I couldn't make out much feature, but I saw his eyes gleaming and his teeth showing, and he had an ugly-looking knife in one hand, and I thought things would be very unpleasant for gentleman number one if the second robber, or robbed, or what you like, caught him up. I can tell you, Phillipps, a fox-hunt is exciting enough, when the horn blows clear on a winter morning, and the hounds give tongue, and the red-coats charge away, but it's nothing to a man-hunt, and that's what I had a slight glimpse of to-night. There was murder in the fellow's eyes as he went by, and I don't think there was much more than fifty seconds between the two. I only hope it was enough.'

Dyson leant back in his arm-chair, relit his pipe, and puffed thoughtfully. Phillipps began to walk up and down the room, musing over the story of violent death fleeting in chase along the pavement, the knife shining in the lamplight, the fury of the pursuer, and the terror of the pursued.

'Well,' he said at last, 'and what was it, after all, that you rescued from the gutter?'

Dyson jumped up, evidently quite startled. 'I really haven't a notion. I didn't think of looking. But we shall see.'

He fumbled in his waistcoat pocket, drew out a small and shining object, and laid it on the table. It glowed there beneath the lamp with the radiant glory of rare old gold; and the image and the letters stood out in high relief, clear and sharp, as if it had but left the mint a month before. The two men bent over it, and Phillipps took it up and examined it closely.

'Imp. Tiberius Cæsar Augustus,'* he read the legend, and then looking at the reverse of the coin, he stared in amazement, and at last turned to Dyson with a look of exultation.

'Do you know what you have found?' he said.

'Apparently a gold coin of some antiquity,' said Dyson coolly.

'Quite so, a gold Tiberius. No, that is wrong. You have found *the* gold Tiberius. Look at the reverse.'

Dyson looked and saw the coin was stamped with the figure of a faun standing amidst reeds and flowing water. The features, minute as they were, stood out in delicate outline; it was a face lovely and yet terrible, and Dyson thought of the well-known passage of the lad's playmate, gradually growing with his growth and increasing with his stature, till the air was filled with the rank fume of the goat.

'Yes,' he said; 'it is a curious coin. Do you know it?'

'I know about it. It is one of the comparatively few historical objects in existence; it is all storied like those jewels we have read of. A whole cycle of legend has gathered round the thing; the tale goes that it formed part of an issue struck by Tiberius to commemorate an infamous excess. You see the legend on the reverse: "Victoria." It is said that by an extraordinary accident the whole issue was thrown into the melting-pot, and that only this one coin escaped. It glints through history and legend, appearing and disappearing, with intervals of a hundred years in time, and continents in place. It was "discovered" by an Italian humanist, and lost and rediscovered. It has not been heard of since 1727, when Sir Joshua Byrde,* a Turkey merchant, brought it home from Aleppo,* and vanished with it a month after he had shown it to the virtuosi,* no man knew or knows where. And here it is!'

'Put it into your pocket, Dyson,' he said, after a pause. 'I would not let any one have a glimpse of the thing if I were you. I would not talk about it. Did either of the men you saw see you?'

'Well, I think not. I don't think the first man, the man who was vomited out of the dark passage, saw anything at all; and I am sure that the second could not have seen me.'

'And you didn't really see them. You couldn't recognise either the one or the other if you met him in the street to-morrow?'

'No, I don't think I could. The street, as I said, was dimly lighted, and they ran like madmen.'

The two men sat silent for some time, each weaving his own fancies of the story; but lust of the marvellous was slowly overpowering Dyson's more sober thoughts.

'It is all more strange than I fancied,' he said at last. 'It was queer enough what I saw; a man is sauntering along a quiet, sober, everyday London street, a street of grey houses and blank walls, and there, for a moment, a veil seems drawn aside, and the very fume of the pit steams up through the flagstones, the ground glows, red-hot, beneath his feet, and he seems to hear the hiss of the infernal caldron. A man flying in mad terror for his life, and furious hate pressing hot on his steps with knife drawn ready; here indeed is horror; but what is all that to what you have told me? I tell you, Phillipps, I see the plot thicken; our steps will henceforth be dogged with mystery, and the most ordinary incidents will teem with significance. You may stand out against it, and shut your eyes, but they will be forced open; mark my words, you will have to yield to the inevitable. A clue, tangled if you like, has been placed by chance in our hands; it will be our business to follow it up. As for the guilty person or persons in this strange case, they will be unable to escape us, our nets will be spread far and wide over this great city, and suddenly, in the streets and places of public resort, we shall in some way or other be made aware that we are in touch with the unknown criminal. Indeed, I almost fancy I see him slowly approaching this quiet square of yours; he is loitering at street corners, wandering, apparently without aim, down far-reaching thoroughfares, but all the while coming nearer and nearer, drawn by an irresistible magnetism, as ships were drawn to the Loadstone Rock in the Eastern tale.'*

'I certainly think,' replied Phillipps, 'that if you pull out that coin and flourish it under people's noses as you are doing at the present moment, you will very probably find yourself in touch with the criminal, or a criminal. You will undoubtedly be robbed with violence. Otherwise, I see no reason why either of us should be troubled. No one saw you secure the coin, and no one knows you have it. I, for my part, shall sleep peacefully, and go about my business with a sense of security and a firm dependence on the natural order of things. The events of the evening, the adventure in the street, have been odd, I grant you, but I resolutely decline to have any more to do with the matter, and, if necessary, I shall consult the police. I will not be enslaved by a gold Tiberius, even though it swims into my ken* in a manner which is somewhat melodramatic.'

'And I, for my part,' said Dyson, 'go forth like a knight-errant in search of adventure. Not that I shall need to seek; rather adventure will seek me; I shall be like a spider in the midst of his web, responsive to every movement, and ever on the alert.'

Shortly afterwards Dyson took his leave, and Mr Phillipps spent the rest of the night in examining some flint arrow-heads which he had purchased. He had every reason to believe that they were the work of a modern and not a palæolithic man; still he was far from gratified when a close scrutiny showed him that his suspicions were well founded. In his anger at the turpitude which would impose on an ethnologist, he completely forgot Dyson and the gold Tiberius; and when he went to bed at first sunlight, the whole tale had faded utterly from his thoughts.

## THE ENCOUNTER OF THE PAVEMENT

MR DYSON, walking leisurely along Oxford Street, and staring with
bland inquiry at whatever caught his attention, enjoyed in all its rare
flavours the sensation that he was really very hard at work. His observation of mankind, the traffic, and the shop windows tickled his faculties
with an exquisite bouquet; he looked serious, as one looks on whom
charges of weight and moment are laid; and he was attentive in his
glances to right and left, for fear lest he should miss some circumstance
of more acute significance. He had narrowly escaped being run over at
a crossing by a charging van, for he hated to hurry his steps, and indeed
the afternoon was warm; and he had just halted by a place of popular
refreshment, when the astounding gestures of a well-dressed individual
on the opposite pavement held him enchanted and gasping like a fish.
A treble line of hansoms, carriages, vans, cabs, and omnibuses was tearing east and west, and not the most daring adventurer of the crossings
would have cared to try his fortune; but the person who had attracted
Dyson's attention seemed to rage on the very edge of the pavement,
now and then darting forward at the hazard of instant death, and at
each repulse absolutely dancing with excitement, to the rich amusement of the passers-by. At last a gap that would have tried the courage
of a street-boy appeared between the serried lines of vehicles, and the
man rushed across in a frenzy, and escaping by a hair's-breadth, pounced
upon Dyson as a tiger pounces on her prey. 'I saw you looking about
you,' he said, sputtering out his words in his intense eagerness; 'would
you mind telling me this! Was the man who came out of the Aerated Bread
Shop* and jumped into the hansom three minutes ago a youngish-
looking man with dark whiskers and spectacles? Can't you speak, man?
For heaven's sake, can't you speak? Answer me; it's a matter of life and
death.'

The words bubbled and boiled out of the man's mouth in the fury of
his emotion, his face went from red to white, and the beads of sweat
stood out on his forehead; he stamped his feet as he spoke, and tore
with his hand at his coat, as if something swelled and choked him, stopping the passage of his breath.

'My dear sir,' said Dyson, 'I always like to be accurate. Your observation was perfectly correct. As you say, a youngish man—a man, I should
say, of somewhat timid bearing—ran rapidly out of the shop here, and
bounced into a hansom that must have been waiting for him, as it went
eastwards at once. Your friend also wore spectacles, as you say. Perhaps
you would like me to call a hansom for you to follow the gentleman?'

'No, thank you; it would be a waste of time.' The man gulped down something which appeared to rise in his throat, and Dyson was alarmed to see him shaking with hysterical laughter; he clung hard to a lamp-post, and swayed and staggered like a ship in a heavy gale.

'How shall I face the doctor?' he murmured to himself. 'It is too hard to fail at the last moment.' Then he seemed to recollect himself; he stood straight again, and looked quietly at Dyson.

'I owe you an apology for my violence,' he said at last. 'Many men would not be so patient as you have been. Would you mind adding to your kindness by walking with me a little way? I feel a little sick; I think it's the sun.'

Dyson nodded assent, and devoted himself to a quiet scrutiny of this strange personage as they moved on together. The man was dressed in quiet taste, and the most scrupulous observer could find nothing amiss with the fashion or make of his clothes; yet, from his hat to his boots, everything seemed inappropriate. His silk hat, Dyson thought, should have been a high bowler of odious pattern, worn with a baggy morning-coat, and an instinct told him that the fellow did not commonly carry a clean pocket-handkerchief. The face was not of the most agreeable pattern, and was in no way improved by a pair of bulbous chin-whiskers of a ginger hue, into which moustaches of like colour merged imperceptibly. Yet, in spite of these signals hung out by nature, Dyson felt that the individual beside him was something more than compact of vulgarity. He was struggling with himself, holding his feelings in check; but now and again passion would mount black to his face, and it was evidently by a supreme effort that he kept himself from raging like a madman. Dyson found something curious, and a little terrible, in the spectacle of an occult emotion thus striving for the mastery, and threatening to break out at every instant with violence; and they had gone some distance before the person whom he had met by so odd a hazard was able to speak quietly.

'You are really very good,' he said. 'I apologise again; my rudeness was really most unjustifiable. I feel my conduct demands an explanation, and I shall be happy to give it you. Do you happen to know of any place near here where one could sit down. I should really be very glad.'

'My dear sir,' said Dyson solemnly, 'the only café in London is close by. Pray do not consider yourself as bound to offer me any explanation, but at the same time I should be most happy to listen to you. Let us turn down here.'

They walked down a sober street and turned into what seemed a narrow passage past an iron-barred gate thrown back. The passage was

paved with flagstones, and decorated with handsome shrubs in pots on
either side, and the shadow of the high walls made a coolness which was
very agreeable after the hot breath of the sunny street. Presently the
passage opened out into a tiny square, a charming place, a morsel of
France transplanted into the heart of London. High walls rose on either
side, covered with glossy creepers, flower-beds beneath were gay with
nasturtiums, geraniums, and marigolds, and odorous with mignonette,*
and in the centre of the square a fountain, hidden by greenery, sent a cool
shower continually plashing into the basin beneath. The very noise made
this retreat delightful. Chairs and tables were disposed at convenient
intervals, and at the other end of the court broad doors had been thrown
back; beyond was a long, dark room, and the turmoil of traffic had become
a distant murmur. Within the room one or two men were sitting at the
tables, writing and sipping, but the courtyard was empty.

'You see, we shall be quiet,' said Dyson. 'Pray sit down here, Mr——?'

'Wilkins.* My name is Henry Wilkins.'

'Sit here, Mr Wilkins. I think you will find that a comfortable seat.
I suppose you have not been here before? This is the quiet time; the
place will be like a hive at six o'clock, and the chairs and tables will
overflow into that little alley there.'

A waiter came in response to the bell; and after Dyson had politely
inquired after the health of M. Annibault, the proprietor, he ordered
a bottle of the wine of Champigny.

'The wine of Champigny,' he observed to Mr Wilkins, who was evidently a good deal composed by the influence of the place, 'is a Tourainian
wine of great merit.* Ah, here it is; let me fill your glass. How do you
find it?'

'Indeed,' said Mr Wilkins, 'I should have pronounced it a fine
Burgundy. The bouquet is very exquisite. I am fortunate in lighting upon
such a good Samaritan as yourself: I wonder you did not think me mad.
But if you knew the terrors that assailed me, I am sure you would no
longer be surprised at conduct which was certainly most unjustifiable.'

He sipped his wine, and leant back in his chair, relishing the drip and
trickle of the fountain, and the cool greenness that hedged in this little
port of refuge.

'Yes,' he said at last, 'that is indeed an admirable wine. Thank you;
you will allow me to offer you another bottle?'

The waiter was summoned, and descended through a trap-door in
the floor of the dark apartment and brought up the wine. Mr Wilkins lit
a cigarette, and Dyson pulled out his pipe.

'Now,' said Mr Wilkins, 'I promised to give you an explanation of my strange behaviour. It is rather a long story, but I see, sir, that you are no mere cold observer of the ebb and flow of life. You take, I think, a warm and an intelligent interest in the chances of your fellow-creatures, and I believe you will find what I have to tell not devoid of interest.'

Mr Dyson signified his assent to these propositions; and though he thought Mr Wilkins's diction a little pompous, prepared to interest himself in his tale. The other, who had so raged with passion half an hour before, was now perfectly cool, and when he had smoked out his cigarette, he began in an even voice to relate the

### Novel of the Dark Valley*

I am the son of a poor but learned clergyman in the West of England——
But I am forgetting, these details are not of special interest. I will briefly state, then, that my father, who was, as I have said, a learned man, had never learnt the specious arts by which the great are flattered, and would never condescend to the despicable pursuit of self-advertisement. Though his fondness for ancient ceremonies and quaint customs, combined with a kindness of heart that was unequalled and a primitive and fervent piety, endeared him to his moorland parishioners, such were not the steps by which clergy then rose in the Church, and at sixty my father was still incumbent of the little benefice* he had accepted in his thirtieth year. The income of the living was barely sufficient to support life in the decencies which are expected of the Anglican parson; and when my father died a few years ago, I, his only child, found myself thrown upon the world with a slender capital of less than a hundred pounds, and all the problem of existence before me. I felt that there was nothing for me to do in the country, and as usually happens in such cases, London drew me like a magnet. One day in August, in the early morning, while the dew still glittered on the turf, and on the high green banks of the lane, a neighbour drove me to the railway station, and I bade good-bye to the land of the broad moors and unearthly battlements of the wild tors.* It was six o'clock as we neared London; the faint, sickly fume of the brickfields about Acton* came in puffs through the open window, and a mist was rising from the ground. Presently the brief view of successive streets, prim and uniform, struck me with a sense of monotony; the hot air seemed to grow hotter; and when we had rolled beneath the dismal and squalid houses, whose dirty and neglected backyards border the line near Paddington, I felt as if I should be stifled in this fainting breath of London. I got a hansom and drove off, and every street increased my gloom; grey houses with blinds drawn

down, whole thoroughfares almost desolate, and the foot-passengers
who seemed to stagger wearily along rather than walk, all made me feel
a sinking at heart. I put up for the night at a small hotel in a street leading from the Strand, where my father had stayed on his few brief visits
to town; and when I went out after dinner, the real gaiety and bustle of
the Strand and Fleet Street could cheer me but little, for in all this
great city there was no single human being whom I could claim even as
an acquaintance. I will not weary you with the history of the next year,
for the adventures of a man who sinks are too trite to be worth recalling.
My money did not last me long; I found that I must be neatly dressed,
or no one to whom I applied would so much as listen to me; and I must
live in a street of decent reputation if I wished to be treated with common civility. I applied for various posts, for which, as I now see, I was
completely devoid of qualification; I tried to become a clerk without
having the smallest notion of business habits; and I found, to my cost,
that a general knowledge of literature and an execrable style of penmanship are far from being looked upon with favour in commercial
circles. I had read one of the most charming of the works of a famous
novelist of the present day, and I frequented the Fleet Street taverns in
the hope of making literary friends, and so getting the introductions
which I understood were indispensable in the career of letters. I was
disappointed; I once or twice ventured to address gentlemen who were
sitting in adjoining boxes, and I was answered, politely indeed, but in
a manner that told me my advances were unusual. Pound by pound, my
small resources melted; I could no longer think of appearances; I migrated
to a shy quarter, and my meals became mere observances. I went out at
one and returned to my room at two, but nothing but a milk-cake had
occurred in the interval. In short, I became acquainted with misfor-
tune; and as I sat amidst slush and ice on a seat in Hyde Park, munching a piece of bread, I realised the bitterness of poverty, and the feelings
of a gentleman reduced to something far below the condition of
a vagrant. In spite of all discouragement I did not desist in my efforts
to earn a living. I consulted advertisement columns, I kept my eyes
open for a chance, I looked in at the windows of stationers' shops, but
all in vain. One evening I was sitting in a Free Library,* and I saw an
advertisement in one of the papers. It was something like this: 'Wanted
by a gentleman a person of literary taste and abilities as secretary and
amanuensis. Must not object to travel.' Of course I knew that such an
advertisement would have answers by the hundred, and I thought my
own chances of securing the post extremely small; however, I applied at
the address given, and wrote to Mr Smith, who was staying at a large

hotel at the West End. I must confess that my heart gave a jump when I received a note a couple of days later, asking me to call at the Cosmopole at my earliest convenience. I do not know, sir, what your experiences of life may have been, and so I cannot tell whether you have known such moments. A slight sickness, my heart beating rather more rapidly than usual, a choking in the throat, and a difficulty of utterance; such were my sensations as I walked to the Cosmopole; I had to mention the name twice before the hall porter could understand me, and as I went upstairs my hands were wet. I was a good deal struck by Mr Smith's appearance; he looked younger than I did, and there was something mild and hesitating about his expression. He was reading when I came in, and he looked up when I gave my name. 'My dear sir,' he said, 'I am really delighted to see you. I have read very carefully the letter you were good enough to send me. Am I to understand that this document is in your own handwriting? He showed me the letter I had written, and I told him I was not so fortunate as to be able to keep a secretary myself. 'Then, sir,' he went on, 'the post I advertised is at your service. You have no objection to travel, I presume?' As you may imagine, I closed pretty eagerly with the offer he made, and thus I entered the service of Mr Smith. For the first few weeks I had no special duties; I had received a quarter's salary, and a handsome allowance was made me in lieu of board and lodging. One morning, however, when I called at the hotel according to instructions, my master informed me that I must hold myself in readiness for a sea-voyage, and, to spare unnecessary detail, in the course of a fortnight we had landed at New York. Mr Smith told me that he was engaged on a work of a special nature, in the compilation of which some peculiar researches had to be made; in short, I was given to understand that we were to travel to the far West.

After about a week had been spent in New York we took our seats in the cars, and began a journey tedious beyond all conception. Day after day, and night after night, the great train rolled on, threading its way through cities the very names of which were strange to me, passing at slow speed over perilous viaducts, skirting mountain ranges and pine forests, and plunging into dense tracks of wood, where mile after mile and hour after hour the same monotonous growth of brushwood met the eye, and all along the continual clatter and rattle of the wheels upon the ill-laid lines made it difficult to hear the voices of our fellow-passengers. We were a heterogeneous and ever-changing company; often I woke up in the dead of night with the sudden grinding jar of the breaks, and looking out found that we had stopped in the shabby street of some frame-built town, lighted chiefly by the flaring windows of the saloon.

A few rough-looking fellows would often come out to stare at the cars, and sometimes passengers got down, and sometimes there was a party of two or three waiting on the wooden sidewalk to get on board. Many of the passengers were English; humble households torn up from the moorings of a thousand years, and bound for some problematical paradise in the alkali desert or the Rockies. I heard the men talking to one another of the great profits to be made on the virgin soil of America, and two or three, who were mechanics, expatiated on the wonderful wages given to skilled labour on the railways and in the factories of the States. This talk usually fell dead after a few minutes, and I could see a sickness and dismay in the faces of these men as they looked at the ugly brush or at the desolate expanse of the prairie, dotted here and there with frame-houses, devoid of garden or flowers or trees, standing all alone in what might have been a great grey sea frozen into stillness. Day after day the waving sky-line, and the desolation of a land without form or colour or variety, appalled the hearts of such of us as were Englishmen, and once in the night as I lay awake I heard a woman weeping and sobbing and asking what she had done to come to such a place. Her husband tried to comfort her in the broad speech of Gloucestershire, telling her the ground was so rich that one had only to plough it up and it would grow sunflowers of itself, but she cried for her mother and their old cottage and the beehives like a little child. The sadness of it all overwhelmed me, and I had no heart to think of other matters; the question of what Mr Smith could have to do in such a country, and of what manner of literary research could be carried on in the wilderness, hardly troubled me. Now and again my situation struck me as peculiar; I had been engaged as a literary assistant at a handsome salary, and yet my master was still almost a stranger to me; sometimes he would come to where I was sitting in the cars and make a few banal remarks about the country, but for the most part of the journey he sat by himself, not speaking to any one, and so far as I could judge, deep in his thoughts. It was, I think, on the fifth day from New York when I received the intimation that we should shortly leave the cars; I had been watching some distant mountains which rose wild and savage before us, and I was wondering if there were human beings so unhappy as to speak of home in connection with those piles of lumbered rock, when Mr Smith touched me lightly on the shoulder. 'You will be glad to be done with the cars, I have no doubt, Mr Wilkins,' he said. 'You were looking at the mountains, I think? Well, I hope we shall be there to-night. The train stops at Reading,* and I dare say we shall manage to find our way.'

A few hours later the breaksman brought the train to a standstill at the Reading depôt, and we got out. I noticed that the town, though of course built almost entirely of frame-houses, was larger and busier than any we had passed for the last two days. The depôt was crowded; and as the bell and whistle sounded, I saw that a number of persons were preparing to leave the cars, while an even greater number were waiting to get on board. Besides the passengers, there was a pretty dense crowd of people, some of whom had come to meet or to see off their friends and relatives, while others were mere loafers. Several of our English fellow-passengers got down at Reading, but the confusion was so great that they were lost to my sight almost immediately. Mr Smith beckoned to me to follow him, and we were soon in the thick of the mass; and the continual ringing of bells, the hubbub of voices, the shrieking of whistles, and the hiss of escaping steam, confused my senses, and I wondered dimly, as I struggled after my employer, where we were going, and how we should be able to find our way through an unknown country. Mr Smith had put on a wide-brimmed hat, which he had sloped over his eyes, and as all the men wore hats of the same pattern, it was with some difficulty that I distinguished him in the crowd. We got free at last, and he struck down a side street, and made one or two sharp turns to right and left. It was getting dusk, and we seemed to be passing through a shy portion of the town; there were few people about in the ill-lighted streets, and these few were men of the most unprepossessing pattern. Suddenly we stopped before a corner house. A man was standing at the door, apparently on the look-out for some one, and I noticed that he and Smith gave sharp glances one to the other.

'From New York City, I expect, mister?'

'From New York.'

'All right; they're ready, and you can have 'em when you choose. I know my orders, you see, and I mean to run this business through.'

'Very well, Mr Evans, that is what we want. Our money is good, you know. Bring them round.'

I had stood silent, listening to this dialogue and wondering what it meant. Smith began to walk impatiently up and down the street, and the man Evans was still standing at his door. He had given a sharp whistle, and I saw him looking me over in a quiet, leisurely way, as if to make sure of my face for another time. I was thinking what all this could mean, when an ugly, slouching lad came up a side passage, leading two raw-boned horses.

'Get up, Mr Wilkins, and be quick about it,' said Smith; 'we ought to be on our way.'

We rode off together into the gathering darkness, and before long I looked back and saw the far plain behind us, with the lights of the town glimmering faintly; and in front rose the mountains. Smith guided his horse on the rough track as surely as if he had been riding along Piccadilly, and I followed him as well as I could. I was weary and exhausted, and scarcely took note of anything; I felt that the track was a gradual ascent, and here and there I saw great boulders by the road. The ride made but little impression on me. I have a faint recollection of passing through a dense black pine forest, where our horses had to pick their way among the rocks, and I remember the peculiar effect of the rarified air as we kept still mounting higher and higher. I think I must have been half asleep for the latter half of the ride, and it was with a shock that I heard Smith saying—

'Here we are, Wilkins. This is Blue Rock Park. You will enjoy the view to-morrow. To-night we will have something to eat, and then go to bed.'

A man came out of a rough-looking house and took the horses, and we found some fried steak and coarse whisky awaiting us inside. I had come to a strange place. There were three rooms—the room in which we had supper, Smith's room, and my own. The deaf old man who did the work slept in a sort of shed, and when I woke up the next morning and walked out I found that the house stood in a sort of hollow amongst the mountains; the clumps of pines and some enormous bluish-grey rocks that stood here and there between the trees had given the place the name of Blue Rock Park. On every side the snow-covered mountains surrounded us, the breath of the air was as wine, and when I climbed the slope and looked down, I could see that, so far as any human fellowship was concerned, I might as well have been wrecked on some small island in mid-Pacific. The only trace of man I could see was the rough log-house where I had slept, and in my ignorance I did not know that there were similar houses within comparatively easy distance, as distance is reckoned in the Rockies. But at the moment, the utter, dreadful loneliness rushed upon me, and the thought of the great plain and the great sea that parted me from the world I knew caught me by the throat, and I wondered if I should die there in that mountain hollow. It was a terrible instant, and I have not yet forgotten it. Of course, I managed to conquer my horror; I said I should be all the stronger for the experience, and I made up my mind to make the best of everything. It was a rough life enough, and rough enough board and lodging. I was left entirely to myself. Smith I scarcely ever saw, nor did I know when he was in the house. I have often thought he was far away, and have been surprised to see him walking out of his room, locking the door behind him, and putting the key in his pocket; and on several occasions, when I fancied he was busy in his room, I have seen him come in with his boots covered with dust and dirt. So far as work went I enjoyed a complete sinecure; I had nothing to do but to walk about the valley, to eat, and to sleep. With one thing and another I grew accustomed to the life, and managed to make myself pretty comfortable, and by degrees I began to venture farther away from the house, and to explore the country. One day I had contrived to get into a neighbouring valley, and suddenly I came upon a group of men sawing timber. I went up to them, hoping that perhaps some of them might be Englishmen; at all events, they were human beings, and I should hear articulate speech; for the old man I have mentioned, besides being half blind and stone deaf, was wholly dumb so far as I was concerned. I was prepared to be welcomed in a rough and ready fashion, without much of the forms of politeness, but the grim glances and the short, gruff answers I received astonished me. I saw the men glancing oddly at each other; and one of them, who had stopped work, began fingering a gun, and I was obliged to return on my path uttering curses on the fate which had brought me into a land where men were more brutish than the very brutes. The solitude of the life began to oppress me as with a nightmare, and a few days later I determined to walk to a kind of station some miles distant, where a rough inn was kept for the accommodation of hunters and tourists. English gentlemen occasionally stopped there for the night, and I thought I might perhaps fall in with some one of better manners than the inhabitants of the country. I found, as I had expected, a group of men lounging about the door of the log-house that served as a hotel, and as I came nearer I could see that heads were put together and looks interchanged, and when I walked up the six or seven trappers stared at me in stony ferocity, and with something of the disgust that one eyes a loathsome and venomous snake. I felt that I could bear it no longer, and I called out—

'Is there such a thing as an Englishman here, or any one with a little civilisation?'

One of the men put his hand to his belt, but his neighbour checked him, and answered me—

'You'll find we've got some of the resources of civilisation before very long, mister, and I expect you'll not fancy them extremely. But, any way, there's an Englishman tarrying here, and I've no doubt he'll be glad to see you. There you are; that's Mr D'Aubernoun.'

A young man, dressed like an English country squire, came and stood at the door, and looked at me. One of the men pointed to me and said—

'That's the individual we were talking about last night. Thought you might like to have a look at him, squire, and here he is.'

The young fellow's good-natured English face clouded over, and he glanced sternly at me, and turned away with a gesture of contempt and aversion.

'Sir,' I cried, 'I do not know what I have done to be treated in this manner. You are my fellow-countryman, and I expected some courtesy.'

He gave me a black look and made as if he would go in, but he changed his mind and faced me.

'You are rather imprudent, I think, to behave in this manner. You must be counting on a forbearance which cannot last very long, which may last a very short time indeed. And let me tell you this, sir, you may call yourself an Englishman, and drag the name of England through the dirt, but you need not count on any English influence to help you. If I were you, I would not stay here much longer.'

He went into the inn, and the men quietly watched my face as I stood there, wondering whether I was going mad. The woman of the house came out and stared at me as if I were a wild beast or a savage, and I turned to her, and spoke quietly—

'I am very hungry and thirsty. I have walked a long way. I have plenty of money. Will you give me something to eat and drink?'

'No, I won't,' she said. 'You had better quit this.'

I crawled home like a wounded beast, and lay down on my bed. It was all a hopeless puzzle to me; I knew nothing but rage, and shame, and terror, and I suffered little more when I passed by a house in an adjacent valley, and some children who were playing outside ran from me shrieking. I was forced to walk to find some occupation; I should have died if I had sat down quietly in Blue Rock Park and looked all day at the mountains; but wherever I saw a human being I saw the same glance of hatred and aversion, and once as I was crossing a thick brake I heard a shot and the venomous hiss of a bullet close to my ear.

One day I heard a conversation which astounded me; I was sitting behind a rock resting, and two men came along the track and halted. One of them had got his feet entangled in some wild vines, and swore fiercely, but the other laughed, and said they were useful things sometimes.

'What the hell do you mean?'

'Oh, nothing much. But they're uncommon tough, these here vines, and sometimes rope is skerse and dear.'

The man who had sworn chuckled at this, and I heard them sit down and light their pipes.

'Have you seen him lately?' asked the humourist.

'I sighted him the other day, but the darned bullet went high. He's got his master's luck I expect, sir, but it can't last much longer. You heard about him going to Jinks's and trying his brass, but the young Britisher downed him pretty considerable, I can tell you.'

'What the devil is the meaning of it?'

'I don't know, but I believe it'll have to be finished, and done in the old style too. You know how they fix the niggers?'

'Yes, sir, I've seen a little of that. A couple of gallons of kerosene 'll cost a dollar at Brown's store, but I should say it's cheap anyway.'

They moved off after this, and I lay still behind the rock, the sweat pouring down my face. I was so sick that I could barely stand, and I walked home as slowly as an old man, leaning on my stick. I knew that the two men had been talking about me, and I knew that some terrible death was in store for me. That night I could not sleep; I tossed on the rough bed and tortured myself to find out the meaning of it all. At last, in the very dead of night, I rose from the bed and put on my clothes, and went out. I did not care where I went, but I felt that I must walk till I had tired myself out. It was a clear moonlight night, and in a couple of hours I found I was approaching a place of dismal reputation in the mountains, a deep cleft in the rocks, known as Black Gulf Cañon. Many years before an unfortunate party of Englishmen and English-women had camped here and had been surrounded by Indians, They were captured, outraged, and put to death with almost inconceivable tortures, and the roughest of the trappers or woodsmen gave the cañon a wide berth even in the daytime. As I crushed through the dense brushwood which grew above the cañon I heard voices; and wondering who could be in such a place at such a time, I went on, walking more carefully, and making as little noise as possible. There was a great tree growing on the very edge of the rocks, and I lay down and looked out from behind the trunk. Black Gulf Cañon was below me, the moonlight shining bright into its very depths from mid-heaven, and casting shadows as black as death from the pointed rock, and all the sheer rock on the other side, overhanging the cañon, was in darkness. At intervals a light veil obscured the moonlight, as a filmy cloud fleeted across the moon, and a bitter wind blew shrill across the gulf. I looked down, as I have said, and saw twenty men standing in a semicircle round a rock; I counted them one by one, and knew most of them. They were the very vilest of the vile, more vile than any den in London could show, and there was murder, and worse than murder, on the heads of not a few. Facing them and me stood Mr Smith, with the rock before him, and on the rock was a great pair of scales, such as are used in the stores. I heard his voice ringing down the cañon as I lay beside the tree, and my heart turned cold as I heard it.

'Life for gold,' he cried, 'a life for gold. The blood and the life of an enemy for every pound of gold.'

A man stepped out and raised one hand, and with the other flung a bright lump of something into the pan of the scales, which clanged down, and Smith muttered something in his ear. Then he cried again—

'Blood for gold, for a pound of gold, the life of an enemy. For every pound of gold upon the scales, a life.'

One by one the men came forward, each lifting up his right hand; and the gold was weighed in the scales, and each time Smith leant forward and spoke to each man in his ear. Then he cried again—

'Desire and lust for gold on the scales. For every pound of gold enjoyment of desire.'

I saw the same thing happen as before; the uplifted hand and the metal weighed, and the mouth whispering, and black passion on every face.

Then, one by one, I saw the men again step up to Smith. A muttered conversation seemed to take place. I could see that Smith was explaining and directing, and I noticed that he gesticulated a little as one who points out the way, and once or twice he moved his hands quickly as if he would show that the path was clear and could not be missed. I kept my eyes so intently on his figure that I noted little else, and at last it was with a start that I realised that the cañon was empty. A moment before I thought I had seen the group of villainous faces, and the two standing, a little apart, by the rock; I had looked down a moment, and when I glanced again into the cañon there was no one there. In dumb terror I made my way home, and I fell asleep in an instant from exhaustion. No doubt I should have slept on for many hours, but when I woke up the sun was only rising, and the light shone in on my bed. I had started up from sleep with the sensation of having received a violent shock; and as I looked in confusion about me, I saw, to my amazement, that there were three men in the room. One of them had his hand on my shoulder, and spoke to me—

'Come, mister, wake up. Your time's up now, I reckon, and the boys are waiting for you outside, and they're in a big hurry. Come on; you can put on your clothes; it's kind of chilly this morning.'

I saw the other two men smiling sourly at each other, but I understood nothing. I simply pulled on my clothes and said I was ready.

'All right; come on, then. You go first, Nichols, and Jim and I will give the gentleman an arm.'

They took me out into the sunlight, and then I understood the meaning of a dull murmur that had vaguely perplexed me while I was dressing. There were about two hundred men waiting outside, and some women too, and when they saw me there was a low muttering growl. I did not know what I had done, but that noise made my heart beat and the sweat come out on my face. I saw confusedly, as through a veil, the tumult and tossing of the crowd, discordant voices were speaking, and amongst all those faces there was not one glance of mercy, but a fury of lust that I did not understand. I found myself presently walking in a sort of procession up the slope of the valley, and on every side of me there were men with revolvers in their hands. Now and then a voice struck me, and I heard words and sentences of which I could form no connected story. But I understood that there was one sentence of execration; I heard scraps of stories that seemed strange and improbable. Some one was talking of men, lured by cunning devices from their homes and murdered with hideous tortures, found writhing like wounded snakes in dark and lonely places, only crying for some one to stab them to the heart, and so end their torments; and I heard another voice speaking of innocent girls who had vanished for a day or two, and then had come back and died, blushing red with shame even in the agonies of death. I wondered what it all meant, and what was to happen; but I was so weary that I walked on in a dream, scarcely longing for anything but sleep. At last we stopped. We had reached the summit of the hill overlooking Blue Rock Valley, and I saw that I was standing beneath a clump of trees where I had often sat. I was in the midst of a ring of armed men, and I saw that two or three men were very busy with piles of wood, while others were fingering a rope. Then there was a stir in the crowd, and a man was pushed forward. His hands and feet were tightly bound with cord; and though his face was unutterably villainous, I pitied him for the agony that worked his features and twisted his lips. I knew him; he was amongst those that had gathered round Smith in Black Gulf Cañon. In an instant he was unbound and stripped naked, borne beneath one of the trees, and his neck encircled by a noose that went around the trunk. A hoarse voice gave some kind of order; there was a rush of feet, and the rope tightened; and there before me I saw the blackened face and the writhing limbs and the shameful agony of death. One after another half a dozen men, all of whom I had seen in the cañon the night before, were strangled before me, and their bodies were flung forth on the ground. Then there was a pause, and the man who had roused me a short while before came up to me, and said—

'Now, mister, it's your turn. We give you five minutes to cast up your accounts, and when that's clocked, by the living God, we will burn you alive at that tree.'

It was then I awoke and understood. I cried out—

'Why, what have I done? Why should you hurt me? I am a harmless man; I never did you any wrong.' I covered my face with my hands; it seemed so pitiful, and it was such a terrible death.

'What have I done?' I cried again. 'You must take me for some other man. You cannot know me.'

'You black-hearted devil,' said the man at my side, 'we know you well enough. There's not a man within thirty miles of this that won't curse Jack Smith when you are burning in hell.'

'My name is not Smith,' I said, with some hope left in me. 'My name is Wilkins. I was Mr Smith's secretary, but I knew nothing of him.'

'Hark at the black liar,' said the man. 'Secretary be damned! You were clever enough, I dare say, to slink out at night and keep your face in the dark, but we've tracked you out at last. But your time's up. Come along.'

I was dragged to the tree and bound to it with chains; I saw the piles of wood heaped all about me, and shut my eyes. Then I felt myself drenched all over with some liquid, and looked again, and a woman grinned at me. She had just emptied a great can of petroleum over me and over the wood. A voice shouted, 'Fire away!' and I fainted, and knew nothing more.

When I opened my eyes I was lying on a bed in a bare, comfortless room. A doctor was holding some strong salts to my nostrils, and a gentleman standing by the bed, whom I afterwards found to be the sheriff, addressed me.

'Say, mister,' he began, 'you've had an uncommon narrow squeak for it. The boys were just about lighting up when I came along with the posse, and I had as much as I could do to bring you off, I can tell you. And, mind you, I don't blame them; they had made up their minds, you see, that you were the head of the Black Gulf gang, and at first nothing I could say would persuade them you weren't Jack Smith. Luckily, a man from here named Evans, that came along with us, allowed he had seen you with Jack Smith, and that you were yourself. So we brought you along and gaoled you, but you can go if you like when you're through with this faint turn.'

I got on the cars the next day, and in three weeks I was in London; again almost penniless. But from that time my fortune seemed to change; I made influential friends in all directions; bank directors courted my company, and editors positively flung themselves into my arms. I had only to choose my career, and after a while I determined that I was meant by nature for a life of comparative leisure. With an ease that seemed almost ridiculous, I obtained a well-paid position in connection with a prosperous political club. I have charming chambers in a central neighbourhood, close to the parks, the club chef exerts himself when I lunch or dine, and the rarest vintages in the cellar are always at my disposal. Yet, since my return to London, I have never known a day's security or peace; I tremble when I awake lest Smith should be standing at my bed, and every step I take seems to bring me nearer to the edge of the precipice. Smith, I knew, had escaped free from the raid of the Vigilantes,* and I grew faint at the thought that he would in all probability return to London, and that suddenly and unprepared I should meet him face to face. Every morning as I left my house I would peer up and down the street, expecting to see that dreaded figure awaiting me; I have delayed at street-corners, my heart in my mouth, sickening at the thought that a few quick steps might bring us together; I could not bear to frequent the theatres or music-halls, lest by some bizarre chance he should prove to be my neighbour. Sometimes I have been forced, against my will, to walk out at night, and then in silent squares the shadows have made me shudder, and in the medley of meetings in the crowded thoroughfares I have said to myself, 'It must come sooner or later; he will surely return to town, and I shall see him when I feel most secure.' I scanned the newspapers for hint or intimation of approaching danger, and no small type nor report of trivial interest was allowed to pass unread. Especially I read and re-read the advertisement columns, but without result; months passed by, and I was undisturbed till, though I felt far from safe, I no longer suffered from the intolerable oppression of instant and ever-present terror. This afternoon, as I was walking quietly along Oxford Street, I raised my eyes and looked across the road, and then at last I saw the man who had so long haunted my thoughts.

Mr Wilkins finished his wine, and leant back in his chair, looking sadly at Dyson; and then, as if a thought struck him, fished out of an inner pocket a leather letter-case, and handed a newspaper cutting across the table.

Dyson glanced closely at the slip, and saw that it had been extracted from the columns of an evening paper. It ran as follows:—

## WHOLESALE LYNCHING
### SHOCKING STORY

A Dalziel telegram* from Reading (Colorado) states that advices received there from Blue Rock Park report a frightful instance of popular vengeance. For some time the neighbourhood has been terrorised by the crimes of a gang of desperadoes, who, under the cover of a carefully planned organisation, have perpetrated the most infamous cruelties on men and women. A Vigilance Committee was formed,* and it was found that the leader of the gang was a person named Smith, living in Blue Rock Park. Action was taken, and six of the worst in the band were summarily strangled in the presence of two or three hundred men and women. Smith is said to have escaped.

'This is a terrible story,' said Dyson; 'I can well believe that your days and nights are haunted by such fearful scenes as you have described. But surely you have no need to fear Smith? He has much more cause to fear you. Consider: you have only to lay your information before the police, and a warrant would be immediately issued for his arrest. Besides, you will, I am sure, excuse me for what I am going to say.'

'My dear sir,' said Mr Wilkins, 'I hope you will speak to me with perfect freedom.'

'Well, then, I must confess that my impression was that you were rather disappointed at not being able to stop the man before he drove off. I thought you seemed annoyed that you could not get across the street.'

'Sir, I did not know what I was about. I caught sight of the man, but it was only for a moment, and the agony you witnessed was the agony of suspense. I was not perfectly certain of the face, and the horrible thought that Smith was again in London overwhelmed me. I shuddered at the idea of this incarnate fiend, whose soul is black with shocking crimes, mingling free and unobserved amongst the harmless crowds, meditating perhaps a new and more fearful cycle of infamies. I tell you, sir, that an awful being stalks through the streets, a being before whom the sunlight itself should blacken, and the summer air grow chill and dank. Such thoughts as these rushed upon me with the force of a whirlwind; I lost my senses.'

'I see. I partly understand your feelings, but I would impress on you that you have nothing really to fear. Depend upon it, Smith will not molest you in any way. You must remember he himself has had a warning; and indeed, from the brief glance I had of him, he seemed to me to be a frightened-looking man. However, I see it is getting late, and if you will excuse me, Mr Wilkins, I think I will be going. I dare say we shall often meet here.'

Dyson walked off smartly, pondering the strange story chance had brought him, and finding on cool reflection that there was something a little strange in Mr Wilkins's manner, for which not even so weird a catalogue of experiences could altogether account.

## ADVENTURE OF THE MISSING BROTHER

MR CHARLES PHILLIPPS was, as has been hinted, a gentleman of pronounced scientific tastes. In his early days he had devoted himself with fond enthusiasm to the agreeable study of biology, and a brief monograph on the Embryology of the Microscopic Holothuria* had formed his first contribution to the *belles lettres*. Later he had somewhat relaxed the severity of his pursuits, and had dabbled in the more frivolous subjects of palæontology and ethnology; he had a cabinet in his sitting-room whose drawers were stuffed with rude flint implements, and a charming fetish from the South Seas was the dominant note in the decorative scheme of the apartment. Flattering himself with the title of materialist, he was in truth one of the most credulous of men, but he required a marvel to be neatly draped in the robes of Science before he would give it any credit, and the wildest dreams took solid shape to him if only the nomenclature were severe and irreproachable. He laughed at the witch, but quailed before the powers of the hypnotist, lifting his eyebrows when Christianity was mentioned, but adoring protyle and the ether.* For the rest, he prided himself on a boundless scepticism; the average tale of wonder he heard with nothing but contempt, and he would certainly not have credited a word or syllable of Dyson's story of the pursuer and pursued, unless the gold coin had been produced as visible and tangible evidence. As it was, he half suspected that Dyson had imposed on him; he knew his friend's disordered fancies, and his habit of conjuring up the marvellous to account for the entirely commonplace; and, on the whole, he was inclined to think that the so-called facts in the odd adventure had been gravely distorted in the telling. Since the evening on which he had listened to the tale he had paid Dyson a visit, and had delivered himself of some serious talk on the necessity of accurate observation, and the folly, as he put it, of using a kaleidoscope instead of a telescope in the view of things, to which remarks his friend had listened with a smile that was extremely sardonic. 'My dear fellow,' Dyson had remarked at last, 'you will allow me to tell you that I see your drift perfectly. However, you will be astonished to hear that I consider you to be the visionary, while I am a sober and serious spectator of human life. You have gone round the circle; and while you fancy yourself far in the golden land of new philosophies, you are in reality a dweller in a metaphorical Clapham;* your scepticism has defeated itself and become a monstrous credulity; you are, in fact, in the position of the bat or owl, I forget which it was, who denied the existence of the sun at noonday,* and I shall be astonished if you do not one day come to me full of contrition for your manifold intellectual errors, with a humble resolution to see things in their true light for the future.' This tirade had left Mr Phillipps unimpressed; he considered Dyson as hopeless, and he went home to gloat over some primitive stone implements that a friend had sent him from India. He found that his landlady, seeing them displayed in all their rude formlessness upon the table, had removed the collection to the dustbin, and had replaced it by lunch; and the afternoon was spent in malodorous research. Mrs Brown, hearing these stones spoken of as very valuable knives, had called him in his hearing 'poor Mr Phillipps,' and between rage and evil odours he spent a sorry afternoon. It was four o'clock before he had completed his work of rescue; and, overpowered with the flavours of decaying cabbage leaves, Phillipps felt that he must have a walk to gain an appetite for the evening meal. Unlike Dyson, he walked fast, with his eyes on the pavement, absorbed in his thoughts, and oblivious of the life around him; and he could not have told by what streets he had passed, when he suddenly lifted up his eyes and found himself in Leicester Square. The grass and flowers pleased him, and he welcomed the opportunity of resting for a few minutes, and glancing round, he saw a bench which had only one occupant, a lady, and as she was seated at one end, Phillipps took up a position at the other extremity, and began to pass in angry review the events of the afternoon. He had noticed as he came up to the bench that the person already there was neatly dressed, and to all appearance young; her face he could not see, as it was turned away in apparent contemplation of the shrubs, and, moreover, shielded with her hand; but it would be doing wrong to Mr Phillipps to imagine that his choice of a seat was dictated by any hopes of an affair of the heart, he had simply preferred the company of one lady to that of five dirty children, and having seated himself, was immersed directly in thoughts of his misfortunes. He had meditated changing his lodgings; but now, on a judicial review of the case in all its bearings, his calmer judgment told him that the race of landladies is like to the race of the leaves, and that there was but little to choose between them. He resolved, however, to talk to Mrs Brown, the offender, very coolly and yet severely, to point out the extreme indiscretion of her conduct, and to express a hope for better things in the future. With this decision registered in his mind, Phillipps was about to get up from the seat and move off, when he was intensely annoyed to hear a stifled sob, evidently from the lady, who still continued her contemplation of the shrubs and flower-beds. He clutched his stick desperately, and in a moment would have been in full retreat, when the lady turned her face towards him, and with a mute entreaty bespoke his attention. She was a young girl with a quaint and piquant rather than a beautiful face, and she was evidently in the bitterest distress. Mr Phillipps sat down again, and cursed his chances heartily. The young lady looked at him with a pair of charming eyes of a shining hazel, which showed no trace of tears, though a handkerchief was in her hand; she bit her lip, and seemed to struggle with some overpowering grief, and her whole attitude was all beseeching and imploring. Phillipps sat on the edge of the bench gazing awkwardly at her, and wondering what was to come next, and she looked at him still without speaking.

'Well, madam,' he said at last, 'I understood from your gesture that you wished to speak to me. Is there anything I can do for you? Though, if you will pardon me, I cannot help saying that that seems highly improbable.'

'Ah, sir,' she said in a low, murmuring voice, 'do not speak harshly to me. I am in sore straits, and I thought from your face that I could safely ask your sympathy, if not your help.'

'Would you kindly tell me what is the matter?' said Phillipps. 'Perhaps you would like some tea?'

'I knew I could not be mistaken,' the lady replied. 'That offer of refreshment bespeaks a generous mind. But tea, alas! is powerless to console me. If you will let me, I shall endeavour to explain my trouble.'

'I should be glad if you would.'

'I shall do so, and I shall try and be brief, in spite of the numerous complications which have made me, young as I am, tremble before what seems the profound and terrible mystery of existence. Yet the grief which now racks my very soul is but too simple: I have lost my brother.'

'Lost your brother! How on earth can that be?'

'I see I must trouble you with a few particulars. My brother, then, who is by some years my elder, is a tutor in a private school in the extreme north of London. The want of means deprived him of the advantages of a University education; and lacking the stamp of a degree, he could not hope for that position which his scholarship and his talents entitled him to claim. He was thus forced to accept the post of classical master at Dr Saunderson's Highgate Academy for the sons of gentlemen, and he has performed his duties with perfect satisfaction to his principal for some years. My personal history need not trouble you; it will be enough if I tell you that for the last month I have been governess in a family residing at Tooting. My brother and I have always cherished the warmest mutual affection; and though circumstances into which I need not enter have kept us apart for some time, yet we have never lost sight of one another. We made up our minds that unless one of us was absolutely unable to rise from a bed of sickness, we should never let a week pass by without meeting, and some time ago we chose this square as our rendezvous on account of its central position and its convenience of access. And indeed, after a week of distasteful toil, my brother felt little inclination for much walking, and we have often spent two or three hours on this bench, speaking of our prospects and of happier days, when we were children. In the early spring it was cold and chilly, still we enjoyed the short respite, and I think that we were often taken for a pair of lovers, as we sat close together, eagerly talking. Saturday after Saturday we have met each other here; and though the doctor told him it was madness, my brother would not allow the influenza to break the appointment. That was some time ago; last Saturday we had a long and happy afternoon, and separated more cheerfully than usual, feeling that the coming week would be bearable, and resolving that our next meeting should be if possible still more pleasant. I arrived here at the time agreed upon, four o'clock, and sat down and watched for my brother, expecting every moment to see him advancing towards me from that gate at the north side of the square. Five minutes passed by, and he had not arrived; I thought he must have missed his train, and the idea that our interview would be cut short by twenty minutes, or perhaps half an hour, saddened me; I had hoped we should be so happy together to-day. Suddenly, moved by I know not what impulse, I turned abruptly round, and how can I describe to you my astonishment when I saw my brother advancing slowly towards me from the southern side of the square, accompanied by another person. My first thought, I remember, had in it something of resentment that this man, whoever he was, should intrude himself into our meeting; I wondered who it could possibly be, for my brother had, I may say, no intimate friends. Then as I looked still at the advancing figures, another feeling took possession of me; it was a sensation of bristling fear, the fear of the child in the dark, unreasonable and unreasoning, but terrible, clutching at my heart as with the cold grip of a dead man's hands. Yet I overcame the feeling, and looked steadily at my brother, waiting for him to speak, and more closely at his companion. Then I noticed that this man was leading my brother rather than walking arm in arm with him; he was a tall man, dressed in quite ordinary fashion. He wore a high bowler hat, and, in spite of the warmth of the day, a plain black overcoat, tightly buttoned, and I noticed his trousers, of a quiet black and grey stripe. The face was commonplace too, and indeed I cannot recall any special features, or any trick of expression; for though I looked at him as he came near, curiously enough his face made no impression on me—it was as though I had seen a well-made mask. They passed in front of me, and to my unutterable astonishment, I heard my brother's voice speaking to me, though his lips did not move, nor his eyes look into mine. It was a voice I cannot describe, though I knew it, but the words came to my ears as if mingled with plashing water and the sound of a shallow brook flowing amidst stones. I heard, then, the words, "I cannot stay," and for a moment the heavens and the earth seemed to rush together with the sound of thunder, and I was thrust forth from the world into a black void without beginning and without end. For, as my brother passed me, I saw the hand that held him by the arm, and seemed to guide him, and in one moment of horror I realised that it was as a formless thing that has mouldered for many years in the grave. The flesh was peeled in strips from the bones, and hung apart dry and granulated, and the fingers that encircled my brother's arm were all unshapen, claw-like things, and one was but a stump from which the end had rotted off. When I recovered my senses I saw the two passing out by that gate. I paused for a moment, and then with a rush as of fire to my heart I knew that no horror could stay me, but that I must follow my brother and save him, even though all hell rose up against me. I ran out, and looked up the pavement, and saw the two figures walking amidst the crowd. I ran across the road, and saw them turn up that side street, and I reached the corner a moment later. In vain I looked to right and left, for neither my brother nor his strange guardian was in sight; two elderly men were coming down arm-in-arm, and a telegraph boy was walking lustily along whistling. I remained there a moment horror-struck, and then I bowed my head and returned to this seat, where you found me. Now, sir, do you wonder at my grief? Oh, tell me what has happened to my brother, or I feel I shall go mad!'

Mr Phillipps, who had listened with exemplary patience to this tale, hesitated a moment before he spoke.

'My dear madam,' he said at length, 'you have known how to engage me in your service, not only as a man, but as a student of science. As a fellow-creature I pity you most profoundly; you must have suffered extremely from what you saw, or rather from what you fancied you saw. For, as a scientific observer, it is my duty to tell you the plain truth, which, indeed, besides being true, must also console you. Allow me to ask you then to describe your brother.'

'Certainly,' said the lady eagerly; 'I can describe him accurately. My brother is a somewhat young-looking man; he is pale, has small black whiskers, and wears spectacles. He has rather a timid, almost a frightened expression, and looks about him nervously from side to side. Think, think! Surely you must have seen him. Perhaps you are an *habitué** of this engaging quarter; you may have met him on some previous Saturday. I may have been mistaken in supposing that he turned up that side street; he may have gone on, and you may have passed each other. Oh, tell me, sir, whether you have not seen him!'

'I am afraid I do not keep a very sharp look-out when I am walking,' said Phillipps, who would have passed his mother unnoticed; 'but I am sure your description is admirable. And now will you describe the person who, you say, held your brother by the arm?'

'I cannot do so. I told you his face seemed devoid of expression or salient feature. It was like a mask.'

'Exactly; you cannot describe what you have never seen. I need hardly point out to you the conclusion to be drawn; you have been the victim of an hallucination. You expected to see your brother, you were alarmed because you did not see him, and unconsciously, no doubt, your brain went to work, and finally you saw a mere projection of your own morbid thoughts—a vision of your absent brother, and a mere confusion of terrors incorporated in a figure which you can't describe. Of course your brother has been in some way prevented from coming to meet you as usual. I expect you will hear from him in a day or two.'

The lady looked seriously at Mr Phillipps, and then for a second there seemed almost a twinkling as of mirth about her eyes, but her face clouded sadly at the dogmatic conclusions to which the scientist was led so irresistibly.

'Ah!' she said, 'you do not know. I cannot doubt the evidence of my waking senses. Besides, perhaps I have had experiences even more terrible. I acknowledge the force of your arguments, but a woman has intuitions which never deceive her. Believe me, I am not hysterical; feel my pulse, it is quite regular.'

She stretched out her hand with a dainty gesture, and a glance that enraptured Phillipps in spite of himself. The hand held out to him was soft and white and warm, and as, in some confusion, he placed his fingers on the purple vein, he felt profoundly touched by the spectacle of love and grief before him.

'No,' he said, as he released her wrist, 'as you say, you are evidently quite yourself. Still, you must be aware that living men do not possess dead hands. That sort of thing doesn't happen. It is, of course, barely possible that you did see your brother with another gentleman, and that important business prevented him from stopping. As for the wonderful hand, there may have been some deformity, a finger shot off by accident, or something of that sort.'

The lady shook her head mournfully.

'I see you are a determined rationalist,' she said. 'Did you not hear me say that I have had experiences even more terrible. I too was once a sceptic, but after what I have known I can no longer affect to doubt.'

'Madam,' replied Mr Phillipps, 'no one shall make me deny my faith. I will never believe, nor will I pretend to believe, that two and two make five, nor will I on any pretences admit the existence of two-sided triangles.'

'You are a little hasty,' rejoined the lady. 'But may I ask you if you ever heard the name of Professor Gregg, the authority on ethnology and kindred subjects.'

'I have done much more than merely hear of Professor Gregg,' said Phillipps. 'I always regarded him as one of our most acute and clear-headed observers; and his last publication, the *Textbook of Ethnology*, struck me as being quite admirable in its kind. Indeed, the book had but come into my hands when I heard of the terrible accident which cut short Gregg's career. He had, I think, taken a country house in the West of England for the summer, and is supposed to have fallen into a river. So far as I remember, his body was never recovered.'

'Sir, I am sure that you are discreet. Your conversation seems to declare as much, and the very title of that little work of yours which you mentioned assures me that you are no empty trifler. In a word, I feel that I may depend on you. You appear to be under the impression that Professor Gregg is dead; I have no reason to believe that that is the case.'

'What?' cried Phillipps, astonished and perturbed. 'You do not hint that there was anything disgraceful? I cannot believe it. Gregg was a man of clearest character; his private life was one of great benevolence; and though I myself am free from delusions, I believe him to have been a sincere and devout Christian. Surely you cannot mean to insinuate that some disreputable history forced him to flee the country?'

'Again you are in a hurry,' replied the lady. 'I said nothing of all this. Briefly, then, I must tell you that Professor Gregg left his house one morning in full health both of mind and body. He never returned, but his watch and chain, a purse containing three sovereigns in gold, and some loose silver, with a ring that he wore habitually, were found three days later on a wild and savage hillside, many miles from the river. These articles were placed beside a limestone rock of fantastic form; they had been wrapped into a parcel with a kind of rough parchment which was secured with gut. The parcel was opened, and the inner side of the parchment bore an inscription done with some red substance; the characters were undecipherable, but seemed to be a corrupt cuneiform.'

'You interest me intensely,' said Phillipps. 'Would you mind continuing your story? The circumstance you have mentioned seems to me of the most inexplicable character, and I thirst for an elucidation.'

The young lady seemed to meditate for a moment, and she then proceeded to relate the

## NOVEL OF THE BLACK SEAL

I must now give you some fuller particulars of my history. I am the daughter of a civil engineer,* Steven Lally by name, who was so unfortunate as to die suddenly at the outset of his career, and before he had accumulated sufficient means to support his wife and her two children. My mother contrived to keep the small household going on resources which must have been incredibly small; we lived in a remote country village, because most of the necessaries of life were cheaper than in a town, but even so we were brought up with the severest economy. My father was a clever and well-read man, and left behind him a small but select collection of books, containing the best Greek, Latin, and English classics, and these books were the only amusement we possessed. My brother, I remember, learnt Latin out of Descartes' *Meditationes*,* and I, in place of the little tales which children are usually told to read, had nothing more charming than a translation of the *Gesta Romanorum*.* We grew up thus, quiet and studious children, and in course of time my brother provided for himself in the manner I have mentioned. I continued to live at home; my poor mother had become an invalid, and demanded my continual care, and about two years ago she died after many months of painful illness. My situation was a terrible one; the shabby furniture barely sufficed to pay the debts I had been forced to contract, and the books I despatched to my brother, knowing how he would value them. I was absolutely alone; I was aware how poorly my brother was paid; and though I came up to London in the hope of finding employment, with the understanding that he would defray my expenses, I swore it should only be for a month, and that if I could not in that time find some work, I would starve rather than deprive him of the few miserable pounds he had laid by for his day of trouble. I took a little room in a distant suburb, the cheapest that I could find; I lived on bread and tea, and I spent my time in vain answering of advertisements, and vainer walks to addresses I had noted. Day followed on day, and week on week, and still I was unsuccessful, till at last the term I had appointed drew to a close, and I saw before me the grim prospect of slowly dying of starvation. My landlady was good-natured in her way; she knew the slenderness of my means, and I am sure that she would not have turned me out of doors; it remained for me then to go away, and to try and die in some quiet place. It was winter then, and a thick white fog gathered in the early part of the afternoon, becoming more dense as the day wore on; it was a Sunday, I remember, and the people of the house were at chapel. At about three o'clock I crept out and walked away as quickly as I could, for I was weak from abstinence. The white mist wrapped all the streets in silence, a hard frost had gathered thick upon the bare branches of the trees, and frost crystals glittered on the wooden fences, and on the cold, cruel ground beneath my feet. I walked on, turning to right and left in utter haphazard, without caring to look up at the names of the streets, and all that I remember of my walk on that Sunday afternoon seems but the broken fragments of an evil dream. In a confused vision I stumbled on, through roads half-town and half-country, grey fields melting into the cloudy world of mist on one side of me, and on the other comfortable villas with a glow of firelight flickering on the walls, but all unreal; red brick walls and lighted windows, vague trees, and glimmering country, gas-lamps beginning to star the white shadows, the vanishing perspectives of the railway line beneath high embankments, the green and red of the signal lamps,—all these were but momentary pictures flashed on my tired brain and senses numbed by hunger. Now and then I would hear a quick step ringing on the iron road, and men would pass me well wrapped up, walking fast for the sake of warmth, and no doubt eagerly foretasting the pleasures of a glowing hearth, with curtains tightly drawn about the frosted panes, and the welcomes of their friends; but as the early evening darkened and night approached, foot-passengers got fewer and fewer, and I passed through street after street alone. In the white silence I stumbled on, as desolate as if I trod the streets of a buried city; and as I grew more weak and exhausted, something of the horror of death was folding thickly round my heart. Suddenly, as I turned a corner, some one accosted me courteously beneath the lamp-post, and I heard a voice asking if I could kindly point the way to Avon Road. At the sudden shock of human accents I was prostrated, and my strength gave way; I fell all huddled on the sidewalk, and wept and sobbed and laughed in violent hysteria. I had gone out prepared to die, and as I stepped across the threshold that had sheltered me, I consciously bade adieu to all hopes and all remembrances; the door clanged behind me with the noise of thunder, and I felt that an iron curtain had fallen on the brief passages of my life, that henceforth I was to walk a little way in a world of gloom and shadow; I entered on the stage of the first act of death. Then came my wandering in the mist, the whiteness wrapping all things, the void streets, and muffled silence, till when that voice spoke to me it was as if I had died and life returned to me. In a few minutes I was able to compose my feelings, and as I rose I saw that I was confronted by a middle-aged gentleman of specious appearance, neatly and correctly dressed. He looked at me with an expression of great pity, but before I could stammer out my ignorance of the neighbourhood, for indeed I had not the slightest notion of where I had wandered, he spoke.

'My dear madam,' he said, 'you seem in some terrible distress. You cannot think how you alarmed me. But may I inquire the nature of your trouble? I assure you that you can safely confide in me.'

'You are very kind,' I replied, 'but I fear there is nothing to be done. My condition seems a hopeless one.'

'Oh, nonsense, nonsense! You are too young to talk like that. Come, let us walk down here, and you must tell me your difficulty. Perhaps I may be able to help you.'

There was something very soothing and persuasive in his manner, and as we walked together I gave him an outline of my story, and told of the despair that had oppressed me almost to death.

'You were wrong to give in so completely,' he said, when I was silent. 'A month is too short a time in which to feel one's way in London. London, let me tell you, Miss Lally, does not lie open and undefended; it is a fortified place, fossed and double-moated with curious intricacies. As must always happen in large towns, the conditions of life have become hugely artificial; no mere simple palisade is run up to oppose the man or woman who would take the place by storm, but serried lines of subtle contrivances, mines, and pitfalls which it needs a strange skill to overcome. You, in your simplicity, fancied you had only to shout for these walls to sink into nothingness,* but the time is gone for such startling victories as these. Take courage; you will learn the secret of success before very long.'

'Alas! sir,' I replied, 'I have no doubt your conclusions are correct, but at the present moment I seem to be in a fair way to die of starvation. You spoke of a secret; for heaven's sake tell it me, if you have any pity for my distress.'

He laughed genially. 'There lies the strangeness of it all. Those who know the secret cannot tell it if they would; it is positively as ineffable as the central doctrine of Freemasonry. But I may say this, that you yourself have penetrated at least the outer husk of the mystery,' and he laughed again.

'Pray do not jest with me,' I said. 'What have I done, *que sais-je?*\* I am so far ignorant that I have not the slightest idea of how my next meal is to be provided.'

'Excuse me. You ask what you have done? You have met me. Come, we will fence no longer. I see you have self-education, the only education which is not infinitely pernicious, and I am in want of a governess for my two children. I have been a widower for some years; my name is Gregg. I offer you the post I have named, and shall we say a salary of a hundred a year?'

I could only stutter out my thanks, and slipping a card with his address, and a bank-note by way of earnest, into my hand, Mr Gregg bade me good-bye, asking me to call in a day or two.

Such was my introduction to Professor Gregg, and can you wonder that the remembrance of despair and the cold blast that had blown from the gates of death upon me made me regard him as a second father. Before the close of the week I was installed in my new duties. The professor had leased an old brick manor-house in a western suburb of London, and here, surrounded by pleasant lawns and orchards, and soothed with the murmur of the ancient elms that rocked their boughs above the roof, the new chapter of my life began. Knowing as you do the nature of the professor's occupations, you will not be surprised to hear that the house teemed with books, and cabinets full of strange, and even hideous, objects filled every available nook in the vast low rooms. Gregg was a man whose one thought was for knowledge, and I too before long caught something of his enthusiasm, and strove to enter into his passion for research. In a few months I was perhaps more his secretary than the governess of the two children, and many a night I have sat at the desk in the glow of the shaded lamp while he, pacing up and down in the rich gloom of the firelight, dictated to me the substance of his *Textbook of Ethnology*. But amidst these more sober and accurate studies I always detected a something hidden, a longing and desire for some object to which he did not allude; and now and then he would break short in what he was saying and lapse into reverie, intranced, as it seemed to me, by some distant prospect of adventurous discovery. The textbook was at last finished, and we began to receive proofs from the printers, which were intrusted to me for a first reading, and then underwent the final revision of the professor. All the while his weariness of the actual business he was engaged on increased, and it was with the joyous laugh of a schoolboy when term is over that he one day handed me a copy of the book. 'There,' he said, 'I have kept my word; I promised to write it, and it is done with. Now I shall be free to live for stranger things; I confess it, Miss Lally, I covet the renown of Columbus; you will, I hope, see me play the part of an explorer.'

'Surely,' I said, 'there is little left to explore. You have been born a few hundred years too late for that.'

'I think you are wrong,' he replied; 'there are still, depend upon it, quaint, undiscovered countries and continents of strange extent. Ah, Miss Lally! believe me, we stand amidst sacraments and mysteries full of awe, and it doth not yet appear what we shall be. Life, believe me, is no simple thing, no mass of grey matter and congeries of veins and muscles to be laid naked by the surgeon's knife; man is the secret which I am about to explore, and before I can discover him I must cross over weltering seas indeed, and oceans and the mists of many thousand years. You know the myth of the lost Atlantis; what if it be true, and I am destined to be called the discoverer of that wonderful land?'

I could see excitement boiling beneath his words, and in his face was the heat of the hunter; before me stood a man who believed himself summoned to tourney with the unknown. A pang of joy possessed me when I reflected that I was to be in a way associated with him in the adventure, and I too burned with the lust of the chase, not pausing to consider that I knew not what we were to unshadow.

The next morning Professor Gregg took me into his inner study, where, ranged against the wall, stood a nest of pigeon-holes, every drawer neatly labelled, and the results of years of toil classified in a few feet of space.

'Here,' he said, 'is my life; here are all the facts which I have gathered together with so much pains, and yet it is all nothing. No, nothing to what I am about to attempt. Look at this'; and he took me to an old bureau, a piece fantastic and faded, which stood in a corner of the room. He unlocked the front and opened one of the drawers.

'A few scraps of paper,' he went on, pointing to the drawer, 'and a lump of black stone, rudely annotated with queer marks and scratches—that is all that drawer holds. Here you see is an old envelope with the dark red stamp of twenty years ago, but I have pencilled a few lines at the back; here is a sheet of manuscript, and here some cuttings from obscure local journals. And if you ask me the subject-matter of the collection, it will not seem extraordinary—a servant-girl at a farm-house, who disappeared from her place and has never been heard of, a child supposed to have slipped down some old working on the mountains, some queer scribbling on a limestone rock, a man murdered with a blow from a strange weapon; such is the scent I have to go upon. Yes, as you say, there is a ready explanation for all this; the girl may have run away to London, or Liverpool, or New York; the child may be at the bottom of the disused shaft; and the letters on the rock may be the idle whims of some vagrant. Yes, yes, I admit all that; but I know I hold the true key. Look!' and he held me out a slip of yellow paper.

*Characters found inscribed on a limestone rock on the Grey Hills*, I read, and then there was a word erased, presumably the name of a county, and a date some fifteen years back. Beneath was traced a number of uncouth characters, shaped somewhat like wedges or daggers, as strange and outlandish as the Hebrew alphabet.

'Now the seal,' said Professor Gregg, and he handed me the black stone, a thing about two inches long, and something like an old-fashioned tobacco-stopper, much enlarged.

I held it up to the light, and saw to my surprise the characters on the paper repeated on the seal.

'Yes,' said the professor, 'they are the same. And the marks on the limestone rock were made fifteen years ago, with some red substance. And the characters on the seal are four thousand years old at least. Perhaps much more.'

'Is it a hoax?' I said.

'No, I anticipated that. I was not to be led to give my life to a practical joke. I have tested the matter very carefully. Only one person besides myself knows of the mere existence of that black seal. Besides, there are other reasons which I cannot enter into now.'

'But what does it all mean?' I said. 'I cannot understand to what conclusion all this leads.'

'My dear Miss Lally, that is a question I would rather leave unanswered for some little time. Perhaps I shall never be able to say what secrets are held here in solution; a few vague hints, the outlines of village tragedies, a few marks done with red earth upon a rock, and an ancient seal. A queer set of data to go upon? Half a dozen pieces of evidence, and twenty years before even so much could be got together; and who knows what mirage or *terra incognita* may be beyond all this? I look across deep waters, Miss Lally, and the land beyond may be but a haze after all. But still I believe it is not so, and a few months will show whether I am right or wrong.'

He left me, and alone I endeavoured to fathom the mystery, wondering to what goal such eccentric odds and ends of evidence could lead. I myself am not wholly devoid of imagination, and I had reason to respect the professor's solidity of intellect; yet I saw in the contents of the drawer but the materials of fantasy, and vainly tried to conceive what theory could be founded on the fragments that had been placed before me. Indeed, I could discover in what I had heard and seen but the first chapter of an extravagant romance; and yet deep in my heart

I burned with curiosity, and day after day I looked eagerly in Professor Gregg's face for some hint of what was to happen.

It was one evening after dinner that the word came.

'I hope you can make your preparations without much trouble,' he said suddenly to me. 'We shall be leaving here in a week's time.'

'Really!' I said in astonishment. 'Where are we going?'

'I have taken a country house in the west of England, not far from Caermaen,* a quiet little town, once a city, and the headquarters of a Roman legion. It is very dull there, but the country is pretty, and the air is wholesome.'

I detected a glint in his eyes, and guessed that this sudden move had some relation to our conversation of a few days before.

'I shall just take a few books with me,' said Professor Gregg, 'that is all. Everything else will remain here for our return. I have got a holiday,' he went on, smiling at me, 'and I shan't be sorry to be quit for a time of my old bones and stones and rubbish. Do you know,' he went on, 'I have been grinding away at facts for thirty years; it is time for fancies.'

The days passed quickly; I could see that the professor was all quivering with suppressed excitement, and I could scarce credit the eager appetence of his glance as we left the old manor house behind us and began our journey. We set out at midday, and it was in the dusk of the evening that we arrived at a little country station. I was tired and excited, and the drive through the lanes seems all a dream. First the deserted streets of a forgotten village, while I heard Professor Gregg's voice talking of the Augustan Legion and the clash of arms, and all the tremendous pomp that followed the eagles; then the broad river swimming to full tide with the last afterglow glimmering duskily in the yellow water, the wide meadows, the cornfields whitening, and the deep lane winding on the slope between the hills and the water. At last we began to ascend, and the air grew rarer. I looked down and saw the pure white mist tracking the outline of the river like a shroud, and a vague and shadowy country; imaginations and fantasy of swelling hills and hanging woods, and half-shaped outlines of hills beyond, and in the distance the glare of the furnace fire on the mountain, growing by turns a pillar of shining flame and fading to a dull point of red. We were slowly mounting a carriage drive, and then there came to me the cool breath and the secret of the great wood that was above us; I seemed to wander in its deepest depths, and there was the sound of trickling water, the scent of the green leaves, and the breath of the summer night. The carriage stopped at last, and I could scarcely distinguish the form of the house as I waited a moment at the pillared porch. The rest of the evening seemed a dream of strange things bounded by the great silence of the wood and the valley and the river.

The next morning, when I awoke and looked out of the bow window of the big, old-fashioned bedroom, I saw under a grey sky a country that was still all mystery. The long, lovely valley, with the river winding in and out below, crossed in mid-vision by a mediæval bridge of vaulted and buttressed stone, the clear presence of the rising ground beyond, and the woods that I had only seen in shadow the night before, seemed tinged with enchantment, and the soft breath of air that sighed in at the opened pane was like no other wind. I looked across the valley, and beyond, hill followed on hill as wave on wave, and here a faint blue pillar of smoke rose still in the morning air from the chimney of an ancient grey farmhouse, there was a rugged height crowned with dark firs, and in the distance I saw the white streak of a road that climbed and vanished into some unimagined country. But the boundary of all was a great wall of mountain, vast in the west, and ending like a fortress with a steep ascent and a domed tumulus clear against the sky.

I saw Professor Gregg walking up and down the terrace path below the windows, and it was evident that he was revelling in the sense of liberty, and the thought that he had for a while bidden good-bye to task-work. When I joined him there was exultation in his voice as he pointed out the sweep of valley and the river that wound beneath the lovely hills.

'Yes,' he said, 'it is a strangely beautiful country; and to me, at least, it seems full of mystery. You have not forgotten the drawer I showed you, Miss Lally? No; and you have guessed that I have come here not merely for the sake of the children and the fresh air?'

'I think I have guessed as much as that,' I replied; 'but you must remember I do not know the mere nature of your investigations; and as for the connection between the search and this wonderful valley, it is past my guessing.'

He smiled queerly at me. 'You must not think I am making a mystery for the sake of mystery,' he said. 'I do not speak out because, so far, there is nothing to be spoken, nothing definite, I mean, nothing that can be set down in hard black and white, as dull and sure and irre-proachable as any blue-book.* And then I have another reason: Many years ago a chance paragraph in a newspaper caught my attention, and focused in an instant the vagrant thoughts and half-formed fancies of many idle and speculative hours into a certain hypothesis. I saw at once that I was treading on a thin crust; my theory was wild and fantastic in the extreme, and I would not for any consideration have written a hint of it for publication. But I thought that in the company of scientific

men like myself, men who knew the course of discovery, and were aware
that the gas that blazes and flares in the gin-palace was once a wild
hypothesis*—I thought that with such men as these I might hazard my
dream—let us say Atlantis, or the philosopher's stone,* or what you
like—without danger of ridicule. I found I was grossly mistaken; my
friends looked blankly at me and at one another, and I could see something of pity, and something also of insolent contempt, in the glances
they exchanged. One of them called on me next day, and hinted that
I must be suffering from overwork and brain exhaustion. "In plain
terms," I said, "you think I am going mad. I think not"; and I showed
him out with some little appearance of heat. Since that day I vowed that
I would never whisper the nature of my theory to any living soul; to no
one but yourself have I ever shown the contents of that drawer. After
all, I may be following a rainbow; I may have been misled by the play of
coincidence; but as I stand here in this mystic hush and silence amidst
the woods and wild hills, I am more than ever sure that I am hot on the
scent. Come, it is time we went in.'

    To me in all this there was something both of wonder and excite-
ment; I knew how in his ordinary work Professor Gregg moved step by
step, testing every inch of the way, and never venturing on assertion
without proof that was impregnable. Yet I divined more from his glance
and the vehemence of his tone than from the spoken word, that he had
in his every thought the vision of the almost incredible continually with
him; and I, who was with some share of imagination no little of a sceptic, offended at a hint of the marvellous, could not help asking myself
whether he was cherishing a monomania, and barring out from this one
subject all the scientific method of his other life.

    Yet, with this image of mystery haunting my thoughts, I surrendered
wholly to the charm of the country. Above the faded house on the hillside began the great forest—a long, dark line seen from the opposing
hills, stretching above the river for many a mile from north to south,
and yielding in the north to even wilder country, barren and savage
hills, and ragged common-land, a territory all strange and unvisited,
and more unknown to Englishmen than the very heart of Africa. The
space of a couple of steep fields alone separated the house from the
wood, and the children were delighted to follow me up the long alleys
of undergrowth, between smooth pleached walls of shining beech, to
the highest point in the wood, whence one looked on one side across the
river and the rise and fall of the country to the great western mountain
wall, and on the other over the surge and dip of the myriad trees of the
forest, over level meadows and the shining yellow sea to the faint coast

beyond. I used to sit at this point on the warm sunlit turf which marked the track of the Roman Road, while the two children raced about hunting for the whin-berries* that grew here and there on the banks. Here beneath the deep blue sky and the great clouds rolling, like olden galleons with sails full-bellied, from the sea to the hills, as I listened to the whispered charm of the great and ancient wood, I lived solely for delight, and only remembered strange things when we would return to the house and find Professor Gregg either shut up in the little room he had made his study, or else pacing the terrace with the look, patient and enthusiastic, of the determined seeker.

One morning, some eight or nine days after our arrival, I looked out of my window and saw the whole landscape transmuted before me. The clouds had dipped low and hidden the mountain in the west; a southern wind was driving the rain in shifting pillars up the valley, and the little brooklet that burst the hill below the house now raged, a red torrent, down to the river. We were perforce obliged to keep snug within-doors; and when I had attended to my pupils, I sat down in the morning-room where the ruins of a library still encumbered an old-fashioned bookcase. I had inspected the shelves once or twice, but their contents had failed to attract me; volumes of eighteenth-century sermons, an old book on farriery,* a collection of *Poems* by 'persons of quality,'* Prideaux's *Connection*,* and an odd volume of Pope,* were the boundaries of the library, and there seemed little doubt that everything of interest or value had been removed. Now, however, in desperation, I began to re-examine the musty sheepskin and calf bindings, and found, much to my delight, a fine old quarto printed by the Stephani,* containing the three books of Pomponius Mela, *De Situ Orbis*,* and other of the ancient geographers. I knew enough of Latin to steer my way through an ordinary sentence, and I soon became absorbed in the odd mixture of fact and fancy—light shining on a little of the space of the world, and beyond, mist and shadow and awful forms. Glancing over the clear-printed pages, my attention was caught by the heading of a chapter in Solinus,* and I read the words:—

'Mira de intimis gentibus Libyae, de lapide Hexecontalitho,'

—'The wonders of the people that inhabit the inner parts of Libya, and of the stone called Sixtystone.'

The odd title attracted me, and I read on:—

'Gens ista avia et secreta habitat, in montibus horrendis fœda mysteria celebrat. De hominibus nihil aliud illi praeferunt quam figuram, ab humano ritu prorsus exulant, oderunt deum lucis. Stridunt potius quam loquuntur; vox absona nec sine horrore auditur. Lapide quo-dam gloriantur, quem Hexecontalithon vocant; dicunt enim hunc lapidem sexaginta notas ostendere. Cujus lapidis nomen secretum ineffabile col-unt: quod Ixaxar.'

'This folk,' I translated to myself, 'dwells in remote and secret places, and celebrates foul mysteries on savage hills. Nothing have they in common with men save the face, and the customs of humanity are wholly strange to them; and they hate the sun. They hiss rather than speak; their voices are harsh, and not to be heard without fear. They boast of a certain stone, which they call Sixtystone; for they say that it displays sixty characters. And this stone has a secret unspeakable name; which is Ixaxar.'

I laughed at the queer inconsequence of all this, and thought it fit for Sinbad the Sailor, or other of the supplementary Nights.* When I saw Professor Gregg in the course of the day, I told him of my find in the bookcase, and the fantastic rubbish I had been reading. To my surprise he looked up at me with an expression of great interest.

'That is really very curious,' he said. 'I have never thought it worth while to look into the old geographers, and I dare say I have missed a good deal. Ah, that is the passage, is it. It seems a shame to rob you of your entertainment, but I really think I must carry off the book.'

The next day the professor called to me to come to the study. I found him sitting at a table in the full light of the window, scrutinising something very attentively with a magnifying glass.

'Ah, Miss Lally,' he began, 'I want to use your eyes. This glass is pretty good, but not like my old one that I left in town. Would you mind examining the thing yourself, and telling me how many characters are cut on it?'

He handed me the object in his hand. I saw that it was the black seal he had shown me in London, and my heart began to beat with the thought that I was presently to know something. I took the seal, and, holding it up to the light, checked off the grotesque dagger-shaped characters one by one.

'I make sixty-two,' I said at last.

'Sixty-two? Nonsense; it's impossible. Ah, I see what you have done, you have counted that and that,' and he pointed to two marks which I had certainly taken as letters with the rest.

'Yes, yes,' Professor Gregg went on, 'but those are obvious scratches, done accidentally; I saw that at once. Yes, then that's quite right. Thank you very much, Miss Lally.'

I was going away, rather disappointed at my having been called in merely to count a number of marks on the black seal, when suddenly there flashed into my mind what I had read in the morning.

'But, Professor Gregg,' I cried, breathless, 'the seal, the seal. Why, it is the stone Hexecontalithos that Solinus writes of; it is Ixaxar.'

'Yes,' he said, 'I suppose it is. Or it may be a mere coincidence. It never does to be too sure, you know, in these matters. Coincidence killed the professor.'

I went away puzzled by what I had heard, and as much as ever at a loss to find the ruling clue in this maze of strange evidence. For three days the bad weather lasted, changing from driving rain to a dense mist, fine and dripping, and we seemed to be shut up in a white cloud that veiled all the world away from us. All the while Professor Gregg was darkling* in his room, unwilling, it appeared, to dispense confidences or talk of any kind, and I heard him walking to and fro with a quick, impatient step, as if he were in some way wearied of inaction. The fourth morning was fine, and at breakfast the professor said briskly—

'We want some extra help about the house; a boy of fifteen or sixteen, you know. There are a lot of little odd jobs that take up the maids' time which a boy could do much better.'

'The girls have not complained to me in any way,' I replied. 'Indeed, Anne said there was much less work than in London, owing to there being so little dust.'

'Ah, yes, they are very good girls. But I think we shall do much better with a boy. In fact, that is what has been bothering me for the last two days.'

'Bothering you?' I said in astonishment, for as a matter of fact the professor never took the slightest interest in the affairs of the house.

'Yes,' he said, 'the weather, you know. I really couldn't go out in that Scotch mist;* I don't know the country very well, and I should have lost my way. But I am going to get the boy this morning.'

'But how do you know there is such a boy as you want anywhere about?'

'Oh, I have no doubt as to that. I may have to walk a mile or two at the most, but I am sure to find just the boy I require.'

I thought the professor was joking, but though his tone was airy enough there was something grim and set about his features that puzzled me. He got his stick, and stood at the door looking meditatively before him, and as I passed through the hall he called to me.

'By the way, Miss Lally, there was one thing I wanted to say to you. I dare say you may have heard that some of these country lads are not over bright; idiotic would be a harsh word to use, and they are usually called "naturals,"* or something of the kind. I hope you won't mind if the boy I am after should turn out not too keen-witted; he will be perfectly harmless, of course, and blacking boots doesn't need much mental effort.'

With that he was gone, striding up the road that led to the wood, and I remained stupefied; and then for the first time my astonishment was mingled with a sudden note of terror, arising I knew not whence, and all unexplained even to myself, and yet I felt about my heart for an instant something of the chill of death, and that shapeless, formless dread of the unknown that is worse than death itself. I tried to find courage in the sweet air that blew up from the sea, and in the sunlight after rain, but the mystic woods seemed to darken around me; and the vision of the river coiling between the reeds, and the silver grey of the ancient bridge, fashioned in my mind symbols of vague dread, as the mind of a child fashions terror from things harmless and familiar.

Two hours later Professor Gregg returned. I met him as he came down the road, and asked quietly if he had been able to find a boy.

'Oh yes,' he answered; 'I found one easily enough. His name is Jervase Cradock, and I expect he will make himself very useful. His father has been dead for many years, and the mother, whom I saw, seemed very glad at the prospect of a few shillings extra coming in on Saturday nights. As I expected, he is not too sharp, has fits at times, the mother said; but as he will not be trusted with the china, that doesn't much matter, does it? And he is not in any way dangerous, you know, merely a little weak.'

'When is he coming?'

'To-morrow morning at eight o'clock. Anne will show him what he has to do, and how to do it. At first he will go home every night, but perhaps it may ultimately turn out more convenient for him to sleep here, and only go home for Sundays.'

I found nothing to say to all this; Professor Gregg spoke in a quiet tone of matter-of-fact, as indeed was warranted by the circumstance; and yet I could not quell my sensation of astonishment at the whole affair. I knew that in reality no assistance was wanted in the housework, and the professor's prediction that the boy he was to engage might prove a little 'simple,' followed by so exact a fulfilment, struck me as bizarre in the extreme. The next morning I heard from the housemaid that the boy Cradock had come at eight, and that she had been trying to make him useful. 'He doesn't seem quite all there, I don't think, miss,' was her comment, and later in the day I saw him helping the old man who worked in the garden. He was a youth of about fourteen, with black hair and black eyes and an olive skin, and I saw at once from the curious vacancy of his expression that he was mentally weak. He touched his forehead awkwardly as I went by, and I heard him answering the gardener in a queer, harsh voice that caught my attention; it gave me the impression of some one speaking deep below under the earth, and there was a strange sibilance, like the hissing of the phonograph* as the pointer travels over the cylinder. I heard that he seemed anxious to do what he could, and was quite docile and obedient, and Morgan the gardener, who knew his mother, assured me he was perfectly harmless. 'He's always been a bit queer,' he said, 'and no wonder, after what his mother went through before he was born. I did know his father, Thomas Cradock, well, and a very fine workman he was too, indeed. He got something wrong with his lungs owing to working in the wet woods, and never got over it, and went off quite sudden like. And they do say as how Mrs Cradock was quite off her head; anyhow, she was found by Mr Hillyer, Ty Coch, all crouched up on the Grey Hills, over there, crying and weeping like a lost soul. And Jervase, he was born about eight months afterwards, and as I was saying, he was a bit queer always; and they do say when he could scarcely walk he would frighten the other children into fits with the noises he would make.'

A word in the story had stirred up some remembrance within me, and, vaguely curious, I asked the old man where the Grey Hills were.

'Up there,' he said, with the same gesture he had used before; 'you go past the Fox and Hounds, and through the forest, by the old ruins. It's a good five mile from here, and a strange sort of a place. The poorest soil between this and Monmouth,* they do say, though it's good feed for sheep. Yes, it was a sad thing for poor Mrs Cradock.'

The old man turned to his work, and I strolled on down the path between the espaliers,* gnarled and gouty with age, thinking of the story I had heard, and groping for the point in it that had some key to my memory. In an instant it came before me; I had seen the phrase 'Grey Hills' on the slip of yellowed paper that Professor Gregg had taken from the drawer in his cabinet. Again I was seized with pangs of mingled curiosity and fear; I remembered the strange characters copied from the limestone rock, and then again their identity with the inscription on the age-old seal, and the fantastic fables of the Latin geographer. I saw beyond doubt that, unless coincidence had set all the scene and disposed all these bizarre events with curious art, I was to be a spectator of things far removed from the usual and customary traffic and jostle of life. Professor Gregg I noted day by day; he was hot on his

trail, growing lean with eagerness; and in the evenings, when the sun
was swimming on the verge of the mountain, he would pace the terrace
to and fro with his eyes on the ground, while the mist grew white in the
valley, and the stillness of the evening brought far voices near, and the
blue smoke rose a straight column from the diamond-shaped chimney
of the grey farmhouse, just as I had seen it on the first morning. I have
told you I was of sceptical habit; but though I understood little or nothing, I began to dread, vainly proposing to myself the iterated dogmas of
science that all life is material, and that in the system of things there is
no undiscovered land, even beyond the remotest stars, where the supernatural can find a footing. Yet there struck in on this the thought that
matter is as really awful and unknown as spirit, that science itself but
dallies on the threshold, scarcely gaining more than a glimpse of the
wonders of the inner place.

There is one day that stands up from amidst the others as a grim red
beacon, betokening evil to come. I was sitting on a bench in the garden,
watching the boy Cradock weeding, when I was suddenly alarmed by
a harsh and choking sound, like the cry of a wild beast in anguish, and
I was unspeakably shocked to see the unfortunate lad standing in full
view before me, his whole body quivering and shaking at short intervals
as though shocks of electricity were passing through him, his teeth
grinding, foam gathering on his lips, and his face all swollen and blackened to a hideous mask of humanity. I shrieked with terror, and
Professor Gregg came running; and as I pointed to Cradock, the boy
with one convulsive shudder fell face forward, and lay on the wet earth,
his body writhing like a wounded blind-worm,* and an inconceivable
babble of sounds bursting and rattling and hissing from his lips. He
seemed to pour forth an infamous jargon, with words, or what seemed
words, that might have belonged to a tongue dead since untold ages,
and buried deep beneath Nilotic mud, or in the inmost recesses of the
Mexican forest. For a moment the thought passed through my mind, as
my ears were still revolted with that infernal clamour, 'Surely this is the
very speech of hell,' and then I cried out again and again, and ran away
shuddering to my inmost soul. I had seen Professor Gregg's face as he
stooped over the wretched boy and raised him, and I was appalled by
the glow of exultation that shone on every lineament and feature. As
I sat in my room with drawn blinds, and my eyes hidden in my hands,
I heard heavy steps beneath, and I was told afterwards that Professor
Gregg had carried Cradock to his study, and had locked the door.
I heard voices murmur indistinctly, and I trembled to think of what
might be passing within a few feet of where I sat; I longed to escape to

the woods and sunshine, and yet I dreaded the sights that might confront me on the way; and at last, as I held the handle of the door nervously, I heard Professor Gregg's voice calling to me with a cheerful ring. 'It's all right now, Miss Lally,' he said. 'The poor fellow has got over it, and I have been arranging for him to sleep here after tomorrow. Perhaps I may be able to do something for him.'

'Yes,' he said later, 'it was a very painful sight, and I don't wonder you were alarmed. We may hope that good food will build him up a little, but I am afraid he will never be really cured,' and he affected the dismal and conventional air with which one speaks of hopeless illness; and yet beneath it I detected the delight that leapt up rampant within him, and fought and struggled to find utterance. It was as if one glanced down on the even surface of the sea, clear and immobile, and saw beneath raging depths, and a storm of contending billows. It was indeed to me a torturing and offensive problem that this man, who had so bounteously rescued me from the sharpness of death, and showed himself in all the relations of life full of benevolence, and pity, and kindly forethought, should so manifestly be for once on the side of the demons, and take a ghastly pleasure in the torments of an afflicted fellow-creature. Apart, I struggled with the horned difficulty, and strove to find the solution; but without the hint of a clue, beset by mystery and contradiction, I saw nothing that might help me, and began to wonder whether, after all, I had not escaped from the white mist of the suburb at too dear a rate. I hinted something of my thought to the professor; I said enough to let him know that I was in the most acute perplexity, but the moment after regretted what I had done when I saw his face contort with a spasm of pain.

'My dear Miss Lally,' he said, 'you surely do not wish to leave us? No, no, you would not do it. You do not know how I rely on you; how confidently I go forward, assured that you are here to watch over my children. You, Miss Lally, are my rearguard; for let me tell you that the business in which I am engaged is not wholly devoid of peril. You have not forgotten what I said the first morning here; my lips are shut by an old and firm resolve till they can open to utter no ingenious hypothesis or vague surmise but irrefragable fact, as certain as a demonstration in mathematics. Think over it, Miss Lally: not for a moment would I endeavour to keep you here against your own instincts, and yet I tell you frankly that I am persuaded it is here, here amidst the woods, that your duty lies.'

I was touched by the eloquence of his tone, and by the remembrance that the man, after all, had been my salvation, and I gave him my hand on a promise to serve him loyally and without question. A few days later the rector of our church—a little church, grey and severe and quaint, that hovered on the very banks of the river and watched the tides swim and return—came to see us, and Professor Gregg easily persuaded him to stay and share our dinner. Mr Meyrick was a member of an antique family of squires, whose old manor-house stood amongst the hills some seven miles away, and thus rooted in the soil, the rector was a living store of all the old, fading customs and lore of the country. His manner, genial, with a deal of retired oddity, won on Professor Gregg; and towards the cheese, when a curious Burgundy had begun its incantations, the two men glowed like the wine, and talked of philology with the enthusiasm of a burgess over the peerage. The parson was expounding the pronunciation of the Welsh *ll*, and producing sounds like the gurgle of his native brooks, when Professor Gregg struck in.

'By the way,' he said, 'that was a very odd word I met with the other day; you know my boy, poor Jervase Cradock. Well, he has got the bad habit of talking to himself, and the day before yesterday I was walking in the garden here and heard him; he was evidently quite unconscious of my presence. A lot of what he said I couldn't make out, but one word struck me distinctly. It was such an odd sound, half-sibilant, half-guttural, and as quaint as those double *ls* you have been demonstrating. I do not know whether I can give you an idea of the sound; "Ishakshar" is perhaps as near as I can get. But the *k* ought to be a Greek *chi* or a Spanish *j*. Now what does it mean in Welsh?'

'In Welsh?' said the parson. 'There is no such word in Welsh, nor any word remotely resembling it. I know the book-Welsh, as they call it, and the colloquial dialects as well as any man, but there's no word like that from Anglesea to Usk. Besides, none of the Cradocks speak a word of Welsh; it's dying out about here.'

'Really. You interest me extremely, Mr Meyrick. I confess the word didn't strike me as having the Welsh ring. But I thought it might be some local corruption.'

'No, I never heard such a word, or anything like it. Indeed,' he added, smiling whimsically, 'if it belongs to any language, I should say it must be that of the fairies—the Tylwydd Têg,* as we call them.'

The talk went on to the discovery of a Roman villa in the neighbourhood; and soon after I left the room, and sat down apart to wonder at the drawing together of such strange clues of evidence. As the professor had spoken of the curious word, I had caught the glint of his eye upon me; and though the pronunciation he gave was grotesque in the extreme, I recognised the name of the stone of sixty characters mentioned by

Solinus, the black seal shut up in some secret drawer of the study, stamped for ever by a vanished race with signs that no man could read, signs that might, for all I knew, be the veils of awful things done long ago, and forgotten before the hills were moulded into form.

When the next morning I came down, I found Professor Gregg pacing the terrace in his eternal walk.

'Look at that bridge,' he said when he saw me; 'observe the quaint and Gothic design, the angles between the arches, and the silvery grey of the stone in the awe of the morning light. I confess it seems to me symbolic; it should illustrate a mystical allegory of the passage from one world to another.'

'Professor Gregg,' I said quietly, 'it is time that I knew something of what has happened, and of what is to happen.'

For the moment he put me off, but I returned again with the same question in the evening, and then Professor Gregg flamed with excitement. 'Don't you understand yet?' he cried. 'But I have told you a good deal; yes, and shown you a good deal; you have heard pretty nearly all that I have heard, and seen what I have seen; or at least,' and his voice chilled as he spoke, 'enough to make a good deal clear as noonday. The servants told you, I have no doubt, that the wretched boy Cradock had another seizure the night before last; he awoke me with cries in that voice you heard in the garden, and I went to him, and God forbid you should see what I saw that night. But all this is useless; my time here is drawing to a close; I must be back in town in three weeks, as I have a course of lectures to prepare, and need all my books about me. In a very few days it will be all over, and I shall no longer hint, and no longer be liable to ridicule as a madman and a quack. No, I shall speak plainly, and I shall be heard with such emotions as perhaps no other man has ever drawn from the breasts of his fellows.'

He paused, and seemed to grow radiant with the joy of great and wonderful discovery.

'But all that is for the future, the near future certainly, but still the future,' he went on at length. 'There is something to be done yet; you will remember my telling you that my researches were not altogether devoid of peril? Yes, there is a certain amount of danger to be faced; I did not know how much when I spoke on the subject before, and to a certain extent I am still in the dark. But it will be a strange adventure, the last of all, the last demonstration in the chain.'

He was walking up and down the room as he spoke, and I could hear in his voice the contending tones of exultation and despondence, or perhaps I should say awe, the awe of a man who goes forth on unknown waters, and I thought of his allusion to Columbus on the night he had laid his book before me. The evening was a little chilly, and a fire of logs had been lighted in the study where we were; the remittent flame and the glow on the walls reminded me of the old days. I was sitting silent in an arm-chair by the fire, wondering over all I had heard, and still vainly speculating as to the secret springs concealed from me under all the phantasmagoria* I had witnessed, when I became suddenly aware of a sensation that change of some sort had been at work in the room, and that there was something unfamiliar in its aspect. For some time I looked about me, trying in vain to localise the alteration that I knew had been made; the table by the window, the chairs, the faded settee were all as I had known them. Suddenly, as a sought-for recollection flashes into the mind, I knew what was amiss. I was facing the professor's desk, which stood on the other side of the fire, and above the desk was a grimy-looking bust of Pitt,* that I had never seen there before. And then I remembered the true position of this work of art; in the furthest corner by the door was an old cupboard, projecting into the room, and on the top of the cupboard, fifteen feet from the floor, the bust had been, and there, no doubt, it had delayed, accumulating dirt, since the early years of the century.

I was utterly amazed, and sat silent still, in a confusion of thought. There was, so far as I knew, no such thing as a step-ladder in the house, for I had asked for one to make some alterations in the curtains of my room, and a tall man standing on a chair would have found it impossible to take down the bust. It had been placed, not on the edge of the cupboard, but far back against the wall; and Professor Gregg was, if anything, under the average height.

'How on earth did you manage to get down Pitt?' I said at last.

The professor looked curiously at me, and seemed to hesitate a little.

'They must have found you a step-ladder, or perhaps the gardener brought in a short ladder from outside?'

'No, I have had no ladder of any kind. Now, Miss Lally,' he went on with an awkward simulation of jest, 'there is a little puzzle for you; a problem in the manner of the inimitable Holmes,* there are the facts, plain and patent; summon your acuteness to the solution of the puzzle. For Heaven's sake,' he cried with a breaking voice, 'say no more about it! I tell you, I never touched the thing,' and he went out of the room with horror manifest on his face, and his hand shook and jarred the door behind him.

I looked round the room in vague surprise, not at all realising what had happened, making vain and idle surmises by way of explanation, and wondering at the stirring of black waters by an idle word and the trivial change of an ornament. 'This is some petty business, some whim on which I have jarred,' I reflected; 'the professor is perhaps scrupulous and superstitious over trifles, and my question may have outraged unacknowledged fears, as though one killed a spider or spilled the salt before the very eyes of a practical Scotchwoman.' I was immersed in these fond suspicions, and began to plume myself a little on my immunity from such empty fears, when the truth fell heavily as lead upon my heart, and I recognised with cold terror that some awful influence had been at work. The bust was simply inaccessible; without a ladder no one could have touched it.

I went out to the kitchen and spoke as quietly as I could to the housemaid.

'Who moved that bust from the top of the cupboard, Anne?' I said to her. 'Professor Gregg says he has not touched it. Did you find an old step-ladder in one of the outhouses?'

The girl looked at me blankly.

'I never touched it,' she said. 'I found it where it is now the other morning when I dusted the room. I remember now, it was Wednesday morning, because it was the morning after Cradock was taken bad in the night. My room is next to his, you know, miss,' the girl went on piteously, 'and it was awful to hear how he cried and called out names that I couldn't understand. It made me feel all afraid; and then master came, and I heard him speak, and he took down Cradock to the study and gave him something.'

'And you found that bust moved the next morning?'

'Yes, miss. There was a queer sort of a smell in the study when I came down and opened the windows; a bad smell it was, and I wondered what it could be. Do you know, miss, I went a long time ago to the Zoo in London* with my cousin Thomas Barker, one afternoon that I had off, when I was at Mrs Prince's in Stanhope Gate, and we went into the snake-house to see the snakes, and it was just the same sort of a smell; very sick it made me feel, I remember, and I got Barker to take me out. And it was just the same kind of a smell in the study, as I was saying, and I was wondering what it could be from, when I see that bust with Pitt cut in it, standing on the master's desk, and I thought to myself, Now who has done that, and how have they done it? And when I came to dust the things, I looked at the bust, and I saw a great mark on it where the dust was gone, for I don't think it can have been touched with a duster for years and years, and it wasn't like finger-marks, but a large patch like, broad and spread out. So I passed my hand over it, without thinking what I was doing, and where that patch was it was all sticky and slimy, as if a snail had crawled over it. Very strange, isn't it, miss? and I wonder who can have done it, and how that mess was made.'

The well-meant gabble of the servant touched me to the quick; I lay down upon my bed, and bit my lip that I should not cry out loud in the sharp anguish of my terror and bewilderment. Indeed, I was almost mad with dread; I believe that if it had been daylight I should have fled hot foot, forgetting all courage and all the debt of gratitude that was due to Professor Gregg, not caring whether my fate were that I must starve slowly, so long as I might escape from the net of blind and panic fear that every day seemed to draw a little closer round me. If I knew, I thought, if I knew what there were to dread, I could guard against it; but here, in this lonely house, shut in on all sides by the olden woods and the vaulted hills, terror seems to spring inconsequent from every covert, and the flesh is aghast at the half-heard murmurs of horrible things. All in vain I strove to summon scepticism to my aid, and endeavoured by cool common-sense to buttress my belief in a world of natural order, for the air that blew in at the open window was a mystic breath, and in the darkness I felt the silence go heavy and sorrowful as a mass of requiem, and I conjured images of strange shapes gathering fast amidst the reeds, beside the wash of the river.

In the morning, from the moment that I set foot in the breakfast-room, I felt that the unknown plot was drawing to a crisis; the professor's face was firm and set, and he seemed hardly to hear our voices when we spoke.

'I am going out for rather a long walk,' he said when the meal was over. 'You mustn't be expecting me, now, or thinking anything has happened if I don't turn up to dinner. I have been getting stupid lately, and I dare say a miniature walking tour will do me good. Perhaps I may even spend the night in some little inn, if I find any place that looks clean and comfortable.'

I heard this, and knew by my experience of Professor Gregg's manner that it was no ordinary business or pleasure that impelled him. I knew not, nor even remotely guessed, where he was bound, nor had I the vaguest notion of his errand, but all the fear of the night before returned; and as he stood, smiling, on the terrace, ready to set out, I implored him to stay, and to forget all his dreams of the undiscovered continent.

'No, no, Miss Lally,' he replied, still smiling, 'it's too late now. *Vestigia nulla retrorsum*,* you know, is the device of all true explorers, though I hope it won't be literally true in my case. But, indeed, you are wrong to alarm yourself so; I look upon my little expedition as quite commonplace; no more exciting than a day with the geological hammers. There is a risk, of course, but so there is on the commonest excursion. I can afford to be jaunty; I am doing nothing so hazardous as 'Arry does a hundred times over in the course of every Bank Holiday.* Well, then, you must look more cheerfully; and so good-bye till to-morrow at latest.'

He walked briskly up the road, and I saw him open the gate that marks the entrance of the wood, and then he vanished in the gloom of the trees.

All the day passed heavily with a strange darkness in the air, and again I felt as if imprisoned amidst the ancient woods, shut in an olden land of mystery and dread, and as if all was long ago and forgotten by the living outside. I hoped and dreaded; and when the dinner-hour came I waited, expecting to hear the professor's step in the hall, and his voice exulting at I knew not what triumph. I composed my face to welcome him gladly, but the night descended dark, and he did not come.

In the morning, when the maid knocked at my door, I called out to her, and asked if her master had returned; and when she replied that his bedroom stood open and empty, I felt the cold clasp of despair. Still, I fancied he might have discovered genial company, and would return for luncheon, or perhaps in the afternoon, and I took the children for a walk in the forest, and tried my best to play and laugh with them, and to shut out the thoughts of mystery and veiled terror. Hour after hour I waited, and my thoughts grew darker; again the night came and found me watching, and at last, as I was making much ado to finish my dinner, I heard steps outside and the sound of a man's voice.

The maid came in and looked oddly at me. 'Please, miss,' she began, 'Mr Morgan the gardener wants to speak to you for a minute, if you didn't mind.'

'Show him in, please,' I answered, and I set my lips tight.

The old man came slowly into the room, and the servant shut the door behind him.

'Sit down, Mr Morgan,' I said; 'what is it that you want to say to me?'

'Well, miss, Mr Gregg he gave me something for you yesterday morning, just before he went off; and he told me particular not to hand it up before eight o'clock this evening exactly, if so be as he wasn't back again home before, and if he should come home before I was just to return it to him in his own hands. So, you see, as Mr Gregg isn't here yet, I suppose I'd better give you the parcel directly.'

He pulled out something from his pocket, and gave it to me, half rising. I took it silently, and seeing that Morgan seemed doubtful as to what he was to do next, I thanked him and bade him good-night, and he

went out. I was left alone in the room with the parcel in my hand—
a paper parcel neatly sealed and directed to me, with the instructions
Morgan had quoted, all written in the professor's large loose hand.
I broke the seals with a choking at my heart, and found an envelope
inside, addressed also, but open, and I took the letter out.

'MY DEAR MISS LALLY,' it began,—'To quote the old logic manual,* the case
of your reading this note is a case of my having made a blunder of some sort,
and, I am afraid, a blunder that turns these lines into a farewell. It is practically
certain that neither you nor any one else will ever see me again. I have made my
will with provision for this eventuality, and I hope you will consent to accept the
small remembrance addressed to you, and my sincere thanks for the way in
which you joined your fortunes to mine. The fate which has come upon me is
desperate and terrible beyond the remotest dreams of man; but this fate you
have a right to know—if you please. If you look in the left-hand drawer of my
dressing-table, you will find the key of the escritoire, properly labelled. In the
well of the escritoire is a large envelope sealed and addressed to your name.
I advise you to throw it forthwith into the fire; you will sleep better of nights if
you do so. But if you must know the history of what has happened, it is all
written down for you to read.'

The signature was firmly written below, and again I turned the page
and read out the words one by one, aghast and white to the lips, my
hands cold as ice, and sickness choking me. The dead silence of the
room, and the thought of the dark woods and hills closing me in on
every side, oppressed me, helpless and without capacity, and not knowing where to turn for counsel. At last I resolved that though knowledge
should haunt my whole life and all the days to come, I must know the
meaning of the strange terrors that had so long tormented me, rising
grey, dim, and awful, like the shadows in the wood at dusk. I carefully
carried out Professor Gregg's directions, and not without reluctance
broke the seal of the envelope, and spread out his manuscript before
me. That manuscript I always carry with me, and I see that I cannot
deny your unspoken request to read it. This, then, was what I read that
night, sitting at the desk, with a shaded lamp beside me.

The young lady who called herself Miss Lally then proceeded to recite

### THE STATEMENT OF WILLIAM GREGG, F.R.S., ETC.

It is many years since the first glimmer of the theory which is now
almost, if not quite, reduced to fact dawned first on my mind. A somewhat extensive course of miscellaneous and obsolete reading had done
a good deal to prepare the way, and, later, when I became somewhat of

a specialist, and immersed myself in the studies known as ethnological, I was now and then startled by facts that would not square with ortho- dox scientific opinion, and by discoveries that seemed to hint at some- thing still hidden for all our research. More particularly I became convinced that much of the folk-lore of the world is but an exaggerated account of events that really happened, and I was especially drawn to consider the stories of the fairies, the good folk of the Celtic races. Here I thought I could detect the fringe of embroidery and exaggeration, the fantastic guise, the little people dressed in green and gold sporting in the flowers, and I thought I saw a distinct analogy between the name given to this race (supposed to be imaginary) and the description of their appearance and manners. Just as our remote ancestors called the dreaded beings 'fair' and 'good' precisely because they dreaded them, so they had dressed them up in charming forms, knowing the truth to be the very reverse. Literature, too, had gone early to work, and had lent a powerful hand in the transformation, so that the playful elves of Shakespeare are already far removed from the true original, and the real horror is disguised in a form of prankish mischief. But in the older tales, the stories that used to make men cross themselves as they sat round the burning logs, we tread a different stage; I saw a widely opposed spirit in certain histories of children and of men and women who vanished strangely from the earth. They would be seen by a peas- ant in the fields walking towards some green and rounded hillock, and seen no more on earth; and there are stories of mothers who have left a child quietly sleeping, with the cottage door rudely barred with a piece of wood, and have returned, not to find the plump and rosy little Saxon, but a thin and wizened creature, with sallow skin and black, piercing eyes, the child of another race. Then, again, there were myths darker still; the dread of witch and wizard, the lurid evil of the Sabbath, and the hint of demons who mingled with the daughters of men. And just as we have turned the terrible 'fair folk' into a company of benignant, if freakish, elves, so we have hidden from us the black foulness of the witch and her companions under a popular *diablerie** of old women and broomsticks and a comic cat with tail on end. So the Greeks called the hideous furies* benevolent ladies, and thus the north- ern nations have followed their example. I pursued my investigations, stealing odd hours from other and more imperative labours, and I asked myself the question: Supposing these traditions to be true, who were the demons who are reported to have attended the Sabbaths? I need not say that I laid aside what I may call the supernatural hypothesis of the middle ages, and came to the conclusion that fairies and devils were of one and the same race and origin; invention, no doubt, and the Gothic fancy of old days, had done much in the way of exaggeration and distortion; yet I firmly believed that beneath all this imagery there was a black background of truth. As for some of the alleged wonders, I hesitated. While I should be very loath to receive any one specific instance of modern spiritualism as containing even a grain of the genuine, yet I was not wholly prepared to deny that human flesh may now and then, once perhaps in ten million cases, be the veil of powers which seem magical to us—powers which, so far from proceeding from the heights and leading men thither, are in reality survivals from the depths of being. The amœba and the snail have powers which we do not possess; and I thought it possible that the theory of reversion might explain many things which seem wholly inexplicable. Thus stood my position; I saw good reason to believe that much of the tradition, a vast deal of the earliest and uncorrupted tradition of the so-called fairies, represented solid fact, and I thought that the purely supernatural element in these traditions was to be accounted for on the hypothesis that a race which had fallen out of the grand march of evolution might have retained, as a survival, certain powers which would be to us wholly miraculous. Such was my theory as it stood conceived in my mind; and working with this in view, I seemed to gather confirmation from every side, from the spoils of a tumulus or a barrow,* from a local paper reporting an antiquarian meeting in the country, and from general literature of all kinds. Amongst other instances, I remember being struck by the phrase 'articulate-speaking men' in Homer,* as if the writer knew or had heard of men whose speech was so rude that it could hardly be termed articulate; and on my hypothesis of a race who had lagged far behind the rest, I could easily conceive that such a folk would speak a jargon but little removed from the inarticulate noises of brute beasts.

Thus I stood, satisfied that my conjecture was at all events not far removed from fact, when a chance paragraph in a small country print one day arrested my attention. It was a short account of what was to all appearance the usual sordid tragedy of the village—a young girl unaccountably missing, and evil rumour blatant and busy with her reputation. Yet I could read between the lines that all this scandal was purely hypothetical, and in all probability invented to account for what was in any other manner unaccountable. A flight to London or Liverpool, or an undiscovered body lying with a weight about its neck in the foul depths of a woodland pool, or perhaps murder—such were the theories of the wretched girl's neighbours. But as I idly scanned the paragraph, a flash of thought passed through me with the violence of an electric shock: what if the obscure and horrible race of the hills still survived, still remained haunting wild places and barren hills, and now and then repeating the evil of Gothic legend, unchanged and unchangeable as the Turanian Shelta,* or the Basques of Spain.* I have said that the thought came with violence; and indeed I drew in my breath sharply, and clung with both hands to my elbow-chair, in a strange confusion of horror and elation. It was as if one of my *confrères* of physical science, roaming in a quiet English wood, had been suddenly stricken aghast by the presence of the slimy and loathsome terror of the icthyosaurus, the original of the stories of the awful worms killed by valorous knights, or had seen the sun darkened by the pterodactyl, the dragon of tradition. Yet as a resolute explorer of knowledge, the thought of such a discovery threw me into a passion of joy, and I cut out the slip from the paper and put it in a drawer in my old bureau, resolved that it should be but the first piece in a collection of the strangest significance. I sat long that evening dreaming of the conclusions I should establish, nor did cooler reflection at first dash my confidence. Yet as I began to put the case fairly, I saw that I might be building on an unstable foundation; the facts might possibly be in accordance with local opinion, and I regarded the affair with a mood of some reserve. Yet I resolved to remain perched on the look-out, and I hugged to myself the thought that I alone was watching and wakeful, while the great crowd of thinkers and searchers stood heedless and indifferent, perhaps letting the most prerogative facts pass by unnoticed.

Several years elapsed before I was enabled to add to the contents of the drawer; and the second find was in reality not a valuable one, for it was a mere repetition of the first, with only the variation of another and distant locality. Yet I gained something; for in the second case, as in the first, the tragedy took place in a desolate and lonely country, and so far my theory seemed justified. But the third piece was to me far more decisive. Again, amongst outland hills, far even from a main road of traffic, an old man was found done to death, and the instrument of execution was left beside him. Here, indeed, there was rumour and conjecture, for the deadly tool was a primitive stone axe, bound by gut to the wooden handle, and surmises the most extravagant and improbable were indulged in. Yet, as I thought with a kind of glee, the wildest conjectures went far astray; and I took the pains to enter into correspondence with the local doctor, who was called at the inquest. He, a man of some acuteness, was dumfounded. 'It will not do to speak of these things in country places,' he wrote to me; 'but frankly, Professor Gregg, there is some hideous mystery here. I have obtained possession of the stone axe, and have been so curious as to test its powers. I took it into the back-garden of my house one Sunday afternoon when my family and the servants were all out, and there, sheltered by the poplar hedges, I made my experiments. I found the thing utterly unmanageable; whether there is some peculiar balance, some nice adjustment of weights, which require incessant practice, or whether an effectual blow can be struck only by a certain trick of the muscles, I do not know; but I assure you that I went into the house with but a sorry opinion of my athletic capacities. It was like an inexperienced man trying 'putting the hammer'; the force exerted seemed to return on oneself, and I found myself hurled backwards with violence, while the axe fell harmless to the ground. On another occasion I tried the experiment with a clever woodman of the place; but this man, who had handled his axe for forty years, could do nothing with the stone implement, and missed every stroke most ludicrously. In short, if it were not so supremely absurd, I should say that for four thousand years no one on earth could have struck an effective blow with the tool that undoubtedly was used to murder the old man.' This, as may be imagined, was to me rare news; and afterwards, when I heard the whole story, and learned that the unfortunate old man had babbled tales of what might be seen at night on a certain wild hillside, hinting at unheard-of wonders, and that he had been found cold one morning on the very hill in question, my exultation was extreme, for I felt I was leaving conjecture far behind me. But the next step was of still greater importance. I had possessed for many years an extraordinary stone seal—a piece of dull, black stone, two inches long from the handle to the stamp, and the stamping end a rough hexagon an inch and a quarter in diameter. Altogether, it presented the appearance of an enlarged tobacco-stopper of an old-fashioned make. It had been sent to me by an agent in the east, who informed me that it had been found near the site of the ancient Babylon. But the characters engraved on the seal were to me an intolerable puzzle. Somewhat of the cuneiform pattern, there were yet striking differences, which I detected at the first glance, and all efforts to read the inscription on the hypothesis that the rules for deciphering the arrow-headed writing would apply proved futile. A riddle such as this stung my pride, and at odd moments I would take the Black Seal out of the cabinet, and scrutinise it with so much idle perseverance that every letter was familiar to my mind, and I could have drawn the inscription from memory without the slightest error. Judge, then, of my surprise when I one day received from a correspondent in the west of England a letter and an enclosure that positively left me thunderstruck. I saw carefully traced on a large piece of paper the very characters of the Black Seal, without alteration of any kind, and above the inscription my friend had written: *Inscription found on a limestone rock on the Grey Hills, Monmouthshire. Done in some red earth, and quite recent.* I turned to the letter. My friend wrote: 'I send you the enclosed inscription with all due reserve. A shepherd who passed by the stone a week ago swears that there was then no mark of any kind. The characters, as I have noted, are formed by drawing some red earth over the stone, and are of an average height of one inch. They look to me like a kind of cuneiform character, a good deal altered, but this, of course, is impossible. It may be either a hoax, or more probably some scribble of the gypsies, who are plentiful enough in this wild country. They have, as you are aware, many hieroglyphics which they use in communicating with one another. I happened to visit the stone in question two days ago in connection with a rather painful incident which has occurred here.'

As may be supposed, I wrote immediately to my friend, thanking him for the copy of the inscription, and asking him in a casual manner the history of the incident he mentioned. To be brief, I heard that a woman named Cradock, who had lost her husband a day before, had set out to communicate the sad news to a cousin who lived some five miles away. She took a short cut which led by the Grey Hills. Mrs Cradock, who was then quite a young woman, never arrived at her relative's house. Late that night a farmer who had lost a couple of sheep, supposed to have wandered from the flock, was walking over the Grey Hills, with a lantern and his dog. His attention was attracted by a noise, which he described as a kind of wailing, mournful and pitiable to hear; and, guided by the sound, he found the unfortunate Mrs Cradock crouched on the ground by the limestone rock, swaying her body to and fro, and lamenting and crying in so heart-rending a manner that the farmer was, as he says, at first obliged to stop his ears, or he would have run away. The woman allowed herself to be taken home, and a neighbour came to see to her necessities. All the night she never ceased her crying, mixing her lament with words of some unintelligible jargon, and when the doctor arrived he pronounced her insane. She lay on her bed for a week, now wailing, as people said, like one lost and damned for eternity, and now sunk in a heavy coma; it was thought that grief at the loss of her husband had unsettled her mind, and the medical man did not at one time expect her to live. I need not say that I was deeply interested in this story, and I made my friend write to me at intervals with all the particulars of the case. I heard then that in the course of six weeks the woman gradually recovered the use of her faculties, and some months later she gave birth to a son, christened Jervase, who unhappily proved to be of weak intellect. Such were the facts known to the village; but to me, while I whitened at the suggested thought of the hideous enormities that had doubtless been committed, all this was nothing short of conviction, and I incautiously hazarded a hint of something like the truth to some scientific friends. The moment the words had left my lips I bitterly regretted having spoken, and thus given away the great secret of my life, but with a good deal of relief mixed with indignation I found my fears altogether misplaced, for my friends ridiculed me to my face, and I was regarded as a madman; and beneath a natural anger I chuckled to myself, feeling as secure amidst these blockheads as if I had confided what I knew to the desert sands.

But now, knowing so much, I resolved I would know all, and I concentrated my efforts on the task of deciphering the inscription on the Black Seal. For many years I made this puzzle the sole object of my leisure moments; for the greater portion of my time was, of course, devoted to other duties, and it was only now and then that I could snatch a week of clear research. If I were to tell the full history of this curious investigation, this statement would be wearisome in the extreme, for it would contain simply the account of long and tedious failure. By what I knew already of ancient scripts I was well equipped for the chase, as I always termed it to myself. I had correspondents amongst all the scientific men in Europe, and, indeed, in the world, and I could not believe that in these days any character, however ancient and however perplexed, could long resist the search-light I should bring to bear upon it. Yet, in point of fact, it was fully fourteen years before I succeeded. With every year my professional duties increased, and my leisure became smaller. This no doubt retarded me a good deal; and yet, when I look back on those years, I am astonished at the vast scope of my investigation of the Black Seal. I made my bureau a centre, and from all the world and from all the ages I gathered transcripts of ancient writing. Nothing, I resolved, should pass me unawares, and the faintest hint should be welcomed and followed up. But as one covert after another was tried and proved empty of result, I began in the course of years to despair, and to wonder whether the Black Seal were the sole relic of some race that had vanished from the world and left no other trace of its existence—had perished, in fine, as Atlantis is said to have done, in some great cataclysm, its secrets perhaps drowned beneath the ocean or moulded into the heart of the hills. The thought chilled my warmth a little, and though I still persevered, it was no longer with the same certainty of faith. A chance came to the rescue. I was staying in a considerable town in the north of England, and took the opportunity of going over the very creditable museum that had for some time been established in the place. The curator was one of my correspondents; and, as we were looking through one of the mineral cases, my attention was struck by a specimen, a piece of black stone some four inches square, the appearance of which reminded me in a measure of the Black Seal. I took it up carelessly, and was turning it over in my hand, when I saw, to my astonishment, that the under side was inscribed. I said, quietly enough, to my friend the curator that the specimen interested me, and that I should be much obliged if he would allow me to take it with me to my hotel for a couple of days. He, of course, made no objection, and I hurried to my rooms and found that my first glance had not deceived me. There were two inscriptions; one in the regular cuneiform character, another in the character of the Black Seal, and I realised that my task was accomplished. I made an exact copy of the two inscriptions; and when I got to my London study, and had the Seal before me, I was able seriously to grapple with the great problem. The interpreting inscription on the museum specimen, though in itself curious enough, did not bear on my quest, but the transliteration made me master of the secret of the Black Seal. Conjecture, of course, had to enter into my calculations; there was here and there uncertainty about a particular ideograph, and one sign recurring again and again on the seal baffled me for many successive nights. But at last the secret stood open before me in plain English, and I read the key of the awful transmutation of the hills. The last word was hardly written, when with fingers all trembling and unsteady I tore the scrap of paper into the minutest fragments, and saw them flame and blacken in the red hollow of the fire, and then I crushed the grey films that remained into finest powder. Never since then have I written those words; never will I write the phrases which tell me how man can be reduced to the slime from which he came, and be forced to put on the flesh of the reptile and the snake. There was now but one thing remaining. I knew, but I desired to see, and I was after some time able to take a house in the neighbourhood of the Grey Hills, and not far from the cottage where Mrs Cradock and her son Jervase resided. I need not go into a full and detailed account of the apparently inexplicable events which have occurred here, where I am writing this. I knew that I should find in Jervase Cradock something of the blood of the 'Little People,' and I found later that he had more than once encountered his kinsmen in lonely places in that lonely land. When I was summoned one day to the garden, and found him in a seizure speaking or hissing the ghastly jargon of the Black Seal, I am afraid that exultation prevailed over pity. I heard bursting from his lips the secrets of the underworld, and the word of dread, 'Ishakshar,' the signification of which I must be excused from giving.

But there is one incident I cannot pass over unnoticed. In the waste hollow of the night I awoke at the sound of those hissing syllables I knew so well; and on going to the wretched boy's room, I found him convulsed and foaming at the mouth, struggling on the bed as if he strove to escape the grasp of writhing demons. I took him down to my room and lit the lamp, while he lay twisting on the floor, calling on the power within his flesh to leave him. I saw his body swell and become distended as a bladder, while the face blackened before my eyes; and then at the crisis I did what was necessary according to the directions on the Seal, and putting all scruple on one side, I became a man of science, observant of what was passing. Yet the sight I had to witness was horrible, almost beyond the power of human conception and the most fearful fantasy. Something pushed out from the body there on the floor, and stretched forth, a slimy, wavering tentacle, across the room, grasped the bust upon the cupboard, and laid it down on my desk.

When it was over, and I was left to walk up and down all the rest of the night, white and shuddering, with sweat pouring from my flesh, I vainly tried to reason with myself: I said, truly enough, that I had seen nothing really supernatural, that a snail pushing out his horns and drawing them in was but an instance on a smaller scale of what I had witnessed; and yet horror broke through all such reasonings and left me shattered and loathing myself for the share I had taken in the night's work.

There is little more to be said. I am going now to the final trial and encounter; for I have determined that there shall be nothing wanting, and I shall meet the 'Little People' face to face. I shall have the Black Seal and the knowledge of its secrets to help me, and if I unhappily do not return from my journey, there is no need to conjure up here a picture of the awfulness of my fate.

Pausing a little at the end of Professor Gregg's statement, Miss Lally continued her tale in the following words:—

Such was the almost incredible story that the professor had left behind him. When I had finished reading it, it was late at night, but the next morning I took Morgan with me, and we proceeded to search the Grey Hills for some trace of the lost professor. I will not weary you with a description of the savage desolation of that tract of country, a tract of utterest loneliness, of bare green hills dotted over with grey limestone boulders, worn by the ravages of time into fantastic semblances of men and beasts. Finally, after many hours of weary searching, we found what

I told you—the watch and chain, the purse, and the ring—wrapped in a piece of coarse parchment. When Morgan cut the gut that bound the parcel together, and I saw the professor's property, I burst into tears, but the sight of the dreaded characters of the Black Seal repeated on the parchment froze me to silent horror, and I think I understood for the first time the awful fate that had come upon my late employer.

I have only to add that Professor Gregg's lawyer treated my account of what had happened as a fairy tale, and refused even to glance at the documents I laid before him. It was he who was responsible for the statement that appeared in the public press, to the effect that Professor Gregg had been drowned, and that his body must have been swept into the open sea.

Miss Lally stopped speaking, and looked at Mr Phillipps, with a glance of some inquiry. He, for his part, was sunken in a deep reverie of thought; and when he looked up and saw the bustle of the evening gathering in the square, men and women hurrying to partake of dinner, and crowds already besetting the music-halls, all the hum and press of actual life seemed unreal and visionary, a dream in the morning after an awakening.

'I thank you,' he said at last, 'for your most interesting story; interesting to me, because I feel fully convinced of its exact truth.'

'Sir,' said the lady, with some energy of indignation, 'you grieve and offend me. Do you think I should waste my time and yours by concocting fictions on a bench in Leicester Square?'

'Pardon me, Miss Lally, you have a little misunderstood me. Before you began I knew that whatever you told would be told in good faith, but your experiences have a far higher value than that of *bona fides*. The most extraordinary circumstances in your account are perfect harmony with the very latest scientific theories. Professor Lodge would, I am sure, value a communication from you extremely; I was charmed from the first by his daring hypothesis in explanation of the wonders of Spiritualism (so called), but your narrative puts the whole matter out of the range of mere hypothesis.'

'Alas! sir, all this will not help me. You forget, I have lost my brother under the most startling and dreadful circumstances. Again, I ask you, did you not see him as you came here? His black whiskers, his spectacles, his timid glance to right and left; think, do not these particulars recall his face to your memory?'

'I am sorry to say I have never seen any one of the kind,' said Phillipps, who had forgotten all about the missing brother. 'But let me ask you a few questions. Did you notice whether Professor Gregg . . .'

'Pardon me, sir, I have stayed too long. My employers will be expecting me. I thank you for your sympathy. Good-bye.'

Before Mr Phillipps had recovered from his amazement at this
abrupt departure Miss Lally had disappeared from his gaze, passing
into the crowd that now thronged the approaches to the Empire.* He
walked home in a pensive frame of mind, and drank too much tea. At
ten o'clock he had made his third brew, and had sketched out the outlines of a little work to be called *Protoplasmic Reversion*.


## INCIDENT OF THE PRIVATE BAR


Mr Dyson often meditated at odd moments over the singular tale
he had listened to at the Café de la Touraine.* In the first place, he
cherished a profound conviction that the words of truth were scattered
with a too niggardly and sparing hand over the agreeable history of
Mr Smith and the Black Gulf Cañon; and secondly, there was the
undeniable fact of the profound agitation of the narrator, and his gestures on the pavement, too violent to be simulated. The idea of a man
going about London haunted by the fear of meeting a young man with
spectacles struck Dyson as supremely ridiculous; he searched his
memory for some precedent in romance, but without success; he paid
visits at odd times to the little café, hoping to find Mr Wilkins there;
and he kept a sharp watch on the great generation of the spectacled
men, without much doubt that he would remember the face of the individual whom he had seen dart out of the aerated bread shop. All his
peregrinations and researches, however, seemed to lead to nothing of
value, and Dyson needed all his warm conviction of his innate detective
powers and his strong scent for mystery to sustain him in his endeavours. In fact, he had two affairs on hand; and every day, as he passed
through streets crowded or deserted, lurked in the obscure districts and
watched at corners, he was more than surprised to find that the affair of
the gold coin persistently avoided him, while the ingenious Wilkins,
and the young man with spectacles whom he dreaded, seemed to have
vanished from the pavements.

He was pondering these problems one evening in a house of call* in
the Strand, and the obstinacy with which the persons he so ardently
desired to meet hung back gave the modest tankard before him an additional touch of bitter. As it happened, he was alone in his compartment,
and, without thinking, he uttered aloud the burden of his meditations.
'How bizarre it all is!' he said, 'a man walking the pavement with the

dread of a timid-looking young man with spectacles continually hovering before his eyes. And there was some tremendous feeling at work, I could swear to that.' Quick as thought, before he had finished the sentence, a head popped round the barrier, and was withdrawn again; and while Dyson was wondering what this could mean, the door of the compartment was swung open, and a smooth, clean-shaven, and smiling gentleman entered.

'You will excuse me, sir,' he said politely, 'for intruding on your thoughts, but you made a remark a minute ago.'

'I did,' said Dyson; 'I have been puzzling over a foolish matter, and I thought aloud. As you heard what I said, and seem interested, perhaps you may be able to relieve my perplexity?'

'Indeed, I scarcely know; it is an odd coincidence. One has to be cautious. I suppose, sir, that you would have no repulsion in assisting the ends of justice.'

'Justice,' replied Dyson, 'is a term of such wide meaning, that I too feel doubtful about giving an answer. But this place is not altogether fit for such a discussion; perhaps you would come to my rooms?'

'You are very kind; my name is Burton, but I am sorry to say I have not a card with me. Do you live near here?'

'Within ten minutes' walk.'

Mr Burton took out his watch, and seemed to be making a rapid calculation.

'I have a train to catch,' he said; 'but after all, it is a late one. So if you don't mind, I think I will come with you. I am sure we should have a little talk together. We turn up here?'

The theatres were filling as they crossed the Strand; the street seemed alive with voices, and Dyson looked fondly about him. The glittering lines of gas-lamps, with here and there the blinding radiance of an electric light, the hansoms that flashed to and fro with ringing bells, the laden 'buses, and the eager hurrying east and west of the foot-passengers, made his most enchanting picture; and the graceful spire of St Mary le Strand* on the one hand, and the last flush of sunset on the other, were to him a cause of thanksgiving, as the gorse blossom to Linnæus.* Mr Burton caught his look of fondness as they crossed the street.

'I see you can find the picturesque in London,' he said. 'To me this great town is as I see it is to you—the study and the love of life. Yet how few there are that can pierce the veils of apparent monotony and meanness! I have read in a paper, which is said to have the largest circulation in the world, a comparison between the aspects of London and Paris, a comparison which should be positively laureat,* as the great master-piece of fatuous stupidity. Conceive if you can a human being of ordinary intelligence preferring the Boulevards* to our London streets; imagine a man calling for the wholesale destruction of our most charming city, in order that the dull uniformity of that whited sepulchre called Paris should be reproduced here in London. Is it not positively incredible?'

'My dear sir,' said Dyson, regarding Burton with a good deal of interest, 'I agree most heartily with your opinions, but I really cannot share your wonder. Have you heard how much George Eliot received for *Romola*? Do you know what the circulation of *Robert Elsmere* was? Do you read *Tit Bits** regularly? To me, on the contrary, it is constant matter both for wonder and thanksgiving that London was not boule-vardised twenty years ago. I praise that exquisite jagged skyline that stands up against the pale greens and fading blues and flushing clouds of sunset, but I wonder even more than I praise. As for St Mary le Strand, its preservation is a miracle, nothing more nor less. A thing of exquisite beauty *versus* four 'buses abreast! Really, the conclusion is too obvious. Didn't you read the letter of the man who proposed that the whole mysterious system, the immemorial plan of computing Easter, should be abolished off-hand, because he doesn't like his son having his holidays as early as March 25th? But shall we be going on?'

They had lingered at the corner of a street on the north side of the Strand, enjoying the contrasts and the glamour of the scene. Dyson pointed the way with a gesture, and they strolled up the comparatively deserted streets, slanting a little to the right, and thus arriving at Dyson's lodging on the verge of Bloomsbury. Mr Burton took a com-fortable armchair by the open window, while Dyson lit the candles and produced the whisky and soda and cigarettes.

'They tell me these cigarettes are very good,' he said; 'but I know nothing about it myself. I hold at last that there is only one tobacco, and that is shag. I suppose I could not tempt you to try a pipeful?'

Mr Burton smilingly refused the offer, and picked out a cigarette from the box. When he had smoked it half through, he said with some hesitation—

'It is really kind of you to have me here, Mr Dyson; the fact is that the interests at issue are far too serious to be discussed in a bar, where, as you found for yourself, there may be listeners, voluntary or involun-tary, on each side. I think the remark I heard you make was something about the oddity of an individual going about London in deadly fear of a young man with spectacles?'

'Yes; that was it.'

'Well, would you mind confiding to me the circumstances that gave rise to the reflection?'

'Not in the least. It was like this.' And he ran over in brief outline the adventure in Oxford Street, dwelling on the violence of Mr Wilkins's gestures, but wholly suppressing the tale told in the café. 'He told me he lived in constant terror of meeting this man; and I left him when I thought he was cool enough to look after himself,' said Dyson, ending his narrative.

'Really,' said Mr Burton. 'And you actually saw this mysterious person?'

'Yes.'

'And could you describe him?'

'Well, he looked to me a youngish man, pale and nervous. He had small black side-whiskers, and wore rather large spectacles.'

'But this is simply marvellous! You astonish me. For I must tell you that my interest in the matter is this. I'm not in the least in terror of meeting a dark young man with spectacles, but I shrewdly suspect a person of that description would much rather not meet me. And yet the account you give of the man tallies exactly. A nervous glance to right and left—is it not so? And, as you observed, he wears prominent spectacles, and has small black whiskers. There cannot be, surely, two people exactly identical—one a cause of terror, and the other, I should imagine, extremely anxious to get out of the way. But have you seen this man since?'

'No, I have not; and I have been looking out for him pretty keenly. But of course he may have left London, and England too, for the matter of that.'

'Hardly, I think. Well, Mr Dyson, it is only fair that I should explain my story, now that I have listened to yours. I must tell you, then, that I am an agent for curiosities and precious things of all kinds. An odd employment, isn't it? Of course, I wasn't brought up to the business; I gradually fell into it. I have always been fond of things queer and rare, and by the time I was twenty I had made half a dozen collections. It is not generally known how often farm-labourers come upon rarities; you would be astonished if I told you what I have seen turned up by the plough. I lived in the country in those days, and I used to buy anything the men on the farms brought me; and I had the queerest set of rubbish, as my friends called my collection. But that's how I got the scent of the business, which means everything; and, later on, it struck me that I might very well turn my knowledge to account and add to my income. Since those early days I have been in most quarters of the world, and some very valuable things have passed through my hands, and I have had to engage in difficult and delicate negotiations. You have possibly heard of the Khan opal—called in the East "The Stone of a Thousand and One Colours"? Well, perhaps the conquest of that stone was my greatest achievement. I call it myself the stone of the thousand and one lies, for I assure you that I had to invent a cycle of folk-lore before the Rajah who owned it would consent to sell the thing. I subsidised wandering storytellers, who told tales in which the opal played a frightful part; I hired a holy man—a great ascetic—to prophesy against the thing in the language of Eastern symbolism; in short, I frightened the Rajah out of his wits. So, you see, there is room for diplomacy in the traffic I am engaged in. I have to be ever on my guard, and I have often been sensible that unless I watched every step and weighed every word, my life would not last me much longer. Last April I became aware of the existence of a highly valuable antique gem; it was in southern Italy, and in the possession of persons who were ignorant of its real value. It has always been my experience that it is precisely the ignorant who are most difficult to deal with. I have met farmers who were under the impression that a shilling of George I. was a find of almost incalculable value; and all the defeats I have sustained have been at the hands of people of this description. Reflecting on these facts, I saw that the acquisition of the gem I have mentioned would be an affair demanding the nicest diplomacy; I might possibly have got it by offering a sum approaching its real value, but I need not point out to you that such a proceeding would be most unbusinesslike. Indeed, I doubt whether it would have been successful; for the cupidity of such persons is aroused by a sum which seems enormous, and the low cunning which serves them in place of intelligence immediately suggests that the object for which such an amount is offered must be worth at least double. Of course, when it is a matter of an ordinary curiosity—an old jug, a carved chest, or a queer brass lantern—one does not much care; the cupidity of the owner defeats its object; the collector laughs and goes away, for he is aware that such things are by no means unique. But this gem I fervently desired to possess; and as I did not see my way to giving more than a hundredth part of its value, I was conscious that all my, let us say, imaginative and diplomatic powers would have to be exerted. I am sorry to say that I came to the conclusion that I could not undertake to carry the matter through single-handed, and I determined to confide in my assistant, a young man named William Robbins, whom I judged to be by no means devoid of capacity. My idea was that Robbins should get himself up as a low-class dealer in precious stones;

he could patter a little Italian, and would go to the town in question and manage to see the gem we were after, possibly by offering some trifling articles of jewellery for sale, but that I left to be decided. Then my work was to begin, but I will not trouble you with a tale told twice over. In due course, then, Robbins went off to Italy with an assortment of uncut stones and a few rings, and some jewellery I bought in Birmingham on purpose for his expedition. A week later I followed him, travelling leisurely, so that I was a fortnight later in arriving at our common destination. There was a decent hotel in the town, and on my inquiring of the landlord whether there were many strangers in the place, he told me very few; he had heard there was an Englishman staying in a small tavern, a pedlar, he said, who sold beautiful trinkets very cheaply, and wanted to buy old rubbish. For five or six days I took life leisurely, and I must say I enjoyed myself. It was part of my plan to make the people think I was an enormously rich man; and I knew that such items as the extravagance of my meals, and the price of every bottle of wine I drank, would not be suffered, as Sancho Panza* puts it, to rot in the landlord's breast. At the end of the week I was fortunate enough to make the acquaintance of Signor Melini, the owner of the gem I coveted, at the café, and with his ready hospitality, and my geniality, I was soon established as a friend of the house. On my third or fourth visit I managed to make the Italians talk about the English pedlar, who, they said, spoke a most detestable Italian. "But that does not matter," said the Signora Melini, "for he has beautiful things, which he sells very very cheap." "I hope you may not find he has cheated you," I said, "for I must tell you that English people give these fellows a very wide berth. They usually make a great parade of the cheapness of their goods, which often turn out to be double the price of better articles in the shops." They would not hear of this, and Signora Melini insisted on showing me the three rings and the bracelet she had bought of the pedlar. She told me the price she had paid; and after scrutinising the articles carefully, I had to confess that she had made a bargain, and indeed Robbins had sold her the things at about fifty per cent below market value. I admired the trinkets as I gave them back to the lady, and I hinted that the pedlar must be a somewhat foolish specimen of his class. Two days later, as I was taking my vermouth at the café with Signor Melini, he led the conversation back to the pedlar, and mentioned casually that he had shown the man a little curiosity, for which he had made rather a handsome offer. "My dear sir," I said, "I hope you will be careful. I told you that the travelling tradesman does not bear a very high reputation in England; and notwithstanding his apparent simplicity, this fellow may turn out to be an arrant cheat. May I ask you what is the nature of the curiosity you have shown him?" He told me it was a little thing, a pretty little stone with some figures cut on it: people said it was old. "I should like to examine it," I replied, "as it happens I have seen a good deal of these gems. We have a fine collection of them in our Museum at London."* In due course I was shown the article, and I held the gem I so coveted between my fingers. I looked at it coolly, and put it down carelessly on the table. "Would you mind telling me, Signor," I said, "how much my fellow-countryman offered you for this?" "Well," he said, "my wife says the man must be mad; he said he would give me twenty lire for it."

'I looked at him quietly, and took up the gem and pretended to examine it in the light more carefully; I turned it over and over, and finally pulled out a magnifying glass from my pocket, and seemed to search every line in the cutting with minutest scrutiny. "My dear sir," I said at last, "I am inclined to agree with Signora Melini. If this gem were genuine, it would be worth some money; but as it happens to be a rather bad forgery, it is not worth twenty centesimi. It was sophisticated, I should imagine, some time in the last century, and by a very unskilful hand." "Then we had better get rid of it," said Melini. "I never thought it was worth anything myself. Of course, I am sorry for the pedlar, but one must let a man know his own trade. I shall tell him we will take the twenty lire." "Excuse me," I said, "the man wants a lesson. It would be a charity to give him one. Tell him that you will not take anything under eighty lire, and I shall be much surprised if he does not close with you at once."

'A day or two later I heard that the English pedlar had gone away, after debasing the minds of the country people with Birmingham art jewellery;* for I admit that the gold sleeve-links like kidney beans, the silver chains made apparently after the pattern of a dog-chain, and the initial brooches have always been heavy on my conscience. I cannot acquit myself of having indirectly contributed to debauch the taste of a simple folk; but I hope that the end I had in view may finally outbalance this heavy charge. Soon afterwards I paid a farewell visit at the Melinis, and the signor informed me with an oily chuckle that the plan I had suggested had been completely successful. I congratulated him on his bargain, and went away after expressing a wish that Heaven might send many such pedlars in his path.

'Nothing of interest occurred on my return journey. I had arranged that Robbins was to meet me at a certain place on a certain day, and I went to the appointment full of the coolest confidence; the gem had been conquered, and I had only to reap the fruits of victory. I am sorry to shake that trust in our common human nature which I am sure you possess, but I am compelled to tell you that up to the present date I have never set eyes on my man Robbins, or on the antique gem in his custody. I have found out that he actually arrived in London, for he was seen three days before my arrival in England by a pawnbroker of my acquaintance consuming his favourite beverage—four ale—in the tavern where we met to-night. Since then he has not been heard of. I hope you will now pardon my curiosity as to the history and adventures of dark young men with spectacles. You will, I am sure, feel for me in my position; the savour of life has disappeared for me; it is a bitter thought that I have rescued one of the most perfect and exquisite specimens of antique art from the hands of ignorant, and indeed unscrupulous persons, only to deliver it into the keeping of a man who is evidently utterly devoid of the very elements of commercial morality.'

'My dear sir,' said Dyson, 'you will allow me to compliment you on your style; your adventures have interested me exceedingly. But, forgive me, you just now used the word morality; would not some persons take exception to your own methods of business? I can conceive, myself, flaws of a moral kind being found in the very original conception you have described to me; I can imagine the Puritan shrinking in dismay from your scheme, pronouncing it unscrupulous—nay, dishonest.'

Mr Burton helped himself very frankly to some more whisky.

'Your scruples entertain me,' he said. 'Perhaps you have not gone very deeply into these questions of ethics. I have been compelled to do so myself, just as I was forced to master a simple system of book-keeping. Without book-keeping, and still more without a system of ethics, it is impossible to conduct a business such as mine. But I assure you that I am often profoundly saddened as I pass through the crowded streets and watch the world at work by the thought of how few amongst all these hurrying individuals, black-hatted, well dressed, educated we may presume sufficiently,—how few amongst them have any reasoned system of morality. Even you have not weighed the question; although you study life and affairs, and to a certain extent penetrate the veils and masks of the comedy of man, even you judge by empty conventions, and the false money which is allowed to pass current as sterling coin. Allow me to play the part of Socrates;* I shall teach you nothing that you do not know. I shall merely lay aside the wrappings of prejudice and bad logic, and show you the real image which you possess in your soul. Come, then. Do you allow that happiness is anything?'

'Certainly,' said Dyson.

'And happiness is desirable or undesirable?'

'Desirable, of course.'

'And what shall we call the man who gives happiness? Is he not a philanthropist?'

'I think so.'

'And such a person is praiseworthy, and the more praiseworthy in the proportion of the persons whom he makes happy?'

'By all means.'

'So that he who makes a whole nation happy is praiseworthy in the extreme, and the action by which he gives happiness is the highest virtue?'

'It appears so, O Burton,' said Dyson, who found something very exquisite in the character of his visitor.

'Quite so; you find the several conclusions inevitable. Well, apply them to the story I have told you. I conferred happiness on myself by obtaining (as I thought) possession of the gem; I conferred happiness on the Melinis by getting them eighty lire instead of an object for which they had not the slightest value, and I intended to confer happiness on the whole British nation by selling the thing to the British Museum, to say nothing of the happiness a profit of about nine thousand per cent. would have conferred on me. I assure you, I regard Robbins as an interferer with the cosmos and fair order of things. But that is nothing; you perceive that I am an apostle of the very highest morality; you have been forced to yield to argument.'

'There certainly seems a great deal in what you advance,' said Dyson. 'I admit that I am a mere amateur of ethics, while you, as you say, have brought the most acute scrutiny to bear on these perplexed and doubtful questions. I can well understand your anxiety to meet the fallacious Robbins, and I congratulate myself on the chance which has made us acquainted. But you will pardon my seeming inhospitality; I see it is half-past eleven, and I think you mentioned a train.'

'A thousand thanks, Mr Dyson, I have just time, I see. I will look you up some evening if I may. Good night.'


## THE DECORATIVE IMAGINATION

IN the course of a few weeks Dyson became accustomed to the constant incursions of the ingenious Mr Burton, who showed himself ready to drop in at all hours, not averse to refreshment, and a profound guide in the complicated questions of life. His visits at once terrified and delighted Dyson, who could no longer seat himself at his bureau secure from interruption while he embarked on literary undertakings, each one of which was to be a masterpiece. On the other hand, it was a vivid pleasure to be confronted with views so highly original; and if here and there Mr Burton's reasonings seemed tinged with fallacy, yet Dyson freely yielded to the joy of strangeness, and never failed to give his visitor a frank and hearty welcome. Mr Burton's first inquiry was always after the unprincipled Robbins, and he seemed to feel the stings of disappointment when Dyson told him that he had failed to meet this outrage on all morality, as Burton styled him, vowing that sooner or later he would take vengeance on such a shameless betrayal of trust.

One evening they had sat together for some time discussing the possibility of laying down for this present generation and our modern and intensely complicated order of society some rules of social diplomacy, such as Lord Bacon* gave to the courtiers of King James I. 'It is a book to make,' said Mr Burton, 'but who is there capable of making it? I tell you, people are longing for such a book; it would bring fortune to its publisher. Bacon's Essays are exquisite, but they have now no practical application; the modern strategist can find but little use in a treatise *De Re Militari*,* written by a Florentine in the fifteenth century. Scarcely more dissimilar are the social conditions of Bacon's time and our own; the rules that he lays down so exquisitely for the courtier and diplomatist of James the First's age will avail us little in the rough-and-tumble struggle of to-day. Life, I am afraid, has deteriorated; it gives little play for fine strokes such as formerly advanced men in the state. Except in such businesses as mine, where a chance does occur now and then, it has all become, as I said, an affair of rough and tumble; men still desire to attain, it is true, but what is their *moyen de parvenir*?* A mere imitation—and not a gracious one—of the arts of the soap vendor and the proprietor of baking-powder. When I think of these things, my dear Dyson, I confess that I am tempted to despair of my century.'

'You are too pessimistic, my dear fellow; you set up too high a standard. Certainly, I agree with you, that the times are decadent in many ways. I admit a general appearance of squalor; it needs much philosophy to extract the wonderful and the beautiful from the Cromwell Road* or the Nonconformist conscience.* Australian wines of fine Burgundy character, the novels alike of the old women and the new women,* popular journalism,—these things, indeed, make for depression. Yet we have our advantages: before us is unfolded the greatest spectacle the world has ever seen—the mystery of the innumerable, unending streets, the strange adventures that must infallibly arise from so complicated a press of interests. Nay, I will say that he who has stood in the ways of a sub-urb, and has seen them stretch before him all shining, void, and deso-late at noonday, has not lived in vain. Such a sight is in reality more wonderful than any perspective of Bagdad or Grand Cairo. And, to set on one side the entertaining history of the gem which you told me, surely you must have had many singular adventures in your own career?'

'Perhaps not so many as you would think; a good deal—the larger part of my business—has been as commonplace as linen-drapery. But, of course, things happen now and then. It is ten years since I estab-lished my agency, and I suppose that a house- and estate-agent who had been in trade for an equal time could tell you some queer stories. But I must give you a sample of my experiences some night.'

'Why not to-night?' said Dyson. 'This evening seems to me admir-ably adapted for an odd chapter. Look out into the street; you can catch a view of it if you crane your neck from that chair of yours. Is it not charming? The double row of lamps growing closer in the distance, the hazy outline of the plane-tree in the square, and the lights of the han-soms swimming to and fro, gliding and vanishing; and above, the sky all clear and blue and shining. Come, let us have one of your *cent nouvelles nouvelles*.'*

'My dear Dyson, I am delighted to amuse you.' With these words Mr Burton prefaced the

### NOVEL OF THE IRON MAID

I think the most extraordinary event which I can recall took place about five years ago. I was then still feeling my way; I had declared for busi-ness, and attended regularly at my office; but I had not succeeded in establishing a really profitable connection, and consequently I had a good deal of leisure time on my hands. I have never thought fit to trouble you with the details of my private life; they would be entirely devoid of interest. I must briefly say, however, that I had a numerous circle of acquaintance, and was never at a loss as to how to spend my evenings. I was so fortunate as to have friends in most of the ranks of the social order; there is nothing so unfortunate, to my mind, as a spe-cialised circle, wherein a certain round of ideas is continually traversed and retraversed. I have always tried to find out new types and persons whose brains contained something fresh to me; one may chance to gain information even from the conversation of city men on an omnibus. Amongst my acquaintance I knew a young doctor, who lived in a far outlying suburb, and I used often to brave the intolerably slow railway journey to have the pleasure of listening to his talk. One night we conversed so eagerly together over our pipes and whisky that the clock passed unnoticed; and when I glanced up, I realised with a shock that I had just five minutes in which to catch the last train. I made a dash for my hat and stick, jumped out of the house and down the steps, and tore at full speed up the street. It was no good, however; there was a shriek of the engine-whistle, and I stood there at the station door and saw far on the long, dark line of the embankment a red light shine and vanish, and a porter came down and shut the door with a bang.

'How far to London?' I asked him.

'A good nine miles to Waterloo Bridge.'* And with that he went off.

Before me was the long suburban street, its dreary distance marked by rows of twinkling lamps, and the air was poisoned by the faint, sickly smell of burning bricks; it was not a cheerful prospect by any means, and I had to walk through nine miles of such streets, deserted as those of Pompeii. I knew pretty well what direction to take, so I set out wearily, looking at the stretch of lamps vanishing in perspective; and as I walked, street after street branched off to right and left, some far-reaching, to distances that seemed endless, communicating with other systems of thoroughfare, and some mere protoplasmic streets, beginning in orderly fashion with serried two-storied houses, and ending suddenly in waste, and pits, and rubbish-heaps, and fields whence the magic had departed. I have spoken of systems of thoroughfare, and I assure you that walking alone through these silent places I felt fantasy growing on me, and some glamour of the infinite. There was here, I felt, an immensity as in the outer void of the universe; I passed from unknown to unknown, my way marked by lamps like stars, and on either hand was an unknown world where myriads of men dwelt and slept, street leading into street, as it seemed to world's end. At first the road by which I was travelling was lined with houses of unutterable monotony, a wall of grey brick pierced by two stories of windows, drawn close to the very pavement; but by degrees I noticed an improvement, there were gardens, and these grew larger; the suburban builder began to allow himself a wider scope; and for a certain distance each flight of steps was guarded by twin lions of plaster, and scents of flowers prevailed over the fume of heated bricks. The road began to climb a hill, and looking up a side street I saw the half moon rise over plane-trees, and there on the other side was as if a white cloud had fallen, and the air around it was sweetened as with incense; it was a may-tree in full bloom. I pressed on stubbornly, listening for the wheels and the clatter of some belated hansom; but into that land of men who go to the city in the morning and return

in the evening the hansom rarely enters, and I had resigned myself once
more to the walk, when I suddenly became aware that some one was
advancing to meet me along the sidewalk. The man was strolling rather
aimlessly; and though the time and the place would have allowed an
unconventional style of dress, he was vested in the ordinary frockcoat,
black tie, and silk hat of civilisation. We met each other under the lamp,
and, as often happens in this great town, two casual passengers brought
face to face found each in the other an acquaintance.

'Mr Mathias, I think?' I said.

'Quite so. And you are Frank Burton. You know you are a man with
a Christian name, so I won't apologise for my familiarity. But may I ask
where you are going?'

I explained the situation to him, saying I had traversed a region as
unknown to me as the darkest recesses of Africa. 'I think I have only
about five miles further,' I concluded.

'Nonsense! you must come home with me. My house is close by; in
fact, I was just taking my evening walk when we met. Come along;
I dare say you will find a makeshift bed easier than a five-mile walk.'

I let him take my arm and lead me along, though I was a good deal
surprised at so much geniality from a man who was, after all, a mere
casual club acquaintance. I suppose I had not spoken to Mr Mathias
half a dozen times; he was a man who would sit silent in an arm-chair
for hours, neither reading nor smoking, but now and again moistening
his lips with his tongue and smiling queerly to himself. I confess he had
never attracted me, and on the whole I should have preferred to continue my walk. But he took my arm and led me up a side street, and
stopped at a door in a high wall. We passed through the still, moonlit
garden, beneath the black shadow of an old cedar, and into an old red-
brick house with many gables. I was tired enough, and I sighed with
relief as I let myself fall into a great leather arm-chair. You know the
infernal grit with which they strew the sidewalk in those suburban districts; it makes walking a penance, and I felt my four-mile tramp had
made me more weary than ten miles on an honest country road. I looked
about the room with some curiosity; there was a shaded lamp, which
threw a circle of brilliant light on a heap of papers lying on an old
brass-bound secretaire of the last century, but the room was all vague
and shadowy, and I could only see that it was long and low, and that it
was filled with indistinct objects which might be furniture. Mr Mathias
sat down in a second arm-chair, and looked about him with that odd
smile of his. He was a queer-looking man, clean shaven, and white to
the lips. I should think his age was something between fifty and sixty.

'Now I have got you here,' he began, 'I must inflict my hobby on you. You knew I was a collector? Oh yes, I have devoted many years to collecting curiosities, which I think are really curious. But we must have a better light.'

He advanced into the middle of the room, and lit a lamp which hung from the ceiling; and as the bright light flashed round the wick, from every corner and space there seemed to start a horror. Great wooden frames, with complicated apparatus of ropes and pulleys, stood against the wall; a wheel of strange shape had a place beside a thing that looked like a gigantic gridiron; little tables glittered with bright steel instruments carelessly put down as if ready for use; a screw and vice loomed out, casting ugly shadows, and in another nook was a saw with cruel jagged teeth.

'Yes,' said Mr Mathias, 'they are, as you suggest, instruments of torture—of torture and death. Some—many, I may say—have been used; a few are reproductions after ancient examples. Those knives were used for flaying; that frame is a rack, and a very fine specimen. Look at this; it comes from Venice. You see that sort of collar, something like a big horse-shoe? Well, the patient, let us call him, sat down quite comfortably, and the horse-shoe was neatly fitted round his neck. Then the two ends were joined with a silken band, and the executioner began to turn a handle connected with the band. The horse-shoe contracted very gradually as the band tightened, and the turning continued till the man was strangled. It all took place quietly, in one of those queer garrets under the leads. But these things are all European; the Orientals are, of course, much more ingenious. These are the Chinese contrivances; you have heard of the 'Heavy Death'? It is my hobby, this sort of thing. Do you know, I often sit here, hour after hour, and meditate over the collection. I fancy I see the faces of the men who have suffered, faces lean with agony, and wet with sweats of death growing distinct out of the gloom, and I hear the echoes of their cries for mercy. But I must show you my latest acquisition. Come into the next room.'

I followed Mr Mathias out. The weariness of the walk, the late hour, and the strangeness of it all made me feel like a man in a dream; nothing would have surprised me very much. The second room was as the first, crowded with ghastly instruments; but beneath the lamp was a wooden platform, and a figure stood on it. It was a large statue of a naked woman, fashioned in green bronze, the arms were stretched out, and there was a smile on the lips; it might well have been intended for a Venus, and yet there was about the thing an evil and a deadly look.

Mr Mathias looked at it complacently. 'Quite a work of art, isn't it?'

he said. 'It's made of bronze, as you see, but it has long had the name of the Iron Maid. I got it from Germany, and it was only unpacked this afternoon; indeed, I have not yet had time to open the letter of advice. You see that very small knob between the breasts? Well, the victim was bound to the Maid, the knob was pressed, and the arms slowly tightened round the neck. You can imagine the result.'

As Mr Mathias talked, he patted the figure affectionately. I had turned away, for I sickened at the sight of the man and his loathsome treasure. There was a slight click, of which I took no notice; it was not much louder than the tick of a clock; and then I heard a sudden whirr, the noise of machinery in motion, and I faced round. I have never forgotten the hideous agony on Mathias's face as those relentless arms tightened about his neck; there was a wild struggle as of a beast in the toils, and then a shriek that ended in a choking groan. The whirring noise had suddenly changed into a heavy droning. I tore with all my might at the bronze arms, and strove to wrench them apart, but I could do nothing. The head had slowly bent down, and the green lips were on the lips of Mathias.

Of course, I had to attend at the inquest. The letter which had accompanied the figure was found unopened on the study table. The German firm of dealers cautioned their client to be most careful in touching the Iron Maid, as the machinery had been put in thorough working order.

For many revolving weeks Mr Burton delighted Dyson by his agreeable conversation, diversified by anecdote, and interspersed with the narration of singular adventures. Finally, however, he vanished as suddenly as he had appeared, and on the occasion of his last visit he contrived to loot a copy of his namesake's *Anatomy*.* Dyson, considering this violent attack on the rights of property, and certain glaring inconsistencies in the talk of his late friend, arrived at the conclusion that his stories were fabulous, and that the Iron Maid only existed in the sphere of a decorative imagination.

## THE RECLUSE OF BAYSWATER

Amongst the many friends who were favoured with the occasional pleasure of Mr Dyson's society was Mr Edgar Russell, realist and obscure struggler, who occupied a small back room on the second floor of a house in Abingdon Grove, Notting Hill. Turning off from the main street, and walking a few paces onward, one was conscious of a certain calm, a drowsy peace, which made the feet inclined to loiter, and this was ever the atmosphere of Abingdon Grove. The houses stood a little back, with gardens where the lilac, and laburnum, and blood-red may blossomed gaily in their seasons, and there was a corner where an older house in another street had managed to keep a back garden of real extent, a walled-in garden, whence there came a pleasant scent of greenness after the rains of early summer, where old elms held memories of the open fields, where there was yet sweet grass to walk on. The houses in Abingdon Grove belonged chiefly to the nondescript stucco period of thirty-five years ago, tolerably built, with passable accommodation for moderate incomes; they had largely passed into the state of lodgings, and cards bearing the inscription 'Furnished apartments' were not infrequent over the doors. Here, then, in a house of sufficiently good appearance, Mr Russell had established himself; for he looked upon the traditional dirt and squalor of Grub Street* as a false and obsolete convention, and preferred, as he said, to live within sight of green leaves. Indeed, from his room one had a magnificent view of a long line of gardens, and a screen of poplars shut out the melancholy back premises of Wilton Street during the summer months. Mr Russell lived chiefly on bread and tea, for his means were of the smallest; but when Dyson came to see him, he would send out the slavey* for six ale,* and Dyson was always at liberty to smoke as much of his own tobacco as he pleased. The landlady had been so unfortunate as to have her drawing-room floor vacant for many months; a card had long proclaimed the void within; and Dyson, when he walked up the steps one evening in early autumn, had a sense that something was missing, and, looking at the fanlight, saw the appealing card had disappeared.

'You have let your first floor, have you?' he said, as he greeted Mr Russell.

'Yes; it was taken about a fortnight ago by a lady.'

'Indeed,' said Dyson, always curious; 'a young lady?'

'Yes; I believe so. She is a widow, and wears a thick crape veil. I have met her once or twice on the stairs and in the street; but I should not know her face.'

'Well,' said Dyson, when the beer had arrived, and the pipes were in full blast, 'and what have you been doing? Do you find the work getting any easier?'

'Alas!' said the young man, with an expression of great gloom, 'the life is a purgatory, and all but a hell. I write, picking out my words, weighing and balancing the force of every syllable, calculating the minutest effects that language can produce, erasing and rewriting, and spending a whole evening over a page of manuscript. And then, in the morning, when I read what I have written——Well, there is nothing to be done but to throw it in the wastepaper basket, if the verso has been already written on, or to put it in the drawer if the other side happens to be clean. When I have written a phrase which undoubtedly embodies a happy turn of thought, I find it dressed up in feeble commonplace; and when the style is good, it serves only to conceal the baldness of superannuated fancies. I sweat over my work, Dyson—every finished line means so much agony. I envy the lot of the carpenter in the side street who has a craft which he understands. When he gets an order for a table he does not writhe with anguish; but if I were so unlucky as to get an order for a book, I think I should go mad.'

'My dear fellow, you take it all too seriously. You should let the ink flow more readily. Above all, firmly believe, when you sit down to write, that you are an artist, and that whatever you are about is a masterpiece. Suppose ideas fail you, say, as I heard one of our most exquisite artists say, "It's of no consequence; the ideas are all there, at the bottom of that box of cigarettes!" You, indeed, smoke tobacco, but the application is the same. Besides, you must have some happy moments; and these should be ample consolation.'

'Perhaps you are right. But such moments are so few; and then there is the torture of a glorious conception matched with execution beneath the standard of the Family Story Paper.* For instance, I was happy for two hours a night or two ago; I lay awake and saw visions. But then the morning!'

'What was your idea?'

'It seemed to me a splendid one: I thought of Balzac and the *Comédie Humaine*, of Zola and the Rougon-Macquart family.* It dawned upon me that I would write the history of a street. Every house should form a volume. I fixed upon the street, I saw each house, and read as clearly as in letters the physiology and psychology of each; the little byway stretched before me in its actual shape—a street that I know and have passed down a hundred times, with some twenty houses, prosperous and mean, and lilac bushes in purple blossom. And yet it was, at the same time, a symbol, a *via dolorosa** of hopes cherished and disappointed, of years of monotonous existence without content or discontent, of tragedies and obscure sorrows; and on the door of one of those houses I saw the red stain of blood, and behind a window two shadows, blackened and faded, on the blind, as they swayed on tightened cords—the shadows of a man and a woman hanging in a vulgar gaslit parlour. These were my fancies; but when pen touched paper they shrivelled and vanished away.'*

'Yes,' said Dyson, 'there is a lot in that. I envy you the pains of trans-muting vision into reality, and, still more, I envy you the day when you will look at your bookshelf and see twenty goodly books upon the shelves—the series complete and done for ever. Let me entreat you to have them bound in solid parchment, with gold lettering. It is the only real cover for a valiant book. When I look in at the windows of some choice shop, and see the bindings of Levant morocco,* with pretty tools and panellings, and your sweet contrasts of red and green, I say to myself, "These are not books, but *bibelots*."* A book bound so—a true book, mind you—is like a Gothic statue draped in brocade of Lyons.'*

'Alas!' said Russell, 'we need not discuss the binding—the books are not begun.'

The talk went on as usual till eleven o'clock, when Dyson bade his friend good night. He knew the way downstairs, and walked down by himself; but, greatly to his surprise, as he crossed the first-floor landing the door opened slightly, and a hand was stretched out, beckoning.

Dyson was not the man to hesitate under such circumstances. In a moment he saw himself involved in adventure; and, as he told him-self, the Dysons had never disobeyed a lady's summons. Softly, then, with due regard for the lady's honour, he would have entered the room, when a low but clear voice spoke to him—

'Go downstairs and open the door and shut it again rather loudly. Then come up to me; and for Heaven's sake, walk softly.'

Dyson obeyed her commands, not without some hesitation, for he was afraid of meeting the landlady or the maid on his return journey. But, walking like a cat, and making each step he trod on crack loudly, he flattered himself that he had escaped observation; and as he gained the top of the stairs the door opened wide before him, and he found himself in the lady's drawing-room, bowing awkwardly.

'Pray be seated, sir. Perhaps this chair will be the best; it was the favoured chair of my landlady's deceased husband. I would ask you to smoke, but the odour would betray me. I know my proceedings must seem to you unconventional; but I saw you arrive this evening, and I do not think you would refuse to help a woman who is so unfortunate as I am.'

Mr Dyson looked shyly at the young lady before him. She was dressed in deep mourning, but the piquant smiling face and charming hazel eyes ill accorded with the heavy garments and the mouldering surface of the crape.

'Madam,' he said gallantly, 'your instinct has served you well. We will not trouble, if you please, about the question of social conventions;

the chivalrous gentleman knows nothing of such matters. I hope I may be privileged to serve you.'

'You are very kind to me, but I knew it would be so. Alas! sir, I have had experience of life, and I am rarely mistaken. Yet man is too often so vile and so misjudging that I trembled even as I resolved to take this step, which, for all I knew, might prove to be both desperate and ruinous.'

'With me you have nothing to fear,' said Dyson. 'I was nurtured in the faith of chivalry, and I have always endeavoured to remember the proud traditions of my race. Confide in me, then, and count upon my secrecy, and if it prove possible, you may rely on my help.'

'Sir, I will not waste your time, which I am sure is valuable, by idle parleyings. Learn, then, that I am a fugitive, and in hiding here; I place myself in your power; you have but to describe my features, and I fall into the hands of my relentless enemy.'

Mr Dyson wondered for a passing instant how this could be, but he only renewed his promise of silence, repeating that he would be the embodied spirit of dark concealment.

'Good,' said the lady, 'the Oriental fervour of your style is delightful. In the first place, I must disabuse your mind of the conviction that I am a widow. These gloomy vestments have been forced on me by strange circumstance; in plain language, I have deemed it expedient to go disguised. You have a friend, I think, in the house, Mr Russell? He seems of a coy and retiring nature.'

'Excuse me, madam,' said Dyson, 'he is not coy, but he is a realist; and perhaps you are aware that no Carthusian monk* can emulate the cloistral seclusion in which a realistic novelist loves to shroud himself. It is his way of observing human nature.'

'Well, well,' said the lady; 'all this, though deeply interesting, is not germane to our affair. I must tell you my history.'

With these words the young lady proceeded to relate the

## NOVEL OF THE WHITE POWDER

My name is Leicester; my father, Major-General Wyn Leicester, a distinguished officer of artillery, succumbed five years ago to a complicated liver complaint acquired in the deadly climate of India. A year later my only brother, Francis, came home after an exceptionally brilliant career at the University, and settled down with the resolution of a hermit to master what has been well called the great legend of the law. He was a man who seemed to live in utter indifference to everything that is called pleasure; and though he was handsomer than most men, and could talk as merrily and wittily as if he were a mere vagabond, he avoided society, and shut himself up in a large room at the top of the house to make himself a lawyer. Ten hours a day of hard reading was at first his allotted portion; from the first light in the east to the late afternoon he remained shut up with his books, taking a hasty half-hour's lunch with me as if he grudged the wasting of the moments, and going out for a short walk when it began to grow dusk. I thought that such relentless application must be injurious, and tried to cajole him from the crabbed text-books, but his ardour seemed to grow rather than diminish, and his daily tale of hours increased. I spoke to him seriously, suggesting some occasional relaxation, if it were but an idle afternoon with a harmless novel; but he laughed, and said that he read about feudal tenures when he felt in need of amusement, and scoffed at the notion of theatres, or a month's fresh air. I confessed that he looked well, and seemed not to suffer from his labours, but I knew that such unnatural toil would take revenge at last, and I was not mistaken. A look of anxiety began to lurk about his eyes, and he seemed languid, and at last he avowed that he was no longer in perfect health; he was troubled, he said, with a sensation of dizziness, and awoke now and then of nights from fearful dreams, terrified and cold with icy sweats. 'I am taking care of myself,' he said, 'so you must not trouble; I passed the whole of yesterday afternoon in idleness, leaning back in that comfortable chair you gave me, and scribbling nonsense on a sheet of paper. No, no; I will not overdo my work; I shall be well enough in a week or two, depend upon it.'

Yet in spite of his assurances I could see that he grew no better, but rather worse; he would enter the drawing-room with a face all miserably wrinkled and despondent, and endeavour to look gaily when my eyes fell on him, and I thought such symptoms of evil omen, and was frightened sometimes at the nervous irritation of his movements, and at glances which I could not decipher. Much against his will, I prevailed on him to have medical advice, and with an ill grace he called in our old doctor.

Dr Haberden cheered me after examination of his patient.

'There is nothing really much amiss,' he said to me. 'No doubt he reads too hard, and eats hastily, and then goes back again to his books in too great a hurry, and the natural consequence is some digestive trouble and a little mischief in the nervous system. But I think—I do indeed, Miss Leicester—that we shall be able to set this all right. I have written him a prescription which ought to do great things. So you have no cause for anxiety.'

My brother insisted on having the prescription made up by a chemist in the neighbourhood; it was an odd, old-fashioned shop, devoid of the studied coquetry and calculated glitter that make so gay a show on the counters and shelves of the modern apothecary; but Francis liked the old chemist, and believed in the scrupulous purity of his drugs. The medicine was sent in due course, and I saw that my brother took it regularly after lunch and dinner. It was an innocent-looking white powder, of which a little was dissolved in a glass of cold water; I stirred it in, and it seemed to disappear, leaving the water clear and colourless. At first Francis seemed to benefit greatly; the weariness vanished from his face, and he became more cheerful than he had ever been since the time when he left school; he talked gaily of reforming himself, and avowed to me that he had wasted his time.

'I have given too many hours to law,' he said, laughing; 'I think you have saved me in the nick of time. Come, I shall be Lord Chancellor* yet, but I must not forget life. You and I will have a holiday together before long; we will go to Paris and enjoy ourselves, and keep away from the Bibliothèque Nationale.'*

I confessed myself delighted with the prospect.

'When shall we go?' I said. 'I can start the day after to-morrow if you like.'

'Ah! that is perhaps a little too soon; after all, I do not know London yet, and I suppose a man ought to give the pleasures of his own country the first choice. But we will go off together in a week or two, so try and furbish up your French. I only know law French myself, and I am afraid that wouldn't do.'

We were just finishing dinner, and he quaffed off his medicine with a parade of carousal as if it had been wine from some choicest bin.

'Has it any particular taste?' I said.

'No; I should not know I was not drinking water,' and he got up from his chair and began to pace up and down the room as if he were undecided as to what he should do next.

'Shall we have coffee in the drawing-room?' I said; 'or would you like to smoke?'

'No, I think I will take a turn; it seems a pleasant evening. Look at the afterglow; why, it is as if a great city were burning in flames, and down there between the dark houses it is raining blood fast, fast. Yes, I will go out; I may be in soon, but I shall take my key; so good night, dear, if I don't see you again.'

The door slammed behind him, and I saw him walk lightly down the street, swinging his malacca cane,* and I felt grateful to Dr Haberden for such an improvement.

I believe my brother came home very late that night, but he was in a merry mood the next morning.

'I walked on without thinking where I was going,' he said, 'enjoying the freshness of the air, and livened by the crowds as I reached more frequented quarters. And then I met an old college friend, Orford, in the press of the pavement, and then—well, we enjoyed ourselves. I have felt what it is to be young and a man; I find I have blood in my veins, as other men have. I made an appointment with Orford for to-night; there will be a little party of us at the restaurant. Yes; I shall enjoy myself for a week or two, and hear the chimes at midnight,* and then we will go for our little trip together.'

Such was the transmutation of my brother's character that in a few days he became a lover of pleasure, a careless and merry idler of western pavements, a hunter out of snug restaurants, and a fine critic of fantastic dancing; he grew fat before my eyes, and said no more of Paris, for he had clearly found his paradise in London. I rejoiced, and yet wondered a little; for there was, I thought, something in his gaiety that indefinitely displeased me, though I could not have defined my feeling. But by degrees there came a change; he returned still in the cold hours of the morning, but I heard no more about his pleasures, and one morning as we sat at breakfast together I looked suddenly into his eyes and saw a stranger before me.

'O Francis!' I cried. 'O Francis, Francis, what have you done?' and rending sobs cut the words short. I went weeping out of the room; for though I knew nothing, yet I knew all, and by some odd play of thought I remembered the evening when he first went abroad to prove his manhood, and the picture of the sunset sky glowed before me; the clouds like a city in burning flames, and the rain of blood. Yet I did battle with such thoughts, resolving that perhaps, after all, no great harm had been done, and in the evening at dinner I resolved to press him to fix a day for our holiday in Paris. We had talked easily enough, and my brother had just taken his medicine, which he had continued all the while. I was about to begin my topic, when the words forming in my mind vanished, and I wondered for a second what icy and intolerable weight oppressed my heart and suffocated me as with the unutterable horror of the coffin-lid nailed down on the living.

We had dined without candles; the room had slowly grown from twilight to gloom, and the walls and corners were indistinct in the shadow. But from where I sat I looked out into the street; and as I thought of what I would say to Francis, the sky began to flush and shine, as it had done on a well-remembered evening, and in the gap between two dark masses that were houses an awful pageantry of flame appeared—lurid whorls of writhed cloud, and utter depths burning, grey masses like the fume blown from a smoking city, and an evil glory blazing far above shot with tongues of more ardent fire, and below as if there were a deep pool of blood. I looked down to where my brother sat facing me, and the words were shaped on my lips, when I saw his hand resting on the table. Between the thumb and forefinger of the closed hand there was a mark, a small patch about the size of a sixpence, and somewhat of the colour of a bad bruise. Yet, by some sense I cannot define, I knew that what I saw was no bruise at all; oh! if human flesh could burn with flame, and if flame could be black as pitch, such was that before me. Without thought or fashioning of words grey horror shaped within me at the sight, and in an inner cell it was known to be a brand. For a moment the stained sky became dark as midnight, and when the light returned to me I was alone in the silent room, and soon after I heard my brother go out.

Late as it was, I put on my bonnet and went to Dr Haberden, and in his great consulting room, ill lighted by a candle which the doctor brought in with him, with stammering lips, and a voice that would break in spite of my resolve, I told him all, from the day on which my brother began to take the medicine down to the dreadful thing I had seen scarcely half an hour before.

When I had done, the doctor looked at me for a minute with an expression of great pity on his face.

'My dear Miss Leicester,' he said, 'you have evidently been anxious about your brother; you have been worrying over him, I am sure. Come, now, is it not so?'

'I have certainly been anxious,' I said. 'For the last week or two I have not felt at ease.'

'Quite so; you know, of course, what a queer thing the brain is?'

'I understand what you mean; but I was not deceived. I saw what I have told you with my own eyes.'

'Yes, yes, of course. But your eyes had been staring at that very curious sunset we had to-night. That is the only explanation. You will see it in the proper light to-morrow, I am sure. But, remember, I am always ready to give any help that is in my power; do not scruple to come to me, or to send for me if you are in any distress.'

I went away but little comforted, all confusion and terror and sorrow, not knowing where to turn. When my brother and I met the next day,

I looked quickly at him, and noticed, with a sickening at heart, that the right hand, the hand on which I had clearly seen the patch as of a black fire, was wrapped up with a handkerchief.

'What is the matter with your hand, Francis?' I said in a steady voice.

'Nothing of consequence. I cut a finger last night, and it bled rather awkwardly. So I did it up roughly to the best of my ability.'

'I will do it neatly for you, if you like.'

'No, thank you, dear; this will answer very well. Suppose we have breakfast; I am quite hungry.'

We sat down, and I watched him. He scarcely ate or drank at all, but tossed his meat to the dog when he thought my eyes were turned away; there was a look in his eyes that I had never yet seen, and the thought flashed across my mind that it was a look that was scarcely human. I was firmly convinced that awful and incredible as was the thing I had seen the night before, yet it was no illusion, no glamour of bewildered sense, and in the course of the morning I went again to the doctor's house.

He shook his head with an air puzzled and incredulous, and seemed to reflect for a few minutes.

'And you say he still keeps up the medicine? But why? As I understand, all the symptoms he complained of have disappeared long ago; why should he go on taking the stuff when he is quite well. And, by the bye, where did he get it made up? At Sayce's? I never send any one there; the old man is getting careless. Suppose you come with me to the chemist's; I should like to have some talk with him.'

We walked together to the shop; old Sayce knew Dr Haberden, and was quite ready to give any information.

'You have been sending that in to Mr Leicester for some weeks I think on my prescription,' said the doctor, giving the old man a pencilled scrap of paper.

The chemist put on his great spectacles with trembling uncertainty, and held up the paper with a shaking hand.

'Oh yes,' he said, 'I have very little of it left; it is rather an uncommon drug, and I have had it in stock some time. I must get in some more, if Mr Leicester goes on with it.'

'Kindly let me have a look at the stuff,' said Haberden, and the chemist gave him a glass bottle. He took out the stopper and smelt the contents, and looked strangely at the old man.

'Where did you get this?' he said, 'and what is it? For one thing, Mr Sayce, it is not what I prescribed. Yes, yes, I see the label is right enough, but I tell you this is not the drug.'

'I have had it a long time,' said the old man in feeble terror; 'I got it from Burbage's in the usual way. It is not prescribed often, and I have had it on the shelf for some years. You see there is very little left.'

'You had better give it to me,' said Haberden. 'I am afraid something wrong has happened.'

We went out of the shop in silence, the doctor carrying the bottle neatly wrapped in paper under his arm.

'Dr Haberden,' I said when we had walked a little way—'Dr Haberden.'

'Yes,' he said, looking at me gloomily enough.

'I should like you to tell me what my brother has been taking twice a day for the last month or so.'

'Frankly, Miss Leicester, I don't know. We will speak of this when we get to my house.'

We walked on quickly without another word till we reached Dr Haberden's. He asked me to sit down, and began pacing up and down the room, his face clouded over, as I could see, with no common fears.

'Well,' he said at length, 'this is all very strange; it is only natural that you should feel alarmed, and I must confess that my mind is far from easy. We will put aside, if you please, what you told me last night and this morning, but the fact remains that for the last few weeks Mr Leicester has been impregnating his system with a drug which is completely unknown to me. I tell you, it is not what I ordered; and what that stuff in the bottle really is remains to be seen.'

He undid the wrapper, and cautiously tilted a few grains of the white powder on to a piece of paper, and peered curiously at it.

'Yes,' he said, 'it is like the sulphate of quinine,* as you say; it is flaky. But smell it.'

He held the bottle to me, and I bent over it. It was a strange, sickly smell, vaporous and overpowering, like some strong anæsthetic.

'I shall have it analysed,' said Haberden; 'I have a friend who has devoted his whole life to chemistry as a science. Then we shall have something to go upon. No, no; say no more about that other matter; I cannot listen to that; and take my advice and think no more about it yourself.'

That evening my brother did not go out as usual after dinner.

'I have had my fling,' he said with a queer laugh, 'and I must go back to my old ways. A little law will be quite a relaxation after so sharp a dose of pleasure,' and he grinned to himself, and soon after went up to his room. His hand was still all bandaged.

Dr Haberden called a few days later.

'I have no special news to give you,' he said. 'Chambers is out of town, so I know no more about that stuff than you do. But I should like to see Mr Leicester if he is in.'

'He is in his room,' I said; 'I will tell him you are here.'

'No, no, I will go up to him; we will have a little quiet talk together. I dare say that we have made a good deal of fuss about very little; for, after all, whatever the white powder may be, it seems to have done him good.'

The doctor went upstairs, and standing in the hall I heard his knock, and the opening and shutting of the door; and then I waited in the silent house for an hour, and the stillness grew more and more intense as the hands of the clock crept round. Then there sounded from above the noise of a door shut sharply, and the doctor was coming down the stairs. His footsteps crossed the hall, and there was a pause at the door; I drew a long, sick breath with difficulty, and saw my face white in a little mirror, and he came in and stood at the door. There was an unutterable horror shining in his eyes; he steadied himself by holding the back of a chair with one hand, his lower lip trembled like a horse's, and he gulped and stammered unintelligible sounds before he spoke.

'I have seen that man,' he began in a dry whisper. 'I have been sitting in his presence for the last hour. My God! And I am alive and in my senses! I, who have dealt with death all my life, and have dabbled with the melting ruins of the earthly tabernacle.* But not this, oh! not this,' and he covered his face with his hands as if to shut out the sight of something before him.

'Do not send for me again, Miss Leicester,' he said with more composure. 'I can do nothing in this house. Good-bye.'

As I watched him totter down the steps, and along the pavement towards his house, it seemed to me that he had aged by ten years since the morning.

My brother remained in his room. He called out to me in a voice I hardly recognised that he was very busy, and would like his meals brought to his door and left there, and I gave the order to the servants. From that day it seemed as if the arbitrary conception we call time had been annihilated for me; I lived in an ever-present sense of horror, going through the routine of the house mechanically, and only speaking a few necessary words to the servants. Now and then I went out and paced the streets for an hour or two and came home again; but whether I were without or within, my spirit delayed before the closed door of the upper room, and, shuddering, waited for it to open. I have said that I scarcely reckoned time; but I suppose it must have been a fortnight after Dr Haberden's visit that I came home from my stroll a little refreshed and lightened. The air was sweet and pleasant, and the hazy form of green leaves, floating cloudlike in the square, and the smell of blossoms, had charmed my senses, and I felt happier and walked more briskly. As I delayed a moment at the verge of the pavement, waiting for a van to pass by before crossing over to the house, I happened to look up at the windows, and instantly there was the rush and swirl of deep cold waters in my ears, my heart leapt up, and fell down, down as into a deep hollow, and I was amazed with a dread and terror without form or shape. I stretched out a hand blindly through folds of thick darkness, from the black and shadowy valley, and held myself from falling, while the stones beneath my feet rocked and swayed and tilted, and the sense of solid things seemed to sink away from under me. I had glanced up at the window of my brother's study, and at that moment the blind was drawn aside, and something that had life stared out into the world. Nay, I cannot say I saw a face or any human likeness; a living thing, two eyes of burning flame glared at me, and they were in the midst of something as formless as my fear, the symbol and presence of all evil and all hideous corruption. I stood shuddering and quaking as with the grip of ague, sick with unspeakable agonies of fear and loathing, and for five minutes I could not summon force or motion to my limbs. When I was within the door, I ran up the stairs to my brother's room, and knocked.

'Francis, Francis,' I cried, 'for Heaven's sake, answer me. What is the horrible thing in your room? Cast it out, Francis; cast it from you.'

I heard a noise as of feet shuffling slowly and awkwardly, and a choking, gurgling sound, as if some one was struggling to find utterance, and then the noise of a voice, broken and stifled, and words that I could scarcely understand.

'There is nothing here,' the voice said. 'Pray do not disturb me. I am not very well to-day.'

I turned away, horrified, and yet helpless. I could do nothing, and I wondered why Francis had lied to me, for I had seen the appearance beyond the glass too plainly to be deceived, though it was but the sight of a moment. And I sat still, conscious that there had been something else, something I had seen in the first flash of terror, before those burning eyes had looked at me. Suddenly I remembered; as I lifted my face the blind was being drawn back, and I had had an instant's glance of the thing that was moving it, and in my recollection I knew that a hideous image was engraved for ever on my brain. It was not a hand; there were no fingers that held the blind, but a black stump pushed it aside, the mouldering outline and the clumsy movement as of a beast's paw had glowed into my senses before the darkling waves of terror had over-whelmed me as I went down quick into the pit. My mind was aghast at the thought of this, and of the awful presence that dwelt with my brother in his room; I went to his door and cried to him again, but no answer came. That night one of the servants came up to me and told me in a whisper that for three days food had been regularly placed at the door and left untouched; the maid had knocked, but had received no answer; she had heard the noise of shuffling feet that I had noticed. Day after day went by, and still my brother's meals were brought to his door and left untouched; and though I knocked and called again and again, I could get no answer. The servants began to talk to me; it appeared they were as alarmed as I; the cook said that when my brother first shut himself up in his room she used to hear him come out at night and go about the house; and once, she said, the hall door had opened and closed again, but for several nights she had heard no sound. The climax came at last; it was in the dusk of the evening, and I was sitting in the darkening dreary room when a terrible shriek jarred and rang harshly out of the silence, and I heard a frightened scurry of feet dashing down the stairs. I waited, and the servant-maid staggered into the room and faced me, white and trembling.

'O Miss Helen!' she whispered; 'oh! for the Lord's sake, Miss Helen, what has happened? Look at my hand, miss; look at that hand!'

I drew her to the window, and saw there was a black wet stain upon her hand.

'I do not understand you,' I said. 'Will you explain to me?'

'I was doing your room just now,' she began. 'I was turning down the bed-clothes, and all of a sudden there was something fell upon my hand, wet, and I looked up, and the ceiling was black and dripping on me.'

I looked hard at her and bit my lip.

'Come with me,' I said. 'Bring your candle with you.'

The room I slept in was beneath my brother's, and as I went in I felt I was trembling. I looked up at the ceiling, and saw a patch, all black and wet, and a dew of black drops upon it, and a pool of horrible liquor soaking into the white bed-clothes.

I ran upstairs, and knocked loudly.

'O Francis, Francis, my dear brother,' I cried, 'what has happened to you?'

And I listened. There was a sound of choking, and a noise like water bubbling and regurgitating, but nothing else, and I called louder, but no answer came.

In spite of what Dr Haberden had said, I went to him; with tears streaming down my cheeks I told him of all that had happened, and he listened to me with a face set hard and grim.

'For your father's sake,' he said at last, 'I will go with you, though I can do nothing.'

We went out together; the streets were dark and silent, and heavy with heat and a drought of many weeks. I saw the doctor's face white under the gas-lamps, and when we reached the house his hand was shaking.

We did not hesitate, but went upstairs directly. I held the lamp, and he called out in a loud, determined voice—

'Mr Leicester, do you hear me? I insist on seeing you. Answer me at once.'

There was no answer, but we both heard that choking noise I have mentioned.

'Mr Leicester, I am waiting for you. Open the door this instant, or I shall break it down.' And he called a third time in a voice that rang and echoed from the walls—

'Mr Leicester! For the last time I order you to open the door.'

'Ah!' he said, after a pause of heavy silence, 'we are wasting time here. Will you be so kind as to get me a poker, or something of the kind.'

I ran into a little room at the back where odd articles were kept, and found a heavy adze-like tool that I thought might serve the doctor's purpose.

'Very good,' he said, 'that will do, I dare say. I give you notice, Mr Leicester,' he cried loudly at the keyhole, 'that I am now about to break into your room.'

Then I heard the wrench of the adze, and the woodwork split and cracked under it; with a loud crash the door suddenly burst open, and for a moment we started back aghast at a fearful screaming cry, no human voice, but as the roar of a monster, that burst forth inarticulate and struck at us out of the darkness.

'Hold the lamp,' said the doctor, and we went in and glanced quickly round the room.

'There it is,' said Dr Haberden, drawing a quick breath; 'look, in that corner.'

I looked, and a pang of horror seized my heart as with a white-hot iron. There upon the floor was a dark and putrid mass, seething with corruption and hideous rottenness, neither liquid nor solid, but melting and changing before our eyes, and bubbling with unctuous oily bubbles like boiling pitch. And out of the midst of it shone two burning

points like eyes, and I saw a writhing and stirring as of limbs, and something moved and lifted up that might have been an arm. The doctor
took a step forward, raised the iron bar and struck at the burning
points; he drove in the weapon, and struck again and again in a fury of
loathing. At last the thing was quiet.

A week or two later, when I had to some extent recovered from the
terrible shock, Dr Haberden came to see me.

'I have sold my practice,' he began, 'and to-morrow I am sailing on
a long voyage. I do not know whether I shall ever return to England; in all
probability I shall buy a little land in California, and settle there for the
remainder of my life. I have brought you this packet, which you may open
and read when you feel able to do so. It contains the report of Dr Chambers
on what I submitted to him. Good-bye, Miss Leicester, goodbye.'

When he was gone I opened the envelope; I could not wait, and proceeded to read the papers within. Here is the manuscript, and if you
will allow me, I will read you the astounding story it contains.

'My dear Haberden,' the letter began, 'I have delayed inexcusably in answering
your questions as to the white substance you sent me. To tell you the truth,
I have hesitated for some time as to what course I should adopt, for there is
a bigotry and an orthodox standard in physical science as in theology, and
I knew that if I told you the truth I should offend rooted prejudices which
I once held dear myself. However, I have determined to be plain with you, and
first I must enter into a short personal explanation.

'You have known me, Haberden, for many years as a scientific man; you and
I have often talked of our profession together, and discussed the hopeless gulf
that opens before the feet of those who think to attain to truth by any means
whatsoever except the beaten way of experiment and observation in the sphere
of material things. I remember the scorn with which you have spoken to me of
men of science who have dabbled a little in the unseen, and have timidly hinted
that perhaps the senses are not, after all, the eternal, impenetrable bounds of
all knowledge, the everlasting walls beyond which no human being has ever
passed. We have laughed together heartily, and I think justly, at the "occult"
follies of the day, disguised under various names—the mesmerisms, spiritualisms, materialisations, theosophies,* all the rabble rant of imposture, with their
machinery of poor tricks and feeble conjuring, the true back-parlour magic of
shabby London streets. Yet, in spite of what I have said, I must confess to you
that I am no materialist, taking the word of course in its usual signification. It
is now many years since I have convinced myself, convinced myself a sceptic
remember, that the old iron-bound theory is utterly and entirely false. Perhaps
this confession will not wound you so sharply as it would have done twenty
years ago; for I think you cannot have failed to notice that for some time
hypotheses have been advanced by men of pure science which are nothing less
than transcendental, and I suspect that most modern chemists and biologists of
repute would not hesitate to subscribe the *dictum* of the old Schoolman, *Omnia*

*exeunt in mysterium*,* which means, I take it, that every branch of human knowledge if traced up to its source and final principles vanishes into mystery. I need
not trouble you now with a detailed account of the painful steps which led me
to my conclusions; a few simple experiments suggested a doubt as to my then
standpoint, and a train of thought that rose from circumstances comparatively
trifling brought me far; my old conception of the universe has been swept away,
and I stand in a world that seems as strange and awful to me as the endless
waves of the ocean seen for the first time, shining, from a peak in Darien.* Now
I know that the walls of sense that seemed so impenetrable, that seemed to loom
up above the heavens and to be founded below the depths, and to shut us in for
evermore, are no such everlasting impassable barriers as we fancied, but thin-
nest and most airy veils that melt away before the seeker, and dissolve as the
early mist of the morning about the brooks. I know that you never adopted the
extreme materialistic position; you did not go about trying to prove a universal
negative, for your logical sense withheld you from that crowning absurdity; but
I am sure that you will find all that I am saying strange and repellent to your
habits of thought. Yet, Haberden, what I tell you is the truth, nay, to adopt our
common language, the sole and scientific truth, verified by experience; and the
universe is verily more splendid and more awful than we used to dream.
The whole universe, my friend, is a tremendous sacrament; a mystic, ineffable
force and energy, veiled by an outward form of matter; and man, and the sun
and the other stars, and the flower of the grass, and the crystal in the test-tube,
are each and every one as spiritual, as material, and subject to an inner working.

'You will perhaps wonder, Haberden, whence all this tends; but I think a little thought will make it clear. You will understand that from such a standpoint
the whole view of things is changed, and what we thought incredible and absurd
may be possible enough. In short, we must look at legend and belief with other
eyes, and be prepared to accept tales that had become mere fables. Indeed, this
is no such great demand. After all, modern science will concede as much, in
a hypocritical manner; you must not, it is true, believe in witchcraft, but you
may credit hypnotism; ghosts are out of date, but there is a good deal to be said
for the theory of telepathy.* Give a superstition a Greek name, and believe in it,
should almost be a proverb.

'So much for my personal explanation. You sent me, Haberden, a phial, stoppered and sealed, containing a small quantity of a flaky white powder, obtained
from a chemist who has been dispensing it to one of your patients. I am not
surprised to hear that this powder refused to yield any results to your analysis.
It is a substance which was known to a few many hundred years ago, but which
I never expected to have submitted to me from the shop of a modern apothecary. There seems no reason to doubt the truth of the man's tale; he no doubt
got, as he says, the rather uncommon salt you prescribed from the wholesale
chemist's; and it has probably remained on his shelf for twenty years, or perhaps longer. Here what we call chance and coincidence begin to work; during
all these years the salt in the bottle was exposed to certain recurring variations
of temperature, variations probably ranging from 40° to 80°. And, as it happens, such changes, recurring year after year at irregular intervals, and with
varying degrees of intensity and duration, have constituted a process, and

a process so complicated and so delicate, that I question whether modern scientific apparatus directed with the utmost precision could produce the same result. The white powder you sent me is something very different from the drug you prescribed; it is the powder from which the wine of the Sabbath, the *Vinum Sabbati*, was prepared. No doubt you have read of the Witches' Sabbath, and have laughed at the tales which terrified our ancestors; the black cats, and the broomsticks, and dooms pronounced against some old woman's cow. Since I have known the truth I have often reflected that it is on the whole a happy thing that such burlesque as this is believed, for it serves to conceal much that it is better should not be known generally. However, if you care to read the appendix to Payne Knight's monograph,* you will find that the true Sabbath was something very different, though the writer has very nicely refrained from printing all he knew. The secrets of the true Sabbath were the secrets of remote times surviving into the Middle Ages, secrets of an evil science which existed long before Aryan man entered Europe.* Men and women, seduced from their homes on specious pretences, were met by beings well qualified to assume, as they did assume, the part of devils, and taken by their guides to some desolate and lonely place, known to the initiate by long tradition, and unknown to all else. Perhaps it was a cave in some bare and wind-swept hill, perhaps some inmost recess of a great forest, and there the Sabbath was held. There, in the blackest hour of night, the *Vinum Sabbati* was prepared, and this evil graal was poured forth and offered to the neophytes, and they partook of an infernal sacrament; *sumentes calicem principis inferorum*,* as an old author well expresses it. And suddenly, each one that had drunk found himself attended by a companion, a shape of glamour and unearthly allurement, beckoning him apart, to share in joys more exquisite, more piercing than the thrill of any dream, to the consummation of the marriage of the Sabbath. It is hard to write of such things as these, and chiefly because that shape that allured with loveliness was no hallucination, but, awful as it is to express, the man himself. By the power of that Sabbath wine, a few grains of white powder thrown into a glass of water, the house of life was riven asunder and the human trinity dissolved, and the worm which never dies,* that which lies sleeping within us all, was made tangible and an external thing, and clothed with a garment of flesh. And then, in the hour of midnight, the primal fall was repeated and re-presented, and the awful thing veiled in the mythos of the Tree in the Garden was done anew. Such was the *nuptiæ Sabbati*.

'I prefer to say no more; you, Haberden, know as well as I do that the most trivial laws of life are not to be broken with impunity; and for so terrible an act as this, in which the very inmost place of the temple was broken open and defiled, a terrible vengeance followed. What began with corruption ended also with corruption.'

Underneath is the following in Dr Haberden's writing:—

The whole of the above is unfortunately strictly and entirely true. Your brother confessed all to me on that morning when I saw him in his room. My attention was first attracted to the bandaged hand, and I forced him to show it me. What I saw made me, a medical man of many years standing, grow sick with loathing, and the story I was forced to listen to was infinitely more frightful than I could have believed possible. It has tempted me to doubt the Eternal Goodness which can permit nature to offer such hideous possibilities; and if you had not with your own eyes seen the end, I should have said to you—disbelieve it all. I have not, I think, many more weeks to live, but you are young, and may forget all this.

JOSEPH HABERDEN, M.D.

In the course of two or three months I heard that Dr Haberden had died at sea shortly after the ship left England.

Miss Leicester ceased speaking, and looked pathetically at Dyson, who could not refrain from exhibiting some symptoms of uneasiness.

He stuttered out some broken phrases expressive of his deep interest in her extraordinary history, and then said with a better grace—

'But, pardon me, Miss Leicester, I understood you were in some difficulty. You were kind enough to ask me to assist you in some way.'

'Ah,' she said, 'I had forgotten that; my own present trouble seems of such little consequence in comparison with what I have told you. But as you are so good to me, I will go on. You will scarcely believe it, but I found that certain persons suspected, or rather pretended to suspect, that I had murdered my brother. These persons were relatives of mine, and their motives were extremely sordid ones; but I actually found myself subject to the shameful indignity of being watched. Yes, sir, my steps were dogged when I went abroad, and at home I found myself exposed to constant if artful observation. With my high spirit this was more than I could brook, and I resolved to set my wits to work and elude the persons who were shadowing me. I was so fortunate as to succeed; I assumed this disguise, and for some time have lain snug and unsuspected. But of late I have reason to believe that the pursuer is on my track; unless I am greatly deceived, I saw yesterday the detective who is charged with the odious duty of observing my movements. You, sir, are watchful and keen-sighted; tell me, did you see any one lurking about this evening?'

'I hardly think so,' said Dyson, 'but perhaps you would give me some description of the detective in question.'

'Certainly; he is a youngish man, dark, with dark whiskers. He has adopted spectacles of large size in the hope of disguising himself effectually, but he cannot disguise his uneasy manner, and the quick, nervous glances he casts to right and left.'

This piece of description was the last straw for the unhappy Dyson, who was foaming with impatience to get out of the house, and would gladly have sworn eighteenth-century oaths, if propriety had not frowned on such a course.

'Excuse me, Miss Leicester,' he said with cold politeness, 'I cannot assist you.'

'Ah,' she said sadly, 'I have offended you in some way. Tell me what I have done, and I will ask you to forgive me.'

'You are mistaken,' said Dyson, grabbing his hat, but speaking with some difficulty; 'you have done nothing. But, as I say, I cannot help you. Perhaps,' he added, with some tinge of sarcasm, 'my friend Russell might be of service.'

'Thank you,' she replied; 'I will try him,' and the lady went off into a shriek of laughter, which filled up Mr Dyson's cup of scandal and confusion.

He left the house shortly afterwards, and had the peculiar delight of a five-mile walk, through streets which slowly changed from black to grey, and from grey to shining passages of glory for the sun to brighten. Here and there he met or overtook strayed revellers, but he reflected that no one could have spent the night in a more futile fashion than himself; and when he reached his home he had made resolves for reformation. He decided that he would abjure all Milesian and Arabian methods of entertainment,* and subscribe to Mudie's for a regular supply of mild and innocuous romance.*

## STRANGE OCCURRENCE IN CLERKENWELL

MR DYSON had inhabited for some years a couple of rooms in a moderately quiet street in Bloomsbury, where, as he somewhat pompously expressed it, he held his finger on the pulse of life without being deafened with the thousand rumours of the main arteries of London. It was to him a source of peculiar, if esoteric, gratification that from the adjacent corner of Tottenham Court Road a hundred lines of omnibuses went to the four quarters of the town; he would dilate on the facilities for visiting Dalston, and dwell on the admirable line that knew extremest Ealing and the streets beyond Whitechapel. His rooms, which had been originally 'furnished apartments,' he had gradually purged of their more peccant parts; and though one would not find here the glowing splendours of his old chambers in the street off the Strand, there was something of severe grace about the appointments which did credit to his taste. The rugs were old, and of the true faded beauty; the etchings, nearly all of them proofs printed by the artist, made a good show with broad white margins and black frames, and there was no spurious black oak. Indeed, there was but little furniture of any kind: a plain and honest table, square and sturdy, stood in one corner; a seventeenth-century settle fronted the hearth; and two wooden elbow-chairs and a bookshelf of the Empire* made up the equipment, with an exception worthy of note. For Dyson cared for none of these things, his place was at his own bureau, a quaint old piece of lacquered-work,* at which he would sit for hour after hour, with his back to the room, engaged in the desperate pursuit of literature, or, as he termed his profession, the chase of the phrase. The neat array of pigeon-holes and drawers teemed and overflowed with manuscript and note-books, the experiments and efforts of many years; and the inner well, a vast and cavernous receptacle, was stuffed with accumulated ideas. Dyson was a craftsman who loved all the detail and the technique of his work intensely; and if, as has been hinted, he deluded himself a little with the name of artist, yet his amusements were eminently harmless, and, so far as can be ascertained, he (or the publishers) had chosen the good part of not tiring the world with printed matter.

Here, then, Dyson would shut himself up with his fancies, experimenting with words, and striving, as his friend the recluse of Bayswater strove, with the almost invincible problem of style, but always with a fine confidence, extremely different from the chronic depression of the realist. He had been almost continuously at work on some scheme that struck him as wellnigh magical in its possibilities since the night of his adventure with the ingenious tenant of the first floor in Abingdon Grove; and as he laid down the pen with a glow of triumph, he reflected that he had not viewed the streets for five days in succession. With all the enthusiasm of his accomplished labour still working in his brain, he put away his papers and went out, pacing the pavement at first in that rare mood of exultation which finds in every stone upon the way the possibilities of a masterpiece. It was growing late, and the autumn evening was drawing to a close amidst veils of haze and mist, and in the stilled air the voices, and the roaring traffic, and incessant feet seemed to Dyson like the noise upon the stage when all the house is silent. In the square the leaves rippled down as quick as summer rain, and the street beyond was beginning to flare with the lights in the butcher's shops and the vivid illumination of the greengrocer. It was a Saturday night, and the swarming populations of the slums were turning out in force; the battered women in rusty black had begun to paw the lumps of cagmag,* and others gloated over unwholesome cabbages, and there was a brisk demand for four-ale. Dyson passed through these night-fires with some relief; he loved to meditate, but his thoughts were not as De Quincey's after his dose;* he cared not two straws whether onions were dear or cheap, and would not have exulted if meat had fallen to twopence a pound. Absorbed in the wilderness of the tale he had been writing, weighing nicely the points of plot and construction, relishing the recollection of this and that happy phrase, and dreading failure here and there, he left the rush and whistle of the gas-flares behind him, and began to touch upon pavements more deserted.

He had turned, without taking note, to the northward, and was passing through an ancient fallen street, where now notices of floors and offices to let hung out, but still about it there was the grace and the stiffness of the Age of Wigs—a broad roadway, a broad pavement, and on each side a grave line of houses with long and narrow windows flush with the walls, all of mellowed brickwork. Dyson walked with quick steps, as he resolved that short work must be made of a certain episode; but he was in that happy humour of invention, and another chapter rose in the inner chamber of his brain, and he dwelt on the circumstances he was to write down with curious pleasure. It was charming to have the quiet streets to walk in, and in his thought he made a whole district the cabinet of his studies, and vowed he would come again. Heedless of his course, he struck off to the east again, and soon found himself involved in a squalid network of grey two-storied houses, and then in the waste void and elements of brickwork, the passages and unmade roads behind great factory walls, encumbered with the refuse of the neighbourhood, forlorn, ill-lighted, and desperate. A brief turn, and there rose before him the unexpected, a hill suddenly lifted from the level ground, its steep ascent marked by the lighted lamps, and eager as an explorer, Dyson found his way to the place, wondering where his crooked paths had brought him. Here all was again decorous, but hideous in the extreme. The builder, some one lost in the deep gloom of the early 'twenties, had conceived the idea of twin villas in grey brick, shaped in a manner to recall the outlines of the Parthenon,* each with its classic form broadly marked with raised bands of stucco. The name of the street was all strange, and for a further surprise the top of the hill was crowned with an irregular plot of grass and fading trees, called a square, and here again the Parthenon-motive had persisted. Beyond, the streets were curious, wild in their irregularities, here a row of sordid, dingy dwellings, dirty and disreputable in appearance, and there, without warning, stood a house, genteel and prim, with wire blinds and brazen knocker, as clean and trim as if it had been the doctor's house in some benighted little country town. These surprises and discoveries began to exhaust Dyson, and he hailed with delight the blazing windows of a public-house, and went in with the intention of testing the beverage provided for the dwellers in this region, as remote as Libya and Pamphylia and the parts about Mesopotamia.* The babble of voices from within warned him that he was about to assist at the true parliament of the London workman, and he looked about him for that more retired entrance called private. When he had settled himself on an exiguous bench, and had ordered some beer, he began to listen to the jangling talk in the public bar beyond; it was a senseless argument, alternately furious and maudlin, with appeals to Bill and Tom, and mediæval survivals of speech, words that Chaucer wrote* belched out with zeal and relish, and the din of pots jerked down and coppers rapped smartly on the zinc counter made a thorough bass for it all. Dyson was calmly smoking his pipe between the sips of beer, when an indefinite-looking figure slid rather than walked into the compartment. The man started violently when he saw Dyson placidly sitting in the corner, and glanced keenly about him. He seemed to be on wires, controlled by some electric machine, for he almost bolted out of the door when the barman asked with what he could serve him, and his hand shivered as he took the glass. Dyson inspected him with a little curiosity. He was muffled up almost to the lips, and a soft felt hat was drawn down over his eyes; he looked as if he shrank from every glance, and a more raucous voice suddenly uplifted in the public bar seemed to find in him a sympathy that made him shake and quiver like a jelly. It was pitiable to see any one so thrilled with nervousness, and Dyson was about to address some trivial remark of casual inquiry to the man, when another person came into the compartment, and, laying a hand on his arm, muttered something in an undertone, and vanished as he came. But Dyson had recognised him as the smooth-tongued and smooth-shaven Burton, who had displayed so sumptuous a gift in lying; and yet he thought little of it, for his whole faculty of observation was absorbed in the lamentable and yet grotesque spectacle before him. At the first touch of the hand on his arm the unfortunate man had wheeled round as if spun on a pivot, and shrank back with a low, piteous cry, as if some dumb beast were caught in the toils. The blood fled away from the wretch's face, and the skin became grey as if a shadow of death had passed in the air and fallen on it, and Dyson caught a choking whisper—

'Mr Davies! For God's sake, have pity on me, Mr Davies! On my oath, I say——' and his voice sank to silence as he heard the message, and strove in vain to bite his lip, and summon up to his aid some tinge of manhood. He stood there a moment, wavering as the leaves of an aspen, and then he was gone out into the street, as Dyson thought silently, with his doom upon his head. He had not been gone a minute when it suddenly flashed into Dyson's mind that he knew the man; it was undoubtedly the young man with spectacles for whom so many ingenious persons were searching; the spectacles indeed were missing, but the pale face, the dark whiskers, and the timid glances were enough to identify him. Dyson saw at once that by a succession of hazards he had unawares hit upon the scent of some desperate conspiracy, wavering as the track of a loathsome snake in and out of the highways and byways of the London cosmos; the truth was instantly pictured before him, and he divined that all unconscious and unheeding he had been privileged to see the shadows of hidden forms, chasing and hurrying, and grasping and vanishing across the bright curtain of common life, soundless and silent, or only babbling fables and pretences. For him in an instant the jargoning of voices, the garish splendour, and all the vulgar tumult of the public-house became part of magic; for here before his eyes a scene in this grim mystery play* had been enacted, and he had seen human flesh grow grey with a palsy of fear; the very hell of cowardice and terror had gaped wide within an arm's-breadth. In the midst of these reflections the barman came up and stared at him as if to hint that he had exhausted his right to take his ease, and Dyson bought another lease of the seat by an order for more beer. As he pondered the brief glimpse of tragedy, he recollected that with his first start of haunted fear the young man with whiskers had drawn his hand swiftly from his greatcoat pocket, and that he had heard something fall to the ground; and pretending to have dropped his pipe, Dyson began to grope in the corner, searching with his fingers. He touched something and drew it gently to him, and with one brief glance, as he put it quietly in his pocket, he saw it was a little old-fashioned notebook, bound in faded green morocco.

He drank down his beer at a gulp, and left the place, overjoyed at his fortunate discovery, and busy with conjecture as to the possible importance of the find. By turns he dreaded to find perhaps mere blank leaves, or the laboured follies of a betting-book, but the faded morocco cover seemed to promise better things, and hint at mysteries. He piloted himself with no little difficulty out of the sour and squalid quarter he had entered with a light heart, and emerging at Gray's Inn Road, struck off down Guilford Street and hastened home, only anxious for a lighted candle and solitude.

Dyson sat down at his bureau, and placed the little book before him; it was an effort to open the leaves and dare disappointment. But in desperation at last he laid his finger between the pages at haphazard, and rejoiced to see a compact range of writing with a margin, and as it chanced, three words caught his glance and stood out apart from the mass. Dyson read

'*the Gold Tiberius,*'

and his face flushed with fortune and the lust of the hunter.

He turned at once to the first leaf of the pocket-book, and proceeded to read with rapt interest the

### HISTORY OF THE YOUNG MAN WITH SPECTACLES

From the filthy and obscure lodging, situated, I verily believe, in one of the foulest slums of Clerkenwell, I indite this history of a life which, daily threatened, cannot last for very much longer. Every day—nay, every hour, I know too well my enemies are drawing their nets closer about me; even now I am condemned to be a close prisoner in my squalid room, and I know that when I go out I shall go to my destruction. This history, if it chance to fall into good hands, may, perhaps, be of service in warning young men of the dangers and pitfalls that most surely must accompany any deviation from the ways of rectitude.

My name is Joseph Walters. When I came of age I found myself in possession of a small but sufficient income, and I determined that I would devote my life to scholarship. I do not mean the scholarship of these days; I had no intention of associating myself with men whose lives are spent in the unspeakably degrading occupation of 'editing' classics, befouling the fair margins of the fairest books with idle and superfluous annotation, and doing their utmost to give a lasting disgust of all that is beautiful. An abbey church turned to the base use of a stable or a bakehouse is a sorry sight; but more pitiable still is a masterpiece spluttered over with the commentator's pen, and his hideous mark 'cf.'

For my part, I chose the glorious career of scholar in its ancient sense; I longed to possess encyclopædic learning, to grow old amongst books, to distil day by day, and year after year, the inmost sweetness of all worthy writings. I was not rich enough to collect a library, and I was therefore forced to betake myself to the Reading-Room of the British Museum.*

O dim, far-lifted, and mighty dome, Mecca of many minds, mausoleum of many hopes, sad house where all desires fail! For there men enter in with hearts uplifted, and dreaming minds, seeing in those exalted stairs a ladder to fame, in that pompous portico the gate of knowledge, and going in, find but vain vanity, and all but in vain. There, when the long streets are ringing, is silence, there eternal twilight, and the odour of heaviness. But there the blood flows thin and cold, and the brain burns adust; there is the hunt of shadows, and the chase of embattled phantoms; a striving against ghosts, and a war that has no victory. O dome, tomb of the quick! surely in thy galleries, where no reverberant voice can call, sighs whisper ever, and mutterings of dead hopes; and there men's souls mount like moths towards the flame, and fall scorched and blackened beneath thee, O dim, far-lifted, and mighty dome!

Bitterly do I now regret the day when I took my place at a desk for the first time, and began my studies. I had not been an *habitué* of the place for many months, when I became acquainted with a serene and benevolent gentleman, a man somewhat past middle age, who nearly always occupied a desk next to mine. In the Reading-Room it takes little to make an acquaintance, a casual offer of assistance, a hint as to the search in the catalogue, and the ordinary politeness of men who constantly sit near each other; it was thus I came to know the man calling himself Dr Lipsius. By degrees I grew to look for his presence, and to miss him when he was away, as was sometimes the case, and so a friendship sprang up between us. His immense range of learning was placed freely at my service; he would often astonish me by the way in which he would sketch out in a few minutes the bibliography of a given subject, and before long I had confided to him my ambitions.

'Ah,' he said, 'you should have been a German. I was like that myself when I was a boy. It is a wonderful resolve, an infinite career. I will know all things; yes, it is a device indeed. But it means this—a life of labour without end, and a desire unsatisfied at last. The scholar has to die, and die saying, "I know very little!"'

Gradually, by speeches such as these, Lipsius seduced me: he would praise the career, and at the same time hint that it was as hopeless as the search for the philosopher's stone,* and so by artful suggestions, insinuated with infinite address, he by degrees succeeded in undermining all my principles. 'After all,' he used to say, 'the greatest of all sciences, the key to all knowledge, is the science and art of pleasure. Rabelais was perhaps the greatest of all the encyclopædic scholars; and he, as you know, wrote the most remarkable book that has ever been written. And what does he teach men in this book? Surely the joy of living. I need not remind you of the words, suppressed in most of the editions, the key of all the Rabelaisian mythology, of all the enigmas of his grand philosophy, *Vivez joyeux*.* There you have all his learning; his work is the institutes of pleasure as the fine art; the finest art there is; the art of all arts. Rabelais had all science, but he had all life too. And we have gone a long way since his time. You are enlightened, I think; you do not consider all the petty rules and by-laws that a corrupt society has made for its own selfish convenience as the immutable decrees of the eternal.'

Such were the doctrines that he preached; and it was by such insidious arguments, line upon line, here a little and there a little, that he at last succeeded in making me a man at war with the whole social system. I used to long for some opportunity to break the chains and to live a free life, to be my own rule and measure. I viewed existence with the eyes of a pagan, and Lipsius understood to perfection the art of stimulating the natural inclinations of a young man hitherto a hermit. As I gazed up at the great dome I saw it flushed with the flames and colours of a world of enticement, unknown to me, my imagination played me a thousand wanton tricks, and the forbidden drew me as surely as a lodestone draws on iron. At last my resolution was taken, and I boldly asked Lipsius to be my guide.

He told me to leave the Museum at my usual hour, half-past four, to walk slowly along the northern pavement of Great Russell Street, and to wait at the corner of the street till I was addressed, and then to obey in all things the instructions of the person who came up to me. I carried out these directions, and stood at the corner looking about me anxiously, my heart beating fast, and my breath coming in gasps. I waited there for some time, and had begun to fear I had been made the object of a joke, when I suddenly became conscious of a gentleman who was looking at me with evident amusement from the opposite pavement of Tottenham Court Road. He came over, and raising his hat, politely begged me to follow him, and I did so without a word, wondering where we were going, and what was to happen. I was taken to a house of quiet and respectable aspect in a street lying to the north of Oxford Street, and my guide rang the bell. A servant showed us into a large room, quietly furnished, on the ground floor. We sat there in silence for some time, and I noticed that the furniture, though unpretending, was extremely valuable. There were large oak presses, two book-cases of extreme elegance, and in one corner a carved chest which must have been mediæval. Presently Dr Lipsius came in and welcomed me with his usual manner, and after some desultory conversation my guide left the room. Then an elderly man dropped in and began talking to Lipsius, and from their conversation I understood that my friend was a dealer in antiques; they spoke of the Hittite seal, and of the prospects of further discoveries, and later, when two or three more persons had joined us, there was an argument as to the possibility of a systematic exploration of the pre-Celtic monuments in England. I was, in fact, present at an archæological reception of an informal kind; and at nine o'clock, when the antiquaries were gone, I stared at Lipsius in a manner that showed I was puzzled, and sought an explanation.

'Now,' he said, 'we will go upstairs.'

As we passed up the stairs, Lipsius lighting the way with a hand-lamp, I heard the sound of a jarring lock and bolts and bars shot on at the front door. My guide drew back a baize door* and we went down a passage, and I began to hear odd sounds, a noise of curious mirth; then he pushed me through a second door, and my initiation began. I cannot write down what I witnessed that night; I cannot bear to recall what went on in those secret rooms fast shuttered and curtained so that no light should escape into the quiet street; they gave me red wine to drink, and a woman told me as I sipped it that it was wine of the Red Jar that Avallaunius* had made. Another asked me how I liked the wine of the Fauns, and I heard a dozen fantastic names, while the stuff boiled in my veins, and stirred, I think, something that had slept within me from the moment I was born. It seemed as if my self-consciousness deserted me; I was no longer a thinking agent, but at once subject and object; I mingled in the horrible sport, and watched the mystery of the Greek groves and fountains enacted before me, saw the reeling dance and heard the music calling as I sat beside my mate, and yet I was outside it all, and viewed my own part an idle spectator. Thus with strange rites they made me drink the cup, and when I woke up in the morning I was one of them, and had sworn to be faithful. At first I was shown the enticing side of things; I was bidden to enjoy myself and care for nothing but pleasure, and Lipsius himself indicated to me as the acutest enjoyment the spectacle of the terrors of the unfortunate persons who were from time to time decoyed into the evil house. But after a time it was pointed out to me that I must take my share in the work, and so I found myself compelled to be in my turn a seducer; and thus it is on my conscience that I have led many to the depths of the pit.

One day Lipsius summoned me to his private room, and told me that he had a difficult task to give me. He unlocked a drawer and gave me a sheet of type-written paper, and bade me read it.

It was without place, or date, or signature, and ran as follows:—

Mr James Headley, F.S.A., will receive from his agent in Armenia, on the 12th inst., a unique coin, the gold Tiberius. It bears on the reverse a faun with the legend VICTORIA. It is believed that this coin is of immense value. Mr Headley will come up to town to show the coin to his friend, Professor Memys, of Chenies Street, Oxford Street, on some date between the 13th and the 18th.

Dr Lipsius chuckled at my face of blank surprise when I laid down this singular communication.

'You will have a good chance of showing your discretion,' he said. 'This is not a common case; it requires great management and infinite tact. I am sure I wish I had a Panurge* in my service, but we will see what you can do.'

'But is it not a joke?' I asked him. 'How can you know—or rather, how can this correspondent of yours know—that a coin has been despatched from Armenia to Mr Headley? And how is it possible to fix the period in which Mr Headley will take it into his head to come up to town? It seems to me a lot of guesswork.'

'My dear Mr Walters,' he replied, 'we do not deal in guesswork here. It would bore you if I went into all these little details, the cogs and wheels, if I may say so, which move the machine. Don't you think it is much more amusing to sit in front of the house and be astonished than to be behind the scenes and see the mechanism? Better tremble at the thunder, believe me, than see the man rolling the cannon-ball. But, after all, you needn't bother about the how and why; you have your share to do. Of course, I shall give you full instructions, but a great deal depends on the way the thing is carried out. I have often heard very young men maintain that style is everything in literature,* and I can assure you that the same maxim holds good in our far more delicate profession. With us style is absolutely everything, and that is why we have friends like yourself.'

I went away in some perturbation; he had no doubt designedly left everything in mystery, and I did not know what part I should have to play. Though I had assisted at scenes of hideous revelry, I was not yet dead to all echo of human feeling, and I trembled lest I should receive the order to be Mr Headley's executioner.

A week later, it was on the sixteenth of the month, Dr Lipsius made me a sign to come into his room.

'It is for to-night,' he began. 'Please to attend carefully to what I am going to say, Mr Walters, and on peril of your life, for it is a dangerous matter,—on peril of your life, I say, follow these instructions to the letter. You understand? Well, to-night at about half-past seven, you will stroll quietly up the Hampstead Road till you come to Vincent Street. Turn down here and walk along, taking the third turning to your right, which is Lambert Terrace. Then follow the terrace, cross the road, and go along Hertford Street, and so into Lillington Square. The second turning you will come to in the square is called Sheen Street; but in reality it is more a passage between blank walls than a street. Whatever you do, take care to be at the corner of this street at eight o'clock precisely. You will walk along it, and just at the bend, where you lose sight of the square, you will find an old gentleman with white beard and whiskers. He will in all probability be abusing a cabman for having brought him to Sheen Street instead of Chenies Street. You will go up to him quietly and offer your services; he will tell you where he wants to go, and you will be so courteous as to offer to show him the way. I may say that Professor Memys moved into Chenies Street a month ago; thus Mr Headley has never been to see him there, and, moreover, he is very short-sighted, and knows little of the topography of London. Indeed, he has quite lived the life of a learned hermit at Audley Hall.

'Well, need I say more to a man of your intelligence? You will bring him to this house, he will ring the bell, and a servant in quiet livery will let him in. Then your work will be done, and I am sure done well. You will leave Mr Headley at the door, and simply continue your walk, and I shall hope to see you the next day. I really don't think there is anything more I can tell you.'

These minute instructions I took care to carry out to the letter. I confess that I walked up the Tottenham Court Road by no means blindly, but with an uneasy sense that I was coming to a decisive point in my life. The noise and rumour of the crowded pavements were to me but dumb-show; I revolved again and again in ceaseless iteration the task that had been laid on me, and I questioned myself as to the possible results. As I got near the point of turning, I asked myself whether danger were not about my steps; the cold thought struck me that I was suspected and observed, and every chance foot-passenger who gave me a second glance seemed to me an officer of police. My time was running out, the sky had darkened, and I hesitated, half resolved to go no farther, but to abandon Lipsius and his friends for ever. I had almost determined to take this course, when the conviction suddenly came to me that the whole thing was a gigantic joke, a fabrication of rank improbability. Who could have procured the information about the Armenian agent? I asked myself. By what means could Lipsius have known the particular day and the very train that Mr Headley was to take? how engage him to enter one special cab amongst the dozens waiting at Paddington? I vowed it a mere Milesian tale, and went forward merrily, turned down Vincent Street, and threaded out the route that Lipsius had so carefully impressed upon me. The various streets he had named were all places of silence and an oppressive cheap gentility; it was dark, and I felt alone in the musty squares and crescents, where people pattered by at intervals, and the shadows were growing blacker. I entered Sheen Street, and found it as Lipsius had said, more a passage than a street; it was a byway, on one side a low wall and neglected gardens, and grim backs of a line of houses, and on the other a timberyard. I turned the corner, and lost sight of the square, and then, to my astonishment, I saw the scene of which I had been told. A hansom cab had come to a stop beside the pavement, and an old man, carrying a handbag, was fiercely abusing the cabman, who sat on his perch the image of bewilderment.

'Yes, but I'm sure you said Sheen Street, and that's where I brought you,' I heard him saying as I came up, and the old gentleman boiled in a fury, and threatened police and suits at law.

The sight gave me a shock, and in an instant I resolved to go through with it. I strolled on, and without noticing the cabman, lifted my hat politely to old Mr Headley.

'Pardon me, sir,' I said, 'but is there any difficulty? I see you are a traveller; perhaps the cabman has made a mistake. Can I direct you?'

The old fellow turned to me, and I noticed that he snarled and showed his teeth like an ill-tempered cur as he spoke.

'This drunken fool has brought me here,' he said. 'I told him to drive to Chenies Street, and he brings me to this infernal place. I won't pay him a farthing, and I meant to have given him a handsome sum. I am going to call for the police and give him in charge.'

At this threat the cabman seemed to take alarm; he glanced round, as if to make sure that no policeman was in sight, and drove off grumbling loudly, and Mr Headley grinned savagely with satisfaction at having saved his fare, and put back one and sixpence into his pocket, the 'handsome sum' the cabman had lost.

'My dear sir,' I said, 'I am afraid this piece of stupidity has annoyed you a great deal. It is a long way to Chenies Street, and you will have some difficulty in finding the place unless you know London pretty well.'

'I know it very little,' he replied. 'I never come up except on important business, and I've never been to Chenies Street in my life.'

'Really? I should be happy to show you the way. I have been for a stroll, and it will not at all inconvenience me to take you to your destination.'

'I want to go to Professor Memys, at number 15. It's most annoying to me; I'm short-sighted, and I can never make out the numbers on the doors.'

'This way, if you please,' I said, and we set out.

I did not find Mr Headley an agreeable man; indeed, he grumbled the whole way. He informed me of his name, and I took care to say, 'The well-known antiquary?' and thenceforth I was compelled to listen to the history of his complicated squabbles with publishers, who had treated him, as he said, disgracefully; the man was a chapter in the Irritability of Authors.* He told me that he had been on the point of making the fortune of several firms, but had been compelled to abandon the design owing to their rank ingratitude. Besides these ancient histories of wrong, and the more recent misadventure of the cabman, he had another grievous complaint to make. As he came along in the train, he had been sharpening a pencil, and the sudden jolt of the engine as it drew up at a station had driven the penknife against his face, inflicting a small triangular wound just on the cheek-bone, which he showed me. He denounced the railway company, heaped imprecations on the head of the driver, and talked of claiming damages. Thus he grumbled all the way, not noticing in the least where he was going; and so unamiable did his conduct appear to me, that I began to enjoy the trick I was playing on him.

Nevertheless, my heart beat a little faster as we turned into the street where Lipsius was waiting. A thousand accidents, I thought, might happen; some chance might bring one of Headley's friends to meet us; perhaps, though he knew not Chenies Street, he might know the street where I was taking him; in spite of his short-sight he might possibly make out the number; or, in a sudden fit of suspicion, he might make an inquiry of the policeman at the corner. Thus every step upon the pavement, as we drew nearer to the goal, was to me a pang and a terror, and every approaching passenger carried a certain threat of danger. I gulped down my excitement with an effort, and made shift to say pretty quietly—

'Number 15, I think you said? That is the third house from this. If you will allow me I will leave you now; I have been delayed a little, and my way lies on the other side of Tottenham Court Road.'

He snarled out some kind of thanks, and I turned my back and walked swiftly in the opposite direction. A minute or two later I looked round, and saw Mr Headley standing on the doorstep, and then the door opened and he went in. For my part, I gave a sigh of relief; I hastened to get away from the neighbourhood, and endeavoured to enjoy myself in merry company.

The whole of the next day I kept away from Lipsius. I felt anxious, but I did not know what had happened, or what was happening, and a reasonable regard for my own safety told me that I should do well to remain quietly at home. My curiosity, however, to learn the end of the odd drama in which I had played a part stung me to the quick, and late in the evening I made up my mind to go and see how events had turned out. Lipsius nodded when I came in, and asked me if I could give him five minutes' talk, We went into his room, and he began to walk up and down, while I sat waiting for him to speak.

'My dear Mr Walters,' he said at length, 'I congratulate you warmly; your work was done in the most thorough and artistic manner. You will go far. Look.'

He went to his escritoire and pressed a secret spring; a drawer flew out, and he laid something on the table. It was a gold coin; I took it up and examined it eagerly, and read the legend about the figure of the faun.

'Victoria,' I said, smiling.

'Yes; it was a great capture, which we owe to you. I had great difficulty in persuading Mr Headley that a little mistake had been made; that was how I put it. He was very disagreeable, and indeed ungentlemanly, about it; didn't he strike you as a very cross old man?'

I held the coin, admiring the choice and rare design, clear cut as if from the mint; and I thought the fine gold glowed and burnt like a lamp.

'And what finally became of Mr Headley?' I said at last.

Lipsius smiled, and shrugged his shoulders.

'What on earth does it matter?' he said. 'He might be here, or there, or anywhere; but what possible consequence could it be? Besides, your question rather surprises me; you are an intelligent man, Mr Walters. Just think it over, and I'm sure you won't repeat the question.'

'My dear sir,' I said, 'I hardly think you are treating me fairly. You have paid me some handsome compliments on my share in the capture, and I naturally wish to know how the matter ended. From what I saw of Mr Headley, I should think you must have had some difficulty with him.'

He gave me no answer for the moment, but began again to walk up and down the room, apparently absorbed in thought.

'Well,' he said at last, 'I suppose there is something in what you say. We are certainly indebted to you. I have said that I have a high opinion of your intelligence, Mr Walters. Just look here, will you?'

He opened a door communicating with another room, and pointed.

There was a great box lying on the floor, a queer, coffin-shaped thing. I looked at it, and saw it was a mummy case, like those in the British Museum, vividly painted in the brilliant Egyptian colours, with I knew not what proclamation of dignity or hopes of life immortal. The mummy swathed about in the robes of death was lying within, and the face had been uncovered.

'You are going to send this away?' I said, forgetting the question I had put.

'Yes; I have an order from a local museum. Look a little more closely, Mr Walters.'

Puzzled by his manner, I peered into the face, while he held up the lamp. The flesh was black with the passing of the centuries; but as I looked I saw upon the right cheek bone a small triangular scar, and the secret of the mummy flashed upon me: I was looking at the dead body of the man whom I had decoyed into that house.

There was no thought or design of action in my mind. I held the accursed coin in my hand, burning me with a foretaste of hell, and I fled as I would have fled from pestilence and death, and dashed into the street in blind horror, not knowing where I went. I felt the gold coin grasped in my clenched fist, and throwing it away, I knew not where, I ran on and on through by-streets and dark ways, till at last I issued out into a crowded thoroughfare and checked myself. Then as conscious-ness returned I realised my instant peril, and understood what would happen if I fell into the hands of Lipsius. I knew that I had put forth my finger to thwart a relentless mechanism rather than a man. My recent adventure with the unfortunate Mr Headley had taught me that Lipsius had agents in all quarters; and I foresaw that if I fell into his hands, he would remain true to his doctrine of style, and cause me to die a death of some horrible and ingenious torture. I bent my whole mind to the task of outwitting him and his emissaries, three of whom I knew to have proved their ability for tracking down persons who for various reasons preferred to remain obscure. These servants of Lipsius were two men and a woman, and the woman was incomparably the most subtle and the most deadly. Yet I considered that I too had some portion of craft, and I took my resolve. Since then I have matched myself day by day and hour by hour against the ingenuity of Lipsius and his myrmidons.* For a time I was successful; though they beat furiously after me in the covert of London, I remained *perdu*,* and watched with some amuse-ment their frantic efforts to recover the scent lost in two or three min-utes. Every lure and wile was put forth to entice me from my hiding-place; I was informed by the medium of the public prints that what I had taken had been recovered, and meetings were proposed in which I might hope to gain a great deal without the slightest risk. I laughed at their endeav-ours, and began a little to despise the organisation I had so dreaded, and ventured more abroad. Not once or twice, but several times, I rec-ognised the two men who were charged with my capture, and I suc-ceeded in eluding them easily at close quarters; and a little hastily I decided that I had nothing to dread, and that my craft was greater than theirs. But in the meanwhile, while I congratulated myself on my cunning, the third of Lipsius's emissaries was weaving her nets; and in an evil hour I paid a visit to an old friend, a literary man named Russell, who lived in a quiet street in Bayswater. The woman, as I found out too late, a day or two ago, occupied rooms in the same house, and I was followed and tracked down. Too late, as I have said, I recognised that I had made a fatal mistake, and that I was besieged. Sooner or later I shall find myself in the power of an enemy without pity; and so surely as I leave this house I shall go to receive doom. I hardly dare to guess how it will at last fall upon me; my imagination, always a vivid one, paints to me appalling pictures of the unspeakable torture which I shall probably endure; and I know that I shall die with Lipsius standing near and gloating over the refinements of my suffering and my shame.

Hours, nay minutes, have become very precious to me. I sometimes pause in the midst of anticipating my tortures, to wonder whether even now I cannot hit upon some supreme stroke, some design of infinite subtlety, to free myself from the toils. But I find that the faculty of combination has left me; I am as the scholar in the old myth, deserted by the power which has helped me hitherto. I do not know when the supreme moment will come, but sooner or later it is inevitable; before long I shall receive sentence, and from the sentence to execution will not be long.

\*     \*     \*     \*     \*

I cannot remain here a prisoner any longer. I shall go out to-night when the streets are full of crowds and clamours, and make a last effort to escape.

\*     \*     \*     \*     \*

It was with profound astonishment that Dyson closed the little book, and thought of the strange series of incidents which had brought him into touch with the plots and counterplots connected with the Gold Tiberius. He had bestowed the coin carefully away, and he shuddered at the bare possibility of its place of deposit becoming known to the evil band who seemed to possess such extraordinary sources of information.

It had grown late while he read, and he put the pocket-book away, hoping with all his heart that the unhappy Walters might even at the eleventh hour escape the doom he dreaded.

## ADVENTURE OF THE DESERTED RESIDENCE

'A WONDERFUL story, as you say, an extraordinary sequence and play of coincidence. I confess that your expressions when you first showed me the Gold Tiberius were not exaggerated. But do you think that Walters has really some fearful fate to dread?'

'I cannot say. Who can presume to predict events when life itself puts on the robe of coincidence and plays at drama? Perhaps we have not yet reached the last chapter in the queer story. But, look, we are drawing near to the verge of London; there are gaps, you see, in the serried ranks of brick, and a vision of green fields beyond.'

Dyson had persuaded the ingenious Mr Phillipps to accompany him on one of those aimless walks to which he was himself so addicted. Starting from the very heart of London, they had made their way westward through the stony avenues, and were now just emerging from the red lines of an extreme suburb, and presently the half-finished road ended, a quiet lane began, and they were beneath the shade of elm-trees. The yellow autumn sunlight that had lit up the bare distance of the suburban street now filtered down through the boughs of the trees and shone on the glowing carpet of fallen leaves, and the pools of rain glittered and shot back the gleam of light. Over all the broad pastures there was peace and the happy rest of autumn before the great winds begin, and afar off London lay all vague and immense amidst the veiling mist; here and there a distant window catching the sun and kindling with fire, and a spire gleaming high, and below the streets in shadow, and the turmoil of life. Dyson and Phillipps walked on in silence beneath the high hedges, till at a turn of the lane they saw a mouldering and ancient gate standing open, and the prospect of a house at the end of a moss-grown carriage drive.

'There is a survival for you,' said Dyson; 'it has come to its last days, I imagine. Look how the laurels have grown gaunt and weedy, and black and bare beneath; look at the house, covered with yellow wash, and patched with green damp. Why, the very notice-board, which informs all and singular that the place is to be let, has cracked and half fallen.'

'Suppose we go in and see it,' said Phillipps; 'I don't think there is anybody about.'

They turned up the drive, and walked slowly towards this remnant of old days. It was a large, straggling house, with curved wings at either end, and behind a series of irregular roofs and projections, showing that the place had been added to at divers dates; the two wings were roofed in cupola fashion, and at one side, as they came nearer, they could see a stableyard, and a clock turret with a bell, and the dark masses of gloomy cedars. Amidst all the lineaments of dissolution there was but one note of contrast: the sun was setting beyond the elm-trees, and all the west and the south were in flames; on the upper windows of the house the glow shone reflected, and it seemed as if blood and fire were mingled. Before the yellow front of the mansion, stained, as Dyson had remarked, with gangrenous patches, green and blackening, stretched what once had been, no doubt, a well-kept lawn, but it was now rough and ragged, and nettles and great docks, and all manner of coarse weeds, struggled in the places of the flower-beds. The urns had fallen from their pillars beside the walk, and lay broken in shards upon the ground, and everywhere from grass-plot and path a fungoid growth had sprung up and multiplied, and lay dank and slimy like a festering sore upon the earth. In the middle of the rank grass of the lawn was a desolate foun-tain; the rim of the basin was crumbling and pulverised with decay, and within the water stood stagnant, with green scum for the lilies that had once bloomed there; rust had eaten into the bronze flesh of the Triton that stood in the middle, and the conch-shell he held was broken.

'Here,' said Dyson, 'one might moralise over decay and death. Here all the stage is decked out with the symbols of dissolution; the cedarn gloom and twilight hangs heavy around us, and everywhere within the pale dankness has found a harbour, and the very air is changed and brought to accord with the scene. To me, I confess, this deserted house is as moral as a graveyard, and I find something sublime in that lonely Triton, deserted in the midst of his water-pool. He is the last of the gods; they have left him, and he remembers the sound of water falling on water, and the days that were sweet.'

'I like your reflections extremely,' said Phillipps; 'but I may mention that the door of the house is open.'

'Let us go in, then.'

The door was just ajar, and they passed into the mouldy hall and looked in at a room on one side. It was a large room, going far back, and the rich, old, red flock paper* was peeling from the walls in long strips, and blackened with vague patches of rising damp; the ancient clay, the dank reeking earth rising up again, and subduing all the work of men's hands after the conquest of many years. The floor was thick with the dust of decay, and the painted ceiling fading from all gay colours and light fancies of cupids in a career, and disfigured with sores of damp-ness, seemed transmuted into other work. No longer the amorini* chased one another pleasantly, with limbs that sought not to advance, and hands that merely simulated the act of grasping at the wreathed flowers; but it appeared some savage burlesque of the old careless world and of its cherished conventions, and the dance of the Loves had become a Dance of Death; black pustules and festering sores swelled and clustered on fair limbs and smiling faces showed corruption, and the fairy blood had boiled with the germs of foul disease; it was a parable of the leaven working, and worms devouring for a banquet the heart of the rose.

Strangely, under the painted ceiling, against the decaying walls, two old chairs still stood alone, the sole furniture of the empty place. High-backed, with curving arms and twisted legs, covered with faded gold leaf, and upholstered in tattered damask,* they too were a part of the symbolism, and struck Dyson with surprise. 'What have we here?' he said. 'Who has sat in these chairs? Who, clad in peach-bloom satin, with lace ruffles and diamond buckles, all golden, a *conté fleurettes* to* his companion? Phillipps, we are in another age. I wish I had some snuff to offer you, but failing that, I beg to offer you a seat, and we will sit and smoke tobacco. A horrid practice, but I am no pedant.'

They sat down on the queer old chairs, and looked out of the dim and grimy panes to the ruined lawn, and the fallen urns, and the deserted Triton.

Presently Dyson ceased his imitation of eighteenth-century airs; he no longer pulled forward imaginary ruffles, or tapped a ghostly snuff-box.

'It's a foolish fancy,' he said, at last; 'but I keep thinking I hear a noise like some one groaning. Listen; no, I can't hear it now. There it is again! Did you notice it, Phillipps?'

'No, I can't say I heard anything. But I believe that old places like this are like shells from the shore, ever echoing with noises. The old beams, mouldering piecemeal, yield a little and groan; and such a house as this I can fancy all resonant at night with voices, the voices of matter so slowly and so surely transformed into other shapes, the voice of the worm that gnaws at last the very heart of the oak, the voice of stone grinding on stone, and the voice of the conquest of Time.'

They sat still in the old arm-chairs, and grew graver in the musty ancient air, the air of a hundred years ago.

'I don't like the place,' said Phillipps, after a long pause. 'To me it seems as if there were a sickly, unwholesome smell about it, a smell of something burning.'

'You are right; there is an evil odour here. I wonder what it is. Hark! Did you hear that?'

A hollow sound, a noise of infinite sadness and infinite pain, broke in upon the silence, and the two men looked fearfully at one another, horror, and the sense of unknown things, glimmering in their eyes.

'Come,' said Dyson, 'we must see into this,' and they went into the hall and listened in the silence.

'Do you know,' said Phillipps, 'it seems absurd, but I could almost fancy that the smell is that of burning flesh.'

They went up the hollow-sounding stairs, and the odour became thick and noisome, stifling the breath, and a vapour, sickening as the smell of the chamber of death, choked them. A door was open, and they entered the large upper room, and clung hard to one another, shuddering at the sight they saw.

A naked man was lying on the floor, his arms and legs stretched wide apart, and bound to pegs that had been hammered into the boards. The body was torn and mutilated in the most hideous fashion, scarred with the marks of red-hot irons, a shameful ruin of the human shape. But upon the middle of the body a fire of coals was smouldering; the flesh had been burnt through. The man was dead, but the smoke of his torment mounted still, a black vapour.

'The young man with spectacles,' said Mr Dyson.

# THE RED HAND

## THE PROBLEM OF THE FISH-HOOKS

'There can be no doubt whatever,' said Mr Phillipps, 'that my theory is the true one; these flints are prehistoric fish-hooks.'

'I dare say; but you know that in all probability the things were forged the other day with a door-key.'

'Stuff!' said Phillipps; 'I have some respect, Dyson, for your literary abilities, but your knowledge of ethnology is insignificant, or rather non-existent. These fish-hooks satisfy every test; they are perfectly genuine.'

'Possibly, but as I said just now, you go to work at the wrong end. You neglect the opportunities that confront you and await you, obvious, at every corner; you positively shrink from the chance of encountering primitive man in this whirling and mysterious city, and you pass the weary hours in your agreeable retirement of Red Lion Square fumbling with bits of flint, which are, as I said, in all probability, rank forgeries.'

Phillipps took one of the little objects, and held it up in exasperation.

'Look at that ridge,' he said. 'Did you ever see such a ridge as that on a forgery?'

Dyson merely grunted and lit his pipe, and the two sat smoking in rich silence, watching through the open window the children in the square as they flitted to and fro in the twilight of the lamps, as elusive as bats flying on the verge of a dark wood.

'Well,' said Phillipps at last, 'it is really a long time since you have been round. I suppose you have been working at your old task.'

'Yes,' said Dyson, 'always the chase of the phrase. I shall grow old in the hunt. But it is a great consolation to meditate on the fact that there are not a dozen people in England who know what style means.'

'I suppose not; for the matter of that, the study of ethnology is far from popular. And the difficulties! Primitive man stands dim and very far off across the great bridge of years.

'By the way,' he went on after a pause, 'what was that stuff you were talking just now about shrinking from the chance of encountering primitive man at the corner, or something of the kind? There are certainly people about here whose ideas are very primitive.'

'I wish, Phillipps, you would not rationalize my remarks. If I recol-lect the phrase correctly, I hinted that you shrank from the chance of encountering primitive man in this whirling and mysterious city, and I meant exactly what I said. Who can limit the age of survival? The troglodyte* and the lake-dweller, perhaps representatives of yet darker races, may very probably be lurking in our midst, rubbing shoulders with frock-coated and finely-draped humanity, ravening like wolves at heart and boiling with the foul passions of the swamp and the black cave. Now and then as I walk in Holborn or Fleet Street I see a face which I pronounce abhorred, and yet I could not give a reason for the thrill of loathing that stirs within me.'

'My dear Dyson, I refuse to enter myself in your literary "trying-on" department. I know that survivals do exist, but all things have a limit, and your speculations are absurd. You must catch me your troglodyte before I will believe in him.'

'I agree to that with all my heart,' said Dyson, chuckling at the ease with which he had succeeded in 'drawing' Phillipps.* 'Nothing could be better. It's a fine night for a walk,' he added, taking up his hat.

'What nonsense you are talking, Dyson!' said Phillipps. 'However, I have no objection to taking a walk with you: as you say, it is a pleasant night.'

'Come along then,' said Dyson, grinning, 'but remember our bargain.'

The two men went out into the square, and threading one of the narrow passages that serve as exits, struck towards the north-east. As they passed along a flaring causeway they could hear at intervals between the clamour of the children and the triumphant *Gloria** played on a piano-organ the long deep hum and roll of the traffic in Holborn, a sound so persistent that it echoed like the turning of everlasting wheels. Dyson looked to right and left and conned the way, and presently they were passing through a more peaceful quarter, touching on deserted squares and silent streets black as midnight. Phillipps had lost all count of direction, and as by degrees the region of faded respectability gave place to the squalid, and dirty stucco offended the eye of the artistic observer, he merely ventured the remark that he had never seen a neighbourhood more unpleasant or more commonplace.

'More mysterious, you mean,' said Dyson. 'I warn you, Phillipps, we are now hot upon the scent.'

They dived yet deeper into the maze of brickwork; some time before they had crossed a noisy thoroughfare running east and west, and now the quarter seemed all amorphous, without character; here a decent house with sufficient garden, here a faded square, and here factories surrounded by high, blank walls, with blind passages and dark corners; but all ill-lighted and unfrequented and heavy with silence.

Presently, as they paced down a forlorn street of two-story houses, Dyson caught sight of a dark and obscure turning.

'I like the look of that,' he said; 'it seems to me promising.' There was a street lamp at the entrance, and another, a mere glimmer, at the further end. Beneath the lamp, on the pavement, an artist had evidently established his academy in the daytime, for the stones were all a blur of crude colours rubbed into each other, and a few broken fragments of chalk lay in a little heap beneath the wall.

'You see people do occasionally pass this way,' said Dyson, pointing to the ruins of the screever's* work. 'I confess I should not have thought it possible. Come, let us explore.'

On one side of this byway of communication was a great timber-yard, with vague piles of wood looming shapeless above the enclosing wall; and on the other side of the road a wall still higher seemed to enclose a garden, for there were shadows like trees, and a faint murmur of rustling leaves broke the silence. It was a moonless night, and clouds that had gathered after sunset had blackened, and midway between the feeble lamps the passage lay all dark and formless, and when one stopped and listened, and the sharp echo of reverberant footsteps ceased, there came from far away, as from beyond the hills, a faint roll of the noise of London. Phillipps was bolstering up his courage to declare that he had had enough of the excursion, when a loud cry from Dyson broke in upon his thoughts.

'Stop, stop, for Heaven's sake, or you will tread on it! There! almost under your feet!' Phillipps looked down, and saw a vague shape, dark, and framed in surrounding darkness, dropped strangely on the pavement, and then a white cuff glimmered for a moment as Dyson lit a match, which went out directly.

'It's a drunken man,' said Phillipps very coolly.

'It's a murdered man,' said Dyson, and he began to call for police with all his might, and soon from the distance running footsteps echoed and grew louder, and cries sounded.

A policeman was the first to come up.

'What's the matter?' he said, as he drew to a stand, panting. 'Anything amiss here?' for he had not seen what was on the pavement.

'Look!' said Dyson, speaking out of the gloom. 'Look there! My friend and I came down this place three minutes ago, and that is what we found.'

The man flashed his light on the dark shape and cried out.

'Why, it's murder,' he said; 'there's blood all about him, and a puddle of it in the gutter there. He's not dead long, either. Ah! there's the wound! It's in the neck.'

Dyson bent over what was lying there. He saw a prosperous gentleman, dressed in smooth, well-cut clothes. The neat whiskers were beginning to grizzle a little; he might have been forty-five an hour before; and a handsome gold watch had half slipped out of his waistcoat pocket. And there in the flesh of the neck, between chin and ear, gaped a great wound, clean cut, but all clotted with drying blood, and the white of the cheeks shone like a lighted lamp above the red.

Dyson turned, and looked curiously about him; the dead man lay across the path with his head inclined towards the wall, and the blood from the wound streamed away across the pavement, and lay a dark puddle, as the policeman had said, in the gutter. Two more policemen had come up, the crowd gathered, humming from all quarters, and the officers had as much as they could do to keep the curious at a distance. The three lanterns were flashing here and there, searching for more evidence, and in the gleam of one of them Dyson caught sight of an object in the road, to which he called the attention of the policeman nearest to him.

'Look, Phillipps,' he said, when the man had secured it and held it up. 'Look, that should be something in your way!'

It was a dark flinty stone, gleaming like obsidian, and shaped to a broad edge something after the manner of an adze. One end was rough, and easily grasped in the hand, and the whole thing was hardly five inches long. The edge was thick with blood.

'What is that, Phillipps?' said Dyson; and Phillipps looked hard at it.

'It's a primitive flint knife,' he said. 'It was made about ten thousand years ago. One exactly like this was found near Abury,* in Wiltshire, and all the authorities gave it that age.'

The policeman stared astonished at such a development of the case; and Phillipps himself was all aghast at his own words. But Mr Dyson did not notice him. An inspector who had just come up and was listening to the outlines of the case, was holding a lantern to the dead man's head. Dyson, for his part, was staring with a white heat of curiosity at something he saw on the wall, just above where the man was lying; there were a few rude marks done in red chalk.

'This is a black business,' said the inspector at length; 'does anybody know who it is?'

A man stepped forward from the crowd. 'I do, governor,' he said, 'he's a big doctor, his name's Sir Thomas Vivian; I was in the 'orspital abart six months ago, and he used to come round; he was a very kind man.'

'Lord,' cried the inspector, 'this is a bad job indeed. Why, Sir Thomas Vivian goes to the Royal Family. And there's a watch worth a hundred guineas in his pocket, so it isn't robbery.'

Dyson and Phillipps gave their cards to the authority, and moved off, pushing with difficulty through the crowd that was still gathering, gathering fast; and the alley that had been lonely and desolate now swarmed with white staring faces and hummed with the buzz of rumour and horror, and rang with the commands of the officers of police. The two men once free from this swarming curiosity, stepped out briskly, but for twenty minutes neither spoke a word.

'Phillipps,' said Dyson, as they came into a small but cheerful street, clean and brightly lit, 'Phillipps, I owe you an apology. I was wrong to have spoken as I did to-night. Such infernal jesting,' he went on, with heat, 'as if there were no wholesome subjects for a joke. I feel as if I had raised an evil spirit.'

'For Heaven's sake say nothing more,' said Phillipps, choking down horror with visible effort. 'You told the truth to me in my room; the troglodyte, as you said, is still lurking about the earth, and in these very streets around us, slaying for mere lust of blood.'

'I will come up for a moment,' said Dyson when they reached Red Lion Square, 'I have something to ask you. I think there should be nothing hidden between us at all events.'

Phillipps nodded gloomily, and they went up to the room, where everything hovered indistinct in the uncertain glimmer of the light from without. When the candle was lighted and the two men sat facing each other, Dyson spoke.

'Perhaps,' he began, 'you did not notice me peering at the wall just above the place where the head lay. The light from the inspector's lantern was shining full on it, and I saw something that looked queer to me, and I examined it closely. I found that some one had drawn in red chalk a rough outline of a hand—a human hand—upon the wall. But it was the curious position of the fingers that struck me; it was like this'; and he took a pencil and a piece of paper and drew rapidly, and then handed what he had done to Phillipps. It was a rough sketch of a hand seen from the back, with the fingers clenched, and the top of the thumb protruded between the first and second fingers, and pointed downwards, as if to something below.

'It was just like that,' said Dyson, as he saw Phillipps's face grow still whiter. 'The thumb pointed down as if to the body; it seemed almost a live hand in ghastly gesture. And just beneath there was a small mark with the powder of the chalk lying on it—as if some one had commenced a stroke and had broken the chalk in his hand. I saw the bit of chalk lying on the ground. But what do you make of it?'

'It's a horrible old sign,' said Phillipps—'one of the most horrible signs connected with the theory of the evil eye.* It is used still in Italy, but there can be no doubt that it has been known for ages. It is one of the survivals; you must look for the origin of it in the black swamp whence man first came.'

Dyson took up his hat to go.

'I think, jesting apart,' said he, 'that I kept my promise, and that we were and are hot on the scent, as I said. It seems as if I had really shown you primitive man, or his handiwork at all events.'

## INCIDENT OF THE LETTER

ABOUT a month after the extraordinary and mysterious murder of Sir Thomas Vivian, the well-known and universally respected specialist in heart disease, Mr Dyson called again on his friend Mr Phillipps, whom he found, not as usual, sunk deep in painful study, but reclining in his easy-chair in an attitude of relaxation. He welcomed Dyson with cordiality.

'I am very glad you have come,' he began; 'I was thinking of looking you up. There is no longer the shadow of a doubt about the matter.'

'You mean the case of Sir Thomas Vivian?'

'Oh, no, not at all. I was referring to the problem of the fish-hooks. Between ourselves, I was a little too confident when you were here last, but since then other facts have turned up; and only yesterday I had a letter from a distinguished F.R.S.* which quite settles the affair. I have been thinking what I should tackle next; and I am inclined to believe that there is a good deal to be done in the way of so-called undecipherable inscriptions.'

'Your line of study pleases me,' said Dyson. 'I think it may prove useful. But in the meantime, there was surely something extremely mysterious about the case of Sir Thomas Vivian.'

'Hardly, I think. I allowed myself to be frightened that night; but there can be no doubt that the facts are patient of a comparatively commonplace explanation.'

'Really! What is your theory then?'

'Well, I imagine that Vivian must have been mixed up at some period of his life in an adventure of a not very creditable description, and that he was murdered out of revenge by some Italian whom he had wronged.'

'Why Italian?'

'Because of the hand, the sign of the *mano in fica*.* That gesture is now only used by Italians. So you see that what appeared the most obscure feature in the case turns out to be illuminant.'

'Yes, quite so. And the flint knife?'

'That is very simple. The man found the thing in Italy, or possibly stole it from some museum. Follow the line of least resistance, my dear fellow, and you will see there is no need to bring up primitive man from his secular grave beneath the hills.'

'There is some justice in what you say,' said Dyson. 'As I understand you, then, you think that your Italian, having murdered Vivian, kindly chalked up that hand as a guide to Scotland Yard?'

'Why not? Remember a murderer is always a madman. He may plot and contrive nine-tenths of his scheme with the acuteness and the grasp of a chess-player or a pure mathematician; but somewhere or other his wits leave him and he behaves like a fool. Then you must take into account the insane pride or vanity of the criminal; he likes to leave his mark, as it were, upon his handiwork.'

'Yes, it is all very ingenious; but have you read the reports of the inquest?'

'No, not a word. I simply gave my evidence, left the court, and dismissed the subject from my mind.'

'Quite so. Then if you don't object I should like to give you an account of the case. I have studied it rather deeply, and I confess it interests me extremely.'

'Very good. But I warn you I have done with mystery. We are to deal with facts now.'

'Yes, it is fact that I wish to put before you. And this is fact the first. When the police moved Sir Thomas Vivian's body they found an open knife beneath him. It was an ugly-looking thing such as sailors carry, with a blade that the mere opening rendered rigid, and there the blade was all ready, bare and gleaming, but without a trace of blood on it, and the knife was found to be quite new; it had never been used. Now, at the first glance it looks as if your imaginary Italian were just the man to have such a tool. But consider a moment. Would he be likely to buy a new knife expressly to commit murder? And, secondly, if he had such a knife, why didn't he use it, instead of that very odd flint instrument?'

'And I want to put this to you. You think the murderer chalked up the hand after the murder as a sort of "melodramatic Italian assassin his mark" touch. Passing over the question as to whether the real criminal ever does such a thing, I would point out that, on the medical evidence, Sir Thomas Vivian hadn't been dead for more than an hour. That would place the stroke at about a quarter to ten, and you know it was perfectly dark when we went out at 9.30. And that passage was singularly gloomy and ill-lighted, and the hand was drawn roughly, it is true, but correctly and without the bungling of strokes and the bad shots that are inevitable when one tries to draw in the dark or with shut eyes. Just try to draw such a simple figure as a square without looking at the paper, and then ask me to conceive that your Italian, with the rope waiting for his neck, could draw the hand on the wall so firmly and truly, in the black shadow of that alley. It is absurd. By consequence, then, the hand was drawn early in the evening, long before any murder was committed; or else— mark this, Phillipps—it was drawn by some one to whom darkness and gloom were familiar and habitual; by some one to whom the common dread of the rope was unknown!

'Again: a curious note was found in Sir Thomas Vivian's pocket. Envelope and paper were of a common make, and the stamp bore the West Central postmark. I will come to the nature of the contents later on, but it is the question of the handwriting that is so remarkable. The address on the outside was neatly written in a small clear hand, but the letter itself might have been written by a Persian who had learnt the English script. It was upright, and the letters were curiously con- torted, with an affectation of dashes and backward curves which really reminded me of an Oriental manuscript, though it was all perfectly legible. But—and here comes the poser—on searching the dead man's waistcoat pockets a small memorandum book was found; it was almost filled with pencil jottings. These memoranda related chiefly to matters of a private as distinct from a professional nature; there were appoint- ments to meet friends, notes of theatrical first-nights, the address of a good hotel in Tours, and the title of a new novel—nothing in any way intimate. And the whole of these jottings were written in a hand nearly identical with the writing of the note found in the dead man's coat pocket! There was just enough difference between them to enable the expert to swear that the two were not written by the same person. I will just read you so much of Lady Vivian's evidence as bears on this point of the writing; I have the printed slip with me. Here you see she says: "I was married to my late husband seven years ago; I never saw any letter addressed to him in a hand at all resembling that on the envelope produced, nor have I ever seen writing like that in the letter before me. I never saw my late husband using the memorandum book, but I am sure he did write everything in it; I am certain of that because we stayed last May at the Hotel du Faisan, Rue Royale, Tours, the address of which is given in the book; I remember his getting the novel 'A Sentinel' about six weeks ago. Sir Thomas Vivian never liked to miss the first- nights at the theatres. His usual hand was perfectly different from that used in the notebook."

'And now, last of all, we come back to the note itself. Here it is in fac-simile. My possession of it is due to the kindness of Inspector Cleeve, who is pleased to be amused at my amateur inquisitiveness. Read it, Phillipps; you tell me you are interested in obscure inscriptions; here is something for you to decipher.'

Mr Phillipps, absorbed in spite of himself in the strange circum-stances Dyson had related, took the piece of paper, and scrutinized it closely. The handwriting was indeed bizarre in the extreme, and, as Dyson had noted, not unlike the Persian character in its general effect, but it was perfectly legible.

'Read it loud,' said Dyson, and Phillipps obeyed.

'Hand did not point in vain. The meaning of the stars is no longer obscure. Strangely enough, the black heaven vanished, or was stolen yesterday, but that does not matter in the least, as I have a celestial globe. Our old orbit remains unchanged; you have not forgotten the number of my sign, or will you appoint some other house? I have been on the other side of the moon, and can bring something to show you.'

'And what do you make of that?' said Dyson.

'It seems to me mere gibberish,' said Phillipps; 'you suppose it has a meaning?'

'Oh, surely; it was posted three days before the murder; it was found in the murdered man's pocket; it is written in a fantastic hand which the murdered man himself used for his private memoranda. There must be purpose under all this, and to my mind there is something ugly enough hidden under the circumstances of this case of Sir Thomas Vivian.'

'But what theory have you formed?'

'Oh, as to theories, I am still in a very early stage; it is too soon to state conclusions. But I think I have demolished your Italian. I tell you, Phillipps, again, the whole thing has an ugly look to my eyes. I cannot do as you do, and fortify myself with cast-iron propositions to the effect that this or that doesn't happen, and never has happened. You note that the first word in the letter is "hand." That seems to me, taken with what we know about the hand on the wall, significant enough, and what you yourself told me of the history and meaning of the symbol, its connec-tion with a world-old belief and faiths of dim far-off years, all this speaks of mischief, for me at all events. No; I stand pretty well to what I said to you half in joke that night before we went out. There are sacra-ments of evil as well as of good about us, and we live and move to my belief in an unknown world, a place where there are caves and shadows and dwellers in twilight. It is possible that man may sometimes return on the track of evolution, and it is my belief that an awful lore is not yet dead.'

'I cannot follow you in all this,' said Phillipps; 'it seems to interest you strangely. What do you propose to do?'

'My dear Phillipps,' replied Dyson, speaking in a lighter tone, 'I am afraid I shall have to go down a little in the world. I have a prospect of visits to the pawnbrokers before me, and the publicans must not be neglected. I must cultivate a taste for four ale; shag tobacco I already love and esteem with all my heart.'

## SEARCH FOR THE VANISHED HEAVEN

FOR many days after the discussion with Phillipps, Mr Dyson was resolute in the line of research he had marked out for himself. A fervent curiosity and an innate liking for the obscure were great incentives, but especially in this case of Sir Thomas Vivian's death (for Dyson began to boggle a little at the word 'murder') there seemed to him an element that was more than curious. The sign of the red hand upon the wall, the tool of flint that had given death, the almost identity between the hand-writing of the note and the fantastic script reserved religiously, as it appeared, by the doctor for trifling jottings, all these diverse and variegated threads joined to weave in his mind a strange and shadowy picture, with ghastly shapes dominant and deadly, and yet ill-defined, like the giant figures wavering in an ancient tapestry. He thought he had a clue to the meaning of the note, and in his resolute search for the 'black heaven,' which had vanished, he beat furiously about the alleys and obscure streets of central London, making himself a familiar figure to the pawnbroker, and a frequent guest at the more squalid pot-houses.

For a long time he was unsuccessful, and he trembled at the thought that the 'black heaven' might be hid in the coy retirements of Peckham, or lurk perchance in distant Willesden, but finally, improbability, in which he put his trust, came to the rescue. It was a dark and rainy night, with something in the unquiet and stirring gusts that savoured of approaching winter, and Dyson, beating up a narrow street not far from the Gray's Inn Road, took shelter in an extremely dirty 'public,' and called for beer, forgetting for the moment his preoccupations, and only thinking of the sweep of the wind about the tiles and the hissing of the rain through the black and troubled air. At the bar there gathered the usual company: the frowsy women and the men in shiny black, those who appeared to mumble secretly together, others who wrangled in interminable argument, and a few shy drinkers who stood apart, each relishing his dose, and the rank and biting flavour of cheap spirit. Dyson was wondering at the enjoyment of it all, when suddenly there came a sharper accent. The folding-doors swayed open, and a middle-aged woman staggered towards the bar, and clutched the pewter rim as if she stepped a deck in a roaring gale. Dyson glanced at her attentively as a pleasing specimen of her class; she was decently dressed in black, and carried a black bag of somewhat rusty leather, and her intoxication was apparent and far advanced. As she swayed at the bar, it was evidently all she could do to stand upright, and the barman, who had looked at her with disfavour, shook his head in reply to her thick-voiced demand for a drink. The woman glared at him, transformed in a moment to a fury, with bloodshot eyes, and poured forth a torrent of execration, a stream of blasphemies and early English phraseology.

'Get out of this,' said the man; 'shut up and be off, or I'll send for the police.'

'Police, you——,' bawled the woman, 'I'll —— well give you something to fetch the police for!' and with a rapid dive into her bag she pulled out some object which she hurled furiously at the barman's head.

The man ducked down, and the missile flew over his head and smashed a bottle to fragments, while the woman with a peal of horrible laughter rushed to the door, and they could hear her steps pattering fast over the wet stones.

The barman looked ruefully about him.

'Not much good going after her,' he said, 'and I'm afraid what she's left won't pay for that bottle of whisky.' He fumbled amongst the fragments of broken glass, and drew out something dark, a kind of square stone it seemed, which he held up.

'Valuable cur'osity,' he said, 'any gent like to bid?'

The habitués had scarcely turned from their pots and glasses during these exciting incidents; they gazed a moment, fishily, when the bottle smashed, and that was all, and the mumble of the confidential was resumed and the jangle of the quarrelsome, and the shy and solitary sucked in their lips and relished again the rank flavour of the spirit.

Dyson looked quickly at what the barman held before him.

'Would you mind letting me see it?' he said; 'it's a queer-looking old thing, isn't it?'

It was a small black tablet, apparently of stone, about four inches long by two and a half broad, and as Dyson took it he felt rather than saw that he touched the secular with his flesh. There was some kind of carving on the surface, and, most conspicuous, a sign that made Dyson's heart leap.

'I don't mind taking it,' he said quietly. 'Would two shillings be enough?'

'Say half a dollar,' said the man, and the bargain was concluded. Dyson drained his pot of beer, finding it delicious, and lit his pipe, and went out deliberately soon after. When he reached his apartment he locked the door, and placed the tablet on his desk, and then fixed himself in his chair, as resolute as an army in its trenches before a beleaguered city. The tablet was full under the light of the shaded candle, and scrutinizing it closely, Dyson saw first the sign of the hand with the thumb protruding between the fingers; it was cut finely and firmly on the dull black surface of the stone, and the thumb pointed downward to what was beneath.

'It is mere ornament,' said Dyson to himself, 'perhaps symbolical ornament, but surely not an inscription, or the signs of any words ever spoken.'

The hand pointed at a series of fantastic figures, spirals and whorls of the finest, most delicate lines, spaced at intervals over the remaining surface of the tablet. The marks were as intricate and seemed almost as much without design as the pattern of a thumb* impressed upon a pane of glass.

'Is it some natural marking?' thought Dyson; 'there have been queer designs, likenesses of beasts and flowers, in stones with which man's hand had nothing to do'; and he bent over the stone with a magnifier, only to be convinced that no hazard of nature could have delineated these varied labyrinths of line. The whorls were of different sizes; some were less than the twelfth of an inch in diameter, and the largest was a little smaller than a sixpence, and under the glass the regularity and accuracy of the cutting were evident, and in the smaller spirals the lines were graduated at intervals of a hundredth of an inch. The whole thing had a marvellous and fantastic look, and gazing at the mystic whorls beneath the hand, Dyson became subdued with an impression of vast and far-off ages, and of a living being that had touched the stone with enigmas before the hills were formed, when the hard rocks still boiled with fervent heat.

'The "black heaven" is found again,' he said, 'but the meaning of the stars is likely to be obscure for everlasting so far as I am concerned.'

London stilled without, and a chill breath came into the room as Dyson sat gazing at the tablet shining duskily under the candle-light; and at last, as he closed the desk over the ancient stone, all his wonder at the case of Sir Thomas Vivian increased tenfold, and he thought of the well-dressed prosperous gentleman lying dead mystically beneath the sign of the hand, and the insupportable conviction seized him that between the death of this fashionable West-end doctor and the weird spirals of the tablet there were most secret and unimaginable links.

For days he sat before his desk gazing at the tablet, unable to resist its loadstone fascination, and yet quite helpless, without even the hope of solving the symbols so secretly inscribed. At last, desperate, he called in Mr Phillipps in consultation, and told in brief the story of the finding the stone.

'Dear me!' said Phillipps, 'this is extremely curious; you have had a find indeed. Why it looks to me even more ancient than the Hittite seal. I confess the character, if it is a character, is entirely strange to me. These whorls are really very quaint.'

'Yes, but I want to know what they mean. You must remember this tablet is the "black heaven" of the letter found in Sir Thomas Vivian's pocket; it bears directly on his death.'

'Oh, no, that is nonsense! This is, no doubt, an extremely ancient tablet, which has been stolen from some collection. Yes, the hand makes an odd coincidence, but only a coincidence after all.'

'My dear Phillipps, you are a living example of the truth of the axiom that extreme scepticism is mere credulity. But can you decipher the inscription?'

'I undertake to decipher anything,' said Phillipps. 'I do not believe in the insoluble. These characters are curious, but I cannot fancy them to be inscrutable.'

'Then take the thing away with you and make what you can of it. It has begun to haunt me; I feel as if I had gazed too long into the eyes of the Sphinx.'

Phillipps departed with the tablet in an inner pocket. He had not much doubt of success, for he had evolved thirty-seven rules for the solution of inscriptions. Yet when a week had passed and he called to see Dyson there was no vestige of triumph on his features. He found his friend in a state of extreme irritation, pacing up and down in the room like a man in a passion. He turned with a start as the door opened.

'Well,' said Dyson, 'you have got it? What is it all about?'

'My dear fellow, I am sorry to say I have completely failed. I have tried every known device in vain. I have even been so officious as to submit it to a friend at the Museum, but he, though a man of prime authority on the subject, tells me he is quite at fault. It must be some wreckage of a vanished race, almost, I think—a fragment of another

world than ours. I am not a superstitious man, Dyson, and you know
that I have no truck with even the noble delusions, but I confess I yearn
to be rid of this small square of blackish stone. Frankly, it has given me
an ill week; it seems to me troglodytic and abhorred.'

Phillipps drew out the tablet and laid it on the desk before Dyson.

'By the way,' he went on, 'I was right at all events in one particular;
it has formed part of some collection. There is a piece of grimy paper
on the back that must have been a label.'

'Yes, I noticed that,' said Dyson, who had fallen into deepest disappointment; 'no doubt the paper is a label. But as I don't much care where
the tablet originally came from, and only wish to know what the inscription means, I paid no attention to the paper. The thing is a hopeless riddle, I suppose, and yet it must surely be of the greatest importance.'

Phillipps left soon after, and Dyson, still despondent, took the tablet
in his hand and carelessly turned it over. The label had so grimed that
it seemed merely a dull stain, but as Dyson looked at it idly, and yet
attentively, he could see pencil-marks, and he bent over it eagerly, with
his glass to his eye. To his annoyance, he found that part of the paper
had been torn away, and he could only with difficulty make out odd
words and pieces of words. First he read something that looked like
'in-road,' and then beneath, 'stony-hearted step——' and a tear cut off
the rest. But in an instant a solution suggested itself, and he chuckled
with huge delight.

'Certainly,' he said out loud, 'this is not only the most charming but
the most convenient quarter in all London; here I am, allowing for the
accidents of side streets, perched on a tower of observation.'

He glanced triumphant out of the window across the street to the
gate of the British Museum. Sheltered by the boundary wall of that
agreeable institution, a 'screever,' or artist in chalks, displayed his brilliant impressions on the pavement, soliciting the approval and the coppers of the gay and serious.

'This,' said Dyson, 'is more than delightful! An artist is provided to
my hand.'


## THE ARTIST OF THE PAVEMENT

MR PHILLIPPS, in spite of all disavowals—in spite of the wall of
sense of whose enclosure and limit he was wont to make his boast—yet
felt in his heart profoundly curious as to the case of Sir Thomas Vivian.
Though he kept a brave face for his friend, his reason could not

decently resist the conclusion that Dyson had enunciated, namely, that the whole affair had a look both ugly and mysterious. There was the weapon of a vanished race that had pierced the great arteries; the red hand, the symbol of a hideous faith, that pointed to the slain man; and then the tablet which Dyson declared he had expected to find, and had certainly found, bearing the ancient impress of the hand of malediction, and a legend written beneath in a character compared with which the most antique cuneiform was a thing of yesterday. Besides all this, there were other points that tortured and perplexed. How to account for the bare knife found unstained beneath the body? And the hint that the red hand upon the wall must have been drawn by some one whose life was passed in darkness thrilled him with a suggestion of dim and infinite horror. Hence he was in truth not a little curious as to what was to come, and some ten days after he had returned the tablet he again visited the 'mystery-man,' as he privately named his friend.

Arrived in the grave and airy chambers in Great Russell Street, he found the moral atmosphere of the place had been transformed. All Dyson's irritation had disappeared, his brow was smoothed with complacency, and he sat at a table by the window gazing out into the street with an expression of grim enjoyment, a pile of books and papers lying unheeded before him.

'My dear Phillipps, I am delighted to see you! Pray excuse my moving. Draw your chair up here to the table, and try this admirable shag tobacco.'*

'Thank you,' said Phillipps, 'judging by the flavour of the smoke, I should think it is a little strong. But what on earth is all this? What are you looking at?'

'I am on my watch-tower. I assure you that the time seems short while I contemplate this agreeable street and the classic grace of the Museum portico.'

'Your capacity for nonsense is amazing,' replied Phillipps, 'but have you succeeded in deciphering the tablet? It interests me.'

'I have not paid much attention to the tablet recently,' said Dyson. 'I believe the spiral character may wait.'

'Really! And how about the Vivian murder?'

'Ah, you do take an interest in that case? Well, after all, we cannot deny that it was a queer business. But is not "murder" rather a coarse word? It smacks a little, surely, of the police poster. Perhaps I am a trifle decadent, but I cannot help believing in the splendid word; "sacrifice," for example, is surely far finer than "murder".'

'I am all in the dark,' said Phillipps. 'I cannot even imagine by what track you are moving in this labyrinth.'

'I think that before very long the whole matter will be a good deal clearer for us both, but I doubt whether you will like hearing the story.'

Dyson lit his pipe afresh and leant back, not relaxing, however, in his scrutiny of the street. After a somewhat lengthy pause, he startled Phillipps by a loud breath of relief as he rose from the chair by the window and began to pace the floor.

'It's over for the day,' he said, 'and, after all, one gets a little tired.'

Phillipps looked with inquiry into the street. The evening was darkening, and the pile of the Museum was beginning to loom indistinct before the lighting of the lamps, but the pavements were thronged and busy. The artist in chalks across the way was gathering together his materials, and blurring all the brilliance of his designs, and a little lower down there was the clang of shutters being placed in position. Phillipps could see nothing to justify Mr Dyson's sudden abandonment of his attitude of surveillance, and grew a little irritated by all these thorny enigmas.

'Do you know, Phillipps,' said Dyson, as he strolled at ease up and down the room, 'I will tell you how I work. I go upon the theory of improbability. The theory is unknown to you? I will explain. Suppose I stand on the steps of St Paul's and look out for a blind man lame of the left leg to pass me, it is evidently highly improbable that I shall see such a person by waiting for an hour. If I wait two hours the improbability is diminished, but is still enormous, and a watch of a whole day would give little expectation of success. But suppose I take up the same position day after day, and week after week, don't you perceive that the improbability is lessening constantly—growing smaller day after day? Don't you see that two lines which are not parallel are gradually approaching one another, drawing nearer and nearer to a point of meeting, till at last they do meet, and improbability has vanished altogether? That is how I found the black tablet: I acted on the theory of improbability. It is the only scientific principle I know of which can enable one to pick out an unknown man from amongst five million.'

'And you expect to find the interpreter of the black tablet by this method?'

'Certainly.'

'And the murderer of Sir Thomas Vivian also?'

'Yes, I expect to lay my hands on the person concerned in the death of Sir Thomas Vivian in exactly the same way.'

The rest of the evening, after Phillipps had left, was devoted by Dyson to sauntering in the streets, and afterwards, when the night grew late, to his literary labours, or the chase of the phrase, as he called it. The next morning the station by the window was again resumed. His meals were brought to him at the table, and he ate with his eyes on the street. With briefest intervals, snatched reluctantly from time to time, he persisted in his survey throughout the day, and only at dusk, when the shutters were put up and the 'screever' ruthlessly deleted all his labour of the day, just before the gas-lamps began to star the shadows, did he feel at liberty to quit his post. Day after day this ceaseless glance upon the street continued, till the landlady grew puzzled and aghast at such a profitless pertinacity.

But at last, one evening, when the play of lights and shadows was scarce beginning, and the clear cloudless air left all distinct and shining, there came the moment. A man of middle age, bearded and bowed, with a touch of grey about the ears, was strolling slowly along the northern pavement of Great Russell Street from the eastern end. He looked up at the Museum as he went by, and then glanced involuntarily at the art of the 'screever,' and at the artist himself, who sat beside his pictures, hat in hand. The man with the beard stood still an instant, swaying slightly to and fro as if in thought, and Dyson saw his fists shut tight, and his back quivering, and the one side of his face in view twitched and grew contorted with the indescribable torment of approaching epilepsy. Dyson drew a soft hat from his pocket, and dashed the door open, taking the stair with a run.

When he reached the street the person he had seen so agitated had turned about, and, regardless of observation, was racing wildly towards Bloomsbury Square, with his back to his former course.

Mr Dyson went up to the artist of the pavement and gave him some money, observing quietly, 'You needn't trouble to draw that thing again.' Then he too turned about, and strolled idly down the street in the opposite direction to that taken by the fugitive. So the distance between Dyson and the man with the bowed head grew steadily greater.

## STORY OF THE TREASURE HOUSE

'THERE are many reasons why I chose your rooms for the meeting in preference to my own. Chiefly, perhaps, because I thought the man would be more at his ease on neutral ground.'

'I confess, Dyson,' said Phillipps, 'that I feel both impatient and uneasy. You know my standpoint: hard matter of fact, materialism if you like, in its crudest form. But there is something about all this affair of Vivian that makes me a little restless. And how did you induce the man to come?'

'He has an exaggerated opinion of my powers. You remember what I said about the doctrine of improbability? When it does work out, it gives results which seem very amazing to a person who is not in the secret. That is eight striking, isn't it? And there goes the bell.'

They heard footsteps on the stair, and presently the door opened, and a middle-aged man, with a bowed head, bearded, and with a good deal of grizzling hair about his ears, came into the room. Phillipps glanced at his features, and recognized the lineaments of terror.

'Come in, Mr Selby,' said Dyson. 'This is Mr Phillipps, my intimate friend and our host for this evening. Will you take anything? Then perhaps we had better hear your story—a very singular one, I am sure.'

The man spoke in a voice hollow and a little quavering, and a fixed stare that never left his eyes seemed directed to something awful that was to remain before him by day and night for the rest of his life.

'You will, I am sure, excuse preliminaries,' he began; 'what I have to tell is best told quickly. I will say, then, that I was born in a remote part of the west of England, where the very outlines of the woods and hills, and the winding of the streams in the valleys, are apt to suggest the mystical to any one strongly gifted with imagination. When I was quite a boy there were certain huge and rounded hills, certain depths of hanging wood, and secret valleys bastioned round on every side that filled me with fancies beyond the bourne of rational expression, and as I grew older and began to dip into my father's books, I went by instinct, like the bee, to all that would nourish fantasy. Thus, from a course of obsolete and occult reading, and from listening to certain wild legends in which the older people still secretly believed, I grew firmly convinced of the existence of treasure, the hoard of a race extinct for ages, still hidden beneath the hills, and my every thought was directed to the discovery of the golden heaps that lay, as I fancied, within a few feet of the green turf. To one spot, in especial, I was drawn as if by enchantment; it was a tumulus, the domed memorial of some forgotten people, crowning the crest of a vast mountain range; and I have often lingered there on summer evenings, sitting on the great block of limestone at the summit, and looking out far over the yellow sea towards the Devonshire coast. One day as I dug heedlessly with the ferrule of my stick at the mosses and lichens which grew rank over the stone, my eye was caught by what seemed a pattern beneath the growth of green; there was a curving line, and marks that did not look altogether the work of nature. At first I thought I had bared some rarer fossil, and I took out my knife and scraped away at the moss till a square foot was uncovered. Then I saw two signs which startled me; first, a closed hand, pointing downwards, the thumb protruding between the fingers, and beneath the hand a whorl or spiral, traced with exquisite accuracy in the hard surface of the rock. Here, I persuaded myself, was an index to the great secret, but I chilled at the recollection of the fact that some antiquarians had tunnelled the tumulus through and through, and had been a good deal surprised at not finding so much as an arrow-head within. Clearly, then, the signs on the limestone had no local significance; and I made up my mind that I must search abroad. By sheer accident I was in a measure successful in my quest. Strolling by a cottage, I saw some children playing by the roadside; one was holding up some object in his hand, and the rest were going through one of the many forms of elaborate pretence which make up a great part of the mystery of a child's life. Something in the object held by the little boy attracted me, and I asked him to let me see it. The plaything of these children consisted of an oblong tablet of black stone; and on it was inscribed the hand pointing downwards, just as I had seen it on the rock, while beneath, spaced over the tablet, were a number of whorls and spirals, cut, as it seemed to me, with the utmost care and nicety. I bought the toy for a couple of shillings; the woman of the house told me it had been lying about for years; she thought her husband had found it one day in the brook which ran in front of the cottage: it was a very hot summer, and the stream was almost dry, and he saw it amongst the stones. That day I tracked the brook to a well of water gushing up cold and clear at the head of a lonely glen in the mountain. That was twenty years ago, and I only succeeded in deciphering the mysterious inscription last August. I must not trouble you with irrelevant details of my life; it is enough for me to say that I was forced, like many another man, to leave my old home and come to London. Of money I had very little, and I was glad to find a cheap room in a squalid street off the Gray's Inn Road. The late Sir Thomas Vivian, then far poorer and more wretched than myself, had a garret in the same house, and before many months we became intimate friends, and I had confided to him the object of my life. I had at first great difficulty in persuading him that I was not giving my days and my nights to an inquiry altogether hopeless and chimerical; but when he was convinced he grew keener than myself, and glowed at the thought of the riches which were to be the prize of some ingenuity and patience. I liked the man intensely, and pitied his case; he had a strong desire to enter the medical profession, but he lacked the means to pay the smallest fees, and indeed he was, not once or twice, but often reduced to the very verge of starvation. I freely and solemnly promised that, under whatever chances, he should share in my heaped fortune when it came, and this promise to one who had always been poor, and yet thirsted for wealth and pleasure in a manner unknown to me, was the strongest incentive. He threw himself into the task with eager interest, and applied a very acute intellect and unwearied patience to the solution of the characters on the tablet. I, like other ingenious young men, was curious in the matter of handwriting, and I had invented or adapted a fantastic script which I used occasionally, and which took Vivian so strongly that he was at the pains to imitate it. It was arranged between us that if we were ever parted, and had occasion to write on the affair that was so close to our hearts, this queer hand of my invention was to be used, and we also contrived a semi-cypher for the same purpose. Meanwhile we exhausted ourselves in efforts to get at the heart of the mystery, and after a couple of years had gone by I could see that Vivian began to sicken a little of the adventure, and one night he told me with some emotion that he feared both our lives were being passed away in idle and hopeless endeavour. Not many months afterwards he was so happy as to receive a considerable legacy from an aged and distant relative whose very existence had been almost forgotten by him; and with money at the bank, he became at once a stranger to me. He had passed his preliminary examination many years before, and he forthwith decided to enter at St Thomas's Hospital, and he told me that he must look out for a more convenient lodging. As we said good-bye, I reminded him of the promise I had given, and solemnly renewed it; but Vivian laughed with something between pity and contempt in his voice and expression as he thanked me. I need not dwell on the long struggle and misery of my existence, now doubly lonely; I never wearied or despaired of final success, and every day saw me at work, the tablet before me, and only at dusk would I go out and take my daily walk along Oxford Street, which attracted me I think by the noise and motion and glitter of lamps.

'This walk grew with me to a habit; every night, and in all weathers, I crossed the Gray's Inn Road and struck westward, sometimes choosing a northern track, by the Euston Road and Tottenham Court Road, sometimes I went by Holborn, and sometimes by way of Great Russell Street. Every night I walked for an hour to and fro on the northern pavement of Oxford Street, and the tale of De Quincey and his name for the Street, "Stony-hearted step-mother,"* often recurred to my memory. Then I would return to my grimy den and spend hours more in endless analysis of the riddle before me.

'The answer came to me one night a few weeks ago; it flashed into my brain in a moment, and I read the inscription, and saw that after all I had not wasted my days. "The place of the treasure house of them that dwell below," were the first words I read, and then followed minute indications of the spot in my own country where the great works of gold were to be kept for ever. Such a track was to be followed, such a pitfall avoided; here the way narrowed almost to a fox's hole, and there it broadened, and so at last the chamber would be reached. I determined to lose no time in verifying my discovery—not that I doubted at that great moment, but I would not risk even the smallest chance of disappointing my old friend Vivian, now a rich and prosperous man. I took the train for the West, and one night, with chart in hand, traced out the passage of the hills, and went so far that I saw the gleam of gold before me. I would not go on; I resolved that Vivian must be with me; and I only brought away a strange knife of flint which lay on the path, as confirmation of what I had to tell. I returned to London, and was a good deal vexed to find the stone tablet had disappeared from my rooms. My landlady, an inveterate drunkard, denied all knowledge of the fact, but I have little doubt she had stolen the thing for the sake of the glass of whisky it might fetch. However, I knew what was written on the tablet by heart, and I had also made an exact facsimile of the characters, so the loss was not severe. Only one thing annoyed me: when I first came into possession of the stone, I had pasted a piece of paper on the back and had written down the date and place of finding, and later on I had scribbled a word or two, a trivial sentiment, the name of my street, and suchlike idle pencillings on the paper; and these memories of days that had seemed so hopeless were dear to me: I had thought they would help to remind me in the future of the hours when I had hoped against despair. However, I wrote at once to Sir Thomas Vivian, using the handwriting I have mentioned and also the quasi-cypher. I told him of my success, and after mentioning the loss of the tablet and the fact that I had a copy of the inscription, I reminded him once more of my promise, and asked him either to write or call. He replied that he would see me in a certain obscure passage in Clerkenwell well known to us both in the old days, and at seven o'clock one evening I went to meet him. At the corner of this by-way, as I was walking to and fro, I noticed the blurred pictures of some street artist, and I picked up a piece of chalk he had left behind him, not much thinking what I was doing. I paced up and down the passage, wondering a good deal, as you may imagine, as to what manner of man I was to meet after so many years of parting, and the thoughts of the buried time coming thick upon me, I walked mechanically without raising my eyes from the ground. I was startled out of my reverie by

an angry voice and a rough inquiry why I didn't keep to the right side
of the pavement, and looking up I found I had confronted a prosperous
and important gentleman, who eyed my poor appearance with a look of
great dislike and contempt. I knew directly it was my old comrade, and
when I recalled myself to him, he apologized with some show of regret,
and began to thank me for my kindness, doubtfully, as if he hesitated to
commit himself, and, as I could see, with the hint of a suspicion as to
my sanity. I would have engaged him at first in reminiscences of our
friendship, but I found Sir Thomas viewed those days with a good deal
of distaste, and replying politely to my remarks, continually edged in
"business matters," as he called them. I changed my topics, and told him
in greater detail what I have told you. Then I saw his manner suddenly
change; as I pulled out the flint knife to prove my journey "to the other
side of the moon," as we called it in our jargon, there came over him
a kind of choking eagerness, his features were somewhat discomposed,
and I thought I detected a shuddering horror, a clenched resolution,
and the effort to keep quiet succeed one another in a manner that puzzled me. I had occasion to be a little precise in my particulars, and
it being still light enough, I remembered the red chalk in my pocket,
and drew the hand on the wall. "Here, you see, is the hand," I said, as
I explained its true meaning, "note where the thumb issues from between
the first and second fingers," and I would have gone on, and had applied
the chalk to the wall to continue my diagram, when he struck my hand
down, much to my surprise. "No, no," he said, "I do not want all that.
And this place is not retired enough; let us walk on, and do you explain
everything to me minutely." I complied readily enough, and he led me
away, choosing the most unfrequented by-ways, while I drove in the
plan of the hidden house word by word. Once or twice as I raised my
eyes I caught Vivian looking strangely about him; he seemed to give
a quick glint up and down, and glance at the houses; and there was
a furtive and anxious air about him that displeased me. "Let us walk on
to the north," he said at length, "we shall come to some pleasant lanes
where we can discuss these matters, quietly; my night's rest is at your
service." I declined, on the pretext that I could not dispense with my
visit to Oxford Street, and went on till he understood every turning
and winding and the minutest detail as well as myself. We had returned
on our footsteps, and stood again in the dark passage, just where I had
drawn the red hand on the wall, for I recognized the vague shape of
the trees whose branches hung above us. "We have come back to our
starting-point," I said; "I almost think I could put my finger on the wall
where I drew the hand. And I am sure you could put your finger on

the mystic hand in the hills as well as I. Remember between stream and stone."

'I was bending down, peering at what I thought must be my drawing, when I heard a sharp hiss of breath, and started up, and saw Vivian with his arm uplifted and a bare blade in his hand, and death threatening in his eyes. In sheer self-defence I caught at the flint weapon in my pocket, and dashed at him in blind fear of my life, and the next instant he lay dead upon the stones.

'I think that is all,' Mr Selby continued after a pause, 'and it only remains for me to say to you, Mr Dyson, that I cannot conceive what means enabled you to run me down.'

'I followed many indications,' said Dyson, 'and I am bound to disclaim all credit for acuteness, as I have made several gross blunders. Your celestial cypher did not, I confess, give me much trouble; I saw at once that terms of astronomy were substituted for common words and phrases. You had lost something black, or something black had been stolen from you; a celestial globe is a copy of the heavens, so I knew you meant you had a copy of what you had lost. Obviously, then, I came to the conclusion that you had lost a black object with characters or symbols written or inscribed on it, since the object in question certainly contained valuable information, and all information must be written or pictured. "Our old orbit remains unchanged"; evidently our old course or arrangement. "The number of my sign" must mean the number of my house, the allusion being to the signs of the zodiac. I need not say that "the other side of the moon" can stand for nothing but some place where no one else has been; and "some other house" is some other place of meeting, the "house" being the old term "house of the heavens." Then my next step was to find the "black heaven" that had been stolen, and by a process of exhaustion I did so.'

'You have got the tablet?'

'Certainly. And on the back of it, on the slip of paper you have mentioned, I read "inroad," which puzzled me a good deal, till I thought of Gray's Inn Road; you forgot the second *n*. "Stony-hearted step——" immediately suggested the phrase of De Quincey you have alluded to; and I made the wild but correct shot, that you were a man who lived in or near the Gray's Inn Road, and had the habit of walking in Oxford Street, for you remember how the opium-eater dwells on his wearying promenades along that thoroughfare? On the theory of improbability, which I have explained to my friend here, I concluded that occasionally, at all events, you would choose the way by Guilford Street, Russell Square, and Great Russell Street, and I knew that if I watched long enough I should see you. But how was I to recognize my man? I noticed the screever opposite my rooms, and got him to draw every day a large hand, in the gesture so familiar to us all, upon the wall behind him. I thought that when the unknown person did pass he would certainly betray some emotion at the sudden vision of the sign, to him the most terrible of symbols. You know the rest. Ah, as to catching you an hour later, that was, I confess, a refinement. From the fact of your having occupied the same rooms for so many years, in a neighbourhood moreover where lodgers are migratory to excess, I drew the conclusion that you were a man of fixed habit, and I was sure that after you had got over your fright you would return for the walk down Oxford Street. You did, by way of New Oxford Street, and I was waiting at the corner.'

'Your conclusions are admirable,' said Mr Selby. 'I may tell you that I had my stroll down Oxford Street the night Sir Thomas Vivian died. And I think that is all I have to say.'

'Scarcely,' said Dyson. 'How about the treasure?'

'I had rather we did not speak of that,' said Mr Selby, with a whitening of the skin about the temples.

'Oh, nonsense, sir, we are not blackmailers. Besides, you know you are in our power.'

'Then, as you put it like that, Mr Dyson, I must tell you I returned to the place. I went on a little farther than before.'

The man stopped short; his mouth began to twitch, his lips moved apart, and he drew in quick breaths, sobbing.

'Well, well,' said Dyson, 'I dare say you have done comfortably.'

'Comfortably,' Selby went on, constraining himself with an effort, 'yes, so comfortably that hell burns hot within me for ever. I only brought one thing away from that awful house within the hills; it was lying just beyond the spot where I found the flint knife.'

'Why did you not bring more?'

The whole bodily frame of the wretched man visibly shrank and wasted; his face grew yellow as tallow, and the sweat dropped from his brows. The spectacle was both revolting and terrible, and when the voice came, it sounded like the hissing of a snake.

'Because the keepers are still there, and I saw them, and because of this,' and he pulled out a small piece of curious gold-work and held it up.

'There,' he said, 'that is the Pain of the Goat.'

Phillipps and Dyson cried out together in horror at the revolting obscenity of the thing.

'Put it away, man; hide it, for Heaven's sake, hide it!'

'I brought that with me; that is all,' he said. 'You do not wonder that I did not stay long in a place where those who live are a little higher than the beasts, and where what you have seen is surpassed a thousandfold?'

'Take this,' said Dyson, 'I brought it with me in case it might be useful'; and he drew out the black tablet, and handed it to the shaking, horrible man.

'And now,' said Dyson, 'will you go out?'

The two friends sat silent a little while, facing one another with restless eyes and lips that quivered.

'I wish to say that I believe him,' said Phillipps.

'My dear Phillipps,' said Dyson as he threw the windows wide open, 'I do not know that, after all, my blunders in this queer case were so very absurd.'

# THE SHINING PYRAMID

## I

### THE ARROW-HEAD CHARACTER

'HAUNTED, you said?'

'Yes, haunted. Don't you remember, when I saw you three years ago, you told me about your place in the west with the ancient woods hanging all about it, and the wild, domed hills, and the ragged land? It has always remained a sort of enchanted picture in my mind as I sit at my desk and hear the traffic rattling in the street in the midst of whirling London. But when did you come up?'

'The fact is, Dyson, I have only just got out of the train. I drove to the station early this morning and caught the 10.45.'

'Well, I am very glad you looked in on me. How have you been getting on since we last met? There is no Mrs Vaughan, I suppose?'

'No,' said Vaughan, 'I am still a hermit, like yourself. I have done nothing but loaf about.'

Vaughan had lit his pipe and sat in the elbow chair, fidgeting and glancing about him in a somewhat dazed and restless manner. Dyson had wheeled round his chair when his visitor entered and sat with one arm fondly reclining on the desk of his bureau, and touching the litter of manuscript.

'And you are still engaged in the old task?' said Vaughan, pointing to the pile of papers and the teeming pigeon-holes.

'Yes, the vain pursuit of literature, as idle as alchemy, and as entrancing. But you have come to town for some time I suppose; what shall we do to-night?'

'Well, I rather wanted you to try a few days with me down in the west. It would do you a lot of good, I'm sure.'

'You are very kind, Vaughan, but London in September is hard to leave. Doré* could not have designed anything more wonderful and mystic than Oxford Street as I saw it the other evening; the sunset flaming, the blue haze transmuting the plain street into a road "far in the spiritual city." '*

'I should like you to come down though. You would enjoy roaming over our hills. Does this racket go on all day and all night? It quite bewilders me; I wonder how you can work through it. I am sure you would revel in the great peace of my old home among the woods.'

Vaughan lit his pipe again, and looked anxiously at Dyson to see if his inducements had had any effect, but the man of letters shook his head, smiling, and vowed in his heart a firm allegiance to the streets.

'You cannot tempt me,' he said.

'Well, you may be right. Perhaps, after all, I was wrong to speak of the peace of the country. There, when a tragedy does occur, it is like a stone thrown into a pond; the circles of disturbance keep on widening, and it seems as if the water would never be still again.'

'Have you ever any tragedies where you are?'

'I can hardly say that. But I was a good deal disturbed about a month ago by something that happened; it may or may not have been a tragedy in the usual sense of the word.'

'What was the occurrence?'

'Well, the fact is a girl disappeared in a way which seems highly mysterious. Her parents, people of the name of Trevor, are well-to-do farmers, and their eldest daughter Annie was a sort of village beauty; she was really remarkably handsome. One afternoon she thought she would go and see her aunt, a widow who farms her own land, and as the two houses are only about five or six miles apart, she started off, telling her parents she would take the short cut over the hills. She never got to her aunt's, and she never was seen again. That's putting it in a few words.'

'What an extraordinary thing! I suppose there are no disused mines, are there, on the hills? I don't think you quite run to anything so formidable as a precipice?'

'No; the path the girl must have taken had no pitfalls of any description; it is just a track over wild, bare hillside, far, even, from a byroad. One may walk for miles without meeting a soul, but it is all perfectly safe.'

'And what do people say about it?'

'Oh, they talk nonsense—among themselves. You have no notion as to how superstitious English cottagers are in out-of-the-way parts like mine. They are as bad as the Irish, every whit, and even more secretive.'

'But what do they say?'

'Oh, the poor girl is supposed to have "gone with the fairies," or to have been "taken by the fairies." Such stuff!' he went on, 'one would laugh if it were not for the real tragedy of the case.'

Dyson looked somewhat interested.

'Yes,' he said, ' "fairies" certainly strike a little curiously on the ear in these days. But what do the police say? I presume they do not accept the fairy-tale hypothesis?'

'No; but they seem quite at fault. What I am afraid of is that Annie Trevor must have fallen in with some scoundrels on her way. Castletown* is a large seaport, you know, and some of the worst of the foreign sailors occasionally desert their ships and go on the tramp up and down the country. Not many years ago a Spanish sailor named Garcia murdered a whole family for the sake of plunder that was not worth sixpence. They are hardly human, some of these fellows, and I am dreadfully afraid the poor girl must have come to an awful end.'

'But no foreign sailor was seen by anyone about the country?'

'No; there is certainly that; and of course country people are quick to notice anyone whose appearance and dress are a little out of the common. Still it seems as if my theory were the only possible explanation.'

'There are no data to go upon,' said Dyson, thoughtfully. 'There was no question of a love affair, or anything of the kind, I suppose?'

'Oh, no, not a hint of such a thing. I am sure if Annie were alive she would have contrived to let her mother know of her safety.'

'No doubt, no doubt. Still it is barely possible that she is alive and yet unable to communicate with her friends. But all this must have disturbed you a good deal.'

'Yes, it did; I hate a mystery, and especially a mystery which is probably the veil of horror. But frankly, Dyson, I want to make a clean breast of it; I did not come here to tell you all this.'

'Of course not,' said Dyson, a little surprised at Vaughan's uneasy manner. 'You came to have a chat on more cheerful topics.'

'No, I did not. What I have been telling you about happened a month ago, but something which seems likely to affect me more personally has taken place within the last few days, and to be quite plain, I came up to town with the idea that you might be able to help me. You recollect that curious case you spoke to me about at our last meeting; something about a spectacle-maker.'

'Oh, yes, I remember that. I know I was quite proud of my acumen at the time; even to this day the police have no idea why those peculiar yellow spectacles were wanted. But, Vaughan, you really look quite put out; I hope there is nothing serious?'

'No, I think I have been exaggerating, and I want you to reassure me. But what has happened is very odd.'

'And what has happened?'

'I am sure that you will laugh at me, but this is the story. You must know there is a path, a right of way, that goes through my land, and to be precise, close to the wall of the kitchen garden. It is not used by many people; a woodman now and again finds it useful, and five or six children who go to school in the village pass twice a day. Well, a few days ago I was taking a walk about the place before breakfast, and I happened to stop to fill my pipe just by the large doors in the garden wall. The wood, I must tell you, comes to within a few feet of the wall, and the track I spoke of runs right in the shadow of the trees. I thought the shelter from a brisk wind that was blowing rather pleasant, and I stood there smoking with my eyes on the ground. Then something caught my attention. Just under the wall, on the short grass, a number of small flints were arranged in a pattern; something like this': and Mr Vaughan caught at a pencil and piece of paper, and dotted down a few strokes.

'You see,' he went on, 'there were, I should think, twelve little stones neatly arranged in lines, and spaced at equal distances, as I have shewn it on the paper. They were pointed stones, and the points were very carefully directed one way.'

'Yes,' said Dyson, without much interest, 'no doubt the children you have mentioned had been playing there on their way from school. Children, as you know, are very fond of making such devices with oyster shells or flints or flowers, or with whatever comes in their way.'

'So I thought; I just noticed these flints were arranged in a sort of pattern and then went on. But the next morning I was taking the same round, which, as a matter of fact, is habitual with me, and again I saw at the same spot a device in flints. This time it was really a curious pattern; something like the spokes of a wheel, all meeting at a common centre, and this centre formed by a device which looked like a bowl; all, you understand, done in flints.'

'You are right,' said Dyson, 'that seems odd enough. Still it is reasonable that your half-a-dozen school children are responsible for these fantasies in stone.'

'Well, I thought I would set the matter at rest. The children pass the gate every evening at half-past five, and I walked by at six, and found the device just as I had left it in the morning. The next day I was up and about at a quarter to seven, and I found the whole thing had been changed. There was a pyramid outlined in flints upon the grass. The children I saw going by an hour and a half later, and they ran past the spot without glancing to right or left. In the evening I watched them going home, and this morning when I got to the gate at six o'clock there was a thing like a half moon waiting for me.'

'So then the series runs thus: firstly ordered lines, then the device of the spokes and the bowl, then the pyramid, and finally, this morning, the half moon. That is the order, isn't it?'

'Yes; that is right. But do you know it has made me feel very uneasy? I suppose it seems absurd, but I can't help thinking that some kind of signalling is going on under my nose, and that sort of thing is disquieting.'

'But what have you to dread? You have no enemies?'

'No; but I have some very valuable old plate.'

'You are thinking of burglars then?' said Dyson, with an accent of considerable interest, 'but you must know your neighbours. Are there any suspicious characters about?'

'Not that I am aware of. But you remember what I told you of the sailors.'

'Can you trust your servants?'

'Oh, perfectly. The plate is preserved in a strong room; the butler, an old family servant, alone knows where the key is kept. There is nothing wrong there. Still, everybody is aware that I have a lot of old silver, and all country folks are given to gossip. In that way information may have got abroad in very undesirable quarters.'

'Yes, but I confess there seems something a little unsatisfactory in the burglar theory. Who is signalling to whom? I cannot see my way to accepting such an explanation. What put the plate into your head in connection with these flint signs, or whatever one may call them?'

'It was the figure of the Bowl,' said Vaughan. 'I happen to possess a very large and very valuable Charles II punch-bowl.* The chasing* is really exquisite, and the thing is worth a lot of money. The sign I described to you was exactly same shape as my punch-bowl.'

'A queer coincidence certainly. But the other figures or devices: you have nothing shaped like a pyramid?'

'Ah, you will think that queerer. As it happens, this punch-bowl of mine, together with a set of rare old ladles, is kept in a mahogany chest of a pyramidal shape. The four sides slope upwards, the narrow towards the top.'

'I confess all this interests me a good deal,' said Dyson. 'Let us go on then. What about the other figures; how about the Army, as we may call the first sign, and the Crescent or Half-moon?'

'Ah, there is no reference that I can make out of these two. Still, you see I have some excuse for curiosity at all events. I should be very vexed to lose any of the old plate; nearly all the pieces have been in the family for generations. And I cannot get it out of my head that some scoundrels mean to rob me, and are communicating with one another every night.'

'Frankly,' said Dyson, 'I can make nothing of it; I am as much in the dark as yourself. Your theory seems certainly the only possible explanation, and yet the difficulties are immense.'

He leaned back in his chair, and the two men faced each other, frowning, and perplexed by so bizarre a problem.

'By the way,' said Dyson, after a long pause, 'what is your geological formation down there?'

Mr Vaughan looked up, a good deal surprised by the question.

'Old red sandstone and limestone,* I believe,' he said. 'We are just beyond the coal measures, you know.'

'But surely there are no flints either in the sandstone or the limestone?'

'No, I never see any flints in the fields. I confess that did strike me as a little curious.'

'I should think so! It is very important. By the way, what size were the flints used in making these devices?'

'I happen to have brought one with me; I took it this morning.'

'From the Half-moon?'

'Exactly. Here it is.'

He handed over a small flint, tapering to a point, and about three inches in length.

Dyson's face blazed up with excitement as he took the thing from Vaughan.

'Certainly,' he said, after a moment's pause, 'you have some curious neighbours in your country. I hardly think they can harbour any designs on your punch-bowl. Do you know this is a flint arrow-head of vast antiquity, and not only that, but an arrow-head of a unique kind? I have seen specimens from all parts of the world, but there are features about this thing that are quite peculiar.'

He laid down his pipe, and took out a book from a drawer.

'We shall just have time to catch the 5.45 to Castletown,' he said.

## II

### THE EYES ON THE WALL

MR DYSON drew in a long breath of the air of the hills and felt all the enchantment of the scene about him. It was very early morning, and he stood on the terrace in the front of the house. Vaughan's ancestor had built on the lower slope of a great hill, in the shelter of a deep and ancient wood that gathered on three sides about the house, and on the fourth side, the south-west, the land fell gently away and sank to the valley, where a brook wound in and out in mystic esses,* and the dark and gleaming alders tracked the stream's course to the eye. On the terrace in that sheltered place no wind blew, and far beyond, the trees were still. Only one sound broke in upon the silence, and Dyson heard the noise of the brook singing far below, the song of clear and shining water rippling over the stones, whispering and murmuring as it sank to dark deep pools. Across the stream, just below the house, rose a grey stone bridge, vaulted and buttressed, a fragment of the Middle Ages, and then beyond the bridge the hills rose again, vast and rounded like bastions, covered here and there with dark woods and thickets of undergrowth, but the heights were all bare of trees, showing only grey turf and patches of bracken, touched here and there with the gold of fading fronds. Dyson looked to the north and south, and still he saw the wall of the hills, and the ancient woods, and the stream drawn in and out between them; all grey and dim with morning mist beneath a grey sky in a hushed and haunted air.

Mr Vaughan's voice broke in upon the silence. 'I thought you would be too tired to be about so early,' he said. 'I see you are admiring the view. It is very pretty, isn't it, though I suppose old Meyrick Vaughan didn't think much about the scenery when he built the house. A queer grey, old place, isn't it?'

'Yes, and how it fits into the surroundings; it seems of a piece with the grey hills and the grey bridge below.'

'I am afraid I have brought you down on false pretences, Dyson,' said Vaughan, as they began to walk up and down the terrace. 'I have been to the place, and there is not a sign of anything this morning.'

'Ah, indeed. Well, suppose we go round together.'

They walked across the lawn and went by a path through the ilex shrubbery to the back of the house. There Vaughan pointed out the track leading down to the valley and up to the heights above the wood, and presently they stood beneath the garden wall, by the door.

'Here, you see, it was,' said Vaughan, pointing to a spot on the turf. 'I was standing just where you are now that morning I first saw the flints.'

'Yes, quite so. That morning it was the Army, as I call it; then the Bowl, then the Pyramid, and, yesterday, the Half-moon. What a queer old stone that is,' he went on, pointing to a block of limestone rising out of the turf just beneath the wall. 'It looks like a sort of dwarf pillar, but I suppose it is natural.'

'Oh, yes, I think so. I imagine it was brought here, though, as we stand on the red sandstone. No doubt it was used as a foundation stone for some older building.'

'Very likely.' Dyson was peering about him attentively, looking from the ground to the wall, and from the wall to the deep wood that hung almost over the garden and made the place dark even in the morning.

'Look here,' said Dyson at length, 'it is certainly a case of children this time. Look at that.'

He was bending down and staring at the dull red surface of the mellowed bricks of the wall. Vaughan came up and looked hard where Dyson's finger was pointing, and could scarcely distinguish a faint mark in deeper red.

'What is it?' he said. 'I can make nothing of it.'

'Look a little more closely. Don't you see it is an attempt to draw the human eye?'

'Ah, now I see what you mean. My sight is not very sharp. Yes, so it is, it is meant for an eye, no doubt, as you say. I thought the children learnt drawing at school.'

'Well, it is an odd eye enough. Do you notice the peculiar almond shape; almost like the eye of a Chinaman?'*

Dyson looked meditatively at the work of the undeveloped artist, and scanned the wall again, going down on his knees in the minuteness of his inquisition.

'I should like very much,' he said at length, 'to know how a child in this out of the way place could have any idea of the shape of the Mongolian eye. You see the average child has a very distinct impression of the subject; he draws a circle, or something like a circle, and puts a dot in the centre. I don't think any child imagines that the eye is really made like that; it's just a convention of infantile art. But this almond-shaped thing puzzles me extremely. Perhaps it may be derived from a gilt Chinaman on a tea-canister in the grocer's shop. Still that's hardly likely.'

'But why are you so sure it was done by a child?'

'Why! Look at the height. These old-fashioned bricks are little more than two inches thick; there are twenty courses from the ground to the sketch if we call it so; that gives a height of three and a half feet. Now, just imagine you are going to draw something on this wall. Exactly; your pencil, if you had one, would touch the wall somewhere on the level with your eyes, that is, more than five feet from the ground. It seems, therefore, a very simple deduction to conclude that this eye on the wall was drawn by a child about ten years old.'

'Yes, I had not thought of that. Of course one of the children must have done it.'

'I suppose so; and yet as I said, there is something singularly unchild-like about those two lines, and the eyeball itself, you see, is almost an oval. To my mind, the thing has an odd, ancient air; and a touch that is not altogether pleasant. I cannot help fancying that if we could see a whole face from the same hand it would not be altogether agreeable. However, that is nonsense, after all, and we are not getting farther in our investigations. It is odd that the flint series has come to such an abrupt end.'

The two men walked away towards the house, and as they went in at the porch there was a break in the grey sky, and a gleam of sunshine on the grey hill before them.

All the day Dyson prowled meditatively about the fields and woods surrounding the house. He was thoroughly and completely puzzled by the trivial circumstances he proposed to elucidate, and now he again took the flint arrow-head from his pocket, turning it over and examining it with deep attention. There was something about the thing that was altogether different from the specimens he had seen at the museums and private collections; the shape was of a distinct type, and around the edge there was a line of little punctured dots, apparently a suggestion of ornament. Who, thought Dyson, could possess such things in so remote a place; and who, possessing the flints, could have put them to the fantastic use of designing meaningless figures under Vaughan's garden wall? The rank absurdity of the whole affair offended him unutterably; and as one theory after another rose in his mind only to be rejected, he felt strongly tempted to take the next train back to town. He had seen the silver plate which Vaughan treasured, and had inspected the punchbowl, the gem of the collection, with close attention; and what he saw and his interview with the butler convinced him that a plot to rob the strong box was out of the limits of enquiry. The chest in which the bowl was kept, a heavy piece of mahogany, evidently dating from the beginning of the century, was certainly strongly suggestive of a pyramid, and Dyson was at first inclined to the inept manœuvres of the detective, but a little sober thought convinced him of the impossibility of the burglary hypothesis, and he cast wildly about for something more satisfying. He asked Vaughan if there were any gypsies in the neighbourhood, and heard that the Romany had not been seen for years. This dashed him a good deal, as he knew the gypsy habit of leaving queer hieroglyphics on the line of march, and had been much elated when the thought occurred to him. He was facing Vaughan by the old-fashioned hearth when he put the question, and leaned back in his chair in disgust at the destruction of his theory.

'It is odd,' said Vaughan, 'but the gypsies never trouble us here. Now and then the farmers find traces of fires in the wildest part of the hills, but nobody seems to know who the fire-lighters are.'

'Surely that looks like gypsies?'

'No, not in such places as those. Tinkers and gypsies and wanderers of all sorts stick to the roads and don't go very far from the farm-houses.'

'Well, I can make nothing of it. I saw the children going by this afternoon, and, as you say, they ran straight on. So we shall have no more eyes on the wall at all events.'

'No, I must waylay them one of these days and find out who is the artist.'

The next morning when Vaughan strolled in his usual course from the lawn to the back of the house he found Dyson already awaiting him by the garden door, and evidently in a state of high excitement, for he beckoned furiously with his hand, and gesticulated violently.

'What is it?' asked Vaughan. 'The flints again?'

'No; but look here, look at the wall. There; don't you see it?'

'There's another of those eyes!'

'Exactly. Drawn, you see, at a little distance from the first, almost on the same level, but slightly lower.'

'What on earth is one to make of it? It couldn't have been done by the children; it wasn't there last night, and they won't pass for another hour. What can it mean?'

'I think the very devil is at the bottom of all this,' said Dyson. 'Of course, one cannot resist the conclusion that these infernal almond eyes are to be set down to the same agency as the devices in the arrow-heads; and where that conclusion is to lead us is more than I can tell. For my part, I have to put a strong check on my imagination, or it would run wild.'

'Vaughan,' he said, as they turned away from the wall, 'has it struck you that there is one point—a very curious point—in common between the figures done in flints and the eyes drawn on the wall?'

'What is that?' asked Vaughan, on whose face there had fallen a certain shadow of indefinite dread.

'It is this. We know that the signs of the Army, the Bowl, the Pyramid, and the Half-moon must have been done at night. Presumably they were meant to be seen at night. Well, precisely the same reasoning applies to those eyes on the wall.'

'I do not quite see your point.'

'Oh, surely. The nights are dark just now, and have been very cloudy, I know, since I came down. Moreover, those overhanging trees would throw that wall into deep shadow even on a clear night.'

'Well?'

'What struck me was this. What very peculiarly sharp eyesight, they, whoever "they" are, must have to be able to arrange arrow-heads in intricate order in the blackest shadow of the wood, and then draw the eyes on the wall without a trace of bungling, or a false line.'

'I have read of persons confined in dungeons for many years who have been able to see quite well in the dark,' said Vaughan.

'Yes,' said Dyson, 'there was the abbé in *Monte Cristo*.* But it is a singular point.'


# III

### THE SEARCH FOR THE BOWL

'Who was that old man that touched his hat to you just now?' said Dyson, as they came to the bend of the lane near the house.

'Oh, that was old Trevor. He looks very broken, poor old fellow.'

'Who is Trevor?'

'Don't you remember? I told you the story that afternoon I came to your rooms—about a girl named Annie Trevor, who disappeared in the most inexplicable manner about five weeks ago. That was her father.'

'Yes, yes, I recollect now. To tell the truth I had forgotten all about it. And nothing has been heard of the girl?'

'Nothing whatever. The police are quite at fault.'

'I am afraid I did not pay very much attention to the details you gave me. Which way did the girl go?'

'Her path would take her right across those wild hills above the house; the nearest point in the track must be about two miles from here.'

'Is it near that little hamlet I saw yesterday?'

'You mean Croesyceiliog,* where the children came from? No; it goes more to the north.'

'Ah, I have never been that way.'

They went into the house, and Dyson shut himself up in his room, sunk deep in doubtful thought, but yet with the shadow of a suspicion growing within him that for a while haunted his brain, all vague and fantastic, refusing to take definite form. He was sitting by the open window and looking out on the valley and saw, as if in a picture, the intricate winding of the brook, the grey bridge, and the vast hills rising beyond; all still and without a breath of wind to stir the mystic hanging woods, and the evening sunshine glowed warm on the bracken, and down below a faint mist, pure white, began to rise from the stream. Dyson sat by the window as the day darkened and the huge bastioned hills loomed vast and vague, and the woods became dim and more shadowy; and the fancy that had seized him no longer appeared altogether impossible. He passed the rest of the evening in a reverie, hardly hearing what Vaughan said; and when he took his candle in the hall, he paused a moment before bidding his friend good-night.

'I want a good rest,' he said. 'I have got some work to do to-morrow.'

'Some writing, you mean?'

'No. I am going to look for the Bowl.'

'The Bowl! If you mean my punch-bowl, that is safe in the chest.'

'I don't mean the punch-bowl. You may take my word for it that your plate has never been threatened. No; I will not bother you with any suppositions. We shall in all probability have something much stronger than suppositions before long. Good-night, Vaughan.'

The next morning Dyson set off after breakfast. He took the path by the garden-wall, and noted that there were now eight of the weird almond eyes dimly outlined on the brick.

'Six days more,' he said to himself, but as he thought over the theory he had formed, he shrank, in spite of strong conviction, from such a wildly incredible fancy. He struck up through the dense shadows of the wood, and at length came out on the bare hillside, and climbed higher and higher over the slippery turf, keeping well to the north, and following the indications given him by Vaughan. As he went on, he seemed to mount ever higher above the world of human life and customary things; to his right he looked at a fringe of orchard and saw a faint blue smoke rising like a pillar; there was the hamlet from which the children came to school, and there the only sign of life, for the woods embowered and concealed Vaughan's old grey house. As he reached what seemed the summit of the hill, he realised for the first time the desolate loneliness and strangeness of the land; there was nothing but grey sky and grey hill, a high, vast plain that seemed to stretch on for ever and ever, and a faint glimpse of a blue-peaked mountain far away and to the north. At length he came to the path, a slight track scarcely noticeable, and from its position and by what Vaughan had told him he knew that it was the way the lost girl, Annie Trevor, must have taken. He followed the path on the bare hill-top, noticing the great limestone rocks that cropped out of the turf, grim and hideous, and of an aspect as forbidding as an idol of the South Seas;* and suddenly he halted, astonished, although he had found what he searched for. Almost without warning the ground shelved suddenly away on all sides, and Dyson looked down into a circular depression, which might well have been a Roman amphitheatre, and the ugly crags of limestone rimmed it round as if with a broken wall. Dyson walked round the hollow, and noted the position of the stones, and then turned on his way home.

'This,' he thought to himself, 'is more than curious. The Bowl is discovered, but where is the Pyramid?'

'My dear Vaughan,' he said, when he got back, 'I may tell you that I have found the Bowl, and that is all I shall tell you for the present. We have six days of absolute inaction before us; there is really nothing to be done.'


## IV

### THE SECRET OF THE PYRAMID

'I HAVE just been round the garden,' said Vaughan one morning. 'I have been counting those infernal eyes, and I find there are fourteen of them. For heaven's sake, Dyson, tell me what the meaning of it all is.'

'I should be very sorry to attempt to do so. I may have guessed this or that, but I always make it a principle to keep my guesses to myself. Besides, it is really not worth while anticipating events; you will remember my telling you that we had six days of inaction before us? Well, this is the sixth day, and the last of idleness. To-night I propose we take a stroll.'

'A stroll! Is that all the action you mean to take?'

'Well, it may show you some very curious things. To be plain, I want you to start with me at nine o'clock this evening for the hills. We may have to be out all night, so you had better wrap up well, and bring some of that brandy.'

'Is it a joke?' asked Vaughan, who was bewildered with strange events and strange surmises.

'No, I don't think there is much joke in it. Unless I am much mistaken we shall find a very serious explanation of the puzzle. You will come with me, I am sure?'

'Very good. Which way do you want to go?'

'By the path you told me of; the path Annie Trevor is supposed to have taken.'

Vaughan looked white at the mention of the girl's name.

'I did not think you were on that track,' he said. 'I thought it was the affair of those devices in flint and of the eyes on the wall that you were engaged on. It's no good saying any more, but I will go with you.'

At a quarter to nine that evening the two men set out, taking the path through the wood, and up the hill-side. It was a dark and heavy night, the sky was thick with clouds, and the valley full of mist, and all the way they seemed to walk in a world of shadow and gloom, hardly speaking, and afraid to break the haunted silence. They came out at last on the steep hill-side, and instead of the oppression of the wood there was the long, dim sweep of the turf, and higher, the fantastic limestone rocks hinted horror through the darkness, and the wind sighed as it passed across the mountain to the sea, and in its passage beat chill about their hearts. They seemed to walk on and on for hours, and the dim outline of the hill still stretched before them, and the haggard rocks still loomed through the darkness, when suddenly Dyson whispered, drawing his breath quickly, and coming close to his companion

'Here,' he said, 'we will lie down. I do not think there is anything yet.'

'I know the place,' said Vaughan, after a moment. 'I have often been by in the daytime. The country people are afraid to come here, I believe; it is supposed to be a fairies' castle, or something of the kind. But why on earth have we come here?'

'Speak a little lower,' said Dyson. 'It might not do us any good if we are overheard.'

'Overheard here! There is not a soul within three miles of us.'

'Possibly not; indeed, I should say certainly not. But there might be a body somewhat nearer.'

'I don't understand you in the least,' said Vaughan, whispering to humour Dyson, 'but why have we come here?'

'Well, you see this hollow before us is the Bowl. I think we had better not talk even in whispers.'

They lay full length upon the turf; the rock between their faces and the Bowl, and now and again, Dyson, slouching his dark, soft hat over his forehead, put out the glint of an eye, and in a moment drew back, not daring to take a prolonged view. Again he laid an ear to the ground and listened, and the hours went by, and the darkness seemed to blacken, and the faint sigh of the wind was the only sound.

Vaughan grew impatient with this heaviness of silence, this watching for indefinite terror; for to him there was no shape or form of apprehension, and he began to think the whole vigil a dreary farce.

'How much longer is this to last?' he whispered to Dyson, and Dyson who had been holding his breath in the agony of attention put his mouth to Vaughan's ear and said:

'Will you listen?' with pauses between each syllable, and in the voice with which the priest pronounces the awful words.*

Vaughan caught the ground with his hands, and stretched forward, wondering what he was to hear. At first there was nothing, and then a low and gentle noise came very softly from the Bowl, a faint sound, almost indescribable, but as if one held the tongue against the roof of the mouth and expelled the breath. He listened eagerly and presently the noise grew louder, and became a strident and horrible hissing as if the pit beneath boiled with fervent heat, and Vaughan, unable to remain in suspense any longer, drew his cap half over his face in imitation of Dyson, and looked down to the hollow below.

It did, in truth, stir and seethe like an infernal caldron. The whole of the sides and bottom tossed and writhed with vague and restless forms that passed to and fro without the sound of feet, and gathered thick here and there and seemed to speak to one another in those tones of horrible sibilance, like the hissing of snakes, that he had heard. It was as if the sweet turf and the cleanly earth had suddenly become quickened with some foul writhing growth. Vaughan could not draw back his face, though he felt Dyson's finger touch him, but he peered into the quaking mass and saw faintly that there were things like faces and human limbs, and yet he felt his inmost soul chill with the sure belief that no fellow soul or human thing stirred in all that tossing and hissing host. He looked aghast, choking back sobs of horror, and at length the loathsome forms gathered thickest about some vague object in the middle of the hollow, and the hissing of their speech grew more venomous, and he saw in the uncertain light the abominable limbs, vague and yet too plainly seen, writhe and intertwine, and he thought he heard, very faint, a low human moan striking through the noise of speech that was not of man. At his heart something seemed to whisper ever 'the worm of corruption, the worm that dieth not,'* and grotesquely the image was pictured to his imagination of a piece of putrid offal stirring through and through with bloated and horrible creeping things. The writhing of the dusky limbs continued, they seemed clustered round the dark form in the middle of the hollow, and the sweat dripped and poured off Vaughan's forehead, and fell cold on his hand beneath his face.

Then, it seemed done in an instant, the loathsome mass melted and fell away to the sides of the Bowl, and for a moment Vaughan saw in the middle of the hollow the tossing of human arms. But a spark gleamed beneath, a fire kindled, and as the voice of a woman cried out loud in a shrill scream of utter anguish and terror, a great pyramid of flame spired up like a bursting of a pent fountain, and threw a blaze of light upon the whole mountain. In that instant Vaughan saw the myriads beneath; the things made in the form of men but stunted like children hideously deformed, the faces with the almond eyes burning with evil and unspeakable lusts; the ghastly yellow of the mass of naked flesh;

and then as if by magic the place was empty, while the fire roared and crackled, and the flames shone abroad.

'You have seen the Pyramid,' said Dyson in his ear, 'the Pyramid of fire.'

# V

## THE LITTLE PEOPLE

'THEN you recognise the thing?'

'Certainly. It is a brooch that Annie Trevor used to wear on Sundays; I remember the pattern. But where did you find it? You don't mean to say that you have discovered the girl?'

'My dear Vaughan, I wonder you have not guessed where I found the brooch. You have not forgotten last night already?'

'Dyson,' said the other, speaking very seriously, 'I have been turning it over in my mind this morning while you have been out. I have thought about what I saw, or perhaps I should say about what I thought I saw, and the only conclusion I can come to is this, that the thing won't bear recollection. As men live, I have lived soberly and honestly, in the fear of God, all my days, and all I can do is believe that I suffered from some monstrous delusion, from some phantasmagoria* of the bewildered senses. You know we went home together in silence, not a word passed between us as to what I fancied I saw; had we not better agree to keep silence on the subject? When I took my walk in the peaceful morning sunshine, I thought all the earth seemed full of praise, and passing by that wall I noticed there were no more signs recorded, and I blotted out those that remained. The mystery is over, and we can live quietly again. I think some poison has been working for the last few weeks; I have trod on the verge of madness, but I am sane now.'

Mr Vaughan had spoken earnestly, and bent forward in his chair and glanced at Dyson with something of entreaty.

'My dear Vaughan,' said the other, after a pause, 'what's the use of this? It is much too late to take that tone; we have gone too deep. Besides you know as well as I that there is no delusion in the case; I wish there were with all my heart. No, in justice to myself I must tell you the whole story, so far as I know it.'

'Very good,' said Vaughan with a sigh, 'if you must, you must.'

'Then,' said Dyson, 'we will begin with the end if you please. I found this brooch you have just identified in the place we have called the

Bowl. There was a heap of grey ashes, as if a fire had been burning, indeed, the embers were still hot, and this brooch was lying on the ground, just outside the range of the flame. It must have dropped accidentally from the dress of the person who was wearing it. No, don't interrupt me; we can pass now to the beginning, as we have had the end. Let us go back to that day you came to see me in my rooms in London. So far as I can remember, soon after you came in you mentioned, in a somewhat casual manner, that an unfortunate and mysterious incident had occurred in your part of the country; a girl named Annie Trevor had gone to see a relative, and had disappeared. I confess freely that what you said did not greatly interest me; there are so many reasons which may make it extremely convenient for a man and more especially a woman to vanish from the circle of their relations and friends. I suppose, if we were to consult the police, one would find that in London somebody disappears mysteriously every other week, and the officers would, no doubt, shrug their shoulders, and tell you that by the law of averages it could not be otherwise. So I was very culpably careless to your story, and besides, there is another reason for my lack of interest; your tale was inexplicable. You could only suggest a blackguard sailor on the tramp, but I discarded the explanation immediately. For many reasons, but chiefly because the occasional criminal, the amateur in brutal crime, is always found out, especially if he selects the country as the scene of his operations. You will remember the case of that Garcia you mentioned; he strolled into a railway station the day after the murder, his trousers covered with blood, and the works of the Dutch clock, his loot, tied in a neat parcel. So rejecting this, your only suggestion, the whole tale became, as I say, inexplicable, and, therefore, profoundly uninteresting. Yes, *therefore*, it is a perfectly valid conclusion. Do you ever trouble your head about problems which you know to be insoluble? Did you ever bestow much thought on the old puzzle of Achilles and the Tortoise!* Of course not, because you knew it was a hopeless quest, and so when you told me the story of a country girl who had disappeared I simply placed the whole thing down in the category of the insoluble, and thought no more about the matter. I was mistaken, so it has turned out; but if you remember, you immediately passed on to an affair which interested you more intensely, because personally. I need not go over the very singular narrative of the flint signs; at first I thought it all trivial, probably some children's game, and if not that a hoax of some sort; but your shewing me the arrow-head awoke my acute interest. Here, I saw, there was something widely removed from the commonplace, and matter of real curiosity; and as soon as I came here I set to work to find the solution, repeating to myself again and again the signs you had described. First came the sign we have agreed to call the Army; a number of serried lines of flints, all pointing in the same way. Then the lines, like the spokes of a wheel, all converging towards the figure of a Bowl, then the triangle or Pyramid, and last of all the Half-moon. I confess that I exhausted conjecture in my efforts to unveil this mystery, and as you will understand it was a duplex or rather triplex problem. For I had not merely to ask myself: what do these figures mean? but also, who can possibly be responsible for the designing of them? And again, who can possibly possess such valuable things, and knowing their value thus throw them down by the wayside? This line of thought led me to suppose that the person or persons in question did not know the value of unique flint arrow-heads, and yet this did not lead me far, for a well-educated man might easily be ignorant on such a subject. Then came the complication of the eye on the wall, and you remember that we could not avoid the conclusion that in the two cases the same agency was at work. The peculiar position of these eyes on the wall made me enquire if there was such a thing as a dwarf anywhere in the neighbourhood, but I found that there was not, and I knew that the children who pass by every day had nothing to do with the matter. Yet I felt convinced that whoever drew the eyes must be from three-and-a-half to four feet high, since, as I pointed out at the time, anyone who draws on a perpendicular surface chooses by instinct a spot about level with his face. Then again, there was the question of the peculiar shape of the eyes; that marked Mongolian character of which the English countryman could have no conception, and for a final cause of confusion the obvious fact that the designer or designers must be able practically to see in the dark. As you remarked, a man who has been confined for many years in an extremely dark cell or dungeon might acquire that power; but since the days of Edmond Dantès,* where would such a prison be found in Europe? A sailor, who had been immured for a considerable period in some horrible Chinese *oubliette*,* seemed the individual I was in search of, and though it looked improbable, it was not absolutely impossible that a sailor or, let us say, a man employed on shipboard, should be a dwarf. But how to account for my imaginary sailor being in possession of prehistoric arrow-heads? And the possession granted, what was the meaning and object of these mysterious signs of flint, and the almond-shaped eyes? Your theory of a contemplated burglary I saw, nearly from the first, to be quite untenable, and I confess I was utterly at a loss for a working hypothesis. It was a mere accident which put me on the track; we passed poor old Trevor, and your mention of his name and of the disappearance of his daughter, recalled the story which I had forgotten, or which remained unheeded. Here, then, I said to myself, is another problem, uninteresting, it is true, by itself; but what if it prove to be in relation with all these enigmas which torture me? I shut myself in my room, and endeavoured to dismiss all prejudice from my mind, and I went over everything *de novo*,* assuming for theory's sake that the disappearance of Annie Trevor had some connection with the flint signs and the eyes on the wall. This assumption did not lead me very far, and I was on the point of giving the whole problem up in despair, when a possible significance of the Bowl struck me. As you know there is a "Devil's Punch-bowl" in Surrey,* and I saw that the symbol might refer to some feature in the country. Putting the two extremes together, I determined to look for the Bowl near the path which the lost girl had taken, and you know how I found it. I interpreted the sign by what I knew, and read the first, the Army, thus: "there is to be a gathering or assembly at the Bowl in a fortnight (that is the Half-moon) to see the Pyramid, or to build the Pyramid." The eyes, drawn one by one, day by day, evidently checked off the days, and I knew that there would be fourteen and no more. Thus far the way seemed pretty plain; I would not trouble myself to enquire as to the nature of the assembly, or as to who was to assemble in the loneliest and most dreaded place among these lonely hills. In Ireland or China or the west of America the question would have been easily answered; a muster of the disaffected, the meeting of a secret society, Vigilantes* summoned to report: the thing would be simplicity itself; but in this quiet corner of England, inhabited by quiet folk, no such suppositions were possible for a moment. But I knew that I should have an opportunity of seeing and watching the assembly, and I did not care to perplex myself with hopeless research; and in place of reasoning a wild fancy entered into judgment: I remembered what people had said about Annie Trevor's disappearance, that she had been "taken by the fairies." I tell you, Vaughan, I am a sane man as you are, my brain is not, I trust, mere vacant space to let to any wild improbability, and I tried my best to thrust the fantasy away. And the hint came of the old name of fairies, "the little people," and the very probable belief that they represent a tradition of the prehistoric Turanian inhabitants* of the country, who were cave dwellers: and then I realised with a shock that I was looking for a being under four feet in height, accustomed to live in darkness, possessing stone instruments, and familiar with the Mongolian cast of features! I say this, Vaughan, that I should be ashamed to hint at such visionary stuff to you, if it were not for that which you saw with your very eyes last night, and I say that

I might doubt the evidence of my senses, if they were not confirmed by yours. But you and I cannot look each other in the face and pretend delusion; as you lay on the turf beside me I felt your flesh shrink and quiver, and I saw your eyes in the light of the flame. And so I tell you without any shame what was in my mind last night as we went through the wood and climbed the hill, and lay hidden beneath the rock.

'There was one thing that should have been most evident that puzzled me to the very last. I told you how I read the sign of the Pyramid; the assembly was to see a pyramid, and the true meaning of the symbol escaped me to the last moment. The old derivation from πυρ,* fire, though false, should have set me on the track, but it never occurred to me.

'I think I need say very little more. You know we were quite helpless, even if we had foreseen what was to come. Ah, the particular place where these signs were displayed? Yes, that is a curious question. But this house is, so far as I can judge, in a pretty central situation amongst the hills; and possibly, who can say yes or no, that queer, old limestone pillar by your garden wall was a place of meeting before the Celt set foot in Britain. But there is one thing I must add: I don't regret our inability to rescue the wretched girl. You saw the appearance of those things that gathered thick and writhed in the Bowl; you may be sure that what lay bound in the midst of them was no longer fit for earth.'

'So?' said Vaughan.

'So she passed in the Pyramid of Fire,' said Dyson, 'and they passed again to the under-world, to the places beneath the hills.'

# THE TURANIANS

THE smoke of the tinkers' camp rose a thin pale blue from the heart of the wood.

Mary had left her mother at work on 'things,' and had gone out with a pale and languid face into the hot afternoon. She had talked of walking across the fields to the Green, and of having a chat with the doctor's daughter, but she had taken the other path that crept down towards the hollow and the dark thickets of the wood.

After all, she had felt too lazy to rouse herself, to make the effort of conversation, and the sunlight scorched the path that was ruled straight from stile to stile across the brown August fields, and she could see, even from far away, how the white dust clouds were smoking on the road by the Green. She hesitated, and at last went down under the far-spreading oak-trees, by a winding way of grass that cooled her feet.

Her mother, who was very kind and good, used to talk to her sometimes on the evils of 'exaggeration,' on the necessity of avoiding phrases violently expressed, words of too fierce an energy. She remembered how she had run into the house a few days before and had called her mother to look at a rose in the garden that 'burnt like a flame.' Her mother had said the rose was very pretty, and a little later had hinted her doubts as to the wisdom of 'such very strong expressions.'

'I know, my dear Mary,' she had said, 'that in your case it isn't affectation. You really *feel* what you say, don't you? Yes; but is it nice to feel like that? Do you think that it's quite *right*, even?'

The mother had looked at the girl with a curious wistfulness, almost as if she would say something more, and sought for the fit words, but could not find them. And then she merely remarked:

'You haven't seen Alfred Moorhouse since the tennis party, have you? I must ask him to come next Tuesday; you like him?'

The daughter could not quite see the link between her fault of 'exaggeration' and the charming young barrister, but her mother's warning recurred to her as she strayed down the shadowed path, and felt the long dark grass cool and refreshing about her feet. She would not have put this sensation into words, but she thought it was as though her ankles were gently, sweetly kissed as the rich grass touched them, and her mother would have said it was not right to think such things.

And what a delight there was in the colours all about her! It was as though she walked in a green cloud; the strong sunlight was filtered through the leaves, reflected from the grass, and made all visible things, the tree-stems, the flowers, and her own hands seem new, transformed into another likeness. She had walked by the wood-path over and over again, but to-day it had become full of mystery and hinting, and every turn brought a surprise.

To-day the mere sense of being alone under the trees was an acute secret joy, and as she went down deeper and the wood grew dark about her, she loosened her brown hair, and when the sun shone over the fallen tree she saw her hair was not brown but bronze and golden, glowing on her pure white dress.

She stayed by the well in the rock, and dared to make the dark water her mirror, looking to right and left with shy glances and listening for the rustle of parted boughs, before she would match her gold with luminous ivory. She saw wonders in a glass as she leaned over the shadowed mysterious pool, and smiled at the smiling nymph, whose lips parted as if to whisper secrets.

As she went on her way, the thin blue smoke rose from a gap in the trees, and she remembered her childish dread of 'the gipsies.' She walked a little farther, and laid herself to rest on a smooth patch of turf, and listened to the strange intonations that sounded from the camp. 'Those horrible people' she had heard the yellow folk called, but she found now a pleasure in voices that sang and, indistinctly heard, were almost chanting, with a rise and fall of notes and a wild wail, and the solemnity of unknown speech. It seemed a fit music for the unknown woodland, in harmony with the drip of the well, and the birds' sharp notes, and the rustle and hurry of the wood creatures.

She rose again and went on till she could see the red fire between the boughs; and the voices thrilled into an incantation. She longed to summon up courage, and talk to these strange wood-folk, but she was afraid to burst into the camp. So she sat down under a tree and waited, hoping that one of them might happen to come her way.

There were six or seven men, as many women, and a swarm of fantastic children, lolling and squatting about the fire, gabbling to one another in their singsong speech. They were people of curious aspect, short and squat, high-cheekboned, with dingy yellow skin and long almond eyes; only in one or two of the younger men there was a suggestion of a wild, almost faunlike grace, as of creatures who always moved between the red fire and the green leaf. Though everybody called them gipsies, they were in reality Turanian metal-workers, degenerated into wandering tinkers; their ancestors had fashioned the bronze battle-axes, and they mended pots and kettles. Mary waited under the tree, sure that she had nothing to fear, and resolved not to run away if one of them appeared.

The sun sank into a mass of clouds and the air grew close and heavy; a mist steamed up about the trees, a blue mist like the smoke of a wood-fire. A strange smiling face peered out from between the leaves, and the girl knew that her heart leapt as the young man walked towards her.

The Turanians moved their camp that night. There was a red glint, like fire, in the vast shadowy west, and then a burning paten* floated up from a wild hill. A procession of weird bowed figures passed across the crimson disk, one stumbling after another in long single file, each bending down beneath his huge shapeless pack, and the children crawled last, goblinlike, fantastic.

The girl was lying in her white room, caressing a small green stone, a curious thing cut with strange devices, awful with age. She held it close to the luminous ivory, and the gold poured upon it.

She laughed for joy, and murmured and whispered to herself, asking herself questions in the bewilderment of her delight. She was afraid to say anything to her mother.

# THE IDEALIST

'DID you notice Symonds while Beever was telling that story just now?' said one clerk to the other.

'No. Why? Didn't he like it?'

The second clerk had been putting away his papers and closing his desk in a grave and business-like manner, but when Beever's story was recalled to him he began to bubble anew, tasting the relish of the tale for a second time.

'He's a fair scorcher, old Beever,' he remarked between little gasps of mirth. 'But didn't Symonds like it?'

'Like it? He looked disgusted, I can tell you. Made a face, something in this style:' and the man drew his features into a design of sour disapproval, as he gave his hat the last polish with his coatsleeve.

'Well, I'm off now,' he said. 'I want to get home early, as there's tart for tea,' and he fashioned another grimace, an imitation of his favourite actor's favourite contortion.

'Well, good-bye,' said his friend. 'You are a hot'un, you are. You're worse than Beever. See you on Monday. What will Symonds say?' and he shouted after him as the door swung to and fro.

Charles Symonds, who had failed to see the humour of Mr Beever's tale, had left the office a few minutes earlier and was now pacing slowly westward, mounting Fleet Street. His fellow clerk had not been much amiss in his observation. Symonds had heard the last phrases of Beever's story, and unconsciously had looked half round towards the group, angry and disgusted at their gross and stupid merriment. Beever and his friends seemed to him guilty of sacrilege; he likened them to plough-boys pawing and deriding an exquisite painted panel, blaring out their contempt and brutal ignorance. He could not control his features; in spite of himself he looked loathing at the three yahoos.* He would have given anything if he could have found words and told them what he thought, but even to look displeasure was difficult. His shyness was a perpetual amusement to the other clerks, who often did little things to annoy him, and enjoyed the spectacle of Symonds inwardly raging and burning like Etna,* but too hopelessly diffident to say a word. He would turn dead man's white, and grind his teeth at an insult, and pretend to join in the laugh, and pass it off as a joke. When he was a boy his mother was puzzled by him, not knowing whether he were sullen or insensible, or perhaps very good-tempered.

He climbed Fleet Street, still raw with irritation, partly from a real disgust at the profane coarseness of the clerks, and partly from a feeling that they talked so because they knew he hated such gross farces and novels. It was hideous to live and work with such foul creatures, and he glanced back fury at the City, the place of the stupid, the blatant, the intolerable.

He passed into the rush and flood of the Strand, into the full tide of a Saturday afternoon, still meditating the outrage, and constructing a cutting sentence for future use, heaping up words which should make Beever tremble. He was quite aware that he would never utter one of those biting phrases, but the pretence soothed him, and he began to remember other things. It was in late November and the clouds were already gathering for the bright solemnity of the sunset, flying to their places before the wind. They curled into fantastic shapes, high up there in the wind's whirlpool, and Symonds, looking towards the sky, was attracted by two grey writhing clouds that drew together in the west, in the far perspective of the Strand. He saw them as if they had been living creatures, noting every change and movement and transformation, till the shaking winds made them one and drove a vague form away to the south.

The curious interest he had taken in the cloud shapes had driven away the thought of the office, of the fetid talk which he so often heard. Beever and his friends ceased to exist, and Symonds escaped to his occult and private world which no one had ever divined. He lived far away down in Fulham, but he let the buses rock past him, and walked slowly, endeavouring to prolong the joys of anticipation. Almost with a visible gesture he drew himself apart, and went solitary, his eyes downcast, and gazing not on the pavement but on certain clear imagined pictures.

He quickened his steps as he passed along the northern pavement of Leicester Square, hurrying to escape the sight of the enamelled strange spectra who were already beginning to walk and stir abroad, issuing from their caves and waiting for the gas-light. He scowled as he looked up and chanced to see on a hoarding* an icon with raddled cheeks and grinning teeth, at which some young men were leering; and one was recalling this creature's great song:

> And that's the way they do it.
> How d'ye fink it's done?
> Oh, *that's* the way they do it.
> *Doesn't* it taike the bun?*

Symonds scowled at the picture of her, remembering how Beever had voted her 'good goods,' how the boys bellowed the chorus under his windows of Saturday nights. Once he had opened the window as they passed by, and had sworn at them and cursed them, in a whisper, lest he should be overheard.

He peered curiously at the books in a Piccadilly shop; now and then when he could save a few pounds he had made purchases there, but the wares which the bookseller dealt in were expensive, and he was obliged to be rather neatly dressed at the office, and he had other esoteric expenses. He had made up his mind to learn Persian and he hesitated as to whether he should turn back now, and see if he could pick up a grammar in Great Russell Street at a reasonable price. But it was growing dark, and the mists and shadows that he loved were gathering and inviting him onwards to those silent streets near the river.

When he at last diverged from the main road he made his way by a devious and eccentric track, threading an intricate maze of streets which to most people would have been dull and gloomy and devoid of interest. But to Symonds these backwaters of London were as bizarre and glowing as a cabinet of Japanese curios; he found here his delicately chased bronzes, work in jade, the flush and flame of extraordinary colours. He delayed at a corner, watching a shadow on a lighted blind, watching it fade and blacken and fade, conjecturing its secrets, inventing dialogue for this drama in *Ombres Chinoises*.\* He glanced up at another window, and saw a room vivid, in a hard yellow light of flaming gas, and lurked in the shelter of an old elm till he was perceived and the curtains were drawn hastily. On the way he had chosen, it was his fortune to pass many well-ordered decent streets, by villas detached and semi-detached,\* half hidden behind flowering-shrubs and evergreens. At this hour, on a Saturday in November, few were abroad, and Symonds was often able, crouching down by the fence, to peer into a lighted room, to watch persons who thought themselves utterly unobserved. As he came near to his home he went through meaner streets, and he stopped at a corner, observing two children at play, regarding them with the minute scrutiny of an entomologist\* at the microscope. A woman who had been out shopping crossed the road and drove the children home, and Symonds moved on, hastily, but with a long sigh of enjoyment.

His breath came quick, in gusts, as he drew out his latch-key. He lived in an old Georgian house, and he raced up the stairs, and locked the door of the great lofty room in which he lived. The evening was damp and chilly, but the sweat streamed down his face. He struck a match, and there was a strange momentary vision of the vast room, almost empty of furniture, a hollow space bordered by grave walls and the white glimmer of the corniced ceiling.

He lit a candle, opened a large box that stood in a corner, and set to work. He seemed to be fitting together some sort of lay figure;* a vague hint of the human shape increased under his hands. The candle sparkled at the other end of the room, and Symonds was sweating over his task in a cavern of dark shadow. His nervous shaking fingers fumbled over that uncertain figure, and then he began to draw out incongruous monstrous things. In the dusk, white silk shimmered, laces and delicate frills hovered for a moment, as he bungled over the tying of knots, the fastening of bands. The old room grew rich, heavy, vaporous with subtle scents; the garments that were passing through his hands had been drenched with fragrance. Passion had contorted his face; he grinned stark in the candlelight.

When he had finished the work he drew it with him to the window, and lighted three more candles. In his excitement, for that night he forgot the effect of *Ombres Chinoises*, and those who passed and happened to look up at the white staring blind found singular matter for speculation.

# WITCHCRAFT

'RATHER left the others behind, haven't we, Miss Custance?' said the captain, looking back to the gate and the larchwood.

'I'm afraid we have, Captain Knight. I hope you don't mind very much, do you?'

'Mind? Delighted, you know. Sure this damp air isn't bad for you, Miss Custance?'

'Oh, d'you think it's damp? I like it. Ever since I can remember I've enjoyed these quiet autumn days. I won't hear of father's going anywhere else.'

'Charmin' place, the Grange. Don't wonder you like comin' down here.'

Captain Knight glanced back again and suddenly chuckled.

'I say, Miss Custance,' he said, 'I believe the whole lot's lost their way. Don't see a sign of them. Didn't we pass another path on the left?'

'Yes, and don't you remember you wanted to turn off?'

'Yes, of course. I thought it looked more possible, don't you know. That's where they must have gone. Where does it lead?'

'Oh, nowhere exactly. It dwindles and twists about a lot, and I'm afraid the ground is rather marshy.'

'You don't say so?' The captain laughed out loud. 'How awfully sick Ferris will be. He hates crossing Piccadilly if there's a bit of mud about.'

'Poor Mr Ferris!' And the two went on, picking their way on the rough path, till they came in sight of a little old cottage sunken alone in a hollow amongst the woods.

'Oh, you must come and see Mrs Wise,' said Miss Custance. 'She's such a dear old thing, I'm sure you'd fall in love with her. And she'd never forgive me if she heard afterwards that we'd passed so close without coming in. Only for five minutes, you know.'

'Certainly, Miss Custance. Is that the old lady there at the door?'

'Yes. She's always been so good to us children, and I know she'll talk of our coming to see her for months. You don't mind, do you?'

'I shall be charmed, I'm sure,' and he looked back once more to see if there were any appearance of Ferris and his party.

'Sit down, Miss Ethel, sit down, please, miss,' said the old woman when they went in. 'And please to sit down here, sir, will you be so kind?'

She dusted the chairs, and Miss Custance enquired after the rheumatism and the bronchitis, and promised to send something from the Grange. The old woman had good country manners, and spoke well, and now and then politely tried to include Captain Knight in the conversation. But all the time she was quietly looking at him.

'Yes, sir, I be a bit lonely at times,' she said when her visitors rose. 'I do miss Nathan sorely; you can hardly remember my husband, can you, Miss Ethel? But I have the Book, sir, and good friends too.'

A couple of days later Miss Custance came alone to the cottage. Her hand trembled as she knocked at the door.

'Is it done?' she asked, when the old woman appeared.

'Come in, miss,' said Mrs Wise, and she shut the door, and put up the wooden bolt. Then she crept to the hearth, and drew out something from a hiding-place in the stones.

'Look at that,' she said, showing it to the young lady. 'Isn't it a picture?'

Miss Custance took the object into her fine delicate hands, and glanced at it, and then flushed scarlet.

'How horrible!' she exclaimed. 'What did you do that for? You never told me.'

'It's the only way, miss, to get what you want.'

'It's a loathsome thing. I wonder you're not ashamed of yourself.'

'I be as much ashamed as you be, I think,' said Mrs Wise, and she leered at the pretty, shy-faced girl. Their eyes met and their eyes laughed at one another.

'Cover it up, please, Mrs Wise; I needn't look at it now, at all events. But are you sure?'

'There's never been a mishap since old Mrs Cradoc taught me, and she's been dead for sixty year and more. She used to tell of her grandmother's days when there were meetings in the wood over there.'

'And you're quite sure?'

'You do as I tell you. You must take it like this'; and the old woman whispered her instructions, and would have put out a hand in illustration, but the girl pushed it away.

'I understand now, Mrs Wise. No, don't do that. I quite see what you mean. Here's the money.'

'And whatever you do, don't you forget the ointment as I told you,' said Mrs Wise.

'I've been to read to poor old Mrs Wise,' Ethel said that evening to Captain Knight. 'She's over eighty and her eyesight is getting very bad.'

'Very good of you, Miss Custance, I'm sure,' said Captain Knight, and he moved away to the other end of the drawing-room, and began to talk to a girl in yellow, with whom he had been exchanging smiles at a distance, ever since the men came in from the dining-room.

That night, when she was alone in her room, Ethel followed Mrs Wise's instructions. She had hidden the object in a drawer, and as she drew it out, she looked about her, though the curtains were drawn close.

She forgot nothing, and when it was done she listened.

# THE CEREMONY

FROM her childhood, from those early and misty days which began to seem unreal, she recollected the grey stone in the wood.

It was something between the pillar and the pyramid in shape, and its grey solemnity amidst the leaves and the grass shone and shone from those early years, always with some hint of wonder. She remembered how, when she was quite a little girl, she had strayed one day, on a hot afternoon, from her nurse's side, and only a little way in the wood the grey stone rose from the grass, and she cried out and ran back in panic terror.

'What a silly little girl,' the nurse had said. 'It's only the . . . stone.' She had quite forgotten the name that the servant had given, and she was always ashamed to ask as she grew older.

But always that hot day, that burning afternoon of her childhood when she had first looked consciously on the grey image in the wood, remained not a memory but a sensation. The wide wood swelling like the sea, the tossing of the bright boughs in the sunshine, the sweet smell of the grass and flowers, the beating of the summer wind upon her cheek, the gloom of the underglade rich, indistinct, gorgeous, significant as old tapestry; she could feel it and see it all, and the scent of it was in her nostrils. And in the midst of the picture, where the strange plants grew gross in shadow, was the old grey shape of the stone.

But there were in her mind broken remnants of another and far earlier impression. It was all uncertain, the shadow of a shadow, so vague that it might well have been a dream that had mingled with the confused waking thoughts of a little child. She did not know that she remembered, she rather remembered the memory. But again it was a summer day, and a woman, perhaps the same nurse, held her in her arms, and went through the wood. The woman carried bright flowers in one hand; the dream had in it a glow of bright red, and the perfume of cottage roses. Then she saw herself put down for a moment on the grass, and the red colour stained the grim stone, and there was nothing else— except that one night she woke up and heard the nurse sobbing.

She often used to think of the strangeness of very early life; one came, it seemed, from a dark cloud, there was a glow of light, but for a moment, and afterwards the night. It was as if one gazed at a velvet curtain, heavy, mysterious, impenetrable blackness, and then, for the twinkling of an eye, one spied through a pin-hole a storied town that flamed, with fire about its walls and pinnacles. And then again the folding darkness, so that sight became illusion, almost in the seeing. So to her was that earliest, doubtful vision of the grey stone, of the red colour spilled upon it, with the incongruous episode of the nursemaid, who wept at night.

But the later memory was clear; she could feel, even now, the inconsequent terror that sent her away shrieking, running to the nurse's skirts. Afterwards, through the days of girlhood, the stone had taken its place amongst the vast array of unintelligible things which haunt every child's imagination. It was part of life, to be accepted and not questioned; her elders spoke of many things which she could not understand, she opened books and was dimly amazed, and in the Bible there were many phrases which seemed strange. Indeed, she was often puzzled by her parents' conduct, by their looks at one another, by their half-words, and amongst all these problems which she hardly recognized as problems, was the grey ancient figure rising from dark grass.

Some semi-conscious impulse made her haunt the wood where shadow enshrined the stone. One thing was noticeable; that all through the summer months the passers-by dropped flowers there. Withered blossoms were always on the ground, amongst the grass, and on the stone fresh blooms constantly appeared. From the daffodil to the Michaelmas daisy* there was marked the calendar of the cottage gardens, and in the winter she had seen sprays of juniper and box, mistletoe and holly. Once she had been drawn through the bushes by a red glow, as if there had been a fire in the wood, and when she came to the place, all the stone shone and all the ground about it was bright with roses.

In her eighteenth year she went one day into the wood, carrying with her a book that she was reading. She hid herself in a nook of hazel, and her soul was full of poetry, when there was a rustling, the rapping of parted boughs returning to their place. Her concealment was but a little way from the stone, and she peered through the net of boughs, and saw a girl timidly approaching. She knew her quite well; it was Annie Dolben, the daughter of a labourer, lately a promising pupil at Sunday school. Annie was a nice-mannered girl, never failing in her curtsy, wonderful for her knowledge of the Jewish Kings. Her face had taken an expression that whispered, that hinted strange things; there was a light and a glow behind the veil of flesh. And in her hand she bore lilies.

The lady hidden in hazels watched Annie come close to the grey image; for a moment her whole body palpitated with expectation, almost the sense of what was to happen dawned upon her. She watched Annie crown the stone with flowers, she watched the amazing ceremony that followed.

And yet, in spite of all her blushing shame, she herself bore blossoms to the wood a few months later. She laid white hothouse lilies upon the stone, and orchids of dying purple, and crimson exotic flowers. Having kissed the grey image with devout passion, she performed there all the antique immemorial rite.

# PSYCHOLOGY

Mr Dale, who had quiet rooms in a western part of London, was very busily occupied one day with a pencil and little scraps of paper. He would stop in the middle of his writing, of his monotonous tramp from door to window, jot down a line of hieroglyphics, and turn again to his work. At lunch he kept his instruments on the table beside him, and a little notebook accompanied him on his evening walk about the Green. Sometimes he seemed to experience a certain difficulty in the act of writing, as if the heat of shame or even incredulous surprise held his hand, but one by one the fragments of paper fell into the drawer, and a full feast awaited him at the day's close.

As he lit his pipe at dusk, he was standing by the window and looking out into the street. In the distance cab-lights flashed to and fro, up and down the hill, on the main road. Across the way he saw the long line of sober grey houses, cheerfully lit up for the most part, displaying against the night the dining-room and the evening meal. In one house, just opposite, there was brighter illumination, and the open windows showed a modest dinner-party in progress, and here and there a drawing-room on the first floor glowed ruddy, as the tall shaded lamp was lit. Everywhere Dale saw a quiet and comfortable respectability; if there were no gaiety there was no riot, and he thought himself fortunate to have got 'rooms' in so sane and meritorious a street.

The pavement was almost deserted. Now and again a servant would dart out from a side door and scurry off in the direction of the shops, returning in a few minutes in equal haste. But foot passengers were rare, and only at long intervals a stranger would drift from the highway and wander with slow speculation down Abingdon Road, as if he had passed its entrance a thousand times and had at last been piqued with curiosity and the desire of exploring the unknown. All the inhabitants of the quarter prided themselves on their quiet and seclusion, and many of them did not so much as dream that if one went far enough the road degenerated and became abominable, the home of the hideous, the mouth of a black purlieu.* Indeed stories, ill and malodorous, were told of the streets parallel, to east and west, which perhaps communicated with the terrible sink beyond, but those who lived at the good end of Abingdon Road knew nothing of their neighbours.

Dale leant far out of his window. The pale London sky deepened to violet as the lamps were lit, and in the twilight the little gardens before the houses shone, seemed as if they grew more clear. The golden laburnum but reflected the last bright yellow veil that had fallen over the sky after sunset, the white hawthorn was a gleaming splendour, the red may a flameless fire in the dusk. From the open window, Dale could note the increasing cheerfulness of the diners opposite, as the moderate cups were filled and emptied; blinds in the higher stories brightened up and down the street when the nurses came up with the children. A gentle breeze that smelt of grass and woods and flowers, fanned away the day's heat from the pavement stones, rustled through the blossoming boughs, and sank again, leaving the road to calm.

All the scene breathed the gentle domestic peace of the stories; there were regular lives, dull duties done, sober and common thoughts on every side. He felt that he needed not to listen at the windows, for he could divine all the talk, and guess the placid and usual channels in which the conversation flowed. Here there were no spasms, nor raptures, nor the red storms of romance, but a safe rest; marriage and birth and begetting were no more here than breakfast and lunch and afternoon tea.

And then he turned away from the placid transparency of the street, and sat down before his lamp and the papers he had so studiously noted. A friend of his, an 'impossible' man named Jenyns, had been to see him the night before, and they had talked about the psychology of the novelists, discussing their insight, and the depth of their probe.

'It is all very well as far as it goes,' said Jenyns. 'Yes, it is perfectly accurate. Guardsmen do like chorus-girls, the doctor's daughter is fond of the curate, the grocer's assistant of the Baptist persuasion has sometimes religious difficulties, "smart" people no doubt think a great deal about social events and complications: the Tragic Comedians* felt and wrote all that stuff, I dare say. But do you think that is all? Do you call a description of the gilt tools on the morocco here an exhaustive essay on Shakespeare?'

'But what more is there?' said Dale. 'Don't you think, then, that human nature has been fairly laid open? What more?'

'Songs of the frantic lupanar* delirium of the mad-house. Not extreme wickedness, but the insensate, the unintelligible, the lunatic passion and idea, the desire that must come from some other sphere that we cannot even faintly imagine. Look for yourself; it is easy.'

Dale looked now at the ends and scraps of paper. On them he had carefully registered all the secret thoughts of the day, the crazy lusts, the senseless furies, the foul monsters that his heart had borne, the maniac phantasies that he had harboured. In every note he found a rampant madness, the equivalents in thought of mathematical absurdity, of two-sided triangles, of parallel straight lines which met.

'And we talk of absurd dreams,' he said to himself. 'And these are wilder than the wildest visions. And our sins; but these are the sins of nightmare.

'And every day,' he went on, 'we lead two lives, and the half of our soul is madness, and half heaven is lit by a black sun. I say I am a man, but who is the other that hides in me?'

# MIDSUMMER

THE old farm-house on the hill flushed rose in the afterglow, and then, as the dusk began to mount from the brook, faded and yet grew brighter, its whitewashed walls gleaming as though light flowed from them, as the moon gleams when the red clouds turn to grey.

The ancient hawthorn tree at the barn-end became a tall black stem and its leaves and boughs a black mass against the pale uncertain blue of the twilight sky. Leonard looked up with a great sigh of relief. He was perched on the stile by the bridge, and as the wind fell, the ripple of the water swelled into a sweeter song, and there was no other sound to be heard. His pipe was finished, and though he knew that his rooms up at the farm looked out on the red rose and the white, he could not make up his mind to leave the view of the shimmering unearthly walls, and the melody of clear running water.

The contrast of it all with London was almost too immense, hardly realized or credible. A few hours before, and his ears seemed bursting with the terrible battle of the streets, with the clangour and jangle of great waggons thundering over the stones, with the sharp rattle of hansoms, the heavy rumble of swaying omnibuses. And during the journey his eyes still saw the thronging crowds, the turbid, furious streams of men that pushed eastward and westward, hurrying and jostling one another, wearying the brain with their constant movement, the everlasting flux and reflux of white faces. And the air, a hot smoke, a faint sick breath as though from a fever-stricken city; the sky, all grey heat that beat upon weary men, as they looked up through the cloud of dust that went before and followed them.

And now he was soothed in the deep silence and soothed by the chanting water, his eyes saw the valley melting into soft shadow, and in his nostrils was the ineffable incense of a summer night, that as a medicine allayed all the trouble and pain of body and mind. He wet his hands in the dew of the long grass and bathed his forehead, as if all the defilement and anguish of the streets should thus be washed utterly away.

He tried to analyse the scent of the night. The green leaves that overshadowed the brook and made the water dark at noon, gave out their odour, and the deep meadow grass was fragrant, a gale of scent breathed from the huge elder-bush that lit up the vague hillside, hanging above the well. But the meadow-sweet was bursting into blossom at his feet, and ah! the wild red roses drooped down from dreamland.

At last he began to climb the hillside towards those white magic walls that had charmed him. His two rooms were at the end of the long low farm-house, and though there was a passage leading to the big kitchen, Leonard's sitting-room opened immediately on the garden, on the crimson roses. He could go and come as he pleased without disturbing the household, or as the pleasant farmer had expressed it, he had a home of his own. He entered and locked the door, and lit the two candles that stood in bright brass candlesticks on the mantelpiece. The room had a low ceiling crossed by a whitewashed beam, the walls were bulging and uneven, decked with samplers, with faded prints, and in a corner stood a glass cupboard, displaying quaint flowery china of some forgotten local pattern.

The room was as quiet, as full of peace, as the air and the night, and Leonard knew that here, at the old bureau, he would find the treasure he had been long vainly seeking. He was tired, but he did not feel inclined to go to bed. He lit his pipe again, and began to arrange his papers, and idly sat down at the bureau, thinking of the task, or rather of the delight, before him. An idea flashed suddenly into his mind, and he began to write hurriedly, in an ecstasy, afraid lest he should lose what he had so happily found.

At midnight his window was still bright on the hill, and he laid down his pen with a sigh of pleasure at the accomplished work. And now he could not go to bed; he felt he must wander into the night, and summon sleep from the velvet air, from the scent of darkness, from the dew. He gently unlocked and locked the door, and walked slowly between the Persian roses, and climbed the stone stile in the garden wall. The moon was mounting to a throne, in full splendour; below, at a little distance, there seemed the painted scene of a village, and higher, beyond the farm-house, a great wood began. And as he thought of the green retreats he had glanced at in the sunlit evening, he was filled with a longing for the wood-world at night, with a desire for its darkness, for the mystery of it beneath the moon. He followed the path he had noted, till on the wood's verge he looked back and found that the shape of the farm-house had fallen into the night and vanished.

He entered the shadow, treading softly, and let the track lead him away from the world. The night became full of whisperings, of dry murmuring noises; it seemed soon as if a stealthy host were beneath the trees, every man tracking another. Leonard quite forgot his work, and its triumph, and felt as though his soul were astray in a new dark sphere that dreams had foretold. He had come to a place remote, without form or colour, made alone of shadow and overhanging gloom. Unconsciously he wandered from the path, and for a time he fought his way through the undergrowth, struggling with interlacing boughs and brambles that dragged back his feet.

At last he got free, and found that he had penetrated into a broad avenue, piercing, it seemed, through the heart of the wood. The moon shone bright from above the tree-tops, and gave a faint green colour to the track which ascended to an open glade; a great amphitheatre amidst the trees. He was tired, and lay down in the darkness beside the turfy road, and wondered whether he had lit on some forgotten way, on some great path that the legions had trodden. And as he lay there watching, gazing at the pale moonlight, he saw a shadow advancing on the grass before him.

'A breath of wind must be stirring some bough behind me,' he thought, but in the instant a woman went by, and then the shadows and white women followed thick.

Leonard gripped hard at a stick he was carrying, and drove his nails into the flesh. He saw the farmer's daughter, the girl who had waited on him a few hours before, and behind her came girls with like faces, no doubt the quiet modest girls of the English village, of the English farm-house.

For a moment they fronted him, shameless, unabashed before one another, and then they had passed.

He had seen their smiles, he had seen their gestures, and things that he had thought the world had long forgotten.

The white writhing figures passed up towards the glade, and the boughs hid them, but he never doubted as to what he had seen.

# THE WHITE PEOPLE

## PROLOGUE

'SORCERY and sanctity,' said Ambrose, 'these are the only realities. Each is an ecstasy,* a withdrawal from the common life.'

Cotgrave listened, interested. He had been brought by a friend to this mouldering house in a northern suburb, through an old garden to the room where Ambrose the recluse dozed and dreamed over his books.

'Yes,' he went on, 'magic is justified of her children. There are many, I think, who eat dry crusts and drink water, with a joy infinitely sharper than anything within the experience of the "practical" epicure.'

'You are speaking of the saints?'

'Yes, and of the sinners, too. I think you are falling into the very general error of confining the spiritual world to the supremely good; but the supremely wicked, necessarily, have their portion in it. The merely carnal, sensual man can no more be a great sinner than he can be a great saint. Most of us are just indifferent, mixed-up creatures; we muddle through the world without realizing the meaning and the inner sense of things, and, consequently, our wickedness and our goodness are alike second-rate, unimportant.'

'And you think the great sinner, then, will be an ascetic, as well as the great saint?'

'Great people of all kinds forsake the imperfect copies and go to the perfect originals.* I have no doubt but that many of the very highest among the saints have never done a "good action" (using the words in their ordinary sense). And, on the other hand, there have been those who have sounded the very depths of sin, who all their lives have never done an "ill deed." '

He went out of the room for a moment, and Cotgrave, in high delight, turned to his friend and thanked him for the introduction.

'He's grand,' he said. 'I never saw that kind of lunatic before.'

Ambrose returned with more whisky and helped the two men in a liberal manner. He abused the teetotal sect* with ferocity, as he handed the seltzer, and pouring out a glass of water for himself, was about to resume his monologue, when Cotgrave broke in—

'I can't stand it, you know,' he said, 'your paradoxes are too monstrous. A man may be a great sinner and yet never do anything sinful! Come!'

'You're quite wrong,' said Ambrose. 'I never make paradoxes; I wish I could. I merely said that a man may have an exquisite taste in Romanée Conti,* and yet never have even smelt four ale.* That's all, and it's more like a truism than a paradox, isn't it? Your surprise at my remark is due to the fact that you haven't realized what sin is. Oh, yes, there is a sort of connexion between Sin with the capital letter, and actions which are commonly called sinful: with murder, theft, adultery, and so forth. Much the same connexion that there is between the A, B, C and fine literature. But I believe that the misconception—it is all but universal—arises in great measure from our looking at the matter through social spectacles. We think that a man who does evil to *us* and to his neighbours must be very evil. So he is, from a social standpoint; but can't you realize that Evil in its essence is a lonely thing, a passion of the solitary, individual soul? Really, the average murderer, *quâ** murderer, is not by any means a sinner in the true sense of the word. He is simply a wild beast that we have to get rid of to save our own necks from his knife. I should class him rather with tigers than with sinners.'

'It seems a little strange.'

'I think not. The murderer murders not from positive qualities, but from negative ones; he lacks something which non-murderers possess. Evil, of course, is wholly positive—only it is on the wrong side. You may believe me that sin in its proper sense is very rare; it is probable that there have been far fewer sinners than saints. Yes, your standpoint is all very well for practical, social purposes; we are naturally inclined to think that a person who is very disagreeable to us must be a very great sinner! It is very disagreeable to have one's pocket picked, and we pronounce the thief to be a very great sinner. In truth, he is merely an undeveloped man. He cannot be a saint, of course; but he may be, and often is, an infinitely better creature than thousands who have never broken a single commandment. He is a great nuisance to *us*, I admit, and we very properly lock him up if we catch him; but between his troublesome and unsocial action and evil—Oh, the connexion is of the weakest.'

It was getting very late. The man who had brought Cotgrave had probably heard all this before, since he assisted with a bland and judicious smile, but Cotgrave began to think that his 'lunatic' was turning into a sage.

'Do you know,' he said, 'you interest me immensely? You think, then, that we do not understand the real nature of evil?'

'No, I don't think we do. We over-estimate it and we under-estimate it. We take the very numerous infractions of our social "bye-laws"—the very necessary and very proper regulations which keep the human company together—and we get frightened at the prevalence of "sin" and "evil." But this is really nonsense. Take theft, for example. Have you any *horror* at the thought of Robin Hood, of the Highland caterans of the seventeenth century, of the moss-troopers,* of the company promoters* of our day?

'Then, on the other hand, we underrate evil. We attach such an enormous importance to the "sin" of meddling with our pockets (and our wives) that we have quite forgotten the awfulness of real sin.'

'And what is sin?' said Cotgrave.

'I think I must reply to your question by another. What would your feelings be, seriously, if your cat or your dog began to talk to you, and to dispute with you in human accents? You would be overwhelmed with horror. I am sure of it. And if the roses in your garden sang a weird song, you would go mad. And suppose the stones in the road began to swell and grow before your eyes, and if the pebble that you noticed at night had shot out stony blossoms in the morning?

'Well, these examples may give you some notion of what sin really is.'

'Look here,' said the third man, hitherto placid, 'you two seem pretty well wound up. But I'm going home. I've missed my tram, and I shall have to walk.'

Ambrose and Cotgrave seemed to settle down more profoundly when the other had gone out into the early misty morning and the pale light of the lamps.

'You astonish me,' said Cotgrave. 'I had never thought of that. If that is really so, one must turn everything upside down. Then the essence of sin really is——'

'In the taking of heaven by storm, it seems to me,' said Ambrose. 'It appears to me that it is simply an attempt to penetrate into another and a higher sphere in a forbidden manner. You can understand why it is so rare. They are few, indeed, who wish to penetrate into other spheres, higher or lower, in ways allowed or forbidden. Men, in the mass, are amply content with life as they find it. Therefore there are few saints, and sinners (in the proper sense) are fewer still, and men of genius, who partake sometimes of each character, are rare also. Yes; on the whole, it is, perhaps, harder to be a great sinner than a great saint.'

'There is something profoundly unnatural about sin? Is that what you mean?'

'Exactly. Holiness requires as great, or almost as great, an effort; but holiness works on lines that *were* natural once; it is an effort to recover the ecstasy that was before the Fall. But sin is an effort to gain the ecstasy and the knowledge that pertain alone to angels, and in making this effort man becomes a demon. I told you that the mere murderer is not *therefore* a sinner; that is true, but the sinner is sometimes a murderer. Gilles de Raiz* is an instance. So you see that while the good and the evil are unnatural to man as he now is—to man the social, civilized being—evil is unnatural in a much deeper sense than good. The saint endeavours to recover a gift which he has lost; the sinner tries to obtain something which was never his. In brief, he repeats the Fall.'

'But are you a Catholic?' said Cotgrave.

'Yes; I am a member of the persecuted Anglican Church.'

'Then, how about those texts which seem to reckon as sin that which you would set down as a mere trivial dereliction?'

'Yes; but in one place the word "sorcerers" comes in the same sentence, doesn't it? That seems to me to give the key-note. Consider: can you imagine for a moment that a false statement which saves an innocent man's life is a sin? No; very good, then, it is not the mere liar who is excluded by those words; it is, above all, the "sorcerers" who use the material life, who use the failings incidental to material life as instruments to obtain their infinitely wicked ends. And let me tell you this: our higher senses are so blunted, we are so drenched with materialism, that we should probably fail to recognize real wickedness if we encountered it.'

'But shouldn't we experience a certain horror—a terror such as you hinted we would experience if a rose tree sang—in the mere presence of an evil man?'

'We should if we were natural: children and women feel this horror you speak of, even animals experience it. But with most of us convention and civilization and education have blinded and deafened and obscured the natural reason. No, sometimes we may recognize evil by its hatred of the good—one doesn't need much penetration to guess at the influence which dictated, quite unconsciously, the "Blackwood" review of Keats*—but this is purely incidental; and, as a rule, I suspect that the Hierarchs of Tophet* pass quite unnoticed, or, perhaps, in certain cases, as good but mistaken men.'

'But you used the word "unconscious" just now, of Keats' reviewers. Is wickedness ever unconscious?'

'Always. It must be so. It is like holiness and genius in this as in other points; it is a certain rapture or ecstasy of the soul; a transcendent effort to surpass the ordinary bounds. So, surpassing these, it surpasses also the understanding, the faculty that takes note of that which comes before it. No, a man may be infinitely and horribly wicked and never suspect it. But I tell you, evil in this, its certain and true sense, is rare, and I think it is growing rarer.'

'I am trying to get hold of it all,' said Cotgrave. 'From what you say, I gather that the true evil differs generically from that which we call evil?'

'Quite so. There is, no doubt, an analogy between the two; a resemblance such as enables us to use, quite legitimately, such terms as the "foot of the mountain" and the "leg of the table." And, sometimes, of course, the two speak, as it were, in the same language. The rough miner, or "puddler," the untrained, undeveloped "tiger-man," heated by a quart or two above his usual measure, comes home and kicks his irritating and injudicious wife to death. He is a murderer. And Gilles de Raiz was a murderer. But you see the gulf that separates the two? The "word," if I may so speak, is accidentally the same in each case, but the "meaning" is utterly different. It is flagrant "Hobson Jobson"* to confuse the two, or rather, it is as if one supposed that Juggernaut and the Argonauts had something to do etymologically with one another. And no doubt the same weak likeness, or analogy, runs between all the "social" sins and the real spiritual sins, and in some cases, perhaps, the lesser may be "schoolmasters" to lead one on to the greater—from the shadow to the reality. If you are anything of a Theologian, you will see the importance of all this.'

'I am sorry to say,' remarked Cotgrave, 'that I have devoted very little of my time to theology. Indeed, I have often wondered on what grounds theologians have claimed the title of Science of Sciences for their favourite study; since the "theological" books I have looked into have always seemed to me to be concerned with feeble and obvious pieties, or with the kings of Israel and Judah. I do not care to hear about those kings.'

Ambrose grinned.

'We must try to avoid theological discussion,' he said. 'I perceive that you would be a bitter disputant. But perhaps the "dates of the kings" have as much to do with theology as the hobnails of the murderous puddler with evil.'

'Then, to return to our main subject, you think that sin is an esoteric, occult thing?'

'Yes. It is the infernal miracle as holiness is the supernal. Now and then it is raised to such a pitch that we entirely fail to suspect its existence; it is like the note of the great pedal pipes of the organ, which is so deep that we cannot hear it. In other cases it may lead to the lunatic asylum, or to still stranger issues. But you must never confuse it with mere social misdoing. Remember how the Apostle, speaking of the "other side," distinguishes between "charitable" actions and charity. And as one may give all one's goods to the poor, and yet lack charity;* so, remember, one may avoid every crime and yet be a sinner.'

'Your psychology is very strange to me,' said Cotgrave, 'but I confess I like it, and I suppose that one might fairly deduce from your premisses the conclusion that the real sinner might very possibly strike the observer as a harmless personage enough?'

'Certainly; because the true evil has nothing to do with social life or social laws, or if it has, only incidentally and accidentally. It is a lonely passion of the soul—or a passion of the lonely soul—whichever you like. If, by chance, we understand it, and grasp its full significance, then, indeed, it will fill us with horror and with awe. But this emotion is widely distinguished from the fear and the disgust with which we regard the ordinary criminal, since this latter is largely or entirely founded on the regard which we have for our own skins or purses. We hate a murderer, because we know that we should hate to be murdered, or to have any one that we like murdered. So, on the "other side," we venerate the saints, but we don't "like" them as we like our friends. Can you persuade yourself that you would have "enjoyed" St Paul's company? Do you think that you and I would have "got on" with Sir Galahad?

'So with the sinners, as with the saints. If you met a very evil man, and recognized his evil; he would, no doubt, fill you with horror and awe; but there is no reason why you should "dislike" him. On the contrary, it is quite possible that if you could succeed in putting the sin out of your mind you might find the sinner capital company, and in a little while you might have to reason yourself back into horror. Still, how awful it is. If the roses and the lilies suddenly sang on this coming morning; if the furniture began to move in procession, as in De Maupassant's tale!'*

'I am glad you have come back to that comparison,' said Cotgrave, 'because I wanted to ask you what it is that corresponds in humanity to these imaginary feats of inanimate things. In a word—what is sin? You have given me, I know, an abstract definition, but I should like a concrete example.'

'I told you it was very rare,' said Ambrose, who appeared willing to avoid the giving of a direct answer. 'The materialism of the age, which has done a good deal to suppress sanctity, has done perhaps more to suppress evil. We find the earth so very comfortable that we have no inclination either for ascents or descents. It would seem as if the scholar who decided to "specialize" in Tophet, would be reduced to purely antiquarian researches. No palæontologist could show you a *live* pterodactyl.'

'And yet you, I think, have "specialized," and I believe that your researches have descended to our modern times.'

'You are really interested, I see. Well, I confess, that I have dabbled a little, and if you like I can show you something that bears on the very curious subject we have been discussing.'

Ambrose took a candle and went away to a far, dim corner of the room. Cotgrave saw him open a venerable bureau that stood there, and from some secret recess he drew out a parcel, and came back to the window where they had been sitting.

Ambrose undid a wrapping of paper, and produced a green pocket-book.

'You will take care of it?' he said. 'Don't leave it lying about. It is one of the choicer pieces in my collection, and I should be very sorry if it were lost.'

He fondled the faded binding.

'I knew the girl who wrote this,' he said. 'When you read it, you will see how it illustrates the talk we have had to-night. There is a sequel, too, but I won't talk of that.'

'There was an odd article in one of the reviews some months ago,' he began again, with the air of a man who changes the subject. 'It was written by a doctor—Dr Coryn, I think, was the name. He says that a lady, watching her little girl playing at the drawing-room window, suddenly saw the heavy sash give way and fall on the child's fingers. The lady fainted, I think, but at any rate the doctor was summoned, and when he had dressed the child's wounded and maimed fingers he was summoned to the mother. She was groaning with pain, and it was found that three fingers of her hand, corresponding with those that had been injured on the child's hand, were swollen and inflamed, and later, in the doctor's language, purulent sloughing set in.'

Ambrose still handled delicately the green volume.

'Well, here it is,' he said at last, parting with difficulty, it seemed, from his treasure.

'You will bring it back as soon as you have read it,' he said, as they went out into the hall, into the old garden, faint with the odour of white lilies.

There was a broad red band in the east as Cotgrave turned to go, and from the high ground where he stood he saw that awful spectacle of London in a dream.

## THE GREEN BOOK

THE morocco binding* of the book was faded, and the colour had grown faint, but there were no stains nor bruises nor marks of usage. The book looked as if it had been bought 'on a visit to London' some seventy or eighty years ago, and had somehow been forgotten and suffered to lie away out of sight. There was an old, delicate, lingering odour about it, such an odour as sometimes haunts an ancient piece of furniture for a century or more. The end-papers, inside the binding, were oddly decorated with coloured patterns and faded gold. It looked small, but the paper was fine, and there were many leaves, closely covered with minute, painfully formed characters.

I found this book (the manuscript began) in a drawer in the old bureau that stands on the landing. It was a very rainy day and I could not go out, so in the afternoon I got a candle and rummaged in the bureau. Nearly all the drawers were full of old dresses, but one of the small ones looked empty, and I found this book hidden right at the back. I wanted a book like this, so I took it to write in. It is full of secrets. I have a great many other books of secrets I have written, hidden in a safe place, and I am going to write here many of the old secrets and some new ones; but there are some I shall not put down at all. I must not write down the real names of the days and months which I found out a year ago, nor the way to make the Aklo letters, or the Chian language, or the great beautiful Circles, nor the Mao Games, nor the chief songs. I may write something about all these things but not the way to do them, for peculiar reasons. And I must not say who the Nymphs are, or the Dôls, or Jeelo, or what voolas mean.* All these are most secret secrets, and I am glad when I remember what they are, and how many wonderful languages I know, but there are some things that I call the secrets of the secrets of the secrets that I dare not think of unless I am quite alone, and then I shut my eyes, and put my hands over them and whisper the word, and the Alala comes. I only do this at night in my room or in certain woods that I know, but I must not describe them, as they are secret woods. Then there are the Ceremonies, which are all of them important, but some are more delightful than others—there are the White Ceremonies, and the Green Ceremonies, and the Scarlet Ceremonies. The Scarlet Ceremonies are the best, but there is only one place where they can be performed properly, though there is a very nice imitation which I have done in other places. Besides these, I have the dances, and the Comedy, and I have done the Comedy sometimes when the others were looking, and they didn't understand anything about it. I was very little when I first knew about these things.

When I was very small, and mother was alive, I can remember remembering things before that, only it has all got confused. But I remember when I was five or six I heard them talking about me when they thought I was not noticing. They were saying how queer I was a year or two before, and how nurse had called my mother to come and listen to me talking all to myself, and I was saying words that nobody could understand. I was speaking the Xu language, but I only remember a very few of the words, as it was about the little white faces that used to look at me when I was lying in my cradle. They used to talk to me, and I learnt their language and talked to them in it about some great white place where they lived, where the trees and the grass were all white, and there were white hills as high up as the moon, and a cold wind. I have often dreamed of it afterwards, but the faces went away when I was very little. But a wonderful thing happened when I was about five. My nurse was carrying me on her shoulder; there was a field of yellow corn, and we went through it, it was very hot. Then we came to a path through a wood, and a tall man came after us, and went with us till we came to a place where there was a deep pool, and it was very dark and shady. Nurse put me down on the soft moss under a tree, and she said: 'She can't get to the pond now.' So they left me there, and I sat quite still and watched, and out of the water and out of the wood came two wonderful white people, and they began to play and dance and sing. They were a kind of creamy white like the old ivory figure in the drawing-room; one was a beautiful lady with kind dark eyes, and a grave face, and long black hair, and she smiled such a strange sad smile at the other, who laughed and came to her. They played together, and danced round and round the pool, and they sang a song till I fell asleep. Nurse woke me up when she came back, and she was looking something like the lady had looked, so I told her all about it, and asked her why she looked like that. At first she cried, and then she looked very frightened, and turned quite pale. She put me down on the grass and stared at me, and I could see she was shaking all over. Then she said I had been dreaming, but I knew I hadn't. Then she made me promise not to say a word about it to anybody, and if I did I should be thrown into the black pit. I was not frightened at all, though nurse was, and I never forgot about it, because when I shut my eyes and it was quite quiet, and I was all alone, I could see them again, very faint and far away, but very splendid; and little bits of the song they sang came into my head, but I couldn't sing it.

I was thirteen, nearly fourteen, when I had a very singular adventure, so strange that the day on which it happened is always called the White

Day. My mother had been dead for more than a year, and in the morning I had lessons, but they let me go out for walks in the afternoon. And this afternoon I walked a new way, and a little brook led me into a new country, but I tore my frock getting through some of the difficult places, as the way was through many bushes, and beneath the low branches of trees, and up thorny thickets on the hills, and by dark woods full of creeping thorns. And it was a long, long way. It seemed as if I was going on for ever and ever, and I had to creep by a place like a tunnel where a brook must have been, but all the water had dried up, and the floor was rocky, and the bushes had grown overhead till they met, so that it was quite dark. And I went on and on through that dark place; it was a long, long way. And I came to a hill that I never saw before. I was in a dismal thicket full of black twisted boughs that tore me as I went through them, and I cried out because I was smarting all over, and then I found that I was climbing, and I went up and up a long way, till at last the thicket stopped and I came out crying just under the top of a big bare place, where there were ugly grey stones lying all about on the grass, and here and there a little twisted, stunted tree came out from under a stone, like a snake. And I went up, right to the top, a long way. I never saw such big ugly stones before; they came out of the earth some of them, and some looked as if they had been rolled to where they were, and they went on and on as far as I could see, a long, long way. I looked out from them and saw the country, but it was strange. It was winter time, and there were black terrible woods hanging from the hills all round; it was like seeing a large room hung with black curtains, and the shape of the trees seemed quite different from any I had ever seen before. I was afraid. Then beyond the woods there were other hills round in a great ring, but I had never seen any of them; it all looked black, and everything had a voor over it. It was all so still and silent, and the sky was heavy and grey and sad, like a wicked voorish dome in Deep Dendo. I went on into the dreadful rocks. There were hundreds and hundreds of them. Some were like horrid-grinning men; I could see their faces as if they would jump at me out of the stone, and catch hold of me, and drag me with them back into the rock, so that I should always be there. And there were other rocks that were like animals, creeping, horrible animals, putting out their tongues, and others were like words that I could not say, and others like dead people lying on the grass. I went on among them, though they frightened me, and my heart was full of wicked songs that they put into it; and I wanted to make faces and twist myself about in the way they did, and I went on and on a long way till at last I liked the rocks, and they didn't frighten me any more.

I sang the songs I thought of; songs full of words that must not be spoken or written down. Then I made faces like the faces on the rocks, and I twisted myself about like the twisted ones, and I lay down flat on the ground like the dead ones, and I went up to one that was grinning, and put my arms round him and hugged him. And so I went on and on through the rocks till I came to a round mound in the middle of them. It was higher than a mound, it was nearly as high as our house, and it was like a great basin turned upside down, all smooth and round and green, with one stone, like a post, sticking up at the top. I climbed up the sides, but they were so steep I had to stop or I should have rolled all the way down again, and I should have knocked against the stones at the bottom, and perhaps been killed. But I wanted to get up to the very top of the big round mound, so I lay down flat on my face, and took hold of the grass with my hands and drew myself up, bit by bit, till I was at the top. Then I sat down on the stone in the middle, and looked all round about. I felt I had come such a long, long way, just as if I were a hundred miles from home, or in some other country, or in one of the strange places I had read about in the 'Tales of the Genie'* and the 'Arabian Nights,' or as if I had gone across the sea, far away, for years and I had found another world that nobody had ever seen or heard of before, or as if I had somehow flown through the sky and fallen on one of the stars I had read about where everything is dead and cold and grey, and there is no air, and the wind doesn't blow. I sat on the stone and looked all round and down and round about me. It was just as if I was sitting on a tower in the middle of a great empty town, because I could see nothing all around but the grey rocks on the ground. I couldn't make out their shapes any more, but I could see them on and on for a long way, and I looked at them, and they seemed as if they had been arranged into patterns, and shapes, and figures. I knew they couldn't be, because I had seen a lot of them coming right out of the earth, joined to the deep rocks below, so I looked again, but still I saw nothing but circles, and small circles inside big ones, and pyramids, and domes, and spires, and they seemed all to go round and round the place where I was sitting, and the more I looked, the more I saw great big rings of rocks, getting bigger and bigger, and I stared so long that it felt as if they were all moving and turning, like a great wheel, and I was turning, too, in the middle. I got quite dizzy and queer in the head, and everything began to be hazy and not clear, and I saw little sparks of blue light, and the stones looked as if they were springing and dancing and twisting as they went round and round and round. I was frightened again, and I cried out loud, and jumped up from the stone I was sitting on, and fell down. When I got up I was so glad they all looked still, and I sat down on the top and slid down the mound, and went on again. I danced as I went in the peculiar way the rocks had danced when I got giddy, and I was so glad I could do it quite well, and I danced and danced along, and sang extraordinary songs that came into my head. At last I came to the edge of that great flat hill, and there were no more rocks, and the way went again through a dark thicket in a hollow. It was just as bad as the other one I went through climbing up, but I didn't mind this one, because I was so glad I had seen those singular dances and could imitate them. I went down, creeping through the bushes, and a tall nettle stung me on my leg, and made me burn, but I didn't mind it, and I tingled with the boughs and the thorns, but I only laughed and sang. Then I got out of the thicket into a close valley, a little secret place like a dark passage that nobody ever knows of, because it was so narrow and deep and the woods were so thick round it. There is a steep bank with trees hanging over it, and there the ferns keep green all through the winter, when they are dead and brown upon the hill, and the ferns there have a sweet, rich smell like what oozes out of fir trees. There was a little stream of water running down this valley, so small that I could easily step across it. I drank the water with my hand, and it tasted like bright, yellow wine, and it sparkled and bubbled as it ran down over beautiful red and yellow and green stones, so that it seemed alive and all colours at once. I drank it, and I drank more with my hand, but I couldn't drink enough, so I lay down and bent my head and sucked the water up with my lips. It tasted much better, drinking it that way, and a ripple would come up to my mouth and give me a kiss, and I laughed, and drank again, and pretended there was a nymph, like the one in the old picture at home, who lived in the water and was kissing me. So I bent low down to the water, and put my lips softly to it, and whispered to the nymph that I would come again. I felt sure it could not be common water, I was so glad when I got up and went on; and I danced again and went up and up the valley, under hanging hills. And when I came to the top, the ground rose up in front of me, tall and steep as a wall, and there was nothing but the green wall and the sky. I thought of 'for ever and for ever, world without end, Amen';* and I thought I must have really found the end of the world, because it was like the end of everything, as if there could be nothing at all beyond, except the kingdom of Voor, where the light goes when it is put out, and the water goes when the sun takes it away. I began to think of all the long, long way I had journeyed, how I had found a brook and followed it, and followed it on, and gone through bushes and thorny thickets, and dark woods full of creeping thorns. Then I had crept up a tunnel under trees, and climbed a thicket, and seen all the grey rocks, and sat in the middle of them when they turned round, and then I had gone on through the grey rocks and come down the hill through the stinging thicket and up the dark valley, all a long, long way. I wondered how I should get home again, if I could ever find the way, and if my home was there any more, or if it were turned and everybody in it into grey rocks, as in the 'Arabian Nights.' So I sat down on the grass and thought what I should do next. I was tired, and my feet were hot with walking, and as I looked about I saw there was a wonderful well just under the high, steep wall of grass. All the ground round it was covered with bright, green, dripping moss; there was every kind of moss there, moss like beautiful little ferns, and like palms and fir trees, and it was all green as jewellery, and drops of water hung on it like diamonds. And in the middle was the great well, deep and shining and beautiful, so clear that it looked as if I could touch the red sand at the bottom, but it was far below. I stood by it and looked in, as if I were looking in a glass. At the bottom of the well, in the middle of it, the red grains of sand were moving and stirring all the time, and I saw how the water bubbled up, but at the top it was quite smooth, and full and brimming. It was a great well, large like a bath, and with the shining, glittering green moss about it, it looked like a great white jewel, with green jewels all round. My feet were so hot and tired that I took off my boots and stockings, and let my feet down into the water, and the water was soft and cold, and when I got up I wasn't tired any more, and I felt I must go on, farther and farther, and see what was on the other side of the wall. I climbed up it very slowly, going sideways all the time, and when I got to the top and looked over, I was in the queerest country I had seen, stranger even than the hill of the grey rocks. It looked as if earth-children had been playing there with their spades, as it was all hills and hollows, and castles and walls made of earth and covered with grass. There were two mounds like big bee-hives, round and great and solemn, and then hollow basins, and then a steep mounting wall like the ones I saw once by the seaside where the big guns and the soldiers were. I nearly fell into one of the round hollows, it went away from under my feet so suddenly, and I ran fast down the side and stood at the bottom and looked up. It was strange and solemn to look up. There was nothing but the grey, heavy sky and the sides of the hollow; everything else had gone away, and the hollow was the whole world, and I thought that at night it must be full of ghosts and moving shadows and pale things when the moon shone down to the bottom at the dead of the night, and the wind wailed up above. It was so strange and solemn and lonely, like a hollow temple of dead heathen gods. It reminded me of a tale my nurse had told me when I was quite little; it was the same nurse that took me into the wood where I saw the beautiful white people. And I remembered how nurse had told me the story one winter night, when the wind was beating the trees against the wall, and crying and moaning in the nursery chimney. She said there was, somewhere or other, a hollow pit, just like the one I was standing in, everybody was afraid to go into it or near it, it was such a bad place. But once upon a time there was a poor girl who said she would go into the hollow pit, and everybody tried to stop her, but she would go. And she went down into the pit and came back laughing, and said there was nothing there at all, except green grass and red stones, and white stones and yellow flowers. And soon after people saw she had most beautiful emerald earrings, and they asked how she got them, as she and her mother were quite poor. But she laughed, and said her earrings were not made of emeralds at all, but only of green grass. Then, one day, she wore on her breast the reddest ruby that any one had ever seen, and it was as big as a hen's egg, and glowed and sparkled like a hot burning coal of fire. And they asked how she got it, as she and her mother were quite poor. But she laughed, and said it was not a ruby at all, but only a red stone. Then one day she wore round her neck the loveliest necklace that any one had ever seen, much finer than the queen's finest, and it was made of great bright diamonds, hundreds of them, and they shone like all the stars on a night in June. So they asked her how she got it, as she and her mother were quite poor. But she laughed, and said they were not diamonds at all, but only white stones. And one day she went to the Court, and she wore on her head a crown of pure angel-gold, so nurse said, and it shone like the sun, and it was much more splendid than the crown the king was wearing himself, and in her ears she wore the emeralds, and the big ruby was the brooch on her breast, and the great diamond necklace was sparkling on her neck. And the king and queen thought she was some great princess from a long way off, and got down from their thrones and went to meet her, but somebody told the king and queen who she was, and that she was quite poor. So the king asked why she wore a gold crown, and how she got it, as she and her mother were so poor. And she laughed, and said it wasn't a gold crown at all, but only some yellow flowers she had put in her hair. And the king thought it was very strange, and said she should stay at the Court, and they would see what would happen next. And she was so lovely that everybody said that her eyes were greener than the emeralds, that her lips were redder than the ruby, that her skin was whiter than the diamonds, and that her hair was brighter than the golden crown. So the king's son said he would marry her, and the king said he might. And the bishop married them, and there was a great supper, and afterwards the king's son went to his wife's room. But just when he had his hand on the door, he saw a tall, black man, with a dreadful face, standing in front of the door, and a voice said—

> Venture not upon your life,
> This is mine own wedded wife.

Then the king's son fell down on the ground in a fit. And they came and tried to get into the room, but they couldn't, and they hacked at the door with hatchets, but the wood had turned hard as iron, and at last everybody ran away, they were so frightened at the screaming and laughing and shrieking and crying that came out of the room. But next day they went in, and found there was nothing in the room but thick black smoke, because the black man had come and taken her away. And on the bed there were two knots of faded grass and a red stone, and some white stones, and some faded yellow flowers. I remembered this tale of nurse's while I was standing at the bottom of the deep hollow; it was so strange and solitary there, and I felt afraid. I could not see any stones or flowers, but I was afraid of bringing them away without knowing, and I thought I would do a charm that came into my head to keep the black man away. So I stood right in the very middle of the hollow, and I made sure that I had none of those things on me, and then I walked round the place, and touched my eyes, and my lips, and my hair in a peculiar manner, and whispered some queer words that nurse taught me to keep bad things away. Then I felt safe and climbed up out of the hollow, and went on through all those mounds and hollows and walls, till I came to the end, which was high above all the rest, and I could see that all the different shapes of the earth were arranged in patterns, something like the grey rocks, only the pattern was different. It was getting late, and the air was indistinct, but it looked from where I was standing something like two great figures of people lying on the grass. And I went on, and at last I found a certain wood, which is too secret to be described, and nobody knows of the passage into it, which I found out in a very curious manner, by seeing some little animal run into the wood through it. So I went after the animal by a very narrow dark way, under thorns and bushes, and it was almost dark when I came to a kind of open place in the middle. And there I saw the most wonderful sight I have ever seen, but it was only for a minute, as I ran away directly, and crept out of the wood by the passage I had come by, and ran and ran as fast as ever I could, because I was afraid, what I had seen was so wonderful and so strange and beautiful. But I wanted to get home and think of it, and I did not know what might not happen if I stayed by the wood. I was hot all over and trembling, and my heart was beating, and strange cries that I could not help came from me as I ran from the wood. I was glad that a great white moon came up from over a round hill and showed me the way, so I went back through the mounds and hollows and down the close valley, and up through the thicket over the place of the grey rocks, and so at last I got home again. My father was busy in his study, and the servants had not told about my not coming home, though they were frightened, and wondered what they ought to do, so I told them I had lost my way, but I did not let them find out the real way I had been. I went to bed and lay awake all through the night, thinking of what I had seen. When I came out of the narrow way, and it looked all shining, though the air was dark, it seemed so certain, and all the way home I was quite sure that I had seen it, and I wanted to be alone in my room, and be glad over it all to myself, and shut my eyes and pretend it was there, and do all the things I would have done if I had not been so afraid. But when I shut my eyes the sight would not come, and I began to think about my adventures all over again, and I remembered how dusky and queer it was at the end, and I was afraid it must be all a mistake, because it seemed impossible it could happen. It seemed like one of nurse's tales, which I didn't really believe in, though I was frightened at the bottom of the hollow; and the stories she told me when I was little came back into my head, and I wondered whether it was really there what I thought I had seen, or whether any of her tales could have happened a long time ago. It was so queer; I lay awake there in my room at the back of the house, and the moon was shining on the other side towards the river, so the bright light did not fall upon the wall. And the house was quite still. I had heard my father come upstairs, and just after the clock struck twelve, and after the house was still and empty, as if there was nobody alive in it. And though it was all dark and indistinct in my room, a pale glimmering kind of light shone in through the white blind, and once I got up and looked out, and there was a great black shadow of the house covering the garden, looking like a prison where men are hanged; and then beyond it was all white; and the wood shone white with black gulfs between the trees. It was still and clear, and there were no clouds on the sky. I wanted to think of what I had seen but I couldn't, and I began to think of all the tales that nurse had told me so long ago that I thought I had forgotten, but they all came back, and mixed up with the thickets and the grey rocks and the hollows in the earth and the secret wood, till I hardly knew what was new and what was old, or whether it was not all dreaming. And then I remembered that hot summer afternoon, so long ago, when nurse left me by myself in the shade, and the white people came out of the water and out of the wood, and played, and danced, and sang, and I began to fancy that nurse told me about something like it before I saw them, only I couldn't recollect exactly what she told me. Then I wondered whether she had been the white lady, as I remembered she was just as white and beautiful, and had the same dark eyes and black hair; and sometimes she smiled and looked like the lady had looked, when she was telling me some of her stories, beginning with 'Once on a time,' or 'In the time of the fairies.' But I thought she couldn't be the lady, as she seemed to have gone a different way into the wood, and I didn't think the man who came after us could be the other, or I couldn't have seen that wonderful secret in the secret wood. I thought of the moon: but it was afterwards when I was in the middle of the wild land, where the earth was made into the shape of great figures, and it was all walls, and mysterious hollows, and smooth round mounds, that I saw the great white moon come up over a round hill. I was wondering about all these things, till at last I got quite frightened, because I was afraid something had happened to me, and I remembered nurse's tale of the poor girl who went into the hollow pit, and was carried away at last by the black man. I knew I had gone into a hollow pit too, and perhaps it was the same, and I had done something dreadful. So I did the charm over again, and touched my eyes and my lips and my hair in a peculiar manner, and said the old words from the fairy language, so that I might be sure I had not been carried away. I tried again to see the secret wood, and to creep up the passage and see what I had seen there, but somehow I couldn't, and I kept on thinking of nurse's stories. There was one I remembered about a young man who once upon a time went hunting, and all the day he and his hounds hunted everywhere, and they crossed the rivers and went into all the woods, and went round the marshes, but they couldn't find anything at all, and they hunted all day till the sun sank down and began to set behind the mountain. And the young man was angry because he couldn't find anything, and he was going to turn back, when just as the sun touched the mountain, he saw come out of a brake in front of him a beautiful white stag. And he cheered to his hounds, but they whined and would not follow, and he cheered to his horse, but it shivered and stood stock still, and the young man jumped off the horse and left the hounds and began to follow the white stag all alone. And soon it was quite dark, and the sky was black, without a single star shining in it, and the stag went away into the darkness. And though the man had brought his gun with him he never shot at the stag, because he wanted to catch it, and he was afraid he would lose it in the night. But he never lost it once, though the sky was so black and the air was so dark, and the stag went on and on till the young man didn't know a bit where he was. And they went through enormous woods where the air was full of whispers and a pale, dead light came out from the rotten trunks that were lying on the ground, and just as the man thought he had lost the stag, he would see it all white and shining in front of him, and he would run fast to catch it, but the stag always ran faster, so he did not catch it. And they went through the enormous woods, and they swam across rivers, and they waded through black marshes where the ground bubbled, and the air was full of will-o'-the-wisps, and the stag fled away down into rocky narrow valleys, where the air was like the smell of a vault, and the man went after it. And they went over the great mountains and the man heard the wind come down from the sky, and the stag went on and the man went after. At last the sun rose and the young man found he was in a country that he had never seen before; it was a beautiful valley with a bright stream running through it, and a great, big round hill in the middle. And the stag went down the valley, towards the hill, and it seemed to be getting tired and went slower and slower, and though the man was tired, too, he began to run faster, and he was sure he would catch the stag at last. But just as they got to the bottom of the hill, and the man stretched out his hand to catch the stag, it vanished into the earth, and the man began to cry; he was so sorry that he had lost it after all his long hunting. But as he was crying he saw there was a door in the hill, just in front of him, and he went in, and it was quite dark, but he went on, as he thought he would find the white stag. And all of a sudden it got light, and there was the sky, and the sun shining, and birds singing in the trees, and there was a beautiful fountain. And by the fountain a lovely lady was sitting, who was the queen of the fairies, and she told the man that she had changed herself into a stag to bring him there because she loved him so much. Then she brought out a great gold cup, covered with jewels, from her fairy palace, and she offered him wine in the cup to drink. And he drank, and the more he drank the more he longed to drink, because the wine was enchanted. So he kissed the lovely lady, and she became his wife, and he stayed all that day and all that night in the hill where she lived, and when he woke he found he was lying on the ground, close to where he had seen the stag first, and his horse was there and his hounds were there waiting, and he looked up, and the sun sank behind the mountain. And he went home and lived a long time, but he would never kiss any other lady because he had kissed the queen of the fairies, and he would never drink common wine any more, because he had drunk enchanted wine. And sometimes nurse told me tales that she had heard from her great-grandmother, who was very old, and lived in a cottage on the mountain all alone, and most of these tales were about a hill where people used to meet at night long ago, and they used to play all sorts of strange games and do queer things that nurse told me of, but I couldn't understand, and now, she said, everybody but her great-grandmother had forgotten all about it, and nobody knew where the hill was, not even her great-grandmother. But she told me one very strange story about the hill, and I trembled when I remembered it. She said that people always went there in summer, when it was very hot, and they had to dance a good deal. It would be all dark at first, and there were trees there, which made it much darker, and people would come, one by one, from all directions, by a secret path which nobody else knew, and two persons would keep the gate, and every one as they came up had to give a very curious sign, which nurse showed me as well as she could, but she said she couldn't show me properly. And all kinds of people would come; there would be gentle folks and village folks, and some old people and boys and girls, and quite small children, who sat and watched. And it would all be dark as they came in, except in one corner where some one was burning something that smelt strong and sweet, and made them laugh, and there one would see a glaring of coals, and the smoke mounting up red. So they would all come in, and when the last had come there was no door any more, so that no one else could get in, even if they knew there was anything beyond. And once a gentleman who was a stranger and had ridden a long way, lost his path at night, and his horse took him into the very middle of the wild country, where everything was upside down, and there were dreadful marshes and great stones everywhere, and holes underfoot, and the trees looked like gibbet-posts, because they had great black arms that stretched out across the way. And this strange gentleman was very frightened, and his horse began to shiver all over, and at last it stopped and wouldn't go any farther, and the gentleman got down and tried to lead the horse, but it wouldn't move, and it was all covered with a sweat, like death. So the gentleman went on all alone, going farther and farther into the wild country, till at last he came to a dark place, where he heard shouting and singing and crying, like nothing he had ever heard before. It all sounded quite close to him, but he couldn't get in, and so he began to call, and while he was calling, something came behind him, and in a minute his mouth and arms and legs were all bound up, and he fell into a swoon. And when he came to himself, he was lying by the roadside, just where he had first lost his way, under a blasted oak with a black trunk, and his horse was tied beside him. So he rode on to the town and told the people there what had happened, and some of them were amazed; but others knew. So when once everybody had come, there was no door at all for anybody else to pass in by. And when they were all inside, round in a ring, touching each other, some one began to sing in the darkness, and some one else would make a noise like thunder with a thing they had on purpose, and on still nights people would hear the thundering noise far, far away beyond the wild land, and some of them, who thought they knew what it was, used to make a sign on their breasts when they woke up in their beds at dead of night and heard that terrible deep noise, like thunder on the mountains. And the noise and the singing would go on and on for a long time, and the people who were in a ring swayed a little to and fro; and the song was in an old, old language that nobody knows now, and the tune was queer. Nurse said her great-grandmother had known some one who remembered a little of it, when she was quite a little girl, and nurse tried to sing some of it to me, and it was so strange a tune that I turned all cold and my flesh crept as if I had put my hand on something dead. Sometimes it was a man that sang and sometimes it was a woman, and sometimes the one who sang it did it so well that two or three of the people who were there fell to the ground shrieking and tearing with their hands. The singing went on, and the people in the ring kept swaying to and fro for a long time, and at last the moon would rise over a place they called the Tole Deol, and came up and showed them swinging and swaying from side to side, with the sweet thick smoke curling up from the burning coals, and floating in circles all around them. Then they had their supper. A boy and a girl brought it to them; the boy carried a great cup of wine, and the girl carried a cake of bread, and they passed the bread and the wine round and round, but they tasted quite different from common bread and common wine, and changed everybody that tasted them. Then they all rose up and danced, and secret things were brought out of some hiding place, and they played extraordinary games, and danced round and round and round in the moonlight, and sometimes people would suddenly disappear and never be heard of afterwards, and nobody knew what had happened to them. And they drank more of that curious wine, and they made images and worshipped them, and nurse showed me how the images were made one day when we were out for a walk, and we passed by a place where there was a lot of wet clay. So nurse asked me if I would like to know what those things were like that they made on the hill, and I said yes. Then she asked me if I would promise never to tell a living soul a word about it, and if I did I was to be thrown into the black pit with the dead people, and I said I wouldn't tell anybody, and she said the same thing again and again, and I promised. So she took my wooden spade and dug a big lump of clay and put it in my tin bucket, and told me to say if any one met us that I was going to make pies when I went home. Then we went on a little way till we came to a little brake growing right down into the road, and nurse stopped, and looked up the road and down it, and then peeped through the hedge into the field on the other side, and then she said, 'Quick!' and we ran into the brake, and crept in and out among the bushes till we had gone a good way from the road. Then we sat down under a bush, and I wanted so much to know what nurse was going to make with the clay, but before she would begin she made me promise again not to say a word about it, and she went again and peeped through the bushes on every side, though the lane was so small and deep that hardly anybody ever went there. So we sat down, and nurse took the clay out of the bucket, and began to knead it with her hands, and do queer things with it, and turn it about. And she hid it under a big dock-leaf for a minute or two and then she brought it out again, and then she stood up and sat down, and walked round the clay in a peculiar manner, and all the time she was softly singing a sort of rhyme, and her face got very red. Then she sat down again, and took the clay in her hands and began to shape it into a doll, but not like the dolls I have at home, and she made the queerest doll I had ever seen, all out of the wet clay, and hid it under a bush to get dry and hard, and all the time she was making it she was singing these rhymes to herself, and her face got redder and redder. So we left the doll there, hidden away in the bushes where nobody would ever find it. And a few days later we went the same walk, and when we came to that narrow, dark part of the lane where the brake runs down to the bank, nurse made me promise all over again, and she looked about, just as she had done before, and we crept into the bushes till we got to the green place where the little clay man was hidden. I remember it all so well, though I was only eight, and it is eight years ago now as I am writing it down, but the sky was a deep violet blue, and in the middle of the brake where we were sitting there was a great elder tree covered with blossoms, and on the other side there was a clump of meadowsweet, and when I think of that day the smell of the meadowsweet and elder blossom seems to fill the room, and if I shut my eyes I can see the glaring blue sky, with little clouds very white floating across it, and nurse who went away long ago sitting opposite me and looking like the beautiful white lady in the wood. So we sat down and nurse took out the clay doll from the secret place where she had hidden it, and she said we must 'pay our respects,' and she would show me what to do, and I must watch her all the time. So she did all sorts of queer things with the little clay man, and I noticed she was all streaming with perspiration, though we had walked so slowly, and then she told me to 'pay my respects,' and I did everything she did because I liked her, and it was such an odd game. And she said that if one loved very much, the clay man was very good, if one did certain things with it, and if one hated very much, it was just as good, only one had to do different things, and we played with it a long time, and pretended all sorts of things. Nurse said her great-grandmother had told her all about these images, but what we did was no harm at all, only a game. But she told me a story about these images that frightened me very much, and that was what I remembered that night when I was lying awake in my room in the pale, empty darkness, thinking of what I had seen and the secret wood. Nurse said there was once a young lady of the high gentry, who lived in a great castle. And she was so beautiful that all the gentlemen wanted to marry her, because she was the loveliest lady that anybody had ever seen, and she was kind to everybody, and everybody thought she was very good. But though she was polite to all the gentlemen who wished to marry her, she put them off, and said she couldn't make up her mind, and she wasn't sure she wanted to marry anybody at all. And her father, who was a very great lord, was angry, though he was so fond of her, and he asked her why she wouldn't choose a bachelor out of all the handsome young men who came to the castle. But she only said she didn't love any of them very much, and she must wait, and if they pestered her, she said she would go and be a nun in a nunnery. So all the gentlemen said they would go away and wait for a year and a day, and when a year and a day were gone, they would come back again and ask her to say which one she would marry. So the day was appointed and they all went away; and the lady had promised that in a year and a day it would be her wedding day with one of them. But the truth was, that she was the queen of the people who danced on the hill on summer nights, and on the proper nights she would lock the door of her room, and she and her maid would steal out of the castle by a secret passage that only they knew of, and go away up to the hill in the wild land. And she knew more of the secret things than any one else, and more than any one knew before or after, because she would not tell anybody the most secret secrets. She knew how to do all the awful things, how to destroy young men, and how to put a curse on people, and other things that I could not understand. And her real name was the Lady Avelin, but the dancing people called her Cassap, which meant somebody very wise, in the old language. And she was whiter than any of them and taller, and her eyes shone in the dark like burning rubies; and she could sing songs that none of the others could sing, and when she sang they all fell down on their faces and worshipped her. And she could do what they called shib-show, which was a very wonderful enchantment. She would tell the great lord, her father, that she wanted to go into the woods to gather flowers, so he let her go, and she and her maid went into the woods where nobody came, and the maid would keep watch. Then the lady would lie down under the trees and begin to sing a particular song, and she stretched out her arms, and from every part of the wood great serpents would come, hissing and gliding in and out among the trees, and shooting out their forked tongues as they crawled up to the lady. And they all came to her, and twisted round her, round her body, and her arms, and her neck, till she was covered with writhing serpents, and there was only her head to be seen. And she whispered to them, and she sang to them, and they writhed round and round, faster and faster, till she told them to go. And they all went away directly, back to their holes, and on the lady's breast there would be a most curious, beautiful stone, shaped something like an egg, and coloured dark blue and yellow, and red, and green, marked like a serpent's scales. It was called a glame stone, and with it one could do all sorts of wonderful things, and nurse said her great-grandmother had seen a glame stone with her own eyes, and it was for all the world shiny and scaly like a snake. And the lady could do a lot of other things as well, but she was quite fixed that she would not be married. And there were a great many gentlemen who wanted to marry her, but there were five of them who were chief, and their names were Sir Simon, Sir John, Sir Oliver, Sir Richard, and Sir Rowland. All the others believed she spoke the truth, and that she would choose one of them to be her man when a year and a day was done; it was only Sir Simon, who was very crafty, who thought she was deceiving them all, and he vowed he would watch and try if he could find out anything. And though he was very wise he was very young, and he had a smooth, soft face like a girl's, and he pretended, as the rest did, that he would not come to the castle for a year and a day, and he said he was going away beyond the sea to foreign parts. But he really only went a very little way, and came back dressed like a servant girl, and so he got a place in the castle to wash the dishes. And he waited and watched, and he listened and said nothing, and he hid in dark places, and woke up at night and looked out, and he heard things and he saw things that he thought were very strange. And he was so sly that he told the girl that waited on the lady that he was really a young man, and that he had dressed up as a girl because he loved her so very much and wanted to be in the same house with her, and the girl was so pleased that she told him many things, and he was more than ever certain that the Lady Avelin was deceiving him and the others. And he was so clever, and told the servant so many lies, that one night he managed to hide in the Lady Avelin's room behind the curtains. And he stayed quite still and never moved, and at last the lady came. And she bent down under the bed, and raised up a stone, and there was a hollow place underneath, and out of it she took a waxen image, just like the clay one that I and nurse had made in the brake. And all the time her eyes were burning like rubies. And she took the little wax doll up in her arms and held it to her breast, and she whispered and she murmured, and she took it up and she laid it down again, and she held it high, and she held it low, and she laid it down again. And she said, 'Happy is he that begat the bishop, that ordered the clerk, that married the man, that had the wife, that fashioned the hive, that harboured the bee, that gathered the wax that my own true love was made of.' And she brought out of an aumbry* a great golden bowl, and she brought out of a closet a great jar of wine, and she poured some of the wine into the bowl, and she laid her mannikin very gently in the wine, and washed it in the wine all over. Then she went to a cupboard and took a small round cake and laid it on the image's mouth, and then she bore it softly and covered it up. And Sir Simon, who was watching all the time, though he was terribly frightened, saw the lady bend down and stretch out her arms and whisper and sing, and then Sir Simon saw beside her a handsome young man, who kissed her on the lips. And they drank wine out of the golden bowl together, and they ate the cake together. But when the sun rose there was only the little wax doll, and the lady hid it again under the bed in the hollow place. So Sir Simon knew quite well what the lady was, and he waited and he watched, till the time she had said was nearly over, and in a week the year and a day would be done. And one night, when he was watching behind the curtains in her room, he saw her making more wax dolls. And she made five, and hid them away. And the next night she took one out, and held it up, and filled the golden bowl with water, and took the doll by the neck and held it under the water. Then she said—

> Sir Dickon, Sir Dickon, your day is done,
> You shall be drowned in the water wan.

And the next day news came to the castle that Sir Richard had been drowned at the ford. And at night she took another doll and tied a violet cord round its neck and hung it up on a nail. Then she said—

> Sir Rowland, your life has ended its span,
> High on a tree I see you hang.

And the next day news came to the castle that Sir Rowland had been hanged by robbers in the wood. And at night she took another doll, and drove her bodkin right into its heart. Then she said—

> Sir Noll, Sir Noll, so cease your life,
> Your heart is piercèd with the knife.

And the next day news came to the castle that Sir Oliver had fought in a tavern, and a stranger had stabbed him to the heart. And at night she took another doll, and held it to a fire of charcoal till it was melted. Then she said—

> Sir John, return, and turn to clay,
> In fire of fever you waste away.

And the next day news came to the castle that Sir John had died in a burning fever. So then Sir Simon went out of the castle and mounted his horse and rode away to the bishop and told him everything. And the bishop sent his men, and they took the Lady Avelin, and everything she had done was found out. So on the day after the year and a day, when she was to have been married, they carried her through the town in her smock, and they tied her to a great stake in the market-place, and burned her alive before the bishop with her wax image hung round her neck. And people said the wax man screamed in the burning of the flames. And I thought of this story again and again as I was lying awake in my bed, and I seemed to see the Lady Avelin in the market-place, with the yellow flames eating up her beautiful white body. And I thought of it so much that I seemed to get into the story myself, and I fancied I was the lady, and that they were coming to take me to be burnt with fire, with all the people in the town looking at me. And I wondered whether she cared, after all the strange things she had done, and whether it hurt very much to be burned at the stake. I tried again and again to forget nurse's stories, and to remember the secret I had seen that afternoon, and what was in the secret wood, but I could only see the dark and a glimmering in the dark, and then it went away, and I only saw myself running, and then a great moon came up white over a dark round hill. Then all the old stories came back again, and the queer rhymes that nurse used to sing to me; and there was one beginning 'Halsy cumsy Helen musty,' that she used to sing very softly when she wanted me to go to sleep. And I began to sing it to myself inside of my head, and I went to sleep.

   The next morning I was very tired and sleepy, and could hardly do my lessons, and I was very glad when they were over and I had had my dinner, as I wanted to go out and be alone. It was a warm day, and I went to a nice turfy hill by the river, and sat down on my mother's old shawl that I had brought with me on purpose. The sky was grey, like the day before, but there was a kind of white gleam behind it, and from where I was sitting I could look down on the town, and it was all still and quiet and white, like a picture. I remembered that it was on that hill that nurse taught me to play an old game called 'Troy Town,'* in which one had to dance, and wind in and out on a pattern in the grass, and then when one had danced and turned long enough the other person asks you questions, and you can't help answering whether you want to or not, and whatever you are told to do you feel you have to do it. Nurse said there used to be a lot of games like that that some people knew of, and there was one by which people could be turned into anything you liked, and an old man her great-grandmother had seen had known a girl who had been turned into a large snake. And there was another very ancient game of dancing and winding and turning, by which you could take a person out of himself and hide him away as long as you liked, and his body went walking about quite empty, without any sense in it. But I came to that hill because I wanted to think of what had happened the day before, and of the secret of the wood. From the place where I was sitting I could see beyond the town, into the opening I had found, where a little brook had led me into an unknown country. And I pretended I was following the brook over again, and I went all the way in my mind, and at last I found the wood, and crept into it under the bushes, and then in the dusk I saw something that made me feel as if I were filled with fire, as if I wanted to dance and sing and fly up into the air, because I was changed and wonderful. But what I saw was not changed at all, and had not grown old, and I wondered again and again how such things could happen, and whether nurse's stories were really true, because in the daytime in the open air everything seemed quite different from what it was at night, when I was frightened, and thought I was to be burned alive. I once told my father one of her little tales, which was about a ghost, and asked him if it was true, and he told me it was not true at all, and that only common, ignorant people believed in such rubbish. He was very angry with nurse for telling me the story, and scolded her, and after that I promised her I would never whisper a word of what she told me, and if I did I should be bitten by the great black snake that lived in the pool in the wood. And all alone on the hill I wondered what was true. I had seen something very amazing and very lovely, and I knew a story, and if I had really seen it, and not made it up out of the dark, and the black bough, and the bright shining that was mounting up to the sky from over the great round hill, but had really seen it in truth, then there were all kinds of wonderful and lovely and terrible things to think of, so I longed and trembled, and I burned and got cold. And I looked down on the town, so quiet and still, like a little white picture, and I thought over and over if it could be true. I was a long time before I could make up my mind to anything; there was such a strange fluttering at my heart that seemed to whisper to me all the time that I had not made it up out of my head, and yet it seemed quite impossible, and I knew my father and everybody would say it was dreadful rubbish. I never dreamed of telling him or anybody else a word about it, because I knew it would be of no use, and I should only get laughed at or scolded, so for a long time I was very quiet, and went about thinking and wondering; and at night I used to dream of amazing things, and sometimes I woke up in the early morning and held out my arms with a cry. And I was frightened, too, because there were dangers, and some awful thing would happen to me, unless I took great care, if the story were true. These old tales were always in my head, night and morning, and I went over them and told them to myself over and over again, and went for walks in the places where nurse had told them to me; and when I sat in the nursery by the fire in the evenings I used to fancy nurse was sitting in the other chair, and telling me some wonderful story in a low voice, for fear anybody should be listening. But she used to like best to tell me about things when we were right out in the country, far from the house, because she said she was telling me such secrets, and walls have ears. And if it was something more than ever secret, we had to hide in brakes or woods; and I used to think it was such fun creeping along a hedge, and going very softly, and then we would get behind the bushes or run into the wood all of a sudden, when we were sure that none was watching us; so we knew that we had our secrets quite all to ourselves, and nobody else at all knew anything about them. Now and then, when we had hidden ourselves as I have described, she used to show me all sorts of odd things. One day, I remember, we were in a hazel brake, overlooking the brook, and we were so snug and warm, as though it was April; the sun was quite hot, and the leaves were just coming out. Nurse said she would show me something funny that would make me laugh, and then she showed me, as she said, how one could turn a whole house upside down, without anybody being able to

find out, and the pots and pans would jump about, and the china would
be broken, and the chairs would tumble over of themselves. I tried it
one day in the kitchen, and I found I could do it quite well, and a whole
row of plates on the dresser fell off it, and cook's little work-table tilted
up and turned right over 'before her eyes,' as she said, but she was so
frightened and turned so white that I didn't do it again, as I liked her.
And afterwards, in the hazel copse, when she had shown me how to
make things tumble about, she showed me how to make rapping noises,
and I learnt how to do that, too. Then she taught me rhymes to say on
certain occasions, and peculiar marks to make on other occasions, and
other things that her great-grandmother had taught her when she was
a little girl herself. And these were all the things I was thinking about in
those days after the strange walk when I thought I had seen a great
secret, and I wished nurse were there for me to ask her about it, but she
had gone away more than two years before, and nobody seemed to know
what had become of her, or where she had gone. But I shall always
remember those days if I live to be quite old, because all the time I felt
so strange, wondering and doubting, and feeling quite sure at one time,
and making up my mind, and then I would feel quite sure that such
things couldn't happen really, and it began all over again. But I took
great care not to do certain things that might be very dangerous. So
I waited and wondered for a long time, and though I was not sure at all,
I never dared to try to find out. But one day I became sure that all that
nurse said was quite true, and I was all alone when I found it out.
I trembled all over with joy and terror, and as fast as I could I ran into
one of the old brakes where we used to go—it was the one by the lane,
where nurse made the little clay man—and I ran into it, and I crept
into it; and when I came to the place where the elder was, I covered up
my face with my hands and lay down flat on the grass, and I stayed there
for two hours without moving, whispering to myself delicious, terrible
things, and saying some words over and over again. It was all true and
wonderful and splendid, and when I remembered the story I knew and
thought of what I had really seen, I got hot and I got cold, and the air
seemed full of scent, and flowers, and singing. And first I wanted to
make a little clay man, like the one nurse had made so long ago, and
I had to invent plans and stratagems, and to look about, and to think of
things beforehand, because nobody must dream of anything that I was
doing or going to do, and I was too old to carry clay about in a tin
bucket. At last I thought of a plan, and I brought the wet clay to the
brake, and did everything that nurse had done, only I made a much
finer image than the one she had made; and when it was finished I did

everything that I could imagine and much more than she did, because it was the likeness of something far better. And a few days later, when I had done my lessons early, I went for the second time by the way of the little brook that had led me into a strange country. And I followed the brook, and went through the bushes, and beneath the low branches of trees, and up thorny thickets on the hill, and by dark woods full of creeping thorns, a long, long way. Then I crept through the dark tunnel where the brook had been and the ground was stony, till at last I came to the thicket that climbed up the hill, and though the leaves were coming out upon the trees, everything looked almost as black as it was on the first day that I went there. And the thicket was just the same, and I went up slowly till I came out on the big bare hill, and began to walk among the wonderful rocks. I saw the terrible voor again on everything, for though the sky was brighter, the ring of wild hills all around was still dark, and the hanging woods looked dark and dreadful, and the strange rocks were as grey as ever; and when I looked down on them from the great mound, sitting on the stone, I saw all their amazing circles and rounds within rounds, and I had to sit quite still and watch them as they began to turn about me, and each stone danced in its place, and they seemed to go round and round in a great whirl, as if one were in the middle of all the stars and heard them rushing through the air. So I went down among the rocks to dance with them and to sing extraordinary songs; and I went down through the other thicket, and drank from the bright stream in the close and secret valley, putting my lips down to the bubbling water; and then I went on till I came to the deep, brimming well among the glittering moss, and I sat down. I looked before me into the secret darkness of the valley, and behind me was the great high wall of grass, and all around me there were the hanging woods that made the valley such a secret place. I knew there was nobody here at all besides myself, and that no one could see me. So I took off my boots and stockings, and let my feet down into the water, saying the words that I knew. And it was not cold at all, as I expected, but warm and very pleasant, and when my feet were in it I felt as if they were in silk, or as if the nymph were kissing them. So when I had done, I said the other words and made the signs, and then I dried my feet with a towel I had brought on purpose, and put on my stockings and boots. Then I climbed up the steep wall, and went into the place where there are the hollows, and the two beautiful mounds, and the round ridges of land, and all the strange shapes. I did not go down into the hollow this time, but I turned at the end, and made out the figures quite plainly, as it was lighter, and I had remembered the story I had quite forgotten before, and in the story the two figures are called Adam and Eve, and only those who know the story understand what they mean. So I went on and on till I came to the secret wood which must not be described, and I crept into it by the way I had found. And when I had gone about half-way I stopped, and turned round, and got ready, and I bound the handkerchief tightly round my eyes, and made quite sure that I could not see at all, not a twig, nor the end of a leaf, nor the light of the sky, as it was an old red silk handkerchief with large yellow spots, that went round twice and covered my eyes, so that I could see nothing. Then I began to go on, step by step, very slowly. My heart beat faster and faster, and something rose in my throat that choked me and made me want to cry out, but I shut my lips, and went on. Boughs caught in my hair as I went, and great thorns tore me; but I went on to the end of the path. Then I stopped, and held out my arms and bowed, and I went round the first time, feeling with my hands, and there was nothing. I went round the second time, feeling with my hands, and there was nothing. Then I went round the third time, feeling with my hands, and the story was all true, and I wished that the years were gone by, and that I had not so long a time to wait before I was happy for ever and ever.

Nurse must have been a prophet like those we read of in the Bible. Everything that she said began to come true, and since then other things that she told me of have happened. That was how I came to know that her stories were true and that I had not made up the secret myself out of my own head. But there was another thing that happened that day. I went a second time to the secret place. It was at the deep brimming well, and when I was standing on the moss I bent over and looked in, and then I knew who the white lady was that I had seen come out of the water in the wood long ago when I was quite little. And I trembled all over, because that told me other things. Then I remembered how sometime after I had seen the white people in the wood, nurse asked me more about them, and I told her all over again, and she listened, and said nothing for a long, long time, and at last she said, 'You will see her again.' So I understood what had happened and what was to happen. And I understood about the nymphs; how I might meet them in all kinds of places, and they would always help me, and I must always look for them, and find them in all sorts of strange shapes and appearances. And without the nymphs I could never have found the secret, and without them none of the other things could happen. Nurse had told me all about them long ago, but she called them by another name, and I did not know what she meant, or what her tales of them were about, only that they were very queer. And there were two kinds, the bright and the dark, and both were very lovely and very wonderful, and some people saw only one kind, and some only the other, but some saw them both. But usually the dark appeared first, and the bright ones came afterwards, and there were extraordinary tales about them. It was a day or two after I had come home from the secret place that I first really knew the nymphs. Nurse had shown me how to call them, and I had tried, but I did not know what she meant, and so I thought it was all nonsense. But I made up my mind I would try again, so I went to the wood where the pool was, where I saw the white people, and I tried again. The dark nymph, Alanna, came, and she turned the pool of water into a pool of fire. . . .

## EPILOGUE

'THAT'S a very queer story,' said Cotgrave, handing back the green book to the recluse, Ambrose. 'I see the drift of a good deal, but there are many things that I do not grasp at all. On the last page, for example, what does she mean by "nymphs"?'

'Well, I think there are references throughout the manuscript to certain "processes" which have been handed down by tradition from age to age. Some of these processes are just beginning to come within the purview of science, which has arrived at them—or rather at the steps which lead to them—by quite different paths. I have interpreted the reference to "nymphs" as a reference to one of these processes.'

'And you believe that there are such things?'

'Oh, I think so. Yes, I believe I could give you convincing evidence on that point. I am afraid you have neglected the study of alchemy? It is a pity, for the symbolism, at all events, is very beautiful, and moreover if you were acquainted with certain books on the subject, I could recall to your mind phrases which might explain a good deal in the manuscript that you have been reading.'

'Yes; but I want to know whether you seriously think that there is any foundation of fact beneath these fancies. Is it not all a department of poetry; a curious dream with which man has indulged himself?'

'I can only say that it is no doubt better for the great mass of people to dismiss it all as a dream. But if you ask my veritable belief—that goes quite the other way. No; I should not say belief, but rather knowledge. I may tell you that I have known cases in which men have stumbled quite by accident on certain of these "processes," and have been astonished by wholly unexpected results. In the cases I am thinking of there could have been no possibility of "suggestion" or sub-conscious action of any kind. One might as well suppose a schoolboy "suggesting" the existence of Æschylus* to himself, while he plods mechanically through the declensions.

'But you have noticed the obscurity,' Ambrose went on, 'and in this particular case it must have been dictated by instinct, since the writer never thought that her manuscripts would fall into other hands. But the practice is universal, and for most excellent reasons. Powerful and sovereign medicines, which are, of necessity, virulent poisons also, are kept in a locked cabinet. The child may find the key by chance, and drink herself dead; but in most cases the search is educational, and the phials contain precious elixirs for him who has patiently fashioned the key for himself.'

'You do not care to go into details?'

'No, frankly, I do not. No, you must remain unconvinced. But you saw how the manuscript illustrates the talk we had last week?'

'Is this girl still alive?'

'No. I was one of those who found her. I knew the father well; he was a lawyer, and had always left her very much to herself. He thought of nothing but deeds and leases, and the news came to him as an awful surprise. She was missing one morning; I suppose it was about a year after she had written what you have read. The servants were called, and they told things, and put the only natural interpretation on them— a perfectly erroneous one.

'They discovered that green book somewhere in her room, and I found her in the place that she described with so much dread, lying on the ground before the image.'

'It was an image?'

'Yes, it was hidden by the thorns and the thick undergrowth that had surrounded it. It was a wild, lonely country; but you know what it was like by her description, though of course you will understand that the colours have been heightened. A child's imagination always makes the heights higher and the depths deeper than they really are; and she had, unfortunately for herself, something more than imagination. One might say, perhaps, that the picture in her mind which she succeeded in a measure in putting into words, was the scene as it would have appeared to an imaginative artist. But it is a strange, desolate land.'

'And she was dead?'

'Yes. She had poisoned herself—in time. No; there was not a word to be said against her in the ordinary sense. You may recollect a story I told you the other night about a lady who saw her child's fingers crushed by a window?'

'And what was this statue?'

'Well, it was of Roman workmanship, of a stone that with the centuries had not blackened, but had become white and luminous. The thicket had grown up about it and concealed it, and in the Middle Ages the followers of a very old tradition had known how to use it for their own purposes. In fact it had been incorporated into the monstrous mythology of the Sabbath. You will have noted that those to whom a sight of that shining whiteness had been vouchsafed by chance, or rather, perhaps, by apparent chance, were required to blindfold themselves on their second approach. That is very significant.'

'And is it there still?'

'I sent for tools, and we hammered it into dust and fragments.'

'The persistence of tradition never surprises me,' Ambrose went on after a pause. 'I could name many an English parish where such traditions as that girl had listened to in her childhood are still existent in occult but unabated vigour. No, for me, it is the "story" not the "sequel," which is strange and awful, for I have always believed that wonder is of the soul.'

# THE BOWMEN

It was during the Retreat of the Eighty Thousand,* and the authority of the Censorship* is sufficient excuse for not being more explicit. But it was on the most awful day of that awful time, on the day when ruin and disaster came so near that their shadow fell over London far away; and, without any certain news, the hearts of men failed within them and grew faint; as if the agony of the army in the battlefield had entered into their souls.

On this dreadful day, then, when three hundred thousand men in arms with all their artillery swelled like a flood against the little English company, there was one point above all other points in our battle line that was for a time in awful danger, not merely of defeat, but of utter annihilation. With the permission of the Censorship and of the military expert, this corner may, perhaps, be described as a salient,* and if this angle were crushed and broken, then the English force as a whole would be shattered, the Allied left would be turned, and Sedan* would inevitably follow.

All the morning the German guns had thundered and shrieked against this corner, and against the thousand or so of men who held it. The men joked at the shells, and found funny names for them, and had bets about them, and greeted them with scraps of music-hall songs. But the shells came on and burst, and tore good Englishmen limb from limb, and tore brother from brother, and as the heat of the day increased so did the fury of that terrific cannonade. There was no help, it seemed. The English artillery was good, but there was not nearly enough of it; it was being steadily battered into scrap iron.

There comes a moment in a storm at sea when people say to one another, 'It is at its worst; it can blow no harder,' and then there is a blast ten times more fierce than any before it. So it was in these British trenches.

There were no stouter hearts in the whole world than the hearts of these men; but even they were appalled as this seven-times-heated hell of the German cannonade fell upon them and overwhelmed them and destroyed them. And at this very moment they saw from their trenches that a tremendous host was moving against their lines. Five hundred of the thousand remained, and as far as they could see the German infantry was pressing on against them, column upon column, a grey world of men, ten thousand of them, as it appeared afterwards.

There was no hope at all. They shook hands, some of them. One man improvised a new version of the battle-song, 'Good-bye, good-bye to Tipperary,'* ending with 'And we shan't get there.' And they all went on firing steadily. The officers pointed out that such an opportunity for high-class fancy shooting might never occur again; the Germans dropped line after line; the Tipperary humourist asked, 'What price Sidney Street?'* And the few machine guns did their best. But everybody knew it was of no use. The dead grey bodies lay in companies and battalions, as others came on and on and on, and they swarmed and stirred and advanced from beyond and beyond.

'World without end. Amen,'* said one of the British soldiers with some irrelevance as he took aim and fired. And then he remembered— he says he cannot think why or wherefore—a queer vegetarian restaurant in London where he had once or twice eaten eccentric dishes of cutlets made of lentils and nuts that pretended to be steak. On all the plates in this restaurant there was printed a figure of St George in blue, with the motto, *Adsit Anglis Sanctus Georgius**—May St George be a present help to the English. This soldier happened to know Latin and other useless things, and now, as he fired at his man in the grey advancing mass—three hundred yards away—he uttered the pious vegetarian motto. He went on firing to the end, and at last Bill on his right had to clout him cheerfully over the head to make him stop, pointing out as he did so that the King's ammunition cost money and was not lightly to be wasted in drilling funny patterns into dead Germans.

For as the Latin scholar uttered his invocation he felt something between a shudder and an electric shock pass through his body. The roar of the battle died down in his ears to a gentle murmur; instead of it, he says, he heard a great voice and a shout louder than a thunder-peal crying, 'Array, array, array!'

His heart grew hot as a burning coal, it grew cold as ice within him, as it seemed to him that a tumult of voices answered to his summons. He heard, or seemed to hear, thousands shouting: 'St George! St George!'

'Ha! messire; ha! sweet Saint, grant us good deliverance!'

'St George for merry England!'

'Harow! Harow!* Monseigneur St George, succour us.'

'Ha! St George! Ha! St George! a long bow and a strong bow.'

'Heaven's Knight, aid us!'

And as the soldier heard these voices he saw before him, beyond the trench, a long line of shapes, with a shining about them. They were like men who drew the bow, and with another shout, their cloud of arrows flew singing and tingling through the air towards the German hosts.

*      *      *      *      *

The other men in the trench were firing all the while. They had no hope; but they aimed just as if they had been shooting at Bisley.*

Suddenly one of them lifted up his voice in the plainest English.

'Gawd help us!' he bellowed to the man next to him, 'but we're blooming marvels! Look at those grey...gentlemen, look at them! D'ye see them? They're not going down in dozens nor in 'undreds; it's thousands, it is. Look! look! there's a regiment gone while I'm talking to ye.'

'Shut it!' the other soldier bellowed, taking aim, 'what are ye gassing about?'

But he gulped with astonishment even as he spoke, for, indeed, the grey men were falling by the thousands. The English could hear the guttural scream of the German officers, the crackle of their revolvers as they shot the reluctant; and still line after line crashed to the earth.

*      *      *      *      *

All the while the Latin-bred soldier heard the cry:

'Harow! Harow! Monseigneur, dear saint, quick to our aid! St George help us!'

'High Chevalier, defend us!'

The singing arrows fled so swift and thick that they darkened the air; the heathen horde melted from before them.

*      *      *      *      *

'More machine guns!' Bill yelled to Tom.

'Don't hear them,' Tom yelled back. 'But, thank God, anyway; they've got it in the neck.'

In fact, there were ten thousand dead German soldiers left before that salient of the English army, and consequently there was no Sedan. In Germany, a country ruled by scientific principles, the Great General Staff decided that the contemptible English* must have employed shells containing an unknown gas of a poisonous nature, as no wounds were discernible on the bodies of the dead German soldiers. But the man who knew what nuts tasted like when they called themselves steak knew also that St George had brought his Agincourt Bowmen* to help the English.

# THE MONSTRANCE

Then it fell out in the sacring* of the Mass that right as the priest
heaved up the Host there came a beam redder than any rose and
smote upon it, and then it was changed bodily into the shape and
fashion of a Child having his arms stretched forth, as he had been
nailed upon the Tree.

*Old Romance.**

So far things were going very well indeed. The night was thick and
black and cloudy, and the German force had come three-quarters of
their way or more without an alarm. There was no challenge from the
English lines; and indeed the English were being kept busy by a high
shell-fire on their front. This had been the German plan; and it was
coming off admirably. Nobody thought that there was any danger on
the left; and so the Prussians, writhing on their stomachs over the
ploughed field, were drawing nearer and nearer to the wood. Once
there they could establish themselves comfortably and securely during
what remained of the night; and at dawn the English left would be hopelessly enfiladed*— and there would be another of those movements
which people who really understand military matters call 'readjustments
of our line.'

The noise made by the men creeping and crawling over the fields was
drowned by the cannonade,* from the English side as well as the German.
On the English centre and right things were indeed very brisk; the big
guns were thundering and shrieking and roaring, the machine guns were
keeping up the very devil's racket; the flares and illuminating shells
were as good as the Crystal Palace in the old days,* as the soldiers said
to one another. All this had been thought of and thought out on the
other side. The German force was beautifully organized. The men who
crept nearer and nearer to the wood carried quite a number of machine
guns in bits on their backs; others of them had small bags full of sand;
yet others big bags that were empty. When the wood was reached the
sand from the small bags was to be emptied into the big bags; the
machine-gun parts were to be put together, the guns mounted behind
the sandbag redoubt, and then, as Major Von und Zu* pleasantly
observed, 'the English pigs shall to gehenna-fire* quickly come.'

The major was so well pleased with the way things had gone that he
permitted himself a very low and guttural chuckle; in another ten minutes

success would be assured. He half turned his head round to whisper a caution about some detail of the sandbag business to the big sergeant-major, Karl Heinz, who was crawling just behind him. At that instant Karl Heinz leapt into the air with a scream that rent through the night and through all the roaring of the artillery. He cried in a terrible voice, 'The Glory of the Lord!' and plunged and pitched forward, stone dead. They said that his face as he stood up there and cried aloud was as if it had been seen through a sheet of flame.

'They' were one or two out of the few who got back to the German lines. Most of the Prussians stayed in the ploughed field. Karl Heinz's scream had frozen the blood of the English soldiers, but it had also ruined the major's plans. He and his men, caught all unready, clumsy with the burdens that they carried, were shot to pieces; hardly a score of them returned. The rest of the force were attended to by an English burying party. According to custom the dead men were searched before they were buried, and some singular relics of the campaign were found upon them, but nothing so singular as Karl Heinz's diary.

He had been keeping it for some time. It began with entries about bread and sausage and the ordinary incidents of the trenches; here and there Karl wrote about an old grandfather, and a big china pipe, and pine woods and roast goose. Then the diarist seemed to get fidgety about his health. Thus:

*April* 17.—Annoyed for some days by murmuring sounds in my head. I trust I shall not become deaf, like my departed uncle Christopher.

*April* 20.—The noise in my head grows worse; it is a humming sound. It distracts me; twice I have failed to hear the captain and have been reprimanded.

*April* 22.—So bad is my head that I go to see the doctor. He speaks of *tinnitus*,* and gives me an inhaling apparatus that shall reach, he says, the middle ear.

*April* 25.—The apparatus is of no use. The sound is now become like the booming of a great church bell. It reminds me of the bell at St Lambart on that terrible day* of last August.

*April* 26.—I could swear that it is the bell of St Lambart that I hear all the time. They rang it as the procession came out of the church.

The man's writing, at first firm enough, begins to straggle unevenly over the page at this point. The entries show that he became convinced that he heard the bell of St Lambart's Church ringing, though (as he knew better than most men) there had been no bell and no church at St Lambart's since the summer of 1914. There was no village either—the whole place was a rubbish-heap.

Then the unfortunate Karl Heinz was beset with other troubles.

*May* 2.—I fear I am becoming ill. Today Joseph Kleist, who is next to me in the trench, asked me why I jerked my head to the right so constantly. I told him to hold his tongue; but this shows that I am noticed. I keep fancying that there is something white just beyond the range of my sight on the right hand.

*May* 3.—This whiteness is now quite clear, and in front of me. All this day it has slowly passed before me. I asked Joseph Kleist if he saw a piece of newspaper just beyond the trench. He stared at me solemnly—he is a stupid fool—and said, 'There is no paper.'

*May* 4.—It looks like a white robe. There was a strong smell of incense today in the trench. No one seemed to notice it. There is decidedly a white robe, and I think I can see feet, passing very slowly before me at this moment while I write.

There is no space here for continuous extracts from Karl Heinz's diary. But to condense with severity, it would seem that he slowly gathered about himself a complete set of sensory hallucinations. First the auditory hallucination of the sound of a bell, which the doctor called *tinnitus*. Then a patch of white growing into a white robe, then the smell of incense. At last he lived in two worlds. He saw his trench, and the level before it, and the English lines; he talked with his comrades and obeyed orders, though with a certain difficulty; but he also heard the deep boom of St Lambart's bell, and saw continually advancing towards him a white procession of little children, led by a boy who was swinging a censer. There is one extraordinary entry: 'But in August those children carried no lilies; now they have lilies in their hands. Why should they have lilies?'

It is interesting to note the transition over the border line. After May 2d there is no reference in the diary to bodily illness, with two notable exceptions. Up to and including that date the sergeant knows that he is suffering from illusions; after that he accepts his hallucinations as actualities. The man who cannot see what he sees and hear what he hears is a fool. So he writes: 'I ask who is singing *Ave Maria Stella*.* That blockhead Friedrich Schumacher raises his crest and answers insolently that no one sings, since singing is strictly forbidden for the present.'

A few days before the disastrous night expedition the last figure in the procession appeared to those sick eyes.

The old priest now comes in his golden robe, the two boys holding each side of it. He is looking just as he did when he died, save that when he walked in St Lambart there was no shining round his head. But this is illusion and contrary to reason, since no one has a shining about his head. I must take some medicine.

Note here that Karl Heinz absolutely accepts the appearance of the martyred priest of St Lambart as actual, while he thinks that the halo must be an illusion; and so he reverts again to his physical condition.

The priest held up both his hands, the diary states, 'as if there were something between them. But there is a sort of cloud or dimness over this object, whatever it may be. My poor Aunt Kathie suffered much from her eyes in her old age.'

          \*       \*       \*       \*       \*

One can guess what the priest of St Lambart carried in his hands when he and the little children went out into the hot sunlight to implore mercy, while the great resounding bell of St Lambart boomed over the plain. Karl Heinz knew what happened then; they said that it was he who killed the old priest and helped to crucify the little child against the church door. The baby was only three years old. He died calling piteously for 'mummy' and 'daddy.'

          \*       \*       \*       \*       \*

And those who will may guess what Karl Heinz saw when the mist cleared from before the monstrance in the priest's hands. Then he shrieked and died.

# N

## I

THEY were talking about old days and old ways and all the changes that
have come on London in the last weary years; a little party of three of
them, gathered for a rare meeting in Perrott's rooms.

One man, the youngest of the three, a lad of fifty-five or so, had
begun to say:

'I know every inch of that neighbourhood, and I tell you there's no
such place.'

His name was Harliss; and he was supposed to have something to do
with chemicals and carboys and crystals.

They had been recalling many London vicissitudes, these three; and
it must be noted that the boy of the party, Harliss, could remember very
well the Strand as it used to be, before they spoilt it all. Indeed, if he
could not have gone as far back as the years of those doings, it is doubtful whether Perrott would have let him into the meeting in Mitre Place,
an alley which was an entrance of the Inn by day, but was blind after
nine o'clock at night, when the iron gates were shut, and the pavement
grew silent. The rooms were on the second floor, and from the front
windows could be seen the elms in the Inn garden, where the rooks
used to build before the war. Within, the large, low room was softly,
deeply carpeted from wall to wall; the winter night, with a bitter dry
wind rising, and moaning even in the heart of London, was shut out by
thick crimson curtains, and the three men sat about a blazing fire in an
old fireplace, a fireplace that stood high from the hearth, with hobs on
each side of it, and a big kettle beginning to murmur on one of them.
The armchairs on which the three sat were of the sort that Mr Pickwick
sits on* for ever in his frontispiece. The round table of dark mahogany
stood on one leg, very deeply and profusely carved, and Perrott said it
was a George IV table, though the third friend, Arnold, held that William
IV, or even very early Victoria, would have been nearer the mark. On
the dark red wall-paper there were eighteenth-century engravings of
'Durham Cathedral' and 'Peterborough Cathedral,' which showed that,
in spite of Horace Walpole and his friend Mr Gray,* the eighteenth
century couldn't draw a Gothic building when its towers and traceries
were before its eyes: 'because they couldn't see it,' Arnold had insisted,

late one night, when the gliding signs were far on in their course, and the punch in the jar had begun to thicken a little on its spices. There were other engravings of a later date about the walls, things of the 'thirties and 'forties by forgotten artists, known well enough in their day; landscapes of the Valley of the Usk, and the Holy Mountain, and Llanthony:* all with a certain enchantment and vision about them, as if their domed hills and solemn woods were more of grace than of nature. Over the hearth was 'Bolton Abbey in the Olden Time.'*

Perrott would apologize for it.

'I know,' he would say. 'I know all about it. It is a pig, and a goat, and a dog, and a damned nonsense—he was quoting a Welsh story—but it used to hang over the fire in the dining-room at home. And I often wish I had brought along "Te Deum Laudamus"* as well.'

'What's that?' Harliss asked.

'Ah, you're too young to have lived with it. It depicts three choirboys in surplices; one singing for his life, and the other two looking about them—just like choir-boys. And we were always told that the busy boy was hanged at last. The companion picture showed three Charity Girls, also singing. This was called "Te Dominum Confitemur." I never heard their story.'

'I know.' Harliss brightened. 'I came upon them both in lodgings near the station at Brighton, in Mafeking year.* And, a year or two later, I saw "Sherry, Sir"* in an hotel at Tenby.'

'The finest wax fruit I ever saw,' Arnold joined in, 'was in a window in the King's Cross Road.'

So they would maunder along, about the old-fashioned rather than the old. And so on this winter night of the cold wind they lingered about the London streets of forty, forty-five, fifty-five years ago.

One of them dilated on Bloomsbury, in the days when the bars were up, and the Duke's porters had boxes beside the gates, and all was peace,* not to say profound dullness, within those solemn boundaries. Here was the high vaulted church of a strange sect, where, they said, while the smoke of incense fumed about a solemn rite, a wailing voice would suddenly rise up with the sound of an incantation in magic. Here, another church, where Christina Rossetti* bowed her head; all about, dim squares where no one walked, and the leaves of the trees were dark with smoke and soot.

'I remember one spring,' said Arnold, 'when they were the brightest green I ever saw. In Bloomsbury Square. Long ago.'

'That wonderful little lion stood on the iron posts in the pavement in front of the British Museum,' Perrott put in. 'I believe they have kept a few and hidden them in museums. That's one of the reasons why the streets grow duller and duller. If there is anything curious, anything beautiful in a street, they take it away and stick it in a museum. I wonder what has become of that odd little figure, I think it was in a cocked hat, that stood by the bar-parlour door in the courtyard of the Bell in Holborn.'

They worked their way down by Fetter Lane, and lamented Dryden's house—'I think it was in '87 that they pulled it down'—and lingered on the site of Clifford's Inn—'you could walk into the seventeenth century'—and so at last into the Strand.

'Someone said it was the finest street in Europe.'

'Yes, no doubt—in a sense. Not at all in the obvious sense; it wasn't *belle architecture de ville.* It was of all ages and all sizes and heights and styles: a unique enchantment of a street; an incantation, full of words that meant nothing to the uninitiated.'

A sort of Litany followed.

'The Shop of the Pale Puddings, where little David Copperfield might have bought his dinner.'*

'That was close to Bookseller's Row—sixteenth-century houses.'

'And "Chocolate as in Spain"; opposite Charing Cross.'

'The *Globe* office,* where one sent one's early Turnovers.'*

'The narrow alleys with steps, going down to the river.'

'The smell of making soap from the scent shop.'

'Nutt's bookshop,* near the Welsh mutton butcher's, where the street was narrow.'

'The *Family Herald*\* office; with a picture in the window of an early type-setting machine, showing the operator working a contraption with long arms, that hovered over the case.'

'And Garden House in the middle of a lawn, in Clement's Inn.'

'And the flicker of those old yellow gas-lamps, when the wind blew up the street, and the people were packing into that passage that led to the Lyceum pit.'

One of them, his ear caught by a phrase that another had used, began to murmur verses from 'Oh, plump head waiter at the Cock.'

'What chops they were!' sighed Perrott. And he began to make the punch, grating first of all the lumps of sugar against the lemons; drawing forth thereby the delicate, aromatic oils from the rind of the Mediterranean fruit. Matters were brought forth from cupboards at the dark end of the room: rum from the Jamaica Coffee House* in the City, spices in blue china boxes, one or two old bottles containing secret essences. The kettle boiled, the ingredients were dusted in and poured into the red-brown jar, which was then muffled and set to digest on the hearth, in the heat of the fire.

'*Misce, fiat mistura*,'* said Harliss.

'Very well,' answered Arnold. 'But remember that all the true matters of the work are invisible.'

Nobody minded him or his alchemy; and after a due interval, the glasses were held over the fragrant steam of the jar, and then filled. The three sat round the fire, drinking and sipping with grateful hearts.


## II


LET it be noted that the glasses in question held no great quantity of the hot liquor. Indeed, they were what used to be called rummers; round, and of a bloated aspect, but of comparatively small capacity. Therefore, nothing injurious to the clearness of those old heads is to be inferred, when it is said that between the third and fourth filling, the talk drew away from central London and the lost, beloved Strand and began to go farther afield, into stranger, less-known territories. Perrott began it, by tracing a curious passage he had once made northward, dodging by the Globe and the Olympic theatres into the dark labyrinth of Clare Market, under arches and by alleys, till he came into Great Queen Street, near the Freemason's Tavern and Inigo Jones's red pilasters. Another took up the tale, and drifting into Holborn by Whetstone's Park, and going astray a little to visit Kingsgate Street—'just like Phiz's plate: mean, low, deplorable; but I wish they hadn't pulled it down'*— finally reached Theobald's Road. There, they delayed a little, to consider curiously decorated leaden water-cisterns that were once to be seen in the areas of a few of the older houses, and also to speculate on the legend that an ancient galleried inn, now used as a warehouse, had survived till quite lately at the back of Tibbles Road—for so they called it. And thence, northward and eastward, up the Gray's Inn Road, crossing the King's Cross Road, and going up the hill.

'And here,' said Arnold, 'we begin to touch on the conjectured. We have left the known world behind us.'

Indeed, it was he who now had the party in charge.

'Do you know,' said Perrott, 'that sounds awful rot, but it's true; at least so far as I am concerned. I don't think I ever went beyond Holborn Town Hall, as it used to be—I mean walking. Of course, I've driven in a hansom to King's Cross Railway Station, and I went once or twice to the Military Tournament, when it was at the Agricultural Hall, in Islington;* but I don't remember how I got there.'

Harliss said he has been brought up in North London, but much farther north—Stoke Newington way.*

'I once knew a man,' said Perrott, 'who knew all about Stoke Newington; at least he ought to have known about it. He was a Poe enthusiast, and he wanted to find out whether the school where Poe boarded when he was a little boy was still standing. He went again and again; and the odd thing is that, in spite of his interest in the matter, he didn't seem to know whether the school was still there, or whether he had seen it. He spoke of certain survivals of the Stoke Newington that Poe indicates in a phrase or two in "William Wilson:"* the dreamy village, the misty trees, the old rambling red-brick houses, standing in their gardens, with high walls all about them. But though he declared that he had gone so far as to interview the Vicar, and could describe the old church with the dormer windows, he could never make up his mind whether he had seen Poe's school.'

'I never heard of it when I lived there,' said Harliss. 'But I came of business stock. We didn't gossip much about authors. I have a vague sort of notion that I once heard somebody speak of Poe as a notorious drunkard—and that's about all I ever heard of him till a good deal later.'

'It is queer, but it's true,' Arnold broke in, 'that there's a general tendency to seize on the accidental, and ignore the essential. You may be vague enough about the treble works, the vast designs of the laboured rampart lines; but at least you knew that the Duke of Wellington had a very big nose. I remember it on the tins of knife polish.'

'But that fellow I was speaking of,' said Perrott, going back to his topic, 'I couldn't make him out. I put it to him; "Surely you know one way or the other: this old school is still standing—or was still standing—or not: you either saw it or you didn't: there can't be any doubt about the matter." But we couldn't get to negative or positive. He confessed that it was strange; "But upon my word I don't know. I went once, I think, about '95, and then, again, in '99—that was the time I called on the Vicar; and I have never been since." He talked like a man who had gone into a mist, and could not speak with any certainty of the shapes he had seen in it.

'And that reminds me. Long after my talk with Hare—that was the man who was interested in Poe—a distant cousin of mine from the country came up to town to see about the affairs of an old aunt of his who had lived all her life somewhere Stoke Newington way, and had just died. He came in here one evening to look me up—we had not met for many years—and he was saying, truly enough, I am sure, how little the average Londoner knew of London, when you once took him off his beaten track. "For example," he said to me, "have you ever been in Stoke Newington?" I confessed that I hadn't, that I had never had any reason to go there. "Exactly; and I don't suppose you've ever even heard of Canon's Park?" I confessed ignorance again. He said it was an extraordinary thing that such a beautiful place as this, within four or five miles of the centre of London, seemed absolutely unknown and unheard of by nine Londoners out of ten.'

'I know every inch of that neighbourhood,' broke in Harliss. 'I was born there and lived there till I was sixteen. There's no such place anywhere near Stoke Newington.'

'But, look here, Harliss,' said Arnold. 'I don't know that you're really an authority.'

'Not an authority on a place I knew backwards for sixteen years? Besides, I represented Crosbies in that district later, soon after I went into business.'

'Yes, of course. But . . . I suppose you know the Haymarket pretty well, don't you?'

'Of course I do; both for business and pleasure. Everybody knows the Haymarket.'

'Very good. Then tell me the way to St James's Market.'

'There's no such market.'

'We have him,' said Arnold, with bland triumph. 'Literally, he is correct: I believe it's all pulled down now. But it was standing during the War:* a small open space with old, low buildings in it, a stone's throw from the back of the Tube station. You turned to the right, as you walked down the Haymarket.'

'Quite right,' confirmed Perrott. 'I went there, only once, on the business of an odd magazine that was published in one of those low buildings. But I was talking of Canon's Park, Stoke Newington——'

'I beg your pardon,' said Harliss. 'I remember now. There is a part in Stoke Newington or near it called Canon's Park. But it isn't a park at all; nothing like a park. That's only a builder's name. It's just a lot of streets. I think there's a Canon's Square, and a Park Crescent, and an Esplanade: there are some decent shops there. But it's all quite ordinary; there's nothing beautiful about it.'

'But my cousin said it was an amazing place. Not a bit like the ordinary London parks or anything of the kind he'd seen abroad. You go in through a gateway, and he said it was like finding yourself in another country. Such trees, that must have been brought from the end of the world: there were none like them in England, though one or two reminded him of trees in Kew Gardens;* deep hollows with streams running from the rocks; lawns all purple and gold with flowers, and golden lilies too, towering up into the trees, and mixing with the crimson of the flowers that hung from the boughs. And here and there, there were little summer-houses and temples, shining white in the sun, like a view in China, as he put it.'

Harliss did not fail with his response, 'I tell you there's no such place.' And he added:

'And, anyhow, it all sounds a bit too flowery. But perhaps your cousin was that sort of man: ready to be enthusiastic over a patch of dandelions in a back-garden. A friend of mine once sent me a wire to "come at once: most important: meet me St John's Wood Station." Of course I went, thinking it must be really important; and what he wanted was to show me the garden of a house "to let" in Grove End Road, which was a blaze of dandelions.'

'And a very beautiful sight,' said Arnold, with fervour.

'It was a fine sight; but hardly a thing to wire a man about. And I should think that's the secret of all this stuff your cousin told you, Perrott. There used to be one or two big well-kept gardens at Stoke Newington; and I suppose he strolled into one of them by mistake, and then got rather wildly enthusiastic about what he saw.'

'It's possible, of course,' said Perrott, 'but in a general way he wasn't that sort of man. He had an experimental farm, not far from Wells,* and bred new kinds of wheat, and improved grasses. I have heard him called stodgy, though I always found him pleasant enough when we met.'

'Well, I tell you there's no such place in Stoke Newington or anywhere near it. I ought to know.'

'How about St James's Market?' asked Arnold.

Then, they 'left it at that.' Indeed, they had felt for some time that they had gone too far away from their known world, and from the friendly tavern fires of the Strand, into the wild No Man's Land of the north. To Harliss, of course, those regions had once been familiar, common and uninteresting: he could not revisit them in talk with any glow of feeling. The other two held them unfriendly and remote; as if one were to discourse of Arctic Explorations, and lands of everlasting darkness.

They all returned with relief to their familiar hunting-grounds, and saw the play in theatres that had been pulled down for thirty-five years or more, and had steaks and strong ale afterwards, in the box by the fire, by the fire that had been finally raked out soon after the new Law Courts were opened.

## III

So, at least, it appeared at the time; but there was something in the tale of this suburban park that remained with Arnold and beset him, and sent him at last to the remote north of the story. For, as he was meditating on this vague attraction, he chanced to light on a shabby brown book on his untidy shelves; a book gathered from a stall in Farringdon Street, where the manuscript of Traherne's *Centuries of Meditations* had been found.* So far, Arnold had scarcely glanced at it. It was called, *A London Walk: Meditations in the Streets of the Metropolis.** The author was the Reverend Thomas Hampole, and the book was dated 1853. It consisted for the most part of moral and obvious reflections, such as might be expected from a pious and amiable clergyman of the day. In the middle of the nineteenth century, the relish of moralizing which flourished so in the age of Addison and Pope and Johnson,* which made the *Rambler* a popular book, and gave fortunes to the publishers of sermons, had still a great deal of vigour. People liked to be warned of the consequences of their actions, to have lessons in punctuality, to learn about the importance of little things, to hear sermons from stones,* and to be taught that there were gloomy reflections to be drawn from almost everything. So then, the Reverend Thomas Hampole stalked the London streets with a moral and monitory glance in his eye: saw Regent Street in its early splendour and thought of the ruins of mighty Rome, preached on the text of solitude in a multitude as he viewed what he called the teeming myriads, and allowed a desolate, half-ruinous house 'in Chancery'* to suggest thoughts of the happy Christmas parties that had once thoughtlessly revelled behind the crumbling walls and broken windows.

But here and there, Mr Hampole became less obvious, and perhaps more really profitable. For example, there is a passage—it has already been quoted, I think, by some modern author—which seems curious enough.

Has it ever been your fortune, courteous reader (Mr Hampole inquired) to rise in the earliest dawning of a summer day, ere yet the radiant beams of the sun have done more than touch with light the domes and spires of the great city? . . . If this has been your lot, have you not observed that magic powers have apparently been at work? The accustomed scene has lost its familiar appearance. The houses which you have passed daily, it may be for years, as you have issued forth on your business or on your pleasure, now seem as if you beheld them for the first time. They have suffered a mysterious change, *into something rich and strange.** Though they may have been designed with no extraordinary exertion of the art of architecture . . . yet you have been ready to admit that they now 'stand in glory, shine like stars, apparelled in a light serene.' They have become magical habitations, supernal dwellings, more desirable to the eye than the fabled pleasure dome of the Eastern potentate,* or the bejewelled hall built by the Genie for Aladdin in the Arabian tale.*

A good deal in this vein; and then, when one expected the obvious warning against putting trust in appearances, both transitory and delusory, there came a very odd passage:

Some have declared that it lies within our own choice to gaze continually upon a world of equal or even greater wonder and beauty. It is said by these that the experiments of the alchemists of the Dark Ages . . . are, in fact, related, not to the transmutation of metals, but to the transmutation of the entire Universe. . . . This method, or art, or science, or whatever we choose to call it (supposing it to exist, or to have ever existed), is simply concerned to restore the delights of the primal Paradise; to enable men, if they will, to inhabit a world of joy and splendour. It is perhaps possible that there is such an experiment, and that there are some who have made it.

The reader was referred to a Note—one of several—at the end of the volume, and Arnold, already a good deal interested by this unexpected vein in the Reverend Thomas, looked it up. And thus it ran:

I am aware that these speculations may strike the reader as both singular and (I may, perhaps, add) chimerical; and, indeed, I may have been somewhat rash and ill-advised in committing them to the printed page. If I have done wrong, I hope for pardon; and, indeed, I am far from advising anyone who may read these lines to engage in the doubtful and difficult experiment which they adumbrate. Still; we are bidden to be seekers of the truth: *veritas contra mundum.**

I am strengthened in my belief that there is at least some foundation for the strange theories at which I have hinted, by an experience that befell me in the early days of my ministry. Soon after the termination of my first curacy, and after I had been admitted to Priest's Orders, I spent some months in London, living with relations in Kensington. A college friend of mine, whom I will call the Reverend Mr S——, was, I was aware, a curate in a suburb of the north of London, S.N. I wrote to him, and afterwards called at his lodgings at his invitation. I found S——in a state of some perturbation. He was threatened, it seemed, with an affection of the lungs, and his medical adviser was insistent that he should leave London for awhile, and spend the four months of the winter in the more genial climate of Devonshire. Unless this were done, the doctor declared, the consequences to my friend's health might be of a very serious kind. S——was very willing to act on this advice, and indeed, anxious to do so; but, on the other hand, he did not wish to resign his curacy, in which, as he said, he was both happy and, he trusted, useful. On hearing this, I at once proffered my services, telling him that if his Vicar approved, I should be happy to do his duty till the end of the ensuing March; or even later, if the physicians considered a longer stay in the south would be advisable. S——was overjoyed. He took me at once to see the Vicar; the fitting inquiries were made, and I entered on my temporary duties in the course of a fortnight.

It was during this brief ministry in the environs of London, that I became acquainted with a very singular person, whom I shall call Glanville.* He was a regular attendant at our services, and, in the course of my duty, I called on him, and expressed my gratification at his evident attachment to the Liturgy of the Church of England. He replied with due politeness, asked me to sit down and partake with him of the soothing cup, and we soon found ourselves engaged in conversation. I discovered early in our association that he was conversant with the reveries of the German Theosophist, Behmen,* and the later works of his English disciple, William Law;* and it was clear to me that he looked on these labyrinths of mystical theology with a friendly eye. He was a middle-aged man, spare of habit, and of a dark complexion; and his face was illuminated in a very impressive manner, as he discussed the speculations which had evidently occupied his thoughts for many years. Based as these theories were on the doctrines (if we may call them by that name) of Law and Behmen, they struck me as of an extremely fantastic, I would even say fabulous, nature, but I confess that I listened with a considerable degree of interest, while making it evident that as a Minister of the Church of England I was far from giving my free assent to the propositions that were placed before me. They were not, it is true, manifestly and certainly opposed to orthodox belief, but they were assuredly strange, and as such to be received with salutary caution. As an example of the ideas which beset a mind which was ingenious, and I may say, devout, I may mention that Mr Glanville often dwelt on a consequence, not generally acknowledged, of the Fall of Man. 'When man yielded,' he would say, 'to the mysterious temptation intimated by the figurative language of Holy Writ, the universe, originally fluid and the servant of his spirit, became solid, and crashed down upon him overwhelming him beneath its weight and its dead mass.' I requested him to furnish me with more light on this remarkable belief; and I found that in his opinion that which we now regard as stubborn matter was, primally, to use his singular phraseology, the Heavenly Chaos,* a soft and ductile substance, which could be moulded by the imagination of uncorrupted man into whatever forms he chose it to assume. 'Strange as it may seem,' he added, 'the wild inventions (as we consider them) of the Arabian Tales give us some notion of the powers of the *homo protoplastus.* The prosperous city becomes a lake, the carpet transports us in an instant of time, or rather without time, from one end of the earth to another, the palace rises at a word from nothingness. Magic, we call all this, while we deride the possibility of any such feats; but this magic of the East is but a confused and fragmentary recollection of operations which were of the first nature of man, and of the *fiat* which was then entrusted to him.'

I listened to this and other similar expositions of Mr Glanville's extraordinary beliefs with some interest, as I have remarked. I could not but feel that such opinions were in many respects more in accordance with the doctrine I had undertaken to expound than much of the teaching of the philosophers of the day, who seemed to exalt rationalism at the expense of Reason, as that divine faculty was exhibited by Coleridge.* Still, when I assented, I made it clear to Glanville that my assent was qualified by my firm adherence to the principles which I had solemnly professed at my ordination.

The months went by in the peaceful performance of the pastoral duties of my office. Early in March, I received a letter from my friend Mr S——, who informed me that he had greatly benefited by the air of Torquay* and that his medical adviser had assured him that he need no longer hesitate to resume his duties in London. Consequently, S——proposed to return at once, and, after warmly expressed thanks for my extreme kindness, as he called it, he announced his wish to perform his part in the Church services on the following Sunday. Accordingly, I paid my final visits to those of the parishioners with whom I had more particularly associated, reserving my call on Mr Glanville for the last day of my residence at S.N. He was sorry, I think, to hear of my impending departure, and told me that he would always recollect our conversational exchanges with much pleasure.

'I, too, am leaving S.N.,' he added. 'Early next week I sail for the East, where my stay may be prolonged for a considerable period.'

After mutual expressions of polite regret, I rose from my chair, and was about to make my farewells, when I observed that Glanville was gazing at me with a fixed and singular regard.

'One moment,' he said, beckoning me to the window, where he was standing. 'I want to show you the view. I don't think you have seen it.'

The suggestion struck me as peculiar, to say the least of it. I was, of course, familiar with the street in which Glanville resided, as with most of the S.N. streets; and he on his side must have been well aware that no prospect that his window might command could show me anything that I had not seen many times during my four months' stay in the parish. In addition to this, the streets of our London suburbs do not often offer a spectacle to engage the amateur of landscape and the picturesque. I was hesitating, hardly knowing whether to comply with Glanville's request, or to treat it as a piece of pleasantry, when it struck me that it was possible that his first-floor window might afford a distant view of St Paul's Cathedral; I accordingly stepped to his side, and waited for him to indicate the scene which he, presumably, wished me to admire.

His features still wore the odd expression which I have already remarked.

'Now,' said he, 'look out and tell me what you see.'

Still bewildered, I looked through the window, and saw exactly that which I had expected to see: a row or terrace of neatly designed residences, separated from the highway by a parterre* or miniature park, adorned with trees and shrubs. A road, passing to the right of the terrace, gave a view of streets and crescents of more recent construction, and of some degree of elegance. Still, in the whole of the familiar spectacle I saw nothing to warrant any particular attention; and, in a more or less jocular manner, I said as much to Glanville.

By way of reply, he touched me lightly with his finger-tips on the shoulder, and said:

'Look again.'

I did so. For a moment, my heart stood still, and I gasped for breath. Before me, in place of the familiar structures, there was disclosed a panorama of unearthly, of astounding beauty. In deep dells, bowered by overhanging trees, there bloomed flowers such as only dreams can show; such deep purples that yet seemed to glow like precious stones with a hidden but ever-present radiance, roses whose hues outshone any that are to be seen in our gardens, tall lilies alive with light, and blossoms that were as beaten gold. I saw well-shaded walks that went down to green hollows bordered with thyme; and here and there the grassy eminence above, and the bubbling well below, were crowned with architecture of fantastic and unaccustomed beauty, which seemed to speak of fairyland itself. I might almost say that my soul was ravished by the spectacle displayed before me. I was possessed by a degree of rapture and delight such as I had never experienced. A sense of beatitude pervaded my whole being; my bliss was such as cannot be expressed by words. I uttered an inarticulate cry of joy and wonder. And then, under the influence of a swift revulsion of terror, which even now I cannot explain, I turned and rushed from the room and from the house, without one word of comment or farewell to the extraordinary man who had done—I knew not what.

In great perturbation and confusion of mind, I made my way into the street. Needless to say, no trace of the phantasmagoria that had been displayed before me remained. The familiar street had resumed its usual aspect, the terrace stood as I had always seen it, and the newer buildings beyond, where I had seen oh! what dells of delight, what blossoms of glory, stood as before in their neat, though unostentatious order. Where I had seen valleys embowered in green leafage, waving gently in the sunshine and the summer breeze, there were now boughs bare and black, scarce showing so much as a single bud. As I have mentioned, the season was early in March, and a black frost which had set in ten days or a fortnight before still constrained the earth and its vegetation.

I walked hurriedly away to my lodgings, which were some distance from the abode of Glanville. I was sincerely glad to think that I was leaving the neighbourhood on the following day. I may say that up to the present moment I have never revisited S.N.

Some months later I encountered my friend Mr S——, and under cover of asking about the affairs of the parish in which he still ministered, I inquired after Glanville, with whom (I said) I had made acquaintance. It seemed he had fulfilled his intention of leaving the neighbourhood within a few days of my own departure. He had not confided his destination or his plans for the future to anyone in the parish.

'My acquaintance with him,' said S——, 'was of the slightest, and I do not think that he made any friends in the locality, though he had resided in S.N. for more than five years.'

It is now some fifteen years since this most strange experience befell me; and during that period I have heard nothing of Glanville. Whether he is still alive in the distant Orient, or whether he is dead, I am completely ignorant.

## IV

ARNOLD was generally known as an idle man; and, as he said himself, he hardly knew what the inside of an office was like. But he was laborious in his idleness, and always ready to take any amount of pains, over anything in which he was interested. And he was very much interested in this Canon's Park business. He felt sure that there was a link between Mr Hampole's odd story—'more than odd,' he meditated—and the experience of Perrott's cousin, the wheat-breeder from the west country. He made his way to Stoke Newington, and strolled up and down it, looking about him with an inquisitive eye. He found Canon's Park, or what remained of it, without any trouble. It was pretty well as Harliss had described it: a neighbourhood laid out in the 'twenties or 'thirties of the last century for City men of comfortable down to tolerable incomes.

Some of these houses remained, and there was an attractive row of old-fashioned shops still surviving. Again, in one place there was the modest cot of late Georgian or early Victorian design, with its trellised porch of faded blue-green paint, its patterned iron balcony, not displeasing, its little garden in the front, and its walled garden at the back; a small coach-house, a small stable. In another, something more exuberant and on a much larger scale: ambitious pilasters and stucco, broad lawns and sweeping drives, towering shrubs, and glass in the back premises. But on all the territory modernism had delivered its assault. The big houses remaining had been made into maisonettes, the small ones were down-at-heel, no longer objects of love; and everywhere there were blocks of flats in wicked red brick, as if Mrs Todgers had given Mr Pecksniff* her notion of an up-to-date gaol, and he had worked out her design. Opposite Canon's Park, and occupying the site on which Mr Glanville's house must have stood, was a Technical College; next to it a School of Economics. Both buildings curdled the blood: in their purpose and in their architecture. They looked as if Mr H. G. Wells's bad dreams had come true.*

In none of this, whether moderately ancient or grossly modern, could Arnold see anything to his purpose. In the period of which Mr Hampole wrote, Canon's Park may have been tolerably pleasant; it was now becoming intolerably unpleasant. But at its best, there could not have been anything in its aspect to suggest the wonderful vision which the clergyman thought he had seen from Glanville's window. And suburban gardens, however well kept, could not explain the farmer's rhapsodies. Arnold repeated the sacred words of the explanation formula: telepathy, hallucination, hypnotism; but felt very little easier. Hypnotism, for example: that was commonly used to explain the Indian Rope Trick. There was no such trick, and in any case, hypnotism could not explain that or any other marvel seen by a number of people at once, since hypnotism could only be applied to individuals, and with their full knowledge, consent, and conscious attention. Telepathy might have taken place between Glanville and Hampole; but whence did Perrott's cousin receive the impression that he not only saw a sort of Kubla Khan,* or Old Man of the Mountain* paradise, but actually walked abroad in it? The SPR* had, one might say, discovered telepathy, and had devoted no small part of their energies for the last forty-five years or more to a minute and thoroughgoing investigation of it; but, to the best of his belief, their recorded cases gave no instance of anything so elaborate as this business of Canon's Park. And again; so far as he could remember, the appearances ascribed to a telepathic agency were all personal; visions of people, not of places: there were no telepathic landscapes. And as for hallucination: that did not carry one far. That stated a fact, but offered no explanation of it. Arnold had suffered from liver-trouble: he had come down to breakfast one morning and had been vexed to see the air all dancing with black specks. Though he did not smell the nauseous odour of a smoky chimney, he made no doubt at first that the chimney had been smoking, or that the black specks were floating soot. It was some time before he realized that, objectively, there were no black specks, that they were optical illusions, and that he had been hallucinated. And no doubt the parson and the farmer had been hallucinated: but the cause, the motive power, was to seek. Dickens told how, waking one morning, he saw his father sitting by his bedside, and wondered what he was doing there. He addressed the old man, and got no answer, put out his hand to touch him: and there was no such thing. Dickens was hallucinated; but since his father was perfectly well at the time, and in no sort of trouble, the mystery remained insoluble, unaccountable. You had to accept it; but there was no *rationale* of it. It was a problem that had to be given up.

But Arnold did not like giving problems up. He beat the coverts of Stoke Newington, and dived into pubs of promising aspect, hoping to meet talkative old men, who might remember their fathers' stories and repeat them. He found a few, for though London has always been a place of restless, migratory tribes, and shifting populations; and now more than ever before; yet there still remains in many places, and above all in the remoter northern suburbs, an old fixed element, which can go back in memory sometimes for a hundred, even a hundred and fifty years. So in a venerable tavern—it would have been injurious and misleading to call it a pub—on the borders of Canon's Park he found an ancient circle that gathered nightly for an hour or two in a snug, if dingy, parlour. They drank little and that slowly, and went early home. They were small tradesmen of the neighbourhood, and talked their business and the changes they had seen, the curse of multiple shops, the poor stuff sold in them, and the cutting of prices and profits. Arnold edged into the conversation by degrees, after one or two visits—'Well, Sir, I am very much obliged to you, and I won't refuse,'—and said that he thought of settling in the neighbourhood: it seemed quiet. 'Best wishes, I'm sure. Quiet; well it was, once; but not much of that now in Stoke Newington. All pride and dress and bustle now; and the people that had the money and spent it, they're gone, long ago.'

'There were well-to-do people here?' asked Arnold, treading cautiously, feeling his way, inch by inch.

'There were, I assure you. Sound men—warm men, my father used to call them. There was Mr Tredegar, head of Tredegar's Bank. That was amalgamated with the City and National many years ago: nearer fifty than forty, I suppose. He was a fine gentleman, and grew beautiful pineapples. I remember his sending us one, when my wife was poorly all one summer. You can't buy pineapples like that now.'

'You're right, Mr Reynolds, perfectly right. I have to stock what they call pineapples, but I wouldn't touch them myself. No scent, no flavour. Tough and hard; you can't compare a crab-apple with a Cox's pippin.'

There was a general assent to this proposition; and Arnold felt that it was slow work.

And even when he got to his point, there was not much gained.

He said he had heard that Canon's Park was a quiet part; off the main track.

'Well, there's something in that,' said the ancient who had accepted the half-pint. 'You don't get very much traffic there, it's true: no trams or 'buses or motor-coaches. But they're pulling it all to pieces; building new blocks of flats every few months. Of course, that might suit your views. Very popular these flats are, no doubt, with many people; most economical, they tell me. But I always liked a house of my own, myself.'

'I'll tell you one way a flat is economical,' the greengrocer said with a preparatory chuckle. 'If you're fond of the Wireless,* you can save the price and the licence. You'll hear the Wireless on the floor above, and the Wireless on the floor below, and one or two more besides when they've got their windows open on summer evenings.'

'Very true, Mr Batts, very true. Still, I must say, I'm rather partial to the Wireless myself. I like to listen to a cheerful tune, you know, at tea-time.'

'You don't tell me, Mr Potter, that you like that horrible jazz, as they call it?'

'Well, Mr Dickson, I must confess . . .' and so forth, and so forth. It became evident that there were modernists even here: Arnold thought that he heard the term 'Hot Blues' distinctly uttered. He forced another half-pint—'very kind of you; mild this time, if you don't mind'—on his neighbour, who turned out to be Mr Reynolds, the pharmaceutical chemist, and tried back.

'So you wouldn't recommend Canon's Park as a desirable residence.'

'Well, no, Sir; not to a gentleman who wants quiet, I should not. You can't have quiet when a place is being pulled down about your ears, as you may say. It certainly was quiet enough in former days. Wouldn't you say so, Mr Batts?'—breaking in on the musical discussion— 'Canon's Park was quiet enough in our young days, wasn't it? It would have suited this gentleman then, I'm sure.'

'Perhaps so,' said Mr Batts. 'Perhaps so, and perhaps not. There's quiet, and quiet.'

And a certain stillness fell upon the little party of old men. They seemed to ruminate, to drink their beer in slower sips.

'There was always something about the place I didn't altogether like,' said one of them at last. 'But I'm sure I don't know why.'

'Wasn't there some tale of a murder there, a long time ago? Or was it a man that killed himself, and was buried at the cross-roads by the Green, with a stake through his heart?'

'I never heard of that, but I've heard my father say that there was a lot of fever about there formerly.'

'I think you're all wide of the mark, gentlemen, if you'll excuse my saying so'—this from an elderly man in a corner, who had said very little hitherto. 'I wouldn't say Canon's Park had a bad name, far from it. But there certainly was something about it that many people didn't like; fought shy of, you may say. And it's my belief that it was all on account of the lunatic asylum that used to be there, awhile ago.'

'A lunatic asylum was there?' Arnold's particular friend asked. 'Well, I think I remember hearing something to that effect in my very young days, now you recall the circumstances. I know we boys used to be very shy of going through Canon's Park after dark. My father used to send me on errands that way now and again, and I always got another boy to come along with me if I could. But I don't remember that we were particularly afraid of the lunatics either. In fact, I hardly know what we were afraid of, now I come to think of it.'

'Well, Mr Reynolds, it's a long time ago; but I do think it was that madhouse put people off Canon's Park in the first place. You know where it was, don't you?'

'I can't say I do.'

'Well, it was that big house right in the middle of the Park, that had been empty years and years—forty years, I dare say, and going to ruin.'

'You mean the place where Empress Mansions are now? Oh, yes, of course. Why they pulled it down more than twenty years ago, and then the land was lying idle all through the war and long after. A dismal-looking old place it was; I remember it well: the ivy growing over the chimney-pots, and the windows smashed, and the "To Let" boards smothered in creepers. Was that house an asylum in its day?'

'That was the very house, Sir. Himalaya House, it was called. In the first place it was built on to an old farmhouse by a rich gentleman from India, and when he died, having no children, his relations sold the property to a doctor. And he turned it into a madhouse. And as I was saying, I think people didn't much like the idea of it. You know, those places weren't so well looked after as they say they are now, and some very unpleasant stories got about; I'm not sure if the doctor didn't get mixed up in a law-suit over a gentleman, of good family, I believe, who had been shut up in Himalaya House by his relations for years, and as sensible as you or me all the time. And then there was that young fellow that managed to escape: that was a queer business. Though there was no doubt that he was mad enough for anything.'

'One of them got away, did he?' Arnold inquired, wishing to break the silence that again fell on the circle.

'That was so. I don't know how he managed it, as they were said to be very strictly kept, but he contrived to climb out or creep out somehow or other, one evening about tea-time, and walked as quietly as you please up the road, and took lodgings close by here, in that row of old red-brick houses that stood where the Technical College is now. I remember well hearing Mrs Wilson that kept the lodgings—she lived to be a very old woman—telling my mother that she never saw a nicer-looking, better-spoken young man than this Mr Vallance—I think he called himself: not his real name, of course. He told her a proper story enough about coming from Norwich, and having to be very quiet on account of his studies and all that. He had his carpet-bag in his hand, and said the heavy luggage was coming later, and paid a fortnight in advance, quite regular. Of course, the doctor's men were after him directly and making inquiries in all directions, but Mrs Wilson never thought for a moment that this quiet young lodger of hers was the missing madman. Not for some time, that is.'

Arnold took advantage of a rhetorical pause in the story. He leant forward to the landlord, who was leaning over the bar, and listening like the rest. Presently, orders round were solicited, and each of the circle voted for a small drop of gin, feeling 'mild' or even 'bitter' to be inadequate to the crisis of such a tale. And then, with courteous expressions, they drank the health of 'our friend sitting by our friend Mr Reynolds.' And one of them said:

'So she found out, did she?'

'I believe,' the narrator continued, 'that it was a week or thereabouts before Mrs Wilson saw there was something wrong. It was when she was clearing away his tea, he suddenly spoke up, and says:

'"What I like about these apartments of yours, Mrs Wilson, is the amazing view you have from your windows."

'Well, you know, that was enough to startle her. We all of us know what there was to see from the windows of Rodman's Row: Fothergill Terrace, and Chatham Street, and Canon's Park: very nice properties, no doubt, all of them, but nothing to write home about, as the young people say. So Mrs Wilson didn't know how to take it quite, and thought it might be a joke. She put down the tea-tray, and looked the lodger straight in the face.

'"What is it, sir, you particularly admire, if I might ask?"

'"What do I admire?" said he. "Everything." And then, it seems, he began to talk the most outrageous nonsense about golden and silver and purple flowers, and the bubbling well, and the walk that went under the trees right into the wood, and the fairy house on the hill; and I don't know what. He wanted Mrs Wilson to come to the window and look at it all. She was frightened, and took up her tray, and got out of the room as quick as she could; and I don't wonder at it. And that night, when she was going up to bed, she passed her lodger's door, and heard him talking out loud, and she stopped to listen. Mind you, I don't think you can blame the woman for listening. I dare say she wanted to know who and what she had got in her house. At first she couldn't make out what he was saying. He was jabbering in what sounded like a foreign language; and then he cried out in plain English as if he were talking to a young lady, and making use of very affectionate expressions.

'That was too much for Mrs Wilson, and she went off to bed with her heart in her boots, and hardly got to sleep all through the night. The next morning, the gentleman seemed quiet enough, but Mrs Wilson knew he wasn't to be trusted, and directly after breakfast she went round to the neighbours, and began to ask questions. Then, of course, it came out who her lodger must be, and she sent word round to Himalaya

House. And the doctor's men took the young fellow back. And, bless my soul, gentlemen; it's close on ten o'clock.'

The meeting broke up in a kind of cordial bustle. The old man who had told the story of the escaped lunatic had remarked, it appeared, the very close attention that Arnold had given to the tale. He was evidently gratified. He shook Arnold warmly by the hand, remarking: 'So you see, Sir, the grounds I have for my opinion that it was that madhouse that gave Canon's Park rather a bad name in our neighbourhood.'

And Arnold, revolving many things, set out on the way back to London. Much seemed heavily obscure, but he wondered whether Mrs Wilson's lodger was a madman at all; any madder than Mr Hampole, or the farmer from Somerset or Charles Dickens, when he saw the appearance of his father by his bed.


## V


ARNOLD told the story of his researches and perplexities at the next meeting of the three old friends in the quiet court leading into the Inn. The scene had changed into a night in June, with the trees in the Inn garden fluttering in a cool breeze, that wafted a vague odour of hay-fields far away into the very heart of London. The liquor in the brown jar smelt of Gascon vineyards and herb-gardens, and ice had been laid about it, but not for too long a time.

Harliss's word all through Arnold's tale was:

'I know every inch of that neighbourhood, and I told you there was no such place.'

Perrott was judicial. He allowed that the history was a remarkable one: 'You have three witnesses,' Arnold had pointed out.

'Yes,' said Perrott, 'but have you allowed for the marvellous operation of the law of coincidences? There's a case, trivial enough, perhaps you may think, that made a deep impression on me when I read it, a few years ago. Forty years before, a man had bought a watch in Singapore— or Hong Kong, perhaps. The watch went wrong, and he took it to a shop in Holborn to be seen to. The man who took it from him over the counter was the man who had sold him the watch in the East all those years before. You can never put coincidence out of court, and dismiss it as an impossible solution. Its possibilities are infinite.'

Then Arnold told the last broken, imperfect chapter of the story.

'After that night at the "King of Jamaica,"' he began, 'I went home and thought it all over. There seemed no more to be done. Still, I felt as

if I would like to have another look at this singular Park, and I went up
there one dark afternoon. And then and there I came upon the young
man who had lost his way, and had lost—as he said—the one who lived
in the white house on the hill. And I am not going to tell you about her,
or her house, or her enchanted gardens. But I am sure that the young
man was lost also—and for ever.'

And after a pause, he added:

'I believe that there is a *perichoresis*,* an interpenetration. It is possible,
indeed, that we three are now sitting among desolate rocks, by bitter
streams.

'. . . And with what companions?'

# THE TREE OF LIFE

## I

THE Morgans of Llantrisant* were regarded for many centuries as among the most considerable of the landed gentry of South Wales. They had been called Reformation *parvenus*, but this was a piece of unhistorical and unjust abuse. They could trace their descent back, without doubt, certainly as far as Morgan ab Ifor, who fought and, no doubt, flourished in his way *c*.980. He, in his turn, was always regarded as of the tribe of St Teilo;* and the family kept, as a most precious relic, a portable altar which was supposed to have belonged to the saint. And for many hundred years, the eldest son had borne the name of Teilo. They had intermarried, now and again, with the Normans, and lived in a thirteenth-century castle, with certain additions for comfort and amenity made in the reign of Henry VII, whose cause they had supported with considerable energy. From Henry, they had received grants of forfeited estates, both in Monmouthshire and Glamorganshire. At the dissolution of the religious houses,* the Sir Teilo of the day was given Llantrisant Abbey with all its possessions. The monastic church was stripped of its lead roof, and soon fell into ruin, and became a quarry for the neighbourhood. The abbot's lodging and other of the monastic buildings were kept in repair, and being situated in a sheltered valley, were used by the family as a winter residence in preference to the castle, which was on a bare hill, high above the abbey. In the seventeenth century, Sir Henry Morgan—his elder brother had died young—was a Parliament man. He changed his opinions, and rose for the King in 1648;* and, in consequence, had the mortification of seeing the outer wall of the castle on the hill, not razed to the ground, but carefully reduced to a height of four or five feet by the Cromwellian major-general commanding in the west. Later in the century, the Morgans became Whigs, and later still were able to support Mr Gladstone,* up to the Home Rule Bill of 1886. They still held most of the lands which they had gathered together gradually for eight or nine hundred years. Many of these lands had been wild, remote, and mountainous, of little use or profit save for the sport of hunting the hare; but early in the nineteenth century mining experts from the north, Fothergills and Renshaws, had found coal, and pits were sunk in the wild places, and the Morgans became wealthy in the modern way. By consequence, the bad seasons of the late 'seventies and the agricultural depression of the early 'eighties hardly touched them. They reduced rents and remitted arrears and throve on their mining royalties: they were still great people of the county. It was a very great pity that Teilo Morgan of Llantrisant was an invalid and an enforced recluse; especially as he was devoted to the memories of his house, and to the estate, and to the interests of the people on it.

The Llantrisant Abbey of his day had been so altered from age to age that the last abbot would certainly have seen little that was familiar to his eyes. It was set in rich and pleasant meadow-land, with woods of oak and beech and ash and elm all about it. Through the park ran the swift, clear river, Avon Torfaen, the stone or boulder-crusher, so named from its furious courses in the mountains where it rose. And the hills stood round the Abbey on every side. Here and there in the southern-facing front of the house, there could be seen traces of fifteenth-century building; but on this had been imposed the Elizabethan gables of the first lay resident, and Inigo Jones* was said to have added the brick wing with the Corinthian pilasters, and there was a stuccoed projection in the sham Gothic of the time of George II. It was architecturally ridiculous, but it was supposed to be the warmest part of the house, and Teilo Morgan occupied a set of five or six rooms on the first floor, and often looked out on the park, and opened the windows to hear the sound of the pouring Avon, and the murmur of the wood-pigeons in the trees, and the noise of the west wind from the mountain. He longed to be out among it all, running as he saw boys running on the hill-side through a gap in the wood; but he knew that there was a gulf fixed between him and that paradise. There was, it seemed, no specific disease but a profound weakness, a *marasmus** that had stopped short of its term, but kept the patient chronically incapable of any physical exertion, even the slightest. They had once tried taking him out on a very fine day in the park, in a wheeled chair; but even that easy motion was too much for him. After ten minutes, he had fainted, and lay for two or three days on his back, alive, but little more than alive. Most of his time was spent on a couch. He would sit up for his meals and to interview the estate agent; but it was effort to do so much as this. He used to read in county histories and in old family records of the doings of his ancestors; and wonder what they would have said to such a successor. The storming of castles at dead darkness of night, the firing of them so that the mountains far away shone, the arrows of the Gwent bowmen dark-ening the air at Crècy,* the battle of the dawn by the river, when it was seen scarlet by the first light in the east, the drinking of Gascon wine in hall from moonrise to sunrise: he was no figure for the old days and works of the Morgans.

It was probable that his feeble life was chiefly sustained by his intense interest in the doings of the estate. The agent, Captain Vaughan, a keen, middle-aged man, had often told him that a monthly interview would be sufficient and more than sufficient. 'I'm afraid you find all this detail terribly tiring,' he would say. 'And you know it's not really necessary. I've one or two good men under me, and between us we manage to keep things in very decent order. I do assure you, you needn't bother. As a matter of fact; if I brought you a statement once a quarter, it would be quite enough.'

But Teilo Morgan would not entertain any such laxity.

'It doesn't tire me in the least,' he always replied to the agent's remonstrances. 'It does me good. You know a man must have exercise in some form or another. I get mine on your legs. I'm still enjoying that tramp of yours up to Castell-y-Bwch* three years ago. You remember?'

Captain Vaughan seemed at a loss for a moment.

'Let me see,' he said. 'Three years ago? Castell-y-Bwch? Now, what was I doing up there?'

'You can't have forgotten. Don't you recollect? It was just after the great snowstorm. You went up to see that the roof was all right, and fell into a fifteen-foot drift on the way.'

'I remember now,' said Vaughan. 'I should think I do remember. I don't think I've been so cold and so wet before or since—worse than the Balkans. I wasn't prepared for it. And when I got through the snow, there was an infernal mountain stream still going strong beneath it all.'

'But there was a good fire at the pub when you got there?'

'Half-way up the chimney; coal and wood mixed; roaring, I've never seen such a blaze: six foot by three, I should think. And I told them to mix it strong.'

'I wish I'd been there,' said the squire. 'Let me see; you recommended that some work should be done on the place, didn't you? Reroofing, wasn't it?'

'Yes, the slates were in a bad way, and in the following March we replaced them by stone tiles, extra heavy. Slates are not good enough, half-way up the mountain. To the west, of course, the place is more or less protected by the wood, but the south-east pine end is badly exposed and was letting the wet through, so I ran up an oak frame, nine inches from the wall, and fixed tiles on that. You remember passing the estimate?'

'Of course, of course. And it's done all right? No trouble since?'

'No trouble with wind or weather. When I was there last, the fat daughter was talking about going to service in Cardiff. I don't think Mrs Samuel fancied it much. And young William wants to go down the pit when he leaves school.'

'Thomas is staying to help his father with the farm, I hope? And how is the farm doing now?'

'Fairly well. They pay their rent regularly, as you know. In spite of what I tell them, they will try to grow wheat. It's much too high up.'

'How do the people on the mountain like the new parson?'

'They get on with him all right. He tries to persuade them to come to Mass, as he calls it, and they stay away and go to meeting. But quite on friendly terms—out of business hours.'

'I see. I should think he would be more at home in one of the Cardiff parishes. We must see if it can't be worked somehow. And how about those new pigsties at Ty, Captain? Have you got the estimate with you? Read it out, will you? My eyes are tired this morning. You went to Davies for the estimate? That's right: the policy of the estate is, always encourage the small man. Have you looked into that business of the marsh?'

'The marsh? Oh, you mean at Kemeys? Yes, I've gone into it. But I don't think it would pay for draining. You'd never see your money back.'

'You think not? That's a pity.'

Teilo Morgan seemed depressed by the agent's judgment on the Kemeys marshland. He weighed the matter.

'Well; I suppose you are right. We mustn't go in for fancy farming. But look here! It's just struck me. Why not utilise the marsh for growing willows? We could run a sluice from the brook right across it. It might be possible to start basket-making—in a small way, of course, at first. What do you think?'

'That wants looking into,' said Captain Vaughan. 'I know a place in Somerset where they are doing something of the kind. I'll go over on Wednesday and see if I can get some useful information. I hardly think the margin of profit would be a big one. But you would be satisfied with two per cent?'

'Certainly. And here's a thing I've been wanting to talk to you about for a long time—for the last three or four Mondays—and I've always forgotten. You know the Graeg on the home farm? A beautiful southern exposure, and practically wasted. I feel sure that egg-plants would do splendidly there. Could you manage to get out some figures for next Monday? There's no reason why the egg-plant shouldn't become as popular as the tomato and the banana; if a cheap supply were forthcoming. You will see to that, won't you? If you're busy, you might put off going to Somerset till next week: no hurry about the marsh.'

'Very good. The Graeg: egg-plants.' The agent made an entry in his note-book, and took his leave soon afterwards. He paced a long corridor till he came to the gallery, from which the main staircase of the Abbey went down to the entrance hall. There he encountered an important-looking personage, square-chinned, black-coated, slightly grizzled.

'As usual, I suppose?' the personage enquired.

'As usual.'

'What was it this time?'

'Egg-plants.'

The important one nodded, and Captain Vaughan went on his way.

## II

As soon as the agent had gone, Teilo Morgan rang a bell. His man came, and lifted him skilfully out of the big chair, and laid him on the day-bed by the window, propping him with cushions behind his back.

'Two cushions will be enough,' said the squire. 'I'm rather tired this morning.'

The man put the bell within easy reach, and went out softly. Teilo Morgan lay back quite still; thinking of old days, and of happy years, and of the bad season that followed them. His first recollections were of a little cottage, snow-white, high upon the mountain, a little higher than the hamlet of Castell-y-Bwch, of which he had been talking to the agent. The shining walls of the cottage, freshly whitened every Easter, were very thick, and sloped outward to the ground: the windows were deep-set in the wall. By the porch which sheltered the front door from the great winds of the mountain, were two shrubs, one on each side, that were covered in their season with orange-coloured flowers, as round as oranges, and these golden flowers were, in his memory, tossed and shaken to and fro, in the breeze that always blew in that high land, when every leaf and blossom of the lower slopes were still. About the house was the garden, and a rough field, and a small cherry orchard, in a shel-tered dip of land, and a well dripping from the grey rock with water very clear and cold. Above the cottage and its small demesne came a high bank, with a hedge of straggling, wind-beaten trees and bramble thickets on top of it, and beyond, the steep and wild ascent of the moun-tain, where the dark green whin bushes bore purple berries, where white cotton grew on the grass, and the bracken shimmered in the sun,

and the imperial heather glowed on golden autumn days. Teilo remembered well how, a long age ago, he would stand in summer weather by
the white porch, and look down on the great territory, as if on the whole
world, far below: wave following wave of hill and valley, of dark wood
and green pastures and cornfields, pale green or golden, the white
farms shining, the mist of blue smoke above the Roman city, and to the
right, the far waters of the yellow sea. And then there were the winter
nights: all the air black as pitch, and a noise of tumult and battle, when
the great winds and driving rain beat upon wall and window; and it was
praise and thanksgiving to lie safe and snug in a cot by the settle near
the light and the warmth of the fire, while without the heavens and the
hills were confounded together in the roaring darkness.

In the white cottage on the high land, Teilo had lived with his mother
and grandmother, very old, bent and wrinkled; with a sallow face, and
hair still black in spite of long years. But he was a very small boy, when
a gentleman who had often been there before, came and took his mother
and himself away, down into the valley; and his next memories were of
the splendours of Llantrisant Abbey, where the three of them lived
together, and were waited on by many servants, and he found that the
gentleman was his father: a cheerful man, always laughing, with bright
blue eyes and a thick, tawny moustache, that drooped over his chin.
Here Teilo ran about the park, and raced sticks in the racing Avon, and
climbed up the steep hill they called the Graeg, and liked to be there
because with the shimmering, sweet-scented bracken it was like the
mountain-side. His walks and runs and climbs did not last long. The
strange illness that nobody seemed to understand struck him down,
and when after many weeks of bitter pains and angry, fiery dreams, the
anguish of day and night left him; he was weak and helpless, and lay
still, waiting to get well, and never got well again. Month after month
he lay there in his bed, able to move his hands faintly, and no more. At
the end of a year he felt a little stronger and tried to walk, and just managed to get across the room, helping himself from chair to chair. There
was one thing that was for the better: he had been a silent child, happy
to sit all by himself hour after hour on the mountain and then on the
steep slope of the Graeg, without uttering a word or wanting anyone to
come and talk to him. Now, in his weakness, he chattered eagerly, and
thought of admirable things. He would tell his father and mother all the
schemes and plans he was making; and he wondered why they looked so
sadly at him.

And then, disaster. His father died, and his mother and he had to
leave Llantrisant Abbey; they never told him why. They went to live in

a grey, dreary street somewhere in the north of London. It was a place full of ugly sights and sounds, with a stench of burning bones always in the heavy air, and an unseemly litter of egg-shells and torn paper and cabbage-stalks about the gutters, and screams and harsh cries fouling the ears at midnight. And in winter, the yellow sulphur mist shut out the sky and burned sourly in the nostrils. A dreadful place, and the exile was long there. His mother went out on most days soon after breakfast, and often did not come back till ten, eleven, twelve at night, tired to death, as she said, and her dark beauty all marred and broken. Two or three times, in the course of the day, a neighbour from the floor below would come in and see if he wanted anything; but, except for these visits, he lay alone all the hours, and read in the few old books that they had in the room. It was a life of bewildered misery. There was not much to eat, and what there was seemed not to have the right taste or smell; and he could not understand why they should have to live in the horrible street, since his mother had told him that now his father was dead, he was the rightful master of Llantrisant Abbey and should be a very rich man. 'Then why are we in this dreadful place?' he asked her; and she only cried.

And then his mother died. And a few days after the funeral, people came and took him away; and he found himself once more at Llantrisant, master of it all, as his mother had told him he should be. He made up his mind to learn all about the lands and farms that he owned, and got them to bring him the books of the estate, and then Captain Vaughan began to come and see him, and tell him how things were going on, and how this farmer was the best tenant in the county, and how that man had nothing but bad luck, and John Williams would put gin in his cider, and drive breakneck down steep, stony lanes on market nights, standing up in the cart like a Roman charioteer. He learnt about all these works and ways, and how the land was farmed, and what was done and what was needed to be done in the farm-houses and farm-buildings, and asked the agent about all his visits of inspection and enquiry, till he felt that he knew every field and foot-path on the Llantrisant estate, and could find his way to every farm-house and cottage chimney corner from the mountain to the sea. It was the absorbing interest and the great happiness of his life; and he was proud to think of all he had done for the land and for the people on it. They were excellent people, farmers, but apt to be too conservative, too much given to stick in the old ruts that their fathers and grandfathers had made, obstinately loyal to old methods in a new world. For example, there was Williams, Penyrhaul, who almost refused to grow roots, and Evan Thomas, Glascoed, who didn't believe in drainpipes, and tried to convince Vaughan that bush drainage was better for the land, and half a dozen, at least, who were sure that all artificials exhausted the soil, and the silly fellow who had brought his black Castle Martins with him from Pembrokeshire, and turned up his nose at Shorthorns and Herefords. Still, Vaughan had a way with him, and made most of them see reason sooner or later; and they all knew that there was not another estate in England or Wales that was so ready to meet its tenants half-way, and do repairs and build new barns and cowsheds very often before they were asked. Teilo Morgan gave his agent all the credit he deserved, but at the same time he could not help feeling that in spite of his disabilities, of the weakness that kept him a prisoner to these four or five rooms, so that he had not once gone over the rest of the Abbey since his return to it; in spite of his invalid and stricken days, a great deal was owing to himself and to the fresh ideas that he had brought to the management of the estate. He took in the farming journals, and was thoroughly well read in the latest literature that dealt with the various branches of agriculture, and he knew in consequence that he was well in advance of his time, in advance even of the most forward agriculturalists of the day. There were methods and schemes and ideas in full course of practical and successful working on the Llantrisant property that were absolutely unheard of on any other estate in the country. He had wanted to discuss some of these ideas in the Press; but Vaughan had dissuaded him; he said that for the present the force of prejudice was too strong. Vaughan was possibly right; all the same Teilo Morgan knew that he was making agricultural history. In the meantime, he was jotting down careful and elaborate notes on the experiments that were being tried, and in a year or two he intended to put a book on the stocks: *The Llantrisant Estates: a New Era in Farming.*

He was pondering happily in this strain; when, in a flash, a brilliant, a dazzling notion came to him. He drew a long breath of delighted wonder; then rang his hand-bell, and told the man that he might now put in the third cushion—'and give me my writing things.' A handy contraption, with paper, ink and the rest was adjusted before him, and as soon as the servant was gone, Teilo began a letter, his eyes bright with excitement.

DEAR VAUGHAN.

I know you think I'm inclined to be rather too experimental in my farming; I believe that this time you will agree that I have hit on a great idea. Don't say a word to anybody about it. I am astonished that it hasn't been thought of long ago, and my only fear is that we may be forestalled. I suppose the fact is that it has been staring us all in the face so long that we haven't noticed it!

My idea is simply this; a plantation, or orchard, if you like, of the Arbor Vitæ;* and I know the exact place for it. You have often told me how Jenkins of the Garth insists on having those fields of his by the Soar down in potatoes, a most unsuitable place for such a crop. I want you to go and see him as soon as you have time, and tell him we want the use of the fields—about five acres, if I remember. Of course, he must be compensated, and, within reason, you can be as liberal as you like. I have understood from you that the soil is a deep, rich loam, in very good heart; it should be an ideal position for the culture I intend. I believe that the Arbor Vitæ will flourish anywhere, and is practically indifferent to climatic conditions: 'makes its own climate,' as one writer rather poetically expresses it. Still, its culture in this county is an experiment; and I am sure Mharadwys—I think that's the old name of those fields by the Soar—is the very spot.

The land must be thoroughly trenched. Get this put in hand as soon as you can possibly manage it. Let them leave it in ridges, so that the winter frosts can break it up. Then, if we give it a good dressing of superphosphate of lime and bone meal in the spring, and plough in September, everything will be ready for the autumn planting. You know I always insist on shallow planting; don't bury the roots in a hole; spread them out evenly within five or six inches of the surface; let them feel the sun. And when it comes to staking; mind that each tree has two stakes, crossed at the top, with the points driven into the ground at a good distance from the roots. I am sure that the single stake, close to the tree stem, with its point driven through the roots is very bad practice.

Of course, you will appreciate the importance of this new culture. The twelve distinct kinds of fruit produced by this extraordinary tree, all of them of delicious flavour, render it absolutely unique. Whatever the cost of the experiment may be, I am sure it will be made good in a very short time. And it must be remembered that while the name, *Tous les mois*, given to a kind of strawberry cultivated on the continent, really only implies that the plants fruit all through the summer and early autumn, in the case of the Arbor Vitæ, the claim may be made with literal truth. As the old writers say: 'The Arbor yielded her fruit every month.' No other cropper, however heavy, can be compared with it. And in addition to all this, the leaves are said to possess the most valuable therapeutic qualities.

Don't you agree with me that this will prove by far the most important and far-reaching of all our experiments?

I remain,
  Yours sincerely,
    Teilo Morgan.

P.S. On consideration; I think it might be better to keep the dressing of super and bone meal till the autumn, just before ploughing.

And you might as well begin to look up the Nurserymen's Catalogues. As we shall be giving a large order, you may have to place it with two or three firms. I think you will find the Arbor Vitæ listed with the Coniferæ.

### III

LONG years after all this, two elderly men were talking together in a club smoking-room. They had the place almost to themselves; most of the members, having lunched and taken their coffee and cigarettes, had strolled away. There was a small knot of men with their heads close together over the table, chuckling and relating and hearing juicy gossip. Two or three others were dotted about the solemn, funebrous room, each apart with his paper, deep in his arm-chair. Our two were in a retired corner, which might have been called snug in any other place. They were old friends, it appeared, and one, the less elderly, had returned not long before from some far place, after an absence of many years.

'I haven't seen anything of Harry Morgan since I've been home,' he remarked. 'I suppose he's still in town.'

'Still in Beresford Street. But he doesn't get out so much now. He's getting a bit stiff in the joints. A good ten years older than I am.'

'I should like to see him again. I always thought him a very good fellow.'

'A first-rate fellow. You know that story about Bartle Frere?* Man was sent to meet him at the station, and asked how he should know him. They told him to look out for an old gentleman with grey whiskers helping somebody—and he found Frere helping an old woman with a big basket out of a third-class carriage. Harry Morgan was like that— except for the whiskers.'

There was a pause; and then the man who had retold the old Sir Bartle Frere story began again.

'I don't suppose you ever heard the kindest thing Morgan ever did—one of the kindest things I've ever heard of. You know I come from his part of the country: my people used to have Plas Henoc, only a few miles from Llantrisant Abbey, the Morgans' place. My father told me all about it; but I don't think many people got to hear of it; Harry kept the thing very dark. Upon my word! what is it about a man not letting his left hand know what his right hand is about? Morgan has lived up to that if any man ever did. Well, it was like this:

'Have you ever heard of old Teilo Morgan? He was a bit before our day. Not an old man, by the way; I don't suppose he was much over forty when he died. Well, he went the pace in the old style. He was very well known in town, not in society, or rather in damned bad society, and not far from here either. They had a picture of him in some low print of the time, with those long whiskers that used to be worn then. They didn't give his name; just called it, "The Hero of the Haymarket." You wouldn't believe it, would you, but in those days the Haymarket was the great place for night-houses—Kate Hamilton and all that lot.* Morgan was in the thick of it all; but that picture annoyed him; he had those whiskers of his cut off at Truefitt's* the very next day. He was the sort of man they got the silver dinner service out for, when he entertained his friends at Cremorne. And "Judge and Jury,"* and the *poses plastiques*,* and that place in Windmill Street where they fought without the gloves—and all the rest of it.

'And it was just as bad down in the country. He used to take his London friends, male and female, down there, and lead the sort of life he lived in town, as near as he could make it. They used to tell a story, true very likely, of how he and half a dozen rapscallions like himself were putting away the port after dinner, and making a devil of a noise, all talking and shouting and cursing at the top of their voices, when Teilo seemed to pull himself together and get very grave all in a minute. "Silence! gentlemen!" he called out. The rest of them took no notice; one of them started a blackguard song, and the others got ready to join in the chorus. "Hold your damned tongues, damn you!" Morgan bawled at them, and smashed a big decanter on the table. "D'you think," he said, "that that's the sort of thing for youngsters to listen to? Have you no sense of decency? Didn't I tell you that the children were coming down to dessert?" With that, he rang a bell that was by him on the table and—so the story goes—six young fellows and six girls came trooping down the big staircase: without a single stitch on them, calling out in squeaky voices: "Oh, dear Papa, what have you done to dear Mamma?" And the rest of it.'

The phrase was evidently an inclusive, vague, but altogether damnatory clause with this teller of old tales.

'Well,' he continued, 'you can imagine what the county thought of all that sort of thing. Teilo Morgan made Llantrisant Abbey stink in their nostrils. Naturally, none of them would go near the place. The women, who were, perhaps, rather more particular about such matters than they are now, simply wouldn't have Morgan's name mentioned in their presence. The Duke cut him dead in the street. His subscription to the Hunt was returned. I don't think he cared. You know Garden Parties were beginning to get fashionable then, and they say Morgan sent out engraved invitation cards, with a picture of a Nymph and a Satyr on them that some artist fellow had done for him—not a nice picture at all according to county standards. And what d'ye think he had at the bottom of the card instead of R.S.V.P.?—'No clothes by request.' He was a damned impudent fellow, if you like. I believe the party came off all right, with more friends from town, and most unusual games and sports on the lawn and in the shrubberies. It was said that Treowen, the Duke's son, was there; but he always swore through thick and thin that it was a lie. But it was brought up against him afterwards when he stood with Herbert for the county.

'And what d'ye think happened next? A most extraordinary thing. Nobody was prepared for it. Everyone said he would just drink and devil and wench himself to death, and a damned good riddance. Well, I'll tell you. There was one thing, you know, that everybody had to confess: in his very worst days Teilo Morgan always left the country girls alone. Never interfered with the farmers' daughters or cottage girls or anything in that way. And then, one fine day when he was up with a keeper looking after a few head of grouse he had on the mountain, what should he do but fall in love with a girl of fifteen, who lived with her mother or grandmother, I don't know which, in a cottage right up there. Mary Trevor, I believe her name was. My father had seen her once or twice afterwards driving with Morgan in his tandem: he said she was a most beautiful creature, a perfectly lovely woman. She was a type that you see sometimes in Wales: very dark, black eyes, black hair, oval face, skin a pale olive—not at all unlike those girls that used to prance up and down Arles in Southern France, with their hair done up in velvet ribbons; I don't know whether you've ever been there? There's something Oriental about that style of beauty; it doesn't last long.

'Anyhow, Teilo Morgan fell flat on the spot. He went straight down to the Abbey and packed the whole company back to town—told them they could go to hell, or bloody Jerusalem, or the Haymarket, for all he cared. As soon as they'd all gone, he was off to the mountain again. He wasn't seen at the Abbey for weeks. I am sure I don't know why he didn't marry the girl straight away; nobody knew. She said that he did marry her; but we shall come to that presently. In due course, the baby came along, and Morgan wanted to pension off the old lady and take the mother and child down to Llantrisant. But the doctors advised against it. I believe Morgan got some very good men down, and they were all inclined to shake their heads over the child. I don't think they committed themselves or named any distinct disease or anything of that kind; but they were all agreed that there was a certain delicacy of constitution, and that the boy would have a much better chance if they kept him up in the mountain air for the first few years of his life. Llantrisant Abbey, I should tell you, is right down in the valley by the river, with woods and hills all round it; fine place, but rather damp and relaxing, I daresay. So, the long and short of it was that young Teilo stayed up with his mother and the old woman, and old Teilo used to come and see them for week-ends, as they say now, till the boy was four or five years old; and then the old lady was looked after somewhere or other, and the mother and son went to live at the Abbey.

'Everything went on all right—except that the county people kept away—for three or four years. The child seemed well and strong, and the tutor they got in for him said he was a tremendous fellow with his books, well in advance of his age, unusually interested in his work and all that. Then he got ill, very ill indeed. I don't know what it was; some brain trouble, I should think, meningitis or something of that sort. It was touch and go for weeks, and it left the unfortunate little chap an absolute wreck at the end of it. For a long time they thought he was paralysed; all the strength had gone out of his limbs. And the worst of it was, the mind was affected. He seemed bright enough, mind you; nothing dull or heavy about him; and I'm told you might listen to him chattering away for half an hour on end, and go away thinking he was a perfect phenomenon of a child for intelligence. But if you listened long enough, you'd hear something that would pull you up with a jerk. Crazy?—yes, and worse than crazy—mixed up in a way with a kind of sense, so that you might begin to wonder which was queer, yourself or the boy. It was a dreadful grief to the parents, especially to his father. He used to talk about his sins finding him out. I don't know, there may have been something in that. "Whips to scourge us"*—perhaps so.

'They got the tutor back after some time; the child begged so hard for him that they were afraid he'd worry himself into another brain fever if they didn't give way. So he came along with instructions to make the lessons as much a farce as he liked, and the more the better; not on any account to press the boy over his work. And from what my father told me, young Teilo nearly drove the poor man off his head. He was far sharper in a way than he'd ever been before, with a memory like Macaulay's*—once read, never forgotten—and an amazing appetite for learning. But then the twist in the brain would come out. Mathematics brilliant; and at the end of the lesson he'd frighten that tutor of his with a new theory of figures, some notion of the figures that we don't know of, the numbers that are between the others, something rather more than one and less than two, and so forth. It was the same with everything: there was the Secret Conquest of England a hundred years ago, that nobody was allowed to mention, and the squares that were always changing their shape in geometry, and the great continent that was hidden because Africa was on top of it, so that you couldn't see it. Then, when it came to the classics, there were fresh cases for the nouns and new moods for the verbs: and all the rest of it. Most extraordinary, and very sad for his father and mother. The poor little fellow took a tremendous interest in the family history and in the property; but I believe he hashed all that up in some infernal way. Well; it seemed there was nothing to be done.

'Then his father died. Of course, the question of the succession came up at once. Poor Mrs Morgan, as she called herself to the last, swore she was married to Teilo, but she couldn't produce any papers—any papers that were evidence of a legal marriage anyhow. I fancy the truth was that they were married in some forgotten little chapel up in the mountains by a hedge preacher or somebody of that kind, who didn't know enough to get in the registrar. Of course, Teilo ought to have known better, but probably he didn't bother at the time so long as he satisfied the girl. He may have meant to make it all right eventually, and left it too late: I don't know. Anyhow, Payne Llewellyn, the family solicitor, gave the poor woman to understand that she and the boy would have to leave Llantrisant Abbey, and off they went. They had one room in a miserable back street in Islington or Barnsbury or some such Godforsaken place and she earned a bare living in a sweater's workshop.

'Meanwhile, the property had passed to a cousin; Harry Morgan. And he hadn't been heard of, or barely heard of, for some years. He had gone off exploring Central Asia or the sources of the Amazon when Teilo Morgan was in his glory—if you can put it that way. He hadn't heard a word of Teilo's reformation or of Mary Trevor and her boy; and when old Llewellyn was able to get at him after considerable difficulty and delay, he never mentioned the woman or her son. When Morgan did come home at last, he found he didn't fancy the old family place; called it a dismal hole, I believe. Anyhow, he let it on a longish lease to a mental specialist—mad doctors, they called them then—and he turned the Abbey into a lunatic asylum.

'Then somebody told Harry about Mary Trevor, and the poor child, and the marriage or no-marriage. He was furious with Llewellyn. He had a search made, and when he found them, it was just too late so far as Mary Trevor was concerned. She had died, of grief and hard work and semi-starvation, no doubt. But Harry took the boy away, and finding how he was longing to go back to the Abbey—he was quite convinced, you see, that he was the owner of it and of all the Morgan estates—Harry got the doctor who was running the place to take Teilo as a patient. He was given a set of rooms to himself in a wing, right away from the other patients. Everything was done to encourage him in his notion that he was Teilo Morgan of Llantrisant Abbey. Going back to the old place had stirred up all his enthusiasm for the family, and the property, and the management of the estates, and it became the great interest of his life. He quite thought he was making it the best-managed estate in the county: inaugurating a new era in English farming, and all the rest of it. Harry Morgan instructed Captain Vaughan, the Estate Agent, to see Teilo once a week, and enter into all his schemes and pretend to carry them out, and I believe Vaughan played up extremely well, though he sometimes found it difficult to keep a straight face. You see, that twist in the brain wasn't getting any better, and when it went to work on practical farming it produced some amazing results. Vaughan would be told to get this bit of land ready for pineapples, and somewhere else they were to grow olives; and what about zebras for haulage? But it kept him happy to the last. D'you know, the very day he died, he wrote a long letter of instructions to Vaughan. What d'you think it was about? You won't guess. He told Vaughan to plant the Tree of Life in a potato patch by the Soar, and gave full cultural directions.'

'God bless me! You don't say so?'

The Major, who had listened to the long story, ruminated awhile. He had been brought up in an old-fashioned Evangelical household, and had always loved 'Revelations.'* The text burned and glowed into his memory, and he said in a strong voice:

'"In the midst of the street of it, and on either side of the river, was there the tree of life, which bare twelve manner of fruits, and yielded her fruit every month: and the leaves of the tree were for the healing of the nations."'

There was only one man besides our two friends left in the darkening room; and he had fallen fast asleep in his arm-chair, with his paper on the ground before him. The Major's clear intonation woke him with a crash, and when he heard the words that were being uttered, he was seized with unspeakable and panic terror, and ran out of the room, howling (more or less) for the Committee.*

But the Major having ended his text, said:

'I always thought Harry Morgan was a good fellow. But I didn't know he was such a thundering good fellow as that.'

And that was his Amen.

# CHANGE

'HERE,' said old Mr Vincent Rimmer, fumbling in the pigeon-holes of his great and ancient bureau, 'is an oddity which may interest you.'

He drew a sheet of paper out of the dark place where it had been hidden, and handed it to Reynolds, his curious guest. The oddity was an ordinary sheet of notepaper, of a sort which has long been popular; a bluish grey with slight flecks and streaks of a darker blue embedded in its substance. It had yellowed a little with age at the edges. The outer page was blank; Reynolds laid it open, and spread it out on the table beside his chair. He read something like this:

$$a \quad aa \quad e \quad ee \quad i \quad e \quad ee$$
$$aa \quad i \quad i \quad o \quad e \quad ee \quad o$$
$$ee \quad ee \quad i \quad aa \quad o \quad oo \quad o$$
$$a \quad o \quad a \quad a \quad e \quad i \quad ee$$
$$e \quad o \quad i \quad ee \quad a \quad e \quad i$$

Reynolds scanned it with stupefied perplexity.

'What on earth is it?' he said. 'Does it mean anything? Is it a cypher, or a silly game, or what?'

Mr Rimmer chuckled. 'I thought it might puzzle you,' he remarked. 'Do you happen to notice anything about the writing; anything out of the way at all?'

Reynolds scanned the document more closely.

'Well, I don't know that there is anything out of the way in the script itself. The letters are rather big, perhaps, and they are rather clumsily formed. But it's difficult to judge handwriting by a few letters, repeated again and again. But, apart from the writing, what is it?'

'That's a question that must wait a bit. There are many strange things related to that bit of paper. But one of the strangest things about it is this; that it is intimately connected with the Darren Mystery.'

'What Mystery did you say? The Darren Mystery? I don't think I ever heard of it.'

'Well, it was a little before your time. And, in any case, I don't see how you could have heard of it. There were, certainly, some very curious and unusual circumstances in the case, but I don't think that they were generally known, and if they were known, they were not understood.

You won't wonder at that, perhaps, when you consider that the bit of paper before you was one of those circumstances.'

'But what exactly happened?'

'That is largely a matter of conjecture. But, anyhow, here's the out-side of the case, for a beginning. Now, to start with, I don't suppose you've ever been to Meirion?* Well, you should go. It's a beautiful county, in West Wales, with a fine sea-coast, and some very pleasant places to stay at, and none of them too large or too popular. One of the smallest of these places, Trenant, is just a village. There is a wooded height above it called the Allt; and down below, the church, with a Celtic cross in the churchyard, a dozen or so of cottages, a row of lodging-houses on the slope round the corner, a few more cottages dotted along the road to Meiros, and that's all. Below the village are marshy meadows where the brook that comes from the hills spreads abroad, and then the dunes, and the sea, stretching away to the Dragon's Head in the far east and enclosed to the west by the beginnings of the limestone cliffs. There are fine, broad sands all the way between Trenant and Porth, the market-town, about a mile and a half away, and it's just the place for children.

'Well, just forty-five years ago, Trenant was having a very successful season. In August there must have been eighteen or nineteen visitors in the village. I was staying in Porth at the time, and, when I walked over, it struck me that the Trenant beach was quite crowded—eight or nine children castle-building and learning to swim, and looking for shells, and all the usual diversions. The grown-up people sat in groups on the edge of the dunes and read and gossiped, or took a turn towards Porth, or perhaps tried to catch prawns in the rock-pools at the other end of the sands. Altogether a very pleasant, happy scene in its simple way, and, as it was a beautiful summer, I have no doubt they all enjoyed them-selves very much. I walked to Trenant and back three or four times, and I noticed that most of the children were more or less in charge of a very pretty dark girl, quite young, who seemed to advise in laying out the ground-plan of the castle, and to take off her stockings and tuck up her skirts—we thought a lot of Legs in those days—when the bathers required supervision. She also indicated the kinds of shells which deserved the attention of collectors: an extremely serviceable girl.

'It seemed that this girl, Alice Hayes, was really in charge of the chil-dren—or of the greater part of them. She was a sort of nursery-governess or lady of all work to Mrs Brown, who had come down from London in the early part of July with Miss Hayes and little Michael, a child of eight, who refused to recover nicely from his attack of measles. Mr Brown had joined them at the end of the month with the two elder children,

Jack and Rosamond. Then, there were the Smiths, with their little family, and the Robinsons with their three; and the fathers and mothers, sitting on the beach every morning, got to know each other very easily. Mrs Smith and Mrs Robinson soon appreciated Miss Hayes's merits as a child-herd; they noticed that Mrs Brown sat placid and went on knitting in the sun, quite safe and unperturbed, while they suffered from recurrent alarms. Jack Smith, though barely fourteen, would be seen dashing through the waves, out to sea, as if he had quite made up his mind to swim to the Dragon's Head, about twenty miles away, or Jane Robinson, in bright pink, would appear suddenly right away among the rocks of the point, ready to vanish into the perilous unknown round the corner. Hence, alarums and excursions,* tiring expeditions of rescue and remonstrance, through soft sand or over slippery rocks under a hot sun. And then these ladies would discover that certain of their offspring had entirely disappeared or were altogether missing from the landscape; and dreadful and true tales of children who had driven tunnels into the sand and had been overwhelmed therein rushed to the mind. And all the while Mrs Brown sat serene, confident in the overseership of her Miss Hayes. So, as was to be gathered, the other two took counsel together. Mrs Brown was approached, and something called an arrangement was made, by which Miss Hayes undertook the joint mastership of all three packs, greatly to the ease of Mrs Smith and Mrs Robinson.

It was about this time, I suppose, that I got to know this group of holiday-makers. I had met Smith, whom I knew slightly in town, in the streets of Porth, just as I was setting out for one of my morning walks. We strolled together to Trenant on the firm sand down by the water's edge, and introductions went round, and so I joined the party, and sat with them, watching the various diversions of the children and the capable superintendence of Miss Hayes.

'Now there's a queer thing about this little place,' said Brown, a genial man, connected, I believe, with Lloyd's. 'Wouldn't you say this was as healthy a spot as any you could find? Well sheltered from the north, southern aspect, never too cold in winter, fresh sea-breeze in summer: what could you have more?'

'Well,' I replied, 'it always agrees with me very well: a little relaxing, perhaps, but I like being relaxed. Isn't it a healthy place, then? What makes you think so?'

'I'll tell you. We have rooms in Govan Terrace, up there on the hillside. The other night I woke up with a coughing fit. I got out of bed to get a drink of water, and then had a look out of the window to see what sort of night it was. I didn't like the look of those clouds in the south-west after sunset the night before. As you can see, the upper windows of Govan Terrace command a good many of the village houses. And, do you know, there was a light in almost every house? At two o'clock in the morning. Apparently the village is full of sick people. But who would have thought it?'

We were sitting a little apart from the rest. Smith had brought a London paper from Porth and he and Robinson had their heads together over the City article.* The three women were knitting and talking hard, and down by the blue, creaming water Miss Hayes and her crew were playing happily in the sunshine.

'Do you mind,' I said to Brown, 'if I swear you to secrecy? A limited secrecy: I don't want you to speak of this to any of the village people. They wouldn't like it. And have you told your wife or any of the party about what you saw?'

'As a matter of fact, I haven't said a word to anybody. Illness isn't a very cheerful topic for a holiday, is it? But what's up? You don't mean to say there's some sort of epidemic in the place that they're keeping dark? I say! That would be awful. We should have to leave at once. Think of the children.'

'Nothing of the kind. I don't think that there's a single case of illness in the place—unless you count old Thomas Evans, who has been in what he calls a decline for thirty years. You won't say anything? Then I'm going to give you a shock. The people have a light burning in their houses all night to keep out the fairies.'

I must say it was a success. Brown looked frightened. Not of the fairies; most certainly not; rather at the reversion of his established order of things. He occupied his business in the City; he lived in an extremely comfortable house at Addiscombe; he was a keen though sane adherent of the Liberal Party; and in the world between these points there was no room at all either for fairies or for people who believed in fairies. The latter were almost as fabulous to him as the former, and still more objectionable.

'Look here!' he said at last. 'You're pulling my leg. Nobody believes in fairies. They haven't for hundreds of years. Shakespeare didn't believe in fairies. He says so.'

I let him run on. He implored me to tell him whether it was typhoid, or only measles, or even chicken-pox. I said at last:

'You seem very positive on the subject of fairies. Are you sure there are no such things?'

'Of course I am,' said Brown, very crossly.

'How do you know?'

It is a shocking thing to be asked a question like that, to which, be it observed, there is no answer. I left him seething dangerously.

'Remember,' I said, 'not a word of lit windows to anybody; but if you are uneasy as to epidemics, ask the doctor about it.'

He nodded his head glumly. I knew he was drawing all sorts of false conclusions; and for the rest of our stay I would say that he did not seek me out—until the last day of his visit. I had no doubt that he put me down as a believer in fairies and a maniac; but it is, I consider, good for men who live between the City and Liberal Politics and Addiscombe to be made to realise that there is a world elsewhere. And, as it happens, it was quite true that most of the Trenant people believed in the fairies and were horribly afraid of them.

But this was only an interlude. I often strolled over and joined the party. And I took up my freedom with the young members by contributing posts and a tennis net to the beach sports. They had brought down rackets and balls, in the vague idea that they might be able to get a game somehow and somewhere, and my contribution was warmly welcomed. I helped Miss Hayes to fix the net, and she marked out the court, with the help of many suggestions from the elder children, to which she did not pay the slightest attention. I think the constant disputes as to whether the ball was 'in' or 'out' brightened the game, though Wimbledon would not have approved. And sometimes the elder children accompanied their parents to Porth in the evening and watched the famous Japanese Jugglers or Pepper's Ghost* at the Assembly Rooms, or listened to the Mysterious Musicians* at the De Barry* Gardens—and altogether everybody had, you would say, a very jolly time.

It all came to a dreadful end. One morning when I had come out on my usual morning stroll from Porth, and had got to the camping ground of the party at the edge of the dunes, I found somewhat to my surprise that there was nobody there. I was afraid that Brown had been in part justified in his dread of concealed epidemics, and that some of the children had 'caught something' in the village. So I walked up in the direction of Govan Terrace, and found Brown standing at the bottom of his flight of steps, and looking very much upset.

I hailed him.

'I say,' I began, 'I hope you weren't right, after all. None of the children down with measles, or anything of that sort?'

'It's something worse than measles. We none of us know what has happened. The doctor can make nothing of it. Come in, and we can talk it over.'

Just then a procession came down the steps leading from a house a few doors further on. First of all there was the porter from the station, with a pile of luggage on his truck. Then came the two elder Smith children, Jack and Millicent, and finally, Mr and Mrs Smith. Mr Smith was carrying something wrapped in a bundle in his arms.

'Where's Bob?' He was the youngest; a brave, rosy little man of five or six.

'Smith's carrying him,' murmured Brown.

'What's happened? Has he hurt himself on the rocks? I hope it's nothing serious.'

I was going forward to make my enquiries, but Brown put a hand on my arm and checked me. Then I looked at the Smith party more closely, and I saw at once that there was something very much amiss. The two elder children had been crying, though the boy was doing his best to put up a brave face against disaster—whatever it was. Mrs Smith had drawn her veil over her face, and stumbled as she walked, and on Smith's face there was a horror as of ill dreams.

'Look,' said Brown in his low voice.

Smith had half-turned, as he set out with his burden to walk down the hill to the station. I don't think he knew we were there; I don't think any of the party had noticed us as we stood on the bottom step, half-hidden by a blossoming shrub. But as he turned uncertainly, like a man in the dark, the wrappings fell away a little from what he carried, and I saw a little wizened, yellow face peering out; malignant, deplorable.

I turned helplessly to Brown, as that most wretched procession went on its way and vanished out of sight.

'What on earth has happened? That's not Bobby. Who is it?'

'Come into the house,' said Brown, and he went before me up the long flight of steps that led to the terrace.

There was a shriek and a noise of thin, shrill, high-pitched laughter as we came into the lodging-house.

'That's Miss Hayes in blaspheming hysterics,' said Brown grimly. 'My wife's looking after her. The children are in the room at the back. I daren't let them go out by themselves in this awful place.' He beat with his foot on the floor and glared at me, awestruck, a solid man shaken.

'Well,' he said at last, 'I'll tell you what we know; and as far as I can make out, that's very little. However. . . . You know Miss Hayes, who helps Mrs Brown with the children, had more or less taken over the charge of the lot; the young Robinsons and the Smiths, too. You've seen how well she looks after them all on the sands in the morning. In the afternoon she's been taking them inland for a change. You know there's beautiful country if you go a little way inland; rather wild and woody;

but still very nice; pleasant and shady. Miss Hayes thought that the all-day glare of the sun on the sands might not be very good for the small ones, and my wife agreed with her. So they took their teas with them and picnicked in the woods and enjoyed themselves very much, I believe. They didn't go more than a couple of miles or three at the outside; and the little ones used to take turns in a go-cart. They never seemed too tired.

'Yesterday at lunch they were talking about some caves at a place called the Darren,* about two miles away. My children seemed very anxious to see them, and Mrs Probert, our landlady, said they were quite safe, so the Smiths and Robinsons were called in, and they were enthusiastic, too; and the whole party set off with their tea-baskets, and candles and matches, in Miss Hayes's charge. Somehow they made a later start than usual, and from what I can make out they enjoyed themselves so much in the cool dark cave, first of all exploring, and then looking for treasure, and winding up with tea by candlelight, that they didn't notice how the time was going—nobody had a watch—and by the time they'd packed up their traps and come out from under-ground, it was quite dark. They had a little trouble making out the way at first, but not very much, and came along in high spirits, tumbling over molehills and each other, and finding it all quite an adventure.

'They had got down in the road there, and were sorting themselves out into the three parties, when somebody called out: "Where's Bobby Smith?" Well, he wasn't there. The usual story; everybody thought he was with somebody else. They were all mixed up in the dark, talking and laughing and shrieking at the top of their voices, and taking every-thing for granted—I suppose it was like that. But poor little Bob was missing. You can guess what a scene there was. Everybody was much too frightened to scold Miss Hayes, who had no doubt been extremely careless, to say the least of it—not like her. Robinson pulled us together. He told Mrs Smith that the little chap would be perfectly all right: there were no precipices to fall over and no water to fall into, the way they'd been, that it was a warm night, and the child had had a good stuffing tea, and he would be as right as rain when they found him. So we got a man from the farm, with a lantern, and Miss Hayes to show us exactly where they'd been, and Smith and Robinson and I went off to find poor Bobby, feeling a good deal better than at first. I noticed that the farm man seemed a good deal put out when we told him what had happened and where we were going. "Got lost in the Darren," he said, "indeed, that is a pity." That set off Smith at once; and he asked Williams what he meant; what was the matter with the place? Williams said there was nothing the matter with it at all whatever but it was "a tiresome place to be in after dark." That reminded me of what you were saying a couple of weeks ago about the people here. "Some damned superstitious nonsense," I said to myself, and thanked God it was nothing worse. I thought the fellow might be going to tell us of a masked bog or something like that. I gave Smith a hint in a whisper as to where the land lay; and we went on, hoping to come on little Bob any minute. Nearly all the way we were going through open fields without any cover or bracken or anything of that sort, and Williams kept twirling his lantern, and Miss Hayes and the rest of us called out the child's name; there didn't seem much chance of missing him.

'However, we saw nothing of him—till we got to the Darren. It's an odd sort of place, I should think. You're in an ordinary field, with a gentle upward slope, and you come to a gate, and down you go into a deep, narrow valley; a regular nest of valleys as far as I could make out in the dark, one leading into another, and the sides covered with trees. The famous caves were on one of these steep slopes, and, of course, we all went in. They didn't stretch far; nobody could have got lost in them, even if the candles gave out. We searched the place thoroughly, and saw where the children had had their tea: no signs of Bobby. So we went on down the valley between the woods, till we came to where it opens out into a wide space, with one tree growing all alone in the middle. And then we heard a miserable whining noise, like some little creature that's got hurt. And there under the tree was—what you saw poor Smith carrying in his arms this morning.

'It fought like a wild cat when Smith tried to pick it up, and jabbered some unearthly sort of gibberish. Then Miss Hayes came along and seemed to soothe it; and it's been quiet ever since. The man with the lantern was shaking with terror; the sweat was pouring down his face.'

I stared hard at Brown. 'And,' I thought to myself, 'you are very much in the same condition as Williams.' Brown was obviously overcome with dread.

We sat there in silence.

'Why do you say "it"?' I asked. 'Why don't you say "him"?'

'You saw.'

'Do you mean to tell me seriously that you don't believe that child you helped to bring home was Bobby? What does Mrs Smith say?'

'She says the clothes are the same. I suppose it must be Bobby. The doctor from Porth says the child must have had a severe shock. I don't think he knows anything about it.'

He stuttered over his words, and said at last:

'I was thinking of what you said about the lighted windows. I hoped you might be able to help. Can you do anything? We are leaving this afternoon; all of us. Is there nothing to be done?'

'I am afraid not.'

I had nothing else to say. We shook hands and parted without more words.

The next day I walked over to the Darren. There was something fearful about the place, even in the haze of a golden afternoon. As Brown had said, the entrance and the disclosure of it were sudden and abrupt. The fields of the approach held no hint of what was to come. Then, past the gate, the ground fell violently away on every side, grey rocks of an ill shape pierced through it, and the ash trees on the steep slopes over-shadowed all. The descent was into silence, without the singing of a bird, into a wizard shade. At the farther end, where the wooded heights retreated somewhat, there was the open space, or circus, of turf; and in the middle of it a very ancient, twisted thorn tree, beneath which the party in the dark had found the little creature that whined and cried out in unknown speech. I turned about, and on my way back I entered the caves, and lit the carriage candle I had brought with me. There was nothing much to see—I never think there is much to see in caves. There was the place where the children and others before them had taken their tea, with a ring of blackened stones within which many fires of twigs had been kindled. In caves or out of caves, townsfolk in the country are always alike in leaving untidy and unseemly litter behind; and here were the usual scraps of greasy paper, daubed with smears of jam and butter, the half-eaten sandwich, and the gnawed crust. Amidst all this nastiness I saw a piece of folded notepaper, and in sheer idleness picked it up and opened it. You have just seen it. When I asked you if you saw anything peculiar about the writing, you said that the letters were rather big and clumsy. The reason of that is that they were written by a child. I don't think you examined the back of the second leaf. Look: 'Rosamond'—Rosamond Brown, that is. And beneath; there, in the corner.

Reynolds looked, and read, and gaped aghast.

'That was—her other name; her name in the dark.'

'Name in the dark?'

'In the dark night of the Sabbath. That pretty girl had caught them all. They were in her hands, those wretched children, like the clay images she made. I found one of those things, hidden in a cleft of the rocks, near the place where they had made their fire. I ground it into dust beneath my feet.'

'And I wonder what her name was?'

'They called her, I think, the Bridegroom and the Bride.'

'Did you ever find out who she was, or where she came from?'

'Very little. Only that she had been a mistress at the Home for Christian Orphans in North Tottenham, where there was a hideous scandal some years before.'

'Then she must have been older than she looked, according to your description.'

'Possibly.'

They sat in silence for a few minutes. Then Reynolds said:

'But I haven't asked you about this formula, or whatever you may call it—all these vowels, here. Is it a cypher?'

'No. But it is really a great curiosity, and it raises some extraordinary questions, which are outside this particular case. To begin with—and I am sure I could go much farther back than my beginning, if I had the necessary scholarship—I once read an English rendering of a Greek manuscript of the second or third century—I won't be certain which. It's a long time since I've seen the thing. The translator and editor of it was of the opinion that it was a Mithraic Ritual;* but I have gathered that weightier authorities are strongly inclined to discredit this view. At any rate, it was no doubt an initiation rite into some mystery; possibly it had Gnostic* connections; I don't know. But our interest lies in this, that one of the stages or portals, or whatever you call them, consisted, almost exactly, of that formula you have in your hand. I don't say that the vowels and double vowels are in the same order; I don't think the Greek manuscript has any *aes* or *aas*. But it is perfectly clear that the two documents are of the same kind, and have the same purpose. And, advancing a little in time from the Greek manuscript, I don't think it is very surprising that the final operation of an incantation in mediæval and later magic consisted of this wailing on vowels arranged in a certain order.

'But here is something that is surprising. A good many years ago I strolled one Sunday morning into a church in Bloomsbury, the head-quarters of a highly respectable sect. And in the middle of a very dignified ritual, there rose, quite suddenly, without preface or warning, this very sound, a wild wail on vowels. The effect was astounding, anyhow; whether it was terrifying or merely funny, is a matter of taste. You'll have guessed what I heard: they call it "speaking with tongues,"* and they believe it to be a heavenly language. And I need scarcely say that they mean very well. But the problem is: how did a congregation of solid Scotch Presbyterians hit on that queer, ancient and not over-sanctified method of expressing spiritual emotion? It is a singular puzzle.

'And that woman? That is not by any means so difficult. The good Scotchmen—I can't think how they did it—got hold of something that didn't belong to them: she was in her own tradition. And, as they say down there: *asakai dasa*: the darkness is undying.'

# RITUAL

ONCE upon a time, as we say in English, or *olim*, as the Latins said in their more austere and briefer way, I was sent forth on a May Monday to watch London being happy on their Whitsun holiday.* This is the sort of appointment that used to be known in newspaper offices as an annual; and the difficulty for the men engaged in this business is to avoid seeing the same sights as those witnessed a year before and saying much the same things about them as were said on Whit-Monday twelve-month. Queuing up for Madame Tussaud's waxworks,* giving buns to diverse creatures in the Zoo,* gazing at those Easter Island gods* in the portico of the British Museum, waiting for all sorts of early doors to open; all these are spectacles of the day. And the patient man who boards the buses from suburbs may chance to hear a lady from Hornsey expounding to her neighbour on the seat, an inhabitant of Enfield Wash, the terrible gaieties that Piccadilly Circus witnesses when the electric signs are fairly lit.

On the Whit-Monday in question, I saw and recorded some of these matters; and then strolled westward along Piccadilly, by the palings of the Green Park. The conventional business of the day had been more or less attended to: now for the unsystematic prowl: one never knows where one may find one's goods. And then and there, I came across some boys, half-a dozen or so of them, playing what struck me as a very queer game on the fresh turf of the Park, under the tender and piercing green of the young leaves. I have forgotten the preliminary elaborations of the sport; but there seemed to be some sort of dramatic action, perhaps with dialogue, but this I could not hear. Then one boy stood alone, with the five or six others about him. They pretended to hit the solitary boy, and he fell to the ground and lay motionless, as if dead. Then the others covered him up with their coats, and ran away. And then, if I remember, the boy who had been ritually smitten, slaugh-tered, and buried, rose to his feet, and the very odd game began all over again.

Here, I thought, was something a little out of the way of the accus-tomed doings and pleasures of the holiday crowds, and I returned to my office and embodied an account of this Green Park sport in my tale of Whit-Monday in London; with some allusion to the curious analogy between the boys' game and certain matters of a more serious nature.

But it would not do. A spectacled Reader* came down out of his glass cage, and held up a strip of proof.

'Hiram Abiff?' he queried in a low voice, as he placed the galley-slip on my desk, and pointed to the words with his pen. 'It's not usual to mention these things in print.'

I assured the Reader that I was not one of the Widow's offspring,* but he still shook his head gravely, and I let him have his way, willing to avoid all *admiratio*.* It was, I thought, a curious little incident, and to this day I have never heard an explanation of the coincidence—mere chance, very likely—between the pastime in the Park and those matters which it is not usual to mention in print.

But a good many years later, this business of the Green Park was recalled to me by a stranger experience in a very different part of London. A friend of mine, an American, who had travelled in many outland territories of the earth, asked me to show him some of the less known quarters of London.

'Do not misunderstand me, sir,' he said, in his measured, almost Johnsonian manner,* 'I do not wish to see your great city in its alleged sensational aspects. I am not yearning to probe the London under-world, nor do I wish to view any opium joints or blind-pigs* for cocaine addicts. In such matters, I have already accumulated more than suffi-cient experience in other quarters of the world. But if you would just shew me those aspects which are so ordinary that nobody ever sees them, I shall be greatly indebted to you.'

I remembered how I had once awed two fellow-citizens of his by taking them to a street not very far from King's Cross Station, and shewing them how each house was guarded by twin plaster sphinxes of a deadly chocolate-red, which crouched on either side of the flights of steps leading to the doorways. I remembered how the late Arnold Bennett* had come exploring in this region, and seen the sphinxes and had noted them in his diary with a kind of dumb surmise, venturing no comment. So I said that I thought I understood. We set out, and soon we were deep in that unknown London which is at our very doors.

'Dickens had been here,' I said in my part as Guide and Interpreter. 'You know "Little Dorrit"? Then this might be Mr Casby's very street,* which set out meaning to run down into the valley and up again to the top of the hill, but got out of breath and stopped still after twenty yards.'

The American gentleman relished the reference and his surround-ings. He pointed out to me curious work in some of the iron balconies before the first floor windows in the grey houses, making a rough sketch of the design of one of them in his note-book. We wandered here and there, and up and down at haphazard, by strange wastes and devious ways, till I, in spite of my fancied knowledge, found myself in a part that I did not remember to have seen before. There were timber yards with high walls about them. There were cottages that seemed to have strayed from the outskirts of some quiet provincial town, off the main road. One of these lay deep in the shadow of an old mulberry, and ripening grapes hung from a vine on a neighbouring wall. The holly-hocks in the neat little front gardens were almost over; there were still brave displays of snapdragons and marigolds. But round the corner, barrows piled with pale bananas and flaming oranges filled the roadway, and the street market resounded with raucous voices, praise of fruit and fish, and loud bargainings, and gossip at its highest pitch. We pushed our way through the crowd, and left the street of the market, and presently came into the ghostly quiet of a square: high, severe houses, built of whitish bricks, complete in 1840 Gothic, all neat and well-kept, and for all sign of life or movement, uninhabited.

And then, when we had barely rested our ears from the market jan-gle, there came what I suppose was an overflow from that region. A gang of small boys surged into the square and broke its peace. There were about a dozen of them, more or less, and I took it that they were playing soldiers. They marched, two and two, in their dirty and shabby order, apparently under the command of a young ruffian somewhat bigger and taller than the rest. Two of them banged incessantly with bits of broken wood on an old meat tin and a battered iron tea tray, and all of them howled as barbarously as any crooner, but much louder. They went about and about, and then diverged into an empty road that looked as if it led nowhere in particular, and there drew up, and formed them-selves into a sort of hollow square, their captain in the middle. The tin pan music went on steadily, but less noisily; it had become a succession of slow beats, and the howls had turned into a sort of whining chant.

But it remained a very horrible row, and I was moving on to get away from the noise, when my American interposed.

'If you wouldn't mind our tarrying here for a few moments,' he said apologetically. 'This pastime of your London boys interests me very much. You may think it strange, but I find it more essentially exciting than the Eton and Harrow Cricket Match* of which I witnessed some part a few weeks ago.'

So we looked on from an unobtrusive corner. The boys, evidently, agreed with my friend, and found their game absorbing. I don't think that they had noticed us or knew that we were there.

They went through their queer performance. The bangs or beats on the tin and the tray grew softer and slower, and the yells had died into a monotonous drone. The leader went inside the square, from boy to boy, and seemed to whisper into the ear of each one. Then he passed round a second time, standing before each, and making a sort of summoning or beckoning gesture with his hand. Nothing happened. I did not find the sport essentially exciting; but looking at the American, I observed that he was watching it with an expression of the most acute interest and amazement. Again the big boy went about the square. He stopped dead before a little fellow in a torn jacket. He threw out his arms wide, with a gesture of embrace, and then drew them in. He did this three times, and at the third repetition of the ceremony, the little chap in the torn jacket cried out with a piercing scream and fell forward as if dead.

The banging of the tins and the howl of the voices went up to heaven with a hideous dissonance.

My American friend was gasping with astonishment as we passed on our way.

'This is an amazing city,' he said. 'Do you know, sir, that those boys were acting all as if they'd been Asiki doing their Njoru ritual.* I've seen it in East Africa. But there the black man that falls down stays down. He's dead.'

A week or two later, I was telling the tale to some friends. One of them pulled an evening paper out of his pocket.

'Look at that,' said he, pointing with his finger. I read the headlines:

MYSTERY DEATH IN NORTH LONDON SQUARE
HOME OFFICE DOCTOR PUZZLED
HEART VESSELS RUPTURED
'PLAYING SOLDIERS'
BOY FALLS DEAD
CORONER DIRECTS OPEN VERDICT

# EXPLANATORY NOTES

### ABBREVIATIONS

| | |
|---|---|
| Danielson | *Arthur Machen: A Bibliography* (1923; New York, 1970) |
| *FOT* | Arthur Machen, *Far Off Things* |
| Frazer | *The Golden Bough: a New Abridgement*, ed. Robert Fraser (Oxford, 1998) |
| Goldstone and Sweetser | *A Bibliography of Arthur Machen* (1965, 1973) |
| Jones | *Horror Stories: Classic Tales from Hoffmann to Hodgson*, ed. Darryl Jones (Oxford, 2014) |
| Joshi | *The White People and Other Weird Stories*, ed. S. T. Joshi (London, 2011) |
| *LA* | Arthur Machen, *The London Adventure* |
| Luckhurst | *Late Victorian Gothic Tales*, ed. Roger Luckhurst (Oxford, 2005) |
| *OCD* | *The Oxford Classical Dictionary*, ed. Simon Hornblower and Antony Spawforth (1996) |
| *ODNB* | *Oxford Dictionary of National Biography* |
| *OED* | *Oxford English Dictionary* |
| Reynolds and Charlton | *Arthur Machen: A Short Account of His Life and Work* (London, 1963) |
| Sweetser | *Arthur Machen* (New York, 1964) |
| *TNF* | Arthur Machen, *Things Near and Far* |
| Trotter | Arthur Machen, *The Three Impostors*, ed. David Trotter (London, 1995) |
| Weinreb and Hibbert | *The London Encyclopedia*, ed. Ben Weinreb and Christopher Hibbert (London, 1983) |

## THE LOST CLUB

First published in 1890 in *The Whirlwind*, 2 (20 December); reprinted in the 1923 collection *The Shining Pyramid* (Covici-McGee; not to be confused with the 1925 Martin Secker collection of the same name; see headnote to 'The Shining Pyramid').

3 *Piccadilly Deserta*: cf. Arabia Deserta ('deserted Arabia'), a classical denomination. Possibly the phrase was in part suggested by the recently published, and much-praised, two-volume work *Travels in Arabia Deserta*, by the explorer Charles Montagu Doughty (1843–1926). Also, the *One Thousand and One Nights* or *Arabian Nights*, which had been translated into English twice in the previous decade (by John Payne in 1882–4 and Richard Burton in 1885), was an important influence on Machen, as was Robert Louis Stevenson's *New Arabian Nights*, published in 1882 ('The

Lost Club' has, indeed, been dismissed by some as little more than an imitation of one of its episodes, 'The Suicide Club').

3  *a true son of the carnation*: the phrase indicates a connection to the Decadent movement; Oscar Wilde had taken the green carnation as his emblem.

  *the Phœnix . . . the Row . . . Hurlingham*: there was a Phoenix Club in St James's Place, though not by this time. 'The Row' refers to Rotten Row (a corruption of 'Route du Roi') in Hyde Park, a track for horse riding and once a fashionable spot. The Hurlingham Club in Fulham, still in operation, was founded in 1869—initially for pigeon shooting, then polo, and finally a broad range of sports and games.

  *bus*: horse-drawn omnibus.

  *'White Horse Cellars'*: old coaching inn.

  *'Badminton'*: the Badminton Club in Piccadilly was founded in 1875.

  *Briar Rose . . . the Beauty . . . was fast asleep*: the briar rose is both a flowering plant (*Rosa rubiginosa*) and the title of a folk tale ('Little Briar Rose' or 'Dornröschen', recorded by the Brothers Grimm), corresponding to the story of 'Sleeping Beauty'.

  *Johnny*: the *OED* quotes an 1889 issue of the *Daily News*: 'An idle and vacuous young aristocrat, of the class popularly known as "Johnnies"'.

4  *a quiet dinner at Azario's*: Luigi Azario's Florence Restaurant, in Rupert Street. Machen dined there in 1890 with Oscar Wilde, who praised his story 'A Double Return' as having 'fluttered the dovecotes' of public opinion.

  *the Junior Wilton*: probably fictitious; there was a Junior Carlton Club in Pall Mall, a Junior Athenaeum Club in Piccadilly, and so on.

  *Green Chartreuse*: a green-tinged liqueur, made by the Carthusian monks.

  *'Hansom!'*: hansom cab (short for 'cabriolet'), a speedy two-wheeled carriage then at the height of its popularity as a mode of urban transport. They are plentiful, for instance, in Arthur Conan Doyle's contemporaneous Sherlock Holmes stories.

## THE GREAT GOD PAN

The first part of what would become 'The Great God Pan' was published in 1890; further chapters were completed at intervals, and the whole published, together with 'The Inmost Light', by John Lane in 1894. 'Pan' has been associated with the Decadent movement since its first appearance when, in Machen's words, 'yellow bookery was at its yellowest'.

9  *phantasmagoria*: a projector-based light show, introduced in Paris at the end of the eighteenth century and in London (where it became very popular) at the beginning of the nineteenth. With its moving ghosts and skeletons which appeared to rush towards the audience, sound effects, and eerie musical accompaniment, the original Phantasmagoria provided an overwhelming, and often terrifying, sensory experience. By extension,

'a rapidly transforming collection or series of imaginary (and usually fantastic) forms, such as may be experienced in a dream or fevered state' (*OED*).

10 *"chases in Arras, dreams in a career"*: from 'Dotage', in *The Temple*, by the Welsh-born clergyman and poet George Herbert (1593–1632). Raymond's exposition to Clarke suggests 'a classic neo-Platonist view of reality' (Luckhurst, 279); Herbert's tropes of the illusory and evanescent, which also include 'Foolish night-fires [will o'wisps] . . . guilded emptinesse, | Shadows well mounted . . . Embroider'd lyes', thus join Raymond's other figures—the phantasmagoria, the lifted veil—as he paints a portrait of the unreality of the material world.

*the god Pan*: Greek (originally Arcadian) deity of shepherds and flocks, half-man and half-goat. Through a false etymology (his name is in fact connected with the word for 'herdsman'), Pan came to be associated with 'the All' ('pan' in Greek). The phrase 'The Great God Pan' had been used by Elizabeth Barrett Browning in her poem 'A Musical Instrument', included in the posthumous collection *Last Poems* (1862).

*grey matter*: one of two kinds of brain tissue (the other being white matter), associated with cerebration.

*Digby's theory, and Browne Faber's discoveries*: fictitious, perhaps suggesting, respectively, the natural philosopher Sir Kenelm Digby (1603–65) and the neurologist Charles Édouard Brown-Séquard (1817–94) (Luckhurst, 279).

11 *this world of ours is pretty well girded now with the telegraph wires and cables*: the first transatlantic telegraph cable was laid in 1858 and promptly failed—to be replaced, successfully, by 1866. After this major hurdle had been cleared, the following decades saw the prodigious extension of a (largely British-dominated) telegraph network across much of the globe, one which formed, by the 1890s, a veritable 'World Wide Web'.

*articulate-speaking men*: a Homeric phrase which often recurs in Machen.

12 *Oswald Crollius*: (*c.*1560–1609) Paracelsian iatrochemist (combination chemist and physician) known for his 'theory of signatures'. Machen came across his writings while working his way through an enormous occult library for which he had to prepare a bookseller's catalogue. Years later he would write:

> Now and then in the older books I came across striking sentences. There was Oswaldus Crollius, for example—I suppose his real name was Osvald Kroll—who is quoted by one of the characters in 'The Great God Pan'. 'In every grain of wheat', says Oswaldus, 'there lies hidden the soul of a star'. A wonderful saying; a declaration, I suppose, that all matter is one, manifested under many forms; and, so far as I can gather, modern science is rapidly coming round to the view of this obscure speculator of the seventeenth century; and, in fact, to the doctrine of the alchemists. (*TNF*, 27)

15 *homœopathic*: in a medical context, curing like with like. The principle of 'homoeopathic magic', by which 'like produces like', is discussed at length by James George Frazer in *The Golden Bough*, first published in 1890.

17 *a place of some importance in the time of the Roman occupation*: the village is near Machen's birthplace of Caerleon, barely disguised here, as in his novel *The Hill of Dreams*, as 'Caermaen'. The town was the site of the *castra* (legionary fortress) of Isca (from the river Usk) Augusta, built around 75 CE. In his twelfth-century *Itinerarium Kambriae*, or 'Journey around Wales', Gerald of Wales wrote:

> Caerleon means the city of Legions, Caer, in the British language, signi-fying a city or camp, for there the Roman legions, sent into this island, were accustomed to winter, and from this circumstance it was styled the city of legions. This city was of undoubted antiquity, and handsomely built of masonry, with courses of bricks, by the Romans. Many vestiges of its former splendour may yet be seen; immense palaces, formerly orna-mented with gilded roofs, in imitation of Roman magnificence, inasmuch as they were first raised by the Roman princes, and embellished with splendid buildings; a tower of prodigious size, remarkable hot baths, relics of temples, and theatres, all inclosed within fine walls, parts of which remain standing. (trans. Richard Colt Hoare (London, 1806), i. 103–4).

No doubt Machen also has in mind the nearby village of Caerwent, of which he wrote, years later: 'Caerwent, also a Roman city, was buried in the earth, and gave up now and again strange relics—fragments of the temple of "Nodens, god of the depths"' (*FOT*, 19). See note to p. 53.

18 *charcoal burners*: the production of charcoal from wood was a traditional occupation in Wales, dating back at least to Roman times.

19 *faun or satyr*: mythological half-human, half-goat creatures. See also note to p. 36.

21 *ET DIABOLUS INCARNATUS EST. ET HOMO FACTUS EST.*: 'And the devil was made incarnate. And was made man'; a travesty of the Nicene Creed, in which Christ 'By the power of the Holy Spirit . . . became incarnate from the Virgin Mary, and was made man' (Luckhurst, 279).

*Wadham*: Wadham College of the University of Oxford, founded in 1610.

*Rupert Street*: see note to p. 4.

23 *Vaughan*: one of several surnames used recurrently in Machen's fiction. He had in mind not the Welsh metaphysical poet Henry Vaughan (1621–95) but his twin brother Thomas (1621–66), the alchemist and hermetic philosopher. The latter, author of the occult treatise *Lumen de Lumine; or a New Magicall Light Discovered and Communicated to the World* (published under the pseudonym 'Eugenius Philalethes'), was an important influence on Machen's fiction. Helen Vaughan's ultimate end, in 'Pan's' denouement, exemplifies the alchemical theories of her seventeenth-century namesake, who

> declare[d] that all human beings are bisexual, and that first matter is a cool slime: 'When I consider the system or fabric of this world I find

it to be a certain series, a link or chain, which is extended "a non gradu ad non gradum" . . . Beneath all degrees of sense there is a certain horrible, inexpressible darkness. The magicians call it "tenebrae activae" ' (Reynolds and Charlton, 46)

26 *the Treasury*: the office of the Director of Public Prosecutions had been combined with that of the Treasury Solicitor in 1884.

29 *model lodging-house*: in response to the squalid and overcrowded conditions of many common lodging houses in the early Victorian era, Prince Albert spearheaded efforts to construct new tenements for the London poor. American novelist Harriet Beecher Stowe wrote from London in 1853: 'This morning Lord Shaftesbury came, according to appointment, to take me to see the Model Lodging Houses. He remarked that it would be impossible to give me the full effect of seeing them, unless I could first visit the dens of filth, disease, and degradation, in which the poor of London formerly were lodged' (*Sunny Memories of Foreign Lands* (Boston, 1854), ii. 209).

35 *Ainu jugs*: the Ainu are a people indigenous to parts of Japan, in particular the island of Hokkaido, and the Russian Far East. Scottish anthropologist Neil Gordon Munro (1863–1942) describes a 'curious' Ainu ceremony involving the ladling out of beer with 'a lacquered jug (*etunup*)' (*Ainu Creed and Cult* (London and New York, 2011), iv. 76). In *The Golden Bough*, James George Frazer discusses 'the bear-sacrifice offered by the Aino or Ainu', which involves the eating of flesh 'in special vessels of wood finely carved' and drinking of blood from a cup. There is no mention here, however, of a jug (Frazer, 524, 530).

*Silet per diem . . . per oram maritimam*: from the *Collectanea Rerum Memorabilum* of classical geographer Gaius Julius Solinus, a work largely plagiarized from Pliny the Elder and Pomponius Mela (*OCD*, 786). The passage 'describes a Bacchic orgy on the seashore beside Mount Atlas', complete with 'Aegipans and Satyres' (Luckhurst, 279).

36 *Walpurgis Night*: English rendering of the German *Walpurgisnacht*, 30 April (May Day's eve). The feast day of the eighth-century St Walpurga, it is associated with the Witches' Sabbath and unholy revelry by the powers of darkness more generally. Frazer writes: 'In Central Europe it was apparently on Walpurgis Night, the Eve of May Day, above all other times that the baleful powers of the witches were exerted to the fullest extent' (Frazer, 574–5).

*Fauns and Satyrs and Ægipans*: there is a strong family resemblance, to say the least, among these mythological caprine hybrids; an Aegipan is described in the *OED* as 'A goat-like creature similar to a satyr.... [also] a Greek god resembling, and sometimes considered to be identical to, the god Pan'. In 'The Fall of the House of Usher', a tale Machen greatly admired, Edgar Allan Poe (1809–49) writes of 'passages in Pomponius Mela, about the old African Satyrs and Œgipans [*sic*], over which Usher would sit dreaming for hours' (*Works of Edgar Allan Poe* (New York, 1861), i. 302).

37 *bachelor's gown*: in other words, a university degree.

37 *Zulu assegais*: one of the relations standing between Charles Aubernoun and the title was presumably an officer killed during the Anglo-Zulu War of 1879, perhaps the disastrous (from a British perspective) Battle of Isandlwana. An assegai is a spear.

38 *the sordid murders of Whitechapel*: a reference to the unsolved 'Ripper' murders of 1888, which remain to this day a source of fascination and seemingly endless speculation. (One wonders what Machen would have thought of the numerous conspiracy theories that arose in the later twentieth century linking the murders to Freemasonry, Black Magic rituals, and other occult matters, explored most famously, perhaps, in Alan Moore's graphic novel *From Hell*.)

40 *the labyrinth of Dædalus*: in Greek mythology, the master artificer Daedalus was responsible for devising such marvels as the Minotaur's labyrinth in Crete—an inescapable maze inhabited by a monstrous man-bull—and the famous waxen wings with which his son Icarus flew too close to the sun.

*the Row*: see note to p. 3.

41 *Carlton Club*: founded in 1832; associated with the Conservative Party.

*Scotland Yard*: the Metropolitan Police force of London, founded in 1829, had moved from Great Scotland Yard to new headquarters (New Scotland Yard) on the Victoria Embankment in 1890.

44 *Queer Street*: slang expression indicating a state of financial embarrassment; a metaphorical place. Here, presumably by extension, Villiers seems to be referring, less figuratively, to a particular seedy locale and its underworldly denizens.

45 *cicerone*: a learned guide, one 'who shows and explains the antiquities or curiosities of a place to strangers'. Derived from the name of the Roman philosopher Cicero (106–43 BCE), with reference to his profound 'learning or eloquence' (*OED*).

50 *paintings which survived beneath the lava*: a reference to Pompeii and/or Herculaneum, Roman cities destroyed in 79 CE by the eruption of Mount Vesuvius.

51 *Caermaen*: see note to p. 17.

53 *the great god Nodens*: alternatively Nodons, a Celtic deity with multiple associations, to whom a temple in Lydney Park, Gloucestershire (3rd century BCE) is dedicated. Described in the *Dictionary of Celtic Mythology* (Oxford, 2004) as the 'British god of healing . . . No physical depiction of Nodons survives, but votive plaques at the shrine indicate his associations with dogs. Another figure appears to show a man hooking a fish. Nodons has been likened to Mars the healer rather than Mars the warrior, as well as to Silvanus, a Roman god, of the hunt.'

## THE INMOST LIGHT

Published with 'The Great God Pan' by John Lane in 1894 (see headnote to 'The Great God Pan'). The story, or at least its most arresting moment, has its origins in what Machen considered to be the hideous suburbanization of London:

> I made the horrid apparition of the crude new houses in the midst of green pastures the seed of my tale, 'The Inmost Light', which was originally bound up with 'The Great God Pan'. And so the man in my story, resting in green fields, looked up and saw a face that chilled his blood gazing at him from the back of one of those red houses that had once frightened me, when I was a sorry lad of twenty, wandering about the verges of London. The doctor of my tale lived in Harlesden. (*FOT*, 123–4)

The tale marks the first appearance of Machen's recurrent character Dyson, who would appear again in *The Three Impostors*, 'The Red Hand', and 'The Shining Pyramid' (all included here).

55 *Rupert Street . . . his favourite restaurant*: see note to p. 4.

56 *salmi*: a stew of roasted game.

*Ratés*: professional failures (French). In his autobiographical *The London Adventure* Machen would write: 'Most of us have always found the career of the *raté*, the artist who misses fire, distinctly comic. The poet who can hardly get into the corner column of his country paper, the novelist whose novels are simply "rot", the painter whose pictures are a joke: we laugh heartily at them all' (*LA*, 113–14). This sounds cruel until one realizes that Machen is self-deprecatingly including himself in this category.

57 *Chaldee roots*: i.e. of the Chaldean language.

*Homers, not Agamemnons. Carent quia vate sacro*: from Horace's *Odes*, 4.9: 'Many brave men lived before Agamemnon; but, all unwept and unknown, are lost in the distant night, since they are without a divine poet (to chronicle their deeds).' London, in other words, does not lack for 'artistic crimes' but for capable chroniclers.

*Harlesden*: once a country village (it is recorded in *Domesday Book*), Harlesden became progressively urbanized in the course of the nineteenth century, particularly in response to the spread of the railway. Machen's story captures this sense of dramatic development in the later decades of the century (see headnote).

*"because it was near the Palace"*: the Crystal Palace, originally erected in Hyde Park for the Great Exhibition of 1851, was moved in 1854 to Sydenham. After this 'the Palace became the centre of [Norwood's] existence. Visitors flocked to the Palace's varied attractions, many of them brought by the Crystal Palace and West End Railway Line, opened in 1856' (Weinreb and Hibbert, 906). Crystal Palace was destroyed by fire in 1936.

58 *city*: the City of London (or Square Mile), the oldest, most historic part of London; also its financial and business centre.

*'bus*: see note to p. 3.

*red lamp*: sign of a doctor's establishment.

59 *"General Gordon"*: a pub named after Major General Charles George Gordon (1833–85), a martyr in the Victorian cultural imagination after his death in Khartoum at the hands of Mahdist forces, a comparatively recent event.

*a fire that is unquenchable*: see note to p. 236.

64 *sudorific*: a perspiration-promoting medicine.

65 *agony column*: newspaper columns devoted to personal advertisements. Sherlock Holmes perused them eagerly in his professional capacity; in 'The Noble Bachelor' he says, 'I read nothing except the criminal news and the agony column. The latter is always instructive', and in 'The Adventure of the Red Circle' we find him '[taking] down the great book in which, day by day, he filed the agony columns of the various London journals. "Dear me!" said he, turning over the pages, "what a chorus of groans, cries, and bleatings! What a rag-bag of singular happenings! But surely the most valuable hunting-ground that ever was given to a student of the unusual!"'

*gimp*: a plaited trimming on furniture.

66 *green rep and the oleographs*: rep is a 'plain-weave fabric (usually of wool, silk, or cotton) with a ribbed surface, used esp. for draperies and upholstery' (*OED*); oleography is a form of lithography that seeks to imitate oil painting ('oleo-' meaning 'relating to oil').

*Benedictine*: a French herbal liqueur, so called because originally made by French monks of that order.

68 *char-woman*: a charwoman or charlady was hired by the day to do cleaning and other domestic work. 'Char' is related etymologically to 'chore'.

70 *pennons*: long, thin flags.

*Paracelsus and the Rosicrucians*: Paracelsus was Theophrastus Bombastus von Hohenheim (*c*.1493–1541), Swiss physician, alchemist, and occultist. (There is a bust of Paracelsus in J. K. Rowling's fictional Hogwarts School of Witchcraft and Wizardry, in the Harry Potter series.) The Rosicrucians were a society, or more properly a number of societies, inspired by a trio of early seventeenth-century manifestoes asserting the existence of a fictitious 'Order of the Holy Cross'; the Order of the Golden Dawn, to which Machen later belonged, had Rosicrucian connections. Machen would write, years later, of his disappointment in learning of the spurious origins of Rosicrucianism:

> It was a sad blow to me to find out afterwards, chiefly through the medium of A. E. Waite's 'Real History of the Rosicrucians', that, as a cold matter of fact, there were no Rosicrucians. A Lutheran pastor who had read Paracelsus, wrote, early in the seventeenth century, a pamphlet describing a secret order which had no existence outside of his brain. Naturally enough, societies arose which imitated, so far as they could, the imaginary organisation described by the fantastic Johannes Valentinus Andrea; I should not be surprised, indeed, to be

told that such societies are now in being in modern London; but these orders are late 'fakes'; the 'seventies and 'eighties of the last century saw their beginnings. There are no Rosicrucians—and there never were any. (*FOT*, 133)

71 *dun*: in this sense, persistently to demand payment.

*Explicit*: Latin; declaration of an ending; cf. *Incipit*, beginning.

73 *Rabelaisian*: François Rabelais (d. 1553), author of the Renaissance classic *Gargantua and Pantagruel*, was on Machen's shortlist of essential authors. 'Rabelaisian' usually suggests the presence of bawdy, earthy comedy; the reference here is to the giant, living sausages encountered by Pantagruel in the fourth book of *Gargantua and Pantagruel*.

74 *penny exercise-books*: blank books used for school exercises.

*story papers*: periodicals containing fiction, especially aimed at a juvenile (male) audience. A prominent example from this period would be the *Boy's Own Paper*.


## THE THREE IMPOSTORS

Published by John Lane in 1895, also as part of the Keynotes Series. In Henry Danielson's 1923 bibliography of his writings to that point, Machen commented:

> The title of this book has a curious history. 'De Tribus Impostoribus' was a book much talked of by the learned in the seventeenth century. As far as I can remember, quoting without book, Browne of the 'Religio Medici' speaks of that 'villain and secretary of hell that wrote the miscreant piece of "The Three Impostors"' . . . the three impostors, by the way, were Christ, Moses and Mohamet. Perhaps there never was such a book, perhaps such a book did exist in manuscript, was seen by a few and talked about by many. Anyhow, I liked the sound of the title, and noted it in '85, and indicated in my notebook the sort of book—a picaresque romance—I should like to write under that head; and so had the title waiting for me in the spring of 1895. (Danielson, 26)

79 *Lipsius*: Machen has likely borrowed the surname (with slight modification) from Prussian archaeologist and Egyptologist Karl Richard Lepsius (1810–84), whose three-year expedition to Memphis and Thebes in 1843–5 filled Berlin's Egyptian Museum with ancient artefacts.

80 *dormer windows . . . Georgian wings; bow windows . . . and two dome-like cupolas*: architectural terms; the house, redolent with unwholesome decay and Gothic menace, is described (yet) more fully in the last chapter of the novel. It is an architectural palimpsest, with later additions (both 'Georgian wings' and bow windows would date from, at least, the eighteenth century) to an original, late seventeenth-century town house.

*a rusting Triton on the rocks*: in Greek mythology, Triton was a sea-god, son of Poseidon, depicted as man above and fish below, and sounding a conch-shell trumpet.

81  *Gold Tiberius*: see note to p. 85.

*Jeremy Taylor*: (bap. 1613, d. 1667) English divine and author of devotional works, particularly *Holy Living* (1650) and *Holy Dying* (1651), which he wrote in south-west Wales. Admirers of Taylor's prose style included favourite Machen authors Thomas De Quincey and William Hazlitt, who wrote of Taylor, 'His style is prismatic. It unfolds the colours of the rainbow; it floats like the bubble through the air; it is like innumerable dew-drops that glitter on the face of the morning, and tremble as they glitter.' When Machen translated Marguerite de Navarre's *Heptameron* into English, he affected a 'composite' Caroline style blending 'Herrick, Taylor, Browne, Pepys, Fuller, and Walton' (Sweetser, 21).

*"The grimy sash an oriel burns"*: from the poem 'All-Saints' Day' by James Russell Lowell (1819–91). An oriel is a recess with a window, but according to Victorian poetic convention could mean a stained-glass window. Lowell is picturing a 'den' of 'Sin and Famine' transfigured by the presence of saints: 'The den they enter grows a shrine, | The grimy sash an oriel burns'.

*cedarn*: made of cedar.

*Bentley's favourite novelists*: George Bentley (1828–95) was scion of one of the Victorian era's great publishing families. His 'favourite novels' series was launched in 1862 with Ellen ('Mrs Henry') Wood's sensational *East Lynne*; other bestselling authors in the series would include Rhoda Broughton and Marie Corelli.

82  *Dyson was addicted to wild experiments in tobacco*: Machen, an enthusiastic smoker, may be said to have begun his literary career with a 'wild experiment in tobacco', his first published book being a learned frolic, in imitation of Robert Burton's *Anatomy of Melancholy*, entitled *The Anatomy of Tobacco: or Smoking Methodised, Divided, and Considered after a New Fashion* (1884).

83  *ethnologist*: 'ethnology' is a term seldom used today; approximately what we would call social or cultural anthropology.

*Bohemianism*: the French had long applied the word 'Bohemian' to gipsies; by extension a 'gipsy of society; one who either cuts himself off, or is by his habits cut off, from society for which he is otherwise fitted; especially an artist, literary man, or actor, who leads a free, vagabond, or irregular life' (*OED*). Popular works like Henri Murger's 1851 *Scènes de la vie de bohème* and its offshoots (most famously Giacomo Puccini's great opera *La Bohème*, first performed in 1896) helped to establish the association between social Bohemianism and grinding poverty, which timely inheritances have helped Dyson and Phillipps to avoid.

*Red Lion Square*: 'a quiet square', as Machen says, 'not far from Holborn', it lies to the south of Theobald's Road. It is named after the Red Lion Inn, where in 1661 Oliver Cromwell's disinterred corpse lay before being hung in chains at Tyburn (Weinreb and Hibbert, 639).

*chiaroscuro*: in painting and other pictorial arts, the treatment of light and shadow.

*the "criticism-of-life" theory*: reference to the critical theory of Victorian poet and critic Matthew Arnold (1822–88), who maintained that 'poetry', alternatively 'literature', 'is a criticism of life'. Machen's own theory of literature, which centred upon the idea of 'ecstasy', would be articulated a few years later in his book *Hieroglyphics*.

84 *a huge pantechnicon warehouse*: the original Pantechnicon (roughly, 'place-of-all-arts'), built in 1830 in Belgrave Square, was part warehouse and part collection of craft shops. Generically, any building serving a similar purpose; a bazaar.

85 *'Imp. Tiberius Cæsar Augustus'*: 42 BCE–37 CE; second emperor of the Roman Empire. While his successors Caligula and Nero may have blacker reputations today, Tiberius was accused by the ancient historians of considerable cruelty and depravity. Both Tacitus (*c.*56–*c.*120) and Suetonius (*c.*70–*c.*130) describe, for instance, infamous orgies on his island retreat of Capreae (Capri). It is not difficult to see how Suetonius' account in particular could have influenced Machen, not only in his conception of Lipsius, but in other tales as well: 'He [Tiberius] furthermore devised little nooks of lechery in the woods and glades of the island, and had boys and girls dressed up as Pans and nymphs, prostituting themselves in front of caverns or grottoes; so that the island was now openly and generally called "Caprineum" ["caper" = "goat"]' (*The Twelve Caesars*, trans. Robert Graves (London, 2003), 132). Tiberius' love of 'prolonged and exquisite tortures' (142) also seems salient in the context of Lipsius and his society.

86 *Sir Joshua Byrde*: invented figure.

*Aleppo*: ancient Syrian city, then one of the most important cities of the Ottoman Empire.

*virtuosi*: plural of virtuoso, in this sense an expert on or connoisseur of antiques.

87 *as ships were drawn to the Loadstone Rock in the Eastern tale*: this story of a ship-destroying magnetic mountain is to be found in the Third Kalendar's Tale in the *One Thousand and One Nights*. As noted earlier (note to p. 3), the work had been translated into English twice in the previous decade: by John Payne in 1882–4 and Richard Burton in 1885. Possibly Machen had this 'Burton' in mind as well as the author of *Anatomy of Melancholy* when he chose Mr Davies's alias (see note to p. 158), though he was far from an admirer of the famous explorer's translation: 'I speak not of Burton, for I found myself unable to read a couple of pages of his detestable English, made more terrible by the imitations of the rhymed prose of the original.' (*FOT*, 39)

*swims into my ken*: Machen frequently invoked John Keats's 1816 sonnet 'On First Looking into Chapman's Homer', in which the poet likens his experience of reading George Chapman's Elizabethan translation of Homer's works first to the exhilaration of an astronomer discovering a new planet, then to the astonishment of an explorer first glimpsing a new ocean.

> Then felt I like some watcher of the skies
> When a new planet swims into his ken;
> Or like stout Cortez when with eagle eyes
> He star'd at the Pacific—and all his men
> Look'd at each other with a wild surmise—
> Silent, upon a peak in Darien.

88 *Aerated Bread Shop*: the Aerated Bread Company was founded in 1861; 'Over the next century hundreds of branches and many tea shops were opened all over the Greater London area' (Weinreb and Hibbert, 8).

90 *mignonette*: *Reseda odorata*, a strongly fragrant flower, popular in Victorian times.

*Wilkins*: perhaps Machen has borrowed the name from New England writer Mary Wilkins Freeman (1852–1930), whose work he praised. (Jane Austen's characters he found 'merely dull' in comparison with those of 'Miss Wilkins', in whose fiction he detected a quality of 'passion' and 'ecstasy' throbbing beneath the surface (*Hieroglyphics* (London, 1926), 152–3).)

*a Touranian wine of great merit*: Machen travelled annually to the Touraine region in France during the 1890s. Of one local vintage he wrote: 'It was scented like flowers in June; it was in its entirely unpretending way quite exquisite. I drank it with relish, and towards the end of the dinner I had accounted for about three-parts of the decanter' (*TNF*, 76). His first wife owned a vineyard there as well (Reynolds and Charlton, 37).

91 NOVEL OF THE DARK VALLEY: after allowing punningly that the novel 'has the machens of a good story in it', *Punch* concluded that 'there is very little worth reading after page 64'—after this episode, in other words (quoted in Trotter, 157). Most readers would probably agree with Machen himself, however, in thinking the story much inferior to those that follow.

*benefice*: churchman's living.

*tors*: rocky peaks or hills.

*the brickfields about Acton*: Acton, then a London suburb, was significantly industrialized in the later nineteenth century, known for both brickyards (where bricks are made) and laundries (earning South Acton the nickname 'Soapsuds Island').

92 *a Free Library*: the appearance in Britain of free public libraries, as opposed to for-profit circulating libraries, was a later nineteenth-century phenomenon, following in the wake of the Public Library Act of 1850. Wilkins's presence in one is a further indication of his poverty.

94 *The train stops at Reading*: fictitious, like all the Colorado place names in this episode.

103 *Vigilantes*: originally members of a vigilance committee. The term is, appropriately, American in origin.

*A Dalziel telegram*: Davison Dalziel, Baron Dalziel of Wooler (1852–1928), founded Dalziel's News Agency in 1890. Its 'specialty was lurid American sensationalism, and nothing was too small or too sensational' (Dennis Griffiths, *Plant Here the Standard* (London, 1996), 185).

105 *Holothuria*: marine animals, a genus within the phylum *Echinodermata* which includes the sea slug; 'they have an elongated form, a tough leathery integument, and a ring of tentacles around the mouth' (*OED*). A tentacular adumbration, perhaps, of the transformation of young Cradock in the ensuing tale.

*protyle and the ether*: a hypothetical primal substance and atmospheric medium respectively.

*a dweller in a metaphorical Clapham*: the Clapham Sect was a group of Anglican Evangelicals including William Wilberforce (1759–1833), Zachary Macaulay (1768–1838), Henry Thornton (1760–1815), and James Stephen (1758–1832), whose religious convictions led them to campaign against the slave trade, among other activities. Dyson is hammering home the point that he considers Phillipps to be the 'true believer' of the two.

*the bat or owl . . . who denied the existence of the sun at noonday*: something like this trope can be found in more than one (theological) context—it is tempting to connect this reference, for instance, with certain remarks of Madame Blavatsky and other Theosophists—but Machen's source seems most likely to have been one of the fables ('The Owl that Wrote a Book') by Victorian writer 'Mrs Prosser' (Sophie Amelia Prosser). In it an owl contends that 'the sun was not full of light; that the moon was in reality much more luminous'. The other night-birds (and bats, to boot) are easily converted to this doctrine, which the wise eagle warns against: 'Children of the light and of the day! beware of night-birds. Their eyes may be large, but they are so formed that they cannot receive the light; and what they cannot see, they deny the existence of' (*The Child's Friend* (London, 1875), 90). This is obviously of a piece with the rest of Dyson's rebuke.

110 *habitué*: habitual visitor.

112 *civil engineer*: as opposed to military engineer.

*Descartes' Meditationes*: the *Mediationes de Prima Philosophia* or *Meditations on First Philosophy* of René Descartes (1596–1650), published in 1641, builds a philosophical system from the ground up after provisionally dismissing all knowledge that can be doubted. Descartes's project thus resonates with the Montaignian query quoted later by Miss Lally (see note to p. 114).

*Gesta Romanorum*: 'Deeds of the Romans', influential collection of tales in Latin, compiled in the late Middle Ages.

114 *it is a fortified place . . . you had only to shout for these walls to sink into nothingness*: an extended conceptual metaphor drawing upon the specialized language of siege warfare.

*que sais-je?*: 'What do I know?'; sceptic's slogan, associated with essayist Michel de Montaigne (1533–92).

118 *Caermaen*: see note to p. 17.

119 *blue-book*: official governmental report or publication (British).

120 *the gas that blazes and flares in the gin-palace was once a wild hypothesis*: Scottish engineer William Murdock (1754–1839) pioneered the use of coal gas for lighting in the 1790s. Early public scepticism is captured by an incredulous question from a parliamentary committee member in 1809: 'Mr. Murdock, do you mean to tell us we can have a light without a wick?' (A. Murdock, *Light without a Wick: A Century of Gas-Lighting* (Glasgow, 1892), 44).

*the philosopher's stone*: legendary substance sought by the alchemists, supposed to have the power to change base metals into gold and confer immortality.

121 *whin-berries*: also whimberry, bilberry, chortleberry (the term 'whinberry' is commonly in use in Wales); a relative of the blueberry.

*farriery*: a farrier is one who shoes horses.

*Poems by 'persons of quality'*: one possibility, given the setting (and author), is an early seventeenth-century collection entitled *A New Miscellany: Being a Collection of Pieces of Poetry . . . Written Chiefly by Persons of Quality. To which is Added, Grongar Hill, a Poem*; 'Grongar Hill' is by Welsh poet John Dyer (1699–1757).

*Prideaux's Connection*: the two-volume *Old and New Testament Connected* by clergyman Humphrey Prideaux (1648–1724) traced the history of the Jews in biblical times. First published in 1716–18, it was still in print in the mid-nineteenth century (*ODNB*).

*an odd volume of Pope*: the poet Alexander Pope (1688–1744).

*fine old quarto printed by the Stephani*: Henri Estienne or, in Latin, Henricus Stephanus was a Parisian printer of the early sixteenth century; his three sons (Estiennes or 'Stephani') carried on the family business. Machen himself possessed 'Pomponius Mela['s] "De Situ Orbis" in a noble Stephanus quarto' (*FOT*, 132).

*Pomponius Mela, De Situ Orbis*: author and title, respectively, of the first Latin geography, also known as *De Chorographia* (written *c*.43 CE). 'Mela is interested in wonders and the mythological past, but little in geographical mathematics' (*OCD*, 1218).

*Solinus*: classical geographer (see note to p. 35). [Silet per diem] Solinus' work *Collectanea rerum memorabilium* (also known as *De mirabilibus mundi*) does speak of a 'sixtystone', but the subsequent passage is fictitious (Joshi, 361).

122 *Sinbad the Sailor, or other of the supplementary Nights*: the adventures of Sinbad, all of them highly fantastical, constitute a later addition to the original *Thousand and One Nights*.

123 *darkling*: here, obscure, in the sense of keeping Miss Lally in the dark.

*Scotch mist*: 'dense, soaking mist characteristic of the Scottish hills' (*OED*).

124 *"naturals"*: as the context suggests, an obsolete term for intellectually impaired persons.

125 *the hissing of the phonograph*: Thomas Edison invented the (cylindrical, tinfoil) phonograph in 1877; wax would later replace the foil, and flat discs begin to compete with cylinders. The invention was little more than a curiosity until the 1890s; as late as 1898, a character in Richard Marsh's story 'The Adventure of the Phonograph' could say, 'It may seem odd, but I suppose there are a good many people—decent, respectable people—who never have seen a phonograph; at any rate, until that moment I had been one of them' (*Curios* (1898; Valancourt Books, 2007), 26).

*Monmouth*: Welsh town, also in Gwent.

*espaliers*: rows of fruit trees trained on stakes.

126 *blind-worm*: not a worm at all (or a snake, which it resembles) but a burrowing lizard, *Anguis fragilis*; also called a 'slow worm'.

128 *the fairies—the Tylwydd Têg*: y tylwyth teg, 'the fair folk' (Welsh); according to MacKillop's *Dictionary of Celtic Mythology*, 'The most usual Welsh name for fairies. They are often known by the euphemism bendith y mamau [Welsh, mother's blessings] to avert kidnapping, especially in Glamorgan. . . . They are described as fair-haired and as loving golden hair, and thus they covet mortal children with blond or fair hair. Their usual king is Gwyn ap Nudd. In general y tylwyth teg are portrayed as benevolent but still capable of occasional mischief.'

130 *phantasmagoria*: see note to p. 9.

*a grimy-looking bust of Pitt*: there is no shortage of likenesses, in various media, of either William Pitt—father (1708–78) or son (1759–1806). The early eighteenth-century contents of the bookcase in the morning room might point towards this being a representation of Pitt the Elder.

*the inimitable Holmes*: there is more than a hint of Sherlock Holmes and John Watson, the immortal creations of Machen's contemporary Arthur Conan Doyle (1859–1930), in Dyson and Phillipps. One reviewer of *The Three Impostors* saw in it 'a mixture of Conan Doyle, Douglas Jerrold, and the author of the Murders in the Rue Morgue [Poe], seasoned with grim touches of German mysticism'. (As for Doyle himself, Machen's story frightened him out of a night's sleep: 'I don't take him to bed with me again') (Trotter, 160, 163).

131 *the Zoo in London*: the Zoological Gardens, one of London's major attractions, were opened in Regent's Park in 1828 by the newly established Zoological Society of London, with the aim of furthering 'the advancements of Zoology and Animal Physiology' (in that spirit, Richard Owen autopsied the collection's first orangutan the following year) (Weinreb and Hibbert, 979).

132  *Vestigia nulla retrorsum*: 'no steps backwards' (Latin).

133  *nothing so hazardous as 'Arry does a hundred times over in the course of every Bank Holiday*: 'Harry' minus the aitch is a 'low-bred fellow . . . of lively temper and manners' (*OED*). Drunkenness and rowdy behaviour were supposed to increase markedly on bank holidays among the lower orders. In 1897 John Lubbock wrote to the Chief Magistrate for London to ask for statistics regarding 'Drunkenness and Assaults' on those days: 'A recent writer has made the extraordinary assertion that from ¼th to ⅛th of the poor (adult) population, including women, get drunk on these occasions' (Horace G. Hutchinson, *Life of Sir John Lubbock, Lord Avebury* (London, 1914), ii. 79).

134  *the old logic manual*: the specific reference, if not invented, is unknown, but Machen owned and relished a number of books on logic, including Richard Whately's *Elements of Logic* (1826).

135  *diablerie*: here, tale of devilry or witchcraft.

    *the hideous furies*: the Erinyes, three terrible, snake-haired goddesses who pursue and torment the guilty. Euphemistically called the 'Eumenides' or 'kind ones' (the title of the final play in Aeschylus' *Oresteia*).

136  *a tumulus or a barrow*: essentially synonymous; a burial mound. The nineteenth-century antiquarian Bernard Bolingbroke Woodward, considering 'The sepulchral mounds or *tumuli*' of ancient Wales, wrote: 'the form of the skulls discovered in these rude tombs . . . is rounder than that of the true Caucasian variety, and approaches the Mongolian type' (*History of Wales* (London, 1859), 21).

    *'articulate-speaking men' in Homer*: see note to p. 11.

137  *Shelta*: 'cryptic jargon used by tinkers, composed partly of Irish or Gaelic words, mostly disguised by inversion or by arbitrary alteration of initial consonants' (*OED*).

    *the Basques of Spain*: ethnic and linguistic group whose historic homeland lies between France and Spain; the Basque language is unrelated to the Indo-European languages, and has been spoken in that region since antiquity, contributing to a characterization of the Basques as an unchanging 'other'.

144  *the approaches to the Empire*: the Royal London Panorama in Leicester Square, built in 1881, was converted into the Empire Theatre in 1884. Not until 1887 did the venue, now reopened as a music hall, become popular.

    *Café de la Touraine*: see note to p. 90.

    *house of call*: place where practitioners of a particular trade gather; often, as here, a public house.

145  *St Mary le Strand*: a Baroque church built in 1714–17 by architect James Gibbs (1682–1754); at the eastern end of the Strand. Charles Dickens's mother and father were married here.

    *as the gorse blossom to Linnæus*: reference to an anecdote involving the reaction of pioneering taxonomist Carl Linnaeus (1707–78) when he encountered a field of gorse, also called furze (*Ulex europæus*), during a visit to England: 'The first time Linnæus crossed Putney Heath the sight of the gorse blossom in its blaze of May made him fall on his knees in rapture to thank God for making anything so beautiful' (Florence Caddy, *Through the Fields with Linnaeus* (Boston and London, 1887), i. 329).

146 *laureat*: crowned, i.e. as victor, with laurels.

*the Boulevards*: in 1853 Georges-Eugène Haussmann was appointed 'Prefect of the Seine' by France's Emperor Napoleon III, and charged with directing a massive public works programme in Paris. A major component of his subsequent transformation of the city involved the construction of a new network of broad avenues and boulevards, replacing the ancient tangle of medieval streets in the city centre. Burton and Dyson are grateful, in the next paragraph, that London has not been similarly 'boulevardised'.

*Romola . . . Robert Elsmere . . . Tit Bits*: *Romola* (1862–3) may not be considered George Eliot's most successful novel, but she is certainly acknowledged today as one of the titans of Victorian prose literature. She was too prosy for the visionary Machen, however, who called her 'poor, dreary, draggle-tailed George Eliot' (*Hieroglyphics*, 58). *Robert Elsmere* (1888) was an enormously successful novel by Mary Augusta ('Mrs Humphry') Ward (1851–1920), treating of that most Victorian of themes, faith and doubt. Machen's view of the novel can be seen in his criticism of Thomas Hardy's *Tess of the D'Urbervilles* as containing 'much pseudo-philosophy of a kind suited to persons who think that *Robert Elsmere* is literature' (*Hieroglyphics*, 112). In 1881 newspaper proprietor George Newnes (1851–1910) founded the weekly magazine *Tit-Bits*, which would become 'the matrix of twentieth-century popular journalism' (*ODNB*).

149 *Sancho Panza*: Don Quixote's squire, in Miguel de Cervantes's great novel *The Ingenious Gentleman Don Quixote of La Mancha* (1605, 1615).

150 *our Museum at London*: established in 1753 by an Act of Parliament, the British Museum initially comprised physician Sir Hans Sloane's (1660–1753) rich and heterogeneous collection of antiquities, manuscripts, natural specimens and other materials. Originally housed in Montagu House in Bloomsbury, the Museum was opened to the public in 1759. Its collections grew steadily over the years through gifts, purchases, and, not to put too fine a point on it, plunder. In the early nineteenth century alone, the Museum acquired the Rosetta Stone and other loot from the British defeat of Napoleon at Alexandria (1802); Charles Townley's famous collection of classical statuary (1805); and the Elgin Marbles, taken from the Parthenon in Athens (1816); among other treasures. A new, larger building with a classical Greek facade, completed in 1847, replaced Montagu House. A Reading Room was constructed during the following decade and became a famous research centre (Karl Marx wrote *Das Kapital* there).

150 *Birmingham art jewellery*: Birmingham has long been a centre of jewellery production. 'Brummagem [Birmingham] ware' once had a reputation for shoddy cheapness, though this appears to be a disparaging reference to the Arts and Crafts design movement, which took early root there.

151 *Socrates*: Burton proceeds to engage Dyson in a process of Socratic dialectic, as depicted in Plato's dialogues. Burton's promise to 'show you the real image which you possess in your soul' particularly echoes the dialogue *Meno*, in which Socrates questions a mathematically ignorant slave boy about geometry.

153 *Lord Bacon*: the first edition of Francis Bacon's *Essayes* appeared in 1597; on one level it is indeed, as Burton and Dyson are suggesting here, a book of advice for courtiers and politicians.

*De Re Militari*: Latin for 'Of Military Matters'. There is a late Roman work of this name, written between 383 and 450 CE by Flavius Renatus Vegetius. '[A] Florentine in the fifteenth century', on the other hand, sounds more like Niccolò Machiavelli (1469–1527), who composed *The Art of War* (*Dell'arte della guerra*)—though not until the early sixteenth century. Or perhaps Burton's example is an invented one.

*moyen de parvenir*: French for 'the way to attain'; the title of a book by Béroalde de Verville (1556–1626), which Machen had translated in 1889. He would later describe this sub-Rabelaisian work as 'one of the most shapeless things ever compounded by the human brain . . . a collection of discourses, in dialogue form, on Reformation politics, on the correct idiom of the French language, on some unknown subject which has been conjectured to be Alchemy—on anything which came into the head of this crazy canon' (Danielson, 18).

*the Cromwell Road*: a comparatively new road, begun in 1855, and given its name by Prince Albert.

*the Nonconformist conscience*: Nonconformists were Protestant dissenters from the Church of England, associated with the evangelizing strain which had such a large impact on mainstream Victorian culture. Dyson implies that theirs is a rigidly moralistic, unimaginative world view.

*novels . . . of the old women and the new women*: 'New Woman' novels by such authors as Sarah Grand and Olive Schreiner (as well as men like Thomas Hardy and Grant Allen) reflected late Victorian debates over issues including contraception, dress, and female suffrage. As Dyson's earlier remark on George Eliot suggests, Machen had little less dislike for at least certain 'old woman' novelists.

154 *cent nouvelles nouvelles*: *Les Cent Nouvelles Nouvelles* is the title of a fifteenth-century collection of French stories.

155 *Waterloo Bridge*: opened in 1817, on the second anniversary of the Battle of Waterloo; demolished in 1936.

158 *his namesake's Anatomy*: Robert Burton's (1577–1640) encyclopedic *Anatomy of Melancholy*, published in 1621, was greatly admired by Machen,

who mimicked Burton's approach and style, in miniature, in his own *Anatomy of Tobacco* (see note to p. 82).

159 *Grub Street*: traditionally associated with hack authors.

*slavey*: (usually male) servant.

*six ale*: bitter ale sold at sixpence a quart.

160 *Family Story Paper*: likely meant in a generic sense here (there was, e.g., a 'New York Family Story Paper' and a 'Daisy Family Story Paper'; this also sounds a good deal like the weekly story paper *Family Herald*).

*Balzac and the Comédie Humaine . . . Zola and the Rougon-Macquart family*: two great nineteenth-century French novelists and their respective (and massive) novel sequences. The 'Human Comedy' of Honoré de Balzac (1799–1850) is a sprawling portrait of French society, comprising some ninety novels and tales, including *Père Goriot* and *Eugénie Grandet*. Naturalist Émile Zola (1840–1902), influenced by Balzac's magnum opus as Russell is by both novelists' projects, wrote twenty novels in his own cycle focusing on the members of a single family tree, including *L'Assommoir* (1877) and *Germinal* (1885).

*via dolorosa*: literally 'way of sorrows' (Latin); in Jerusalem, the supposed route taken by Jesus on his way to Calvary.

*These were my fancies; but when pen touched paper they shrivelled and vanished away*: compare with Machen's description of his own experiences confronting 'the horrid gulf that yawns between the conception and the execution'. Every writer, he concludes, 'dream[s] in fire', but 'work[s] in clay' (*FOT*, 100–1).

161 *Levant morocco*: metonymically, 'morocco' denotes the leather originally imported from there, associated with bookbinding; 'Levant morocco' refers to 'a high-grade morocco, with a large grain, properly made from the skin of the Angora goat' (*OED*).

*bibelots*: trinkets, curios.

*brocade of Lyons*: the French city of Lyons is historically associated with textile, particularly silk, production.

162 *Carthusian monk*: the Carthusians are a monastic order, originating in France; see note to p. 4.

164 *Lord Chancellor*: high-ranking officer in the British Government, responsible for administration of the court system. Until 2005 the Lord Chancellor also presided over the House of Lords.

*Bibliothèque Nationale*: France's National Library, which had taken up new quarters in the Rue de Richelieu in Paris in 1868.

165 *malacca cane*: Malacca or Melaka, a Malaysian state, was then a British colony. A 'malacca cane' is 'a rich brown, often clouded or mottled, walking stick made from the stem of any of several Malaysian palms' (*OED*).

*and hear the chimes at midnight*: from *Henry IV, Part Two*, 3.2; Justice Shallow is reminiscing with Sir John Falstaff about their old college days.

Falstaff replies, 'We have heard the chimes at midnight, Master Shallow.' There is a clear suggestion of sexual dalliance on Leicester's part here (Shallow gleefully reminds an irritated Falstaff of the pair's former patronage of London brothels).

168 *quinine*: drug, derived from cinchona bark, used to treat malaria.

169 *the earthly tabernacle*: from 2 Corinthians 5:1, in which the mortal body is likened by St Paul to a temporary dwelling (the original meaning of 'tabernacle'): 'For we know that if our earthly house of *this* tabernacle were dissolved, we have a building of God, an house not made with hands, eternal in the heavens' (King James Version). Machen's tale of corporeal 'dissolution' thus grotesquely literalizes Paul's words.

173 *mesmerisms, spiritualisms, materialisations, theosophies*: mesmerism is the theory of 'animal magnetism' associated with Franz Anton Mesmer (1734–1815). Spiritualism, premised on the belief that the spirits of the dead not only live on but also wish to speak with the living, was extremely popular in the Anglosphere during the nineteenth century and beyond (the phenomenon of spirits 'materializing' belongs also to this belief system). 'Theosophies' could refer to 'Any system of speculation which bases the knowledge of nature upon that of the divine nature' (in this sense Thomas Vaughan spoke of 'The Ancient, reall Theosophie of the Hebrewes and Egyptians' (quoted in the *OED*)); however, the predominant association at this time would have been with the doctrines of Madame Blavatsky (1831–91) and her Theosophical Society. Rejection of such 'occult' doctrines—and there was much cross-pollination between and among all of these—establish the bona fides of the two men of science as hard-headed sceptics.

174 *Omnia exeunt in mysterium*: 'All things pass into mystery' (Latin). Machen's source for the quotation is likely Coleridge's *Aids to Reflection* (Jones, 501).

*a peak in Darien*: see note to p. 87.

*the theory of telepathy*: the word had been coined in the 1880s by one of the founders of the Society for Psychical Research (SPR) (see note to p. 313), a newly formed body which sought to apply scientific methods to the study of what we should today term paranormal phenomena.

175 *Payne Knight's monograph*: Richard Payne Knight (1751–1824), British writer and art collector. Of this episode Machen would write: 'The general hypothesis of "The White Powder" is obtained, very distantly, from Payne Knight; the special *machina*, the magical division of personality, is, to the best of my belief, my own' (Danielson, 27). (The magical, or at least chemical, 'division of personality' does, however, recall Stevenson's Dr Jekyll and Mr Hyde.) The relevant passage in Payne Knight's *Account of the Remains of the Worship of Priapus* (1786) reads: 'The ineffable name [of God] also, which, according to the Massorethic punctuation, is pronounced *Jehovah*, was anciently pronounced *Jaho* . . . which was a title of BACCHUS, the nocturnal sun; as was also *Sabazius*, or *Sabadius*, which is the same word as *Sabaoth*, one of the scriptural titles of the true God, only adapted to the pronunciation of a more polished language' (Jones, 501).

*Aryan man entered Europe*: during the nineteenth century the linguistic category of 'Aryan' (Indo-European) became conceptualized as a racial one as well, with an ancient migration or invasion imagined from the East—or, in the case of Madame Blavatsky and the Theosophists, the West (i.e., Atlantis).

*sumentes calicem principis inferorum*: 'taking from the chalice of the prince of the shades below' (Latin), invented by Machen (Jones, 501–2).

*the worm which never dies*: see note to p. 236.

177 *Milesian and Arabian methods of entertainment*: the original 'Milesian Tales', written in the 2nd century BCE by Aristides of Miletus, were a collection of short stories, often salacious, often set in the Asia Minor city of Miletus; afterwards a group of stories resembling Aristides'. This genre has been linked with the practice of interpolating shorter, subordinate tales within a larger frame narrative, as in Apuleius' *Golden Ass* (which begins, 'I would like to tie together different sorts of tales for you in that Milesian style of yours')—and, of course, *The Three Impostors*. 'Arabian methods of entertainment' refers, once more, to the *One Thousand and One Nights* (see note to p. 3).

*subscribe to Mudie's for a regular supply of mild and innocuous romance*: the famous lending library established in 1842 by Charles Mudie (1818–90) was the Netflix of its day; for a guinea a year, one could borrow unlimited material, one volume at a time. Owing to the censoriousness of its founder, 'Mudie's' was synonymous with inoffensive reading matter.

178 *bookshelf of the Empire*: from the period of Napoleonic rule (1800–15).

*lacquered-work*: work covered with lacquer, a wood varnish.

*cagmag*: unwholesome meat.

*De Quincey's after his dose*: as a boy of around 12, Machen saw Thomas de Quincey's *Confessions of an English Opium Eater* at the railway station in Pontypool, Wales: 'This . . . I instantly bought and as instantly loved, and still love very heartily' (*FOR*, 41).

179 *Parthenon*: the temple of Athena on the Acropolis in Athens.

180 *Pamphylia and the parts about Mesopotamia*: Pamphylia, 'land of all tribes', was a region in Asia Minor. The 'parts about' Mesopotamia (the region between the Tigris and Euphrates rivers, as its name signifies) included the kingdoms of Assyria and Babylonia, perhaps leading associatively to the 'babble of voices' in the next sentence.

*words that Chaucer wrote*: late medieval poet Geoffrey Chaucer (*c*.1330–1400) used a number of words ('ers', 'queynte', 'pisse' come to mind) seldom to be found in the pages of Victorian books, even Decadent ones.

181 *mystery play*: medieval vernacular plays dramatizing such biblical episodes as the events connected with the Crucifixion and Resurrection.

182 *the Reading-Room of the British Museum*: see note to p. 150.

183 *philosopher's stone*: see note to p. 120.

183 *Rabelaisian . . . Vivez joyeux*: 'Live joyfully', motto on the title page of Rabelais's *Gargantua* (see note to p. 73). (Cf. the French expression *joie de vivre*.)

185 *baize door*: door lined with baize, a woollen cloth also used to cover billiard tables.

*Avallaunius*: invented by Machen, or rather altered from a Romano-British name, Vallaunius: 'Machen thought the word should be Avallanius, meaning the man of Avalon, a reference to the mystical region beyond the veil in Arthurian legend' (Susan Johnston Graf, *Talking to the Gods* (Albany, NY, 2015), 74). *The Garden of Avallaunius* was Machen's original title for the novel that would become *The Hill of Dreams*, and he took the name 'Frater Avallaunius' when initiated into the Order of the Golden Dawn.

186 *Panurge*: major character in Rabelais's *Gargantua and Pantagruel* (see note to p. 73). He is companion to Pantagruel, knavish and resourceful. Etymologically (ultimately from the Greek) the name suggests one 'ready to do anything', or who 'knows how to do everything'.

*style is everything in literature*: suggests the followers of Walter Pater, author and aesthete, among them Oscar Wilde.

189 *Irritability of Authors*: proverbial. Machen likely has in mind a chapter in the collection *Curiosities of Literature* by Isaac D'Israeli (1766–1848), a work he called 'that singular magazine of oddities' (*FOT*, 132).

191 *myrmidons*: in Homer's *Iliad*, the Myrmidons were warriors led by Achilles; by extension, devoted followers or (as here) private gang or army.

*they beat furiously after me in the covert of London, I remained perdu*: Walter's terms, and overarching metaphor, are drawn from the language of the chase; he is like a fox in hiding, with Lipsius' crew hunting him.

194 *flock paper*: wallpaper with a raised pattern, akin to velvet in texture, made by applying dyed 'flock', a powdered wool, to the paper. Once a luxury item.

*amorini*: cupids.

195 *damask*: defined in *Chambers's Encyclopaedia* as 'the name given to all textile fabrics in which figures of flowers, fruits, or others not of geometrical regularity, are woven. The word is supposed to be derived from the city of Damascus having been an early seat of these manufactures' (Philadelphia, 1875), iii. 406.

*a conté fleurettes to*: i.e., flirting with.

## THE RED HAND

First appeared in *Chapman's Magazine* in December 1895; published in book form in *The House of Souls* (1906).

198 *troglodyte*: caveman.

*'drawing' Phillipps*: i.e. inducing him to go out; alternatively, irritating him (or perhaps both).

*Gloria*: the greater doxology of the Roman Catholic and Anglican Masses, 'Gloria in Excelsis Deo', here performed on a street-organ.

199 *screever's work*: a screever is an 'Artist in chalks', as Machen later tells us; a pavement artist. Derived ultimately from *scribere* (Latin, 'to write').

*Abury*: Avebury, name of village in Wiltshire and site of Neolithic henge. Sometimes called 'Abury', as by antiquarian William Stukeley (1687–1765) in his *Abury: a Temple of the British Druids* (1743). John Lubbock, author of *Pre-Historic Times as Illustrated by Ancient Remains* (1865), was made the first Lord Avebury in 1900.

202 *the theory of the evil eye*: a curse delivered by a look. The same year 'The Red Hand' first appeared, philologist Frederick Thomas Elworthy (1830–1907) published his book *The Evil Eye: An Account of this Ancient and Widespread Superstition*, in which he writes, sounding very like Phillipps, 'The origin of the belief is lost in the obscurity of prehistoric ages. The enlightened call it superstition; but it holds its sway over the people of many countries, savage as well as civilised, and must be set down as one of the hereditary and instinctive convictions of mankind' (London, 1895), 3. Elworthy also discusses the 'horrible old signs' (in Phillipps's words) used to avert the evil eye, such as the 'mano pantea' and the one mentioned here, the 'mano fica' (the quasi-obscene 'fig hand').

*F.R.S.*: Fellow of the Royal Society, the national academy of science in the UK.

*mano in fica*: see note above.

208 *spirals and whorls . . . the pattern of a thumb*: in a notebook of approximately this period, Machen records his musings on the recurrence of 'the whorl, the spiral, Maori decoration. . . . Why was this form common to all primitive art' (*LA*, 107). It may also be worth noting that Francis Galton had just published three pioneering books on fingerprints, in 1892, 1893, and 1895.

211 *shag tobacco*: a strong tobacco also favoured by Sherlock Holmes.

216 *"Stony-hearted step-mother"*: from *Confessions of an English Opium Eater*; Part II begins: 'So then, Oxford-street, stony-hearted stepmother! thou that listenest to the sighs of orphans, and drinkest the tears of children, at length I was dismissed from thee' (London, 1845), 20.

## THE SHINING PYRAMID

First published in 1895 in the short-lived journal *The Unknown World*, edited by Machen's close friend, the occult writer A. E. Waite. The story subsequently appeared in two separate collections, both entitled *The Shining Pyramid* (published in 1923 and 1925 respectively), leading to a somewhat embarrassing situation for which Machen's carelessness, and perhaps impecuniousness, seem to have been responsible. Machen himself spoke deprecatingly of the story, but it has been called 'one of the most terrifying of all Machen's horror tales' (Carole Silver, *Strange and Secret Peoples* (Oxford, 1999), 146).

222 *Doré*: painter and illustrator Gustave Doré (1832–83) produced illustrations for editions of Milton's *Paradise Lost*, Dante's *Divine Comedy*, and the Bible, among other works. Doré did in fact depict London itself in a series of engravings (*London: A Pilgrimage*, published in 1872), but it is unlikely that Machen has these pictured scenes of poverty and squalor in mind, given the sublime effect described by Dyson. (Five years before writing 'The Shining Pyramid', Machen had travelled to the French province of Touraine, and been disappointed by its failure to live up to 'Doré's wonderful illustrations to [Honoré de Balzac's] "Contes Drolatiques" ', with their representations of 'enchanted heights . . . profound and somber valleys, [and] airy abysses') (*TNF*, 71).

*"far in the spiritual city"*: from 'The Holy Grail', one of Tennyson's *Idylls of the King* (1859–85). The words are spoken by Percivale's sister to Galahad before he sets out on his quest: 'Go forth, for thou shalt see what I have seen, | And break through all, till one will crown thee king | Far in the spiritual city.'

223 *Castletown*: presumably a stand-in for Newport, Wales, port city near Caerleon and site of Newport Castle.

226 *Charles II punch-bowl*: a silver punchbowl from the reign of the 'Merry Monarch' (1660–85) would have been, then as now, extremely valuable.

*chasing*: design engraved on metal.

227 *Old red sandstone and limestone*: the geological description of this region of south-west Wales is accurate.

*mystic esses*: plural of 'ess' ('The name of the letter S; anything in the shape of an S', *OED*). A favourite Machen word.

229 *almost like the eye of a Chinaman*: see note to p. 240.

232 *the abbé in Monte Cristo*: in Alexandre Dumas's *The Count of Monte Cristo* (serialized in 1844–5), the wrongfully imprisoned Edmond Dantès is aided in his escape from the Château d'If by his fellow prisoner, the Abbé Faria, a character Dumas based on a real historical figure.

*Croesyceiliog*: now a suburb of Cwmbran, a new town established in 1949 and comprising six villages. It lies to the north of Caerleon and Newport.

233 *idol of the South Seas*: the context suggests the great stone moai of Easter Island (see note to p. 347).

235 *the awful words*: i.e. of the consecration. Cf. Anglican theologian Edward Pusey's description of 'the awful words, whereby He consecrated for ever elements of this world to be His Body and Blood' (*The Holy Eucharist a Comfort to the Penitent* (Oxford, 1843), 20).

236 *'the worm of corruption, the worm that dieth not'*: a reference to the eternal punishment of hell, described in Mark 9:48 ('Where their worm dieth not, and the fire is not quenched'), a passage which itself looks back to Isaiah

66:24 ('for their worm shall not die, neither shall their fire be quenched; and they shall be an abhorring unto all flesh').

237 *phantasmagoria*: see note to p. 9.

238 *the old puzzle of Achilles and the Tortoise*: famous paradox proposed by the pre-Socratic philosopher Zeno of Elea (active early fifth century BCE). Aristotle summarized it thus: 'the so-called "Achilles" [argument] amounts to this, that in a race the quickest runner can never overtake the slowest, since the pursuer must first reach the point whence the pursued started, so that the slower must always hold a lead' (*Physics* 6.9).

239 *the days of Edmond Dantès*: see note to p. 232.

*oubliette*: 'secret dungeon with access only through a trapdoor in its ceiling' (*OED*).

240 *de novo*: from the beginning.

*there is a "Devil's Punch-bowl" in Surrey*: natural amphitheatre. At a nearby Gibbet Hill, a memorial stone commemorates the 1786 murder of the 'Unknown Sailor'. Perhaps Machen had in mind the site's lurid history, as well as its shape, in conceiving of his own infernal 'punch-bowl' in Gwent; as a lover of Dickens, he would certainly have remembered Nicholas and Smike's visit to the spot in *Nicholas Nickleby* (serialized in 1838–9).

*Vigilantes*: see note to p. 103.

*prehistoric Turanian inhabitants*: for his conception of the Welsh *Tylwyth Teg*, Machen drew upon a rich and heady brew of speculation and theorizing that bubbled up in the nineteenth century, mingling new scientific ideas with ancient folk legend and lore. A particularly salient example of this intellectual ferment was the hypothesis, advanced by antiquarian David MacRitchie in his *Testimony of Tradition* (1890), 'that the fairies of Scotland and Ireland were really non-Aryan, Finno-Ugaric peoples . . . that there had been little, yellow, slant-eyed devils all over northern Europe' (Silver, *Strange and Secret Peoples*, 138). The racial category invoked here is the 'Turanian'—an all but unknown term today, but one which in the nineteenth century stood alongside 'Aryan' and 'Semite' in a widely used taxonomical triad (though other classificatory schemes existed as well). These designations could be applied in various contexts; indeed, the conceptual evolution of 'Turanian' makes for an exemplary case of the way in which language, culture, and race tended to be blurred together in the nineteenth century. Originally it was a philological category, a posited family of languages—and a deeply flawed one, a kind of omnium-gatherum of leftovers, 'comprising the dialects of the nomad races scattered over Central and Northern Asia, the Tungusic, Mongolic, Turkic, Samoyedic, and Finnic' (Max Müller, *Science of Language* (London, 1885), i. 35). (Hence the connection here with 'Mongolians' and 'Chinamen'.) The category was employed also in the comparative study of religion, as well as in systems of racial classification. Within the latter it was promiscuously employed; to give but one example in a British anthropological context, John Beddoe in his *Races of Britain* presented evidence of two distinct racial groups in

Wales, one of which bears an 'aspect . . . suggestive of a Turanian origin' (London, 1885), 260). This idea may be responsible for the ambivalence or inconsistency one finds in Machen's treatment of his own Celtic ancestry; sometimes the Celt is explicitly classified as 'Aryan' (as in *Things Near and Far*), while elsewhere Machen flirts with the notion of personal descent from the Little People (as in *The Hill of Dreams*). The Aryan–Semite–Turanian triad also appeared in occult texts with which Machen would likely have been familiar; Madame Blavatsky, for instance, borrowing from Ignatius Donnelly, presented the Turanians as one of her 'root races' which emigrated from Atlantis.

241 *The old derivation from* πυρ: accepted by Samuel Johnson in his *Dictionary* ('Pýramid. n.s. [*pyramide*, Fr. πύραμις, from πῦρ, fire; because fire always ascends in the figure of a cone]'), but presented as an exemplary case of etymological spuriousness by renowned Victorian philologist Richard Chenevix Trench: 'the Greeks assumed that the pyramids were so named from their having the appearance of *flame* going up into a point, and so they spelt "pyramid", that they might find πῦρ or "pyre" in it; while in fact "pyramid" has nothing to do with flame or fire at all; being, as those best qualified to speak on the matter declare to us, an Egyptian word of quite a different signification' (*English Past and Present* (New York, 1858), 213–14).

## THE TURANIANS

This and the five following short pieces ('The Idealist', 'Witchcraft', 'The Ceremony', 'Psychology', 'Midsummer') were all written in 1897, and all first appeared in book form in *Ornaments in Jade* (1924).

For information about the word Turanians, see note to p. 240.

244 *paten*: during the Eucharist, a gold or silver plate to hold the host.

## THE IDEALIST

245 *yahoos*: in Part IV of Jonathan Swift's *Gulliver's Travels* (1726), Lemuel Gulliver encounters two races: the Houyhnhnms (intelligent, articulate horses) and the Yahoos (coarse, filthy humanoids). To Symonds, in other words, the other clerks are little better than subhuman brutes.

*Etna*: Mount Etna in Sicily (in Latin *Aetna*); the highest active volcano in Europe. The Greek fire-god Hephaestus, and later his Roman equivalent Vulcan, were supposed to reside underneath.

246 *hoarding*: a fence on which advertisements or bills are posted, or in this case the 'icon' (meaning, here, a portrait) of, apparently, a music-hall performer (prominent real-life woman singers of the time include Marie Lloyd, Bessie Bellwood, and Jenny Hill).

*And that's the way they do it . . . taike the bun?*: lyrics, apparently of Machen's invention, parodying a typical music-hall song in cockney dialect. I am grateful to Barry Faulk for identifying some hits of the day which Machen may have had in mind here, such as 'The boy I love is up in the gallery'

(1885) (this less for its dialect than its depiction of adoring male fans), 'Wot Cher Ria' (1885), and 'Knocked 'em on the Old Kent Road' (1891).

247 *Ombres Chinoises*: 'Chinese shadows' (French); a shadow-puppet show.

*detached and semi-detached*: a semi-detached house is one of a pair of single-family dwellings sharing a wall, as opposed to a stand-alone ('detached') house.

*entomologist*: scientist who studies insects.

248 *lay figure*: a 'jointed wooden figure of the human body, used by artists as a model for the arrangement of draperies, posing, etc.' (*OED*).

## THE CEREMONY

253 *Michaelmas daisy*: the *aster amellus*, a small, star-shaped flower ranging in colour from purple to pink to blue, which blooms near Michaelmas (29 September). 'From the daffodil to the Michaelmas daisy' thus spans the natural 'calendar' of rural life from early spring to autumn.

## PSYCHOLOGY

Besides its inclusion in *Ornaments in Jade*, 'Psychology' also appeared, entitled 'Fragments of Paper', in *The Glorious Mystery* (1924).

255 *purlieu*: originally land bordering a forest; here, 'a poor or disreputable area of a city, town, or district; a slum' (*OED*).

256 *Tragic Comedians*: title of an 1880 George Meredith novel, mentioned by Machen in his work of criticism *Hieroglyphics*.

*lupanar*: a brothel.

## THE WHITE PEOPLE

Written in 1899, 'The White People' first appeared in *Horlick's Magazine* in 1904, and was published in book form in the 1906 collection *The House of Souls*.

261 *ecstasy*: a key Machen term; his theory of literature, for instance, as articulated in his book *Hieroglyphics*, is centred upon the concept.

*forsake the imperfect copies and go to the perfect originals*: a quintessentially Platonic formulation.

*teetotal sect*: non-drinkers. The term derives from the Total Abstinence Society, founded in 1832 by Joseph Livesey (1794–1884).

262 *Romanée Conti*: a highly esteemed vineyard in Burgundy.

*four ale*: cheap ale, originally sold at fourpence a quart.

*quâ*: 'as being'; in other words, insofar as the killer merely kills, he does not qualify as a 'sinner' in Ambrose's spiritual sense, since a soulless animal may do as much.

263 *Highland caterans of the seventeenth century . . . moss-troopers*: both terms refer to gangs of Scots marauders.

263 *company promoters*: those who solicit investors for a new corporation. An example from Victorian fiction is Augustus Melmotte, in Anthony Trollope's *The Way We Live Now* (1875).

264 *Gilles de Raiz*: the Baron de Retz, Rais, or Raiz (*c.*1404–40) fought the English alongside Joan of Arc during the Hundred Years War and was made marshal of France, but achieved historical immortality for the ritualized torture, rape, and murder of children. He has been suggested as the original of the serial uxoricide Bluebeard, made famous by Charles Perrault's fairy tale, though as French novelist Joris-Karl Huysmans points out in his 1891 novel of Satanism *Là-bas*, there is little similarity between the two. One reason to suppose that Machen may have read Huysmans's novel (and may have been thinking of it here) lies in its description of de Rais, and of the fine line between 'saint' and 'Satanist': 'this man . . . was a true mystic. . . . Association with Jeanne d'Arc certainly stimulated his desires for the divine. Now from lofty Mysticism to base Satanism there is but one step. In the Beyond all things touch. He carried his zeal for prayer into the territory of blasphemy' (trans. Keene Wallace (New York, 1972), 52–4).

*the "Blackwood" review of Keats*: both the *Quarterly Review* and *Blackwood's Magazine* reviewed Keats's *Endymion* (1818) with great harshness; the reference here is to John Gibson Lockhart's review, in which, gibing at Keats's vocation, he wrote: 'it is a better and a wiser thing to be a starved apothecary than a starved poet; so back to the shop, Mr John, back to the "plasters, pills, and ointment boxes"'. Shortly before Keats's death from tuberculosis, Shelley would write: 'Poor Keats was thrown into a dreadful state of mind by this review, which, I am persuaded, was not written with any intention of producing the effect, to which it has, at least, greatly contributed, of embittering his existence, and inducing a disease from which there are now but faint hopes of his recovery' (*Letters from Italy*, in *Works* (London, 1847), 147).

*Hierarchs of Tophet*: Tophet or Topheth is a place near Jerusalem associated in the Bible with child sacrifice; in extended use, hell itself. A 'hierarch' is a high priest.

265 *flagrant "Hobson Jobson"*: originally a British corruption of the Arabic 'Yā Ḥasan! Yā Ḥusayn!', the phrase can refer, as here, to the linguistic phenomenon described by H. L. Mencken as

> a familiar effort to bring a new and strange word into harmony with the language—an effort arising from what philologists call the law of Hobson-Jobson. This name was given to it by Col. Henry Yule and A. C. Burnell, compilers of a standard dictionary of Anglo-Indian terms. They found that the British soldiers in India, hearing strange words from the lips of the natives, often converted them into English words of similar sound, though of widely different meaning. Thus the words *Hassan* and *Hosein*, frequently used by the Mohammedans of the country in their devotions, were turned into *Hobson-Jobson*. The same process is constantly in operation elsewhere. By it the French

*route de roi* has become *Rotten Row* in English, *écrevisse* has become *crayfish*, and the English *bowsprit* has become *beau pré* (= *beautiful meadow*) in French (*The American Language* (New York, 1921), 51–2).

Perhaps it is the oblique invocation of Yule and Burnell's glossary which suggests to Ambrose the word 'Juggernaut' (which is indeed included therein) for his subsequent example of superficial linguistic resemblance.

266 *the Apostle . . . distinguishes between "charitable" actions and charity . . . one may give all one's goods to the poor, and yet lack charity*: in 1 Corinthians 13, Paul famously says, 'And though I bestow all my goods to feed the poor, and though I give my body to be burned, and have not charity, it profiteth me nothing.' Feeding the poor is a charitable action; yet unaccompanied by true 'charity' (*agape*, the highest form of Christian love), it will not lead to salvation.

*De Maupassant's tale*: 'Qui sait' ('Who Knows') by Guy de Maupassant (1850–93), first published in 1890 in the newspaper *L'Écho de Paris*.

268 *morocco binding*: see note to p. 161.

*the Aklo letters . . . or what voolas mean*: an incantatory litany of inventions, singled out for mention by Lovecraft, who wrote admiringly in his influential essay on supernatural horror: 'Mr. Machen's narrative, a triumph of skilful selectiveness and restraint, accumulates enormous power as it flows on in a stream of innocent childish prattle; introducing allusions to strange "nymphs", "Dôls", "voolas", "White, Green, and Scarlet Ceremonies", "Aklo letters", "Chian language", "Mao games", and the like' (*Supernatural Horror in Literature* (Mineola, NY, 1973), 91). Subsequent fantastical nomenclature in the tale is similarly invented, unless otherwise noted.

271 *'Tales of the Genie'*: eighteenth-century imitation of the *One Thousand and One Nights* (then known, in England, as the *Arabian Nights' Entertainments*) by clergyman James Ridley (1736–65) (its full title was *The Tales of the Genii, or, The Delightful Lessons of Horam, the Son of Asmar*, and its title page announced it to be 'Faithfully translated from the Persian Manuscript; and Compared with the French and Spanish editions Published at Paris and Madrid').

272 *'for ever and for ever, world without end, Amen'*: the conclusion of the *Gloria Patri* ('glory to the Father') doxology. As a young man Machen, climbing in Welsh hills, encountered

> grey limestone rocks, something dread, threatening, Druidical about them. . . . And so onward, slope rising to a still higher slope and no end or limit that the eye could see. . . . And I remember—I was only twenty then—feeling that there was an expression for all this in words: 'For ever and ever. Amen'. It was not till very many years afterwards that I learnt that the Welsh for 'and ever shall be' is 'ac yn y wastad'—and into the waste, the waste of time being understood. (*LA*, 118–19)

284 *aumbry*: cupboard, with archaic flavour.

286 *'Troy Town'*: name given to a number of turf labyrinths throughout Britain. In his 1922 book *Mazes & Labyrinths: Their History and Development*,

W. H. Matthews traces several specifically Welsh connections. Particularly close to home for Machen would have been the 'oral tradition of a maze of some kind on a particular hill above [Caerleon] . . . quite distinct from the well-known Roman mosaic labyrinth' (Mark Valentine, 'Arthur Machen and the Maze Theme', *Caerdroia* (1991), 57).

292  *Æschylus*: Greek dramatist (*c*.525–*c*.456 BCE).


## THE BOWMEN

First appeared in 1914 in the *Evening News*. Published in book form in the 1915 collection *The Angels of Mons*.

294  *the Retreat of the Eighty Thousand*: British retreat from the Battle of Mons in 1914. Machen is surely also invoking the famous 'Retreat of the Ten Thousand' Greek mercenaries from deep in Persian territory, as narrated by Xenophon (*c*.430–*c*.355 BCE) in his *Anabasis*.

*the Censorship*: the Defence of the Realm Act of 1914 gave the British Government power 'to prevent the spread of reports likely to cause disaffection, or alarm'. 'The censorship' plays a significant role in Machen's 1917 novel *The Terror*, in which the animal kingdom revolts against humanity in wartime Britain.

*salient*: here, 'a spur-like area of land, esp. one held by a line of offence or defence, as in trench-warfare; spec[ifically] . . . that at Ypres in western Belgium, the scene of severe fighting in the war of 1914–18' (*OED*).

*Sedan*: that is, a catastrophic defeat, as of the French by German forces in 1870, during the Franco-Prussian War.

295  *good-bye to Tipperary*: from 1912 music-hall song 'It's a long way to Tipperary', popular with British soldiers during the war. The original song concludes: 'It's a long long way to Tipperary, | But my heart's right there'.

*'What price Sidney Street?'*: the 1911 'Siege of Sidney Street', witnessed by Winston Churchill when he was Home Secretary (and also by Machen, in his capacity as a reporter), was a stand-off, and shootout, between the Metropolitan Police and a pair of Latvian anarchists holed up in a house in Stepney, ending in their fiery deaths. The sense here, given the context, seems to be something like, 'Those anarchist chappies had nothing on us', or 'That was a picnic compared to this'.

*'World without end. Amen'*: see note to p. 272.

*a queer vegetarian restaurant . . . Adsit Anglis Sanctus Georgius*: Machen may not have had a particular restaurant in mind, but historian of vegetarianism James Gregory tells me that 'there were turn of the century vegetarians who might have made connections with saintly intervention'. In his introduction to *The Angels of Mons* Machen wrote:

> It was at about this period that variants of my tale began to be told as authentic histories. At first, these tales betrayed their relation to their original. In several of them the vegetarian restaurant appeared,

and St. George was the chief character. In one case an officer—name and address missing—said that there was a portrait of St. George in a certain London restaurant, and that a figure, just like the portrait, appeared to him on the battlefield, and was invoked by him, with the happiest results.

*Harow! Harow!*: a call for aid, ultimately from Old French. Machen's bowmen sound like Anglo-Normans, though it is not 'likely that the Agincourt bowmen, most of whom came from Wales, would use the French expressions Machen evokes from them' (Reynolds and Charlton, 117).

296 *shooting at Bisley*: site of the National Shooting Centre, approximately 30 miles from London.

*the contemptible English*: Kaiser Wilhelm II was supposed to have spoken dismissively of England's 'contemptible little army'.

*Agincourt Bowmen*: the Battle of Agincourt, immortalized by Shakespeare in *Henry V*, was fought on St Crispin's Day (25 October) 1415. King Henry's longbowmen, who as noted were largely from Machen's own county of Gwent, played an important role in the English victory over a larger French force.


## THE MONSTRANCE

First appearance in *The Angels of Mons* (see headnote to 'The Bowmen'). The Monstrance is a receptacle for the Eucharistic host, or alternatively for the display of relics.

297 *Then it fell out in the sacring of the Mass . . . Old Romance*: apparently Machen's invention.

*sacring*: consecration of the bread and wine during Mass.

*enfiladed*: subjected to gunfire along their entire line.

*cannonade*: continuous cannon fire.

*the Crystal Palace in the old days*: from 1865 to 1936—with a hiatus during the 1910s—the Brock's fireworks company put on annual displays ('Brock's benefits') at the Crystal Palace site (see note to p. 57). Interestingly, in the 1920s the phrase 'Brock's benefit' would begin to be used to describe artillery battles in the Great War (*OED*).

*Von und Zu*: literally 'of and at'; a joke involving German nobiliary nomenclature.

*gehenna-fire*: hellfire.

298 *tinnitus*: ringing in the ears.

*St Lambart on that terrible day*: widespread reports of what came to be known as 'the German atrocities', both real and inflated in Allied propaganda, followed in the wake of the German invasion of Belgium and France. Machen, inventing his own war atrocity, has out-Heroded Herod.

299 *Ave Maria Stella*: more likely the medieval plainsong hymn to Mary, 'Ave Maris Stella', 'Hail Star of the Sea'.

N

First appeared as the only new story in the 1936 collection *The Cosy Room and Other Stories*.

301 *of the sort that Mr Pickwick sits on*: describes the frontispiece to Charles Dickens's *The Posthumous Papers of the Pickwick Club* (1836–7), by Hablot Knight Browne ('Phiz') (1815–82).

*Horace Walpole and his friend Mr Gray*: Walpole was responsible for the first Gothic romance, *The Castle of Otranto* (1764), and the Gothic Revival house Strawberry Hill, at Twickenham; the poetry of Thomas Gray (1716–71) anticipated the Gothic movement in literature, while as a scholar he turned his attention from classical to medieval history, particularly the study of Gothic architecture.

302 *landscapes of the Valley of the Usk, and the Holy Mountain, and Llanthony*: all located in south-east Wales. The 'Holy Mountain' is a local name for Ysgyryd Fawr (Skirrid Fawr in English), Llanthony a village with an important medieval priory.

*'Bolton Abbey in the Olden Time'*: engraving of a popular painting by Sir Edwin Landseer (1802–73).

*"Te Deum Laudamus"*: title and opening words of Latin hymn of praise; the words 'Te Dominum Confitemur' immediately follow, and together are translated as, 'You are God: we praise you | You are the Lord: we acclaim you.' The pair of prints seems to be invented, though Machen seems to suggest a family resemblance with the work of Frith (see note below).

*Mafeking year*: the Siege of Mafeking, during the Second Boer War, lasted from October 1899 to May 1900.

*"Sherry, Sir"*: after a painting by William Powell Frith (1819–1909). The title (properly 'Sherry, Sir?') was coined specifically for the engraving.

*Bloomsbury, in the days when the bars were up, and the Duke's porters had boxes beside the gates, and all was peace*: before 1890, that is, when 'parliament authorised the newly established London County Council to order the removal of London's many private gates and bars, five of which were in the Duke of Bedford's Bloomsbury' (Rosemary Ashton, *Victorian Bloomsbury* (New Haven, 2012), 282). This is a good place to note that, in this story, subsequent glossing of London place names will be selective.

*Christina Rossetti*: (1830–94), poet associated with the Pre-Raphaelite Brotherhood, sister of Dante Gabriel Rossetti, and devout Anglican.

303 *'The Shop of the Pale Puddings, where little David Copperfield might have bought his dinner'*: Machen means to call to mind the following passage, from chapter 11 of the novel:

> I remember two pudding shops, between which I was divided, according to my finances. One was in a court close to St Martin's Church—at the back of the church,—which is now removed altogether. The pudding at that shop was made of currants, and was rather a special

pudding, but was dear, twopennyworth not being larger than a penny-worth of more ordinary pudding. A good shop for the latter was in the Strand—somewhere in that part which has been rebuilt since. It was a stout pale pudding, heavy and flabby, and with great flat raisins in it, stuck in whole at wide distances apart.

*The Globe office*: the young Machen had sold his first articles to *The Globe*—which were, indeed, 'turnovers'—before finding in early 1890 that the *St James's Gazette* paid better.

*Turnovers*: a newspaper item (as Machen well knew from his experience as a reporter) that continues overleaf.

*Nutt's bookshop*: the David Nutt bookshop was founded in Fleet Street in 1829 before moving to the Strand in 1848.

*Family Herald*: see note to p. 160.

*Jamaica Coffee House*: founded in the seventeenth century in Cornhill; became the Jamaica Wine House in 1869.

304 *'Misce, fiat mistura'*: 'Mix to make a mixture' (Latin). The following remark by Arnold, as Machen indicates, employs the lingo of the alchemists.

*Kingsgate Street—'just like Phiz's plate . . . I wish they hadn't pulled it down'*: the street, demolished in 1902–6, had been home to Dickens's Mrs Gant. 'Phiz's plate' likely refers to Hablot Browne's illustration, 'Mr Pecksniff on his Mission', plate 16 in Part 8 of *Martin Chuzzlewit*.

305 *the Military Tournament, when it was at the Agricultural Hall, in Islington*: the 'Royal Tournament', annual pageant by the British Armed Forces, was first held in 1880, at the Royal Agricultural Hall.

*Stoke Newington way*: area in the northern part of Hackney; described in *The London Encyclopedia* (1983) in this way: 'one of the ancient villages engulfed in the tide of London's growth, but a rural atmosphere persists ... it still does not quite belong to London and at times presents the aspect of an 18th-century village with a hinterland of Victorian suburb' (827–8). The 'at times' is interesting in this context (as is 'does not quite belong to London'); one wonders whether the writer of this entry had read 'N'.

*the school where Poe boarded . . . a phrase or two in "William Wilson"*: the Manor House boarding school was demolished in 1880. In the passage from 'William Wilson' here referred to, Poe describes Stoke Newington as

a misty-looking village of England, where there were a vast number of gigantic and gnarled trees, and where all the houses were excessively ancient. In truth, it was a dream-like and spirit-soothing place, that venerable old town. At this moment, in fancy, I feel the refreshing chilliness of its deeply-shadowed avenues, inhale the fragrance of its thousand shrubberies, and thrill anew with undefinable delight, at the deep hollow note of the churchbell, breaking, each hour, with sullen and sudden roar, upon the stillness of the dusky atmosphere in which the fretted Gothic steeple lay imbedded and asleep. (*Works of Edgar Allan Poe* (New York, 1861), i. 418)

306 *the War*: the First World War.

307 *Kew Gardens*: Royal Botanic Gardens, in what was then the London suburb of Kew. The gardens have eighteenth-century origins but became
a national botanical garden in 1840. An 1838 report by the botanist John
Lindley noted the 'many fine Exotic Trees and Shrubs' to be found there.

*Wells*: cathedral city in Somerset.

308 *where the manuscript of Traherne's Centuries of Meditations had been found*:
Thomas Traherne (c.1637–74), clergyman and metaphysical poet, might
well have been forgotten had not a number of manuscripts of his writings
been discovered in the late nineteenth and early twentieth centuries.

*A London Walk: Meditations in the Streets of the Metropolis*: this fictitious
work, and its author the Revd Thomas Hampole, had first been used by
Machen in his 1933 novel *The Green Round*.

*Addison and Pope and Johnson*: a reference to the demand for moral instruc-
tion in literature in the eighteenth century; the aim of Joseph Addison's
and Richard Steele's *Spectator* (1711–12, 1714) was to 'enliven Morality
with Wit, and to temper Wit with Morality'. Samuel Johnson's *Rambler*
(1750–2) was in the same tradition. Alexander Pope's *Moral Essays* in verse
appeared between 1731 and 1735.

*to hear sermons from stones*: Oscar Wilde said of William Wordsworth, 'He
found in stones the sermons he had already hidden there'.

*'in Chancery'*: title of the first chapter of Dickens's *Bleak House* (1852–3);
also 1920 novel by John Galsworthy (hence the quotation marks); meaning
in the possession of the Court of Chancery.

*something rich and strange*: from Shakespeare's *The Tempest*; Ariel is
describing the radical 'sea-change' of a submerged corpse.

309 *the fabled pleasure dome of the Eastern potentate*: in the Mongol city of
Shang-tu ('Xanadu'), as immortalized by Coleridge in 'Kubla Khan': 'In
Xanadu did Kubla Khan | A stately pleasure-dome decree'.

*Aladdin in the Arabian tale*: famous tale in the *One Thousand and One
Nights*.

*veritas contra mundum*: 'truth against the world' (Latin).

310 *Glanville*: no doubt a nod to the seventeenth-century English philosopher
Joseph Glanvill, who produced a mighty counterblast to unbelief in the
supernatural, and witchcraft in particular, in his *Sadducismus Triumphatus*
(1681), a book quoted in tales by Poe, Aleister Crowley, and Lovecraft.

*the German Theosophist, Behmen*: Jakob Böhme (1575–1624).

*his English disciple, William Law*: (1686–1761) devotional writer. 'Law had
long been a reader of mystical writers, but at some point in the mid-1730s
his understanding of Christianity was profoundly altered by his reading of
the German protestant mystic Jacob Boehme' (*ODNB*).

*Heavenly Chaos*: cf. Thomas Vaughan's *Cœlum Terræ, or the Magician's
Heavenly Chaos* (1650).

*Reason, as that divine faculty was exhibited by Coleridge*: cf. his *Aids to Reflection*, in which he sets out to 'substantiate and set forth at large the momentous distinction between reason and understanding'.

311 *Torquay*: seaside resort town in Devon.

*parterre*: ornamental garden.

313 *Mrs Todgers . . . Mr Pecksniff*: characters in Charles Dickens's *Martin Chuzzlewit*. Mrs Todgers is proprietress of a boarding house in a claustrophobic, labyrinthine neighbourhood near the Monument; the hypocritical Seth Pecksniff is ostensibly an architect.

*Both buildings curdled the blood . . . They looked as if Mr H. G. Wells's bad dreams had come true*: these imagined products of 1930s British Modernist architecture put Machen in mind of, perhaps, such Wellsian prophetic works as *A Modern Utopia*: 'The place has been designed by an architect happily free from the hampering traditions of Greek temple building, and of Roman and Italian palaces. . . . The material is some artificial stone with the dull surface and something of the tint of yellow ivory; the colour is a little irregular, and a partial confession of girders and pillars breaks this front of tender colour with lines and mouldings of greenish gray, that blend with the tones of the leaden gutters and rain pipes from the light red roof' (London, 1905), 215.

314 *Kubla Khan*: see note to p. 309.

*Old Man of the Mountain*: according to legend (one told, most famously, by Marco Polo), this 'Mountain Sheik' converted men into desperate assassins by first bestowing, then withholding, the pleasures of his paradisaical garden.

*SPR*: the Society for Psychical Research, founded in 1882.

315 *the Wireless*: radio, first developed as the 'wireless telegraph' at the end of the nineteenth century; in the UK at this time, a wireless licence was required to receive broadcasts.

320 *perichoresis*: interpenetration, with particular reference to the special relationship which is supposed to obtain between and among the Persons of the Trinity (Father, Son, and Holy Spirit). From Greek for 'going round'; 'circumsession' is the Latinate equivalent.

## THE TREE OF LIFE

One of the six new stories written for the 1936 collection *The Children of the Pool and Other Stories*. One could fill an entire book glossing the nearly universal mytheme of 'The Tree of Life'. In the context of this story, and Machen's known interests, some of the more salient connections are these: in the Garden of Eden there is a 'tree of life' as well as the better-known 'tree of the knowledge of good and evil'; another biblical connection is the passage from the Book of Revelation quoted at the end of the story. In esoteric Judaism, the phrase refers to a mystical symbol made up of the ten Sephiroth or 'emanations' in Kabbalah, subsequently adopted within the Hermetic tradition—particularly, in Machen's time, by the Order of the Golden Dawn. Perhaps Machen had read one of the recent hermetic works addressing the topic, such as Israel Regardie's *The Tree of Life* in 1932, or *Mystical Qabalah*, by Welsh occultist Dion Fortune (another erstwhile member of the Order), which appeared in 1935. He had himself dilated on the subject in *Things Near and Far* (1923). Finally, coniferous trees of the genus *Thuja* are also called *arbor vitæ*, Latin for 'tree of life' (so named in 1558).

321 *Llantrisant*: town in South Wales; the name means 'Parish of the Three Saints'.

*St Teilo*: important sixth-century Welsh saint, invoked elsewhere by Machen, for instance in *The Secret Glory*. Interestingly, according to the Latin *Vita sancti Teiliaui*, Teilo and St Samson are supposed to have planned, and planted, an orchard of fruit-bearing trees extending for 3 miles.

*the dissolution of the religious houses*: Henry VIII disbanded the Roman Catholic monasteries in Britain between 1536 and 1541.

*rose for the King in 1648*: for Charles I, in other words, and the losing side, during the English Civil War.

*Mr Gladstone*: Liberal prime minister William Ewart Gladstone (1809–98) was one of the towering figures of the Victorian political world, and an advocate of Irish home rule.

322 *Inigo Jones*: (1573–1652) celebrated architect.

*marasmus*: vague designation for any wasting disease.

*the arrows of the Gwent bowmen darkening the air at Crècy*: like the later Battle of Agincourt, the Battle of Crécy (1346) represented an English victory during the Hundred Years War; cf. 'The Bowmen'.

323 *Castell-y-Bwch*: 'Buck's Castle'.

329 *Arbor Vitæ*: see headnote to 'The Tree of Life'.

330 *Bartle Frere*: Sir Henry Bartle Frere (1815–84), colonial administrator; the anecdote can be found in *The Life and Correspondence of Sir Bartle Frere* (London, 1895), 131.

331 *night-houses—Kate Hamilton and all that lot*: a 'night house' was an all-night public house, such as the disreputable 'Kate Hamilton's'.

*Truefitt's*: the self-described 'Oldest Barbershop in the World', still in existence; founded in 1805.

*"Judge and Jury"*: parlour game.

*poses plastiques*: Victorian practice of posing as 'living statues', a mode of performance with risqué associations.

333 *"Whips to scourge us"*: Lord Byron is quoted as having said to Walter Scott, 'Our pleasant vices are but whips to scourge us', echoing *King Lear* 5.3.161–2: 'The gods are just, and of our pleasant vices | Make instruments to plague us' (Quarto reads 'instruments to scourge us'). Perhaps

Machen got the not-quite-right phrasing from Stevenson, who had used it in his essay on Villon.

*a memory like Macaulay's*: Thomas Babington Macaulay (1800–59); as Francis Galton wrote in *Hereditary Genius*, 'He was able to recall many pages of hundreds of volumes by various authors, which he had acquired by simply reading them over' (London, 1869), 23.

335 *'Revelations'*: from Revelation 22.

*the Committee*: i.e. of the club.

## CHANGE

Like 'The Tree of Life', newly written for the 1936 collection *The Children of the Pool and Other Stories*. The perceptive reader may notice that the shift from the frame story to Rimmer's narrative (on p. 338) is accompanied by the dropping of the quotation marks indicating that he is speaking to Reynolds; these return, rather awkwardly, at the end of his story (on p. 344).

337 *Meirion*: the description suggests the historic county of Meirionnydd (Merionethshire), within which the coastal tourist village Portmeirion was constructed in 1925. 'Meirion' also appears in *The Terror*, along with several of the place names which follow.

338 *alarums and excursions*: Elizabethan stage direction; by extension uproar or commotion.

339 *City article*: financial reporting appeared in the London daily newspapers, including *The Times*.

340 *Pepper's Ghost*: optical illusion, named after inventor John Henry Pepper (1821–1900).

*Mysterious Musicians*: probably a reference to a scene (set in a Welsh castle) in the popular musical comedy *Florodora*.

*De Barry*: the De Barrys were an ancient Norman-Welsh family.

342 *the Darren*: commonly found in Welsh place names, 'tarren' or 'darren' meaning 'knoll' or 'rock' in Welsh.

345 *Mithraic Ritual*: Mithraism, an originally Iranian religion, was popular in the Roman Empire before Constantine's adoption of Christianity.

*Gnostic*: reference to Gnostic Christianity, i.e. early Christian sects professing special, mystic knowledge.

*"speaking with tongues"*: glossolalia (from the Greek for 'speaking in tongues') refers to ecstatic, unintelligible utterance taking place, typically, at religious gatherings.

## RITUAL

First published in the anthology *Path and Pavement*, edited by John Rowland (London, 1937). According to Goldstone and Sweetser, Machen's original MS is titled 'London Sports'.

347 *Whitsun holiday*: the weekend of Whitsunday, the seventh Sunday following Easter.

*Madame Tussaud's waxworks*: in 1802 Anna Maria Tussaud (bap. 1761, d. 1850) brought some thirty wax figures from Napoleonic France to London. Her first exhibition there, a 'Grand European Cabinet of Figures', took place at the Lyceum Theatre on the Strand. By 1835 she and her portraits in wax were established in Baker Street. In 1884 the museum was moved to the Marylebone Road, where it became, and remains, a major tourist attraction (particularly famous is its 'Chamber of Horrors', containing waxworks of murderers and other notorious figures from history).

*Zoo*: see note to p. 131. 'Ritual' was published shortly after the introduction of penguins there, and before the arrival of a panda.

*those Easter Island gods*: moai are large stone statues depicting human figures, carved between 1400 and 1600 by the Rapa Nui people. The British Museum (see note to p. 150) possesses two moai, one being the celebrated *Hoa Hakananai'a* (meaning 'hidden or stolen friend'), taken by British Navy Commodore Richard Ashmore Powell in 1869 and offered to Queen Victoria, who gave it in turn to the Museum. Both were displayed outside, beneath the Museum's front portico, until the Second World War.

348 *Reader*: proofreader, who examines the printed 'galley slip' or 'proof' for errors (or, as here, the incautious revelation of Masonic secrets).

'*Hiram Abiff*' . . . *not one of the Widow's offspring*: references to Freemasonry. In the Masonic legend, Hiram Abiff or Abif, the architect of Solomon's Temple, is killed by three masons ('ruffians' in the Masonic account) when he refuses to divulge his secrets. His murder, burial, and resurrection form part of Masonic ritual. (The legendary figure is also called 'the Widow's son', a reference to one of the multiple biblical 'Hirams' mentioned in connection with the Temple.)

*admiratio*: Latin, 'wonder' or 'astonishment'; perhaps here closer to 'regard', in the sense of attracting unwanted attention.

*Johnsonian manner*: reminiscent of the mode of speaking of writer and lexicographer Samuel Johnson (1709–84), as recorded by his friend James Boswell in his immortal *Life of Johnson*. (The 'Sir' is a particularly Johnsonian touch.) There is some irony in Machen's choice of an American as a modern-day avatar of Johnson, considering his (Johnson's) view of that people: 'Sir, they are a race of convicts, and ought to be thankful for anything we allow them short of hanging'. Machen himself enjoyed formulating 'Johnsonisms', as when (and here, too, Johnson's view of Americans is part of the joke) the United States entered the First World War: 'Why, Sir, it is difficult to deny the Americans merit: if it be a merit to have saved the world from destruction' (Reynolds and Charlton, 99).

*blind-pigs*: a speakeasy (American slang).

*Arnold Bennett*: (1867–1931), British writer born in Staffordshire (where such well-known works as *The Old Wives' Tale* are set); he moved to London in 1889 as a young man.

*"Little Dorrit"*... *Mr Casby's very street*: Christopher Casby, landlord of Bleeding Heart Yard, 'lived in a street in the Gray's Inn Road, which had set off from that thoroughfare with the intention of running at one heat down into the valley, and up again to the top of Pentonville Hill; but which had run itself out of breath in twenty yards, and had stood still ever since' (book 1, chapter 13).

349 *Eton and Harrow Cricket Match*: the first match between the two venerable public schools took place in 1805 at Lord's Cricket Ground. By the early twentieth century the annual contest had become itself a kind of ritual, conjuring up an image of a vanished English past.

350 *Asiki doing their Njoru ritual*: Machen takes the name 'Asiki' from *Fetichism in West Africa*, a 1904 book by the missionary Robert Hamill Nassau; there the 'Asiki' are a supernatural race of 'little beings' analogous if not identical (as Machen had suggested in an essay collected in the 1926 collection *Dreads and Drolls*) to the 'little people' of Celtic lore. There is an 'Asiki tribe' in H. Rider Haggard's 1908 novel *The Yellow God*; perhaps Haggard was also familiar with Nassau's book. Presumably Machen has invented the 'Njoru ritual'.